PRAISE FOR CATHERINE COULTER'S
FBI THRILLER SERIES

"Fast-paced."   —*People*

"A good storyteller . . . Coulter always keeps the pace brisk."
                                        —*Fort Worth Star-Telegram*

"With possible blackmail, intra-judiciary rivalries, and personal pecca-
dilloes, there's more than enough intrigue—and suspects—for full court
standing in this snappy page-turner. . . . A zesty read."   —*BookPage*

"Twisted villains . . . intriguing escapism. . . . The latest in the series featur-
ing likable . . . FBI agents Lacey Sherlock and Dillon Savich."
                                        —*Lansing State Journal*

"Coulter takes readers on a chilling and suspenseful ride . . . taut, fast-paced,
hard to put down."   —*Cedar Rapids Gazette*

"The perfect suspense thriller, loaded with plenty of action."
                                        —The Best Reviews

"The newest installment in Coulter's FBI series delivers . . . a fast-moving
investigation, a mind-bending mystery. . . . The mystery at the heart . . . is
intriguing and the pacing is brisk."   —*Publishers Weekly*

"Fast-paced. . . . Coulter gets better and more cinematic with each of her
suspenseful FBI adventures."   —*Booklist*

DOUBLE JEOPARDY

CATHERINE COULTER

BERKLEY
NEW YORK

BERKLEY
An imprint of Penguin Random House LLC
penguinrandomhouse.com

Copyright © 2008 by Catherine Coulter
The Target copyright © 1998 by Catherine Coulter
The Edge copyright © 1999 by Catherine Coulter

BERKLEY and the BERKLEY & B colophon are registered trademarks of
Penguin Random House LLC.

Second Berkley trade paperback ISBN: 9780593546512

The Library of Congress has catalogued the first Berkley trade paperback edition of
this book as follows:

Coulter, Catherine.
[Target]
Double jeopardy / Catherine Coulter.—Berkley trade pbk. ed.
p.   cm.
ISBN: 978-0-425-22435-9 (alk. paper)
1. United States. Federal Bureau of Investigation—Fiction.   2. Savich, Dillon
(Fictitious character)—Fiction.   3. Sherlock, Lacey (Fictitious character)—Fiction.
4. Suspense fiction, American.   I. Coulter, Catherine. Edge.   II. Title.
PS3553.O843T3   2008
813'.54—dc22   2008011878

First Berkley trade paperback edition / June 2008
Second Berkley trade paperback edition / September 2022

PRINTED IN THE UNITED STATES OF AMERICA

1st Printing

CONTENTS

THE TARGET

To Dr. Anton Pogany,
who has the instincts,
the patience, a light
touch. In other words,
he's got the right
stuff. Let's keep
on cooking.

My thanks to Alex McClure, Esquire, for her intrepid assistance on the workings of the federal justice system.

PROLOGUE

He saw the man clearly: tall, with dark clothes, a stark figure against the misty gray sky. He was walking into the big granite building, ugly and flat-looking, with scores of windows that didn't look out over much except if you were up high. Then, suddenly, he was behind the man, just over his shoulder, keeping pace with him, watching him take the elevator to the nineteenth floor. He was nearly beside him as he walked down the long corridor and opened the door to a large office. A smiling receptionist greeted him, laughing at something he said. He watched the man greet two other people, a young man and a young woman, both well dressed, both obviously subordinate to him. He went into a large office with the man, saw a United States flag, a huge desk with its computer on top, the built-in bookshelves behind him, the windows beside him. He punched up the computer. Then, he was right behind the man; he could have reached out and helped him put on the long black robe. He watched him fasten the two clips closed. The man opened a door and walked into a big room, the look on his face somber, becoming cold, all the earlier humor wiped clean. There was a buzz. It stopped abruptly when he came into the room. Then the place went deathly silent.

Suddenly the room began to spin, faces blurred into one another, the very air of the room turned dark and darker still, and then the great main doors burst open and three men slammed into the room. They were carrying guns, assault guns like Russian AK47s. They were shooting, people were screaming, blood was spewing everywhere. He saw the man's face tighten with horror and fury. He saw the man suddenly leap over the railing that had separated him from the rest of that roomful of people, his black robe swirling. His leg was up, he was turning, striking out, his motion so fast it was hard to see it clearly. Someone screamed loudly.

He was right behind the man now, heard him breathe, could feel the controlled rage in him, the vicious tension and determination, and wondered.

Suddenly, the man whirled about again, turning this time to face him. He stared at himself, looked deeply into the eyes of a man who had just killed and would kill again. He felt the spit pool in his mouth, the coiled muscles, and felt his arm fly out, striking a man's throat.

He jerked up, flailing at the single sheet that was wound tightly around him like a mummy's shroud, a yell dying on his lips. He was soaked with sweat, his hair plastered to his head. His heart was pounding so fast and hard he thought he'd explode. Again, he thought, that bloody dream yet again. He didn't think he could stand it.

An hour later, he let himself out of his house, carefully locking the door behind him. He was on the way to his car when a man jumped out of the bushes and blinded him with a good half dozen photo flashes. It was too much.

He grabbed the photographer, hauled him up by his shirtfront, and yelled right in his face, "You've gone over the line, you little bastard." He grabbed his camera, pulled the film out, and threw him aside. He tossed the camera to the man, who was lying on his back, gaping at him.

"You can't do that!"

"I just did. Get off my property."

The man scrambled to his feet, holding his camera to his chest. "I'll sue you! The public has a right to know!"

He wanted to beat the guy senseless. The urge was so strong he was shaking with it. It was then he knew he had to leave. Otherwise it might not stop before he went nuts and really hurt one of the jerks. Or he simply just went nuts.

ONE

Rocky Mountains
Spring

He stood at the edge of the mountain that sheered down a good two hundred feet before smoothing out into tree-covered ledges and gentle wildflower-covered slopes and sharp gaping ridges. He breathed in the thin air that was so fresh it burned his lungs, but, truth be told, it burned less today than it had yesterday. Soon, the frigid clean air at nearly six thousand feet would become natural to him. It had been only yesterday that he'd realized he hadn't thought all day about a telephone, a TV, a radio, a fax machine, the sound of other voices coming at him from all sides, about people grabbing at him, shouting questions six inches from his face. And those blinding explosions of white from the ever-present flashbulbs. Now, he figured, at last he was beginning to let go, to forget for stretches of time what had happened.

He looked across the valley at the massive, raw mountains that stretched mile upon mile like unevenly spaced jagged teeth. Mr. Goudge, the owner of the Union 76 gas station down in Dillinger, had told him that many of the locals, lots of them Trekkies, called the whole mess of knuckle-shaped mountains the Ferengi Range. The highest peak rose to twelve thousand feet, bent slightly to the south, and looked like a misshapen phallus. He wondered if he'd hurt himself if he climbed that mountain. The folks down in Dillinger joked about that peak, saying it was a sight with snow dropping off it in the summer.

He was aware again as he was so often of being utterly alone. At this elevation there were thick forests of conifers, mainly birch, fir, and more ponderosa pine than anyone could begin to count. He'd seen lots of quaking aspen too. No logging companies had ever devoured this land. On the higher-elevation peaks across the valley, there were no trees, no flowers as there were here in his alpine meadow, just snow and ruggedness, so much savage beauty, untouched by humans.

He looked toward the small town of Dillinger at the far end of the valley that stretched from east to west below. It claimed fifteen hundred and three souls. Silver mines had made it a boomtown in the 1880s, nearly bursting the valley open with more than thirty thousand people—miners, prostitutes, store owners, crooks, an occasional sheriff and preacher, and very few families. That was a long time ago. The descendants of those few locals who had stuck it out after the silver mines had closed down now catered to a trickle of summer tourists. There were cattle in the valley, but they were a scruffy lot. He'd seen bighorn sheep and mountain goats coming down the slopes really close to the cattle, pronghorn antelope grazing at the lower elevations, and prowling coyotes.

He'd driven his four-wheel-drive Jeep down there just once since he'd been here to stock up on groceries at Clement's grocery. Had it been Tuesday? Two days ago? He'd bought a package of frozen peas, forgetting that he didn't have a freezer, just a small high-tech refrigerator that was run off a generator sitting just outside the cabin. He'd cooked those frozen peas on his wood-burning stove, then eaten the entire package in one sitting next to the one bright standing lamp that also worked off the generator.

He stretched, caught a glimpse of two hawks flying low, looking for a snack, and took his ax back to the stump beside the cabin where he was splitting logs. It didn't take him long to pull off his down jacket, then his flannel shirt, then his undershirt. And still he worked up a sweat. His rhythm sped up. The sun felt hot and good on his skin, seeping in to warm his muscles. He felt strong and healthy. He was in business. He knew he had more logs than he could use for the next week, but he just kept to that hard, smooth rhythm, feeling his muscles flex and loosen, grow tight with power, and release.

He stopped a moment to wipe the sweat off his face with a sleeve of his shirt. Even his sweat smelled fresh, as if his innards were clean.

He heard something.

A very faint sound. It had to be an animal. But he'd gotten used to the owls and the sparrow hawks, to the chipmunks and the skunks, and to the wolves. This sound wasn't one of them. He hoped it wasn't another person invading his mountain. His was the only cabin in the high meadow. There were other cabins, but they were lower, at least a half mile away. No one came up here except maybe in the summer to hike. It was mid-April. No hikers yet. He hefted his ax again. He froze in midswing when the sound came again.

It was like the desperate cry of something—a kitten? No, that was crazy. Still, he pulled on his flannel shirt, and the down jacket. He leaned down and picked up his ax. The weight felt good. Had another man come onto his mountain?

He paused, holding perfectly still, letting the silence invade him until he was part of it. He felt the cool afternoon breeze stir the hair on his head. At last it came again, a soft mewling sound that was fainter this time, broken off into two distinct parts, as if suddenly split apart.

As if a creature was nearly dead.

He ran fast over the flat meadow where his cabin stood. He ran into the pine forest that surrounded the high meadow, slowing because of the undergrowth, praying he was going in the right direction, but uncertain even as he ran.

He heard his own hard breathing and stopped. Little sun could cut through the dense trees. Now that it was late afternoon, it was nearly dark here deep in the forest, where there were suddenly no sounds at all. Nothing. He calmed his breathing and listened. Still nothing. He heard a slithering sound. He whipped around to see a small prairie rattlesnake winding its way under a moss-covered rock. The snake was higher up than it should be.

He waited silent as the trees on all sides of him. He felt a cramp in his right bicep. Slowly he lowered the ax to the ground.

Suddenly he heard it again, off to his left, not too far away, muffled and faint, a sound that was almost like an echo of itself, a memory of what it had been.

He moved slowly now, eyes straight ahead, his stride long. He came to a small clearing. The afternoon sun was still bright overhead. There was rich high grass waving in the breeze. Blue columbine, the Colorado state flower, was blooming wildly, soft and delicate, already welcoming spring. It was a beautiful spot, one he hadn't yet found on his daily treks.

He waited now, his face upturned to the slanting sun, listening. There was a squirrel running up a tree, a distinct sound, one he'd learned very quickly to identify. The squirrel scampered out on a narrow branch, making it wave up and down, its leaves rustling with the weight and movement.

Then there wasn't anything at all, just silence.

He knew the sun wouldn't be shining on him much longer; shadows were already lengthening, swallowing the light. Soon it would be as dark as Susan's hair in the forest. No, he wouldn't think about Susan. Actually it had been a very long time since he'd thought about Susan. It was time to go home, back to his cabin where he'd laid wood for a fire that morning, still waiting for a single match. He'd gotten good at building fires both in the fireplace and in the woodstove. He'd slice up some fresh tomatoes and shred some iceberg lettuce he'd bought two days before at Clement's. He'd heat up some vegetable soup. He stepped back into the thick pine forest.

But what had he heard?

It was darker now than it had been just two minutes before. He had to walk carefully. His sleeve caught on a pine branch. He stopped to untangle himself. He had to lay down the ax.

It was then he saw the flash of light yellow off to his right. For a moment, he just stared at that light yellow. It didn't move and neither did he.

He quickly picked up his ax. He walked toward that light yellow patch, pausing every few seconds, his eyes straining to make out what it was.

It was a lump of something.

He saw from three feet away that it was a child, unmoving, lying on her stomach, her dark brown hair in tangles down her back, hiding her face.

He fell on his knees beside her, afraid for an instant to touch her. Then he lightly put his hand to her shoulder. He shook her lightly. She didn't move. The pulse in her throat was slow but steady. Thank God she was unconscious, not dead. He felt each of her arms, then her legs. Nothing was broken. But she could be injured internally. If she was, there was nothing he could do about it. He carefully turned her over.

There were two long scratches on her cheek, the blood dried and smeared. Again, he placed his finger against the pulse in her neck. Still slow, still steady.

He picked her up as carefully as he could, and grabbed his ax. He curved her in against him to protect her from the low pine branches and underbrush. She was small, probably not older than five or six. He realized then she wasn't wearing a jacket, only the thin yellow T-shirt and dirty yellow jeans. There were white sneakers on her feet, one of the laces unfastened and dangling. No socks, no gloves, no jacket, no cap. What was she doing out here alone? What had happened to her?

He stopped. He could have sworn that he heard the sound of a heavy foot snapping through leaves and small branches. No, he was imagining things. He pulled her closer and quickened his step, the sound of that crunching step hovering just behind him.

It was heavy dusk by the time he walked through the door of his cabin. He laid the little girl on the sofa and covered her with an afghan, an old red-and-blue-checked wool square that was probably older than he was, and very warm. He lit the lamps throughout the cabin.

He turned to look at the front door. He frowned at it, then walked to the door, locked it, and turned the dead bolt. His hand paused as he lifted the chain. Better to be certain. He secured it. Then he lit the fire in the fireplace. Within ten minutes the single large room was warm.

The child was still unconscious. He lightly patted her cheeks, and sat back, waiting, but she didn't stir.

His day certainly wasn't ending as it had begun. "Who are you?" he said to the child. Her face was turned away from him. The scratches were bright and ugly in the lamplight.

He fetched a bowl of tepid water that had been sitting on the wood-stove all afternoon, a clean pair of white gym socks, and a bar of soap. He washed her face, as carefully as he could with a gym sock pulled over his hand, blotting the blood off the long scratches.

He brought one of his white undershirts that was warm and soft after years of laundering, and began to strip her. He had to examine her as best he could. He was shocked, then furious, at what he saw.

She was covered with bruises and welts, some of them crusted with dried blood. Blood was smeared between her legs. Oh, God. He closed his eyes a moment.

He bathed her thoroughly, examining her as well as he could, but he didn't see any signs of wounds or cuts, just abrasions and deep bruises. He turned her onto her stomach. Long thin welts scored her child's flesh, from her shoulders to her ankles, welts that didn't overlap, as if made by a care-less enraged hand, but that had been carefully placed by someone who wanted to mark every inch of the child, to obtain a certain result, a certain effect. She was thin and as white as the clean undershirt he pulled over her head. The undershirt came to her ankles. He smoothed the covers back over her, and spread out her hair about her head on the pillow with his fingers, gentle as he could be, easing out the worst of the tangles. It was just as well that she wasn't awake while he'd taken care of her. He sat back, staring at the silent child.

He realized he was shaking with fury. What monster had done this to a child? He knew, from firsthand experience, that there were many monsters out there, but to come face-to-face with this made him want to puke and kill at the same time.

He willed her to wake up. She didn't move. He considered whether to take her to the hospital now. He had no phone so he couldn't call. He'd even left his cell phone at home. It was late. He didn't know where the hospital was, how far. And he didn't know who had done this to her, who'd abused and beaten her, or where they were. No, tomorrow he'd take her, and he'd stay with her. He wouldn't leave her alone. Tomorrow, he'd drive with her to the sheriff. There had to be a sheriff in Dillinger. Tonight he'd take care of her himself. If she awoke, if she was hurting, then he'd take her to the hospital, no matter what the hour. But not now.

Had she saved herself, escaped somehow, and run into the forest? Had she tripped on a root or a rock and struck her head? Or had the monster who'd hurt her dumped her, leaving her to die in the forest? He leaned over her and gently ran his fingers over her head. He couldn't feel any lumps. The pulse in her throat was still slow and steady.

If she had escaped the man who'd done this to her, that meant he was still out there looking for her. Of course he'd known this in his gut when he'd brought her into the cabin and that was why he'd locked the door. He checked his Browning Savage 99 lever action rifle. It was already chambered with a .243 Win. On the table by the sofa was his Smith & Wesson .357 Magnum revolver. He loved that gun, had since his father had given it to him on his fourteenth birthday and taught him how to use it. It was called the Black Magic because of its black finish on stainless steel. He liked to shoot it, but he'd never used it on a person.

He picked it up. It was fully loaded, as always. He looked toward the door, the revolver in his hand, gauging the distance there.

What man had done this?

He fixed himself a salad and ate it, never taking his eyes off the child. Then he heated the soup. It smelled very good. He waved a spoonful beneath her nose. "Come on now, wouldn't you like to have a taste? Campbell's is good stuff and it's hot, right off an old-fashioned woodstove. It takes a while to heat anything, but it does work. Come on now, sweetheart, wake up."

Her mouth moved. He got a smaller spoon, dipped it into the soup, and lightly pressed it against her bottom lip. To his surprise and relief, her mouth opened. He dribbled in the soup. She swallowed, and he gave her more.

She ate nearly half a bowl. Only then did she open her eyes. She looked confused. Slowly, she turned her face toward him, and stared up at him. He smiled and said, "Hello, don't be afraid. My name's Ramsey. I found you. You're safe now."

She opened her mouth and there came the strange noise he'd heard, a soft mewling that sounded of bone-deep fright and helplessness.

"It's all right. No one will hurt you. You're safe now with me."

Her mouth opened but no sound came out this time. Her arms came out from under the afghan and she flailed at him, the only sound her small mouth made was that awful mewling that made him want to pull this little scrap of humanity against him and protect her.

He quickly set down the spilled soup and grabbed her wrists. Her eyes fluttered closed, but not before he saw the flash of pain. He released her wrists. Both wrists were raw. She'd been tied up. "I'm sorry, sweetheart. I'm really sorry. Don't fight me, please. I won't hurt you."

She huddled into a small ball and turned her back to him, her arms over her head, and didn't move.

He sat there wondering what he should do. She was terrified. Of him. He couldn't blame her.

Why didn't she scream at him? She'd just made those strange sounds. Was she mute?

He said very quietly, hoping she could hear him, "Your wrists and ankles are in bad shape. Can I bandage them for you? They'll feel better."

Had she heard him? She still didn't move. He pulled an old undershirt from beneath the pile of clothes he'd brought and ripped it into strips. He felt every scrap of fear in her as he washed her wrists and ankles really well, smeared on some Neosporin, then wrapped the soft material around them, knotting the bandages off. There, he'd done everything he could. He stood slowly, knowing now he shouldn't make any abrupt moves, and stared down at her. She was still in a tight little ball, her hands, now freed of him, tucked inside the covers.

She'd eaten a good bit of the soup. She wouldn't starve. She was warm. She was clean. He'd smoothed antibiotic cream on the worst of the scratches and cuts. He looked toward the front door, then the front windows. He pulled down the shades and closed the curtains. Now no one could see in. He slid the bolts home on the windows. To get in, someone would have to shatter them. He walked to the back door in the kitchen and flipped the dead bolt. The door didn't have a chain. He pulled one of the kitchen chairs over and shoved it beneath the doorknob. Someone could shove the door open, but the chair feet would screech on the floor and certainly wake him up.

He looked at her one last time. "If you wake up, just call me. My name's Ramsey. I'll be here with you. You're safe now. All right? If you have to use the bathroom, it's just beyond the kitchen, behind you. It's clean. I just washed up in there yesterday."

The covers moved just a little bit. Good, she'd heard him. But she didn't make a sound, not even that gut-wrenching mewling noise.

His bed was on the far side of the single room. He remained fully clothed. He put both the rifle and his Smith & Wesson on the small table by the bed, right next to the reading lamp. He carefully marked the page of the thriller he was reading and set it on the floor.

He left the single lamp lit. If she awoke during the night, he didn't want her to be terrified in the dark.

He didn't sleep for a long time. When he did finally, he dreamed there was a man's face staring in through the window at the little girl. He awoke and walked to the window, stumbling with fear and panic, but there wasn't any face staring in. The curtains were tightly drawn. He couldn't help it, he pulled the curtains open. He looked into the darkness and saw instead the contorted face of someone else, the woman in the courtroom who'd screamed at him that she would kill him.

He awoke at dawn at the sound of that ghastly mewling.

TWO

The child's face was leached of color, he could tell that even in the early-morning light that was mixed with the stark overlay of lamplight. Her eyes were wide open, staring up at him, her fear so palpable he could feel it crawling inside his skin.

"No," he said very slowly, not moving. "It's all right. It's me. Ramsey. I'm here to take care of you. I won't hurt you. Did you have a nightmare?"

She didn't move, just lay there, staring up at him. Then, very slowly, she shook her head. He saw her arms move beneath the covers, saw her small hands come up over the top. The small hands were clenched. The bandages on her thin wrists looked obscene.

"Don't be afraid. Please."

It was getting lighter quickly. He turned the lamp off. Her eyes were light blue, large in her thin face, her pupils dilated. She had a thin straight nose, dark lashes and eyebrows, a rounded chin, and two dimples. She was a pretty little girl, and she'd be beautiful when she smiled and those dimples deepened. "Are you in any pain?"

She shook her head.

He felt profound relief. "Can you tell me your name?"

She just stared at him, all frozen and tense, as if she were just waiting for her chance to run, to escape him.

"Would you like to go to the bathroom?"

He saw it in her eyes and smiled. Her kidneys were working. Everything seemed to be working fine except she couldn't speak. He started to touch her, to help her up, but didn't. He kept his voice low, utterly matter-of-fact. "The bathroom is on the other side of the kitchen. The kitchen's just behind you. Do you need any help?"

Slowly, she shook her head. He waited. She didn't move. Then he realized she didn't want to get up with him watching her.

He smiled and said, "I'm going to make some coffee. I'll see what I have that a little kid would like to eat, all right?"

Since he knew she wasn't going to answer, he just nodded and left her.

He didn't hear anything until the bathroom door shut. He heard the lock click into place.

He shook some Cheerios into one of the bright blue painted bowls and set the skimmed milk beside it. At least it wouldn't clog her arteries. He went to his store of fresh fruit. There were only two peaches left. He'd bought a half dozen, but eaten all the rest. He sliced one on the cereal.

He waited. He'd heard the toilet flush, then nothing more. Had something happened?

He waited some more. He didn't want to terrify her by knocking on the door. But finally too much time had passed. He lightly tapped his knuckles against the pine bathroom door. "Sweetheart? You all right?"

He heard nothing at all. He frowned at the locked door. Well, he'd been stupid. She probably believed she was safe from him now. She'd probably never come out willingly.

He poured himself a large mug of black coffee and sat down beside the bathroom door, his long legs stretched out nearly reaching the opposite wall. His black boots were scuffed and comfortable as old slippers. He crossed his ankles.

He began to talk. "I'd sure like to know your name. 'Sweetheart' is all right, but it's not the same as a real name. I know you can't talk. That's no problem now that I understand. I could give you a pencil and a piece of paper and you could write your name down for me. That sounds good, doesn't it?"

Not a whisper of sound.

He drank his coffee, rolled his shoulders, then relaxed against the wall, and said, "I'll bet you've got a mom who's really worried about you. I can't help you until you come out and write down your name and where you're from. Then I can call your mother."

He heard that soft mewling again. He took another drink of coffee. "Yeah, I bet your mom is really worried about you. Wait a minute. You're too young to know how to write, aren't you? Maybe you're not. I don't know. I don't have any kids."

Not a sound.

"Well, so much for that. Okay. Come on out now and have some break-fast. I have Cheerios and a sliced peach. All I bought was skimmed milk, but you can't tell any difference by the taste. You just don't want to look at it. It's all runny and thin. The peach is really good, sweet as anything. I ate four of them since I bought them two days ago. You're getting the second to the last one. I'll make you some toast too, if you'd like. I've got some straw-berry jam. Come on out. I'll bet you're getting hungry.

"Listen, I'm not going to hurt you. I didn't hurt you yesterday, did I? Or last night? No, and I didn't hurt you this morning. You can trust me. I was a Boy Scout when I was young, a real good one. That person who hurt you, he won't come anywhere near here. If he does, I'll shoot him. Then I'll beat the crap out of him. Well, I didn't mean to say that exactly, but you know, I'm not around kids very often. I've got three nieces and two nephews I see at least once a year and I like them. They're my brothers' kids. I taught the girls how to play football last Christmas. Do you like football?"

No sound.

He remembered his sister-in-law Elaine cheering when Ellen, her ten-year-old daughter, had caught a ten-yard pass in the makeshift end zone. "I'll try to be careful with my language. But you can count on this. If that monster comes anywhere close, I'll make him real sorry for hurting you. I promise.

"Please come out. The sunrise is beautiful. Would you like to see it? There are lots of pinks and soft grays and even some oranges. It's going to happen pretty quick now."

The lock clicked open. The door slowly opened. She stood there wear-ing his undershirt that came to her small feet and was nearly falling off her shoulders.

"Hi," he said easily, not moving a muscle. "You want some cereal now?"

She nodded.

"Can you help me up?" He held out his hand to her.

He saw the fear, the wild panic in her eyes. She looked at his hand as if it were a snake about to bite her. She scooted around him and ran into the kitchen. Okay, it was too soon for her to begin to trust him. "The milk's on the counter," he called out. "Can you reach it?"

He walked very slowly back into the kitchen. She was sitting in the cor-ner, pressed against the wall, the bowl of cereal hugged to her chest. Her face was very nearly into that bowl, her dark brown hair in thick tangles, hiding her face.

He said nothing, poured himself some more coffee, slid two slices of wheat bread into the long-handled metal toaster, and held it over the wood-stove. It only took about two minutes to brown the toast on each side. He sat down in one of the two kitchen chairs, straddling the back. The other one was still shoved beneath the back doorknob.

It came to him quite clearly at that moment that he wasn't about to give her over to strangers. She was his responsibility and he willingly shouldered it. No, he couldn't begin to imagine what they'd do to her in a hospital: doctors, nurses, lab people, all of them poking around, terrifying her, shrinks showing her dolls and asking what the man had done to her, male doctors not understanding, treating her as if she were like any other little girl, when she wasn't. No, none of that, not now. And then the sheriff would get involved. Well, he would speak to the sheriff, but not yet. Let her ease a bit more. Let her come to trust him, just a little.

"Would you like a slice of toast? I've learned how to work this toast holder really well. I haven't burned any bread now for nearly a week."

The small head shook back and forth.

"Okay, I'll eat both slices. If you change your mind, I've got some really good strawberry jam, made right down there in Dillinger by a Mrs. Harper. She's been here for all of her sixty-four years.

"I've been here for nearly two weeks now. I come from San Francisco. This cabin was built by the grandfather of a friend of mine. He loaned it to me. I've never been here before. It's a beautiful place. Maybe later you can tell me where you come from. I wanted to be alone, to be completely away from everything and everyone, to be isolated, you know what I mean? No, I don't guess you'd have any idea, would you?

"Who said that life is too much with us? Maybe I did and just forgot. So much stuff can happen to you when you're grown-up, but then you're supposed to be able to handle it. But you're a little kid. Nothing bad should have happened to you. I'll fix things if I can.

"But you know," he continued slowly, eyeing the strips of undershirt on her wrists and ankles, thinking of that small battered body, knowing she'd been raped, "I think we should see a doctor, maybe in a couple of days, then we should see the sheriff. I hope Dillinger has a sheriff."

The mewling sounds began. She laid the empty cereal bowl on the floor beside him and raised her face. She began shaking her head, back and forth, back and forth, the mewling sounds coming from the back of her throat, raw and ugly.

He felt goose bumps rise on his arms. "You don't want to see a doctor?"

She pressed hard against the wall, her legs up, the undershirt wrapped around her like a white tent, her head tucked in, and she was rocking.

"Okay, we won't go anywhere at all. We'll stay right here all safe and snug. I've got lots of food. Did I tell you that I went into Dillinger just two days ago? I got stuff even a kid would like. I've got hot dogs and some of those old-fashioned buns that don't taste like anything, French's mustard, and some baked beans. I cut up onions in the beans, add mustard and some catsup, then put it in a pot on the stove for about twenty minutes. That sounds good, doesn't it?"

She stopped rocking.

Slowly, she turned her face toward him. She pushed back her hair.

"You like hot dogs?"

She nodded.

"Good. I do too. I bought some of those old-fashioned potato chips. The real greasy kind that makes your hands all oily. Do you like potato chips?"

She nodded again. She eased a little bit.

The kid liked food. It was a start. "Did you mind the skimmed milk?"

She shook her head.

What now? "Do you mind if I eat my toast? It's getting cold." He didn't wait for her to nod again, just smiled at her and began to butter his toast. When he'd slathered strawberry jam on one slice, he held it out to her. "You want to try this?"

She stared at that piece of toast with a glob of jam about ready to fall over the edge. "Let me put it on a napkin." Thank heaven he'd bought napkins.

He handed it to her. She took three fast bites, hardly chewing, then sighed and ate more slowly. She licked strawberry jam off her lower lip. For the first time she looked happy.

"Has it been a long time since you've eaten?"

She was chewing slowly on a bite of toast. She seemed to think about it. Then she nodded slowly.

"I see I've got to ask you only yes or no questions. Do you feel better this morning?"

Fear washed all the color from her face.

She was looking at her bandaged wrist holding the half slice of toast.

"I'll put some more medicated cream on your wrists and ankles after you finish your toast." He said nothing more, ate his own toast. What about the rest of her body? He knew he should examine her again but he didn't want to, not with her awake and terrified.

When they'd both finished, he rose and said as he walked away from her into the living area, "Would you like to have a bath? I can heat some water over the stove and pour it into the tub. I've got a couple of really big pans that work fine." He knew without looking at her that she was probably shaking her head, pressed against the kitchen wall. "You're a big girl. You can bathe yourself, right?" He turned, smiling toward her.

Slowly, she rose. She nodded.

"I've got some shampoo in the bathroom. Can you wash your own hair? Good. Then I can put more cream on your wrists and ankles. There are a couple of other spots that need some medicated cream too. Now we've got a clothing problem. Tell you what. When you're through, put the undershirt back on. I'll see what I can scrounge up for you."

He'd gotten so used to silence over the past two weeks that hearing himself talk on and on felt strange. He felt the echo of his own voice inside himself.

After he'd heated enough hot water and poured it into the tub, he heated more for her to rinse her hair and set the pots beside the tub. While she was in the bathroom, he sat down at the old Olivetti typewriter that had belonged to his mom. It felt comfortable hammering away at those dinosaur keys. He put on his glasses and began reading what he'd written the day before.

He didn't know how long he read. But suddenly he looked up to see her standing there beside his desk, making no noise, just standing there, her hair wet and tangled around her face, her wrists and ankles raw and ugly, her face shiny and clean, wearing his undershirt.

"Hi," he said, taking off his glasses. "I'm sorry I didn't hear you come out. When I work I tend to forget where I am. Why don't you come over and sit on the couch."

He took his own comb, washed it first, then spent the next ten minutes combing the tangles out of her hair. Then he put more medicated cream on her wrists and ankles and bandaged them again. He knew he had to check her over but he couldn't see himself pulling off that undershirt. No, he'd have to be more devious. He rose. "Now, clothes for you."

He wasn't about to put her back into what she was wearing when he'd found her. He could only begin to imagine what sorts of memories those clothes would bring her.

"You're going to be a Ralph Lauren Polo girl. What do you think?" It was a long-sleeved soft wool pullover sweater. At least it would keep her warm. No underwear, no pants, no shoes.

He handed her the sweater. "Why don't you change in the bathroom?"

She left him. This time she came back in five minutes. He was gaining ground. The sweater came to her ankles, the sleeves flopping a foot beyond her hands. He rolled the sleeves up to her elbows. She looked ridiculous and endearing.

What was one to do with a little kid?

"Do you know the capital of Colorado?"

She nodded. He pulled out a map then realized he didn't know if she could read. Well, it didn't matter. She pointed to Denver. It had a red star beside it. So she lived in Colorado.

"That's really good. I don't think my nieces and nephews know the capital of any state, even Pennsylvania, where they live. Do you know where we are?"

Fear, cold, frozen fear.

He said easily, "We're in the Rockies, about a two-hour drive southwest of Denver. There aren't any ski resorts close by, so it's pretty empty. Still, it's a really pretty place. Do you watch *Star Trek?*"

She nodded, some color coming back into her face.

"I'm told the local folks call the mountain peaks opposite us the Ferengi Range."

She opened her mouth and rubbed her fingers over her teeth.

He laughed. "That's it. All the peaks are jagged and crooked and spaced funny. Ferengi teeth."

The sleeves of his shirt were dragging on the floor again. He leaned forward to roll them up. She made that deep mewling sound and ran over to the wall by the fireplace. She curled up just as she had in the kitchen.

He'd scared her. Slowly, he got up and walked to the sofa. He sat down.

"I'm sorry I scared you. All I wanted to do was roll up your sleeves. Your arms aren't quite as long as mine yet. I should have told you what I intended. Can I roll up your sleeves? I think there are some safety pins in the kitchen drawer. If I can pin them up, you won't have to worry about them."

She got up and started to walk to him. One step, and she paused. Another step. Another pause, studying him, weighing if she could trust him, wondering if he wouldn't turn on her. Finally she was beside him. She looked up at his face. He smiled and slowly lifted his hand. He rolled up the sleeves. Then he said, "I can try to braid your hair. It won't be great but at least you won't have your hair in your face."

The braid wasn't all that bad. He fastened the end with a rubber band that had come around the bag of peaches.

"The sun's really bright. It's not too cold out. If I bundle you up, would you like to go outside?"

He should have known. She was gone in a flash, into the kitchen. He knew she was against the damned wall. At least she didn't lock herself in the bathroom.

What to do?

Whatever he did with her, he had to do it slowly, really slowly.

Thank God there were some old magazines in the cabin. He said, "Would you like to look at the photos? If you like, we could look at them together and I could read to you what they say about the photos."

Finally, she nodded slowly. "First let me get those safety pins and fasten your arms up."

Then she followed him into the living area. It was tough because she didn't want to get anywhere close to him. The magazine ended up between them on the sofa. At least he got her to wrap the afghan around her.

He looked over at her and said, "Socks."

She blinked and cocked her head to one side.

"I was worried about you walking around in your bare feet. Do you want to try some of my socks? They'll look funny and come up to your neck. Maybe you could practice to be a clown. You could wear my socks and see if I laugh. What do you say?"

The socks were a big hit. She didn't try to be funny, but she did give one tiny smile when she pulled them over her knees.

It took them nearly an hour to get through a *People* magazine from the previous October. He didn't think he ever wanted to see a picture of Cindy again. She was on every other page. He looked up after reading about a movie star's painful reunion with her long-lost brother. She was asleep, her cheek on her hands, resting on the arm of the sofa. He smoothed the afghan around her and went back to his typewriter.

He nearly knocked his glasses off, he roared up out of his chair so quickly. That horrible low mewling sound was louder this time. She was having a nightmare, twisting inside the afghan, her small face flushed, strained with fear. He had to touch her, no choice.

He shook her shoulder. "Wake up, sweetheart. Come on, wake up."

She opened her eyes. She was crying.

"Oh no." He didn't think, just sat down and pulled her onto his lap. "I'm so sorry, baby. It's all right now." He held her close, gently pressing her head against his chest, pulling the afghan around her to keep her warm. One of his socks was dangling off her left foot. He pulled it back up and tucked her in tighter against him.

"It's all right now. I won't let anyone hurt you. I swear it to you. No one will ever hurt you again."

He realized she was frozen against him. He'd terrified her but good. But he didn't let her go. If ever she needed another person, it was now, and he was the only one available. He kept whispering to her, telling her over and over that she was safe, that he'd never let anyone hurt her again. He spoke on and on until he finally felt her begin to loosen. Finally, he heard her give a huge sigh, then, miracle of miracles, she was asleep again.

It was early afternoon. He was getting hungry, but it could wait. He wasn't about to disturb her. She was nestled against him, her head nearly in his armpit. He rearranged her just a bit, then picked up his book. She whimpered in her sleep. He pulled her closer. She smelled sweet, that unique child sweet. His eyes feral, he said low toward the window, "You come anywhere close, you bastard, and I'll blow your head off."

THREE

The morning rain slammed against the cabin windows, driven hard by a gusting westerly wind. Ramsey sat beside her on the sofa, a good foot between them, one of the many novels he'd brought with him to the cabin in his hand, reading quietly to her as he'd done for the past three days. She was getting more at ease with him, not jerking away from him anymore if he happened to startle her.

His voice was quiet and deep as he read to her. "Mr. Phipps didn't know what he was going to do. He could go back to his wife and deal with her, or he could give up and leave her to all the men who wanted her, all the rich men who would give her what she wanted. But then, he'd never given up in his life." He paused. What was coming, he saw in a quick scan, wouldn't be good for a child. No, thinking about killing his wife wouldn't be cool for her to hear. He should never have begun this one. He cleared his throat.

The words blurred as he said quietly, pretending still to read, "But he realized that he had another choice. His little girl was waiting at home for him. He loved her more than he loved himself, and that was saying something. In fact, he loved his little girl more than he'd loved anything or anyone in his life."

She was sitting very quietly beside him. That foot was still between them. He had no idea whether or not she was listening to him. At least she was warm. She was wearing one of his undershirts, a gray one with a V-neck, a cardigan sweater over it that nearly touched the floor, and the afghan pulled to her chin against the chill of the incessant rain and wind. He was getting better at braiding her hair. If she weren't so very silent, perhaps with a small smile on her face, you could take her for any kid, sitting next to her dad, while he read her a story.

But she wasn't like any kid. Slowly, he looked back down at the book. He said with a feeling that was suddenly crystal clear and true inside him, "He wanted his little girl to know that she would always be safe with him. He would protect her and love her for as long as he lived. She was sweet and gentle and he knew she loved him. But she was scared and he understood that. She'd been through so much, too much for a little girl to have to bear. But she'd come through it. She was the bravest little girl he'd ever known. Yes, she'd survived it, and now she would be with him.

"He thought of the little mountain cabin in the Rockies with its meadow of brightly blooming columbine and Indian paintbrush. He knew she'd like it there. She'd be free and he'd hear her laugh again. It had been a long time since he'd heard her laugh. He walked into the house, saw her standing there by the kitchen door, holding a small stuffed monkey. She smiled at him and held out her arms."

He turned to her and very slowly, very lightly, touched his fingertips to her ear. "Do you have a stuffed animal?"

She didn't look at him, just kept staring straight ahead out the cabin windows, at the gray rain he wondered would ever stop. Then she nodded.

"Is it a monkey?"

She shook her head.

"A dog?"

She turned to him then and tears pooled in her eyes. She nodded.

"It's all right. Hey, he's not stuffed, is he? He's a real dog? I promise, you'll be back soon enough with your dog. What kind is he?"

This time she reached over for the pen and paper he'd set on the table by the sofa the previous evening. This was the first time she'd paid any attention to it. He felt a leap of hope. She drew a dog with lots of spots on it.

"A Dalmatian?"

She nodded, then she smiled, a very small smile, but that's what it was, a smile. She tugged at his sleeve. She actually touched him.

"You want the story to go on?"

She nodded. She moved just a little bit closer to him and snuggled down into the afghan. He said, "Funny thing, she wanted a dog, but she loved her stuffed monkey more than anything. His name was Geek. He had very long arms and a silly brown hairy face. She took him everywhere with her. One day when she and her daddy were walking across their meadow in the mountains, they heard this loud sound. It was a milk delivery truck. 'Why did it come up here on our mountain?' the little girl asked her papa.

" 'He's bringing us our weekly milk supply,' her father said. Sure enough there was milk in the truck, but what the man had really brought was a litter of puppies, all of them pure white. Soon the six puppies were yapping at each other and chasing each other around the meadow, hiding in among the flowers, rolling over on their backs, all in all having a wonderful time.

"But Geek wasn't happy. He sat on the porch, his long arms at his side, watching the puppies steal the little girl's attention. He heard her laugh and saw her play with the puppies, saw them climbing all over her, licking her face, whining when she didn't scratch their tummies quickly enough. His monkey head dropped to his legs. He was very unhappy.

"Then suddenly she came back to where he was sitting on the porch. She picked him up and gave him a big kiss on his hairy face. 'Come and play with the babies, Geek,' she said to him. 'Daddy said they have to go back to their own home soon. The milkman brought them here so we could play with them.'

"When Geek thought about it later, he realized that he'd liked the puppies, once he'd gotten used to them. They were sort of cute. Now that he thought about it, maybe he could find a puppy and bring it to the little girl. He went to sleep snuggled up next to her, and he dreamed about a little white puppy that would have black spots appear on it when it was older."

Ramsey made a big production of closing the novel. "There, what do you think of Geek the monkey?"

She picked up the pen and paper. She labored over it a moment, then sat back. He looked down to see a stick figure little girl holding what must be Geek. She was hugging him tightly and she was smiling.

"That's great," he said. Was she sitting right next to him? Hot damn, she was.

It was he who fell asleep, his head flopped back against the sofa. When he awoke several hours later, she was snuggled against him, her head on his chest, boneless as children are when they are utterly relaxed. He leaned down and kissed the top of her head. She smelled like his shampoo mixed with little kid. He liked it. He eased her off him, covered her well, and went to the kitchen. He made himself some coffee, sat down at the kitchen table, and listened to the rain pelt against the cabin roof.

She'd been with him nearly four days now. There'd been no sign of anybody near the cabin. He'd rather wanted the man who'd abused her to show up. He'd like to have the chance to kill him himself. Where was that bastard? Probably long gone. How much longer should he keep her with him, hidden away from the outside world? At least he didn't have to worry about her health. The second day he'd given her a third of one of his sleeping pills. When she was deeply asleep, he'd examined her again, checked all the bruises and welts, applied more antibiotic cream, then covered her again. She was healing nicely. She'd never stirred, thank God.

He wondered if she really had a Dalmatian. He realized, too, that he'd put himself in the place of her real father. Well, too bad. As long as she was with him, she was his. But what about her parents? Had they been there when she'd been taken? Maybe they were responsible, maybe they'd allowed it to happen? What were they like? No, it didn't matter, at least not yet. But, of course, it did matter.

He felt good. This was the first time she'd actually gotten close to him. It had taken his falling asleep for her to get closer, but it was a start, a definite start.

He smiled toward the stove, got up, and opened a can of chicken noodle soup. She liked the soup with toasted cheese sandwiches.

THAT evening after they'd roasted the last two hot dogs, eaten the rest of the baked beans, and he'd managed to make some strawberry Jell-O that wasn't rubbery at the bottom, he said to her, "Why don't I say some girl names. If I happen to hit your name, you can nod three times or pull on my arm or kick me in my shin. Okay?"

She didn't move. Her expression didn't change. Her lack of enthusiasm didn't bode well.

"Okay, let's give it a shot. How about Jennifer? That's a really pretty name. Is it yours?"

She didn't move.

"How about Lindsey?"

Nothing.

"Morgan?"

She turned her back on him. That made her feelings clear enough. She didn't want to play a name game. But why?

"Draw me a picture of your mommy."

She turned back in an instant. Her fingers fluttered over the blank sheet of paper. She didn't look at him, just stared at that paper. Then she began to draw. It was a stick figure wearing a skirt, sneakers, and a head of curly hair. The figure was holding what looked like a box with a knob in the front of it.

He said then, "That's just excellent. Is her hair dark brown like yours?"

She shook her head.

"Red?"

She smiled hugely and nodded. Then she drew more curly hair around the stick woman's head.

"I guessed red because it's my favorite color. She's got really curly hair? Is it long?"

She shrugged her shoulders.

"Okay, it's medium. Is she holding a box?"

She shook her head. She pointed to people on the cover of a magazine on the coffee table. Then clicked her index finger again and again to her thumb.

"Ah," he said. "That's a camera. She's a photographer?"

She nodded, again pointing to the pictures.

"And she photographs people?"

She nodded happily. Then, suddenly, her face fell. She was thinking about her mother, missing her, wondering where she was, and there was not a thing he could do about it. He said, "Now draw me a picture of your daddy."

She clutched the pen the way one would a dagger. Then she made that horrible mewling sound in her throat.

"It's all right, sweetheart. I'm here. You're safe."

Then, somewhat to his surprise, she began to draw a man stick figure and he was playing a guitar and his mouth was open. Her father was a singer? Then she pressed down so hard the pencil tip broke. So could her father have been the one who'd left her vulnerable? Abused her? No, certainly a father wouldn't do that to his own kid. Yeah, right. With everything he knew about life, everything he'd watched and dealt with, he knew, of course, it was very possible. He wanted to ask her questions about her dad, but seeing her reaction, he let it wait.

She wadded up the paper. She slowly pulled away from him and drew up into a ball, pressed against the back of the sofa.

It would take time, he knew. Time. But how much should he take?

"I'M not going to leave you here in the Jeep. It's not safe. You're going to come with me. Here, hold my hand. Can you do that?" He paused a moment, and lightly touched her cheek with his fingertips. "It's all right, sweetheart, I know you're worried about this, but it'll be all right. No one's going to hurt you. You've got me now and I'm big and strong. I know karate. I'm good at it. Sort of like Chuck Norris. You ever hear of him? He can lay flat more bad guys than Godzilla."

She made some chopping motions with her hands.

"Yeah, that's right. I know you don't want to wear those clothes, but it'll just be for a little while, until I can buy you some new things. Then you can change immediately and we'll throw these out. Better yet, we'll leave them here at the store." He'd washed the yellow jeans and the light yellow shirt in the bathtub along with his own T-shirts and underwear. He'd hated having her put the clothes on, but there was no choice. He couldn't very well take her into Mr. Peete's Lucky General Store wearing one of his sweaters or undershirts, and barefoot. He chucked her under the chin. "Now, let's go. This will be an adventure. Don't worry. I'll keep you safe. Think of me as your own Geek the monkey, only much bigger. Can you imagine what Geek would do if someone tried to hurt you? I'm sure you can. Geek and I, we're the good-guy monkeys. You ready?"

She smiled, a very brief smile, but he knew she didn't want to leave the Jeep. But he wasn't about to leave her in here, even with the doors locked. He said, "The faster we get in there the faster we can leave."

Finally, she nodded. He lifted her out of the Jeep and set her onto the rough sidewalk. He locked the Jeep door and held out his hand to her. Slowly, she took his hand.

"Real good," he said and lightly squeezed her hand. "Let's go shop 'til we drop."

The Lucky General Store wasn't a Kmart; it wasn't even close, only about one-twentieth the size. When they walked in the door, she shrank against his leg. He smiled down at her. "You're doing great. Now, let's get you some jeans first, then some shirts. Yeah, it's this way. You point when you see something you like." He could feel her trembling against his leg. He picked her up. In moments, she eased.

The pants she was wearing were a five tall. And the shirt was a 4–6. There was a smiling woman in the kids' section, heavy and pretty, with really white teeth. Ramsey said with a friendly smile, "We need some clothes for my little girl."

It didn't take long. Mildred looked her over and started selecting clothes. "His little girl," as Mildred called her, even pointed to a lime green T-shirt. They ended up with two pairs of jeans, one red, the other plain blue jeans, and four tops, all in bright colors. Her new sneakers were orange. Her socks were green, red, and blue. The lightweight jacket she liked was orange and green patterned. That was a mixed blessing. On the one hand, she'd stand out like a beacon. On the other hand, seeing her go for the vivid colors was positive. He wasn't about to object.

Mildred smiled really big when she showed off her new clothes. "You look a treat, honey. What's your name?"

Ramsey said easily, "She doesn't talk, but she hears everything. She does look pretty, doesn't she?"

"Orange and green are sure your colors. How old are you, honey?"

She held up six fingers.

"Six years old. Aren't you a bright girl. And so pretty. Your mama is going to be so pleased."

She froze. Ramsey said quickly, picking up a bright blue down jacket that looked as though it would fit her, "It might get really cold still. It's still only the middle of April."

"You're right about that. We'll have at least two more snowstorms before it finally decides to heat up."

He nodded. "Yes, better not take any chances." He helped her on with the jacket. He then stepped back and stroked his chin. "You look great in it. You like it? The arms are a bit on the long side, but you'll grow into it soon enough."

She was smiling. She fingered the jacket sleeves. She nodded.

"Your family up here for the week?"

"Yes," he said. "Beautiful country. We're really enjoying ourselves."

"I've lived here all my life. You can lay a twenty on two more snowstorms. Maybe they'll hit after you're gone. You never know."

He didn't know what else to say. They'd been here too long. He wanted to get her back to the cabin. He gave Mildred a big smile, then said, "Wave good-bye to Mildred."

She nodded to Mildred instead.

He leaned down, saying quietly so Mildred couldn't hear, "Can I pick you up now?"

To his pleasure, she raised her arms. He tossed a bottle of baby shampoo into the cart on the way to the checkout counter. No one had given them one strange look. Everyone had been open and friendly. No more than ten people had seen them together.

Mr. Peete, the owner, was at the checkout counter. "Goodness, kid, you'll be the best-dressed little girl in the Ferengi Range. Here, have a Tootsie Pop on the house, since your daddy's paid our overhead for the week."

They were out of the store after one hundred and sixty-nine dollars, and thirty-five minutes. He put the packages in the Jeep then said, "Now, I've got a surprise for you. See that bookstore? Let's go." Again, she let him carry her.

This stop took nearly as long before they got back to the Jeep. He unlocked the door and put her inside. Then he straightened and stopped cold. Someone was looking at him.

FOUR

The hair prickled on the back of his neck. He slowly turned but didn't see anyone who seemed out of place or overly interested in them. There, in the alley beside the Union 76 gas station, was there a movement? He stared hard, not moving, feeling a light breeze ruffle his hair. There was nothing at all.

Still he didn't like it. He'd never before ignored his gut. He quickly climbed into the Jeep. She hadn't noticed anything, thank God. She'd pulled the afghan he'd brought to keep her warm close around her, nearly hiding her face. She looked like she was ready to fall asleep. Was she tired or did she just want to escape her fear in sleep?

He looked toward the sheriff's office down Boulder Street. Cops might be looking for her. He knew he couldn't keep her with him indefinitely. She had parents. At least she had a mother she loved, if her smile was any clue. He'd asked her if her mom was as cute as she was and she'd smiled. Her father? He'd find out eventually. But her mother, at least, had to be worried sick about her. But he couldn't do it, not quite yet. What the hell had happened? He'd teased over the questions for the past six days, but hadn't found any answers. He had to do something soon, but watching her small face pinch with fear when he turned her over to strangers wasn't in him yet. The more time she had with him, hopefully, the stronger she'd be. Actually, it was she herself holding him back.

He looked down at the sleeping child. There was some color in her cheeks. The taut gray look she'd had even in sleep since he'd found her was finally gone. She looked like a normal little girl. He smiled at the bright colors she was wearing. He remembered the previous evening when they'd settled down for him to read to her after dinner. He'd brought up seeing the sheriff again.

This time she hadn't just shaken her head. She'd grabbed his hand and clung to him. And then shaken her head. He hated that awful empty fear in her eyes.

"All right," he'd said. "We'll give it a while longer. But your parents, kiddo, they've got to be frantic for you."

She lowered her head and began to cry.

He wanted to curse, but he didn't. He hadn't snarled a nice meaningful curse in four days, at least out loud, in her hearing.

She seemed terrified that if anyone knew where she was, parents included, she would be hurt again. And she just might. How had he gotten her the first time? Had her parents been careless with her? Left her alone in a shopping mall? Or had the kidnapper simply walked into the girl's yard and taken her?

Maybe he'd go to the sheriff in a couple of days. Almost as soon as he thought it, he was shaking his head. No, she needed more time to trust, to see that he wouldn't let anything happen to her.

But when she was back with her parents, he wouldn't see her again. He wouldn't be able to protect her. They'd failed to protect her before. It could happen again. But the bottom line was, she wasn't his. He'd saved her, but she wasn't his. He didn't know what to do.

He shook his head at himself and speeded up. The Jeep was a work-horse. He loved it. It was a beautiful day, a bit on the cool side, not more than fifty-five degrees, but the sun was bright overhead. There'd been lots of people on the streets. He remembered the feeling of being watched. Had it been real?

He turned at the sound of a low moan. Another nightmare. He leaned over and touched her face. She moved her cheek against his palm, then stilled. He ruffled her hair and cupped her small chin in his palm. She opened her beautiful light blue eyes and blinked up at him. He saw her fear slowly disappear. Her eyes warmed. In that instant he knew he wasn't going to let anyone else have her until he knew for certain that she'd be safe.

"Yeah, yeah, so I'm a big Jell-O. But you know what? Jell-O isn't bad. Another thing, not only are you the best-dressed kid in the Ferengi Range, you're the cutest."

THE next afternoon when he came in from out of doors carrying an arm-ful of logs, she flinched and ducked back behind the sofa.

He stopped immediately. "What's up? What's the matter?"

She tried to smile, but it fell away.

"I surprised you?"

She nodded, relieved that he'd explained it as she'd wanted him to. He smiled. "I'll knock next time. I cut us some more wood for the fireplace and the woodstove. Now, after I get this all set, how about you and I go out into the meadow? I want to show you your surprise. While you were trying on your jeans, I got you something really neat." It was, he knew, the only way he was going to get her outside. Since they were in town, she'd refused even to step out onto the front porch. It was time to get her into the fresh air.

Still, she hung back, her small face pale, her expression wary.

"It's really neat," he said again, not acting all that excited, "your sur-prise, I mean. You need your blue down jacket. It's a little cold out there."

She looked adorable in her stiff new jeans, her orange sneakers as bright as neon lights, red socks, and a bright orange shirt with lime green apples all over it. He was braiding her hair better each time he tried. She looked fresh and sweet and scared. He hated this fear in her, but it had only been a week since he'd found her. Both of them had made strides.

Had the man gotten her easily because she was mute and couldn't scream for help?

"It's a really great surprise. Hey, would I lie to you? Nah, put on your jacket. You can take it off when you work up a good sweat."

She still hesitated. He set the fire, rose, and waited, leaning his shoulders against the mantel.

Finally, she nodded and ran to fetch her jacket that was hanging next to his. Of course she couldn't reach it. He got it down for her and helped her into it. It fit her great, except for the too-long sleeves that he rolled up.

"Your surprise is going to have you running around. Soon you'll want to take it off."

He led her out into the middle of the meadow and pointed to a dragon-tail kite. He'd spread it out on the ground in all its glory. She stood there and stared, then smiled, a huge smile that deepened her dimples. It was the first time he'd seen a smile like that.

"You ever fly a kite before?"

Even without her squealing with pleasure, he knew he'd scored big. She was so excited she could barely keep still. He handed her the rod, waited until she picked up the red diamond body, and arranged the long glittery dragon tail out behind. She let out some of the string.

"You're good at this."

She smiled and let out some more string.

She knew what she was doing. Who had taught her? Her mother? He yelled, "Okay, let her rip!"

She began running across the flat meadow, feeding out the line. He released the kite when he felt it catch the wind. He shouted, "You've got liftoff!" She stopped running, drew back a bit, and turned the rod a bit to the left. The long multicolored tail whirled about in a big circle.

"Great, let's see you do some more."

She was a lot better at flying it than he would have been. The kid was really good. He watched her move her hand first this way, then that, then flip her wrist, and the dragon's tail whipped about and whirled around and around, turning back in on itself, then streaming out again, long and shining in the wind. He didn't know how she did it, but she turned her wrist back, wiggled it a bit, and that shimmery tail rippled just like a real dragon's tail.

Whoever had taught her was an expert.

She made no sound at all, but she seemed to be having the time of her life. He stood back and watched her. It was the best twelve-dollar investment he'd ever made.

He ended up sitting on the steps of the cabin, not letting her out of his sight.

Time and his thoughts slowed, leaving only the child who was flying the dragon kite amid the meadow of bright columbine.

Then, suddenly, there was a shot, startling and clear in the silence. The kite dipped and plowed earthward, landing in a bush. She didn't hesitate for an instant, not even to look around. She started to run back toward him as fast as she could.

He was to her in a moment, grabbed her up on the run, and turned back, carrying her into the cabin. Another shot rang out from behind him just as he slammed the door with his foot. He set her down behind the couch. "Stay here. Don't move."

He shoved his pistol into his belt and picked up his rifle. He crouched next to the window, scanned the far forest, searching for something that was different, something that didn't belong in his world. There came another shot, then another, but he couldn't hear any bullet impacts.

He heard a man shout and another man answer. They were some distance away, maybe fifty yards from the front of the cabin, at the edge of the forest. There were no other voices. There were two men, then. He said quietly to her, "Stay behind the sofa, sweetheart. It will be all right. Just stay there. Remember what I told you. I'm big and strong. I'm also mean when I have to be. Nobody will get to hurt you."

He looked back out the window. To his surprise, two men stumbled out of the thick fir trees, each carrying a rifle. He had the closer one in his sights when he saw they were laughing, leaning into each other, one of the men dragging his rifle. He cursed viciously. The idiots were drunk. There was no hunting allowed anywhere near here and here they were shooting and drinking.

The closer man was very tall and thin, he could tell that even though he was wearing thick dark corduroy pants and a heavy dark brown down jacket. He had a plaid hunter's hat on his head. He was waving toward the cabin, yelling, "Hey! Anybody there? We're sorry, we didn't mean anything." Then he giggled as the other man, short, bowlegged, wearing cowboy boots, said, "Yeah, we thought you was a couple of deer. I told Tommy here that deer didn't fly kites."

Ramsey put down his rifle, but held the pistol at his side as he came through the front door out onto the porch.

He was so angry he was shaking. He wanted to bang their heads together, the morons. He yelled at them, "What do you think you're doing firing guns up here? Didn't you see my little girl?"

They waved at him. The drunken idiots actually waved, as if he'd invited them up for a beer. The tall guy called out, "Hey, buddy, it was an accident. Who are you? We didn't think anybody lived up here. We're sorry, real sorry."

The bowlegged guy didn't say a word, just walked along toward him, looking at his rifle or his snakeskin boots, or both.

"You up here a long time?"

When the tall guy asked him the question, Ramsey looked away from the shorter man for an instant, long enough for the man to raise the rifle and aim it at him.

Ramsey didn't think, he fired. He caught the bowlegged guy in his shooting arm as he felt a numbing cold slam against his left thigh. The tall man had his rifle up in an instant, but Ramsey was faster this time. He got him in the shoulder, a clean hit that knocked him backward, off his feet, to the ground.

Ramsey started toward them, then stumbled. He'd been shot in the leg. He hadn't realized it. He yelled, "What the hell do you want? Who are you?"

They were both wounded, cursing, one of the rifles on the ground. The tall guy on the ground managed to jump up, and the two of them had turned and were stumbling back toward the forest. Ramsey raised his Smith & Wesson and fired. He saw a chunk of tree bark fly into the air. He fired again. He heard one of the men yell. Good, he'd gotten one of them with two bullets. He couldn't see them now. They were gone deep into the forest. He wanted to go after them, but he couldn't. He looked down at his thigh. Blood was seeping through the denim. He realized in that instant that he hurt like hell.

Ramsey quickly turned and ran as fast as he could with his gimp leg to the cabin. One of the men still had his gun. He was still at risk. He was in the open and they were hidden in the trees. He saw an old .22 on the ground where the bowlegged guy had dropped it. It was banged up, not very powerful, thank God, but powerful enough to do the job, accurate as hell from close range.

He made the cabin and looked up in shock to see her standing there on the porch, frozen, staring at him. He grabbed her up, ran inside, slamming the door behind him. He felt a new shock of pain in his left leg. He looked down to see his jeans ripped through the outside of his thigh, the blood oozing through the thick denim to run slowly down his leg. He eased her down. She clutched his right leg. She was making those gut-wrenching mewling noises again.

He kept her against his right leg. He didn't want to get any blood on her, that would be all she needed to freak her out all over again. But she'd overcome her fear to come outside to see if he was okay. "I'm all right, sweetheart. The bad men are gone, at least I hope they are. You're really brave, you know that? I'm proud of you. You run really fast and that's good too.

"I didn't lie to you. We kicked butt, didn't we? We beat the bad guys. They're gone." But for how long? What the hell did they want? Who were they? What did they want?

HE was seated on the single chair in the living room. She stood over him when he pulled down his jeans to examine his leg. The bullet had gouged a gash through the outside of his thigh, ripping away skin, a bit of muscle. Not deep, maybe two inches long. It wasn't bad. He was very lucky.

He poured vodka over the wound. It burned like hell, but she was standing right there, so scared, her face whiter than high mountain snow, and he wasn't about to yell. He gritted his teeth and kept pouring until he was as certain as he could be that the wound was clean. It probably needed to be stitched, but he couldn't do that, no way, since he couldn't sterilize a needle and thread. The last thing he needed was an infection. He pulled the skin tightly together over the gash, then put some sterilized gauze over it. Then he ripped some adhesive tape off with his teeth, stretched the tape tight to hold the edges of skin together beneath the gauze, and pressed it down. Pain hissed out between his gritted teeth. She made a small mewling sound. He saw her lay her hand on his right knee. "It's all right. It just hurt a little bit, not bad. That was the worst of it, putting that tape over it." He laid down more tape, making it tighter. He rose slowly, turned slightly away from her, and pulled up his jeans. "Now, sweetheart, let's get some aspirin down my gullet." He took four generic aspirin from Clement's and drank a full glass of orange juice. He laughed and wiped his mouth. "Vitamin C is good stuff, maybe even helpful for a gunshot wound."

His leg hurt, but that was the least of his problems.

He knew she was watching him, fear leaving her face as pale as new snow. He locked the front door, shot home the dead bolt, and fastened the chain. Maybe later he'd go get that old .22 rifle. He knew the men weren't coming back. They had no idea he had no ability to contact the outside world. They'd think he'd called in the troops immediately. He doubted they'd hang around. It would be too dangerous for them. Besides, they were both wounded. They'd have to get help. He had bought himself some time.

He looked down at her, standing there, not an inch from him, and he knew he had to deal with this and he had to deal with it now.

"Let's sit down," he said, and held out his hand. There were some flecks of blood on the back of his hand. He hoped she wouldn't see it.

Slowly, she gave him her hand. He sat beside her on the sofa. He carefully moved the bowl of bloody vodka to the far side of the sofa.

"I don't know who those men were," he said, looking at her full face, willing her not to be afraid, not to worry so much. "Did you recognize either of them?"

She cocked her head to one side. She was thinking, he knew that look. He wore one remarkably like it on occasion. Finally, she shook her head, but he could tell she wasn't completely certain. Well, that was good enough for now.

Maybe it hadn't been only one man who'd taken her. Maybe it had been two men. Maybe it was the men who'd shown up pretending to be drunk to get him out of the cabin, then shooting. Maybe they'd both stayed masked when they'd had her. That meant they hadn't planned to kill her. What was their plan then? Keep her a prisoner and play with her until they were tired of her?

It made the blood pound in his temple. They'd been willing to kill him to get her back? But this time they weren't wearing masks. They wanted her dead now?

That first shot they'd fired hadn't been at him, had it? He couldn't remember. He'd think about it later, go over his memories second by second. Still, it was weird. What was going on? How the devil had they found him?

He'd been a fool. He should have left her in the Jeep in town and told her to keep hidden. Well, he'd done it and there was no undoing it now. It was likely they'd seen him with her in Dillinger the day he'd bought her clothes, the day he'd had her with him, holding her hand while walking to the store, carrying her. He felt the aspirin kick in.

About time.

At the end of it, they'd been shooting to kill. He took her hand in his. "We've got to be really careful now. Okay? I want you to stay close to me." As if she'd stray six inches from him, he thought.

She nodded solemnly.

"We'll get out of this, sweetheart. I promise you that."

Again, she nodded, her little face so serious, so pale and tight that he wanted to cry.

FIVE

The aspirin hadn't worked worth a damn. His thigh was throbbing big time. He couldn't get comfortable and he couldn't get back to sleep. He knew he had a low-grade fever. It was nearly two o'clock in the morning. He got up finally, listened for her breathing, heard it, and knew she was deeply asleep because he was used to the rhythms of her breathing now. He walked as quietly as he could to the kitchen and sat down at the kitchen table, balancing the flashlight so it shone on his leg. He knew he had to get that tape and gauze off to see if the wound was infected. If it was, he would be in the Jeep on his way to the hospital within five minutes. And that would mean the cops since it was a gunshot wound. No hope for it. And he would have to bring her into it, giving her over to the authorities, relinquishing all his protection of her.

He was wearing loose sweats. He pulled down the pants and looked at his swelled thigh. It felt warm to the touch, but that seemed normal to him under the circumstances.

It hurt like hell to pull off the tape and lift the gauze, that had, naturally, stuck to the wound, but he took a long swig of vodka, gritted his teeth, and did it. He stared down at his leg. It was swelled and warm, but there was no redness, no pus, thank God. He poured more vodka over the gash, hissing between his teeth.

He felt her presence, then her small hand on his shoulder. He prayed he didn't look as bad as the wound looked when he said, turning slowly, "Hi, sweetheart. I'm sorry I woke you up. I decided to check my leg. It isn't bad, maybe swelled a bit, and warm, but nothing scary. I'm trying to be really careful. Now, let me bandage it up again."

She carefully took a thick pad of gauze, then waited. With both hands, he pushed the flesh tightly together on the exit wound, then nodded to her. She laid the gauze over it. Then she pulled out a length of tape, laid it over the gauze and his flesh, and pulled it taut. Then she flattened it down with her palm. He couldn't have done it better himself.

"Maybe you're going to be a doctor," he said, wanting to howl from the pain. He felt sticky sweat on his face, imagined he was as gray as one of his old nightshirts. He took several quick deep breaths. "Thanks, sweet-heart. I'm okay, really. Let me get some more tape over this to make sure it holds." He pressed down four more strips.

She stood back, but kept her hand on his shoulder. Every once in a while, she patted him. He appreciated it.

When it was done, he pulled his sweats back up again. "I'd say tomor-row night my leg's going to be all black and blue. Hopefully the swelling will go down a bit by then. Now, let me take some more aspirin." He took three this time.

"You want to go back to bed now?"

She shook her head.

"Me either. You want me to read you a story?"

She shook her head, then mimicked talking.

"You want me to tell you a story?"

She nodded, then, to his delight, she took his hand. He stretched out on the sofa, with her beside him on top of the blanket that covered him, and pulled two more blankets and the afghan over them. The pistol was right beside him on the floor. He settled her against him, feeling the warmth of her against his side, her cheek against his neck. "Once upon a time there was a little princess named Sonya who knew how to fly kites better than anyone in her father's kingdom. One year, her father decided he would have a contest. He knew no one could beat her. She had a special kite, you see, a dragon-tailed kite that could fly higher and make more figures than an ice-skater. There was just one competitor her father worried about. It was Prince Luther from a neighboring kingdom. But he knew she could beat anyone, even Luther, who was a bully and a loudmouth. Do you know what happened at the contest?"

She was lightly snoring. He leaned down and kissed the top of her head. He realized that he'd forgotten all about his damned thigh. He also realized that to this point, his story was pretty bad, probably because he was so tired, his brain woozy. It was lucky she'd fallen back asleep or he would have bored her into yawns.

HE tried to stay off his leg throughout the next day. He stuck to the cabin, sitting by the front window, scanning, forever scanning the meadow and the forest that crept up to the edge. He saw nothing out of the ordinary, and no one.

He was going to lay low today, let himself get stronger, then he'd decide what to do.

He knew she was frightened. He knew it and couldn't do a thing about it. He told her half a dozen stories, and none of them too bad, about the little princess named Sonya who beat the nasty little boy, Luther, in the kite-flying contest, then went on to save her father's life, and cook excellent mushrooms and . . . well, he wouldn't think ahead to the next story. He found it was better if he opened his mouth and let the story come out unrehearsed.

She sat on the floor next to his chair by the window, drawing with one of his pencils. The afternoon shadows were lengthening. He looked down to see a stick woman with curly hair holding a kite, a little stick girl standing next to her, holding a kite the same size as she was. A curved-up line was the woman's smile; there was a curved-up line for the little girl as well.

Her mother had taught her to fly a kite. He praised the drawings. Perhaps he could get her to draw him pictures of the man or men who'd taken her and where they'd taken her, what they'd done to her. But he balked at that. He wasn't a shrink. The last thing he wanted to do was make things worse.

"It's time to make dinner. You hungry, kiddo?"

She nodded enthusiastically and gathered up her pages and the three pencils he'd given her. She laid them carefully on the coffee table, lining up the pages neatly. He realized he did the same thing. Then she held out her hand to him.

He took her hand and made a big deal of her helping him up. His leg hurt like the devil, but that was no surprise. The fever was gone. His wound was still swelled up and warm to the touch. The skin near the wound was turning a little black and blue. He wasn't about to pull off the tape again. Best to leave the leg alone to heal. At least until tomorrow.

They didn't have much left in the larder. Tomorrow he'd either have to go in to Clement's grocery, exposing her yet again, or he'd pack up the Jeep early and they'd get out of here. No matter how he cut it, their location was known. Even if there wasn't danger from the two men he'd wounded, the people who'd sent them now knew where she was. He knew he should drive right to the sheriff's office. He knew it. He also knew he wasn't going to do it, not yet anyway. He remembered those desperate mewling noises she'd made. She might snap. But the bigger issue was: How could he send her back home where she could be kidnapped again?

Now that the danger was clear, he had to get off this mountain. He wanted to call his friend Dillon Savich at the FBI to ask his advice. Of course Savich would tell him to call the FBI. He might even know about her if she'd been abducted. Ever since the Lindbergh baby's kidnapping back in the early '30s, and the resulting tragedy, kidnapping had been the purview of the FBI. But until he could get to Savich, he knew his bottom line was to keep her safe, and that meant, to him, to keep her with him.

Tomorrow, he thought, tomorrow early, they'd get out of here. He did a checklist in his mind of everything he needed to do in the interim before they could leave.

As he opened a can of vegetable soup, he looked at her tearing pieces of lettuce into a big bowl. She had a look of intense concentration on her small face.

"You want French dressing or Italian?"

She picked up the bottle of French dressing.

"Good choice. That was always my favorite when I was your age." He wasn't going to tell her they were leaving until he was ready to load her into the Jeep.

She cocked her head to one side. He realized he did the same thing in just the same way. Had she picked it up from him in only a week? He shook his head, smiling at her. "Yeah, I was once your age. A long time ago. Don't make fun of me because I'm old."

She gave him an impudent grin that was as kid-normal as kicking a soccer ball.

They ate the soup and salad in front of the fireplace. The evening had turned cold, really cold once the sun went down. It was probably in the low forties.

A coyote howled.

JUST after dawn, he unbolted the door, unfastened the chain, and as quietly as he could, he went out into a silent world where he could see his breath. He needed to chop wood for the fireplace and the wood-burning stove. He stood very still, looking everywhere for any sign of something that shouldn't be here. Nothing. He finally laid his Browning Savage down on the ground, really close to his left foot. He looked around again but couldn't see anything out of the ordinary.

He split half a dozen logs before his leg began throbbing so much he had to stop. It would be enough. He'd agreed to leave the cabin the way he'd found it, and that included a goodly amount of split logs. He was cursing softly as he cradled the logs in his arms, pressed his rifle against his side, and carried it all back inside.

The dawn light was gray, the forest line blurred and indistinct. There was no movement, not even an early-morning squirrel dashing between trees. He crossed the cabin threshold to see her jerk bolt upright, mewling deep in her throat, her face ashen.

He quickly set the logs and his rifle down by the fireplace, then went to her. He sat beside her on the sofa. Slowly, because he'd learned never to make any unexpected or quick moves, he gathered her against him. He kissed the top of her head. "It's all right, sweetheart. I had to get some more logs." He wouldn't tell her yet that they were leaving. "You snuggle down again and I'll get the fire going really strong. Okay?"

He laid her back down, the covers in his hands to pull up to her small chin.

"Don't you touch her, you filthy bastard. Step away from her now!"

He and the child both froze at the sound of the woman's voice. He was the stupidest human alive. He'd left the cabin door unlocked. He looked at his Smith & Wesson on the table beside the sofa.

A shot rang out and his gun went flying off the table, skidded across the wooden floor until it was stopped by one of the Indian rugs.

"Try anything at all and the next bullet will go in your head. I promise you that. Get away from her now."

He backed away from her and stood. He turned to see a woman standing in the open doorway, wearing a black down jacket, black jeans and boots, a black knit cap on her head. Her face was very white, her irises showing huge and black. She was holding a Detonics .45 ACP, a nasty little pistol that could blow a man's brains out if he was within twenty feet, which he was.

She looked strung out and quite ready to kill him, but her voice was calm, quiet, filled with hatred. "Move, you creep. I'm not going to tell you again. I don't want you anywhere near her. If I have to blow your head off, I'll do it. Damn you, get away from her!"

"You don't want to kill me. I'm not the one who took her, I swear it to you."

"You perverted piece of filth, just shut up. I saw you touching her. What would you have done to her if I hadn't shown up? Move!" He stepped two feet away from the sofa. She had the gun trained on his chest.

Her eyes darted to the sofa. "Baby, are you all right?"

It was her mother. But how had she found them?

He said, "You really should believe me about this. I'm not the one who hurt her."

"Shut up! Em, are you okay?"

"I found her a week ago in the forest near this cabin. I didn't kidnap her."

"Shut up! Em? What's wrong, baby? Listen to me, he can't hurt you anymore. I'm holding a gun on him. Come here, Em, come to Mama."

She was mewling deep in her throat. She threw back the blankets, looking from him to her mother.

"Get away from him, Em. I want you to come over here to me. I'm going to tie him up and take him to the sheriff. Then neither of us will ever have to be afraid again. I know you understand. Come here now, Em."

The woman raised the gun. She said more to herself than to him, "You're very big. You're not going to let me even get near you, are you? No, the instant I try to tie you up, you're going to attack me. It won't ever be over, not until you're dead. I have no choice, none at all."

"Sure you do. You don't want to shoot me. I didn't kidnap her. I saved her."

"Shut up! No, I won't have you lurking about in the shadows, hanging over our lives ever again. I'll do it. I know I can do it. You're evil. You're a monster. Oh God, you abused her, didn't you? I'd prayed and prayed that the kidnapper hadn't hurt her, but you did, didn't you? You don't deserve to live. Em, come here, now. What's wrong with you? Come here so I can make you safe again." She steadied the gun. It was trained right on his chest.

Suddenly, the child threw herself in front of him, her small hands grabbing at his knees. She yelled, "No, Mama, it's Ramsey! He saved me. Don't hurt him!"

Both of them froze. Both of them looked into each other's eyes.

She spoke before he did. "Now, Em, you know he took you away from me. He's using you, he's—"

"No, I didn't kidnap her. I haven't hurt her. But I will tell you that this is the first time she's spoken since I found her in the forest more than a week ago." Slowly, he came down on his haunches, his thigh screaming from the exertion, but he ignored it.

"Your name's Em? Is that short for Emily?"

"No, Emma," she whispered. She was wearing one of his gray T-shirts, washed so many times it was softer than goat leather. She turned to the woman. "Mama, it's all right. Ramsey saved me. Really." She put her hand on his shoulder. She said again in that small tired voice, "He saved me, Mama. He wouldn't let anybody hurt me again. He gets really mad whenever he even thinks about it."

The woman slowly lowered the pistol, but he could tell she didn't want to. "Who are you?"

He picked up Emma and rose, aware that his leg wanted very much to give out under him. "Forgive me, but I've got to sit down. My leg hurts pretty bad."

The Detonics pistol jerked up again. "Don't you move, damn you. Put her down."

SIX

He ignored her. She wouldn't shoot him now. He was holding her daughter. He carried Emma to the sofa and sat down. Only then did he say to her, "I've got lots to tell you. My name's Ramsey Hunt. You can trust me. Please."

"Give me my daughter. Let her go."

He set Emma on her feet, and she ran to her mother. The woman came down on her knees. He watched her as she crushed Emma to her. Tears streaked down her face. She kissed Emma, all over her face, ran her hands all over her, smoothing her hands over her hair, squeezing her until she squeaked.

Emma finally pulled back. She lifted her hand to her mother's hair and lightly patted it. "I'm okay, Mama, really. Ramsey saved me. He took care of me. You look like G.I. Joe. I like those black gloves."

The woman laughed as she pulled off the black leather gloves. "I'm your mama again and not a soldier." He watched Emma lace her fingers through her mother's. He saw the close-clipped nails, several broken off. The back of her hands were red and chafed from the cold.

He felt incredibly relieved. And suddenly very tired. He sat back, stretching his leg out in front of him, watching them. Finally, when she was sitting across from him, Emma in her lap, held tightly against her chest, the woman raised her head and said, "Thank you. I'm sorry I nearly killed you. If I had, it would have been wrong." She sounded only mildly sorry. He didn't mind. He could imagine something of what she'd gone through, what she'd thought.

"Yes, very wrong. I'm glad that Emma isn't mute. But you know, we've gotten along fine. She draws really well."

"Why didn't you say anything, Em?"

Emma shook her head, then frowned. She whispered, "Nothing would come out. Nothing until I thought you'd shoot Ramsey. I couldn't let you shoot Ramsey. I didn't know what to do so I talked. Ramsey wanted me to write my name but I couldn't do that either. He didn't think I could write. I couldn't do anything, Mama, except draw pictures."

"You did well," her mother said and kissed her not once, but half a dozen times. "Oh, Emma, I love you so much." She settled the child again in her lap.

"I'm glad to see you, Mama. I didn't think I'd ever see you again until Ramsey found me. It was scary, Mama. I was so afraid." Emma threw her arms around her mother's neck. She was crying now, deep low sobs that rent the silence.

"It's all right, baby. We're together again. It's all right. I'll never let you go again, I swear it. Oh, Emma, I love you. Oh, God, I nearly lost hope."

He turned away, giving them what privacy he could, but he listened to them both crying, Emma's sobs, strangely, deeper than her mother's. He waited until they'd begun to quiet, listened to the sniffs, then tossed her a blanket. She pulled it over both of them. She said blankly, "Emma's wearing a man's undershirt."

"Yes, I forgot to buy her some pajamas. At least she doesn't trip over the undershirt."

Ramsey rose, his leg screaming. "Let me lock the door. We can't take any chances."

She didn't say anything, content to wait, he supposed, since she had her daughter back. He knew she watched him closely as he stared through the window, then fastened the chain and flipped the dead bolt. When he turned, he watched her pull off a close-fitting black knit cap. Red curly hair spouted out, most of it in a braid, the rest a riot around her thin face, a pretty face, one that was changing even as he watched. The tension was leaving her face, bringing color to her cheeks. Her mouth was curving into a smile, her eyes were growing lighter even as he stared at her.

There was so much to say, so much to ask, but what came out of his mouth was, "Would you like some coffee? It will just take a minute to make. We're really basic here."

She nodded. "That would be wonderful. I'm so cold I think it's permanent now."

He walked to the kitchen. He felt Emma's hand on his knee. She'd followed him out, his gray T-shirt nearly dragging on the floor and a pair of white gym socks pooling around her skinny ankles. He watched her walk to the small table and measure the coffee into the waiting pan. Then he poured the water over the coffee and set it on the stove. They'd gotten this routine down as of four days ago.

He looked over to the woman standing in the doorway, staring at them, more dazed than not. He didn't even know her name, but at this moment, it didn't seem to matter. What mattered was creating an air of normality. He said to her, "Emma and I are a good act. We got the coffee thing down first thing. We're just about ready to take it on the road. Hey, Emma, who gets top billing?"

"I don't know what that means, Ramsey."

"Does your name go first on the signs or does mine?"

"I'm the youngest. I should go first."

He laughed and ruffled her hair. He looked over at her mother. She was standing there trying to make sense of things, not just coming to understand the relationship between her daughter and this man she didn't know, but she was also trying to come to grips with the fact that Emma was safe, that she actually had her daughter back.

She didn't say anything. She looked strung out and very tired. He said, "You'd think that boiled coffee would rot your fillings out, and it just might, come to think of it, but it doesn't taste too bad and it does zing your brain. As I said, we're basic here. We've got a small refrigerator and the lights in the living room, due to a generator. But it's a wood-burning stove and we heat the water for a bath."

Emma said, "We toast bread with a metal thing that has a long handle."

The woman shook her head, still trying, he knew, to understand what was happening here. "I'd drink anything that passed for coffee at this point. I've been sitting out there waiting and waiting for daylight, waiting for you to come outside, but when you did, you had that rifle and I was too far away to do anything with my Detonics."

"I shouldn't have left the cabin door unlocked. It was stupid. If it hadn't been you, it could have been them."

"Well, it wasn't. I didn't see anyone else out there. Who's them? Who are you talking about?"

"Let's hold that for a little bit," he said, and nodded toward Emma. He poured her a cup of coffee that was still bubbling. "Sit down and try to drink it. If anything it'll keep you buzzing until noon, when you'll probably crash. Emma, I'm going to fix you a bowl of Cheerios. You want peaches or bananas?"

"A banana. I don't really like peaches."

"But you've eaten them without complaint."

She said as she took the cereal box from him and poured Cheerios into her bowl, "I didn't want to hurt your feelings. But I do like bananas better."

He sliced the banana over her cereal while she got the milk out of the small refrigerator. "Look, Mama," she said, pointing. "It doesn't have a freezer. We make everything fresh, just the way we do at home."

"I've never seen one that fancy before. It's neat." She didn't know how the words, such ordinary words, had come out of her mouth. She'd passed from blankness to disbelief. Here she'd expected to come in and fight her daughter's abductor and deal with a hysterical hurt child, and now she was drinking boiled coffee at a kitchen table, looking into a high-tech refrigerator, listening to her daughter chew her Cheerios. She looked at the big man who needed to shave. He'd saved her daughter? He'd protected her with his life? Nothing made sense yet.

Emma was eating Cheerios with a banana on top, nicely sliced by that stranger. She didn't say anything more until Emma was down to her last bite of cereal and he was drinking his second cup of coffee, seated across from her at the table. "I've been tracking her for two weeks. When I showed Emma's picture down in Dillinger, I couldn't believe it. Several people told me she was Ramsey's little girl. I didn't know what to think. I've been watching since yesterday, but I couldn't get to you without taking a chance of hurting Emma. You never came out of the cabin. Neither of you did."

"Who are you?"

"I'm Molly Santera."

Emma looked up as she swallowed a banana circle. "Mama says it sounds like a made-up band's name—our last name—but it's real. It's my dad's name."

Molly smiled at her daughter and leaned close to touch her. "That's true enough. But I'll bet you there are lots of Santeras in the New York phone directory."

"I've never been to New York," Emma said.

"We'll go when you're a bit older, Em. We'll have a great time. We'll stay at the Plaza and walk right over to FAO Schwarz. It's really close."

Santera. The name was vaguely familiar. He remembered Emma's drawing of a man holding a guitar and his jaw dropped. He said slowly, "Santera. You mean Louey Santera? The rock star?"

"One and the same," Molly said, her voice clipped, colder than a late-spring freeze.

Ramsey wanted to know more about Emma's father, ask her why the hell the guy wasn't tracking with her, even though he was a famous rock star. But he could tell that Molly didn't want to say more about him right now. There would be time enough for her to answer all his questions and for him to answer all of hers. Emma had eaten her cereal, all the while smiling at her mother, then smiling at him, like any happy well-adjusted kid.

Molly said, "I know who you are now."

He cocked his head at her. "Me? How?"

"I recognize you now that I've thought about your name. You're the famous Ramsey Hunt?"

Again, for Emma's sake, he used a light hand. "Infamous is more accurate."

"In your dreams."

He sputtered in his coffee, raised his head, and stared at her. "Men," she said, her hands wrapped around her coffee mug, "if they have a choice, would rather have the world believe them infamous—you know, rogues and bad boys—not heroes, not known for something worthy or moral they've done or tried to do."

"No," he said. "That's not me."

She sighed, and shrugged, looking away from him. "This is tough to believe. You're a federal judge from San Francisco, but you're here. You found Emma."

"Yes," he said.

"Given what you did in your courtroom, I suppose Emma couldn't have been safer."

He said nothing, took another sip of the afterburner coffee.

A federal judge who was also famous, a hero truth be told, despite his reticence, and here both she and Emma were with him. Life had kicked her so much in the teeth for the past two weeks that she supposed she shouldn't be shocked at this latest surprise. She said to her daughter, "Em, you look beautiful. How are you, love?"

Emma kept her head down. Reality had crashed in suddenly and she wasn't ready yet. Molly had sounded too serious, too strident. She felt stupid and so very tired. She could have kissed Ramsey Hunt when he said, his voice still light and calm, his attention seemingly on Emma, "She had to have other stuff to wear than my T-shirts. I put off leaving the cabin for as long as possible, but she had to have some clothes. And that's how you found us. When Emma and I went shopping in Dillinger."

"As I said, I showed her photo around and the town folks all believed she was your little girl. Truth be told, I didn't expect to learn anything at Dillinger. It was the last stop. I guess then I would have had to let the cops and the FBI deal with things. Naturally, they are dealing with things, in their own way. They didn't solve a thing, didn't turn up a thing. I gave them two days, then hit the road. I heard they called off the manhunt for her after four days."

"Where do you live?"

"In Denver." She picked up a spoon and fiddled with it, her eyes down on the white-and-red-checked tablecloth, "Her father is in Europe. He's on tour and couldn't leave, but he'll be back soon now." She turned to her daughter and took her small hand. "I speak to him nearly every day, Em. He's very worried about you, really."

Emma stared down into her bowl that had one banana slice floating in a bit of milk. She said, never looking up, "I don't know why he'd come. I haven't seen him for two years."

Ramsey realized her daughter had knocked her flat. He said quickly, "I see. You're divorced."

"Yes," Molly said. She'd gotten herself together again. "Emma, it doesn't have anything to do with the divorce. Your daddy loves you. It's just that he's so very busy."

"Yes, Mama."

Time to move along, quickly, Ramsey thought, and said, "So you gave the cops all of two days then you struck out on your own?"

"Yes. There was nothing I could do at home except go quietly nuts."

He wanted to tell her that if the kidnappers called, they'd have wanted to speak to her. Then he realized that any female police officer could do that duty. He didn't say anything. Emma was all ears.

"I've been traveling from Aspen to Vail to Keystone and all the places in between. Dillinger was my final try."

"You lucked out. As I said, if she hadn't needed clothes, I wouldn't have taken her to Dillinger. I'd been here at the cabin for nearly two weeks before I found Emma."

"Why were you here of all places?"

He shrugged, looking down at his coffee. "It got to be too much," he said at last. "Just too much. The tabloids wouldn't let up. The paparazzi were leaping out from behind my bushes to catch me unawares."

"They call you Judge Dredd."

"It's ridiculous, all of it." He started to curse, realized that Emma was staring up at him, and took a deep breath. "I took three months off and got away from everything—people, phones, TVs, everything. Then I found Emma." He leaned over and cupped Emma's chin in his palm. There was color in her cheeks. She looked little-kid beautiful, and healthy. "Why don't you go wash up and put on your jeans and a real bright shirt. Your mom and I will talk and decide what we should do."

She looked worried. "Mama, you won't try to shoot Ramsey again, will you?"

"I never drink a man's coffee then hurt him, honey. It's not done."

"Mama, you made a joke." Emma beamed at her.

"Yes, a good joke," Ramsey said. "Go, Emma."

He sat back in his chair and looked at the woman across from him. "Emma drew several pictures of you. In all of them you were smiling really big." But now she wasn't smiling. She was pale and thin and had the reddest hair he'd ever seen, all curly, just like Emma's drawings. Her eyes were a sort of green-grayish color, a bit tilted at the corners, sort of exotic. She didn't have any freckles, and she didn't look a thing like Emma.

"I've been calling her 'sweetheart.' I like Emma. It suits her."

"It was my grandmother's name."

She sat forward, intent, then suddenly jumped to her feet and began pacing the small kitchen, hyper now from the coffee, alert, and ready for answers. "How did you find Emma?"

"It was exactly eight days ago. I was out chopping logs when I heard this strange sound, you know, a sound I shouldn't have heard here. I tracked it down and found her unconscious in the woods. I spotted her only because she was wearing a bright yellow T-shirt. I brought her back here and took care of her. She didn't speak until she yelled at you."

He saw the question in her eyes and slowly nodded. "Yes, she'd been beaten and sexually assaulted. There wasn't any sodomy that I could tell, but then again, I'm not a doctor. She's much better now, even though last night she had a nightmare." He stopped and shook his head. "It took her a good four days to trust me. She's a great kid."

Tears were running out of her eyes and down her cheeks, dripping off her lips. She sniffled. He handed her a napkin and she blew her nose and wiped her eyes.

"She's only six years old. She was kidnapped by a child molester and it was all my fault. If only—"

"Stop it, just stop it. I've known you for an hour and I know you didn't leave her unattended, wouldn't do anything to jeopardize her. Now, I don't want to hear any more of that crap." He sighed, knowing deep down that she'd probably never stop blaming herself for the rest of her life. "Believe me, I've never felt so helpless in my life. She's such a sweet little girl. She was terrified of me, a man, and I couldn't blame her at all. When she didn't speak, I became convinced she was mute."

He'd kept talking so she could get a hold on herself, which she finally did. He watched her shoulders square. "Maybe it was the trauma. Maybe she felt safer if she didn't say anything and didn't write down her name for me. Maybe she really couldn't speak until it became a matter of life and death. Would you have shot me?"

"In a heartbeat if you'd so much as moved a finger."

"I'm rather relieved Emma remembered her voice. You've had a hard time of it. It must have been very difficult to go into all the towns and show her picture."

"No, everyone was very nice, all except for the local cops. Almost to the man, they treated me like a hysterical female, all patronizing and pats on the shoulder and leave it to them, the big macho guys. I nearly punched one guy out in Rutland. When I finally found your cabin, I thought a lot about what I was going to do. I know enough about how law enforcement works to realize that if I only captured the man who'd abducted her, he'd probably be out on bail at some point. Would he come after Emma again? Say the judge denied bail, they kept him in jail, then even convicted him.

He'd probably get out sooner or later and then be out again to prey on other children or come after Emma again. I'd have to worry about him for the rest of my life. So would Emma, and that's worse. A child molester, a kidnapper. A monster like that doesn't deserve to live."

She met his eyes squarely. "If that monster had been you, I would have at least wounded you. That way, at least, you couldn't have been out on bail. You would have been in a hospital. There maybe someone would have screwed up your medicine and maybe you would have croaked."

He drained the last of his coffee, an eyebrow arched. "You don't have much faith in our system."

"No, not a scintilla of faith. The system, even if it weren't screwed up, is so backed up that plea bargains are the only way to keep criminals moving. Why am I saying the obvious to you, a judge who lives this every day?

"You know that this guy, even if he were caught, might plea-bargain down to seven years then get out in three. It's not right, but of course the trial lawyers aren't about to let anybody change anything. They don't care about justice, just about getting their hands on as much money as they can. Then they put all the focus on the poor criminal and how screwed up his childhood was, as if that excuses his brutality. It's not right. You're part of it. You know it's not right."

He said mildly, "No, it's not right. Look, no one wants the bad guys on the streets. Most of us work really hard to keep them in prison." He shrugged. "But sometimes wrong things happen."

"Spoken like the person you are."

He shrugged. "I guess none of us can escape what we are for very long."

"You said you came here to hide out."

He looked mildly embarrassed. "Things were out of control. I came here to get myself back together again and to give people time to forget, which they will, soon enough."

"You're a federal judge. You have to know lots of people. You must believe in the system. Why didn't you immediately take Emma to the police? The hospital?"

"I couldn't," he said simply. "She was terrified. I couldn't bear the thought of strangers all over her." His eyes dropped to his running shoes. "I also worried that she could be taken again if she went home."

She looked at him for a very long time, then, slowly, she nodded. "If I'd been in your shoes, I wouldn't have given her over to strangers either. I wouldn't have sent her home either, not until I knew she'd be protected. Thank you for keeping her safe. She's the most important person in the whole world. I don't know if I could have gone on if she'd been killed."

He thought she would cry, but instead, she shook herself, and stood up. "And that's why I don't want to go back to Denver."

SEVEN

"If I were in your shoes, I'd feel the same way." He sat forward, his elbows on the scarred tabletop. "I worried about *not* notifying the police, not taking her to a hospital, but, bottom line, I couldn't give her over to the care of strangers. Did you see the sheriff in Dillinger?"

"No, I stopped seeing the local cops as of six towns ago. I took Emma's photo around and asked and asked. I didn't know what else to do. I had this feeling that the kidnapper had taken her west, not up north toward Fort Collins and Cheyenne. No, I knew it was here in the Rockies."

"Why?"

"The Denver police had this hotline for anyone who had seen anything. They were flooded with calls, none of them relevant, but there was this one, an old woman who claimed she'd seen a white van heading west. The cops thought she was senile and ignored it, but I went to see her. She lives up the block from me. She has really bad arthritis and so she spends a lot of time sitting in her chair, looking out the window. If there was anything to see I knew she'd have seen it. I told the cops this, but they blew it off."

"How could she know the van was going west?"

"We live on a hill facing west and facing the 70. From her deck, she saw the van turn onto the freeway going west. She swears she saw a little girl in the van."

"No ransom note?"

She shook her head. "No, at least not since yesterday morning. That's the last time I checked in. That's what the FBI agents were counting on. They kept telling me over and over that I had to be patient, just sit there by the phone and be patient. I was to let them tell me what to do since they knew everything and I was stupid. I nearly smacked this one agent. I waited for two days and nothing. Still, the FBI agents just kept shaking their heads saying that I had to wait, wait, wait. I was going crazy. Finally I just headed out at dawn the morning of the third day. I call in every day and let them yell at me.

"I've visited more places than I can remember. Really, this one was the last stop. When I came into Dillinger, I couldn't believe it when everyone nodded and said she was Ramsey's little girl. If I'd seen you then, without Emma, I would probably have cleaned out my Detonics on you."

"You would have gone to jail."

"Yeah, some justice."

"If you had shot me, sending you to jail would have indeed been justice. For my sake, I hope they wouldn't have plea-bargained you down." Of course that wasn't the point. She didn't say anything to that, but he could practically see the hackles rising. He wanted to ask how Emma had been taken, about Emma's father, and a dozen other things, but now Emma was standing in the doorway, looking bright and clean, a hairbrush in her hand. She walked to him and held out the brush. He heard Molly suck in her breath. He smiled, took the brush, and brought Emma to stand between his knees. He combed out the tangles, then began the braid.

Emma said, "Mama, could you teach Ramsey how to French-braid my hair?"

"Yes, I can. He's doing pretty well with your regular braid, though."

"You should have seen the first braid he did. It was all spiky and crooked, like it was broken in the middle."

When he got to the end of the braid, she handed back a rubber band. "There." He turned her around, his hands on her shoulders. "You look great. Everyone is going to ask you who your hairdresser is. I'm the best."

"That was well done," Molly said in a calm voice, but both of them recognized that it was tough for her, this unquestioned trust and affection Emma had for another human being, one she hadn't even known until a week ago. "Can I show Ramsey how to French-braid it tomorrow for you, Em?"

"Yes, Mama."

Ramsey leaned forward in his chair, taking her hands. "I want you to gather up all your clothes, Em, and stuff everything in a pillowcase. Don't forget anything. It's important. If those men come back, I don't want them to see anything that has to do with any of us in here. The three of us are leaving in fifteen minutes. All right?"

She gave him a long look, then nodded slowly.

He waited until he heard Emma rummaging around in the living room, then said to Molly, "I told you that I was relieved you weren't the bad guys. We had visitors, two of them."

Emma said from the doorway, a half-filled pillowcase in her hands, "Are you going to look at your leg, Ramsey?"

He'd forgotten. He should, just to make sure there was no infection. He nodded slowly. "I'll get the tape," she called.

"What's going on?"

"Two guys stumbled out of the forest into the meadow yesterday, firing their rifles, pretending to be drunk. I got Emma inside and came back out with my rifle and handgun. I got hit in the leg, but I managed to hit both of them. One of them twice. They ran off. I have one of their rifles. Maybe the police can run a check on it.

"I don't know who they were or why they were here. My feeling is they were after Emma." Then, Emma was standing there, beside him. He said easily, "Emma, hand me a sterile gauze." He rose and pulled down his sweatpants. He heard Molly suck in her breath. He said as he sat back down again, "Let me get this tape and gauze up. There, that's not too bad. It's supposed to turn black and blue. Okay, Emma, give me the gauze. You know, I think the swelling's down a bit."

"I hope so, Ramsey," Emma said, leaning close. "It doesn't smell bad, so that's good."

Molly said as she watched the two of them work smoothly together, Emma handing him strips of adhesive tape, then helping him pull it tight over the gauze, keeping the flesh together, "How'd you know about that, Em?"

"I know lots of things, Mama. I watched an ancient history show, the one Mr. Spock does, and they talked about how this one phara—"

"Pharaoh?"

"Yeah. He had his leg rot and ooze because someone hit him with a spear, and then he died."

"You mean gangrene?" Molly asked.

"Yes, that's it. I don't see any red, Ramsey."

"No, I don't either."

"Is it still real warm?" She didn't wait for him to answer, lightly pressed her palm next to the bandage. "Yes, it is. How much longer will it be warm?"

"I don't know. Not much longer. I'm a real quick healer."

"But it is better, isn't it?"

He heard the crawling fear in her voice, and came up with a big grin. He rubbed his knuckles on her cheek. "I'm nearly ready to go skiing, sweetheart. You want to go to Vail?"

"Mama likes to ski at Vail. I'm just learning."

"You can be my mascot. I'll carry you around on my shoulders. When I fall, I'll toss you in a snowbank and you can be a snow angel." Still, she looked profoundly worried. She lightly pressed a hand on either side of the bandage.

"It's okay, Em, I promise. If I wasn't sure, I'd be in the ER quicker than I could get the Jeep started."

A small calm voice said, "He said there wasn't a hospital close to here, just a nice big church."

Molly and Ramsey stared at her, not breathing. The air in the kitchen seemed to dry up.

Ramsey sat forward. He'd wanted desperately to question her about the man who'd kidnapped and abused her, but he hadn't. He had no experience in this kind of thing. There was no way he'd risk freaking her out. He said calmly, his voice utterly matter-of-fact, "Who said that, Emma? What man?"

She began shaking her head back and forth so violently the braid slapped her cheek. She said over and over, "No one, no one, no one."

"It's okay, Em." Molly went down on her knees and pulled her daughter against her. Emma was leaning heavily against his thigh, pulling her mother with her, but he didn't feel any pain from the weight. "I love you. It's okay."

He met Molly's eyes over Emma's head. He saw murder. He prayed that if they ever caught the guy they'd have time to get information out of him before Molly managed to sneak in and kill him. On the other hand, maybe he'd kill the monster himself before Molly could.

"Em, you got your stuff ready?"

She pulled back, looking at him. Her face was pale, the cheekbones looking as if they were ready to poke through her skin, she was drawn so tightly. "Yes, Ramsey. I'm nearly ready. I can't find one of my red socks."

"We're out of here in five minutes, red sock or not. Bring the tape with you. Let's leave the leg alone for another day. Come on, you guys, let's get moving."

THEY didn't see a soul. Of course anyone could be hiding in the forest, watching them. Ramsey herded them into the Jeep as fast as he could.

"Where's your car?" he asked Molly as he slipped into the driver's seat. In one quick motion he'd inserted the key and turned it. The engine was loud in the early-morning silence.

"It's down about a half a mile, on the side of the road. It's a rental, a Chevrolet." She paused a moment, never stopped looking out the windshield, and said calm as a clam, "Look, Ramsey, you're a federal judge. You're part of the system. I don't believe in the system. I'm not about to call the cops or go back to Denver. Why don't you drop me and Emma off and then go about your life?"

"What do you mean by that?" He swung the wheel too far in his surprise and instant anger, and nearly went off the rutted narrow road.

"I mean," she said, still looking out the dirty windshield, and not once at him, "that you don't know us. I'm here now. Emma's my responsibility. I'll take over."

"No."

"I'm not calling in the damned cops."

"Fine. For the time being. But I disagree." He knew there was something else holding her back, something she hadn't told him, not that she'd told him hardly anything at all.

"I don't care. I'm calling the shots here. If you can't accept that, then leave."

"Mama, you don't want Ramsey to stay with us?"

Molly kissed her daughter's ear. "He's an innocent bystander, Em. This isn't his trouble."

"How did you reach that brilliant conclusion?" The Jeep crunched over rocks and lurched to the side. "Some guys tried to take me out at the cabin. Chances are they just wanted to get me out of the way."

"I don't suppose you considered that it could have been you they were after?"

He wanted to strangle the steering wheel. "Emma," he said, "stop listening, as of now. Put your hands against your ears. Yes, that's good. Now, I'm going to speak my mind to your mother."

Molly said, "I don't want to hear any more. It doesn't matter. You've done your good deed. You've even been hurt protecting Emma. It's enough, more than enough. You're now out of our lives. When we trade cars, I'll be really careful to make certain no one follows us. I've gotten very good at being sneaky. I'm not going back to Denver, so you don't have to worry that Emma will be in any danger again. Oh yeah, I'll call the cops and the FBI and tell them it's over. I'll tell them where you found Emma so maybe they can find the cabin where the kidnapper was holding Emma. Then I'll tell them what a dynamite job they all did."

Emma sat perfectly still on her mother's lap, her hands over her ears. But she was making those horrible mewling sounds in her throat.

Molly looked like she'd been punched in the stomach. She gathered Emma close, rocking her. "Baby, it's all right. Oh, God, I'm sorry, Emma. Please, trust me. I promise I'll take care of you. It was my fault that he got you that first time, but we're not going back there. I'll keep you safe. I won't yell at Ramsey again."

Ramsey stopped the Jeep. He turned in his seat to face them. "Emma," he said matter-of-factly, "take your hands away from your ears. Now listen to me. You won't make those sounds anymore, do you hear me? If you have something to say, you'll say it, not scare the devil out of me making those sounds. They make my leg hurt more. Now, I'm not leaving you and your mom. Your mom can yell at me if it makes her feel better. I might even yell back. But nothing could make me leave you. Do you hear me?"

A loud silence, and then, "You promise you won't leave, Ramsey?"

"I promise. I don't break my promises. Your mom will get used to me just as you did. She won't talk me out of it, no matter what kind of reasons she comes up with. I'll even play by her rules, for the time being. You're going to talk from now on, all right?"

She nodded slowly. "I don't like to hear you yelling."

"No, we don't either. But it'll happen sometimes. You can tell us both to be quiet. Now, enough said."

Molly didn't say a word. She looked as if she wanted to fold up on herself. She looked near the edge. He felt like taking a strip off her, but he didn't. She might just crumble. Or, she might shoot him. He lightly patted her shoulder and said in that calm deep voice that served him well in the courtroom, "It will be all right, Molly. You'll see. There's nothing wrong with needing backup, and that's how you can think of me. Now, let's get out of here. Emma, look out the rear window. If you see a car behind us, you tell me."

"Yes, Ramsey."

"I'm counting on you. Keep sharp."

"I will."

"About those men," Molly said. "Do you think it's possible they could have been after you and not Emma?"

"I don't know."

"You've made enemies. I read you'd gotten threats, particularly from that one woman whose husband died that day in the courtroom."

"That's right, I have, but no one has tried to kill me before."

"That would mean that there were two men with Emma, not just the one who abducted her."

"That's right. Could you please pour me a cup of coffee from the thermos?"

She knew he didn't want to talk about it in front of Emma. But there was so much dammed up inside her. For nearly two weeks, she'd been filling up with anger and hatred and helplessness. She'd wait, she had to. The last thing she wanted was to terrify her daughter even more than she already was. She handed the cup to Ramsey Hunt, a man she'd read about, a man she'd wondered about in odd moments along with the rest of the country. Until two weeks ago when her world was blown apart.

She hugged Emma tightly to her.

"Let me loose, Mama. I've got to keep looking out the back window. The Jeep's dirty, Ramsey. We should stop and get it washed."

"That's a good idea. Who would be looking for a spanking clean Jeep?"

They left Molly's rental car where it sat. Molly took all the papers out of the glove compartment. "I'll call them and tell them where the car is. They may not mind too much if I tell them to charge anything extra on my credit card."

They had the Jeep washed when they stopped for lunch in Rappahoe, a small town just off the 70. No one was following them as best Ramsey could tell.

"How's your leg?"

"Stiffening up on me," he said, taking a big bite of his hamburger. He closed his eyes as he chewed. When he swallowed, he groaned and said, "Fat. There's nothing better in life."

"I heard my dad say that sex was the best thing in life," Emma said, and chewed on a French fry coated with catsup.

"I think kittens and little girls are about the two best things," Molly said without skipping a beat.

He admired her for that. He himself was aware that his mouth had dropped open.

"Did you bring my kite, Ramsey?"

"Oh yes. This kid's a pro," he added to Molly, who'd taken all of one spoonful of her vegetable soup. "You taught her, didn't you?"

She nodded, picked up her spoon, and began stirring the soup. There was a film of grease over the top. She dropped the spoon and took a slice of white bread. She spread butter and jam on it. At least she was eating that.

"Ramsey, two guys came in. They're looking over here. One of them has a rifle."

MELISSA Shaker watched her father move smoothly and steadily on the rowing machine. She wanted to tell him he looked really good for a guy his age, that he should hang around in jock T-shirts and shorts. The minute he dressed in one of his expensive Savile Row suits, he looked faintly ridiculous. The bottom line was, he looked like a thug, really. The more expensive the clothes, the more they seemed to reduce him to a stereotype of a Hollywood movie Mafia character. But strip her old man down, and he looked just fine.

She said, "I noticed that you've stopped taking Eleanor around to the clubs."

He grunted, never missing his rhythmic pull, release, pull, release. "Yeah, she's so classy she makes me look like a bodyguard."

She blinked at that. She didn't realize he'd known. Eleanor, classy?

He continued after a moment, his voice smooth and calm, despite his exertion, "The younger, the more beautiful the girl, the more like a gargoyle I look."

Melissa laughed. "You're right, but I wouldn't have said it out loud. I saw you with a really beautiful girl out by the swimming pool the other day. You were wearing a bikini and so was she. You looked better than she did. Wear shorts, Dad, and you'll look great."

He grunted, slowly easing down on his speed. This was his cooldown. He'd been on the rowing machine for forty minutes. Sweat was dripping off him and his muscles were pumped and glistening. If he hadn't been her father, she would have at least looked him over.

The phone rang. He said without looking up, "Answer it, but don't say anything."

She did. When she handed him the phone, he'd finally come to a halt. He was breathing a bit on the fast side. He listened, then said, "What's the status?"

He listened. Melissa wished she could pick up the extension. She walked over to the weight rack and picked up two five-pound free weights. She began to do bicep curls.

She turned only when she heard him place the phone back into the cradle. He said, "It shouldn't be long now. We'll get three for the price of one."

"I wish it could be different."

He looked at her closely, doing the slow bicep curls, like pulling through water, just as he'd taught her. "No you don't. You enjoy all this crap. But I promised you. You know I always keep my promises."

She put down the free weights and walked to him. She hugged him close, not caring that he was sweaty. "Thanks, Daddy. I know. I appreciate it."

He lightly pushed her away and toweled himself off. "You're a good girl, Mellie, but sometimes you get strange ideas." He raised his hand. "No, it's okay. It keeps life interesting."

Rule Shaker was whistling when he walked into the huge shower stall in the marble bath off his private gym.

EIGHT

"Emma, keep your head down and eat your French fries. Molly, don't go for your gun, listen to me. I want you and Emma to go through that doorway that says TELEPHONES & TOILETS. If there's an exit, go on out to the Jeep, otherwise, stay in the bathroom. If you get to the Jeep, lock yourselves in. I'll be out as soon as I pay the bill. Go. Act as naturally as you can. Don't look back."

Molly didn't move. "Em, did you see the two men that came to the cabin?"

"Not really."

"So you wouldn't recognize them?"

"No, Mama, but Ramsey would."

"That's right, I would. Go, Molly. There's no time for any more discussion. If they're the guys I'll be out as soon as I can, probably walking really fast."

"Molly gave him a final long look, grabbed her purse, kept her attention on Emma, and walked with her to the back of the small restaurant, through the doorway. Slowly, Ramsey turned around and raised his hand to the waitress. They were standing with their backs to him. One was tall and thin, the other short. He couldn't tell if he was bowlegged or not. He didn't think they were the same guys who'd come to the cabin. How could they be? He'd shot both the bastards. He didn't have his Smith & Wesson. The restaurant was pretty crowded. He prayed the men wouldn't do anything stupid.

The waitress smiled down at him. He said without looking at her, "Is there a back way out of here?"

"Yeah, there's a back door beside the men's room."

"Good. How much do I owe you?"

She wrote down a couple of more things, frowned as she added, then ripped off the paper and handed it to him, saying, "You guys didn't eat all that much so I took a bit off the bill."

"That's really nice of you. My wife was feeling a bit on the edge. She's pregnant."

"Oh, well, congratulations. It happens to the best of us, getting sick that is."

"Hey, Elsa, how's tricks?"

The guy looked like a cowboy with a gut. He was standing behind the waitress. Ramsey couldn't see his face because Elsa was large, had very big hair, and was standing squarely between them. But it wasn't one of the men at the cabin. He didn't know whether to be relieved or worried over a possible new threat.

"I'm mean and pretty as ever," she said, turning to face the man, blocking Ramsey's view of him. "You're new, aren't you? You move here or something?"

"Yeah. Me and the missus came down from Wyoming. Nice around here."

"Yeah. You want some lunch, then go sit with your friend at that booth." She pointed with the pencil then stuck it behind her ear.

"Hey, mister, what happened to that pretty little girl I was smiling at?"

Ramsey slowly rose. Elsa stepped out of the way, alarm suddenly hitting her brain. Ramsey towered over the man, who was middle-aged, losing the war to fat, and looked as sincere and nice as Ted Bundy had probably looked.

"Hey, buddy, that your kid?"

"Yes, she's my kid. Why do you want to know?"

"No reason. She's cute, like one of my little granddaughters."

Ramsey handed the waitress a twenty, saying to both of them, "Have a good day. Bye now." He went to the front door, but not before he looked for the other man. He didn't see him. Not seeing him bothered him a lot more. Where was the bastard?

His gut was dancing double time. He looked back again. There was no single guy in the restaurant. Why had the man wanted to know about Emma?

It was then he heard the screech of brakes. He was out the door in an instant to see Molly backing up the Jeep, then slamming on the brakes again to miss a parked pickup truck, by about four inches. He saw a man running toward her. She gunned the engine and the Jeep shot forward. The man shouted and dived into the scrawny bushes that lined the wall of the restaurant.

"Molly!"

He grabbed the passenger door, pulled it open, and jumped in.

She was onto the entrance ramp to the 70 before he even got the door closed.

He looked back to see the man dusting off his pants, staring after them. Then the man he'd been speaking to came out. The two men conferred, heads bent close. He lost sight of them as Molly veered onto the 70, tires screaming.

"Ramsey."

He heard the small voice and looked down. Emma was scrunched on the floor at his feet. "Come here, kiddo. We're fine. Your mama's a heroine. She saved us. Come here and hug me. I need some attention and a kiss. A kiss would make my heart slow down and put my stomach back where it belongs."

Emma crawled up and let him lift her onto his lap. Now wasn't the time to worry about his seat belt. She kissed him on the cheek. "That's better. Thanks." He said calmly to Molly, "Slow down, and go out at this next exit."

"But—oh, yes, you're right. Then we'll see if they follow."

"Slow down. We don't want to attract any attention. When you get off, make a sharp right, and drive behind that Mobil gas station. Emma, hug me tighter. Yeah, that's better."

"If I see them, I'm going to get back on the highway. Maybe we can see their license plate. You'd be able to find out who it belongs to, won't you?"

He nodded. She looked calm and steady, handling the Jeep well enough. Emma was hanging onto him like a leech. It felt good, those skinny little arms of hers choking his neck. The kid had grit.

Molly was off the highway, veering right, then turning sharply right toward the back of the Mobil station, all in the space of about twenty seconds. "Well done," he said. "Now, kiddo," he said to Emma, "I want you to look with me back up to the highway. We want to see if those two men are following us."

"I should have waited to see what car they were driving," Molly said. She hit the steering wheel with her fist. "I didn't think it through."

"It's okay. We'll recognize them. Keep looking." A dark green Corolla went by with two women inside. Then a truck with a single guy and a big German shepherd, his head out the window, his tongue hanging long. There was a space of five heartbeats, then a filthy black truck, its bed empty. In the cab were two men.

"That's them," Ramsey said. "Okay, Molly, ease back onto the highway. Keep a minimum of three cars back."

She was already driving out from behind the Mobil station. There was a small white Honda in front of her. She wanted to honk, to run over it, to yell at the older woman driving, but she managed to keep herself calm and steady, but she was whispering, "Move, move, move."

Ramsey kept his arms loosely around Emma. "You okay, kiddo?"

"I'm scared, Ramsey."

His arms tightened. He kissed the top of her head. "I wish I could give you the power not to be afraid of anything, Emma, but I can't. Fear isn't bad, as long as it doesn't freeze you up. I know you don't like to think about it, but you didn't freeze up that time. You managed to escape and run into the woods and I found you. You were extraordinarily brave. And so you see that if you keep thinking, if you don't give up, then you can help yourself. You've got a chance." He knew Molly was listening. "You won't forget that, will you, Em?"

"No," she whispered. "I won't forget. There's the truck, Ramsey. Mom's close now."

"Can you see the license number?"

"It's really dirty, but I can see it."

Then he laughed. "You can see it but you can't tell me the letters or numbers. I'm going to teach you how to read tomorrow, okay, kiddo?"

"I know how to read a little. Mama points her finger at the words while she's reading. You think it'll only take one day?"

"With you, maybe half a day." He said to Molly, "It looks to me like it's a *B*, then an *L*, then mud's all smeared over the next letter. There's a space, then three-eight-eight-something. That last number's too smeared to make out."

"You'll find a cell phone in my bag. Since you're a federal judge, you're bound to know someone who can tell us who owns the truck. Once you find that out, I promise I'll call the cops in Denver and tell them. You don't have to tell anybody anything. Now, I'll hang back until you find out."

A cell phone. She had a cell phone and hadn't told him until they were holding on by their teeth. He wanted to yell at her, but he didn't. He pulled out the slim phone. He started to call Virginia Trolley in San Francisco, then paused. No, she couldn't do anything. He needed someone with an inside track who wouldn't butt in, but would give him all the help he could. He dialed the main number to the FBI in Washington, D.C., and asked for Dillon Savich in the Criminal Apprehension Unit.

In two minutes he was talking to Savich. "Why don't you ever use my e-mail, Ramsey? You know I hate phones. I think when I was a kid a phone cord must have wrapped around my neck and nearly choked me to death."

"Sorry, I don't have my laptop and modem with me. Long story. I need help, Savich."

"Talk to me."

No hesitation, no questions. Ramsey said, "I need to know who belongs to this license plate." He gave Savich the information. "I'm on a cell phone." He gave him the phone number. "Yeah, I'll keep it on. I owe you one, Savich."

A grunt, nothing more. Ramsey smiled into the cell phone. He hung up but left the phone button on.

"Who did you call? The police in San Francisco?"

"No. I called a friend of mine in Washington, D.C."

"A good friend, if he didn't ask you any questions."

"Yes, a good friend. We met about four years ago at a law-enforcement conference in Chicago. At that time I was with the U.S. Attorney's office. Savich is into karate, does an exhibition now and again. He got married about six months ago to another agent named Sherlock. Keep farther back, Molly."

"Oh no."

The truck was slowing. The man in the passenger seat was looking back. "They've gone far enough to know we're not ahead of them. Slow down more, Molly. Yeah, let that Chevy get ahead of you. Good."

He pressed Emma against him. "I don't want them catching sight of you, kiddo. Keep down."

"They're pulling out, Ramsey," Molly said.

He wanted to follow. So did Molly, probably. But they couldn't, not with Emma such an open target.

"It won't matter," Ramsey said. "Once we know who owns the truck, we'll have what we need. We don't have to do everything."

"I don't know about that," she said, her voice all rough and low. Then she smiled at Emma and said, "Sure thing," and slowed down even more.

"They're hanging on the side, the way we did." He weighed the options. "Drive like a bat out of hell, Molly. In a couple of exits, we're out of here."

She didn't hesitate for an instant. She floored the gas pedal. The Jeep hit ninety miles an hour quickly. They sped by two exits, Molly weaving in and out like a pro, then she slowed and swung off at the third exit onto a high arcing road that flattened finally, headed due south.

"Good going. Keep driving, then pull over about a mile toward—what's the name of the town in this direction?"

"Paulson, according to the sign we just passed."

"Yeah, it's about three miles to Paulson. Let's go nearly to the town, then take a side road. We'll sit there for a while. I'll bet everyone's thirsty. We'll have to buy a bottle of water."

"I have to go to the bathroom," Emma said.

"I do, too," Ramsey said, hugging her. "Hold it three more minutes, Em."

The cell phone beeped.

"Savich?"

"Yes. Since you didn't have a clean set, we have three possibilities."

"Okay. I've got a pen and paper." Molly watched him pull a pad from the glove compartment and write down names and addresses. She heard him say, "Thanks, Savich. I owe you big time." There was a long pause, then, "I'll tell you everything when I can, but not yet. Say hello to Sherlock for me."

He shut down the phone.

"It appears we've lost those guys from the restaurant. I still think we should call the cops, Molly."

"No, not yet. Please, not yet."

He sighed deeply. The last thing he wanted was for her to try to take Emma and go off on her own. He had a strong feeling she'd do that if he didn't play by her rules. It wasn't only that she didn't trust the police. It was something more, something she hadn't told him. "Well, hell," he said, "let's go to Aspen and stay at the Jerome. I'll take you guys to the Cantina for a good Mexican meal."

Molly pulled off the road a minute later. She took Emma to the cover of some bushes. Molly met his eyes over a tangle of blackberries. He had eyes nearly as black as his hair, thick hair a bit on the long side since he'd been away from civilization for three weeks. He had a strong face, high cheekbones, an olive complexion. She wondered if he didn't have some Italian blood lurking somewhere. He also had the beginnings of a five-o'clock shadow. Actually, now that she was really looking at him for the first time, she realized he was handsome, not drop-dead handsome like a film star, but handsome in a way that was calm and strong, a handsome that you could trust. She owed him the rest of the truth, but not yet.

She thought, as she helped Emma with her clothes, that it felt rather strange not to be alone anymore. She'd known him for less than one day. It seemed longer, but the fact was that she didn't really know him at all. She knew his reputation, but not the man. He'd saved Emma. That was really the beginning and the end of it. He'd have her gratitude forever.

She smiled at him.

Ramsey did a double take. He smiled back at her automatically. He'd been wishing that he'd gotten a look at the other man at the restaurant. Were they dealing with two new men entirely? Probably so. There'd been no sign that either of them had been wounded. If they were new on the scene, then there might be a lot more going on here. What was Molly keeping from him?

He handed Molly the cell phone when she and Emma got back to the Jeep. "It's time to call the Denver police. It's time to tell them that Emma's safe. Whatever else you don't want to tell them, then keep it to yourself. But at least do that much."

She pulled a small notebook from her large shoulder bag. She looked up a number, then dialed it in. He handed her the paper with the three names and addresses on it. He moved to the driver's side, watching Emma crowd close to her.

She gave no greeting, said, "I've got my daughter back, Detective Mecklin."

"Is that you, Mrs. Santera? What did you say? Are you all right? Are you injured?"

"No I'm not hurt. I said that I've got my daughter back, Detective." She could practically see those wide blue eyes of his narrowing as he stared at the phone, wondering if she'd lost it or not. She really didn't care. She rather hoped she'd never have to deal with Mecklin again, but here she was on the phone to the jerk. She'd thought he believed it was her fault that Emma was taken. She had hated him for helping to pile that guilt on her. She still did. She'd felt enough guilt on her own.

There was a very long silence, then, "I don't understand how that can be possible."

She laughed, the tension beginning to lighten. She was beginning to enjoy herself. The sexist jerk. "It is, believe me. Would you like me to tell you what's happened?"

"But we just got a ransom note last night. The kidnappers want $500,000."

"Don't let anyone pay it. I've got my daughter right here, Detective. Emma, say hello to the detective."

"Hello, Detective Mecklin. I'm with my mom and Ramsey. He saved me and then my mommy found us. We're okay."

"Ramsey? Who the hell's this Ramsey?"

Molly pulled the phone back up. "That's not important for the moment, Detective Mecklin. Listen to me. I've got three names and addresses that go with these license plate letters and numbers. You need to see which of these fits with Emma's kidnappers. One of them does, count on it."

"I don't understand this, Mrs. Santera. You need to come back to Denver and talk to us. If you really have Emma, you need to bring her in to see us. We've got doctors here for her, a shrink trauma team, everything she'll need. Was that really Emma? Are you all right, Mrs. Santera? Where are you?"

"Will you do anything with the information if I give it to you, Detective Mecklin, or am I wasting my time?"

There was another long pause with very controlled breathing. "Give me the info," he said.

She read out the names and addresses very slowly, occasionally repeating. "I don't recognize any of these names myself, but one of them has to be involved with the kidnappers. Now maybe you've got a chance to catch them. Surely there's a drop site indicated on the note. Well, now you don't have to worry about Emma. You can forget the trauma team. Do your job,

Detective. Nail the bad guys. Oh yeah, the guy who kidnapped Emma took her to a cabin not far from Dillinger. I'm sure he's not there anymore but you may find out something."

"Are you in Dillinger, Mrs. Santera?"

"No, Detective, I'm not, so please don't bother siccing any local cops on me."

"This sure puts a mighty different spin on things, Mrs. Santera."

"Sure does," she agreed. "You've got everything?"

"Yeah, I've got it. But you've got to tell me what's going on. The FBI agents just walked in. They want to talk to you. They don't think—"

She spoke over him, slowly and clearly. "The license is on a dirty black pickup truck. It's fairly new. A Chevy. You've got that?"

"Yes, yes. Hold on. Don't hang up, Mrs. Santera. You need us. Here's Agent Anchor."

"I don't think so, Detective. Give them the information. They'll drool, if they bother to believe it."

"We would have gotten this information in a very short time. Now, I believe you, Mrs. Santera, but . . . well, you see, this is very irregular." It was Agent Anchor, a man with a great deal of experience with kidnappings. He was also a dictator who believed everyone except himself had a brain the size of a pea. He'd ordered the Denver cops around as if they were his personal chattel.

"No buts, Agent Anchor. Catch the men who took my daughter."

"You have no idea if any of these license plates has anything to do with the kidnappers, do you? Look, I don't understand any of this. Tell me where you are. Do you understand what I'm saying to you, Mrs. Santera? You may be in danger. Tell me where you found Emma. You can't just call in and order us around and—"

"Agent Anchor, go catch the kidnappers. Ah, that pickup truck was last seen just west of Rappahoe on Highway 70." Molly smiled as she pushed the *Off* button. "I hated to tell him that because he's not stupid and he'll know that's where we are, too. But I had to, otherwise, how could they catch them? I hope they can locate that cabin quickly, maybe find something helpful."

"No, you're right. You had to tell them. By the time they get themselves together, we'll be tucked safely away in Aspen. They really shouldn't care all that much about us, and where we are, but who knows? At least our perps don't know we got them tagged. They shouldn't be hiding out. Were the Fed agents a big pain?"

"Yes. If I hadn't been so terrified about Emma, I would have felt sorry for the local cops. The Feds treated them like gofers. Detective Mecklin isn't really all that much of a jerk, but he's also not what you'd call very flexible. He's got this big handlebar mustache, dyed really black, you know? It droops around his mouth, makes him look something like a basset hound. He's also very fat. I hope he doesn't have a heart attack." Then she just shook her head. "He didn't want to believe that I had Emma. He even asked me if that was really Emma who'd spoken to him. As for Agent Anchor, he has a God complex."

A lot of the Federal people did, but they were getting better, or at least some of them were, like Dillon Savich. He'd like to meet this Agent Anchor when this was over. He'd like to pin Agent Anchor's ears back. "You did well, Molly. At least we had to do that much. Let's go to Aspen. Let's forget both of them for now. We'll call Detective Mecklin back tomorrow and see what he's got."

"A ransom note arrived last night. The kidnappers wanted a half a million."

"Their bluff," he said. "It's a good try." He looked quickly at Emma, who looked to be nearly asleep, but he wasn't fooled for an instant. "Just a bluff," he said again. "But it gives the cops a real chance at them now. So there are at least four other guys besides the kidnapper. I wonder how many people are involved in this? And why? It isn't just a kidnapping, Molly."

"I don't like it," Emma said, snuggling close to her mother. "I don't like it at all."

Their eyes met. "Neither do we, Emma. Neither do we," Molly said.

Ramsey pulled back onto the highway. There was no sign of the black pickup, thank the good Lord.

NINE

After Molly showed him a weighty wad of one-hundred-dollar bills and assured him she had lots more in her bra, Ramsey got them a junior suite at the Jerome, providing them a false name and paying cash. They were shown to a huge single room filled with Victorian furniture, long red or gold fringe on the lamps, and wall-to-wall carpeting woven with big cabbage roses and copious vines. There was violent red wallpaper in the bathroom, which had been updated to a rich pink marble. The old with the new—it was a fascinating combination. There was a sitting area at one end of the big room, with the bed, dresser, and a couple of more chairs at the other. There were tall windows with rich velvet draperies. "I always wanted to stay here," Ramsey said, standing back. "I saw the place way back when I was a kid here on a ski break. It's something, isn't it?"

"Yes," Molly said. "They didn't have two beds? Just this king?"

"We're married, remember? Don't look at it too long, it'll make you bilious. Also, don't worry about it. They're bringing up a cot for me." The spread was a bright blue velvet with red tassels that screamed Victorian Wild West.

Emma said, "What's 'bilious'?"

"Bad liver stuff."

He saw her repeat the word a couple of more times beneath her breath. He smiled as he watched Molly go down on her knees and hug Emma until, suddenly, she squealed. Molly let her loose and the both of them began to laugh. "It's a game we play," Molly said. "If Emma can let me hug her for a whole minute without making a single sound, then she gets an ice cream. Actually, she usually wins. Are you feeling sorry for me, kiddo?"

"I just wanted to see you smile really big, Mama."

"Then you won the smile out of me."

Molly had a single duffel bag, Emma had her stuffed pillowcase, and Ramsey had two suitcases. He'd locked his mom's old Olivetti typewriter and all the pages he'd managed to write during his stay before Emma, and some books and novels in the Jeep. The hotel brought up a cot for him, too short, but he shook his head at her when she would have protested.

Actually, Ramsey didn't care if he slept on the floor. His leg hurt like hell, he had a headache, and he felt as if he'd hit a brick wall. Molly looked as if she had her nose pressed against that same brick wall. She was standing in the middle of the room, running her hand through her rioting red hair.

He smiled. "You want me to give Emma a bath? No, I take that back. She can bathe herself."

"She's really not very good at it, but she does try." Molly grabbed Emma up and sniffed behind her ear. "Smells sweet. You did a good job. You want me to bathe you this time, Em? For a change?"

Emma nodded happily.

Molly turned to Ramsey, who looked ready to fall over. "You lie down. I'll bring you some aspirin. Do you put an ice pack on the leg?"

"I hadn't thought of that. Why not?"

"Good. Lie down, Ramsey. I'll be right back."

After she'd watched him wash down three aspirin and she'd laid the ice wrapped in a towel over his bandaged leg, she said, "Do you mind if we don't go to the Cantina?"

"I'll see if they deliver."

They did, for a fifty-buck service charge. It was Aspen, he thought, as he ate a ten-dollar taco.

EXHAUSTION hit big time after they'd consumed a good half dozen beef tacos, and enough chips and salsa for a football team. Emma had some guacamole smeared on her chin when it was all over and she'd looked wonderful. She was asleep ten minutes later, next to her mother, just after they'd gotten her to brush her teeth.

She beat them to sleep by five minutes.

Molly awoke at midnight at the final stroke from a big grandfather clock in the corner out in the corridor. There was a quarter moon sending a white shaft of light through the open window. It wasn't too cold, just cold enough to make you pull the covers to your chin and let the fresh air hit your face.

It was the first time she'd slept over three hours in more than two weeks. Sixteen days, she thought, suddenly sitting up just to look over to see Emma curled up into a ball, the pillow hugged to her chest, her beautiful hair, free of its braid, tangled about her head. She was safe.

Molly felt tears sting her eyes, felt them ooze out and slowly trickle over her cheeks. They'd been so very lucky. As it turned out, she hadn't been the important one in the equation, not that she'd ever really believed she actually would be.

Ramsey Hunt. He'd saved her daughter. He would have continued to protect her until he'd gotten her back safely.

The tears came more freely. She sobbed. Oh no, that was humiliating. She stuffed her fist into her mouth.

"Molly? It's okay."

How had he heard her? Emma was still sound asleep. He said quietly, "Cry, it's good for you. I'll bet this is the first time you've had the luxury to let go. Think you can?"

She kept crying and he kept talking, saying nothing really, just nonsense. Then, "Mama, what's wrong?"

Emma sounded terrified.

Ramsey said quickly, "It's all right, Emma. Roll over and hug your mama. She's crying because she's so relieved you're safe. She's been on the edge for a really long time. She's been really scared for you."

Molly was hiccuping, crying, and now laughing. Emma had wrapped her arms around her.

"I feel better now. Thanks, Em." She kissed her daughter's neck, and felt as happy as she'd ever felt in her life. In that instant, she remembered another moment, a long time ago, when she'd believed there was no way she could have been happier. It had been a lie.

The three of them went back to sleep, Ramsey's feet hanging off the end of the cot. It was Ramsey who woke near three o'clock in the morning.

Maybe he'd heard something. His brain was still turned inward to a pleasant dream. It was about Susan. She was wearing her uniform and smiling. She saluted him, then poked him in the belly. Once he was fully awake, though, bittersweet memories flooded through him. Then suddenly, it all just faded back into time. He wanted no more dreams about Susan.

He heard it again. Could they be that good?

Very slowly, he stood up. He saw that both Emma and Molly were still asleep. He heard only Molly's deep, even breathing. He was glad for that. He didn't want them frightened.

He stood up, felt his stiff leg lock on him, and grabbed one of the high chair backs. Not unexpected. He held very still and listened.

It was a shuffling sound. It was coming from the corridor, right outside their room door. He picked up his pistol from the small circular table beside the cot. He forced his leg to move, one step at a time, quietly, toward the door, pausing every few steps to listen.

He heard voices. No, it wasn't possible that it could be trouble. There was no way they could have found out where they were. The hotel registration hadn't demanded an ID. There was no way anyone could know they were here. But they had seen the Jeep. They could have easily traced the license plate, or even spotted it coming into town. He cursed. He was an idiot. Tomorrow, he'd have to turn it in, maybe buy a used car, another Jeep, or any four-wheel-drive vehicle. He heard the voices again, too low for him to make out what they were saying.

He held his Smith & Wesson ready.

It was a man's voice, low and urgent, clear now. "Listen, Doris, you want to sneak back in there, you do it. But your old man could be awake even as we speak. I don't want him to blow my head off. No, don't go in there. If you do, at least wait until I get out of here."

He leaned his head against the door, relief pouring through him. It was a wife screwing around on her husband.

It wasn't anybody after Emma.

He heard a woman's voice, with a touch of hysteria in it. It would be better if she didn't try to sneak back in, he thought, but thank goodness, it wasn't any of his business. He silently checked the lock and the chain.

He laid the Smith & Wesson back on the circular table. When he turned to the cot, he saw Molly sitting up, staring toward him.

He whispered, "It's a wife cheating on her husband."

Emma said in a sleepy voice, "It couldn't be him, could it, Ramsey? He didn't see really good. He didn't wear his glasses all of the time. That's how I got away. I made my pillow look like me when he was out smoking a cigarette on the front steps. When he came back, he looked for me, and thought he saw me. I crawled out the front door when he was drinking a glass of whiskey. He really liked whiskey. He kept saying he didn't like it, that it rotted his soul, but he drank it, lots of it."

Molly said, "Do you know his name, Em?"

But Emma folded, just shut down again, her breathing even and slow. She was sound asleep.

They looked at each other. Molly said, "What am I going to do?"

"I told you, Molly. I'm in for the long haul. Now the question is, what are *we* going to do? Tell you what. We're both still too tired to think straight. I've got some ideas. We'll discuss it tomorrow."

She was shaking her head back and forth, her red hair moving in concert. "I can't go back to Denver. I'm never going back to Denver. I don't understand what's going on here. How many people are involved in this? Who are they? How, why, could Emma's kidnapping be a conspiracy?"

"Conspiracy," he repeated slowly. "Why do you call it a conspiracy?"

She shrugged, one corner of her sleep shirt falling off her shoulder.

"I guess kidnapping could end up being a conspiracy if the parents were in on it, or if it was done for another purpose. But you didn't mean that. Did you?"

"I just said the word. It seemed it might be possible. We already know about up to five different men."

"An elaborate scheme then. But a conspiracy? That smacks of something darker, something beneath the surface. It might mean it would involve people around you."

She was silent. He watched her pull up the shoulder of her sleep shirt. It said on the front: *BIGFOOT WAS HERE.* Her hair was corkscrewed and wild around her pale face. She looked inutterably weary. And also very pretty, he thought, somewhat amazed that he'd noticed and here it was in the middle of the night. Her skin was very white, unlike his, with his olive skin tone. He wanted to put his hand on her, to compare the color difference between them. He was losing it. "Let's get some sleep. We're out of here tomorrow."

HE returned to the Jerome at noon. Molly and Emma were playing Old Maid seated cross-legged opposite each other, the card pile in the middle.

"No, don't get up. We're the proud owners of a 1989 Toyota 4Runner with lots of miles on it. It's a two-door model, on the beat-up side, but who cares? It's got four-wheel drive, nearly all the comforts of the Jeep."

He'd gotten the maximum allowed from AMEX and paid the car dealer in cash. He added, "Even if they've tracked down the Jeep, it'll take them a good long time to find it in that long-term parking lot over by the lift." But he knew they weren't safe, not by a long shot.

He said quickly, "It's time we checked out of here. Fifteen minutes okay with everybody? We shop and then we're heading west."

They'd spoken about it briefly that morning when they'd awakened. "It's our next destination," Ramsey had said, "it gets us closer to my home and my turf."

Molly had said quietly, afraid that Emma would awaken, "I know we can't stay here. Where west do you want to go?"

"Truckee. I know the area very well. Let's get ourselves lost for the time being in the Sierras. I had a friend from college who lived on Lake Tahoe."

Molly didn't say anything more until she got him in the bathroom with the door shut, Emma in the bedroom packing her pillowcase.

He said, "Anyone with a brain could trace the money withdrawal from AMEX that I used to pay for the Toyota, and I think we've got professionals here. So our best bet is to get ourselves lost for the time being. The Sierras are beautiful and out of the way. Any problem with that?"

"I've never been to Lake Tahoe," she said, fiddling with a towel that was wadded up. She was methodically folding it, arranging it back on the rack.

"It's a little town, quaint, all rigged out for the skiers in the winter and the hikers in the summer. Emma'll like it. It'll be safe."

She looked up at him. "How's your leg?"

"Better this morning. You and Emma were both standing over me when I took up the tape and gauze. The skin's staying together, a good sign. The flesh is pink. Very little swelling. It just aches."

"You wouldn't lie to me?"

"Yes, but not about this."

"All right. Let's go." She turned away, her hand on the bathroom door-knob, and said over her shoulder, "You don't have to do this, you really don't. I have money. Not just the cash I showed you. I have lots of money, family money and money from my divorce from Louey. I could get Emma to safety."

"Don't, Molly. I couldn't leave Emma in danger."

She sighed as she twisted a corkscrew curl around her index finger. "I know."

She opened the bathroom door and walked out, calling, "Em, love, are you ready? Do you know what? I'm going to buy you a duffel bag, just like mine."

"Can it be a Mingus Raiders duffel? Yours looks like a soldier's."

"Okay, Mingus Raiders it is." She said over her shoulder to Ramsey, "The Mingus cartoon good guys also include Mingus cartoon good girls. They're hot stuff."

THEY drove all that day and night, spelling each other, and reached Truckee the next evening at just after six o'clock. They spent that night at a Best Western Motel.

The next morning Ramsey went to a local Realtor's office and looked over the rental houses available. They didn't want a condo, too many people around, they told the woman. They were a family on vacation. They'd saved their money for this and didn't want to use credit cards.

If the woman didn't believe this, she didn't argue, just showed them properties. Emma fell in love with the third one, a small two-bedroom house that sat off by itself, backed against a forest and fronting a small creek. Tree-covered mountains rose all around it. Lake Tahoe was only about four miles distant. It was safe. Everyone was pleased.

They paid five hundred for the week, including the security deposit. They stocked up for a week at Food Giant.

When they returned to Nathan's Creek, it was well into the afternoon. Emma was asleep in Molly's arms. Ramsey took her and carried her up to the larger of the two bedrooms.

When he met Molly downstairs in the kitchen, she handed him a glass of iced mineral water.

"Come in the living room," he said. "It's time."

"All right," she said. "You're right. It is time. We've got to do some talking and some planning."

He waited until she sat down in a big recliner that was well worn, a real guy's chair, then said, "Now, no more stalling. Who are you, Molly? What are you still keeping from me?"

"It's impossible that Emma's kidnapping has anything to do with what you don't know."

"Molly, I'm going to throw this water glass at you."

"I was Margaret Lord before I married."

He just stared at her, then breathed out hard. His leg started hurting. "Shit," he said. "Your daddy is Mason Lord?"

JOE Elders loved those few precious minutes just before the sun arched up over the low-lying barren hills just a mile or so from his farm. He stood there, breathing in the fifty-degree air, filling his lungs, letting the silence and soft air fill him.

The sun struck his eyes with brilliant light and he smiled into it, closing them. He heard Millie moo. She was soon joined by half a dozen of her cousins. It was time to begin his day, and that meant milking his girls. He whistled as he walked to the cow barn, brand-new, just completed a month before, with all the new technology they told him would at least put him in the same ballpark as the big dairy outfits. And he'd had the money to pay for it all. He'd been smart, really smart. They hadn't taken advantage of him, no they hadn't. After his deal, he hadn't had to borrow anything. He paused, sniffing the air.

He could swear it was the sweet clinging scent of marijuana. He kicked one of the goat's favorite old chewing gloves out of his path. He cursed. It was pot he smelled. Nancy was smoking and carrying on again, and after she promised him and her mother that she would straighten up. Pot, of all things. She was sixteen years old, popular at school. He hoped she wasn't that popular. No, she was too young to really have the hots for any of the boys he'd seen around. But pot, hell and damnation.

He opened the barn door. He was greeted with a chorus of moos, most of them welcoming, a couple pissed, he could tell. They didn't like all the new equipment that relieved them of their milk.

Shirley was the one who hated the machines the most. Since she was one of his old girls, he'd decided just the week before to milk her himself. She enjoyed that, turning her head to look at him while he pulled on her teats.

He got all the other cows set up. It still took him a while. Well, he'd get better and faster at it soon. Then he took his old stool down to where Shirley was standing, still and fat with milk, watching him come closer.

"Good morning, old girl," he called out, giving her a wink like the one he'd given her every dawn for the past seven years.

He began to whistle as he set the stool down beside her. "Now, let's make you a couple of pounds lighter."

He heard a soft whooshing sound. It was close, real close. He wrenched around on the stool. There was a man standing over him. He was black, his eyes hard and wide, his head bald. Joe never even had a chance to ask the man who he was.

He felt a huge hand on his shoulder, and saw a big hammer part the air. He felt the blow throughout his body, but it wasn't exactly painful, just a numbing jarring that made his eyes blink once in surprise. The large hand released his shoulder.

Joe Elders fell beside Shirley's stool, his eyes staring up at her milk-swelled teats.

TEN

"I heard Emma moving around upstairs. We've only got a few minutes before she comes down. We'll get back to your daddy a bit later. Now our immediate problems: We've got to assume they're professionals. And that means we've also got to assume they have a backup organization to be on us in a flash if we use credit cards. If we're careful, your three thousand and my two thousand should last us until this mess is cleaned up."

Molly figured she'd been frugal for a total of thirteen months in her life. She'd gone from one wealthy home to taking care of herself, and she'd done it, not that it had lasted long. Then she'd gone to another one. From a rich father to a rich husband. But for the past two years, she'd been on her own again. She loved it. She grinned. Actually, it was the first time she'd smiled in a very long time. "I'm going to go scrub a toilet."

"Mama, you're joking."

Emma had arrived, full of energy. Molly hauled her up in a big hug, kissed her small ear, and said, "No, sweetie, this time I'm not. Well, maybe. I'm thinking that if I can take Ramsey in poker, then he can scrub the john. What do you think?"

Emma looked very serious, her head cocked to one side. "I think you could beat him in Old Maid. I beat you last time we played poker."

"Thanks for the support, kiddo. All right, I'll think about it. Maybe I can play him to a draw."

"That's chess, Mama."

"Yes, but maybe I can figure out how to apply it to poker. Hey, you want some hot dogs for supper?"

"Oh yes. Ramsey makes the best. We stuck them on coat hangers and held them over the fire in the fireplace."

Ramsey was sitting in that big recliner, his hands folded over his stomach, a pillow under his leg. "You'll have to go a long way to beat my hot dogs, Molly."

"I know how to make the *secret relish,* handed down from my mother's family in Italy. The relish will make her jump off your bandwagon quick enough."

"We'll see about that. I've got secret other things, like good cheap yellow mustard." He said to Emma, "How come you know about draws and chess?"

"My boyfriend taught me."

"You've got a boyfriend, Emma?"

"His name's Jake. He's my nerd boyfriend."

Ramsey rolled his eyes. "You also got a jock boyfriend?"

"Oh no, Ramsey, they're gross."

"Hey now, I was once a jock and I wasn't gross. Well, maybe I was for a while, when I was real young."

"Young as me?"

He stared down into that small intent upturned face. "No, Em, I was never as young as you."

She giggled, actually giggled. It warmed him to his toes. Molly looked up, smiling. Emma said, "I'm just glad you're not as young as me right now." She lightly touched her palm to the wound in his thigh. "It's not warm anymore."

"Nope, all of me is at room temperature again."

She patted him, then skipped off to the small kitchen to help her mother.

It was an easy evening, with no talk at all about the sword of Damocles that was hanging over their heads, no talk just yet about Molly's criminal father. They played word games, then Ramsey gave Emma a reading lesson using the sets of letters and numbers he'd bought at the bookstore in Dillinger.

The kid was smart and fast. She was writing his name in full sentences, along with her name and her mother's by nine o'clock. "You put the best teacher in the world with the smartest kid in the world, and just look what you've got." He leaned down to stare at the last word Emma had printed: *john*.

Both of them tucked her up in the small single twin bed.

"You want a night-light on, Em?"

"No, Mama. Are you going to sleep with me again?"

"Yes," Molly said easily. "If Ramsey wakes up and gets lonesome, he can talk to us through the wall."

Emma was smiling even as her eyes closed. They stood looking down at her, this child who had changed both their lives.

"She wrote my name," Ramsey said. "It was legible. She wrote it in a whole sentence. Amazing."

"She's got her mother's brains." Molly grinned up at him. "*My Ramsey is smart.* Yep, that has a real ring to it. Can you believe she spelled *john*?"

"And she did it well. It made her laugh, Molly. Where'd she get the hair?"

"Her father." Her voice was clipped. She didn't say anything else. Why hadn't he come back here after Emma had been kidnapped? He'd teased himself with that question at least half a dozen times now. He simply couldn't imagine any father not being frantic about his child. That the parents were divorced made no difference. He said, "Let's go downstairs. Now that Emma's in bed, I want you to tell me everything about Daddy."

"I should call Detective Mecklin and Agent Anchor first. I forgot."

"No, you didn't, but it doesn't matter. Let's do it. Who knows, maybe they've got something."

"Don't bet your gym socks on it."

She asked for Detective Mecklin and got put on hold. She stared down at the phone, then suddenly banged down the receiver. "They were trying to trace the call," she said. "I know it. The bastards."

"You're probably right. Let's call in the morning. They didn't have enough time. Don't worry."

"I guess you'd know all about that."

"Enough. It's not as if we really have to hide from the cops, Molly."

"I don't want to let them near Emma. Don't you see? They might take her away and give her over to a battery of doctors, strangers, all of them. She's doing so well. I can't take that risk. You didn't want to do it either. Just leave it alone."

"All right. Tell you what. Let me call Dillon Savich, my friend in Washington, D.C. See if he knows what's going on."

"Who is this friend, exactly?"

"He's a computer expert who happens to be an FBI agent. Trust me on this, he's not like Agent Anchor. Actually, he and his partner—who's now his wife, Sherlock—were the ones who broke The Toaster case in Chicago. Do you remember that?"

"That was the young guy who'd killed those families?"

"Yeah. Russell Bent."

"They won't ever let him out, will they?"

"Trust the system on this one, Molly. Russell will be in a psychiatric hospital until he dies."

"Yeah, but I also remember the killer in Boston who escaped when the judge ordered that he be let out of restraints while he was being evaluated by the psychiatrists. The String Killer, wasn't that the moniker the press gave him?"

"Yes, that's what happened."

She gave him a long look. "Some system."

"You know, Molly, our legal system works well most of the time. Since people run it, sure there are screwups now and again. You need to be a bit more objective."

Molly sighed, then rose and walked to the French windows that looked out over a small sloping lawn to Nathan's Creek, full and rushing from melting mountain snow. The half-moon made the snow glisten. "This is a beautiful place. Aren't you going to call Dillon Savich?"

"Yep. You got me sidetracked. I want to tell him what's going on. I want to tell him who you are. He won't do anything unless I ask him to. All right?"

Molly nodded.

He used the house phone and punched the speaker button. The phone was picked up on the third ring in Washington, D.C. Ramsey identified himself.

A very alert Savich said, "You know it's one A.M. here? Never mind. Where are you? You've got the speaker on. Are you finally ready to tell me what's going on?"

"You know about that kidnapping case in Denver? Emma Santera?"

"Yes. Wait, don't tell me. You're somehow involved in that?"

Ramsey gave him an unedited version of what had happened until they'd arrived in California. "We're all right, hopefully, safely hidden. Mrs. Santera doesn't want anyone to know exactly where we are."

"Including the FBI? Including the cops? This is all very strange, Ramsey."

"Yeah, I know. Bear with me. Can you tell me what's happening there? Has an Agent Anchor said anything that's filtered back?"

Savich laughed. "Has Bud said anything? He's been yelling his head off, claiming he's going to bring in Mrs. Santera for hampering his investigation. It's going to be hard to keep my mouth shut, Ramsey, but I will until you give me the 'go' signal. Can you begin to imagine what folks here would say if they knew you were a part of this and you were getting inside information from me?"

"What about the owner of the truck? We gave the Denver PD and Agent Anchor the three names and license numbers you gave me."

"The truck was reported stolen last month from a dairy farmer in Loveland, Colorado. The wife reported it. Then the husband said it hadn't been stolen, he'd sold it, and hadn't told his wife. Who knows? Did he sell it to the kidnappers? That plays for me."

"Yeah, it does for me too." Ramsey sighed.

"You might consider coming in now. Any more attempts to get the kid?"

"Not since we've come to our new location."

"Come in, Ramsey. It sounds dicey. I agree that this isn't just a simple kidnapping. You got any ideas?"

"Maybe. Look, Savich, let me keep us hidden awhile longer. I'll check in on Friday unless something happens sooner. Listen, thanks. I owe you."

"You can bet on it."

"Is that Sherlock I hear? Give her a kiss for me."

"Not on your life. You're too much like the kind of man she likes, all hard and tough. Given your macho demonstration a while back in your courtroom, I'd be hard-pressed to keep her away from you, especially if she's having a bad day and not thinking clearly. No, all kisses are from me. Take care of yourself, Ramsey, and call if there's anything I can do."

"Thanks, Savich." Ramsey slowly hung up the phone. "You heard everything?"

She nodded.

"Now, no more procrastinating. It's time. On to Daddy."

She started shaking her head.

"Listen, Molly, your father is Mason Lord. It's time we thought about him. I don't think it's possible he could be involved directly in any of this, but it's very possible that from what we've seen, maybe some of your father's enemies had Emma kidnapped to use as leverage against your father."

She didn't turn, ran her fingers over the thick fabric of the light tan drapes. "I think he would have warned me if someone he was dealing with might consider such a thing."

"Yes, he probably would have, if he'd had warning. Do you agree that perhaps some of his enemies are involved up to their gum lines to get leverage on him, to milk him? You wondered about all the guys who seemed to be involved in this, so far. Well, that could be our answer."

She still didn't turn around. Slowly, she pulled the drapes shut over the French windows and stood there, head down, saying nothing.

He noticed that she was barefoot. Her toes were painted a pale pink and were chipping. "When did you last speak to your father?"

"Last week."

"And you told him what was going on?"

She nodded.

"Tell me something, Molly. When was the last time you saw your father?"

"That's none of your business. It has nothing to do with this. Stop pushing me on this."

"I want us to stay alive. You're making that difficult by holding out on me. When, Molly? I deserve to know." He rubbed his leg.

"All right, but it doesn't make any difference. The last time I saw him was three years ago."

He slammed the recliner forward and stood, staring at her. "Three years ago? What's been going on?"

She turned then to face him, but she didn't move from her stand by the windows. "The last time I saw him was when Emma had just turned three years old. He flew to Denver for her birthday. But that wasn't the real reason he came. He was angry at my husband. He came to Denver to see him."

"And did he see your husband?"

"Yes, he saw him. Louey ended up with two broken ribs, a fractured kidney, and bruises everywhere except on his face, that lasted until the next Christmas."

"What had Louey done?"

"I don't want to talk about it. It has nothing to do with this."

"You have no clue what does or what doesn't have to do with anything at all."

"Listen, as I told you, Louey is my ex-husband. We've been divorced for two years. I didn't lie to Emma about her father being worried about her. Louey did call once when he heard that she was missing, which was a big surprise to me. He called me before I even considered contacting him. As Emma already told you, he hasn't bothered to see her since he left.

"It was right after one of his concerts in Berlin. I remember clearly that he asked about Emma, said he'd heard from somebody in Denver that she'd been snatched, and wondered if I had her back yet. When I said no, he acted all sorry and depressed for about a minute. Then he sort of laughed and said that my daddy would pay the moon to get her back, and not to worry. He told me how the tour was going. He said this *fräulein* reporter—yeah, that's what he called her—from the *Berliner Zeitung* compared him to Bruce Springsteen. He told me the Europeans had better taste than the Americans—in other words they like him better—said he just might spend most of the year in Europe. He talked about his conquests in Europe, in great detail. I don't think you need to know any of that. He never mentioned Emma after the first time.

"The policewoman listening with me just stared at me. She worshiped Louey, prayed he'd call so she could just hear his sexy voice. Or rather, she worshiped him until she heard what that sexy voice said. She patted my shoulder when I hung up.

"I started crying and she kept patting. She thought I was sorry about Louey leaving me, sorry that he was bragging about all these women."

"I remember now," he said after a moment. "There was press about the divorce, but never any details, no hints of infidelity or drugs or anything at all. Just a quiet announcement of irreconcilable differences, something like that. It was out of the public eye very quickly."

"My father is powerful. In this instance it was a good thing. No one had much to say about anything. There were a couple of days of speculation in the tabloids, but even they dropped it. I was very grateful to my father." She looked down at her fingernails. There was mustard from the hot dogs on her index finger. She licked it off.

"Molly?"

"Louey, her biological father, didn't ever want her. After we split up, I think he was relieved to be out of the daddy business. A child didn't go with the sexy footloose image he had of himself. Funny thing is, she's probably just as talented musically as he is. Maybe more so."

"How did Louey know Emma had been kidnapped? You said he called you before you called him."

"I wondered later about that. One of his friends in Denver probably called him. Louey undoubtedly thought that if it hit the press, he should act the concerned papa so he wouldn't be seen in a bad light. Who knows?"

"I wonder which friend in Denver bothered to call him."

"He didn't say and I was too upset to ask. But you know, Louey is friends with a lot of folks in the media, from TV to newspapers. It was probably one of his newspaper buddies."

"Is there a special buddy?"

"Yes, his name is James Hicks and he's with the *Denver Post*. Why?"

"No reason. I like to gather information. Now, are you going to call your papa and tell him Emma's safe?"

"Yes, I should. He's been very worried. I called him right away when Emma was kidnapped. I knew he'd have some of his people on it right away, and he did. A man and two women came by six hours after I'd called. It drove the local cops nuts. Lots of suspicion. I ignored the cops' bitching about outsiders. I told them everything I could, why not? They wanted to help; my father was paying them to find Emma. I don't know what his people actually did. I saw them several more times. We discussed leads, possibilities. If they found out anything, I don't know about it."

"Did you tell them you were taking off to find Emma yourself?"

"No, I didn't. I'll call him right now. At least he won't try to trace the call." She paused a moment, then said, turning to face him, "I wonder if my father suspected Emma's kidnapping had anything to do with him? I bet he has. I know one thing: If he found out who did this, he wouldn't hesitate to sanction a kill."

ELEVEN

Sanction a kill. She'd said it so easily, so naturally.

How many times had she heard it said when she was a kid?

"All right, I'm going to call. Hey, wait a minute. What if those men were there to rescue Emma and they thought you were the kidnapper? Of course they'd try to get rid of you. Of course they'd follow you. Oh goodness, there's no end to the possibilities. I've got a headache, Ramsey."

"That goes really well with my leg ache. That theory could fly until you showed up. You think they haven't at least seen a photo of you? You think that there's any way they wouldn't know you're the boss's daughter? Call, Molly. I want to hear what he has to say. Use your cell phone. Come over here so I can hear."

She sat down on the arm of the recliner and began dialing. Area code 312. Chicago and outlying residential areas, like Oak Park. Sure, that was where Mason Lord lived, only the best. He saw her hand tighten around the phone.

Why hadn't she seen her father for three years?

The phone rang twice, then a man answered, his voice deep and mellifluous.

"Miles? It's me, Molly."

"Yes, Molly. You've got news about Emma?"

"She's fine, Miles. She's back with me. Thank you for asking. I want to give Dad the news."

"Just a moment. Goodness, this is a relief. Mr. Lord's been on a real tear."

"You heard that?" she asked Ramsey. Ramsey was three inches from the receiver.

"Yeah, I heard."

There was a good twenty more seconds of silence, then, "Molly? Emma's safe?"

"Hello, Dad. Yes, I've got her with me. I found her. She's fine."

"I don't understand. I haven't heard a word from my people. Do the Denver police know you've got Emma back?"

"Yes, they know. They don't like the fact that I got her back without them."

"Tell me."

She took a deep breath. "You know I went looking when the cops and the FBI didn't get anywhere. I would have thought your people would know. Well, I found her. A guy had saved her and I came upon both of them. She's safe. We're going to stay out of sight for a while."

"There's no reason to, Molly. Come home. You can bet I'll protect the both of you."

"No, not yet. There are a lot more people involved than just a single kidnapper. I don't want to take any chances. I'm going to keep Emma hidden as long as those people are still out there and looking for her." Her knuckles were white she was clutching the phone so tightly. "It's not a simple kidnapping, Dad."

"But they got a ransom note."

"Yes, but that ransom note arrived after I already had Emma back. It was a lie. Do you understand any of this?"

"No, but I'll speak to Buzz about it. We've already discussed the possibility of some enemy of mine being involved. But the important thing is you've got Emma back. I'm tremendously relieved." He sighed. She could picture him running his fingers lightly through his hair, never enough to mess it up. "We've got nothing as of yet. But I don't like the feel of this at all. How many people have you seen?"

"Probably four different men, but we've managed to get away from them. We're safely tucked away now."

"All right. I'll speak to Buzz Carmen immediately. He's still in Denver. How exactly did you find out about these other men?"

"I knew they were following so I pulled off at an exit. When they went by, I got the license. I checked with a friend who found out for me that the truck was reportedly stolen from a farmer in Loveland, Colorado. The wife reported it; then the husband said he'd sold it. It sounds like maybe he did sell it—to the kidnappers. I phoned in the license plate to the Denver PD and the FBI. I'd appreciate your checking as well, Dad, then I'd know it got done right." She gave him the license and the name of the farmer.

"I've got it. I don't suppose you'll tell me who gave you this information?"

"I can't."

He sighed. "Very well. Come home, Molly."

"I'll call tomorrow. Emma's fine. Don't worry. Those men won't find us."

"About this man who found Emma. Who is he? How can you be sure you can trust him?"

"If we can't trust him, Dad, then it's all over. Believe me, he's the most trustworthy man in the world. Tomorrow, Dad." She pushed the *Off* button and laid the phone on the table.

"At least you don't call him Godfather."

She smiled at him. It was a charming smile, warm and full. She had a wide mouth and very white teeth. His father was a dentist. Ramsey always noticed a person's teeth. His old man would really like what he saw.

Ramsey liked that smile, too. It was almost as if she was ready to stop being afraid. She said, "Mason Lord is very good-looking. He's black Irish: fair skinned, hair like ink, straight and thick, just a dabbling of gray at his temples. His eyes are such a startling blue, women stare at him. He doesn't appreciate having a grown daughter, much less a grandchild, but he copes. My mother was the one who told me I should call him by his first name, but I couldn't get the hang of it. Neither could he. I remember thinking Mason jar every time I used his first name. When I told him that, he threw up his hands, laughed, and said to forget it. He's been Dad for a very long time, actually since I was eight years old and moved away with my mother."

"I've never thought of Mason Lord as having human qualities, like a sense of humor. You don't look a thing like him."

"No, I'm the picture of my grandmother. She was an actress in the fifties. Never got very far with it because she wasn't beautiful or very photogenic. Boy, but could she act. It turned out not to be enough."

"You're far from plain, Molly."

She smiled at him, that same gorgeous smile. "You should see my mother. Now she's what you'd call a looker. She's fifty-five now and still a head-turning beauty. Both she and Father were appalled, I think, when I turned out the way I did."

She honestly believed what she was saying. It amazed him. Didn't she look in a mirror once in a while? "Where's your mother? What's her name?"

"Her name is Alicia and she lives near Livorno, Italy. That's where her family is. She and Dad divorced when I was just a kid. I lived with her in Italy nine months out of the year and the other three months with Dad. I came back to the United States to go to college at Vassar. I've only seen her once a year for the past seven or eight years."

"Does she know about Emma's kidnapping?"

"I don't think so, not unless she read about it in an Italian newspaper, and I strongly doubt the story made it there. I saw no reason to worry her."

"Your father hasn't remarried."

"Oh yes he has, nearly three years ago. Her name's Eve and she's two years younger than me."

"You said that Emma's musical. Does she play the piano or something yet?"

"Don't want to know about Eve, huh? I don't blame you. She'd take one gander at you and lick her chops, but not while my dad was looking. One of my mother's old friends called me and filled my ears with tales of Eve Lord. My mother's friend is a Sunday school teacher, so I guess she's trustworthy. Although maybe she wanted Dad for herself. Who knows? Emma plays the piano."

"I'll buy her one of those two-octave portable pianos tomorrow. I'd like to hear her play."

"Thank you, Ramsey."

"Why haven't you seen your father for three years?"

He swore he could see her stiffen from across the room. He said, "Was it because he'd hurt your husband?"

"You're good at your job."

"Yeah, I am, but this hasn't a thing to do with my job. I'm not being nosy, Molly, only trying to figure out what's going on here. Help me."

"That was part of it."

"That's a lie. I can hear it in your voice."

"All right. Louey said he'd take Emma away from me if I ever saw my father again. He called him a son of a bitch, as I remember."

"Why?"

"Louey hated my father because he found out about him."

"Found out what?"

She sighed deeply. "Louey beat me."

He started to jump out of the chair, grabbed his leg, and sank back down. "That scrawny little fucker beat you? As in he hit you?"

"Yes. Don't think I'm some sort of victim here. I told him if he ever touched me again I'd kill him. To be honest, I don't know if he believed me, but I believed me and I'm sure he must have picked up on that."

"If he had a brain he picked up on it really fast."

"This was three years ago. What happened was that one of my friends found out and called my father. Mason came to Denver and personally beat the daylights out of Louey.

"He told Louey that if he ever touched me again, he'd kill him. So Louey knew that he was in deep trouble, but he hated being helpless, so he told me not to see my father again."

"Would you have killed him if he'd hit you again?"

"Probably not, but I would have left in a flash. That first time, he was drunk, he'd gotten a bad review on his newly released CD, *Danger Floats Deep*, and was really angry. That same day I got a notice from a magazine that they wanted to buy some of my photos. He was jealous, which is ridiculous, if you just think about the relative proportion of things. But it didn't matter. Louey took his anger out on me."

"I don't remember hearing a thing about Louey Santera being hurt."

"No, there was no coverage on it. My dad had a doctor come over and check him out. I kicked Louey out the next year."

"Ah," he said. "What took you so long?"

She sighed, realizing how easy it was to talk to him. "I wanted to try to make a go of it for Emma's sake. Not a smart idea. Actually, when he did officially leave, it was just a formality since he'd moved out of the house and in with one of his girlfriends." Then she laughed. "My father made sure Louey gave me more money in the settlement than Louey even had at the time. He was royally pissed, but there was nothing he could do about it. He tried the threat again, about Emma, but I wasn't buying it. I told him I'd kill him if he tried to take Emma, and this time, he believed me."

"Why didn't you see your father again? After you and your husband split up?"

"There are two truths. The one I tell people if they ask is that Eve doesn't want to be seen with a stepdaughter who is older than she is. And a step-granddaughter? Please."

"And the other truth? The real truth?"

She began rubbing her arms. "To most people, if they've even heard of my father, they think he's a very rich successful businessman. He's in Silicon Valley, into communications, he owns lumber mills in the Northwest, he has a chain of restaurants in the South, lots of other enterprises. He's never been convicted of or indicted for anything. His accountants are top-notch, so he'll never go down on a tax-evasion charge. People like you know that he's a lot more than that. He's a kingpin in extortion, gambling, prostitution, just about everything except drugs. He hates drugs.

"My mother was very wise. After the divorce, she took me far away from him, all the way to Italy. I wasn't raised with his influence. I remember how she'd cry every time she had to put me on an airplane to come to the United States, to him, for those summer months every year. I don't want Emma near him. My mother kept me away from him and I intend to do the same for Emma."

"*Sanction a kill.* That's what you said."

"You're right. It came right out. It's insidious, that kind of influence. Can you believe I ever want Emma to even know those words go together? A child growing up with a man like my father—I'd fear for that child and I'd be afraid of the adult that child would become. Now, that's enough. No more for you, Mr. Hunt. I think we should get some sleep. You don't know Emma. She'll be awake and raring to go at six o'clock in the morning."

"I know. She waited until seven after I got shot in the leg, I'd wake up with this soft little hand on my forearm, lightly stroking up and down." He was silent a moment. "She's a great kid, Molly."

"I know," she said. "I know."

"We'll keep her safe."

"I know we will," she said.

It was deep in the middle of the night when a loud piercing scream brought Molly straight up in bed.

She grabbed her daughter and shook her. "Em, wake up, honey. Come on, wake up!"

She shook her again. Ramsey stood in the doorway, his heart pounding, his Smith & Wesson in his hand. He watched Molly sit up and pull Emma onto her lap. "Come on, love, wake up. It's all right. I'm here with you. Ramsey's here too. Wake up, Emma."

Emma suddenly arched then twisted around, throwing her arms around her mother. She was shuddering and sobbing. Ramsey quickly sat down beside them and held them both tightly. After a few moments, he eased his hold and leaned back. He pushed back Emma's tangled hair from her ear. "It's okay, really, Emma, it's okay. We're here. No bad guys, just us."

She slowly stopped sobbing. She hiccuped. He looked at Molly over Emma's head. Her eyes were shadowed, then he saw her mouth was tight, saw the pain deep within her, visible now to him, and he knew what that pain felt like because he felt it as well. Emma said in a flat singsong voice, "I dreamed about him, Mama. He tied my hands and feet to the bed. He used twine. He said he didn't need rope because I was just a little girl. He said I was perfect and that he needed me more than God needed him. Only me. He took that twine and he wrapped me like a package." She fell silent. Ramsey and Molly waited, stiff, enraged, but she said nothing more.

They held Emma between them for a very long time. Finally, Molly said quietly, "She's asleep. Thank you, Ramsey. I'll hold her real close the rest of the night."

It was a very long time before Molly fell asleep again. When she awoke, she felt Emma's wet kiss on her cheek. Emma took her arm and pulled it and she naturally turned over to curl around her daughter's back.

When Ramsey awoke early in the morning, he thought about Emma's nightmare, her flat dead words. Twine. He'd tied her with twine, as he would a package. He hadn't needed rope. She was just a little girl.

Not that it mattered. If Ramsey could get his hands on that man, he would probably kill him. Would he send the man through the system, confident that he'd be punished as he should be? He didn't know. He just didn't know. And he should know. He walked to the other bedroom, stood quietly in the open doorway, watching Emma and Molly sleep.

"Ramsey?"

A little whisper of a voice.

"Good morning, Emma. Did you sleep well?"

"Oh yes. Mama's all snuggled in behind me. This is nice, but I have to go to the bathroom."

He heard Molly giggle.

He saw Molly kissing Emma's neck, telling her they'd both go and then they'd get her a bowl of cereal, with bananas, or maybe some chocolate kisses.

He went back to bed and pulled the covers to his chin. Louey Santera had beaten her. He didn't blame Mason Lord one bit for taking the bastard down. He'd have taken him down himself. He wondered, as he got up to go to the bathroom himself, if Molly had loved her husband before that.

TWELVE

Emma was jumping out of her skin she was so excited. She started playing the two-octave piano as soon as she saw it, Ramsey standing just behind her, so surprised he couldn't speak.

She was playing a Mozart piano concerto that had been the title song to an old film called *Elvira Madigan*.

All the salespeople in the toy store were beginning to gather around along with children and their parents. No one was saying anything, just watching Emma play on that little excuse for a piano and listening to the incredible music she was making.

He looked over at Molly. He could see she was humming to herself along with Emma's playing. She looked as if it was nothing out of the ordinary.

He bought the piano. The saleswoman said, "It's a pity she can't have a regular piano. She's quite talented. How long has she been playing?"

Molly answered. "Since she was three. We're vacationing here and forgot to bring her portable piano. We'll make do nicely with this one."

"Amazing," the saleswoman said. "You've got a lovely, talented little girl."

Ramsey nodded. "Yes, she is amazing."

He felt Emma's hand slip into his. He hugged her against his leg, which was feeling nearly back to normal again. He was down to about four aspirin a day. He wondered if Emma remembered her nightmare. He wanted to ask her about it but thought better of it. No, they needed to talk to a professional. He realized he could call and get a reference.

He said low to Molly when he opened the car door, "Do you think Emma's doing okay?"

"I don't know. I haven't asked her. After last night, I'm more afraid than before."

"I could probably find out the name of a local shrink, one who deals only with children. What do you think?"

She chewed on that so hard he could practically see her thinking. Finally, she shook her head. "We don't dare take a chance. I think that for the time being we should just keep her close and let her know she's safe."

But she knew Emma wasn't safe from those terrifying dreams. Molly forced a frown because she wanted to cry.

He nodded, still uncertain. He looked into the backseat of the Toyota. Emma was holding the big box with her piano inside really close. Her eyes were closed. What was she thinking? Or was she playing music in her mind? He prayed it was music there and nothing else, at least for the time being.

He noticed the Honda Civic a half mile from the shopping center. There weren't many cars on 89, the road to Lake Tahoe from Truckee. It was another seven miles, give or take a mile, to Alpine Meadows Road, their turnoff. He didn't say anything, just kept checking every couple of minutes in the rearview mirror.

Finally, when he was certain they were being followed, he said quietly, "Molly, look back and see if you can get the license plate number on the Civic two cars behind us. It's fairly new and gray. Be as discreet as you can. We don't want them to notice us looking."

She didn't even change expression, but he saw the panic in her eyes, followed by a hard coldness, the look she'd given him when she'd burst into the cabin that first morning.

She looked back at Emma. She was staring out the window, her piano box still hugged to her chest. She didn't appear to have overheard them.

They were nearly to their turnoff when she could finally make out the license. "It's F A R B three-three-three. That's too easy. Are you sure they're following us? It's a ridiculous plate."

"No. But I'm not about to take any chances. You got your gun?"

"Oh yes. What do you want to do?"

"Let's turn and see what they do. It's two guys, right?"

"As best I can make out. They're being really careful to hang back. I can't tell yet if it's the same two guys. My cell phone is at home getting recharged."

"That's all right. We'll call in the number as soon as we get home." *If we go home* hung silently in the air between them.

Emma said, "We shouldn't have gone out for my piano. That's how they got us. It's all my fault." Her small face was pale.

Ramsey said clearly, "Nothing is your fault. Don't say that again or I'll have to keep you away from hot dogs for a week. Don't be afraid, Emma. We'll take care of you."

"Listen to me, Emma," Molly said, turning in the front seat to face her daughter. "If anyone tries to get you again, I'll shoot them, even if it's the president. Do you understand?"

"Yes, Mama."

"Make sure your seat belt's tight."

They turned right onto Alpine Meadows Road. The River Ranch Motel was sprawled out on the left-hand corner, a landmark for some time, a ski shop of nearly equal age on the right. It looked closed down. There was still some spring skiing, but not enough to lure more than half a dozen cars into the parking lot of the River Ranch Motel. He prayed the car wouldn't turn right after them.

The day was bright and would warm to about sixty degrees. Ramsey said, "Hey, Emma, you want to go hiking with me this afternoon? We might get lucky and see some neat wildlife—foxes, deer, lots of birds, rabbits."

The clothes he'd bought her were perfect. He was trying to distract her, but it wasn't working. "You game, Molly?"

"Maybe. We'll see. Are you hungry, Emma?"

"I don't know, Mama. I'm still trying to see the men in that car. Do you think they're the same men who were in Colorado, at that restaurant?"

"I don't know," Molly said. "They're not close enough to tell yet."

Ramsey looked behind him. The car had turned, dammit. There wasn't another car between them now. They were hanging back about forty yards. "Okay, they're after us. I'm going all the way down to the ski resort. There's a big turnaround. Then we'll head to Tahoe City. It's only a couple of more miles east. I'm not about to let them get anywhere near our house."

He saw that Molly had taken her Detonics out and was holding it loosely by her leg. He'd put his Smith & Wesson underneath the front seat, loaded and ready to go. There were only about fifty cars at the ski resort and a couple of dozen four-wheel-drive vehicles parked up close to the ticket windows. The snow already looked slushy. The people who were here were either really serious skiers, or didn't know better. He slowly drove by the front of the resort, making the large lazy circle back onto Alpine Meadows Road, heading back toward the main road again.

The Honda Civic paused at the row of ticket windows, but didn't stop. He knew they wouldn't stop. He wondered if they knew they'd been spotted.

He gunned the Toyota as soon as they got back onto the road. When they got to the intersection with Highway 89, he took a right toward Tahoe City. No one had said a word.

He was thinking about how the hell he could lose the Honda behind them in very small touristy Tahoe City with its endless restaurants, ski rental shops, and souvenir kiosks. There was a shopping center. It was good sized. There were walkways all around the indoor center. He didn't know where most of them led, but he was fairly certain he could get them lost there.

It was on the right, he remembered, as you drove into town. He'd have to get rid of the Toyota. Pity, but no choice now. He didn't see them behind him for the moment. He turned into the huge parking lot and eased the Toyota right up front.

"Out. Quickly!"

He grabbed Emma's piano and they were through the shopping center doors in five seconds. "Go directly out the back, Molly. There's a walkway out there. Take the nearest one to the back door. I'll be with you in just a second."

There were just a handful of people in the shopping enclosure. He saw

Molly weave her way through, Emma pressed against her side, moving as quickly as they could.

He didn't need to wait long before the Honda pulled around. They saw the Toyota and stopped. It was all he needed to know. He was out the back door in ten seconds, several unhappy people behind him.

He took the nearest walkway and started running. He caught them behind a small Louisiana-type restaurant.

"Molly, you and Emma go into this restaurant and stay in the bathroom. In five minutes, I'll pull up out front. Be there. Five minutes, by your watch."

He ran back toward the shopping center. He didn't see them. He walked quickly around the north side, into the parking lot. There was the Honda, double-parked right out front. It was empty.

He smiled.

Four and a half minutes later, he was in front of the restaurant, and Molly was opening the passenger side.

"Excellent. Emma, you all set back there?"

"Yes, Ramsey. My piano's okay, too." She was hugging that box so tightly her knuckles were white.

It was hard to smile, but he managed it. "Hold on, kiddo. We're outta here."

"Will they follow?"

He looked over at Molly as he pulled back onto 89. "No, they're going to be a while. I took the distributor cap. They probably have a cell phone and will make some calls. Since they know where we are, we can't take the chance of going back to the house."

They were on Highway 80 ten minutes later, heading west.

"We never got to hike, Ramsey."

"We will, Emma, we will."

THEY drove over the Golden Gate Bridge three hours and thirty-five minutes later. The day was sharp and clear, a picture-postcard day. The fog was just beginning to curl through the arches of the bridge.

"Are you sure this is a good idea, Ramsey?"

"I don't know, but I'm tired of running. My base is here, Molly. It's time we got help. We discussed this before. You didn't disagree."

"But the men who are after us, surely they'll find out who you are very soon. When they find out, they'll be on us like a shot."

He cursed under his breath. "You're right. I'll just bet they already know what I like to eat for breakfast. Okay. Let's stop at my house so I can change, pack, and make arrangements. We'll fly to your father this afternoon. Sorry, Molly, but I can't see any other choice unless you want to go to the cops right here in San Francisco."

"No." Molly cursed under her breath. "There are no good alternatives, are there? Let's go to Chicago, then. I'd still rather have her with me than being questioned by police psychologists, hordes of cops, not to mention the FBI. If Special Agent Anchor is representative, then the FBI is scary."

"He's not representative. All right, let's go to Chicago. When the time is right to bring in the cops, we can call them from there."

"I probably should have gone to him sooner. My old man's got more ability to protect Emma than the cops and the FBI. He may be a big criminal, but he'll do his best to keep Emma safe."

"All right, then. Let's use your father, if he'll let us. We'll let him keep Emma safe."

She closed her eyes a moment, then nodded to herself, coming to a decision. Then she smiled as she said to Emma, "Look over there, Em. It's Alcatraz Island. It was a prison for really bad guys until sometime in the 1950s."

"It's pretty. I wouldn't mind being a prisoner there."

"I read they fed the prisoners about six thousand calories a day, to make them fat, so they'd be less likely to try to escape and swim to shore. I think it was a whole lot of hot dogs and beans. They didn't let them exercise much."

Emma's eyes brightened.

He grinned at her in the rearview mirror. "They didn't cook them on hangers in a fireplace, Emma. They were boiled."

"Yuck."

Ramsey turned onto Scenic Drive in a beautiful old section of the city called Sea Cliff. "We're the closest houses to the bay. My house is number twenty-seven, right there on the end."

"I knew federal judges must be paid pretty well, but not that well. This place must have cost a bundle, Ramsey."

"It's worth quite a lot, but I didn't buy it. It was bequeathed to me by my grandparents along with a nice inheritance. I'm not as rich as you, but I won't starve. The views are incredible. We'll come back, Emma, and barbecue. We can sit in the backyard and watch the fog roll in. It floats through the Golden Gate Bridge like soft white fingers. I've always loved the fog. I've even got a piano for you, an old baby grand that my grandfather played. He was a great old man."

Ramsey's nose twitched the instant he unlocked the front door and stepped into the tiled foyer. It smelled like rotten food, but that didn't make any sense. He stepped into the living room and quickly stepped back.

The room had been trashed. His high-tech stereo equipment was ripped open and stomped on. CDs were strewn all over the hardwood floor. All the furniture had been slashed. He walked numbly into the kitchen. The stench was pretty bad.

The refrigerator door stood open. Someone had flung food all over the floor, not that there'd been very much. Dishes were smashed, in shards everywhere. Drawers were pulled out, silverware all over the floor. A violent hand had simply swept everything out of the cabinets.

"Don't come in here, Emma," he said.

"Oh no," was all Molly said from the doorway, holding Emma back.

It took him only minutes to see that whoever had done this hadn't forgotten a single room.

He walked into his study, a magnificent dark oak-paneled room that looked toward the Marin Headlands. His antique rolltop desk had been gouged, the drawers pulled out and smashed, all his papers in shredded heaps everywhere. Books lay in broken piles on the Tabriz carpet. His favorite leather chair had been ripped open with a knife. His grandfather's baby grand piano had its legs sawed off. It lay drunkenly on its side, most of the keys stomped in. Someone had even cut the piano wires.

Devastation everywhere.

What had they been looking for? Something to tie him to Molly and Emma?

"I'm sorry, Ramsey," she said at his elbow. "I'm really very sorry. We brought this to you."

He realized then what she'd said, the full impact of it. He turned slowly, took her upper arms in his big hands, and said, "I was feeling equal parts enraged and sorry for myself. But now, after what you just said, I realize that this place, no matter how nice, is still just a place. When we get the person responsible for this, I look forward to kicking his butt, but Emma means more to me than a pile of stupid possessions. There's no contest. Do you understand me, Molly?"

She nodded. "I don't understand why someone would do this. They could have searched, if they wanted to find some sort of connection between us. They didn't have to destroy everything."

"I don't understand either, but we're going to find out."

"I hope so." She leaned down and picked up an atlas, its pages ripped, the spine broken. She tried to smooth the pages. She looked numb.

He gently took the book from her. "Help me pack, then we're out of here. I'll make some phone calls from a pay phone." But there weren't any undamaged clothes left. Even his leather luggage, a Christmas present from his folks, was mutilated.

Ramsey made four calls from a public phone on the corner of California and Gough. The first was to a cleaning service, the second was to Dillon Savich, the third was to an airline, and the fourth was to Virginia Trolley of the San Francisco Police Department. He made one stop: his bank.

"Let's go," he said, grinning at Emma as he came out of the bank. "This is going to be exciting, kiddo. At least now I'm as rich as your mama." He handed her a twenty-dollar bill. "Keep this, Emma. Tuck it away somewhere safe."

Molly gave him a quizzical look but didn't say anything, just watched her daughter very carefully fold the twenty-dollar bill and slip it inside her piano.

"I think I've had enough exciting things happen, Ramsey," Emma said and hugged her piano to her chest.

Molly said, "Maybe we can buy her some more clothes at the airport."

Ramsey frowned. "I'm thinking. I don't remember any kids' clothes there. T-shirts, but that's about it. We don't have time to stop. We'll get her a new T-shirt at the airport, and work on her wardrobe in Chicago. Ours, too, for that matter."

THIRTEEN

There wasn't a sound, only the slow movement of a finger, a gentle silent stroke, and an instant later, the whoosh of rending paper. The man's chest exploded outward, the sharp, jagged edges fanning out from a huge hole, smelling of char.

Gunther nodded to himself, turning away. He said under his breath, "Not bad."

"What do you mean, 'Not bad'?" she said, staring at the target as she walked closer. "How about perfect?" She watched Gunther blow on the muzzle of his Spanish Star Ten, one of the very few European 10mm auto caliber pistols, Gunther had told her in an unusual show of pride. Of all his acquaintances he had the only one, he'd said, which was just as well since he'd also be the only one to shoot it right. She watched him blow on the muzzle again. Naturally there was no smoke to blow away. She imagined he did it because it was symbolic, a move reminiscent of the gunslingers in the Old West.

He gave her an irritated look but didn't say anything.

"Don't you like to be perfect, Gunther?" She came closer, running her fingers down his forearm, over his hand, to stroke the barrel of the gun.

He stayed silent. She was doing this to make him crazy, he knew that, but it was tough not to respond in some way, a small push, a tiny shove away from him. But he wasn't stupid. He couldn't lay a finger on her, no matter what the provocation. No, he wouldn't even acknowledge that she was playing a game with him.

He had a feeling that Mr. Lord enjoyed these games of hers, even encouraged her. Maybe he was standing in the shadows at the back of the gallery, watching, chewing on an unlit cigarillo, a habit he'd developed since he'd stopped smoking the year before. Gunther slowly pulled away, cradling his gun in his big hands. He liked the feel of the cold smooth steel against his warm palm.

She shook her head, laughing at him. "The way you hold that gun of yours. What is it with you, Gunther? You think that gun is a woman?"

"No," he said very precisely, "I think this gun is a tool to get my job done." He nodded to her, politely, as always, and turned away from her. He said over his shoulder, pausing just a moment in the gallery doorway, "Mr. Lord appreciates my tool."

She stared at him an instant, then doubled over, hooting with laughter. "I sure hope not," she said. "I sure hope you're wrong about that."

His jaw locked. Embarrassment flooded him from the inside out, as if his guts had turned red before his face. He hated the feeling. A soft voice said, "Yes, Gunther, I do appreciate your tool. Why don't you go clean your gun. You've used it a great deal today and with excellent effect."

"Yes, sir."

Mason Lord watched his man leave the gun gallery before turning to his wife. His look was indulgent, his voice amused as he said, "You torment poor Gunther."

"Yes, but he's really too easy, Mason. Did you bring my Lady Colt?"

He nodded. "I wish you'd let me teach you how to shoot a real gun, not this ridiculous toy."

Her voice hardened. It was disconcerting in that she looked like an angel, from that smooth thick pale blond hair of hers to the soft blue eyes, the fragile blue of a summer sky. "If I'm close enough, it'll get the job done. I don't want a tool like poor Gunther's. It's not elegant."

He had to agree with that. The recoil from the Spanish Star Ten would also knock her on her butt. He handed her the Lady Colt, stood back, and watched her put six bullets straight through the chest of the target.

She turned, her eyes sparkling, removed her earmuffs, and said in a wicked voice, "And I didn't even have to fondle it."

"No," he said, drawing her to him, "I'm the only thing you fondle."

But though he spoke the words, he wasn't responding to her the way he usually did. Usually she would have been on her back by now. She stepped back, laying her Lady Colt on the counter. "I wonder what your daughter is doing?"

He shook his head. "I called Buzz Carmen in Denver a little while ago. He said the cops are still acting like idiots, mad at her for saving her own daughter, trying to track her down and this man with her. Buzz and three others have fanned out now, looking for her. Molly's an amateur. Buzz and his people aren't. They'll find her. He admitted he hadn't known she'd left Denver. He said they'd kept their distance because the cops had hassled them."

"No one's found her except whoever did this. Maybe the bad guys got them, Mason. You have to consider that."

"Molly's smart. She may be an amateur, but she's smart."

"I thought she was like your wife."

He stared at her, then laughed. "Like Alicia? Molly thinks of herself as the ugly duckling compared to my former wife. No, Molly might look like a railroad tie, but she's smart." He frowned a bit. "I suppose she's like me in that. I wish she'd just admit she needs me and get over here. She knows I can protect her and Emma."

"I'll bet this guy who's with them is calling the shots. Don't you think?"

"I don't even have an idea yet who he is." He took her arm. "Let's have one of Miles's margaritas."

It was during that first delicious margarita that Miles said from the doorway, "Sir, Molly's here. Emma too, and a man I don't know."

"It took her long enough to come," Mason Lord said, rising slowly. He set his glass on the marble tabletop as Miles went back out. Then he heard a child's voice, soft, high, not frightened, but wary?

"This is a very big house, Mr. Miles."

"Yes, Emma, it is."

"It's even bigger than the one we had with Daddy. This ceiling just goes up and up."

Then the three of them were standing in the open doorway, Miles behind them, his look questioning. "It's all right, Miles. I'll call if I need you."

Then his daughter turned, her hand on Miles's arm. "Can Emma have a glass of water, Miles?"

Miles looked down at the little girl, who was standing very close to her mother, her hand now held by the big man on her other side. "How about some lemonade instead?"

"Oh yes, Mr. Miles, that would be wonderful."

The three of them turned back to face Mason Lord. Three years since he'd seen Molly or her daughter. The little girl was the picture of Alicia, but her dark brown hair was her father's, that low-life runty little scum sucker who'd always reminded him of Mick Jagger when he'd been younger. She was six now, tall and skinny, her skin that pearly white that only children seemed to have. She'd be at least as beautiful as Alicia when she grew up.

He'd wanted Molly to come here. He'd told her to come here. Yet now that she was here, her child with her, and that man, whoever the hell he was, he didn't know how to respond. What was he to say to her? Three years. It had been a long time and she'd been the one who wanted to keep a goodly distance between them. But now things were different. Things had changed, irrevocably.

"Hello, Molly."

"Hello, Dad. You're looking well." She looked beyond at Eve, who was sitting elegant as a Parisian model on a soft yellow brocade love seat. She was wearing tight black jeans and a white blouse tied in a knot over her smooth midriff. "Hello, Eve. I presume you're Eve? I believe we spoke once on the telephone a long time ago."

"Oh, yes, I remember. How delightful to finally meet you in the flesh. And you are Molly, I presume?"

"Yes. Dad, Eve, this is Ramsey Hunt. He's the one who saved Emma. Then I came along. There are maybe five men after us, and they're very good at tracking us. We don't know why they're after us, but we wanted you to know this right away."

The man cleared his throat and said, "We decided to come here, Mr. Lord, because they know who I am now. We just couldn't keep Emma safe. The people hunting us are good, too good. We trust you to keep Emma safe better than the authorities can."

Mason Lord walked to the man and extended his hand. "This is an honor. It's a pleasure to meet you, Judge Hunt."

Ramsey shook the man's hand. "Thank you. We're here because we believe you're our best shot at keeping Emma safe."

"I didn't imagine for a moment that you were here to visit me, Judge Hunt. Yes, yes, I know who you are. You're a famous man. It's quite a surprise that you're the one who found Emma."

Molly could only stare at them, all civilized on the outside, but she could see each sizing up the other, weighing, assessing. She gathered Emma closer to her. She hadn't wanted to be here, hadn't wanted her daughter exposed to her father, but it was the safest place for Emma.

Mason Lord wouldn't allow anyone to get close to his granddaughter, even though he hadn't seen her since she'd been a toddler. No, Emma carried his blood. He would protect her with every weapon in his arsenal.

Her father finally said, his voice smooth and deep, "You saved Molly and her daughter. I thank you. You brought her home when she refused. You will all be safe here. No one, cops or anyone else, will get near Emma."

"Thank you," Ramsey said. He squeezed Emma's hand, then said to the crook he was trusting with all their lives, "Actually, sir, Emma had saved herself. She'd escaped from the man and run into the forest. I found her there and took her to my cabin. Some days later, Molly found both of us." Ramsey looked down a moment at Emma, who was staring at a huge rhinoceros head, complete with a shining tusk, above the mantel, her mouth open. She was tugging on his hand. He gave hers a squeeze, looked at the rhino, and said, "I wonder what kind of polish they used on the tusk. What do you think, Emma?"

She squeezed his hand tighter. "Soap and water," she said. "Mama always says that soap and water's the best."

Ramsey said, "I would imagine that the men after us have already tracked us to the airport. We had to show photo ID. Someone will remember, no doubt about that, even though Molly bought her ticket singly and I bought Emma's ticket with mine. Yes, the men will be here very soon."

"You took a cab from O'Hare?"

"Yes, to downtown, Michigan Avenue. Emma needed some clothes, as did Molly and I. None of us were very presentable. Then we took another cab to the Jefferson Police Station, wandered in and spoke to the desk sergeant about nothing in particular, then we got a third cab out here. But they'll find us. I'm convinced of that. They probably already know we're here with you. As I said, they're good, and, as Molly and I have agreed, there's got to be an organization behind them."

Mason Lord nodded, then said, "That was smart of you to go to a police station. It will give them pause. Please, all of you, sit down. As to any organization behind all this, we'll speak of it later. Ah, here's Miles with some lemonade."

"I brought enough for all of you, sir."

"Thank you, Miles," Molly said.

"And I brought some chocolate cake I baked this morning." He looked at Emma as he poured her a glass. "You like chocolate cake?"

"Oh yes, Mr. Miles. It's the best."

Ramsey laughed. "Be careful or she'll eat the whole cake. She hasn't had many goodies for a while."

Miles smiled as he ruffled Emma's hair, even as Mason Lord frowned. He watched his daughter wipe the child's hands on one of the little wet towels Miles had brought. How had Miles known to do that? He was like one of those hovering smiley-faced airline attendants. He was silent until everyone had drunk the lemonade and eaten some of Miles's chocolate cake. He hadn't known of any cake. He loved chocolate cake but Miles hadn't offered him any, either for lunch or right now. He'd had a low-cal, low-fat flan for dessert the previous night. It hadn't even tasted very good. He looked at his beautiful wife. She wasn't looking at the cake. She was looking at Molly. Her face was perfectly still. No expression at all. What was she thinking?

Ramsey Hunt was big, tall, and very well built, but that made sense, of course, given what he'd done in his own courtroom. He was a man who obviously worked out, who took good care of himself, a man who looked as if he could deal with anything that happened to cross his path. Mason supposed he was good-looking enough, his features regular, his coloring olive, his eyes a green color that argued against Italian blood. But who knew in America? All of them were mongrels, himself included. At least he had more good Irish blood than anything else. As for his beautiful Eve, she was Swedish, every beautiful blond inch of her. She'd told him stories about her father falling in love with a German countess, but he hadn't married her. Too many control-freak genes, he'd said. No, Eve was pure Scandinavian. He'd chosen well this time.

He looked again, hard, at the man sitting opposite him. Judge Ramsey Hunt of the Ninth Federal District Court—who would have imagined that he'd be the one to find Emma?

What were the odds of this man's finding Molly's daughter and saving her? He cleared his throat and said, "Judge Hunt, you said you found Emma in the forest. Did she willingly come with you to your cabin?"

"She was unconscious." He saw that Emma had stopped eating. Those ears of hers were on full alert. He said easily, "I can tell you all about it after we've got Emma settled in, all right?"

Mason Lord said, "Very well. Miles, give them three rooms."

"Emma and I will stay together, Dad."

"Very well, two bedrooms."

Ramsey turned to Molly, and said low, "Your father wants to grill me. Take Emma upstairs, all right?"

She didn't want to go; he knew it. "Please, Molly, go. I'll set your father straight."

"No," she said. "Emma is my daughter. You won't send me off to the kitchen to make tea."

He understood. He said to Mason Lord, "Let's make it a bit later, sir. Molly and I will settle in. If Emma is content to stay with Miles, then we'll come see you as soon as we can."

Mason Lord turned to his daughter. "What's wrong with you? Take your child upstairs. I want to speak to him. You had little enough to do with any of this. I want to thank him for saving you, for bringing you here. You haven't got the sense of a goat. Now, take your child upstairs. Judge Hunt and I need to talk things over."

Molly rose. She was shaking. Odd, she thought, how he could push the buttons so easily, so quickly. Only this time, she wasn't going to fold her tent and slink away. She fought the urge to lower her head, her eyes at her feet, like a whipped dog. She jerked her head up. She'd been through too much ever to let anyone take control of her again. But she had to keep calm, not let him see how she had to fight the hold he still had on her, the pull she was still fighting.

"I see," she said slowly, cutting him off, for he would have continued, she knew. She touched Emma's shoulder. "Emma, love, are you full? Yes, then let me wipe your mouth. Now, we're leaving this place. As it turns out, we just came for a short visit. Come along, Emma." She smiled at Ramsey. "You coming?"

"In a flash," he said. He nodded to Miles. "Thank you for the cake and lemonade. It was delicious."

"You don't talk to me like that, Molly."

"I didn't talk to you in any way at all. Good-bye, Dad. A pleasure to finally meet you in person, Eve. You're a knockout stepmom."

"Stop it. What do you think you're doing? Where do you think you're going?"

He'd used that cold harsh voice with her countless times when she was growing up. She turned, saying easily, "We're out of here, Dad. It's obvious that only one of us is welcome and that isn't your daughter or your grand-daughter."

"Damn you, I just want to find out what's happened, what his plans are."

"Anything that's happened, any plans made, we've made them together. I'm sorry, Dad, but just because you're men doesn't mean you rule my world."

"Yeah, well, if a man hadn't been around, Louey would still be beating the crap out of you."

Molly knew Emma had heard that. "Be quiet," she said as calmly as she could manage. "Just be quiet."

Mason watched the little girl turn, obviously puzzled, and stare at him. He saw she didn't understand, but she would soon. He saw she was gripping both their hands. Had Molly already taken Ramsey Hunt as a lover? Despite her daughter's presence?

He said to Judge Ramsey Hunt, "Damn you, come back here. There's no way you're leaving my house now and taking them with you. Besides, given who you are, your chances of getting away unrecognized are about zip."

Suddenly, Eve uncurled from her chair and rose. She smiled at all of them indiscriminately and said in a charming hostess voice, "How about some more lemonade? It will make everyone feel better."

IT had been a long day, too long a day without Ingrid. Louey Santera rubbed the back of his neck, feeling the painful knots. The performance had hurled him to the heights, the crowd's applause still rang in his ears, as always, but now that it was over, he'd fallen into the pits. He needed Ingrid's clever hands on him.

But he'd given Ingrid the day off. She was with her parents in Frankfurt. Maybe one of his groupie girls could rub him down. He walked to the door and pulled it open.

"Alenon! Get in here!"

A skinny young guy with acne and stringy blond hair stuck his head around the corner. "Yes, boss?" Even the kid's voice was stringy, with little substance.

"Get me one of the girls, one who just might know how to unknot my neck and shoulders."

Alenon was back in under five minutes towing a small black-haired girl who couldn't have been more than sixteen. She looked like a baby. Was she one of the groupies who trailed after him like a pack of puppies? He didn't recognize her.

"This is Karolina, sir. She says her mother's a masseuse. She says she knows what to do."

Louey looked into the girl's eyes. She might be sixteen in years, but not in experience. He nodded. "Hello, Karolina. Can you help me?"

She said in excellent English, "It is my pleasure to help you, Mr. Santera. Is your daughter all right? I read in the newspaper that she was kidnapped."

What the hell was this? "What newspaper?"

"The *Berliner Zeitung*. There was an article about you. At the bottom, there was a sentence about your daughter being kidnapped. The reporter wrote it happened somewhere out in America's Wild West. I'm very sorry."

How had the reporter known? Hell, when she wasn't listening to him speak or writing down what he said or wrapping her legs around him, there hadn't been any time for her to find out anything. He'd just muttered something about Emma, not even a complete sentence. She must have called Denver. He turned to Karolina. "You speak English better than that reporter did."

"My mother is American."

"Oh," Louey said, rubbing his neck. He watched as Karolina efficiently covered the massage table with its soft flannel sheet. She stood back. Louey smiled. Slowly, he undressed for her. She didn't say a word. When he started to pull down his jockey shorts, she stepped forward, holding a towel out wide in front of him.

When she was rubbing his feet, she said, "I'm in Al-Anon. It's for children whose parents are alcoholics. Why do you use it as a name for Rudy?"

Rudy. That was the kid's name? He shrugged, a small movement because he was lying flat on his stomach. "Because it amuses me."

"I see," Karolina said as she moved up the table. He felt her hands dig into his shoulders. He closed his eyes.

It was the best massage of his life. When he woke up two hours later, Karolina was gone.

Alenon was standing there, watching him. For how long? Had he snored? Drooled? "What do you want?"

"I have a message from Mr. Lord for you."

"Oh no," Louey said and sat up, pulling the sheet to his waist. "When did the old man call? What did he want?"

"It was actually a man who said he was calling for Mr. Lord. He said he didn't need to speak to you. He said that your daughter is safe again, with Mr. Lord, at his house. That was all."

Rudy Brinker watched one of the most talented men in the world lower his head in his hands. He looked sad, broken. But his voice, when he spoke, was vicious. Rudy listened to him curse for a good thirty seconds. Then he quietly let himself out of Mr. Santera's room. He went down the hall to Mr. Murdock's room and knocked twice.

The ugliest man Rudy had ever seen answered the knock.

FOURTEEN

Mason Lord swirled the rich golden brandy in the Waterford snifter, watched it lightly veil the sides of the glass. It was magnificent brandy, coating his tongue and his throat as well when he swallowed. He allowed himself one snifter at night, an hour after dinner.

Eve was sitting on the sofa, watching television. He thought it was an idiotic show like *Wheel of Fortune*, only worse. Although he'd felt contempt for her taste even before he'd married her, he hadn't felt anything but lust for her body, and in his way of thinking, contempt couldn't begin to catch up with lust.

She looked up. It must be a commercial. "What are you going to do with them, Mason?"

He took the last drink of his brandy, carefully set the snifter down on a marble-topped side table, then said slowly, "I wanted them to come here. You heard me tell Molly when she called that she was to come here."

"Yes, so she listened to you."

"But she didn't want to. It was the man. It was Ramsey Hunt." He looked at the gold Rolex on his wrist. "He said he would come down to speak to me. Miles told him he wasn't to bring Molly."

"When did he say that?"

"Miles told him what he had to do if he wanted my protection. He'll do as I ask. He knows he needs me." He streaked his long fingers through his hair. Eve stared at him. She'd never seen him do that. "What's wrong?"

"She needs to be controlled. The way she spoke to me. I nearly struck her, Eve."

"But you didn't. When she threatened to leave, you backed off and told her what she wanted to hear—that you wanted to know what she had to say as well as this Ramsey Hunt." Eve paused a moment. The show was coming back on. Then she said, "You flattered her and she fell for it. You did control her, Mason."

"No," he said, "really, she didn't fall for anything. She's scared for her daughter. She'd make a deal with the devil to keep her daughter safe, even if the devil is me." But he knew if he hadn't backed off, she'd have been out of there, and that man would have gone with her. She had to be sleeping with him, to have him so pussy whipped. He looked at his wife. She'd turned back to her game show. He walked to the door of the immense living room and quietly opened the beautiful French doors that gave onto a walled-in, quite lovely English garden. The air was soft, redolent with the intermingling scents of hyacinths, roses, and star jasmine. The jasmine he'd selected himself for the garden. There were no sounds to break the quiet. Very few people knew that half a dozen men were stationed in and around the house. As soon as Molly, Emma, and Ramsey Hunt had arrived, he'd added more guards. He turned to see Miles coming from across the hall, toward him.

"Emma liked the spaghetti I made for her," he said. "The pasta was shaped like Jurassic Park dinosaurs."

Mason Lord could only stare at a man who'd been loyal only to him, at his beck and call only, for twenty-two years. He'd begun here when Molly was a little girl, but he'd never paid her much attention. Why Emma? Sure she was pretty, she was the very picture of Alicia, but so what? He'd never paid any attention to Alicia either.

He saw Ramsey Hunt coming down the wide staircase to his right. He was dressed well in black slacks and a white shirt. No tie, but that was all right. They'd been on the run. He called to him, "Did you deal with Molly?"

"Yes."

"You told her how she was to behave in my house?"

Ramsey wanted to laugh at the heavy-handed tactics. He smiled. "She knows exactly what to do. Now, I hear from Miles that you want to speak to me."

"Yes, but just you, not Molly. She doesn't understand either business or strategy."

"Last I knew, Molly was in her bedroom, giving Emma another reading lesson. The kid's really bright."

"I read *Moby Dick* when I was five years old."

"I understand that Molly was reading very early on as well. That's remarkable."

Mason Lord had forgotten that. He nodded. "Come to my study. It's quiet there." He shut the double oak doors, cutting off the repulsive sound of that game show in the living room and all those shouting low-class slugs.

Ramsey said without preamble, "I understand that when you heard that Louey Santera had beaten Molly you were out there like a flash. That was well done."

Mason Lord stared at the big man standing in front of his desk, at ease, his face open, his expression even admiring.

He wouldn't have even gone to Denver if it hadn't been for what Louey had done. "I wasn't about to let that little creep hurt one of mine."

And that was the bottom line for Mason Lord, Ramsey thought, relieved and pleased. "And naturally you'd feel the same about Emma. She's also one of yours. Who do you think is behind this?"

"It's a kidnapping. Louey is rich—well, not as rich as he was before my daughter divorced him, but he's doing very well. His European tours net him literally millions, the wretched little shit."

"No, it's not just a kidnapping. I told you there were a lot more men after us. How many more people would you need to mount a tracking operation like that? Say at least two more, all of them professionals. Not a kidnapping, sir. Something else. I'd stake a lot on that." Ramsey paused a moment, then said, "I'm sorry to have to tell you, but you don't know yet that Emma was taken to a cabin in the woods, high in the Rockies, and sexually abused and beaten. It's another thing we have to think about. Emma needs to see a doctor and a child psychiatrist. She has nightmares. Neither Molly nor I have spoken about this because we're afraid of making things worse."

The blood drained from Mason Lord's face. For a moment Ramsey thought he'd be sick—that, or explode. He did neither. Gradually the color returned. His breathing was slow now, calm.

He looked directly at Ramsey. "The bastards have signed their death warrants."

"I shouldn't, but I feel the same way."

"You're supposed to uphold justice and the precious laws that protect scum like that."

"Yes," Ramsey said. "I'm supposed to uphold the rights of all sorts of scum."

Mason Lord looked at him sharply, but Ramsey's expression didn't change. "As much as I don't want to even consider it, you're probably right that there's got to be either a connection to me or to Louey. I will think about that. Actually, I'd already spoken to Buzz Carmen about my enemies being behind this. We'll see."

"I want to leave Molly and Emma here with you. At least here I know they'll be safe."

"What will you do that I can't?"

"Your people didn't do much of anything in Colorado. No, my resources are more far-reaching."

"Who are your resources other than a whole bunch of cops and lawyers in San Francisco?"

Ramsey shook his head. "You wouldn't approve, so I'll keep that information under my collar."

Mason Lord felt red creeping up his neck. He rose slowly, his palms flat on the beautiful mahogany desktop, but he didn't have time to say anything, The door opened and his daughter walked in. She was smiling. She said to her father, "Have I missed much? I'm sorry for being late, but Emma wasn't ready to go to sleep. You know, it's true—a mother's work is never done. Now, tell me what you're thinking and I'll tell you what I think."

Ramsey winked at Mason Lord. "Might as well, sir. She's got a really good brain. It'd be stupid not to use it. You should have seen her drive the getaway car."

Mason Lord heard the mindless music from the game show. He shouldn't have, not in his soundproofed study. Had she turned the volume up? He looked at his daughter's face. "Go back to see to your daughter."

"Your granddaughter is peachy. She's with Miles. Let's talk."

"Go watch the game show with Eve."

"I don't know Eve. I don't like game shows. Actually, on my list of priorities at this moment, neither of those is very high."

He wanted to tell her to butt out, that this was his home and he was the boss here. Then he looked at her eyes, filled with pain and defiance and determination.

"Well, hell," he said.

Ramsey Hunt smiled and nodded at him. He still had to tell Molly that he was leaving her and Emma here. He'd been avoiding it. He wondered if she'd take him apart. But he had to do something.

Molly smiled at him, patting his arm. "Don't even think it," she said. "I overheard you speaking to Dad. No, Ramsey, no way am I letting you go out there on your own."

Ramsey looked at Mason Lord. "Well, hell," he said.

DILLON Savich said to Agent Sherlock, who happened to be his wife of six months, two weeks, and three days, "This whole thing doesn't make any sense. I've tried lots of different approaches with MAX but he can't seem to get a reasonable handle on it."

MAX was Dillon's laptop and partner, so he called him. Dillon's reputation in the Bureau was that he could make the laptop dance, and he did, that was true enough. Sherlock patted MAX's case. "You've got lots of suppositions, but only a few facts. Unfortunately MAX likes solid facts, not wussy guesses from the ether."

"That true, MAX?" Savich punched a key on his laptop. A deep mellow voice said, "Right, boss."

Sherlock laughed. "I still can't get used to that voice. You're a sicko, Dillon. You're going to have to change the voice when MAX has a sex change again to MAXINE."

"You want to audition?"

"Do I strike you as a Maxine type?"

He stared up at her face and shook his head. "No, but don't worry, I'll think of something when the inevitable sex change happens. You should see Jimmy Maitland's face when I ask MAX a prearranged question. The first time he nearly fainted. Now he sits forward, like a kid waiting for a Spiderman cartoon to come on." As a matter of fact, she had seen his boss's face when MAX had come out with "Actually, Savich, I don't think I wish to deal with this confusion anymore." Maitland had run out of his office, shouting for everyone in the vicinity to come in and hear this.

She poked him lightly on the shoulder and said, "We've got to get more information. Ramsey called you this morning from San Francisco to check in. Has he called since then?"

"No. But at least we know where he is."

"Imagine Ramsey Hunt—a federal judge—at Mason Lord's house in Oak Park. It boggles the mind."

"Imagine that Molly's his daughter. Now that's got to be a real shock to Ramsey's system, having to go to Mason Lord. At least the little girl should be safe now. I hear that place is a fortress." He sighed. "Unfortunately, with Mason Lord's resources, I don't blame Ramsey a bit for wanting to try his protection. I did try to talk him into calling the FBI, but he refused, said this was the safest way to go for the moment, and he's probably right. He also wants the little girl protected from the cops asking her questions, psychologists all over her. At least until we find out who's behind all this." Savich sighed again. "You want to see some photos we just got from a military satellite?"

She smiled at him. "Do you know something of interest, sir?"

"A bit." He punched buttons on MAX, waited a moment, and then the two of them watched photos of Mason Lord's huge house come onto the screen. Dillon hit another button and the photo changed to another view, this one from east of the vast grounds. "These shots just came in. I counted six different men stationed around the grounds. Now on to the boss man himself." He hit a key and Mason Lord's lean, very handsome face appeared on the screen. "He ain't bad, is he?"

"No. Who's that? His daughter?"

"Nope, that's his new wife. She's younger than the daughter."

Sherlock made a rude noise. They looked at more photos. Finally, he hit a key and said, "This is Molly Santera and Emma, her daughter."

Sherlock was silent for several moments. Then she said, "We've got to do more, Dillon."

Special Agent Dillon Savich, chief of the Criminal Apprehension Unit at the FBI, tilted back his chair, looked up, and said, "What do you suggest, Sherlock?"

"For starters I'd go see that farmer in Loveland, Colorado. You know, the one who said he'd sold the truck that later turned up being driven by the guys chasing Ramsey."

He felt a tingling down his spine. He sat forward, his eyes never leaving her face. "You think this guy knows who they are."

"Yes, it makes sense. I think we should go there, talk to him, have a really serious talk. Besides, at the moment, there aren't any other leads."

"Agreed. I'm with you on this one—that farmer knows. One of the guys from the field office in Denver can take a ride up there and talk to the farmer."

She was shaking her head. "No, Agent Anchor is already involved. I'll bet he's also already verified to his own satisfaction that the farmer didn't have a clue that he'd sold his truck to the kidnappers. In other words, his mind is already made up and I doubt he'd change it unless something smashed him in the nose. The word about Agent Anchor is that he's got an attitude problem. He brown-noses up the chain of command at the Bureau and tromps on local law enforcement. Nope, it's got to be one of us who goes. We're not on the FBI's side. We're on the kid's side."

"And that makes a difference?"

"Maybe this time it does," she said thoughtfully, lightly stroking her fingers over two thick black strips that were MAX's speakers. She remembered hearing Dillon hoot when MAX had made his first statement, which was, if she remembered correctly, "Hooray for the Redskins."

She said, "If it were a simple kidnapping, that would be different. But this is big, Dillon, and no one has a clue who's behind it and what they want. Well, maybe Mason Lord does. You know, that's got to be one of the reasons Ramsey's there."

"All right. I'll phone the field office and let Agent Anchor know we're coming." Savich swiveled his chair back, pulled out his directory, and punched out some numbers on his telephone. The phone rang busy. "Damned thing. I think e-mail should be mandatory for everybody in every department and in every field office in the FBI, maybe even everybody in the world."

She shook her head at him, picked up the phone, and punched in the same numbers. When it was answered, she asked to speak to Agent Anchor. She said to Dillon, "Phones hate you. It's time to face up to it. Let me do the dialing from now on. Oh yes, hello, Agent Anchor. Agent Sherlock here from the CAU in Washington. I'm fine, you? Good. I wanted to ask you about the Santera kidnapping. Un-huh. Now, about that farmer you interviewed who claimed he'd sold his truck after his wife had reported it stolen?" In an instant she was staring at the phone as if it had bitten her. "You're kidding me."

She waited some more, nodded, then said, "When? How? Any leads?"

She asked more questions, then listened for a couple of more minutes. Slowly, she hung up.

"What happened?" Savich's voice was tense, low.

"You won't believe this," she said. "The farmer's dead. He was found three days ago after dawn by his teenage daughter. His head had been bashed in with a hammer. Whoever did it dropped the hammer by the body. No clues, no leads as of yet. Of course no fingerprints. As for other forensic evidence, we've got to wait to see. Agent Anchor said he'd call us when he found out anything more. He said they found out about it from the local cops.

"The locals said that no one saw anything or anyone. His wife said he always went to the barn before dawn to milk the cows."

"And someone was waiting for him."

She stared out the window. "He had three other kids besides the teenage daughter who found him."

"Of course it has to be tied to the kidnapping, or whatever the hell it is."

"Agent Anchor thinks so, at least he now thinks there might be a connection. What do we do now, Dillon?"

Savich pressed one of MAX's buttons and said in a throaty FBI interview voice that imitated MAX's, "We're going to kick butt, Sherlock."

FIFTEEN

"I'll say it again. No way are you going out there on your own. We're in this together."

He grinned down at her. "Before we get into it, let me compliment you first. You did really well with your dad. You hung in there, didn't lose your temper, and finally he caved. He's pretty smart himself. What I'm thinking now is that I should go to Denver, get personally involved, work with both the local cops and the FBI. As for you and Emma, you'll both stay here." He saw the fear draining the brilliance from her eyes. "I can handle myself, Molly. I won't get killed. I promise."

The emptying fear left her eyes and anger moved right in. She took three deep breaths.

"Good. You're getting good at control. When my mom gets really mad at my dad, she throws something at him. My father can still move faster than any human I've ever seen."

"I'm trying hard not to kick you in the shin. Listen to me, Ramsey. I know you mean well, but there's no way I'm going to let you go out there alone and put yourself on the line." She smiled at him. "It's all for one and one for all. We're the Three Musketeers. Call me D'Artagnan."

"He was the fourth musketeer."

"His is the only name I know."

"I remember Aramis was one of them. Tell me, Molly, which one is Emma? Do we give her a sword or a gun, in this case, and let her fight right alongside us?"

She walked away from him, rubbing her hands over her arms. Then she hugged herself. "You and I have done a good job of protecting Emma. Besides, I can't begin to imagine what she'd do if you just up and left. Don't you understand? Emma needs us, both of us."

He cursed under his breath and ran his fingers through his dark hair. "Okay. So you're right. I agree. And I really don't want to leave Emma in any case. Now here's what we'll do first thing. You're going to call Louey in Germany and get him back here. It's very possible he's involved. How? I don't know, but it's possible. We need to talk to everyone."

"I can try," she said and walked to the phone. Three minutes later, the speaker on, they were listening to the phone ring at the Bristol Hotel Kempinski in Berlin.

Ramsey asked, "It's what? Six A.M. there?"

"Something like that." She asked for Louey Santera's room.

The phone rang three times, then, "Mr. Santera's suite. Rudy here. May I help you? It's just past dawn here, by the way."

"Good morning to you, too, Rudy. This is Mrs. Santera. I don't know if Louey happened to mention it, but his daughter was kidnapped. Please put him on the phone."

There was a miserable silence.

"Now, Rudy."

"Yes, ma'am."

After a three-minute wait, Louey Santera said, "Molly, that you? What the hell's going on? Is Emma all right? I heard she was safe."

"Yeah, she's fine. However, all is not what it seems, Louey. You've got to come home right now. Today."

"I can't. I have a concert tonight. Three more before I come back to the U.S."

"Look, Louey, this is important. It's about your daughter's life. Doesn't that mean anything to you?"

"Dammit, Molly, I could probably come back by the end of the week, but not before then. I—"

"Today, Louey," said Mason Lord, his voice soft and very gentle.

"Who's that?"

"Hello, Louey," Mason Lord said. "This is your ex-father-in-law. How are you feeling this morning? It is morning, isn't it?"

"Yes, damn you, it's morning. So Molly went home to Daddy, did she?"

"I suggest you get yourself back here, Louey. You can make the Lufthansa flight from Frankfurt to Chicago."

"I can't, I—"

"Today, Louey. There are many things we need to talk about. Perhaps you have some explaining to do."

They heard a woman's voice in the background. "Who is that, Louey? Why are you breathing so hard?"

Molly laughed. "Bring her along, Louey. No one wants you to get lonesome." She hung up.

Ramsey looked ready to burst into laughter. He said, "If it were between a grand jury and your father, I'd bet any day on your dad getting him home."

"Oh yes," she said, and yawned. "He's good at scaring people's socks off."

"I like your hair," he said, surprising both of them.

She blinked at him. "My hair? What did you say? You like my hair?"

"Yes," he said. "I do. It's substantial, your hair. I like all those curls. It's good hair."

"Well, I like your hair too."

He began to laugh. She joined him. The door opened and Mason Lord looked in. "What is going on here? Why are you two laughing?"

Molly shook her head. "Will we be picking Louey up at O'Hare?"

Mason Lord looked back and forth between them. "I think Judge Hunt should pick Louey up. That would catch the little bastard off guard."

Ramsey merely nodded. "I'd be delighted. I've got lots to say to Mr. Santera. I'll use my old prosecutorial style."

"My daughter," Mason Lord said precisely, "doesn't have nice hair. She looks like a grown-up Little Orphan Annie. She has her grandmother's hair."

He'd had it. Ramsey walked up to Mason Lord. He got right in his face. "Why don't you tell Molly how happy you are to see her after three years? Why don't you tell her that she's got brains and grit and you're about the luckiest guy alive to have her for your daughter?"

Mason Lord turned on his heel and left the bedroom. Ramsey knew he'd gone too far. Mason Lord was enraged, nearly over the edge. But when he turned in the doorway, it wasn't Ramsey he went after. He said, his voice low and vicious, "Don't bother wasting your time sleeping with her. Louey said she was a cold lump in bed. No fun at all. Of course I had to have him disciplined when it got back to me what he'd said, but there it is anyway."

Molly didn't fold at all from the hurt of his words. Instead, she said, her voice filled with amusement, "Well, Louey's the expert, isn't he? Bottom line, Dad, I'm really glad I didn't get some disease from him."

She saw her father pause a moment, and then he was gone from her view.

Ramsey said, "The two of you are quite the duo. Look, Molly, you're an adult. I know it must hurt when he goes after you, but kiss it off. It's not important. There are lots more important things to think about and the most important is standing right there."

"Mama, why is Grandfather angry?"

Emma was standing in the doorway, her hair long and tousled, her nightgown with its pink bows nearly to the floor. She was clutching her piano against her chest. It was nearly as big as she was.

Ramsey said, "She needs a doll."

"Your grandfather wasn't what you'd call really angry, Em. It's late and he's older, you know? Older people get cross quickly when they get tired."

"Boy, what a whopper."

"Be quiet. Em, Ramsey is trying to make a joke. I'm going to give him lessons. Now, come back to bed. I'll tuck you in."

"I'll come with you." Ramsey walked to Emma and picked her up in his arms. "This piano weighs a ton, Emma. I think I'll have to remove an octave."

Emma reared back in his arms and looked at him closely. "That was funny, Ramsey. Not as funny as Mama, but funny. Has she given you a lesson already?"

"Thank you, Emma. She hasn't yet given me any lessons at all. Actually, I came out with that one all on my own." He took the piano, handed it to Molly. Emma sprawled against him, her head on his shoulder. She sucked her fingers.

There was a queen bed in the bedroom. It was Molly's old room, he realized. There wasn't a ruffle to be had. What there was were bookshelves all up and down one wall, filled with paperbacks and hardcovers, piled indiscriminately. On the other wall were photos, dozens and dozens of photos. Many were framed, most were arranged lovingly and carefully on corkboards.

"Mama takes pictures," Emma said to Ramsey when he laid her on her back. "She took all these when she was young."

"I see," he said, and leaned down and kissed Emma's forehead. He stroked her hair back from her face. "You go to sleep now, Emma. I don't want you worrying about anything, all right?"

"You won't leave, will you, Ramsey?"

He'd already made that decision, with Molly's help, but still, what if something happened? Something he couldn't foresee made him leave?

She whispered, "You don't know if you should tell me the truth. It's all right. Everybody lies. Except Mama. She never lies."

"Is that so?"

"Yes," Emma said. "Mama, will you come to bed soon?"

"Yes, love, in a little while. Ramsey and I have bunches of things to discuss."

She turned off Emma's light, but left the door ajar. A slice of light shone into the room from the three Tiffany lamps standing at intervals in the wide corridor.

Ramsey said, "I won't leave you, Emma, unless I have to, and then I'll tell you first."

Emma didn't say anything.

"We can hear her if she has a nightmare," Molly said quietly as she followed Ramsey back to his room.

"Now," he said once they were in his bedroom, "tell me what you think we should do."

"Beat up Louey Santera again."

"After we beat him up."

She sighed. "I don't know, Ramsey. So much has happened."

"One of the first things is to take Emma to a doctor and to a child shrink."

"Yes," she said. "I've been thinking about that. I don't want to take her to her regular pediatrician. He's a man. I want to take her to a woman."

"That's probably smart."

"I'll make calls tomorrow, get some names. Where do you think those men are, Ramsey?"

"If they're here, they're cursing a blue streak. There's no way in here. Miles told me he has six men patrolling the grounds around the clock. I think this place is more secure than the White House."

"I heard Mason tell Gunther to bring in another three men to patrol. He's not taking any chances."

"He loves you and Emma."

"Yeah, right. It's all a matter of possession. He doesn't want anyone messing with something he sees as his."

"Whatever it is, it's still a start. We'll see. Tomorrow—" He rubbed his hands together. "Tomorrow I'll get to meet dear Louey face-to-face."

"It won't be one of the high points of your day. Trust me."

"As Emma would say, you made a joke."

"Sometimes truth's funnier than fiction."

LOUEY Santera was furious and it showed. His mouth was tight, his lips a skinny pursed line. Then he saw a reporter and the fury was masked immediately by a charming smile and a little-boy shrug. "Hi," he said to the reporter, turned, and gave a smile to the accompanying photographer, then saw Molly and gave a wave.

The reporter, a longtime friend of Ramsey's, said cheerfully, "I hear you flew back, breaking concert dates, when you heard your little girl was kidnapped."

"I couldn't leave immediately," Louey said, nose sharp, on the alert instantly. "I naturally came back as soon as I could."

"Is it true your little girl is safe and at her grandfather's house? Her grandfather is Mason Lord, isn't that right?"

"Yeah, he is her grandfather, and yeah I heard she was at his house. It's over now, thank God. Did you hear? My concerts went great, too."

"I've heard you've had your problems with Mr. Lord. Is that right, Mr. Santera?"

A man came from behind Louey Santera to plant himself directly in front of the reporter. He was a young guy, stringy, with acne scars. "Mr. Santera just flew in from Germany. He wants to be reunited with his little girl. He's tired. He's said all he's going to say. Good day."

The reporter said, "Come on, Mr. Santera, what's going on here? Your little girl was kidnapped over two weeks ago. You're coming back a little late, aren't you?"

"No comment."

The young guy with Louey actually shoved the reporter. The photographer flashed a photo.

Louey Santera was white-faced. Ramsey smiled as he stepped up to him. "Mr. Santera? I'm here to greet you. I'm Ramsey Hunt, currently residing with Mr. Mason Lord. Do come this way, out of all this crowd of people. Ah, yes, here's Molly."

"Get out of his face," the young guy said, and gave Ramsey a shove. The guy might look scrawny and too young, but Ramsey spotted the moves immediately, the watchful eyes, the stance.

"That isn't polite," Ramsey said, and in a move that was subtle and smooth, he gently clasped the young man's hand and twisted his thumb back. The guy gasped with pain. He didn't move.

"Now, back off," Ramsey said very quietly. "I'm not a reporter." He applied a bit more pressure on the thumb. "All right?"

"Leave be, Alenon," Louey Santera said.

The young guy nodded. There was cold hatred in his dark eyes. It seemed to be awfully easy to make enemies these days. Ramsey released his thumb. "Now, let's get out of here. Molly, say hello to your ex-husband."

"Hi, Louey. How's tricks? Hey, I don't see your girlfriend. She doesn't have a passport?"

"How did you find Emma?"

She batted her eyelashes at him and put her hand on her hip. "I used my considerable sex appeal, naturally."

Ramsey stared at her. Louey Santera barked out a vicious laugh. "Hey, that's a joke," he said. "You're always telling jokes, never serious. You didn't find Emma at all, did you? It's all hype."

"Why do you think that? I don't have enough brainpower? Not enough guts?"

"Come off it, Molly. You know you didn't have a thing to do with getting Emma back. You wouldn't know where to find square one if it hit you in the nose. What really happened?"

She leaned close. "Okay, Louey, the game's over." She leaned over to whisper in his ear. "Listen, you selfish jerk, I found my daughter, all by myself. You want to know what happened? The man who took her sexually abused her and beat her. What do you think of that, Louey?"

"That can't be true. I didn't hear anything like that. No, you're lying, trying to make me look bad."

"No one could make you look worse than you already look. You call from Europe and start bragging about your success there and all the women you're screwing. You're a toad, Louey, you don't give a damn about Emma."

"Then why am I here?"

"Because my father scares you all the way down to your crooked little toes. If he told you to be celibate for a week, I bet you'd really try to do it."

"He shouts to the world he's a big legitimate businessman, but he's nothing but a big-time crook, and you know it. You're no better. You took me for everything in the divorce, you're nothing but a—"

Ramsey broke in. "All right, enough of the emotional sentimental reunion. It's time to get out of here before more reporters show up." He turned to the acne-faced young guy who was Louey Santera's bodyguard. "You get Mr. Santera's luggage. You can drop it off at Mason Lord's place in Oak Park. Then you can go to a motel or something. I don't think you're included on Mr. Lord's houseguest list."

Louey looked over at the reporter who'd been so rude. He recognized him. His name was something like Marzilac. He was from the *Chicago Sun-Times*. Hell. He was just standing there, speaking low to his photographer. What were they talking about? Maybe they were talking about whether to print any of this. Just his luck. Now he had to face Mason Lord. His kidney hurt just thinking about it.

"Let's go," Ramsey said.

"Do as he says, Alenon," Louey said. "Call the house and tell me where you're staying."

SIXTEEN

An hour and a half later, Louey Santera faced his ex–father-in-law across the huge mahogany desk in Mason Lord's study.

"This cretin—" He motioned toward Ramsey, who was standing by the door. "He accosted me. He nearly broke my bodyguard's thumb. In fact, I'll bet you he got a reporter to come there and ask me stupid questions. It cost me a bundle to leave Germany. I was busy, everything was going great with the crowds. Besides, there's nothing I can do for you. I've thought about it, and I don't know of anyone who could have done this."

Mason Lord didn't rise. He sat there, tall and straight in his chair, weaving his black Mont Blanc pen, heavy with gold trim, expertly between his long fingers. He let Louey talk and talk. Finally, when he'd heard more than enough, he said, smoothly, "You're looking thin, Louey. Your eyes look too bright, the pupils too large. I hope you're well."

"Touring is hard work, real long hours. Sometimes I have to take sleeping pills to calm me down. Listen, I didn't want to come here. What can you possibly want from me?"

"I do hope you're not doing cocaine again. I really hate drugs, you know that. I told you that when you were married to Molly. If the coke doesn't kill you, then it's usually something else. Like the guys selling it to you getting pissed off. I've never seen simple sleeping pills dilate your pupils."

"I'm not doing drugs."

"Did you meet Ramsey Hunt?" Mason Lord waved a hand toward Ramsey, who was still standing by the door, arms crossed over his chest.

"I told you, he was the bastard who—"

"It's Judge Ramsey Hunt. Perhaps you've heard of him?"

"No. Who is he? Some gigolo your young wife wanted?"

"Ah, Louey, you do like to push the envelope, don't you? I suggest you think a bit before you open your mouth. If you ever mention my wife again, I'll have Gunther cut off the end of your tongue. Your singing wouldn't benefit from that. Now, since you appear to be ignorant as well as unwise, I'll tell you that Ramsey Hunt is the San Francisco Federal District Court judge whose picture was on the covers of both *Newsweek* and *Time* magazines a while back. He's a real hero, they say. Don't you remember? The big drug murder case in San Francisco? What Judge Hunt did all by himself when they tried to break the defendants out of the courtroom?" Louey looked blank. Mason Lord sighed. "Ah, Louey, I do pray that Emma didn't inherit your brains, your inability to recognize the importance of anything that doesn't pertain directly to you. It would be a pity."

Ramsey said, "Ignorance isn't the same as stupidity."

"In Louey's case, it seems to be."

"She's got his talent, Dad," Molly said, coming into the room to stand beside Ramsey. "In fact, she's got all the talent that he could ever claim. And his talent is good even if his brain isn't."

"Impossible," Louey Santera said, whirling around to see Molly standing beside that damned judge. The guy was too young to be a judge. She'd come in very quietly. How long had she been standing there? "Emma? She's a little kid, only what, five years old?"

"Six, Louey. Your daughter is six years old."

"Yeah, well, what talent?"

"She can play the piano for you. She's incredible."

"Enough!"

Everyone looked at Mason Lord. He relaxed slowly, saying nothing more, knowing that he had all their attention again.

Louey said, "Why did you want me to come back? You got Emma. What else is there?"

"It appears there's a conspiracy afoot. Not just one kidnapper, Louey. Judge Hunt believes there are a goodly number of men involved since it appears to be a very professional operation, and they're all after Emma. Indeed, the men tracked Molly and Ramsey all across Colorado into California. Do you know anything about this, Louey?"

"That's ridiculous! What would I know about that? Emma's my daughter, for God's sake. I don't know anything about any conspiracy."

"Well, there's a problem," Mason Lord continued, his voice suddenly soft, oily with sincerity. It reminded Ramsey of Bill Matthias's voice, a lawyer in San Francisco unoriginally called Slick Willie. "I'm not behind any conspiracy, Louey, and there, quite simply, isn't anybody else. There's another little point that's really very disturbing. The man who had Emma. He abused her sexually and beat her."

Louey lunged to his feet, his face white. "No! That's impossible. Molly said that, but I didn't believe her. There must be a mistake . . . not Emma, no one would dare touch Emma like that."

Mason Lord sat slightly forward. "Didn't you bother to make sure that the man you hired to hold Emma in that cabin in the Rockies wasn't a child molester?"

Louey collapsed back into the chair. "Listen, I didn't hire anybody! I don't know anything about any of it. Dammit, she's my daughter. I wouldn't have my own daughter kidnapped."

"Oh?" It was Molly's voice coming from behind him, cold and hard. "You'd do anything for money, Louey. Anything. I'll bet you owe some big shot lots of money and you left the country because you couldn't pay. Is that it?"

He turned on her, so furious the pulse pounded wildly in his thin neck. "You have the gall to talk high and mighty about money. You took me for every dime I had. You didn't deserve anything at all. All you managed to do was get pregnant. Dammit, I didn't have Emma kidnapped!"

Mason Lord slowly rose. He pressed his palms against the desktop. He said in that same soft, oily voice, "I think Molly's right. You're in big debt to somebody and this was your way of paying them off. Tell us the names of the men, Louey. Tell us who helped you pull this off. Tell us why they're still after Emma."

"I don't know about any men! I don't know anything! Molly's dead wrong."

"Gunther, please come here."

Gunther, huge and menacing, his big hands relaxed at his sides, said, "Yes, Mr. Lord?"

"Gunther, please take Mr. Santera to one of our guest rooms. He's weary from his long journey. He flew in from Germany today, you know. Yes, he's tired and needs to rest. Take him upstairs and put him to bed. Stay with him, Gunther. Remind him that life is sometimes very difficult. Remind him that I forgave him once, but patience is a precious commodity. Remind him that I'm not always such a patient man. Oh yes, he doesn't need to speak to that creature who is supposedly his bodyguard. Keep Mr. Santera quiet and apart. He needs to rest."

"I didn't have Emma kidnapped!"

"I'll see you after you've had a nice rest, Louey," Mason Lord said. He rose and watched Gunther wrap one huge hand around Louey Santera's upper arm and pull him toward the study doors.

Louey jerked around at the door. "If it's Molly who's claiming I did that, she's crazy. She hates me. Maybe this judge character is her lover and they wanted the money. Yeah, maybe Molly did it."

Gunther quietly closed the study doors, and there was silence.

Ramsey whistled. He said, "I sometimes forget the awesome power people like you wield. Every day I deal with people claiming that they're as innocent as their dear grannies, but you know they're lying through their teeth, you know that most of them are thugs, cons, just plain scum, and many times much worse.

"And the thing is, of course, that in our justice system you can't beat the crap out of them even though you know they're so guilty they're bulging with it. No, we play by rules that seem absurd in their gentleness, in their lack of focus and force. We use compromise and negotiation, not metaphorical thumb screws." Ramsey shrugged. "On the other hand, your performance hasn't yet resulted in anything, except to terrify one skinny little man. Molly would probably disagree with me on how often we get to it, but the truth is always there, somewhere. Don't beat the crap out of him yet, sir. Your threats are just as potent. I'd like a chance to talk to him myself. From what I could see, Molly should probably keep her distance. She's quite good with that pistol of hers."

Mason Lord said easily, "Of course I know my threats are potent, Ramsey. They wouldn't be potent, however, if occasionally I didn't back them up, and the knowledge of that got around. Talk to Louey, see what you can dig out of the little bastard."

Ramsey nodded, then said to Molly, "I'm thirsty. Would you like to drink a glass of lemonade with me and Emma?"

"Yes. Then I've got phone calls to make."

DR. Eleanor Loo, a tall Chinese-American woman in her mid-thirties, was wearing a leg cast. She rose clumsily when they came into her office. Molly had gotten her name from Emma's new pediatrician. Her fingers were crossed when, after introductions were made, Dr. Loo turned to Emma. She smiled at her, then said, "Let me sit down, Emma. My leg makes me a bit awkward and the cast is heavy. At least it doesn't hurt much anymore. I broke it skiing. It was a beautiful fall, right off a twelve-foot cliff. Everyone said I looked so graceful sailing off that cliff. I don't suppose you ski?"

"My mama does. I'm learning." Emma didn't move, just stood there between Ramsey and Molly.

"You've had three lessons, kiddo," Molly said. "You're going to be very good. Maybe you'll be lucky and not go sailing off a cliff, but it happens. Remember when I strained the ligaments in my right knee?"

"Yes, Mama. You had to have physical therapy."

"Me too," said Dr. Loo. "I'll ski again, but not for another year. I miss it. Now, Emma, why don't you come over here and sit by me?"

Emma didn't move. She tightened her hold on Ramsey's hand.

Ramsey said easily, "Tell you what, Dr. Loo, why don't I let Emma sit on my lap for a while. Is that all right?"

"Sure thing. I understand that you're a very smart girl, Emma. Your mama told me you escaped from this bad man all by yourself, that you thought it all through and figured out what to do."

Emma was frozen. Ramsey couldn't even hear her breathe. But he forced himself to keep quiet, to wait. He supposed he'd expected the shrink to go easier, to ease into Emma's experience, not dive in, face first.

Dr. Loo said, "How did you figure out how to escape?"

Emma licked her lips. It was the first movement she'd made. Ramsey wanted so much to pull her against him and cover her with his arms, protect her, but he knew there was no protection when the wound was raw and deep, all on the inside. He looked at Molly. Her face was white and set. She was trying to look relaxed, but she wasn't succeeding. Her hands were fists on the chair arms.

Emma said in a small reflective voice, "I thought and thought."

Ramsey felt as if he'd been punched in the gut. Emma's voice was a whisper of sound. He was surprised any of them even heard her words.

Dr. Loo waited for more, but Emma didn't say any more. Dr. Loo said then, "You thought well. How long did you think about it?"

"All that day. But I didn't know how I could get the string off my hands, and then he forgot. He just forgot and went outside to smoke."

"Then what did you do?"

Emma was pressed so tightly against his chest that Ramsey wondered if he shouldn't intervene. He was on the point of opening his mouth when Emma said in that same whispery soft little voice, "I jumped off the bed. It was real dirty. He wasn't wearing his glasses. When he came back he thought the pillow was me. I crawled out the front door."

"You were barefoot?"

Emma thought. "No, I knew I had to run, so I put on my sneakers. I put them on after I was outside."

"Did he drink very much?"

"I counted four empty bottles. I didn't have anything to do, so I counted them. They were really big."

"How long did it take him to drink those four bottles?"

"Five days."

"That's how many days it was until you escaped?"

"Yes," Emma said, her voice not quite so choked now.

"Were there certain times of the day or night that he drank out of those bottles?"

It was loud, that mewling sound that ripped Ramsey's guts. She was trembling, wheezing for breath, making those awful sounds. "No, no, sweetheart," Ramsey said, pressing his cheek to hers, holding her tightly, rocking her, keeping her close and closer still. "It's all right. You're safe now, with me and your mama. If Dr. Loo had been there I bet she would have kicked that miserable man in his butt."

"That's right, Em. She would have kicked him with her cast. That would really hurt."

The mewling sounds stopped.

"Emma?" It was Dr. Loo. Emma didn't say anything, pressed closer to Ramsey's chest. "I would have kicked him really hard. Count on it."

Emma jerked. Then, slowly, she raised her head. She looked at her mother, at Ramsey, then at Dr. Loo. "Mama wanted to shoot him," she said at last. "She might have shot Ramsey if I hadn't said something."

"You did well, kiddo," Molly said. "You did really well."

"Can you answer another question for me, Emma?"

The little girl looked at her clearly now. "I don't want to but I know that my mama wants me to, and Ramsey."

"Yes, but only if it doesn't make you sick afraid. Okay?"

"Okay."

"Was this man who kept you at the cabin for five days the same man who took you?"

"Yes."

"How did he get you?"

"Mama was taking pictures in the park in front of our house. I was with Scooter—he's the neighbor's dog. Mama said I could get one just like him. I was throwing his stick. It took me a long time to teach him to bring me back the stick because Mama said that Dalmatians weren't genius dogs, just dumb dogs and really cute. I threw the stick and when Scooter didn't come back I went to him. There was a man petting him. I heard Mama call my name and I called back and said I was getting Scooter. Then the man smiled at me and he hit me on the head. I tried to call my mama but I couldn't."

Ramsey thought: It was that easy. It took only an instant, only one instant when the adult believed everything was all right. And then it was too late.

He glanced over at Molly. She looked stricken, guilt ridden. He'd have to shake her out of it. It hadn't been her fault, but he knew just how deeply self-blame could burrow in and corrode.

Then Emma turned her face in against Ramsey's chest. It was as if she'd frozen, stiff and cold. He held her, kissing her hair.

Molly rose slowly at a nod from Dr. Loo. "Thank you, Dr. Loo."

"It was nice to meet you, Mrs. Santera, Mr. Hunt. I like you, Emma. You've got guts. You've got a good mind. You're going to do fine. Now, I want us to talk some more when you're feeling less overwhelmed with bad memories. All right?"

Emma slowly turned to face the doctor. She said finally, "I don't know, Dr. Loo. Maybe we can talk next week?"

Ramsey noticed that Molly was flushed with relief.

Emma slipped off his lap and went to her mother. She took her hand and held it hard. She dragged Molly out of the office.

"Mr. Hunt, a moment, please."

He turned and smiled. "You did that very well. I was wondering about your approach, but it worked."

"Emma's a smart child. You've always got to take a chance, though, on your initial reading. I don't know your part in all of this, but Emma certainly trusts you. So, whatever you and her mother have done, it's been good. It's up to me to get it all out of her so she can look at it, dismantle it, study it, then come to terms with it. Are the police in any way involved?"

He shook his head. "Not right now. Neither Molly nor I wanted to give her over to strangers. This is just for Emma. She's had some doozy night-mares."

"No wonder. I understand you had her examined?"

"Yes, the pediatrician put her under, at our request, then examined her. She'd been sexually abused, she'd been beaten, as we thought, but she's healed nicely, at least on the outside. Oh, yes, one other thing. A couple of times, coming out of a nightmare, Emma said things about this man. She talked about him tying her up with twine because she was just a little girl. She mentioned that he told her he needed her more than God needed him."

"Now that's a real lead. Give the FBI this information, Mr. Hunt, if you haven't already."

"I will."

Dr. Loo nodded. "You and Mrs. Santera keep doing what you're doing. I'll see you on Tuesday?"

"Yes, that's fine." It was only four days away. "There was something else."

She reached out to pick up a scratching stick. He watched her ease it down into the cast. She smiled. "Ah, that feels good. You never realize how important scratching is until it's a pain to be able to do it. Now, your something else—you think I'm going too fast. I am. But you see, you want to get all the poison out of her as quickly as possible before it has a chance to fester. Talking about all the hideousness is like the psychological equiva-lent of using a stomach pump. Don't worry, I'll pull back if I think it's too much at a time."

She stuck out her hand. "Tell her mother she's doing a great job. Tell her mother, too, that if she continues to blame herself for what happened then she won't be much good to Emma in the long run. All right, Judge Hunt? Don't look so surprised. You're a famous man."

"I'll tell Molly what you said." He turned, then said over his shoulder, "Dr. Loo, what I am really is a very frightened man."

SEVENTEEN

Molly came out of the kitchen to see Emma standing beside a hallway table, one of Miles's chocolate-chip cookies in her hand, staring up at her father. Louey looked profoundly uncomfortable.

"I remember you," Emma said slowly, and took a bite of cookie. "You're my papa. Mama said you were coming to see me."

"Yeah, well, here I am all right. You've really grown, kid."

"You haven't seen me for a long time," Emma said, staring at a man she dimly recognized. He looked tired and nervous. "Mama says I grow taller than a Dr Pepper can every month. That's my favorite drink."

"You look pretty tall to me. Look, Emma, I've got to go. I've got to see some people, do some things, you know?"

"Yes, Papa," she said slowly, her eyes never leaving his face. "I know."

Molly caught up to Louey in the upstairs hallway after she'd tucked Emma into bed an hour later. He was coming out of his bedroom. Gunther stood some twenty feet away, his arms crossed over his chest, chewing on a toothpick.

"You saw Emma for all of two minutes, Louey. The first time you've seen her, I might add, in two years. I was thinking you could have her play her new piano for you. You'll be impressed, I promise."

Louey Santera looked more harassed than scared at the moment, and he knew he had good reason to be scared. "Look, Molly, I saw her. What was I supposed to do, for God's sake? She's fine. Oh, all right. The next time I see her, I'll ask her to play that ridiculous piano."

"All right, how about this, after she's played for you—how about telling her you love her? You are her father, and she needs you, although that's a concept that never really took root in your brain."

"You wanted her, I didn't. You were a lot more fun before you had a kid, Molly. Remember those photos you took of me that *Rolling Stone* featured? Now those could have made you, but what did you do? You just laughed and said they were okay, not all that great. The editor at *Rolling Stone* said you were terrific, but you wouldn't hear about doing any more work for them."

"Louey, you're not remembering quite right. I was pregnant with Emma at the time and puking my toenails up on a very regular basis. I've been getting back into it since Emma's older."

"No one has ever photographed me as well as you did."

So that was it. As usual, Louey was thinking about himself. She wanted to roll her eyes and smack him. She did neither, just smiled at him. She really didn't hate him most of the time, actually; she really didn't even think of him except rarely, and even on those rare occasions she felt only mild dislike simply because she understood the bone-deep fears that always festered beneath the surface in him. They occasionally even overwhelmed his remarkable conceit and ego. Because she was sometimes so weak-headed, she forgot about the damage he could wreak. It was fear that was driving him now and so she said without rancor, "You're an excellent subject, Louey. You know how to mate with the camera. Don't be impatient. There are lots of terrific photographers out there, but that's neither here nor there." She stopped, then shook her head. "Never mind. Sometimes I'm a fool. Now, tell me what you know about Emma's kidnapping, if you want me to help you before my father gets nasty. And he will, Louey, he'll get nastier than anything you can begin to imagine, nastier than he was to you in Denver three years ago."

"You weren't in Denver when he showed up three years ago, so how would you know what your dear daddy does?"

"I remember one summer when I was here. I was twelve years old and I woke up late, probably about midnight, and walked downstairs to the kitchen. I saw a light under his study door and I could hear men's voices. I pushed the door open and looked inside." She shuddered from the force of the memory, but she said only, "Tell him, Louey. Don't be cute. When he sets a goal, his focus never falters. His patience is formidable, but when it's gone, it's well and truly gone. Tell him. Or tell me. How were you involved in this? Tell me the names of the men you owe money to."

Ramsey pulled back around the corner. He'd come up the stairs to go to bed. It was late. There stood Molly and Louey Santera facing off like two gunslingers in the hallway outside his bedroom door. He'd heard her last few words. He knew she didn't really think that Louey had had anything to do directly with Emma's kidnapping. But he was involved indirectly. She was covering all the bases, which was really smart. He wondered if Louey was buying it.

Louey cast a furtive look at Gunther, who hadn't moved a muscle, then leaned against the door, crossing his arms over his chest. "I sure made a big mistake marrying you, didn't I? You were Little Miss Sweet Innocence with a big crook for a father. But I found that out too late."

"What do you mean?"

"You want some truth? I'll give you some truth." He stared down at her, his mouth twisting. "I wanted to fuck you, Molly, not marry you. But your daddy found out about us. He left me no choice."

"That's not true, Louey, you know it's not. He didn't even know I was dating you until I told him we were going to get married. Stop looking at me like I'm an idiot. I tell you, he didn't know a thing until I told him. I re-member the surprise on his face. I'm not making it up. He *was* surprised."

He laughed, a nasty laugh that nearly froze Molly where she stood.

"It's not true," she said again. She was crumbling inside. Was nothing as it had seemed in her life? "You're making this up, after all these years, to hurt me."

"Sure, Molly Dolly, sure I am. It turns out your old man had us followed—you didn't know that, did you? Of course you didn't. Yeah, and he had me followed to protect his little girl from the scummy coke-snorting rock star. He probably knew to the minute when you lost your virginity to me. And I got a visit from him the very next day. That was the day I really understood who your daddy actually is."

"You're not lying? My father made you propose marriage to me?"

"You don't think it was because I could have possibly wanted a wife, do you? Come on, Molly, even you're not that stupid. I always liked fresh-faced eager girls. You looked at me like I was a god. I wasn't about to deny myself. So I had to be patient and play a few games with you so that you'd fall on your back for me. I wanted to take your virginity. I've always preferred virgins. And so I did, but then there was Daddy standing at my front door after you left that morning." Louey shrugged. "I remember one of his goons—a guy who got his head shot off a while back—he had huge hands. He grabbed my neck between his hands and lifted me off the ground. Then your daddy told me how things would be. He told me I'd better be real sincere when I proposed to his daughter. He told me if I wasn't faithful to his daughter, he'd make my face so ugly nobody would want to see it. I believed him."

"You were very sincere," she said, and wondered how she could even form the words, much less get them out of her mouth. "I remember that evening very well. But you slept with lots of women."

Louey shrugged. "Yeah, well, what was I supposed to do when I was married to you? Finally, I called your daddy and confessed that I was having sex on the side. I told him you weren't interested. What was I to do?"

Louey laughed, actually laughed. "Your daddy finally gave me his permission. He told me to be discreet."

Humiliation and rage mingled and flowed over. She drew back her arm and struck him as hard as she could with her fist in his belly. The air whooshed out of him. He gasped, clutching his stomach, bent over.

"You bastard," she said low. "You complete and utter bastard. You'd do anything, wouldn't you? It's true that you're the only man I've ever slept with so I have no comparisons, but let me tell you, Louey, it wasn't ever any fun at all. From what I hear from other women, you were a pig at sex, and I bought it because I didn't know any better.

"You have nothing in you but greed and ego. And you've got street smarts, enough anyway to keep you alive, enough to realize that my father would have annihilated you if you hadn't done what he told you to do. Did you have Emma kidnapped? You need money. You always need money. You knew Mason would be the one to pay for her release, but you didn't care where it came from." She paused, panting, then smacked her palm against her forehead. "How could I be so stupid? You didn't want my dad involved. You wanted me alone to pay the ransom. You viewed it as getting your money back.

"I really didn't think you'd done it, but I've changed my mind. You don't owe big bucks to anyone, do you? No, you're the one who had her kidnapped. You wanted your money back."

She hit him again in his stomach. "And you got a child molester to take her. *You did that to your own daughter!* What kind of a man are you?"

She punched him yet again. He was still bent over, gasping for air. "No," he managed to get out. "I didn't. Don't hit me again, Molly, I mean it. Remember how I hit you three years ago? I'll do it again."

"You try it, you worm, just try it." She started to say something else, then just shook her head and walked away.

Ramsey didn't move for some time. People did the most incredible things to each other. He, Judge Ramsey Hunt, without hesitation, walked quickly down the corridor to where Louey Santera was still standing, alternately looking at Gunther and at his own toes.

"Hey, Louey. How's tricks?"

Louey managed to raise his head. "What do you want, you prick?"

Ramsey smiled at him and said in the mildest of voices, "Molly creamed you good. I knew she was strong, but that was quite a demo. You must have really pissed her off."

"She's really tough when her father's nearby or one of his goons. Can you imagine what Gunther would have done if I'd so much as breathed too hard on her? She knew. I had to stand here and let her hit me."

Ramsey kept that smile on his mouth. He lifted Louey Santera up by his shirtfront, straightened him, and sent his fist into his jaw. Louey yowled, staggering back. Ramsey let him go and he hit the wall.

"You're a real piece of work, you know that, Louey? There, that should give you something else to think about. I can't wait to see the back of you. And Molly's right, you know. Mason's about ready to snap. I have a feeling that when he does, you'll be dead meat."

"You're a bloody judge, a bloody federal judge, and listen to you. Some officer of the court you are. I'll get you for assault and battery. I'll get you impeached and disbarred, you bastard. I'll get you."

"Hey, you want to try to get me now? I'd sure welcome that, Louey. Anytime you want to play some more, you come see me." He shook his head. "It looks right now like you hired a child molester to kidnap your own daughter. You probably didn't know that, but it shows what a real winner you are. You're going to do big time for this, Louey, if you're involved, and that, only if you're lucky. Who knows, maybe I'll see you in my courtroom."

"You're in San Francisco, idiot."

"Yeah, but I've got lots of judge friends." Ramsey walked away whistling. He said over his shoulder, "Sleep well, Louey. Tomorrow will be here soon enough."

He went to his bedroom. He didn't bother turning on the lights. He knew his way around now. He walked to the bed, lay down, and stared up at the black ceiling. Was Louey involved? It seemed fantastic to him. But on the other hand, the man didn't seem to have a moral bone in his skinny body.

"You heard everything he said, didn't you?"

He jerked to a sitting position. "Molly? Why are you here, in the dark?"

"Waiting for you. I saw you lift him off the ground and hit him in the jaw."

"Between the two of us pounding him, maybe he might dredge up a bit of humanity, although I doubt he can. Why did you ever think you loved him?"

"I was nineteen years old and stupid."

"And he was the big rock star."

"Yes, and I was super-impressed. A friend of mine who knew him introduced us. You heard him. The only reason he asked me to go out with him was because I was Little Miss Sweet Innocence. I didn't go to bed with him that first night, and that was probably why he asked me out again. I didn't go to bed with him at all until one night I smoked marijuana, drank too much—Oh God, that sounds pathetic. Anyway, I just floated off with him to his bed." She shuddered with the memory of it.

"Leave it be, Ramsey. At least he gave me Emma. I would have danced with the devil if the result was Emma."

"Of course you would have," he said, and rose from the bed. He could see her now, standing by the open window. There was a quarter moon, sending a sliver of white light into the bedroom.

She turned to face him. "You did hear everything he said, didn't you?"

"Yes. It felt good to hit him, Molly. He's a miserable human being."

"Do you really think he had something to do with Emma's kidnapping?"

"Maybe. If he did, you hit it right on the head. He wanted his money back. But you know, I keep coming back to the same questions. Why all the professionals? Who was tracking us? Remember, the ransom note arrived after we'd gotten Emma back. I got the distinct impression that if they'd found us, we'd all be dead. Why? That wouldn't give them any ransom."

"I know."

They heard a scream, a high piercing cry that had them out of his bedroom in an instant and down the hall into Emma and Molly's bedroom.

Ramsey stood back while Molly gathered Emma to her and rocked her. "It's all right, baby, really, it's all right. That's right, breathe deeply now for Mama. You're okay. I'm here. Ramsey's here too."

He sat down on the other side of the bed and rubbed Emma's back, saying nothing.

"Was it that awful man, Em?"

Emma nodded against her mother's shoulder. "I woke up when there was this noise. I looked over. He was at the window. He was staring in at me. He was grinning. He had bad teeth, just like before."

Ramsey went immediately to the window and stared out. He didn't see anything. He unlocked the window and raised it. They were on the second floor. There was a ledge outside, wide enough for a man to stand on. He looked and looked but there was no movement in the bushes or trees, no shifts in the shadows, no sounds. He didn't see a single one of Mason Lord's guards.

He turned to Emma as she said in a small broken voice, "He won't go away. He's always there, waiting for me. I knew he'd come back for me, and he did. He followed us all the way from California. He's here now."

Molly looked up at him. He shook his head.

"You sure you saw him at the window, Em?"

"Yes. He was grinning at me. I was so scared."

Molly pulled her tightly against her again. "I know, sweetheart. But you're all right. Both Ramsey and I are here with you."

Ramsey said, "He won't come back again, Emma. And he won't be there for much longer, I promise. Now, I'm going downstairs and we're going to look for this character."

He was at the door when Emma called out his name. He turned to her. "Yes, Emma?"

"Thank you for believing me."

He smiled. "If he's still out there, we'll get him."

She didn't look as if she believed him. Actually, he didn't either since he believed she had indeed dreamed him up out of a nightmare, but he and the guards would all look anyway. He couldn't imagine that anyone could sneak onto the estate without one of the guards seeing him. But it couldn't hurt to look around, to talk to the guards, to make sure they were on their toes.

Emma was sucking her fingers, hiccuping. Molly said, "I'm going to come to bed now, Emma, we can play spoons. We can snuggle real close."

"Can Ramsey come, too?"

He didn't even hesitate. "Sure, Emma. Tell you what, you get settled with your mom and I'll be in soon. I'll hug you both until you fall asleep. I'm going to go look for that guy."

She sucked harder on her fingers, then pulled them out of her mouth and whispered, "Please be careful, Ramsey. He's a bad man. He even smokes."

"I'll be back soon, Emma. I'll be careful as a judge."

The sucking slowed. She sniffed and swallowed. "That was kind of funny, Ramsey."

MILES knocked lightly on the bedroom door, then quietly opened it. Emma was lying pressed against Molly. Ramsey was sleeping in a chair next to the bed, an afghan pulled up to his chin.

It was late, after eight o'clock in the morning. He paused, not knowing what to do.

"Is that you, Miles?"

"Yes, Ramsey. Should I come back?"

"No, it's time for us all to get up." He sat up in the chair and stretched. "I'm a damned pretzel," he said, and rubbed his neck. He started to get up, then Emma's hand shot out from under the covers and grabbed his hand. Molly awoke. She tried to sit up and not disturb Emma at the same time.

"I'm awake, Mama. I've got Ramsey."

"I see that you do. Miles?"

"Yes, Molly." He suddenly broke off and turned. "Oh, good morning, sir. As you can see, Ramsey and Molly were protecting Emma."

"This is ridiculous," Mason Lord said. "What the hell are you doing in here, Ramsey?"

Ramsey said quietly, Emma's hand still held in his, "If the two of you will please leave, Molly and I will get ourselves together. In case you're wondering why I'm in here, Emma had a nightmare. I stay close. It makes her feel safe again. Let me go now, Em. That's right." He leaned down and kissed her, then lightly patted her cheek.

Mason Lord turned away. They heard him say, his voice hard and cold and very smooth, "Good morning, Louey. I trust you have a whole lot to say to me this morning."

"So she's sleeping with him, huh?"

"You have a very plebeian mind, Louey. I suggest you go downstairs, have some bacon and toast, then prepare to tell me all about the recent happenings in your miserable life."

"I tell you, I didn't kidnap Emma. She's my daughter, too. Why do you call her Molly's daughter? Listen, you've got to believe me, I—"

Miles, thankfully, closed the door.

RAMSEY called Dr. Loo, telling her about Emma's nightmare that had seemed so real to her. Dr. Loo would see them right away.

Mason Lord stopped Ramsey on the way to the breakfast room and drew him aside. "I had Gunther bring the Mercedes around for you. You can drive it to the doctor's. I also heard about the search last night."

"We didn't find any evidence of an intruder, and no one really expected to. Emma dreamed about the man, then half woke up and saw him in the window. Adults could do that. It shouldn't be too much of a stretch to imagine a six-year-old seeing the bad man at the window. That's why we're seeing Dr. Loo right away while it's still fresh in Emma's mind." Ramsey frowned, looking past Mason Lord's shoulder.

"What is it?"

"It's very likely Emma could describe the kidnapper. I'd thought about it before, but I decided she didn't need that kind of stress. It was too soon. Maybe she could do it now. We could get a police artist out here."

"No police. They poke where they shouldn't. I'll get an artist and have him make arrangements to see you at Dr. Loo's."

Ramsey nodded and walked into the breakfast room. Only Emma and Molly were there. It was a charming room done in the Colonial style, with bowed windows looking over the back lawn with its glittering blue swimming pool. He sat down at the cherry-wood table with its hand-embroidered tablecloth, covered dishes set for them.

"I like Dr. Loo," Emma said as she started on her bowl of the special oatmeal Miles had made for her. "Do you really believe I saw him?"

"It's possible you didn't really see him, sweetheart. I hope we can find out what you really saw. Do you mind?"

"No." She sighed deeply. Ramsey hadn't ever thought a child could sigh like that.

Molly stood up and walked behind Emma. "Let me French-braid your hair, Em. It looks a bit ratty."

While Emma ate her cereal, Ramsey drank coffee, watching Molly do the French braid, her hands sure, her motions smooth. He'd have to learn how to do that. He remembered the pathetic braids he'd managed after he'd found Emma.

"You said you'd teach me how to do that," he said to Molly, who was twisting a rubber band around the bottom of the braid. She wrapped a pretty yellow puffy bow around that.

"Sure, no problem. Emma, do you mind Ramsey practicing on you?"

"No, Mama. Ramsey can learn anything."

"Such faith," Molly said and kissed her daughter's ear. "If you're finished, sweetheart, it's nearly time to go. I'll call Miles to get the car."

"Gunther already brought it around earlier, according to your father."

They went out of the house five minutes later to see the car parked on the far side of the wide circular drive.

Suddenly, Louey Santera bolted from behind a thick row of bushes, rushed to the car, and jerked open the driver's-side door of the Mercedes.

"He's trying to escape," Ramsey said, shaking his head. "The idiot."

He yelled, "Come back here, Louey. You can't get out of here, you know that. The drive is gated. There are two guys there, with guns. Stop, you moron. For God's sake, Mason isn't going to pull your fingernails out. All you've got to do is tell him the truth and nobody's going to hurt you."

Louey gave them the finger. He twisted the key in the ignition.

It was his last act.

EIGHTEEN

The car exploded in a ball of flame. Tongues of fire and metal swept upward and outward from the car, shooting into the air, hurtling toward them. Molly grabbed Emma and threw her to the ground, falling over her. Ramsey flung himself on top of them both, gathering them in with his arms, covering them as best he could. He felt the fierce heat of the flames, heard the whoosh of the fire and chunks of metal striking the sidewalk and gravel. Suddenly he felt as if a boulder had slammed into the middle of his back. It was hard and heavy and hot. The pain was intense. Whatever had hit him was still on his back, burning through his sports jacket and shirt. "Hold still, Molly." He quickly rolled off them onto his back. A smoking fragment of upholstery fell to the ground beside him. The pain immediately lessened. He'd stopped the burning.

He looked back at Molly and saw a sharp piece of metal that looked like a spear jutting out of her arm, right above the elbow. "Oh Jesus, Molly, hold still. Emma, you okay?"

"Yes, Ramsey."

"Good. Don't either of you move yet. It's still too dangerous." He ripped off the sleeve of his shirt, took a deep breath, and without saying a word to Molly, he jerked the metal spear out of her arm. "Good," he said. "Don't move, I'm going to wrap it up."

Molly hadn't made a sound. He didn't know how she'd managed it, but she did. The next minutes ground slowly by. Emma was fidgeting. He said things, silly meaningless things, to quiet her. Finally, the car was burning down, consuming itself, the flames collapsed into plumes of black smoke, which then fell, blanketing everything. The smell of burning rubber was nauseating. The Mercedes was a burning corpse. And what was left of Louey was inside it.

Emma twisted onto her back when Ramsey finally moved and looked up at him and her mother, who was holding her arm. "What happened? Why did our car blow up?"

"It's all right, Emma." He couldn't answer her, not yet. He helped Molly to her feet. "You hanging in there?"

"Yes, don't worry about me. I'm lucky I was wearing a long-sleeved dress. Not much protection, but some." Her sleeve was seared off, the blood from the wound soaking his makeshift bandage and snaking down her forearm.

"Both of us need a doctor."

She was staring at him. "Are you all right, Ramsey? I know you're hurt. How bad is it?"

"I'm all right. Come on, Molly."

She looked away toward the burning car. She turned perfectly white. "Oh God, Louey!" She ran toward the burning wreck, holding her hurt arm. "Louey!"

Ramsey grabbed her around her waist, pulling her back. "No, Molly. He's dead." He blinked. It hit him that Emma's father had just been blown up in front of her. He and Molly were both in shock, not thinking clearly or quickly, but now here was Emma, staring at the car. He came down on his knees in front of her and gathered her against him. "It will be all right, Emma, I promise. I'm real sorry, sweetheart. Someone put a bomb in the car. It exploded when he turned it on."

He heard people's voices behind him, coming from the house, but he didn't turn to see who was there.

There was nothing left of the car. Nothing left either of Louey Santera. Then he saw that the Mercedes hood ornament was still recognizable. He turned then to see everyone standing on the front steps gaping at the twisted, blackened car. There were still small spurts of flame eating into the metal, bursting up now and then into glittering showers.

Emma's piano was smashed. Still she held it against her chest. She looked at her mother, then back at him. "I don't understand."

"He's dead, Emma," Molly said.

"Oh," she said finally. She looked at the gutted car, at the licking flames. "I don't see him, Ramsey."

"No," he said. He wasn't about to tell her that her father could be picked up in a wastebasket.

Then everyone seemed to be talking at once, patting, soothing, Mason Lord even holding Molly close to his side for a moment. Gunther had his gun out. Miles was trying to edge close to Emma. Guards had swarmed to the burning wreck, their guns at the ready. All of them were young men, fit and strong, each carrying an automatic weapon. Even they stopped to stare at the devastation.

Eve Lord said slowly, her eyes on Emma, "You three were supposed to be in that car, not Louey Santera."

"It was that bad man," Emma said. "He came back to get me, but he killed Daddy instead."

She looked at her smashed piano, and gently laid it on the grass. "Look at all the broken keys." She came down on her knees beside it and gently pressed the middle C. A sharp tinny sound pinged out. Her face went very still. She picked up the piano again, clutched it to her chest, and walked back into the house. Molly caught her in a moment, and pulled her up into her arms.

"I'll call the police," Ramsey said to Mason Lord.

"There will be no police on my property."

"Oh, yes, there will."

MOLLY didn't make a sound as Mason Lord's own personal physician, Dr. Theodore Otterly, sewed up her arm. Ramsey felt the ripples of pain, the tensing of her muscles, but she didn't complain. He'd put two chairs together, sitting on the back one to support Molly in front of him. Dr. Otterly asked him to help support her, so Ramsey put his arm around her, under her chin, his hand cupping her shoulder. She leaned her chin on his arm. Emma was holding her hand. Her wounded arm was resting on the kitchen table. All of Dr. Otterly's medical stuff was spread out on the table. Molly flinched, then drew a deep fast breath.

Suddenly Emma made a small mewling sound. Ramsey said easily, "I know, Em. This is tough, but your mom's hanging in there. If you want to say something, say it."

"Are you all right, Mama?"

Her voice was small and thin, her fear stark. Molly didn't know where she got a smile, but she managed to manufacture one. "Hey, Em, this is nothing. I'm mean and tough, just like Ramsey. I can take these little hits. I'm a macha. Don't you worry, kiddo, I'm fine."

He felt her shudder again and tightened his arm around her. She leaned back, letting him support her weight. Dr. Otterly had helped him off with his jacket, probed at his shirt a moment, then said he'd deal with Molly first. He was vastly relieved. He didn't want an injury that would shut him down for even a short time. Events had gotten out of control, and he couldn't afford to be out of control as well. But damn, his back hurt.

He was aware that Mason Lord was standing back by the kitchen door, his arms folded across his chest. He hadn't said a word, just stood there. Miles was seated beside Emma, holding her other hand. He knew the police had arrived. He'd heard sirens and voices, running feet.

"Ramsey, your back is all black. I mean your shirt is all black. I hope you're not black underneath."

"Dr. Otterly just grunted when he saw it, told me not to whine, that he wanted to see to your mom first. He knows I'm okay, Emma." Ramsey was glad he couldn't see exactly what that crashing piece of upholstery had done to him.

Dr. Otterly set the last stitch in Molly's arm. He wet a thick cotton ball with alcohol and dabbed it against the stitches, getting off the last of the blood. He straightened. "That's good, Mrs. Santera. All over now. Now a couple of shots. Let me get you bandaged up and then we'll see to Judge Hunt."

Molly ended up with a sling. "To keep those stitches from pulling even a little bit," Dr. Otterly said.

When it was Ramsey's turn, he felt Emma take his hand. "I'm here, Ramsey. It's okay."

"Thanks, sweetheart. I need you to be here."

The pain was bad, but he managed to keep himself still. It felt as if a year had passed, a very painful one, before Dr. Otterly got his shirt off and his back cleaned. He said, "It's not as bad as I thought it would be. Your jacket saved your bacon. You've got a small second-degree burn on your back which means it'll blister and take a little bit longer to heal. You've also got some bruising. I'm going to apply some antibiotic ointment and put a bandage over the area. Leave it be for a day or two. You'll be fine, Judge Hunt.

"If either of you has any problems, give me a call. Oh yes, here are some more pain pills like the ones I've already given you. Mrs. Santera, you'll need them for the next three days or so."

Dr. Otterly smiled down at Emma. "Now, young lady, I've got a treat for you."

Emma didn't believe that for an instant. She took a step back. He laughed. "No, no, I promise nothing horrible. I just want you to drink some orange juice." He nodded to Miles. In a couple of minutes Miles handed her a half glass of orange juice. "Now, Emma, you need to drink it down."

She clearly didn't want to.

Ramsey said, "How can you make sure that your mama and I take care of ourselves if you're not in top-flight form?"

He saw she wasn't sure what that meant, but it was enough. She drank down the juice. Dr. Otterly patted her head, nodding to Molly.

"Em, will you see me upstairs? I'm a little bit shaky. No, I'm all right, but I've got to say that my arm isn't very happy with me. I'm also kind of worried about Ramsey. Yes, I need to lie down for a little while. Will you come with me?"

After Molly and Emma left the kitchen, Mason Lord said, "Will my daughter be all right?"

"I didn't lie to her, sir. The metal didn't slice that deeply, so I didn't have to repair the muscle. I gave her a tetanus shot and an antibiotic.

"Don't get me wrong. Although Judge Hunt's back wound isn't as severe as I feared it would be, your daughter's wound is bad enough. I'd say they were both very lucky with all the burning car fragments hurtling around."

"And Molly's daughter? What did you give her in that orange juice?"

Dr. Otterly had to think a moment, then nodded. He said, "Oh, you mean your granddaughter. Emma's okay. I slipped a bit of a sedative in the orange juice. She'll start feeling sleepy in a little while."

He turned back to Ramsey. "Both you and Mrs. Santera need to rest. It's the best thing for both of you. No heroics. As I said, take the pills. Rest." He eyed Ramsey's back, frowned, and pressed down another strip of tape over the bandage. "There, that should hold it. I hope you've got a good psychologist for the little girl?"

"Yes, we do. We were on our way to see her when all this happened. One other thing, Dr. Otterly. I got a gunshot in my left thigh some two weeks ago. Do you think you could take a look at it?"

"Here I thought that a judge's life was pretty staid. Drop your pants, Judge Hunt, and let me take a look."

When Dr. Otterly was done prodding and probing, he said, "You're fine. Whatever you did, it worked. The flesh has grown together nicely, not even much of a scar. Have you got full strength back yet in the leg?"

"Not all of it."

"Another week or so and you'll be running again. I wish you luck, Judge Hunt. Call me if there's any sort of problem." He nodded to Mason Lord.

Ramsey thanked him again and held himself still while Miles helped him on with a clean shirt. It didn't hurt.

Thank God Emma had escaped being hurt. Only she hadn't escaped, not really. It was another blow, a really big one.

Ramsey walked slowly with Mason Lord to the living room where Eve was answering questions for the police until they got there. Ramsey was relieved that Mason Lord hadn't put up much of a fight about their coming, had even agreed to speak to them. Not even he could try to kiss them off through his lawyers after a homicide. Neither Ramsey nor Molly had seen the police yet. He wasn't surprised that Molly had gone straight upstairs with Emma to try to keep her from the police. He wished he could have gone with her, too.

Three plainclothes officers sat on the edges of their chairs, looking uncomfortable, as if they had hemorrhoids, amid the stiff opulence and, naturally, in the company of Mason Lord's gorgeous young wife. All three of them rose when Ramsey and Mason walked into the living room.

Mason introduced himself, nodded coolly to each of the three men, then sat down beside his wife. He looked down at his fingernails and began to swing his leg.

Immediately, one of the men turned to Ramsey. "Judge Hunt? I'm Riley O'Connor. It's a pleasure and an honor to meet you, sir." Detective O'Connor was at least fifteen years older than Ramsey, skinny as a one-sided board, and bald. His dark eyes glittered with intelligence and humor. "We're very pleased that you're all right." The two men shook hands. Detective O'Connor introduced the other two officers, Sergeant Burnside and Detective Martinez.

Mason Lord cleared his throat. "Do you have all the information you need, officers?"

Detective O'Connor arched a very black eyebrow. "No, sir, we've actually only started. We've got a murder on our hands, a particularly violent murder. Mrs. Lord hasn't really had time to tell us much. And you just got here. However, I'd like to speak to Judge Hunt first. Then perhaps you'd be free, sir?"

Mason gave Detective O'Connor an infinitesimal regal nod, rose, and walked to the sideboard to pour himself a brandy.

"Fine," Ramsey said. "Let's go to Mr. Lord's study. Is that all right, sir?"

Mason didn't look happy. But he had no choice. He nodded. The other two detectives rose to go back out to the burned-out Mercedes, to join the forensics team combing the remains. Ramsey overheard one of them say, "I heard there isn't much left of him, after the blast and fire."

Detective Martinez said to Sergeant Burnside, "The three of them were lucky beyond belief. This is a weird one, Tommy, really weird. That guy, Gunther, didn't tell us a thing. I've got this feeling that we're not going to find out anything at all from anyone who works here."

"Yeah, and I wonder what Judge Hunt is doing here, with a guy like Mason Lord? Talk about a straight arrow."

Ramsey couldn't make out any more words. A straight arrow, was he? He rather liked that.

Beside him, Riley O'Connor laughed. "This is really something for us, Judge Hunt. I'm really sorry, but it's all going to come out now, everything about the kid's kidnapping, you guys being followed all over the West, and now this. Yeah, both fact and supposition. But I guess you know firsthand what the media spotlight can do. You can be a devil or a saint, depending on the reporters' likes and dislikes, and how nice you've been to them. As for the photographers, I'll bet you've wanted to slug some of them."

"Oh yes," Ramsey said, remembering the paparazzo outside hiding in his bushes, the final straw that had sent him to the Rockies where he'd found Emma and discovered that he really hadn't had any problems worth a damn. "On the other hand, this does need to come out. I want the press to have a field day. I'll personally cheer them on."

"Why?" Detective O'Connor cocked his head, his eyes trained on Ramsey's face.

"One reason: to protect Emma. Maybe the people who are after her will back off once everyone knows there's some sort of conspiracy afoot and that the press is going to plunk themselves in the middle of it."

"Conspiracy?"

Ramsey smiled at him. "A moment, Detective."

They went into the study and Ramsey closed the door. His back was beginning to ache. He must have winced because Detective Riley O'Connor said, "I heard it was a nasty hit you took in the back."

"Yeah, a slice of burning car upholstery. It's not so bad as the cut Mrs. Santera took on the arm. It landed flat on me, didn't slice the skin. She's with her daughter." Even as he was saying the words, there was a knock on the door. It opened. Molly appeared, pale, her arm in the sling, her hair a wild nimbus around her thin face. Her eyes were large, calm, and very green, not even a speck of gray. He noticed, for the first time, that she had a faint line of freckles across the bridge of her nose. He liked them.

He realized she was near the edge. He took a step toward her, then stopped. "Molly, what are you doing here? Is Emma all right?"

She raised her hand and lightly touched her fingers to his mouth. "It's all right. Emma's fine. She's asleep or I wouldn't have left her. Miles is keeping watch over her. I wanted to meet the police, tell them everything I know. There's no reason for them to have to repeat everything separately with me. Besides, I imagine you and I will be the only forthcoming witnesses in this household. When we tell the detective the whole story, maybe I'll remember something you forget and vice versa." She walked forward, her hand out. "I'm Molly Santera."

Detective O'Connor looked at a loss. "The dead man—Louey Santera, the rock star—he was your husband?"

"Ex-husband. Louey and I had been divorced for two years."

"Molly, would you like a brandy?"

She started to shake her head, then paused. "You know, that might work some magic."

Ramsey poured all three of them a small amount of brandy and handed it around. Detective O'Connor smiled at him, gave a mournful look at the brandy, and set the glass down on an end table. "Thank you," he said. "Perhaps later."

"This will take some time, Detective."

O'Connor took a small tape recorder out of his coat pocket. "May I record our conversation? That'll be best." They listened to him identify himself, them, the date, the place. Then he said clearly, "What I was saying about the media, Judge Hunt, is that with Mr. Santera's death, there'll be almost as many TV vans here as there were in L.A. covering the O.J. trial.

When all the stuff about your daughter's kidnapping gets out, the good Lord only knows what will happen."

"It can't be helped," Ramsey said. "Now, I think we should all start with you, Molly. Detective O'Connor needs the whole story. Whoever blew up Louey Santera meant to kill the three of us."

"Yes," she said, her voice just a whisper of sound. She drank some more brandy, and set the nearly empty snifter on a side table. She cleared her throat. "It started with Emma's kidnapping. Goodness, Ramsey, that was only about three and a half weeks ago."

"Emma was taken from your house, Mrs. Santera?"

"No, from the small park just behind our house. I was photographing there." She stopped, just stopped cold. Her hands were clasped in her lap, her knuckles white.

Ramsey said, his voice sharp, "It wasn't your fault, Molly. Tell Detective O'Connor exactly what happened."

The door opened again.

Special Agent Dillon Savich and Special Agent Lacey Sherlock Savich, both of the FBI, walked into the room.

Savich said, "Hi, Ramsey. I'm real happy to see you in one piece. Things have really turned ugly. We heard about the explosion on the ride in. You remember Sherlock, don't you?"

Dillon Savich looked over at Riley O'Connor, smiled, and stuck out his hand. "We're with the FBI. Don't worry. We're not here to bigfoot you. We're friends of Judge Hunt's. We want to help."

DR. Loo looked at Emma's new piano, fresh out of its box. She plunked a couple of keys. She smiled. "Do you know how to play 'Twinkle Twinkle Little Star'?"

"Yes, Dr. Loo. But it's been a long time."

Ramsey grinned at Emma. "Why don't you give her the theme and some variations, Emma?"

Emma gave him a small smile before she looked down at her new piano. The finish was so glossy she could see her face in it. She swallowed hard. She laid one finger gently over F. She didn't press the key down. Slowly, she turned to Dr. Loo. "I'm sorry, but I can't play right now. It doesn't feel right. My old piano just died."

Ramsey thought he'd cry. Oh, shit. He beat Molly to it. He picked

Emma up, leaving the piano on the small table, and gathered her to his chest. "You're right, Emma, you should mourn your old piano for a while. Dr. Loo can hear you play on your next visit."

Dr. Loo, who'd heard from Molly exactly what had happened, didn't mention the violent death of Emma's father. Rather, she said, "Mason Lord sent an artist over, Emma. We would like you to describe that man who kidnapped you, that same man you saw look in your bedroom window at your grandfather's house. Can you do that?"

Emma looked worried, then, slowly, she nodded. "I can try, Dr. Loo."

An elderly bald man was shown into Dr. Loo's office by the receptionist. His name was Raymond Block and he'd been a police artist for twenty-seven years. "Don't worry," he said to all of them. "I've worked with children all my career." He sat down beside Emma and opened his drawing pad.

"Are you ready, Emma? No, wait a moment, Mr. Block. I need to scratch inside my cast."

Dr. Loo didn't leave them until it was done. It took Mr. Block forty-five minutes of drawing, erasing, widening, elongating, more drawing, more erasing. Finally, Emma said, "That's him."

Mr. Block turned the drawing so that Dr. Loo, Ramsey, and Molly could see it.

"Oh, dear," Molly said, staring at the excellent drawing. "Are you sure that's the man you saw at the window, Emma? The man who kidnapped you?"

"Yes, he was the man who stole me. And then he came back and he smiled at me through the window."

Ramsey shook his head back and forth, quelling a weird desire to laugh and cry at the same time. "Well, this fellow isn't any pool man who works down the street from your house in Denver, Molly. No, I think he resembles someone who lives in a much more prestigious place."

It was an excellent rendering of Bill Clinton, only he had very bad teeth.

NINETEEN

Two hours later, Ramsey and Molly sat opposite Dillon Savich and Sherlock in the small breakfast room off the kitchen. Miles had served coffee and some special nut bread he said he'd baked that morning. He said Emma had told him she liked nut bread, but only with walnuts. Miles and Gunther stood in the shadows back by the outside door.

"Yeah," said Ramsey. "It was an excellent likeness of Bill Clinton."

Sherlock, who was drinking some of Miles's rich Jamaican coffee, choked.

Savich slapped her on the back. "Get a hold, Sherlock. It may not have been a coincidence. It may have been a mask. But he wore a mask the whole time? That would get real uncomfortable."

"Yes," Molly said, handing Sherlock a glass of water, "but it also means that they—whoever they are—wanted Emma alive, and they continued the disguise so she wouldn't be able to identify that man later."

"It still doesn't make sense," Ramsey said, picking a big chunk of walnut out of the bread. "Then why the attempts on our lives? Believe me, Savich, someone wanted Emma, alive? Dead? I'm not sure which."

Sherlock took another sip of her coffee, then shuddered. She said, "This coffee is delicious but I think it's trying to kill me."

"You shouldn't drink it in any case. You're pregnant. It's not good for you."

"Thanks for announcing it," Sherlock said, grabbed her stomach, and flew through the door Miles quickly opened for her. "Down the hall on the left," he shouted.

Savich shook his head. "I forgot. You won't believe this, but usually she's fine. But when I mention the word *pregnant* in front of her, she has to heave."

Ramsey started to say something, then shook his head, smiling. "I'm not going to go there, Savich." He stuck out his hand. "Congratulations."

"Me too," Molly said.

"She'll be just fine when she gets back, and I'll try harder to watch my mouth. Poor Sherlock. She hates it when she loses control."

"She married you," Ramsey said. "She can't hate losing control all that much."

Savich laughed. "Point that out to her and see what she has to say."

Molly said, "You're both FBI agents, you're married, and she's pregnant. You have a transgender laptop and you took a week off to come and help us. Why?"

Suddenly serious, Savich leaned forward, resting his chin on his clasped hands, his elbows on the table. "I've known Ramsey for a while now. We were both in law enforcement, Ramsey with the U.S. Attorney's office in San Francisco, and I with the FBI. We found we had a lot in common.

"We've kept in touch. I admire him, Mrs. Santera. I don't like what's happening. As for Sherlock, she's been a special agent less than a year now, but she's tough and bright, and although she's pregnant, she wouldn't have dreamed of not coming. Uh, if you could not mention the word *pregnant* in front of her, both of us would appreciate it."

"So it's anyone who says the word *pregnant*?"

Savich grinned at Ramsey. "As in she blames any messenger or just the guy who got her in this condition?"

"That's it."

"I don't know. I thought it was just me. Maybe you could drop the word by accident and we'll run a small scientific experiment."

"I wouldn't do that to another woman," Molly said. "Thank you both for coming."

"No problem. This is a royal mess. Sherlock doesn't like what's happening to you guys, either. So, this guy was either wearing a Clinton mask or he was a master at makeup and disguises. But it'd have to be a really good mask for Emma not to have realized it was a mask. I vote for a guy who's really good at disguises."

"Yes, that sounds more reasonable," Molly said. "Emma even put bad teeth in Clinton's mouth. Emma's bright."

Ramsey said, "I'm not her mother, but she's right. Emma's three dozen points sharper than Molly's razor."

"I told you not to use it."

"I was lucky not to cut my throat." He turned to Savich. "Did you mean it? You're not here to take over the case from the locals?"

"Nope. Sherlock and I are off for a week. But I've got MAXINE—"

"MAX experienced another sex change just three days ago," Sherlock said from the doorway, a wet washcloth in her hand. She daubed at her forehead, but she was smiling. "It's happened twice since I've known Dillon."

"I might have thought it meant MAX didn't know how to relate to her," Savich said. "That he was trying to make an accommodation since he knew she was here to stay. But the fact is he's gone back and forth now for about four years."

Ramsey said simply, "Molly and I both appreciate your help."

"We know that, Ramsey." He smiled up at his wife. "You okay, Sherlock?"

She nodded. "Just a brief brush with the devil." She turned to Molly. "That's what Dillon calls it every time I'm sick. Now, we'll put every scrap of information we can get our hands on into MAXINE and see what she comes up with." She saw that Molly didn't understand. "Dillon is the chief of the Criminal Apprehension Unit or CAU at the FBI. We don't do profiling, but we work with the profilers and with local law enforcement to catch serial killers. We use a number of programs that Dillon's developed. We plug in all the information we can get our hands on, including everything from the local police, the forensic reports, the autopsy reports, witness statements, you name it. MAXINE isn't better at figuring things out than real people, but he or she, depending on the month, is faster and looks at the data in many different ways. In just the first year, we solved six cases along with the local cops. We think we can apply that experience to help us catch this monster."

Savich said, "Ramsey, I'll speak to Agent Anchor and get all the reports on the cabin where Emma was kept. There's bound to be some physical evidence left. I'll get MAXINE to work on child molesters who have an M.O. using disguises."

Ramsey said, "Emma said he smoked, had bad teeth, and drank. Once when she was coming out of a nightmare, she remembered he'd said that he needed her more than God needed him."

Molly said, "He also used twine to tie her up." She swallowed and looked down. "He used twine because she was just a little girl."

"That's a start," Savich said.

Sherlock patted Molly's shoulder as she said, "Dillon and I took a week's vacation. We're at your command."

"I already told them," Savich said, pulling her down onto his lap. "They haven't applauded yet, but when they see what we can do, they'll do handsprings. I'll also speak to the police in Denver. We can add stuff from forensics from the explosion. Sherlock can help us by translating what you know into data for MAXINE."

"Then we push a button and MAXINE becomes the brightest Cuisinart on the planet," Sherlock said. "While Dillon talks to the cops, why don't we make a list of all the things you guys can remember.

"Where," Sherlock began, "do you think Louey Santera planned to go if he did manage to get the Mercedes off the estate?"

"Nowhere," Molly said. "He hadn't thought that far ahead. He was scared and he lost it. He did that sometimes."

"This time it was fatal," Ramsey said. "Poor bastard."

"Not a poor bastard if he was the one who staged Emma's kidnapping," Molly said, her voice hard. "How will we prove it if he was behind it?"

"Follow the money," Savich said. "I'll get a warrant to search through all Santera's financial records. There's always something there, always."

"You don't need a warrant. I'll get the records." Mason Lord stood in the kitchen doorway, Gunther standing right behind his right shoulder.

"I'd prefer you didn't do anything, Mr. Lord," Savich said. "It's our job. Let us do it on the up and up. Admittedly it takes a bit longer. On the other hand, it's legal. There are advantages to being really legal in this situation."

Mason said, "I know Louey's accountant. I will speak personally with him. Warren will plead to tell me everything he knows, to show me every record he's ever entered. Warren has always been useful and informative."

"You know," Sherlock said slowly, eyeing Mason Lord, wondering how he could be so utterly different from her own father yet look so remarkably like him. Both men had power, but they were on opposite sides of the law. "Maybe since Mr. Lord and Mr. Santera's accountant are such good acquaintances, it wouldn't be a bad thing. What do you think, Judge Hunt? Does that sound kosher enough to you? Would evidence from such a source give the defense a shot at an appeal?"

"Not that I can see. Hey, why not? We're on Mason Lord's turf. Let him glean information for the case." He grinned at Lord. "I would discourage breaking and entering, though."

In that instant Molly realized her father had been standing there stiff as a poker. Now she saw him ease up, saw those aristocratic hands unclench, the long lean fingers uncurl. The cops were admitting him. They wanted to involve him. He didn't smile, no, he'd never go that far, but there was something in his expression that held at least some degree more warmth than usual.

WARREN O'Dell was completely bald—probably through shaving—and looked like a longshoreman, exactly the opposite from what you'd expect of an accountant. He did wear wire-rimmed glasses, though. He had something of the look of Michael Jordan.

When he spoke, you saw he had yellow teeth from too much smoking. He had calluses on the pads of his fingers and his palms. He spared one glance for Ramsey, his full attention on Mason Lord. Then he did a double take. "I know you," he said, staring hard.

Ramsey smiled and said, "I'm Ramsey Hunt."

"You're that federal judge in California who jumped over the railing and chopped up a group of terrorists in your courtroom."

"That's the way things worked out. It was just a little group."

Mason Lord cleared his throat, and suddenly Warren O'Dell turned pale. "Uh, sir," he said, nodding his head and making a sweeping gesture with his hand toward an expensive white leather sofa. "Please, sit down. I was devastated at the news of Louey's death. I was going to call you."

"Were you now, Warren?" Mason said. "Why?"

It was obvious that Warren O'Dell was scared spitless. He was standing in the middle of his beautifully furnished office on the nineteenth floor of the McCord Building on Michigan Avenue looking as if he wanted to jump out a window.

"Yes, sir," he said finally. "I would have called you as soon as it happened, but it was such a shock, you know. I couldn't pull myself together until just this morning. Louey's dead, blown up by a car bomb. I can't believe it. It doesn't seem possible. I heard you allowed the cops to investigate?"

Ramsey felt a small ripple of surprise in his gut. Did O'Dell consider Mason Lord to be some sort of god with total immunity?

"It was murder, Warren. I'm a law-abiding citizen," Mason said, his voice austere, as if he'd been the one to insist on the cops coming in. He looked toward Ramsey. "Judge Hunt is the man who saved Molly's daughter."

"Oh, yes, now I see. I couldn't imagine why he was here, with you, seeing me. It's the shock of Louey's death. It's shaken me badly. I gave my girl the day off I was so upset."

"I see you have some boxes shoved behind your desk, Warren. I don't suppose you were planning to destroy some documents? Perhaps in preparation for a nice long vacation?"

"Oh no, sir. I was cleaning house. Nothing more."

"I'll see that you get any assistance you require," Mason said.

"No, sir, I'm fine, really."

Mason Lord barely raised his voice. "Gunther."

The huge man was there in the doorway, looking dead on at Warren O'Dell. As if O'Dell were a bug, Ramsey thought.

"Yes, Mr. Lord?"

"We need to assist Mr. O'Dell. See those boxes shoved behind that impressive mahogany desk of his? We'll take those and have a look at them. Ramsey, maybe you would be so kind as to look through Mr. O'Dell's file cabinets."

"I have some questions first," Ramsey said.

"Please, Mr. Lord, there's really nothing—"

Mason Lord raised his hand. O'Dell was instantly silent. "Judge Hunt wants to ask you some questions, Warren. You will answer them completely and honestly."

Warren O'Dell's bald head glistened with perspiration. He watched Gunther carrying out the boxes. He licked his lips. "Yes, sir."

Ramsey felt exceedingly strange. Here he was with a powerful criminal boss who had a potential witness nearly pissing in his pants, and he, Ramsey, a federal judge, was a co-conspirator in what was probably extortion, at least duress. Who cared? "Mr. O'Dell, tell me about Mr. Santera's finances."

Warren O'Dell swallowed. He looked again toward Gunther, who was coming back into the office, his gun in its shoulder holster clearly visible because his coat was open.

"Louey was broke," he said at last. "Dead broke. He was doing this tour to try to pay off his debts. There's nothing now that he broke his contract, not even loose change."

"Louey was broke?" Ramsey repeated. "Did he owe a lot of money?"

"Louey wasn't ever big on denying himself. Then he got butt-deep in debt. There's this small consortium in Las Vegas. I think they arranged for Louey to lose heavily at the craps table, which he did. He was a lousy gambler, but he wouldn't admit it. He thought he was the greatest in just about everything. No, in everything. He was into them for nearly a million dollars. They kept him gambling and he couldn't begin to pay them off. They just kept adding on interest. They made threats. On him, on your daughter, sir, and on your granddaughter."

"Names, please, O'Dell," Ramsey said. "Give me names and then give me records."

Mason rose and walked to the small bar, a chrome-and-glass affair on wheels with three gold leaf-framed glass levels. He picked up the brandy decanter and poured an inch into a snifter. He never turned, just stood there, looking out the wide windows, sipping on the brandy. He said quietly, "I know who it is."

"Who, sir?" Ramsey asked.

"Rule Shaker. Am I right, Warren?"

"Mr. Rule Shaker's the main player, yes sir. Louey had turned him down on a long engagement to play in Las Vegas. Mr. Shaker insisted, Louey kept saying no, even after he was in for all that money. That's when he decided to go on tour in Europe. He thought he could make back all the money. He's very popular in Europe, much more so than here in the U.S. He would have been able to repay Mr. Shaker if he'd stayed on his tour."

Ramsey said quietly, "You must have heard that Emma and Molly were the targets of that bomb, not Louey."

"Yeah, I heard. That's why I was heading out of town, until things settled down, just as Mr. Lord said. Mr. Shaker told Louey that no one he knew was safe. He was the one behind the car blowing up, there's no doubt in my mind about that. But he didn't want to kill Louey. He was after Louey's kid. He wanted to use the kid to show Louey he was serious."

"You think then Mr. Shaker also ordered Emma taken?"

Warren O'Dell said, "Louey was sure it was him. Didn't surprise me either. Louey called me from Germany. He didn't know what to do. I didn't either."

"Yes," Mason said. "Rule Shaker had Emma kidnapped. Rule killed Louey by mistake. I wonder why?"

Mason had spoken very quietly, but Ramsey had heard him. He said to Warren O'Dell, "How much money did Louey make before he died?"

"About three hundred thousand. There would have been taxes, of course, and some extra overhead we hadn't figured in, but he was getting there. If he'd been able to finish his tour, he might have been able to pay back every cent."

"Where's the money?"

"I don't know."

"You're his accountant," Mason said, his voice soft and clear as he turned from the huge glass window. "His accountant. Louey was particularly feckless, couldn't even seem to understand the most basic concept of how the dollar worked. I'm sure you must have been the one who guided him after he and my daughter divorced. I know that she handled all the finances during their marriage, but after? No, Warren, it was you. Now, tell Judge Hunt where the money went."

"I'm not lying, sir. I swear to you, I don't know. Louey wouldn't tell me. I've got the records, sir. Withdrawals from the bank, nearly all of it. He took it out, didn't say a thing to me."

"When did he withdraw the money, Mr. O'Dell?" Ramsey asked.

"Before he went to Germany. He was broke, but he still managed to talk the backers out of a huge advance, nearly two hundred thousand, if I remember correctly. Another hundred thousand was coming later, after he was in Germany performing, and that's gone too. Louey took all of it. He didn't tell me a thing, I swear it."

Gunther stood by the door, silent.

"You have all of Mr. O'Dell's papers?"

"Yes, sir."

"Then we'll be off. Judge Hunt, do you have more questions for Warren?"

"Yes. Where were you early this morning?"

Warren O'Dell looked as if he was going to faint. He cleared his throat. He swallowed and made himself cough. He said at last, "I was home in bed."

"Was anyone with you?"

"Yes, my girlfriend, Glennis."

"Give me her phone number."

In another four minutes, Ramsey was on the phone speaking to Glennis Clark, a waitress at the Downtown Diner over on O Street. He spoke quietly for several minutes. Finally, he hung up. "Unless you have excellent

ESP, Mr. O'Dell, and a very strong connection to Ms. Clark, it appears you're telling the truth."

Ramsey nodded and walked with Mason Lord to the door of the opulent office. He turned and said, "Who are you hiding from, Mr. O'Dell?"

"Mr. Shaker. He already called me. He's very angry, claims I'm responsible for Louey being in that car. Now that Louey's dead, he won't get his money back."

"A million bucks is a spit in the ocean for the likes of Mr. Shaker. Why is he really so angry?"

"Because he can't have Louey," Warren O'Dell said finally. "He really wanted Louey. When he realized that Louey would earn back the money and he couldn't use the debt as leverage, then he kidnapped the kid. Jesus, he'd kill me if he knew I'd told anybody."

"He wanted Louey to perform in his casino?"

"That too."

TWENTY

It was after nine o'clock that evening. Everyone had finally moved from the dining room into the huge living room for coffee and some of Miles's low-fat apricot tarts. Emma had begged to stay up so she could help Miles load the dishwasher. After she'd left in Miles's wake for the kitchen, Ramsey told everyone about their encounter with Warren O'Dell. When he said, "And then Mr. O'Dell said Rule Shaker really wanted Louey," Molly stared at him, disbelieving.

"He's gay? This Mr. Rule Shaker wanted Louey Santera for a lover? Is that what he meant?"

"Yeah," said Sherlock. "What's all this about?"

Ramsey smiled. Both Sherlock and Molly had understood it just as he had. Their incredulity was as great as his had been.

Savich sat back in his chair and said, "I'll bet there's an unexpected punch line here. Come on, Ramsey, spit it out."

Ramsey smiled wider, nodding to Mason as he said, "As it turns out, it was Mr. Shaker's daughter who wanted Louey. Her name is Melissa and apparently she's the apple of her daddy's eye. Anything she wants, Daddy gets for her. It was Louey she wanted, and so Mr. Shaker went after him."

"And ended up killing him." Molly was tired to her bones, worried sick about Emma, and now some gangster's daughter had wanted Louey? She continued, "So her daddy rigged a craps game so Louey would lose big time? And when that didn't work, you're saying this Mr. Shaker had Emma kidnapped to make Louey fall into line? Then he sent men after the three of us? Finally he tried to blow Emma and me up and killed Louey by mistake?" Molly jumped up from her chair, nearly knocking it over. She began pacing up and down, her eyes fastened on the toes of her black Bally loafers. "No, that's as nuts as this Shaker guy being gay. What kind of monster is he? That's sick."

Mason narrowed his eyes on his daughter, "Get a hold of yourself, Molly. Louey could have had his own daughter kidnapped so he could get his hands on my money and pay back Rule Shaker. It would further seem that finally Rule Shaker tried to kill Emma so that Louey would be frightened enough to do as he wanted him to do. It was business."

"Mason's right," Eve said. She gracefully set down her coffee cup. "If there's something you want badly enough, then you must be prepared to do whatever is necessary to gain it."

"Despite the costs?" Molly asked.

"Costs are part of doing business," Mason said.

"No," Ramsey said. "Louey didn't have a thing to do with any of it. Don't you see? There wasn't enough time to get another team in there working for a different master. Emma was kidnapped; I found her; then the two men came to the mountain cabin and tried to shoot us. Then two others probably followed us all the way here. No one knew where Emma was except the people who took her. All these acts seem connected, they're all part of the same piece of cloth."

Mason was chewing on an unlit cigarillo. He said slowly, "Well, it's a lot simpler to think that Louey wasn't involved at all."

"I've got a headache," Molly said, going toward the door. "It's late and I don't think I can help us anymore. I'm going to go to bed."

"I'll come with you," Ramsey said. "Sherlock? Savich?"

"I want to speak to MAXINE about all this a bit longer," Dillon said from where he was sitting near the fireplace in a massive leather chair, his laptop on a small table in front of him. "She's been chewing over some information while we were talking."

Sherlock said, "When she's finished chewing, then, doubtless, MAXINE will want to speak to me. When she's a female, she communicates better with another female. We'll be up soon."

Mason held out his hand to Eve. "Shall we go up, my dear?"

"Certainly, Mason," Eve said, smoothing the silk of her dress over her hip. Every man's eyes followed that move.

Mason Lord turned at the doorway, slight bewilderment in his voice, "I have a judge and two FBI agents staying in my house. This isn't what I'm used to."

He left without another word. Ramsey would have laughed, but he felt too much tension. He rubbed his neck. Emma would have remarked that her granddaddy had made a joke. Mason Lord knew this Rule Shaker, or at least he knew of him. What did he really think of all this? He as well as all his staff had been politely unhelpful to the police. What would Mason do?

Savich stood and said to Ramsey, "You want to go work out? That is, if your back's up to it?"

Sherlock said to Ramsey, "Working out is great for his stress. I usually work out with him. I used to let him throw me around, under the pretext of teaching me karate. He tromped me regularly until he found out I was in this interesting condition, then he refused even to let me watch him. You two go; it'll be good for both of you. I'm beat. Molly, I'll head on upstairs with you."

Molly gave Ramsey a worried look, but he just smiled, nodding at her. "I'll be up later," he said. "Tell Emma I'll be in to kiss her good night." He knew she was thinking about Emma, whose father had been blown up, and it had to be dealt with.

"Let's do it," Ramsey said. They didn't have to leave the compound or even Mason Lord's house. Gunther took them to the downstairs of the west wing to a state-of-the-art gym, actually more like a sports facility.

Ramsey said when they came out of the locker room, "Look at this. You think we're in the wrong line of work, Savich?"

Savich fastened on a weight belt. "Nah, it doesn't matter. Hey, the equipment might be the best, the mats might be the thickest, the bottled water might be from France, but the end result is still sweat. Let me help you tape your back up really well before we get the kinks out. I can even make you waterproof."

After Savich taped him, they both stretched for five minutes, then, as if of one mind, they began circling each other, poised and focused. Ramsey made the first move, a high clean kick with his right foot. Savich stepped three inches to the left, grabbed the ankle with his right hand, and pushed. Ramsey went flying to the floor, only to roll to the side and be back in position in an instant. He felt a twinge in his back, and Savich noticed.

"You're a bit faster than Sherlock, but not much, Ramsey. I don't think your back's ready for this. Why don't we just spot each other on the equipment?"

After thirty minutes, they ended up on their backs on the mat, their arms flung out, sweating and feeling better. After twenty laps in the swimming pool, they felt even better.

"Not bad," Ramsey said as he hauled himself out of the pool onto the cool pale blue tile apron. "I'd forgotten how busting my butt relieves the tension. My back doesn't feel so bad either."

"It's always worked for me."

Ramsey gave Savich a hand out of the pool. They sat in silence, soaking in the sweet still air in the huge enclosed pool room. "This place is something," Savich said. "So much foliage, it looks like a rain forest."

"As long as it doesn't have any boa constrictors under those palm fronds."

"Look," Savich said quietly, nodding only slightly upward. "It's a TV camera. Well, what did I expect—our host to give us a welcome kiss and let us roam at will? I'll bet there are microphones as well."

"Who cares? I'll have to ask Miles to show me the equipment," Ramsey said. "It looks like high-grade stuff from here."

"Think he has any female security people?"

"No," Ramsey said, "not Mason Lord. He's not what you'd call a major employer of women. I've seen him look at his wife. There's actually lust in his eyes and a sort of immense satisfaction that she's his and no one else's. I'm a bit surprised that he bothered to marry her, except that maybe he wants to get himself a son." Ramsey shook his head. "Mason probably had to marry her just to get into her pants. Eve's very smart."

Savich said, "Safe bet, huh?"

"As for Molly, well, she seems to deal with him pretty well. When we showed up here, I could practically taste her fear of him, the pressure to be the helpless little girl grateful for her daddy's help, but at the first insult from him, she dug in her heels."

"You backed her up, I assume?"

"Yeah, even though I didn't know the players then. I didn't realize then what a big deal it was for him to back down. I do now. And he did back down, Savich."

"You'd have to be blind not to notice what he thinks of her. That's got to have been tough on her. Jesus, I hope he doesn't show his stripes too obviously in front of Sherlock. She'd take a strip off him."

"I bet she would. Good choice, Savich. I like her. She's tough and she's smart and she seems to think you're pretty hot."

"Ramsey, what do you really think is going on here?"

Ramsey slowly rose. He was nearly dry. His back was beginning to hurt. He'd probably pay for the exercise, but right now, he was still glad he'd done it. He picked up a big dark gold towel and wrapped it around his shoulders. It was very soft, money soft. He shook his head, lifted an end of the towel, and wiped his face. "What's going on here?" he repeated, still drying his left ear. "I don't know, Savich, any more than you do. I'm too close. I care too much for the players. I do know one thing: To put a bomb in that Mercedes means that someone here on the premises had to have done it. No one could have gotten in here and planted that bomb without being seen. But nobody's coming right out and saying it. I wonder what Mason Lord is going to do."

"How much do you know about Molly Santera?"

Ramsey cocked a dark eyebrow not at the question itself, but the seriousness of Savich's voice. He said slowly, "I know she's fiercely protective of Emma. I know she's brave and tough, just like Sherlock. I know she can focus on one main thing and disregard everything else. She's also got great hair. Red like Sherlock's, but not at all the same shade. It's more like a sunset I once saw when I was on the west coast of Ireland."

Savich didn't say anything to that. He looked away, wishing things could be different, but, of course, they weren't. He said finally. "Did you know that one summer when she was about twelve years old she supposedly let her younger brother drown?"

Ramsey dropped the towel. He stared at Savich. He was shaking his head. "No," he said, "oh no. I can't believe that, Savich. That's not at all like her."

"I'm sorry. Sherlock discovered it in fifteen-year-old records. I'm sorry if you think she was spying on something that wasn't her business, but Sherlock is a professional to her fingertips. She looks at everything."

"I have no problem with Sherlock checking out my birthmark if she thinks it's relevant to this case, but I'm telling you that this thing with Molly's brother, it had to be an accident. Molly could never watch her own flesh and blood die. No way. And that includes that son-of-a-bitch father of hers."

Savich shrugged. "There was an investigation, of course, but the results were inconclusive. The general belief at the time was that she hated her younger brother because Daddy made it clear he was the favorite, the heir, the only one worth anything. You told me yourself Mason doesn't have much use for his daughter. Maybe you're right, maybe that's one reason he married Eve. He wants another boy child.

"Mason and his first wife, Alicia, were divorced when Molly was around eight years old and her brother was six," Savich continued. "She went with the mother back to her mother's home in Italy and the boy stayed with the father. Molly was visiting here one summer when this happened. When she was eighteen, she went to Vassar. She left after a year and moved in here with her father.

"You can't dismiss it out of hand, Ramsey. Molly Santera has a past. She may have been innocent, but you know there was a question about it. We can't afford to ignore it."

Ramsey said, "Are you suggesting she'd have anything to do with Emma's kidnapping?"

"No, I don't believe that. But how about Louey's murder. What if Louey was the target after all?"

Ramsey said, "Listen, she divorced his worthless ass. There was no reason to kill him. Besides, she couldn't have known that he would try to escape. It was a spontaneous thing; Louey lost it and ran."

Savich rose to stand facing Ramsey. "What if she convinced him that her father was going to kill him? What if she told him he'd best clear out and he could take the Mercedes that Gunther had just brought up? Isn't that possible? Think about it, Ramsey. None of us have known any of these people for very long. Don't sweep it under the rug because you happen to admire the lady, because you think her hair's cool."

Ramsey felt his heart pounding against his chest. It made his back ache even more. He didn't believe it. He was a good judge of character. He'd seen Molly in crunch situations. She hadn't faltered, hadn't broken, hadn't flipped out. He said aloud, "She would have no clue how to fashion a bomb. That means she would have had to hire someone in a very short length of time. Not likely."

"She's Mason Lord's daughter, but maybe you're right about her. You really seem to know this woman very well, even though it's only been for a short time." He sighed, and rubbed the back of his neck. "What better person to bring someone onto the estate in secret? And how do you know she wouldn't know how to rig a bomb?"

Ramsey just stared at him. He shook his head. Then he turned and walked away. His back was throbbing.

TWENTY-ONE

The night was dark with thick clouds hanging low, the air heavy with coming rain and sweet with the scent of the late-spring flowers. Ramsey shifted to his side, pulling the covers with him. He'd flung the pillow on the floor some hours earlier.

He flipped onto his back again, his left arm over his head. Then, suddenly, he was thrust into a dark room where there were blurred images, voices that overlapped one another, growing louder and louder. Suddenly the room was clear, the images sharp. He was in his courtroom, jumping over the guardrail, his black robes flying, his legs straight out, his foot kicking the semiautomatic out of a man's arms, sending it spinning across the oak floor. He heard the snap of the man's humerus, heard his howl of rage, saw the wild pain in his eyes. Then he saw terror and panic, saw him leap toward the gun even as he held his broken arm.

He was on him again, with a back-fist punch to his ribs that sent him sprawling to the floor. The din of screaming people filled his mind. A second man whirled around to face him, the semiautomatic raised, ready, and he'd rolled, coming up to twist his hips as he parried, seizing the man's wrist so he wasn't in the line of fire. With his free hand he went after the man's throat, crushing his windpipe, watching him gag, hearing his gun slam against the spectator railing. The screams were high and loud. They went on and on, filling the courtroom, filling his mind, seeping into his brain. He saw the third man now, whirling around in a slow, very precise movement, saw the point when failure registered in his brain, saw him raise his gun and fire randomly, striking the shoulder of one of the defense team, a young man in a pristine white shirt that was instantly shredded and soaked red. The force of the bullet flung him back against three women who were cowered down in the first row of spectators. The man turned back to him, his eyes filled with panic and death. Ramsey felt the heat of a bullet as it passed an inch from his temple, and rolled, picking up the semiautomatic, aiming it even as he lay on his side, and pulled the trigger. He saw the man flung hard against the wall, his blood splattering against the wainscotting. The screams wouldn't stop, just grew louder and louder.

Ramsey jerked up in bed, breathing hard, sweat sheening his forehead, and covered his face with his hands. So much blood, as if it had rained blood.

"It's all right, Ramsey."

It was Emma. She was sitting beside him, her small fingers lightly stroking his forearm. "It's all right. It was a nightmare, a bad one, like mine sometimes. Don't worry. I won't leave you, not until you're okay again."

"Emma," he said, surprised that he could even get the word out of his mouth. He swung his legs off the side of the bed, pulled the little girl onto his lap, and drew her close.

"I heard you," she said against his shoulder. "I was scared for you."

"Thank you for coming. It was a bad one. It happened three months ago. I haven't dreamed about it for several weeks now."

"I'm sorry it came back. What was it, Ramsey?"

"I had to kill someone, Emma."

She drew back and gazed up at him. His eyes were used to the darkness and he could see her clearly. She looked at him with calm and utter certainty. "You must have had to, that's all. Did they deserve it?"

He stared down into that child's face with her eyes that had felt far too much pain and seen horrible evil. He owed her the truth.

"Yes," he said slowly, never looking away from her. "They deserved it. They broke into my courtroom. They had guns. They wanted to free the drug dealers the jury had just found guilty. They started shooting jurors. So I stopped the carnage."

"What's carnage?"

"Emma? What are you doing here, love?"

She turned toward the door. "Mama, Ramsey had a nightmare. I heard him and knew he needed me. He dreamed about car-nage."

Molly blinked at that.

"Hello, Molly," Ramsey said. "I'm okay now. Emma's made me see things a bit differently."

"Can we help you get to sleep, Ramsey?"

"I smell like sweat, Emma. You don't want to stay close to a sweaty guy."

"You're drying off, Ramsey. It's not too bad." Emma yawned, her head falling forward to Ramsey's chest. He looked toward Molly, who was standing in the doorway, wearing a white sleep shirt that had across the front in blue lettering, *F-Stops Are My Specialty*.

Molly shrugged. "Why not? Emma and I can stay on top of the covers. Here's another blanket I can cover us with. I'm surprised I didn't hear you. I just realized Emma was gone a moment ago."

As Molly climbed in next to Ramsey, pulling Emma next to her, she said, "Next time it'll be my turn to have a nightmare."

"Are you all right, Ramsey?"

"I'm much better now, Em, that you're here."

"Tell me about the nightmare, Ramsey," Emma said, leaning up over her mother. "Mama says it helps when you say everything out loud," and he did. It was easier this time.

Molly said, "How did they get into the courthouse with guns?"

"A guard was bribed. He's in jail." He felt himself begin to ease. He had no more words. The shadows were reclaiming the blood and the death.

"Yes, I remember now. That was in the articles I read. Well, it's over now. Does your back hurt?"

"No. It wasn't much of a burn, Molly."

"Good," Molly said. Emma was breathing deeply in sleep. Molly lightly touched her hand to his shoulder. "I'm very glad you weren't hurt."

He tightened like a spring. He cleared his throat and said, "I'm sorry I'm sweaty."

"There are three blankets between you and us. You haven't sweated them through."

He heard Emma's rhythmic breathing. She'd crashed. He hated himself, but he couldn't stop the words. "Tell me about your little brother, Molly."

He felt her stiffen, then felt the whisper of her sigh in the silence. "He was such a sweet little boy. He was just ten years old that summer. He was a good swimmer, which was why I was on the dock, not really paying all that much attention. I was probably thinking about some thirteen-year-old boy, I was about at that age. Then he was yelling and going under. I swam to him as fast as I could but he never woke up.

"It was a reporter who first wrote that it might not have been an accident. My father was a ruthless criminal. Why would his daughter be any different? I was devastated. Teddy was dead and I was some sort of evil seed."

"If there's one thing I'm sure about, Molly, it's the quality of your seed."

She laughed, sadness and relief in her voice, then she leaned over and kissed his shoulder.

He was content when he fell asleep.

"THE police have already interviewed Rule Shaker, with his lawyer present, of course," Savich said to a full audience the following morning just after they'd finished breakfast and trooped into the living room. "Detective O'Connor called me a while ago. He said Rule Shaker is giving them all the same kind of cooperation the president gives to Congress. That approach stretches things out forever and ends up leading anybody anywhere.

"Rule Shaker sat there behind his big chrome-and-glass desk, smoking his Cuban cigars, and swore he only wanted Louey Santera to come play in his casino. He freely admitted that Louey lost a good deal of money at the craps table, so what? What reasonable man, what reasonable businessman, he asked, would kill a man who owed him money?

"When the cops pointed out that Louey might not have been the target, Mr. Shaker very politely informed them that any operation he ever undertook was done right. A screwup would have been impossible with him running it. Then he offered both O'Connor and the Las Vegas detective a cigar."

Everyone stared morosely at Savich. Mason Lord said, "That sounds like Shaker. He's an arrogant little bastard."

"Sorry, guys," Savich said, "ain't nothing easy in this life, even when it involves bastards."

Miles cleared his throat at the door. "Detective O'Connor is here."

O'Connor looked very tired; he had bags under his eyes that hadn't been there two days before. He tried to smile, but didn't make it. "Hello. I got by the reporters and photographers intact. Your men are dealing well with them, Mr. Lord, no violence, but they're firm. There aren't more than a dozen out there today. Ah, I see that Agent Savich is giving you all a run-down of what I didn't accomplish in Las Vegas." He turned to Savich. "Do you have anything for us?"

"MAXINE might, Detective O'Connor," Savich said, grinning. "Actually, we've had her plugged in all night. We're just waiting for her to cough something up."

Mason Lord cleared his throat. "My dear, would you ask Miles to bring in coffee?"

"Of course, Mason," Eve Lord said and rose gracefully from the elegant wing chair she'd been sitting in. She hadn't said a word until that moment, hadn't really called any attention at all to herself. But when she stood, all the men's eyes began to swing toward her. She was wearing tight white jeans, a top tied beneath her breasts, her pale blond hair long and loose, smooth as a silk swatch down her back. Every male eye in the room watched Eve Lord walk to the door, open it, and leave the living room. There was nearly a collective sigh of lust.

Ramsey smiled as he said, "Detective O'Connor, we didn't mean to interrupt you."

"Well, I can tell you that we spoke to Mr. Santera's accountant, Warren O'Dell, last evening, after you'd seen him. He was telling the truth, as far as we can tell. Louey Santera did personally remove three hundred thousand dollars from his account. We won't know what he did with it.

"About the bomb," Detective O'Connor continued. "It was hooked directly to the ignition switch. The parts are common, but we're checking for leads. It was professional, no doubt about that. Mr. Lord, we'd like to speak to your staff again, at some length, beginning with Gunther. You said, Mr. Lord, that he was the man who brought the Mercedes up from the garage."

"Yes, that's right. He brought it around at about five o'clock in the morning. I was awake and so was he. He had the time, so he washed the car. Gunther does that. When he finished, he brought it around. He doesn't know anything more or he would have told me. This is my estate, and I know everything that goes on here."

"Evidently not," Molly said, ignoring the look her father gave her.

O'Connor said, "Someone could have rigged the bomb in the car, but not turned it on until they were sure who would be in the car. Unless, of course, Gunther told anyone who he was bringing the car around for. You must realize, Mr. Lord, that someone on the estate must have been involved."

There, it was said out in the open.

Mason Lord said in his mildest voice, "That is one opinion, Detective O'Connor. Now, there is, of course, the man who works here to take care of my cars. I have a fleet of six. He also lives on the premises. But I know you've already spoken to him. It's possible that Gunther would have said something to him, I suppose. I'll send him to see you, Detective."

"I would appreciate some cooperation from your people, Mr. Lord."

Mason Lord looked at him, one eyebrow arched. Then he rose and left the living room, saying nothing more.

"Judge Hunt, can you think of anything else?"

Ramsey said slowly, "I remember vividly when the car blew up. For an instant you don't register that it's really happening. Your brain doesn't want to accept it as real. It's like this special effect in a movie. Then it hits. It becomes real and terrifying.

"As to whether there was anyone else, no, I saw only Louey rush out of the bushes and yank the car door open. I remember he was wearing a blue shirt, short sleeves, no jacket. He looked frantic."

O'Connor said to Ramsey, "Of course we've searched those bushes. We'll look again. Anything else?"

Ramsey shook his head. "I asked Mason about Rule Shaker, but he refused to say anything much about him."

"I wouldn't expect him to, Ramsey," Molly said. He suddenly remembered that kiss on his shoulder blade in the night. He wished now it had been his mouth. He'd told Savich what Molly had told him about her little brother, Teddy. And Savich had looked off into the distance, thinking his own private thoughts, and finally nodded.

"Yeah, whichever way you want to translate that," Detective O'Connor said. "The point is, though, that Mr. Shaker wouldn't ever let a trail, particularly a murder trail, lead anywhere near him. If he was responsible for Louey Santera's death, we don't have what I'd call a very good chance of connecting him personally to it.

"We've got court orders to take a narrow look at his financial records, to see if there's anything to indicate that he had dealings with Louey Santera, and if he did, what they were. The cops in Las Vegas told us he goes out of his way to keep his nose clean. Even the IRS is happy with him at the moment."

Detective O'Connor rose. "I'm really sorry, Mrs. Santera, but we're no closer to finding out who took your little girl and abused her. It really bums me out."

Molly nodded as she rose to face him. "If we're right about what happened, the danger's over simply because Louey's dead. I don't want to live with that, but I guess I'll have to learn how to. Emma's safe now, thank God. But I want that monster who abused her, raped her, and beat her. I want him. I want him to burn for what he did."

"I promise, Mrs. Santera," Detective O'Connor said, taking her hand, "we're just getting started with this." Molly thought there wasn't much hope in his voice.

After Detective O'Connor left, Molly looked around and said, "I've got to get things together for a small memorial service for Louey. I owe it to Emma. He was her father." She and Sherlock left the living room, speaking quietly to each other.

"It's down to us two," Ramsey said. "I'm depressed."

Savich said, "Miles never brought any coffee." He leaned his head back against the sofa. "How's your back, Ramsey?"

"What? Oh, it's fine. I only took two aspirin yesterday."

"I didn't want to tell Molly, but we really don't have much," Savich said. "MAXINE agreed with Detective O'Connor, indicates there's a high probability that Rule Shaker in Las Vegas is behind all of it. But MAXINE needs facts, and we're short on them."

"You were here, and I appreciate it. Let's go scare up some coffee."

"You know, I was thinking that Sherlock and I might as well fly to Paris," Savich said. "We've still got five days." He laughed. "Doubtless Mr. Lord will be relieved to see us law-enforcement types out of his digs."

"I still wish we could catch the guy who abused Emma."

"I'm sure O'Connor isn't lying to make Molly feel better. No one likes that kind of scum on the loose. We'll all keep working, but for now, well, we can hope that it's over."

TWENTY-TWO

Ramsey and Molly were standing in his bedroom, he by the window, she at the door. It was early morning, and the house was still quiet. His suitcase was open on the bed, some of his clothes packed. He looked up to see her standing there.

"You're leaving, then?"

Ramsey shrugged, looking over at the suitcase on the bed. "Yes, I think so. I couldn't sleep, decided I might as well start to pack." He paused. "Did you know I was trying to write a novel? It seems like a million years ago."

"No, I had no idea."

"That's why I was there at that isolated cabin in the Rockies. I took a leave of absence for five months. Like I told you, I had to get away from all the media hype, all the reporters. One guy even stuck his head in my bathroom window one morning when I was shaving. I nearly sliced my own throat. That's when I decided to leave town for a while. I decided to write the novel I'd thought about for the past year."

"What's it about?"

"A courtroom novel, about a judge in the federal court system. It's a subject I should know well enough, a subject I'd like to say a few things about."

"I see. So you want to go back to Colorado? To write?"

"Yes, I suppose so." He fiddled with a loose thread on his pale blue sweater, remembering her kiss on his shoulder. He looked at her. "Actually, I was wondering when you would be going back to Colorado."

"I hadn't really thought about it, not yet. All this is still sinking in. I'm willing to accept intellectually that this awful man, Rule Shaker, from Las Vegas, is behind everything that's happened, but there's still that monster who abused Emma. I won't ever forget that. I've got lots of money. I think I'll spend some of it trying to find him myself."

She looked defensive, as if she expected him to argue with her. He said, "I'd do the same thing. In fact, I'm going to be putting the word out as soon as I get home. Pedophiles have networks; they seem to either know one another or of one another. I've got several friends who spend a lot of time on the Internet. I'll see where that leads." He drew a deep breath. "Savich will keep the fire lit by alerting all the FBI field offices. He's not happy about this either."

She looked down at the soft nap of the carpet beneath her feet. "Well, I guess I should thank you, Ramsey. Emma will miss you."

He looked up at her, at the dark shadows in her eyes, and that dancing line of freckles across the bridge of her nose. He said, "I told Savich that your hair isn't at all the same color as Sherlock's, although most people would just say you've both got red hair. I told Savich your hair was the color of a sunset I saw once in Ireland."

The nap lost her attention. She blinked up at him. "A sunset in Ireland? When were you in Ireland?"

"Two years ago. I was staying in Ballyvaughan. Nearly every day I went to the Cliffs of Moher. You really can't describe how awesome they are, because you just say something like they're rugged cliffs with waves crashing and billowing up against the rocks, that they dip and then push right to the very edge of the sea, but that really doesn't tell you." He shrugged again. "You see what I mean? You haven't got a clue really how it actually makes you feel just to be there, to look over the water into the distance where there's no sign of anything."

"I'm beginning to," she said.

He ran his fingers through his hair, standing it straight on end. "Dammit, you're nice, Molly."

"Tell me about this sunset."

He looked mildly embarrassed. She grinned at his hair, though he was now smoothing it back down. He hadn't shaved yet. He looked tough and hard and she saw him in that moment with Emma on his lap, holding her against his chest, his big hands stroking her back, her face against his shoulder. He was wearing slacks and a T-shirt, his feet bare. She had intruded. He was going to leave.

It didn't matter. It couldn't matter. He had his own life. Hers and Emma's had intersected his briefly and violently. It was time.

He was going to leave.

It wasn't what she wanted, but she wasn't going to try to change it. He said quietly, "I'll never forget this one evening I was at the Cliffs of Moher. The air was crisp and dry and the sky perfectly clear. No Irish rain that day. I sat there and watched that red ball of sun slowly sink into the Atlantic. You almost expected the water to hiss and boil when the sun sank into it. People around me were talking and laughing and joking around, until that precise moment. Then there was a hush and everyone went silent and still, staring at that red ball sinking under the horizon." He shook his head, bemused at the memory. "I'll never forget that sight as long as I live." He paused a moment, then looked at her. "I remember the next day it rained so hard it was like payback time for that incredible sunset. You know, Molly, I was thinking that maybe you'd like it as well, both you and Emma. Not the rain, although that's beautiful too, no, the sunsets."

"Emma and I? Go to Ireland?"

"Yes. With me. I don't want to leave you."

The morning light was dim and gray. Her expression wasn't clear to him, as she kept her head down. After a very long moment, she raised her head and looked across the room at him. She said, smiling, "Yes, I'd like that. I'll bet Emma would too."

He felt a shock of pleasure. The strength of it surprised him. He smiled back at her. "Savich and Sherlock are going to Paris. They're leaving from O'Hare this morning."

"They're very good people."

"Do you think we could go to Ireland soon? We could all just get away for a while. I think it would be good for Emma."

"I don't have our passports. They're at the house in Denver."

"Mine's in San Francisco. We could pick them up and meet in New York. Or back here in Chicago. Or best yet, I could go with you and Emma to Denver and then all of us could go on to San Francisco. How about that?"

She started laughing, her hands splayed in front of her. "I didn't know you a month ago."

"No, you didn't. On the other hand, we've probably been through more in the past weeks than most people have in a decade, or at all, for that matter."

"You really think my hair is the color of that sunset?"

He gave her a slow smile. "Yeah, that's what I think."

"Is your back really all right?"

"Yes. Your arm?"

"It still throbs sometimes, but it's not too bad. These stitches aren't the kind they have to take out. They'll resorb by themselves, Dr. Otterly said. I couldn't believe you went to the gym with Savich, though. You could have hurt yourself more."

"My back has barely blistered. Besides, I was careful. Savich taped me up pretty well so I wouldn't stress anything, and so I could swim." Then he grinned at her. "Yeah, I was stupid."

She laughed at him, shaking her head. "I didn't say that."

He smiled at her. "I'm worried about Emma. Is she asleep?"

"I hope so. She wakes up a lot. Three times this last night. Still the same dreams. And she dreams about the car exploding."

"I suppose we need to ask Dr. Loo about taking Emma to Ireland this soon."

"We can ask her this morning how Emma's doing, if she thinks a trip would be good for her. I can't think of anything better."

He was surprised how giddy he felt that she was going to go to Ireland with him. It was as if a knot he felt in his belly were loosening. It had come out of his mouth, unplanned. He really hadn't thought about it at all.

Well, maybe without knowing it. He hadn't really wanted to be separated from either Molly or Emma.

"What time is her appointment?"

"Ten o'clock this morning."

"Let's see what she says before we make definite plans, then."

Molly straightened the sash on her robe, a glamorous peach silk thing she'd obviously borrowed from her stepmama. He wondered what she'd look like without it. She gave him another smile. "Ireland, huh? Did you go there alone before?"

"No," he said. "I didn't."

"No," she said, "I don't suppose you'd do anything alone unless you wanted to."

"What's that supposed to mean?"

"Even with a burn on your back, Ramsey, a lot of women would find you an appealing kind of guy."

"Thank you. Go back to bed, Molly. It's too early to be up and about yet."

"What about you?"

"Yeah, now that we've made some plans, I think I'll sack out for another hour myself. I'm not nervous and uptight anymore. It's a miracle."

She nodded, then her smile fell away. "Oh yes. I've made the arrangements for a small memorial service for Louey this afternoon, here on the estate. I even found a Presbyterian minister to come and give a service."

"It's good," he said. "It's good for Emma."

"I hope so."

"EMMA, are you ready to play 'Twinkle Twinkle Little Star' for me?"

"Yes, Dr. Loo, I think so. But I haven't played a piano seriously for a long time."

"It's okay. I don't mind."

Emma straightened her new piano on the low coffee table. Dr. Loo sat in a chair, Ramsey and Molly on a love seat opposite her.

"Don't forget the variations, Emma," Ramsey said.

This time Emma didn't hesitate. She took a deep breath, one that sounded appallingly adult, and played with one hand the simple notes of the song, beginning with F. Once she'd played through the tune, she added the left hand. It sounded classical, like Mozart. The next time through, she changed it to a jazz sound, then to a definite John Lennon feel.

Dr. Loo blinked. She looked shell-shocked. When Emma finished, she leaned forward, took Emma's small hands between hers, and looked her in the eye. "Thank you, Emma. You've given me great pleasure. I hope someday to hear you perform at Carnegie Hall."

"What's Carnegie Hall?"

"It's where great artists from all over the world come to perform. It's in New York City. I heard Liam McCallum play the violin there. It was an incredible experience. You could be there too, Emma."

"Yes," Molly said, "I think she might."

"My papa never played at Carnegie Hall," Emma whispered, not looking up from her keyboard. "But he was a great artist, Mama said so."

"Yes, he was," Molly said. She looked as if she was going to burst into tears.

Ramsey sat forward. "I have one of your dad's CDs, Emma. Even though he didn't make it to Carnegie Hall, everyone in the world can hear him. All his music will live on."

"That's what Mama said."

"And when was the last time your mama was wrong?" Ramsey said, lightly stroking his fingers over her French braid, one that he'd done himself. It wasn't bad, hardly crooked at all, and the plaiting looked pretty smooth.

Emma raised her face then. She thought really hard. "It's been a long time," she said finally. "Maybe two months ago."

Ramsey laughed.

"Now," Dr. Loo said. "It's time we talked about you going to Ireland with your mama and Ramsey."

Emma said, "I don't know what Ireland is, Dr. Loo."

"It's a beautiful wild country that's across the ocean. It's a place to enjoy, Emma, a place where you can look at things and maybe see them in a different light. It's a place where you can stop being afraid, where you can play your piano, where you can run in the mornings with Ramsey and play Frisbee with your mama, and have picnics. It's very beautiful, Emma. You can sit on the rocks and dangle your toes into the water. It's so cold you yip in surprise. You'll be with two people who love you and want you to be safe and happy. What do you think?"

Emma drew back between Ramsey's knees. "Will that bad man be there?"

Ramsey rubbed his hands lightly up and down her thin arms. "No, he won't. We'll never let him get close to you again. I promise, Emma."

Emma turned to face him. "He's close, Ramsey. He's real close now. He killed my daddy. He wants me now."

"No, Emma, he doesn't. He's very afraid, and he's running and hiding now because he knows the police are after him. I'd like him to be caught. Then he'd be in jail for the rest of his life. Everyone is trying really hard to catch him.

"I do know one thing for sure, Emma. We won't ever let him come near you again. Do you believe me?"

Emma looked up at him for a very long time. Molly was aware she was holding her breath. Emma continued to be silent, but she finally released her breath, letting it out slowly and quietly. She looked at Dr. Loo, who smiled and shook her head slightly.

Dr. Loo took a quick look at her watch and stood. She pulled Molly aside. "It will take time. Don't push her. I can already see that both you and Judge Hunt are dealing with this very well. I think Ireland is a fine idea. However, I think Emma and I should meet tomorrow. When had you expected to leave?"

"It doesn't matter," Molly said, her eyes on her daughter. "Emma's what's important. We'll leave when you think it's right and not before."

"She's doing well, Mrs. Santera. She really is. But this sort of thing—it will be with her forever. You must face that and find a way to deal with it. Her feelings about it will change as she grows up. Most of it will fade into blurry vague memories, and that's good, but it won't ever disappear. But now, she's just a little girl. She doesn't have a clue about the concept of rape. She knows this bad man hurt her badly, and that it wasn't right, but there are no grown-up connotations. What you're dealing with right now are feelings of fear and remembered helplessness.

"Eventually, she'll have to understand that what happened to her can't be changed, that it was real, and that the trick is for her to learn to deal with it so that it doesn't ruin the rest of her life. It's not going to be easy for either of you. You'll put out a fire then another one will crop up in some other context.

"She's lucky that you're her mother. I know that Judge Hunt has known Emma for a very short time, but they trust each other, their affection seems to be deep and abiding."

"It will be difficult when Judge Hunt returns to his home," Molly said.

Dr. Loo let a couple of seconds go by, then said in that comfortable, matter-of-fact voice, "Well, these things have a way of working out. Tomorrow I'll meet with Emma alone. I want to speak to her about the abuse, try to make her see that the man wasn't normal, that it wasn't in any way her fault, that this didn't happen to her because she was bad."

"But how could she possibly feel that way?"

"Children, Mrs. Santera, children can bring almost everything back onto themselves. Also, we have no idea what the man said to her, how he manipulated her, how he terrorized her, or how he hurt her. It's always the adults who screw up royally. I have to deal with Emma now from the inside of her head. I'm telling you not to worry, but of course you will, both of you."

"You won't want either Judge Hunt or me here?"

"I think it would be better between the two of us. You would find it very upsetting. I can see Judge Hunt becoming quite enraged. No, just Emma and me."

"If you think that's best, Dr. Loo. You will call me, won't you?"

"Of course." Dr. Loo turned back to Emma with a smile. She leaned over and patted her shoulder. "I'll see you tomorrow, Emma. In the meantime I want you to get a lot of rest and try to smile at least three times a day at your mama."

"How about me?"

"And at least six times for Ramsey. I've found that guys need more smiles than girls do. Remember that."

RAMSEY smiled down at Emma. It was early afternoon, two hours before Louey Santera's memorial service. He'd brought her upstairs for a nap, just tucked her in. "I like your jazz variation, Emma. Did you know that Mr. Savich plays the guitar and sings? Yep, country and western. He performs in a club. It isn't Carnegie Hall, but it's a neat place, he told me. He also has a friend who plays the saxophone. He and Sherlock want us to visit them."

"I wish they didn't have to leave. Sherlock told me she hoped she was going to have a little girl like me. She said that Mr. Savich felt the same way. She said they both thought I was really neat. I told her that wasn't a good idea. I'm not very good anymore."

Ramsey looked down at the child he'd give his life for. He'd kissed her forehead, complimented her on her music, and now this. He gently pushed her hair back from her face. Before he could think of what to say, Emma continued, "Sherlock's face turned red. She was really mad, but she said she wasn't mad at me."

"You, my perfect Emma, not good? Where'd you get a weird idea like that?"

She looked away, into a past that still had a hammerlock on her, a past that hemorrhaged into the present. "That man said I would save him. I didn't know what he was talking about."

Ramsey wanted to kill. He forced down a deep breath, slowed it, tried to calm himself. This was something for Dr. Loo, but she wasn't here, he was, and the rage he felt couldn't help her. "Listen to me, Em. This man who kidnapped you, he's sick in the head, really sick. What he thinks, what he does, it has nothing to do with you—Emma Santera. He would have hurt any little girl he could find. You weren't Emma to him. Do you understand?"

"No," she said finally. "I don't understand. It's scary, Ramsey."

He leaned down, his forehead touching hers. He kissed the tip of her nose. "Listen up, Emma. We're on a roll here. The three of us together, we'll take on the scariest thing you can dream up. You're a very good little girl. In fact, you're so good that the thought of not having you with me makes a big dent in my heart. That's how good you are."

She gave him a big smile. One small hand stroked his cheek. "You won't leave, Ramsey, will you? You won't go back to your house?"

He took both of her hands between his and kissed her fingers. They tasted like the gingerbread that Miles had baked for her at lunchtime. He didn't really know what the future would bring, but he knew he couldn't tell that to her. Her life had been smashed, her father murdered, and he said now, without hesitation at all, "I won't leave you, ever, Emma."

"Good," she said, and yawned.

"Emma?"

"Yes, Ramsey?"

"Will you be a brat for me just once? Maybe when you get up from your nap? Or this evening? I know, you could whine about having to drink your milk or finish your dinner or having to go to bed? Throw a kid fit?"

She smiled at him. "Sure."

"You want to take a nap now?"

"Okay." She closed her eyes, then opened one and squinted up at him. "But maybe I won't go to bed tonight."

"Fair enough." Actually, he just wanted to get her through her father's memorial service. He hoped they could continue to keep out all the reporters, the local TV stations, and the paparazzi. The guards had ably assisted one reporter back up over the compound wall and out onto the road. He prayed that Emma wouldn't pay any attention to the impertinent questions that flew at him and Molly whenever they went outside the gates.

TWENTY-THREE

Melissa Shaker was crying so hard she nearly tripped down the steps leading into the garage. It had been two days now but she still couldn't believe it, didn't want to believe it. That damned ex-wife of his had held a dipshit little memorial service, no actual funeral because there'd been nothing to cremate or bury.

Louey was gone, just simply gone, and nobody cared. Except her. She tripped again, grabbing the handrail to steady herself as she stepped into the underground garage. A car horn honked loudly. She felt its hot exhaust as it whooshed past her, the driver yelling at her to pay attention.

She wiped her eyes. There was nothing to do. Just nothing. Her father had sworn he hadn't killed Louey, but she'd looked into his eyes and seen guilt. She would never forgive him, ever.

"Miss Shaker."

She didn't want Greg anywhere near her. She wanted to be alone. She wanted to drive out into the desert and let the sun burn into her. She kept walking toward her car.

"Miss Shaker! Please, wait up. You know your father's orders, particularly now."

She waited for him simply because she didn't want to get Greg fired when all he was trying to do was his job.

She stopped by her BMW roadster, painted James Bond blue. It was exactly like the one he'd driven in a movie, except hers was more powerful. She loved that little car.

"Thank you," Greg said as he trotted up to her. "Listen, Miss Shaker, I'm really sorry."

"Thank you," she said, and got into the car. Greg came around the other side.

"Don't try to lose me, Miss Shaker. It's important that I stick close to you, particularly during the next week."

"They gave him a measly memorial service," she said, and turned the key. The car exploded into flames.

IT came on the local Las Vegas news brought in via satellite at twelve-twenty in the afternoon.

Melissa Shaker, twenty-three, daughter of Rule Shaker, Las Vegas casino owner, was killed at ten A.M. this morning when she and a friend were in an explosion involving Ms. Shaker's car that was parked in the underground parking lot beneath the Sirocco Casino.

Arson experts say a bomb was involved. Police haven't yet said if there are any suspects. Details at five o'clock.

Ramsey dropped his fork, and a thin slice of ham slithered off his plate. He'd heard the TV playing from the kitchen, wondered why it was even on, wondered why it was turned up loud enough to hear in the dining room, wondered why it was on satellite to get a local Las Vegas station, and now this. And now all his questions were answered.

Obviously someone had known it would make the local Las Vegas noon news. Obviously someone had been waiting for this.

There was an instant of shocked silence, then everyone was talking. He heard Eve gasp, heard her say something, but he couldn't make out her words. There was a crash of a pan that Miles must have dropped in the kitchen. At the head of the table, Mason Lord continued to eat his casaba melon, not missing a beat. There was a slight flush on his cheeks, but he said nothing, did nothing out of the ordinary at all.

Molly had been saying something to Emma. She stopped in mid-sentence. She looked over at her father and said quietly, "An eye for an eye, Dad?"

Mason Lord chewed on the bite of melon, gracefully laid down his fork, and looked at his daughter. "I suggest you refrain from such talk, Molly, particularly in front of your daughter."

Emma, attuned to the change in the most important person in her world, pulled on her mother's sleeve. "Mama? What happened?"

Ramsey watched Molly pull herself together for Emma's sake. She banked the horror in her eyes and smoothed her expression into nothing more than a soft smile for her daughter. She turned to Emma, hugged her close for a moment, and said, "I taste something strange in Miles's quiche. What do you think?"

Emma gave her that weary adult look. "The quiche has bacon in it, Mama, and fresh spinach. I watched Mr. Miles make it. He even let me add the eggs. The quiche is fine."

Molly looked as if she'd just been smashed on the head with a cannon-ball. She was having a tough time getting it together. "I'm sorry, Emma. You're right, of course. I don't know, love, I guess I don't feel well."

Molly looked over at Eve Lord, who sat to her right at the foot of the table, her face tight, as white as the tablecloth. She was staring at her husband. Then, suddenly, Eve turned to Emma, and her face was again as smooth as a Madonna's. "I gave the quiche recipe to Miles. My mother was an excellent cook. I'm sorry your mother doesn't like it."

"I think it's time we had coffee," Mason said. "Miles?"

Ramsey said, controlling his voice, "I would like to speak with you, Mason. Shall we take our coffee to the living room?"

"It's a beautiful day," Eve Lord said, staring again at her husband. "Mason said we would go out on the yacht, Ramsey. Perhaps you can speak with him later?"

They heard the phone ring. Miles appeared around the door of the dining room. "Judge Hunt, it's Agent Savich. He, uh, wants to speak with you."

Ramsey tossed his napkin on his plate and walked quickly to the kitchen where Miles stood patiently, holding the phone.

"Sherlock and I are at O'Hare. We just heard about the murders in Las Vegas. I can't believe this, Ramsey. The man has balls, I'll say that for him. You want us to come back?"

Ramsey wanted them back in the worst way, but there was nothing they could do, nothing anyone could do, really. How selfish did he want to be? "No, Savich. Take Sherlock off somewhere and make her happy. Just let me know where you're staying in Paris so I can call if there's occasion to sound the cavalry trumpet."

"It's a little pension on the Left Bank," Savich said. "Sherlock wants to show it to me. We'll let you know the number. Did Mason say anything? Have you seen him?"

"Oh yes. We all heard it on the news at the dining table. It didn't even touch him that there were a federal judge and FBI agents in his house when he gave the orders."

"Here's what I think. Get out of there, Ramsey. Take Molly and Emma, and check out of the Bates Motel. You don't need this. It's vengeance. Don't get involved. There's nothing you can do in any case."

"I can't believe you're saying that."

"I'm saying it as Molly and Emma's friend. You don't want them in the middle of something that could shape up into a nice little personal war. There's been tit for tat. Don't stay to see if it goes another round. Just get out."

Ramsey said slowly, "You're right, of course." He rubbed his hand over his forehead. "I feel that I should question Mason, handcuff Gunther. No, you're right. It's Molly and Emma's safety that's most important. I'll call you in a couple of days, let you know what's going on."

They spoke a bit longer, and then Ramsey laid the phone slowly back into its cradle. It was an old-fashioned black rotary, one that Miles had picked out specifically for his kitchen, he'd told Ramsey when he was whipping up pancakes for breakfast one morning.

Ramsey turned slowly to see Miles standing at the island, chopping celery. A chopped red apple stood in a bright pile to one side. Green grapes, sliced in half, formed another pile. Miles said in a very precise voice, "I'm making Waldorf salad."

"Did you know this was going to happen, Miles?"

"You know I can't say anything, Ramsey. Leave, sir, that's my best advice to you. Take Molly and Emma and leave. Since this man Shaker was behind everything, you're safe now that Louey's dead. Just leave."

"Unless Shaker plans his own vengeance now. Unless he plans to escalate. If he does, we're in really deep."

Miles shook his head, chopped some more celery in sure quick strokes, and said, "It doesn't work that way. It's over. One player knocked down, one opposing player knocked down. Everything's even again. Those are the rules. Nobody breaks the rules."

The horror of it bubbled out of him. Ramsey slammed his fist down on the counter. "That's sick and you know it."

Miles shrugged. "No one will miss Louey Santera. No one will miss this Rule Shaker's daughter. Leave it alone, Ramsey. Get Molly and Emma out of here."

Ramsey, his jaw locked hard from disbelief and tension, left the kitchen. He looked only at Molly when he reached the dining room. "Come upstairs with me, will you?"

"Yes, certainly."

Then he realized that Emma was sitting there, quiche on her fork, staring at them. Ramsey calmed himself. "Em, would you do me a favor?"

She wanted to ask him questions, he could see that, but he shook his head at her. "Would you come upstairs with your mom and me?"

Five minutes later, after they'd settled Emma with a book on animal husbandry for children in her bedroom, all of them knowing it was a ploy, especially Emma, Molly and Ramsey were standing alone in his bedroom.

He said without preamble, "I see no reason to stay. Do you?"

"No, no reason at all," Molly said, pulling a silver ring off her pinkie finger, then pushing it back on. "He's a monster, Ramsey. My father just blew up a twenty-three-year-old woman."

"That's the league he plays in, Molly. The media should be back here anytime, if they haven't already pulled up to the front gates. Let's fly to Denver today, to your house. You and Emma can pack stuff for Ireland, then we'll go to San Francisco. Okay?"

Molly said more to herself than to him, "Ireland would be beautiful, I've seen pictures." Then he saw a sparkle in her eyes. "I could begin work again. I could take my cameras."

He realized it would be a new beginning for Molly. And for himself as well. "Yes, bring all you need. Will you take a photo of Emma for me?"

"You don't think the media will follow us, do you?"

"I doubt we're interesting enough."

"You know that's not true."

"All right, so we'll have to be smarter than they are."

"YOU'RE leaving," Mason said, no particular regret or surprise in his voice. "Miles said you'd ordered a taxi." He smiled. "I can understand why you wouldn't want to take one of my cars or have one of my people drive you."

It was a joke Ramsey hoped Emma hadn't understood. He'd dealt with men like Mason Lord in his professional life. They were men to whom a designated death was just another move on a chessboard. "Yes," Ramsey said, "we're leaving. Molly is ready to return to Denver." He wasn't about to tell Mason Lord where they were really going.

"Eve wanted to go out on Lake Michigan. We didn't go. I knew you'd leave if I left."

"You stayed and we're still leaving. It doesn't matter, Mason. Thank you for your hospitality."

Eve Lord came up behind her husband and said that Detective O'Connor had arrived.

Ramsey cursed under his breath. He should have foreseen this, but he hadn't. He'd been focused on getting the Hell Out of Dodge. He turned to Molly. "You and Emma stick close for a moment. I want to speak to Detective O'Connor." Ramsey got to him before he'd stepped into the living room.

"I was just leaving. Mrs. Santera and Emma are going with me."

Detective O'Connor looked as if he'd slept in somebody else's face. The skin didn't fit, it was loose over his jowls. There were bags under his eyes. "I don't blame you, Ramsey. Before you head out, do you know anything about this?"

"I heard it on the TV. We were all at lunch. I remember wondering why a local Las Vegas station was on the TV in the kitchen, why it was so loud. Then, of course, it was clear. You know as well as I do that Mason Lord arranged for the explosion. I've been told that now things are even again and there won't be any more violence."

Detective O'Connor whistled between his teeth. "I feel like a fly buzzing around with no place to land. I don't suppose Mr. Lord admitted to you that he'd done it?"

"No, he didn't say a word. But you know, he had a glimmer of satisfaction in his eyes that he couldn't quite hide. Sure he ordered it. This place is like an alternate universe."

"The cops down in Las Vegas say they ain't got dip. Everything was neat and tidy, except for the two bodies left over."

"You'll be checking to see if any of Lord's men took a quick trip down to Las Vegas?"

"Yeah, but it won't matter if they did. Lots of folks go to Las Vegas. Besides, the chances of Mr. Lord bringing the murders this close to home are slim to none. These guys don't operate like that. It's like dogs and their own backyards. But I got to talk to everyone, go through all the motions, just the way homicide did with me down in Las Vegas. Maybe some of the Las Vegas detectives will come up here, who knows?"

"I still have trouble with what Miles told me about the even-up rules. If it were me, I'd want to up the ante myself, not walk away, not just wipe my hands and say, well, that's how it is. My daughter's dead, but hey."

"Probably Shaker knew when he had that bomb planted that he was putting his daughter's life on the line. It does make him sound like he's not the greatest dad, doesn't it? These guys aren't like you or me, Ramsey. There's something missing somewhere in how they're put together. But they don't get where they are by being stupid. He probably thought Mr. Lord would try for him, only he didn't."

"Let's say he didn't expect Mason to go that far. Let's say he doesn't consider things even. What happens then?"

"Listen, go home, Ramsey. I'd say for you it's over. Rule Shaker isn't about to make another mistake. He can't afford to; he's got too much to protect.

"Send the little girl and her mother home. The Denver cops will take care of them.

"It's over now. You can leave the rest of it to us. We'll let you know if we find out anything that would fill a cereal box."

TWENTY-FOUR

At six-thirty in the evening a taxi pulled up to Molly's house on Shrayder Drive. It was a small, lovely house with white window frames and window boxes painted a soft blue. Flowers bloomed wildly over the fence, in bordered flower beds, and in half a dozen flower boxes attached to the porch railing.

The house faced the park where Emma had been kidnapped while Molly was taking pictures. All the front yards were filled with trees and bushes, but no other house had such beautiful flowers.

Emma was a silent ghost. She was holding her piano against her chest, looking straight ahead. She was so very still, as if the quieter she became, the less likely the chance that anything bad would happen to her. He could tell her again that she need not be frightened, but that wasn't true, not really, and both of them knew it. The man was still out there. Probably he was far away, in hiding, but to Emma, he was lurking close, just as he had been, waiting to take her again. It broke his heart.

He looked out over the park, with its small dips and rises, its clusters of flowers and bushes, and banks of elm and pine trees. He wondered where the man had waited for Emma to get close enough to take her.

He saw that Molly was gazing toward a knot of trees at the west corner of the park. So that was where it happened. Her face was tense, drawn, and thin. Even her glorious red hair seemed flat and lank, pulled back and fastened with a pale green clip that matched the color of her silk blouse. He'd bet that if she'd had a piano like Emma's, she'd be carrying it too.

"Emma, we're home." Molly spoke very softly, not wanting to frighten her, just gain her attention slowly and gently. "Remember, we're just going to pack our things and then we're going with Ramsey to San Francisco."

"And then Ramsey is coming with us to Ireland?" Emma said, pressed against her mother's side, not an inch between them. Molly wondered what had gone on between Dr. Loo and Emma. That morning Emma saw her for the final time. She must remember to call her.

"Yes, he is," Molly said. "He wants to go back and he really, really wants us to go with him. He begged, Emma. I'm a nice person, I had to say yes."

"Did you really beg, Ramsey?" Emma asked, shooting a look at him.

"I can beg with the best of them, Emma," Ramsey said, going down on his haunches in front of her. "I decided I didn't want to let you out of my sight. I decided not seeing you would make me very unhappy. Do you mind my staying with you at your house until tomorrow?"

"You can stay with us, Ramsey. I think it's a good idea." She marched through the open gate toward the front door, her piano hugged against her. She said over her shoulder, "Dr. Loo showed me Ireland in her atlas. She said it was so green you had to brush your teeth at least twice a day or they'd turn green too."

"Emma, was that a joke?"

To his delight, Emma gave him a wicked little smile over her shoulder.

He said quietly, "The park, over there?"

"Yes. I used to love this house. We lived with Louey in one of those estate areas in the western part of Denver. After the divorce, I sold the house and found this one. The thing is, I don't love it anymore. I can tell that Emma's terrified. To be honest, I am too."

"Let's give it time," he said and knew it was a worthless thing to have said. "Actually, we only have to give it the next few minutes, just time enough for you and Emma to pack. We don't even have to spend the night if you don't want to."

"No, we won't," she said.

"Also, there's no reason you can't sell the place, Molly. There's no reason at all why you couldn't, say, move to San Francisco."

The words came out of his mouth, and his eyes fastened on a rosebush just beyond Molly's left shoulder. "I didn't mean what you could maybe think I meant."

"No, certainly not," Molly said, all cool and calm and together. "Men rarely do."

"What's that supposed to mean?"

"Nothing. I'm sorry. It's been a long day. It was a lot of years with Louey. We're coming, Emma."

Emma stood patiently in front of the door while Molly pulled out her key. She slipped it into the lock and turned it easily. "Things look so beautiful because I've had a person coming to garden for me. One of my neighbors waters the indoor flowers and plants. Still, it's bound to be a bit on the musty side and—"

Molly got no farther. The stench hit them full in the face the moment they stepped into the small foyer.

"Mama, this isn't good," Emma said, backing up. "It smells like there's bad food everywhere. It smells like Ramsey's house did when we went there."

Ramsey caught Emma as she raced back out the front door. "Get behind me, Emma. That's right. Your mother and I will go see what's going on. You stay right here."

"OH, no." Molly's once-colorful very cozy living room with high ceilings open to the dining room through an arch, filled with fat silk pillows, framed watercolors and photographs, and restored furniture painted in bright colors, all of it was trashed. Even the ivy had been pulled from its pots and dashed to the wooden floor.

"Let's see if your clothes and Emma's are all right. Pack up and get your passports, if they're still here, then we're out of here. We'll call the police from the hotel."

"I want to call my neighbors, too, and a cleaning service. Who did this and why? Is it ever going to stop?"

"It will. It has. This was done days ago."

An hour and a half later, the police met them at the hotel, in their two-bedroom suite on the ninth floor of the Brown Palace. The suite was huge, but the rooms were too warm. Ramsey had opened all the windows and complained to the front desk that the air conditioner was on the fritz. It was finally beginning to cool down a bit. Emma was seated on one of the sofas, watching a cartoon on TV. Ramsey, Molly, and Detective Mecklin of the Denver PD were sitting at the circular table at the other end of the living room. A pot of coffee and a plate of cookies were on the table.

Detective Mecklin was chewing on an oatmeal cookie from the Brown Palace kitchen.

"As I told you," Molly said, "I had a neighbor coming in to water my plants. Everything was fine three days ago. One of your people is speaking to her, right?"

"Yeah, right. But I doubt she saw anything, or we'd have gotten a call by now. Whoever did it, had guts. We didn't clear out of there until about five days ago."

The hotel doorbell rang.

An officer who'd accompanied Detective Mecklin answered it. He walked into the living room, a stoic look on his young face. Behind him stood FBI Special Agent Anchor, decked out in his dark suit, white shirt, dark thin tie, and wing tips.

Molly wanted to groan. Mecklin was enough. Now the both of them?

"Hello, Mrs. Santera. I'm still considering whether or not to arrest you."

"That's nice, Agent Anchor," Molly said, feeling the tension in her replaced by anger. It felt good, that wave of rage. She sat back in her chair and smiled at him. She realized she'd seen her father do this. She'd wanted to fry this guy since he'd first walked into her house after Emma had been kidnapped. He was arrogant and overbearing. "Hey, have you decided on the charge? Was it saving my daughter from a kidnapper? Was it perhaps escaping to avoid getting murdered? Or maybe it was keeping my child out of your incompetent hands? No, I've got it. You're going to arrest me for doing your job."

She'd got him. His face was red and his hands were stiff at his sides. He looked ready to explode. She loved it. "Oh, how about this—you want to arrest me because I trashed my own house?"

Agent Anchor managed to control himself. He even managed a very stiff smile at Molly. Ramsey was surprised and hopeful that perhaps the man would stop being a jerk. Agent Anchor said finally, "Your attitude isn't helping your case, Mrs. Santera." He then looked at Ramsey, a dark eyebrow raised. The raised eyebrow was met with silence.

Agent Anchor said finally, "You look familiar."

"He should," Detective Mecklin said between chews on another oatmeal cookie. "He's Judge Ramsey Hunt, you know the guy we've been hearing about from San Francisco and Chicago."

Agent Anchor froze. He was used to being in charge and then Molly Santera and this guy Hunt had treated him like he was a Keystone Kop. "What are you doing here?"

Ramsey smiled at him. "Well, you know, my house in San Francisco was trashed just like Mrs. Santera's. We were thinking that there might be some parallels. What do you think? Maybe Mr. Shaker is a very thorough man?"

"I don't appreciate your humor," Agent Anchor said. "I know all this. But she shouldn't have taken off to look for her daughter. She shouldn't have refused to return to Denver after she'd found her. She shouldn't have hindered my investigation." He stared at Molly, his thin nostrils flared wide with dislike. "And she shouldn't have insulted me when I walked in now. Maybe if she'd done what I told her to, she wouldn't have ended up with a dead husband. But then, you got a live judge, didn't you?"

Molly shot a quick look toward Emma, who looked to be glued to the TV cartoon. Then she stood up in one smooth motion and kicked Agent Anchor hard in the shin. He gasped, grabbed his leg, then very slowly, he straightened. "I'm arresting you for assaulting a federal officer," he said when he could speak again.

"I don't think so," Ramsey said. "Actually, she beat me to it. Stop being an ass, Agent Anchor." He gracefully slid his hand to the man's elbow. He said close to his ear, "I think you're laboring under a severe misapprehension here. Listen up: *She's not her father*. You'd best get that right away. Now, why don't you put on your human clothes, sit down, and we can try to work together. If that isn't to your liking, then I'll call up your boss and Agents Savich and Sherlock, who worked the case with us in Chicago, and we'll all have a talk. Your call, Agent."

Agent Anchor wasn't happy. On top of everything, the case of the murdered farmer in Loveland wouldn't ever officially get solved now. They hadn't even found the man who'd abused the little girl, and it had all started when she'd up and left Denver and gone out to hot-dog on her own. Ramsey Hunt was wrong about her. She was just like her father, he'd known it the minute he'd set eyes on her. She'd made the case go sour. And now this damned judge had taken her side. And he knew Savich.

Detective Mecklin pushed back from the table and rose. There were cookie crumbs on his solid red tie and on the white shirt that gaped over his belly. "Listen, we're not getting anywhere with all this crap. Agent Anchor, sit down, if Judge Ramsey will let you."

Molly said, "There's also my daughter, Agent Anchor. Children hear most things adults say. I think we've said enough."

Agent Anchor looked over at Emma, who was chewing gum, too fast. He had two kids. He knew when a kid was hearing things she shouldn't. And now he had this judge in the mix.

"Yeah," Agent Anchor said, and sat down.

There was dead silence. Detective Mecklin picked up another oatmeal cookie and said as he took a big bite, "If all this is connected, it took power, men, and money, all of which this Mr. Shaker has in abundance."

Molly said, "Why do you think they trashed my house? Just for the fun of it?"

"Say it happened two or three days ago, Mrs. Santera," Detective Mecklin said. "That was about the same time your ex-husband was getting blown up. Maybe it was all part of the same puzzle. The word is that you and your daughter were the intended victims, to bring Mr. Santera in line. Yeah, it's gotta all be part of the same effort."

"All that," Molly said. "All that for some money, or to get Louey for his daughter? It sounds crazy."

Agent Anchor poured himself a cup of coffee. He hadn't said a word. He drank a bit, then poured in some cream. Finally, he said, "People like Shaker can't allow anyone to stiff them for a million bucks. He relies too much on people being afraid of him. God knows the money was there to hire the best."

Detective Mecklin said, "Shaker did it, all right. Trust me on this. It's over."

"You're probably right," Ramsey said. "There is no other answer." He turned to Agent Anchor. "Unless you can come up with something?"

Agent Anchor shook his head. "No, it's just my gut. Did Savich discover anything on that damned laptop?"

"Nothing solid yet," Ramsey said.

Agent Anchor shook his head. He had a buzz haircut, which was just as well since he was mostly bald. "I remember once when I was in Washington, I got to be in a meeting with Savich, and the person recording the minutes asked him what sex the laptop was currently enjoying. Nobody laughed."

Ramsey didn't particularly like to have a person start to turn human on him when he'd made the decision that the person was a jerk. Still, maybe the guy would relapse again.

Ramsey saw that Emma had curled up on the sofa, her piano clutched to her, sound asleep. One leg of her jeans was rucked up and he could see the pink sock over her Nike sneaker. He wasn't really shocked at the strength of his feelings for her, not anymore. He swallowed. Then he saw that her other sock was white. Well, it had been a hard day for all of them. He rose, still looking at Emma. "I can't see that this is leading anywhere. Maybe we shouldn't even have bothered to call you. Waste of time for all of us."

"No," Detective Mecklin said, rising as well. "All of it is part of the investigation. Maybe we'll turn up something at the house. Sooner or later, we'll snag that guy who hurt Emma. The Feds want him real bad. Hey, Agent Anchor, maybe you can get him on tax evasion, huh?"

TWENTY-FIVE

It was sixty-two degrees and breezy in San Francisco, with a big unclouded sky overhead. Ramsey breathed in the clean air deeply and smiled. He looked through the half-open window of his study that gave onto a small lawn and the Golden Gate Bridge beyond, off in the distance: He loved Sea Cliff, which was considered by many, himself included, to be the most spectacular area in the city. His house was among the first tier of homes that sat atop the line of the cliffs at the northwestern tip of the city. The ocean rolled in from the left, the Golden Gate stood guardian at the entrance of the bay to the right, connecting the city to the bleak naked Marin Headlands directly across from him. The Headlands stood stark in the afternoon sunlight. There was still some green on the hills. But it wouldn't be long now, deep into summer, until the Headlands would be unrelieved brown, seemingly barren of life. If the fog rolled in during the late afternoon, it would settle over the Headlands, and look for all the world like the setting for a Gothic movie.

His house had been photographed, fingerprinted, thoroughly cleaned up, and repaired. He'd spoken to his secretary and both of his externs, the two law clerks assigned to him as a federal district judge. The three of them had volunteered to refurbish his house. He'd given them color schemes, the type of furniture he liked, and a budget. They'd gone over budget, but given the furniture and draperies that had been delivered and lovingly arranged throughout the house, he wasn't about to bitch. He wondered what else would be arriving. It was interesting to see himself through other people's eyes. His study was more domineering and masculine now, full of leather and rich earth colors. They'd spent a small fortune on the leather sofa and chairs and the immense mahogany desk, and he'd approved that as well. The walls were still empty. They couldn't have bought the art he would like.

Given that less than a month had passed, they'd accomplished miracles.

"Ramsey?"

"Yes, Emma?"

"I like your house. The water makes me feel good."

He grinned as he leaned down and picked her up in his arms. He carried her to his huge leather chair and sat down. He put his feet up on the sinfully rich leather hassock, something he'd never had before. "Let's look at the view together, okay? We can let our souls commune with nature. Hey, where's your piano?"

"Upstairs. But my piano's not important right now." She sighed, that adult sigh. "I'm worried about Mama. I don't think she feels good even though she told me she was fine."

"What's wrong?"

"She's sick. She sent me down here to keep you busy, to keep you away. She doesn't want you to know, but I'm worried. Can you fix it, Ramsey?"

"Oh, damn. Sorry, Emma. Will you stay here and commune with nature for me?"

"Yes, but just for a little while. Mama's face is kind of green."

"I'll take care of her. You stay put, all right, Emma?"

"I won't go outside by myself, Ramsey."

"Good girl," he said, kissed her forehead, and took off upstairs. He heard her retching from the top of the stairs. There were three rooms on the second floor—his master suite, a study, and a guest room, where she and Emma were sleeping. She was in the bathroom attached to the guest room. The door was pulled to, but not closed all the way. He inched it open. Molly was on her knees, her head over the toilet, heaving.

He didn't say anything, gently reached down to rub her shoulders, then hunched down on his knees beside her. He pulled back her hair. She sank back against him. "You okay now?"

She moaned. "I don't want to talk. I want to die."

He flushed the toilet. "Hold still, let me get you some water to wash out your mouth."

She moaned again. "I wish you hadn't come up here. I should have known Emma would get you. This is humiliating."

He handed her a glass of water. She eyed it, then rose slowly. "Let me brush my teeth."

"I've got some antacid. You want some? Oh yes, Emma was really worried. I'm glad she had sense enough to fetch me. More sense than her mother."

"Go away," she said, pushing him out the door and closing it. He heard her rinse her mouth out with mouthwash. Five minutes later, he was walking beside her to the bed. There wasn't a great view in the guest room, but the row of three windows that were there gave a glimpse of the Golden Gate.

"At least while I'm lying here dying, the last thing I see will be beautiful."

"Nah, the last thing you'll see is my ugly face. That's enough right there to get you well again."

"I must have eaten something bad on the airplane."

She'd had the linguine with clam sauce. Both he and Emma had chewed through the chicken. "Could be. That or it's stress." He gently cupped her face with his palm. She was sweaty and damp. He frowned. "I'm going to call my doctor, see what he has to say."

"I'm not going to any doctor, Ramsey. Forget it. My stomach's empty now. I'll be fine."

"We'll see," he said, in the same adult tone she used naturally with a child when she wanted to clamp down on any further arguments.

He brought her a couple of pills and a glass of water. "Take these."

She didn't even ask what they were. When she'd swallowed them, she leaned back against the pillows.

"How's your arm?"

"It's fine. How's your back?"

He smiled at her. "I'm okay. Can you still see the stitches in your arm?"

"Some of them, but they're on their way. How's your leg?"

"Long healed. I want to see your arm." She suffered his rolling up the sleeve of her pale cream-colored blouse. He gently pulled back the bandage. The skin was a healthy pink, the stitches obscene in her white arm, but the wound was much better, the remaining stitches disintegrating. He grunted and pressed the bandage down again. "Well, your heaving isn't from this wound."

"Where's Emma?"

"She's in my big leather chair staring out the French doors toward the bridge. But let me go check." He brought her back up five minutes later.

"Look who I found with her cute little nose pressed to the window."

"My beautiful little princess?"

"Nah, she's mine, but I'll be willing to share her for a couple of minutes. You can see for yourself, Emma. Your mom's okay."

"Can I stay with her, Ramsey? I'll try to make her laugh. She says laughing always makes anybody feel better."

"Okay, but if she gets sick again, you holler and I'll get somebody over here with some needles to stick in her."

"Yuck," said Emma.

Three hours later, Molly was chewing on some dry toast and drinking hot plain Earl Grey tea. She still looked pale. At least she hadn't vomited again. The nausea had been gone for an hour, but his hand still hovered over the phone. He wanted to call Jim Haversham, an internist with privileges at San Francisco General.

"I don't think we're going anywhere tomorrow," he said at nine o'clock that evening. Both Emma and Molly were lying in the guest-room bed, the brand-new TV on low, providing background noise.

The doorbell sounded. Ramsey turned to leave. "It's a friend of mine from the San Francisco PD. I called her. She's going to brief me on anything they've turned up."

"About your house being trashed?" Molly asked, moving the wet washcloth a bit to the left on her forehead.

"That and other things. You guys relax. Emma, if your mom needs anything, you come and tell me. Can I count on you to mind me and not her?"

Emma looked worried. "I don't know, Ramsey, she's my mom. She's been around since I was born."

"I know, but right now she's on the pathetic side. She doesn't know what's good for her. Call me, all right?"

Emma still looked uncertain. She pulled her piano onto her lap. Molly groaned. She groaned again, a big funny groan that made Emma smile.

Good for you, Molly, he thought, gave them a salute, and took off downstairs.

Virginia Trolley was at the door, wearing her signature black boots, black slacks, black turtleneck, and a red blazer. "I'm glad you're home, Ramsey. All hell's broken loose."

He invited her into his study. There was a fire in the fireplace and the new heavy pale gold draperies were drawn, making the room darker, more intimate.

"I love your house. The new stuff looks great. Did they bankrupt you refurbishing it?"

"The insurance will cover most of it."

"Good. Now that everything's brand-new, do you think we could get married, then we could get divorced and I'd get the house?"

"No way you'd get the house unless you bribed a judge," Ramsey said, and poured her a cup of coffee from the Thermos on a side table.

She sighed. "My husband might not understand, either. Would you consider adopting me?"

"You're older than I am."

"Ah, so have you heard of age discrimination?"

"Not me. Thanks for coming by, Ginny. What's going on downtown?"

"You know everyone still calls you Judge Dredd. It really fits now, what with all your flirting with the underworld. The media has been going nuts about all of it. I'm surprised they haven't found out you're home. Be thankful for small favors. It won't last."

He brought her up-to-date, finishing with, "Molly, Emma, and I are all going to Ireland day after tomorrow. We were going to leave first thing tomorrow, but Molly was throwing up her toenails all afternoon. She seems better now, but it doesn't seem too bright to fly right now. I think it was what she ate on the plane. I'm praying it's not gastritis or an ulcer, though an ulcer wouldn't surprise me what with all she's been through."

Virginia Trolley rose from her chair, walked to the wide French doors, and pulled back the drapes. The clouds were hanging black and low. There was no sign of a moon or any stars. She sighed deeply. "We've all been talking about what's happened. This Shaker guy is bad stuff, Ramsey. If he is behind all of it, the chances of getting enough for an indictment are about the same as the Raiders winning another Super Bowl anytime soon. The odds are astronomical." She grinned. "Actually, it's looking like the Forty-niners aren't going to come up smelling like roses either for a long time."

Ramsey sat down in the big leather chair behind his desk. He leaned back, cradling his head on his arms. "I'm hoping it is Shaker because it means the three of us are probably out of danger. Anyway, it's what the Feds think, it's what the Denver cops think. They're all still looking for the creep who took Emma.

"I'm praying we're out of here before the media discover we're back. I think all of us being out of the country for a while would be a healthy thing. Have you got anything new?"

Virginia turned from the French doors, letting the drapes drop back into place. "You're probably right. No leads as to who trashed your house. The neighbors saw nothing. There weren't any prints." She paused, looking around the man's study—dark wainscotting, rich leather furniture, and highly polished oak floor. "The cleaning service took real pride in fixing Judge Ramsey Hunt's house all right and tight. The *Chronicle* even wanted a photo of this room after your people refurbished it. It do sparkle, don't it?"

"Yeah, it do."

"Any problems?"

"No, everything is fine, at least for the moment. But I'm thinking it might be smart to have some protection."

"Agreed. I'll schedule a patrol to come by every half hour or so. Oh yes, I need to show you this, though we don't think it's much of anything. Anonymous, of course. It was shoved under your office door." She pulled it out of her purse and handed it to him.

It was short and to the point.

YOU ARE A MURDERER. YOU WILL DIE.

It was printed carefully with a thick-tip black pen. Ramsey handed it back to her, "No verbosity—it can't be a lawyer. Any reason to think it's more than the usual crank stuff?"

"Not much different from what you got right after you destroyed the scum in your courtroom. You haven't gotten anything else recently, have you?"

"No, not that anyone has told me about."

"All right, it's probably nothing. But be careful, Judge Dredd. One of the undercover cops was telling his buddies he'd pulled a Hunt maneuver. In other words, he kicked some butt. He said he'd just wished he'd been wearing a black robe, that would have made him the ultimate cool. Sorry, Ramsey, you're in the cop lexicon now." Virginia Trolley looked up to see a little girl standing in the doorway, holding a large portable piano against her chest. The thing came down to her knees. She was clutching it really tightly. She had beautiful thick mahogany-colored hair that was straggling out of a fat French braid.

"Hi," Ginny said easily. "Are you Emma Santera?"

"Yes, ma'am. Ramsey, Mama's throwing up again. She told me not to tell you, but I'm worried. Would you make it stop again?"

"Yes, Emma, I'll take care of it right now." He turned to Ginny. "I'm going to call Jim Haversham. He owes me. I'll never forget Savich telling me that it's always a good thing to have a physician on your debt list."

"He's your FBI friend?"

"Yeah. Listen, Ginny, I'll keep in touch. If anything comes up, you can fax me in Ireland. We'll be staying at Dromoland Castle just north of Shannon Airport for a couple of days. I don't remember the county name. I'll let you know after that."

"Okay. You keep yourself safe, Ramsey. Good-bye, Emma. Take care of your mama and Ramsey, okay?"

"Yes, ma'am." Emma slipped into the room and stood by Ramsey while Ginny went out. As soon as she'd left the study, Ramsey picked up the phone.

When he hung up, he swung Emma and her piano up in his arms. "Let's go tell your mom that she's lucky. No going to any hospital. Nope, she's going to have a real live doctor make a house call to see her."

DR. James Haversham was forty-two, divorced twice, a man who sailed every free minute. He straightened and rubbed his jaw, a habit of long standing. He said finally, still looking down at Molly, still rubbing his jaw, "I need to do some tests."

"No. Forget it. If I ever go to the hospital, I'll be dead and I won't know about it. No tests."

He sighed. "All right, then. My best guess is that you ate something spoiled. Ramsey told me you had linguine with clams on the plane. From what he told me, nearly all of it is out of your system. But you're still having bowel spasms and that's why you started vomiting again. I'm going to give you a shot and some pills. They will help calm your stomach, make you drowsy, and take away the nausea. It'll take time for your bowels to straighten out. You're getting dehydrated. I want you to drink plenty of fluids tonight and tomorrow. Okay, the shot's for your butt. Turn over, please."

"Ramsey, please take Emma outside."

But Emma wasn't about to budge. "No, Mama, you need me. I'll hold your hand."

"You need me, too. I'll hold your other hand. It's your hour of need, Molly."

Emma looked up at him. "Was that a joke, Ramsey?"

"All right," Dr. Haversham said, "both of you turn around so my patient isn't embarrassed."

They turned to face the television that was showing a rerun of M*A*S*H, without sound.

They heard a yelp, then Dr. Haversham's voice. "Now, two of these pills, Mrs. Santera. You're going to stay in bed, sleep and eat through tomorrow. Drink enough water so that you're in the bathroom every fifteen minutes. Any more vomiting, though, and you're coming to the ER. I mean it. Unless you feel better soon, it means there's something going on here other than food poisoning." She was shaking her head even as he leaned down and said, "You have a beautiful little girl who needs you. Pick something else to be stubborn about."

She sighed. "You're right, of course. Thank you for coming."

"You're welcome."

He had turned to leave when Molly called out, "What did Ramsey do for you? He said you owed him and that's why you came to the house."

"He saved my life."

"What did he do?"

"When my first ex-wife got drunk and was going to beat up my other ex-wife, but not ex then, Ramsey stepped in. He distracted Melanie and had her dancing the rest of the night."

Molly laughed. "That's quite a debt you've paid off."

Dr. Haversham wasn't about to tell her that he'd made that up. She was a lovely woman with an easy smile on her face. And he'd put the smile there, brought the laugh. It was probably as effective as his pills and shot. "It sure was. Take care, Mrs. Santera."

She was nearly asleep. He smiled and shook Ramsey's hand.

"I heard what you said," Ramsey said. "I didn't know you could think that fast on your feet. We're even now."

"Oh, no. I still owe you another two or three more favors. I remember that water sure was cold. If you hadn't gotten me out of there, I wouldn't be doing favors for anybody."

He leaned down and automatically put his palm against Emma's forehead. She gasped and leaped back. Ramsey just smiled and patted her shoulder. "It's all right, sweetheart. Dr. Haversham just wants to make sure you're not sick like your mama. He's always checking everybody around him. Foreheads are his specialty."

Then Dr. Haversham remembered. This was the little girl who'd been kidnapped and sexually abused. He smiled down at her. "You seem to be in great health to me. You've got a fine forehead. You stick close to your mom, okay?"

"Yes, sir, I will," Emma said, but she kept back, staying close to Ramsey. He felt her hand slide into his. She was holding the piano up with only one arm. He quickly reached down and picked her and her piano up. "Let's see Dr. Haversham out, Emma. Then we can bring some water to your mama."

"She won't like having to go to the bathroom all the time, Ramsey."

"I wouldn't either, but it's her fate for a while."

TWENTY-SIX

Molly slept through the night. The next morning, she felt weak, but her stomach was settled. Ramsey gave her three slices of toast, thick with strawberry jam. Both Ramsey and Emma sat on the end of her bed, watching her take every bite. Finally, Molly laughed and said, "Enough. Look, two slices. I'm stuffed to my tonsils."

"You don't have any tonsils, Mama."

"Close enough. Now, I need a shower to feel really human. Ramsey, can you get us out of here today?"

He shook his head. "Let's give it another day, Molly. You've got orders to stay close and rest. Take those pills and keep drinking your water. I got you the bottled stuff. If you're good, if you're feeling even better this afternoon, we can go over to my favorite Mexican restaurant on Lombard Street for dinner."

Molly groaned and clutched her stomach.

"Okay then. Chicken soup it is."

She was exhausted by the time she'd blow-dried her hair and dressed. She looked at the bed, freshly made, the comforter turned back, at Ramsey, who was just smiling at her, and flopped down. "A woman picked out this bed set. It's so bright and whimsical. Am I right?"

"Yep. Probably my secretary. I like it. Here, drink this entire glass, all twelve ounces. Then, take a nap. I'm going to take Emma over to Cliff House. The beach there is wonderful, right below what we call The Great Highway. She'll see some seals. We'll build a sand castle and throw a Frisbee for one of the many dogs that hang out with their owners over there. I'll bring her back dirty and happy. I want that bottle to be empty."

They'd been on the beach only twenty minutes when a huge panting black Lab came trotting over to Ramsey and butted his head against Ramsey's leg. A woman called out, "Just tell him to eat dirt if you don't want to throw that Frisbee for him."

But Ramsey patted the Lab's big head. "You up for this, fella?" He pulled his ancient chewed-up yellow Frisbee out of the old duffel bag that also held his and Emma's sandwiches, potato chips, and soft drinks, and flung it a good thirty yards. The Lab raced after it.

"Now Bop's never going to leave you," a young woman said, striding up to where Ramsey and Emma stood. Emma's eyes were on Bop as he hurled himself into the air, but couldn't extend far enough to catch the Frisbee.

"He'll get it next time. He has to learn your style. Tell me when you're tired of throwing for him. This your little girl?"

Emma quietly slipped her hand into Ramsey's. She pressed against his side.

"Yes," Ramsey said. "This is my little girl, Emma."

"I'm Betty Conlin," the young woman said and thrust out her hand. Ramsey shook it. The woman knelt down in front of Emma. "Hi. How old are you?"

Emma gave her a long assessing look. She said finally, "Bop's coming back. My mama's home in bed. We're here so I can play and try to forget about things. We're here so Mama can rest and get well."

"I see," Betty said and rose, and, naturally, she did indeed see. She smiled. "Here, Bop!"

Ramsey snapped his wrist and sent the Frisbee flying again. Bop had already begun running. He caught it on a three-foot leap. Ramsey yelled out, "Nice goin', boy, well done!"

He was laughing. There was dog slobber on his hands. Emma was playing in the sand one foot away from him. The sun was bright, making the ocean surface gleam like light blue diamonds. The sound of the waves sweeping onto shore was a constant rumble behind all the human voices. All they needed was Molly with them, lying on a blanket, drinking lots and lots of water and probably needing a bathroom, of which there were none anywhere close. He looked down at Emma and saw that she was staring at Betty Conlin. He didn't need to worry about any woman coming on to him. Emma would protect him. Well, for the moment they couldn't have Bop without Betty. Bop came dashing back, played tug-on-the-Frisbee with Ramsey, dropped it, and took off running. Ramsey let loose with a really long throw, skimming low toward the water. He shaded his eyes, watching Bop. The Frisbee caught a sliver of upward air and went flying even farther. Maybe fifty yards?

He turned when he heard Betty say something. He nodded and watched Bop finally catch the Frisbee well into the surf. He bounded back through a spray of water that looked like diamond droplets beneath that crystal sunlight.

"Did you see that, Emma?" He was grinning as he turned.

Emma was gone.

He felt instant overwhelming panic.

"What's wrong?" Betty was saying even as she was patting Bop.

"Emma," he said. "Emma." He whirled about searching. He heard a cry, jerked about toward the Cliff House, but saw a little boy fighting with his sister.

He yelled again at the top of his lungs, "Emma!"

Oh God no. This couldn't be happening. No, she had to be close. They couldn't have taken her far, not in just the couple of minutes Ramsey hadn't been looking at her. The sun was in his eyes.

Then he saw a man walking quickly down the beach, heading south. He was wearing a long dark brown overcoat. There was a huge bulge in that overcoat. He had Emma under that overcoat. How had he done it so fast?

Ramsey took off after him. He didn't say a word, didn't scream at the man, just sprinted. The man stumbled suddenly, lurching toward the water. Emma's head poked out of the side of the overcoat.

She yelled at the top of her lungs. "Ramsey! Ramsey!"

Now he did call back. "It's over!" He was nearly on him. The man jerked back his head, saw that it was over, dropped Emma, and took off back up the beach to the high concrete retaining wall. Ramsey started after him, then heard someone yell. He whipped back and saw Emma.

She was lying motionless on the beach. Two little girls were standing over her, one of them holding a blue bucket in her hand. A woman was running toward them. He ran back, gently pulled the little girls back, and knelt down beside Emma. She was drawn up in the fetal position, her eyes closed, her hair slashed across her forehead, strands stuck to her cheeks.

"Emma." He lightly touched his hand to her shoulder. "Emma, love. It's me, Ramsey. Are you all right?"

She moaned low in her throat. Slowly, she turned to face him, staring up at him.

"Are you hurt?"

She shook her head. "Well, a little. He covered my face and hit me on my head."

The bastard had struck her, put her under his coat, and simply walked away. He looked toward the retaining wall. There were a lot of people milling around up there, but no man wearing an overcoat. Of course he could have just taken it off, and probably had.

He gathered Emma up against him, hugged her tightly, and kissed her. He'd nearly lost her. No more than three, maybe four minutes, and he'd nearly lost her. A woman said, "Did that man try to steal her?"

"Yes, he did. Did you happen to see what happened to him once he made the retaining wall?"

The woman shook her head. "No, I was looking right here."

"It happened so fast," Betty said, running up. Bop was pushing his head against Ramsey's legs, the Frisbee in his mouth. "From one instant to the next. She was gone. I'm so sorry."

The woman didn't say anything more, just gathered her two little girls close. "We're leaving," she said. The children whined and argued, but the woman had a firm hold on their arms and dragged them away.

"Do you want me to call the cops?"

"No," Ramsey said, slowly rising. He still held Emma tightly against him. He was kissing the top of her head. "I'm so sorry, Emma, so sorry." He turned to Betty Conlin. "Bop can have the Frisbee and the sandwiches."

The police would question the people on the beach, all the people on the sidewalk at the top of the retaining wall, but Emma was burrowed against him, she was shuddering, he had to get her home. He kept her pressed against him even in the front seat of his old Porsche. It was a tight squeeze but he didn't care.

He was still holding her when he stood at his desk, calling Virginia Trolley. When she came on the line, he said, "Ramsey here. A man just tried to steal Emma on the beach near Cliff House. He dropped her when he saw I was about to catch him. I couldn't go after him because Emma was down. He was wearing a long brown overcoat, scuffed black-and-white running shoes, a brown knit cap on his head, dark sunglasses. He moved like he was over forty. Not all that tall, maybe five-ten. Yeah, he was white. If you could send some people over there to find someone who saw the bastard. Yeah, thanks. See you in a few minutes."

He was still holding Emma when he hung up the phone. "Now, sweetheart, let me take a look at your head."

"Mama," Emma said against his jacket. "Mama."

"You're right. Let's go see that she's all right."

But Molly wasn't there.

Ramsey stared dumbly down at the empty bed. The water bottle beside the bed was empty. He yelled her name. He even looked in the bathroom shower.

"Molly!"

"Where's Mama, Ramsey?"

"I don't know, Emma, I don't know."

He ran back downstairs, Emma clinging to him like a limpet. He called her name again and again.

What the hell had happened?

He ran outside. There were two older people walking on the sidewalk. They knew him and waved. He waved back, even as he was turning to look the other way. No one else was around.

Emma was shuddering in his arms, crying, deep and low, harsh ugly sobs. "It's all right, Emma. She must have gone for a walk, that's all." He continued speaking nonsense to her, and that's what it was—nonsense. Where was Molly? He'd never been so afraid in his life.

Virginia Trolley pulled up with a young cop in her white Plymouth.

"Molly's gone," he said. "She's just gone."

Virginia Trolley saw the shock on his face, saw the little girl nearly hysterical in his arms. She said quietly, "Let's go inside and make some calls. It will be all right, Ramsey. Come along."

Virginia got on the phone. Ramsey started rocking Emma in his big desk chair. They heard a woman yell.

"Mama!"

Emma jerked out of Ramsey's arms and ran to the front door. It opened and Molly nearly fell inside, the young cop right behind her, his arm outstretched to grab her.

"Mama!"

Molly was on her knees in the foyer, Emma crying against her neck. The young cop said to Virginia, "I'm sorry, she wouldn't say who she was."

"It's okay. Now that Molly's here, you can go on over to Cliff House, Joe, and join the questioning."

Ramsey stood slowly. He waited until Emma had quieted a bit, waited until Molly finally raised her head.

"What happened to you?"

He sounded furious, at the end of his rope. Molly saw the policewoman standing by his desk. For a moment, she was so relieved she simply couldn't speak. She held Emma close.

"I got a phone call," she said, her voice strained and thin. "It came about ten minutes ago. I was sound asleep. It was a man. His voice was muffled, as though he was talking through a handkerchief. At first I was too asleep to realize what he was saying. But then he said everything again. He said something about the beach and he'd gotten her and I'd never see her again."

"Mama," Emma whispered. For a moment, Molly just held her daughter close. She rose finally, lifting Emma in her arms. She staggered. Ramsey walked to her and gathered them both close. He said against Molly's hair, "Thank God you're all right."

"Yes," Molly said. "What happened?"

Ramsey walked both of them to the sofa and sat down, holding each of them very close. He kissed Emma's forehead, then Molly's. "It's all right. We're all together. What happened is that a man did grab Emma, but I saw him running away with her and got her back. He ran away. Virginia's got police at the beach questioning people." He paused a moment, not releasing his hold on either of them. "But why did he call you? Ten minutes ago? That means he called you after I got Emma back. Why'd he do that?"

Virginia said, "He did it to terrorize Molly. Now, who would like a glass of water?"

Ramsey started to say that Molly would, but he didn't. He realized that he was feeling very strange, as though his brain had slowed to a stumbling walk.

"I've been stupid," he said. "Even though I asked you about protection and you volunteered a patrol car, I still thought it was all over. I didn't really think there was any more danger. I never thought that man would come back."

"We've all been stupid," Molly said. "I didn't think there was any more danger either. The man's insane."

"That's probably very true," Virginia said. "Now, let's get down to it." Virginia asked him questions. She was infinitely patient, her voice pitched low. Ramsey realized, of course, that she'd played through scenes like this before, only most of them hadn't ended as well as this one had.

They sat close together, Emma on his lap, her face against her mother's shoulder, his arms around both of them.

Virginia said, "Mrs. Santera, please think back. Oh, I'm sorry. I'm Virginia Trolley, of the SFPD. I've known Ramsey for a while."

Molly nodded at the woman who was dressed all in black with a bright red blazer. "Call me Molly."

"All right. Good. Now, the man called at about—" She looked at her watch, did some calculations. "He called about ten after three. He said what exactly?"

"He said he had Emma. He said that stupid judge had left her on the beach, didn't care about her at all, that he was flirting with this girl and throwing a Frisbee for her dog. He said it was a piece of cake. He said he'd never let her escape him again. He said I'd never see her again. Then he laughed. He said he was going to drive close to the house so maybe I could see him and Emma. He said he'd let Emma wave good-bye to me. Then he hung up. I was staring at the phone. I couldn't think of anything to say. Then I thought if I went outside maybe I could catch him. I ran outside. I've been running all through Sea Cliff. I'm surprised neighbors haven't called the cops to report a crazy woman."

"He called her after I got Emma back," Ramsey said slowly. "To frighten her?"

"Like I said," Virginia repeated, "he wanted to terrorize Molly. He wanted to make himself feel powerful. He'd failed to get Emma, but by calling Molly, he could win, at least for a while, until the both of you got back here."

His brain was beginning to function again, thank God. He could tell that Molly, too, was getting herself back together. As for Emma, he didn't know what they'd be facing with her. "Emma says he hit her on the head."

Molly patted her daughter's shoulder. "Em, does your head hurt?"

Emma sat up on Ramsey's lap. Slowly, she lifted her hand to touch above her left ear. "It's just a little lump."

"I saw you poke your head out of his overcoat."

Emma nodded. "I bit him through his shirt, too. Real hard. You told me never to give up and I didn't."

Virginia said, "In his side, Emma?"

"Yes."

"Which side?"

"His right side. I think it hurt him."

"Good for you." Ramsey cupped her face between his hands and kissed her nose. "Good for you, Em." He looked into that small face that had become so inexpressibly dear to him. It broke him. "Oh, Emma, I'm so sorry." He touched his forehead to hers. He felt the panic well up again, and that awful foreboding of sheer helplessness.

Slowly, Emma raised her small hand and lightly ran her fingers over his cheek. "I'm okay, Ramsey. You didn't do anything wrong. He was so fast. I was patting down one of my sand castle walls, and then he hit me."

Virginia Trolley turned away, cleared her throat, and said over her shoulder, "Emma, does your head hurt?"

"No, ma'am. It's just sore."

"Perhaps we should call Dr. Haversham again, Ramsey."

"All right. I'd sure feel better."

"I'm like my mama. I hate hospitals."

Ramsey and Molly exchanged glances.

"He wasn't wearing a mask this time, but he still had bad teeth."

Her voice sounded almost normal. She was sitting up straight now on Ramsey's legs. She was looking at Virginia.

"Did you notice anything else about him, Emma?"

"He smelled funny, like the way he did before."

"Funny how?" Virginia asked, taking a small pad of paper out of her purse and writing on it.

Emma shrugged. "Strong. Not nice."

"Whiskey," Ramsey said. "Was it whiskey?"

Emma wasn't certain. Ramsey lifted her in his arms and carried her over to the sideboard. He pulled the cork out of a bottle and lifted it to her nose. "Is this the smell?"

She scrunched up her face and jerked back. "Yes, Ramsey, like that. It's not a nice smell."

"No, it's not."

"And he had bad teeth?"

"Yes, ma'am, all black and yucky. I remember one was missing." She pulled open her lip and pointed to one of the incisors on the left.

"Good," Virginia said as she wrote. "Did he say anything to you, Emma?"

She shook her head. Ramsey returned to the sofa with her and sat back down beside Molly. "Think, Em. What were you doing just before he hit you on the head?"

"I was packing down sand."

"Then what?"

"I heard something. I looked up but something hit me and I don't remember."

"That's fine, Emma," Molly said. "All done in an instant of time." Emma slipped her hand into her mother's.

Virginia Trolley quietly closed her small notebook. She nodded to Ramsey. "He's made a mistake. He's close. Now maybe we can get this monster. Emma, you're the greatest. Ramsey told me you got away from this jerk before. You did it again. Now, you need to take care of Ramsey and your mom, okay? They aren't doing so well right now."

"Yes, Officer, I will."

Ramsey said, "Emma, can you give a police artist a description of the man? This time he wasn't wearing a mask."

"I can try, Ramsey."

Virginia Trolley said, "I'll send someone right over. You're a good girl, Emma. I'll see you later."

"I don't think you should ever go to the bathroom again, Mama, unless I go with you. Ramsey either."

Virginia Trolley heard Mrs. Santera laugh as she walked out the front door. It was a shaky thin sound, but still a laugh.

TWENTY-SEVEN

Both Emma and Molly were openmouthed when they stepped into the reception area of Dromoland Castle, with its circular, gray stone inside the same as outside, and its giant windows, ancient tapestries, and smiling Irish. Dromoland had once been the stronghold of the O'Briens and was now a huge, turreted Gothic-style stone building that had been turned into a hotel in the early part of the century. It was a sprawling grand mass of stone, set amid the most beautiful park they'd ever seen. They were in the Speath Suite, a vast square room with tall windows that gave onto the beautifully mowed sloping lawns, formal gardens, and a lake. There were two queen beds. They'd ordered a rollaway cot for Emma, but when it arrived with the smiling bellman Tommy, and Ramsey had turned to ask Emma where she wanted the bed, the lost panicked look on her face had made him quickly turn back to Tommy and order the cot taken away. Emma slept with her mother. She'd had no more nightmares since they'd arrived.

On their third full day in Ireland, the first day it wasn't raining heavily, the sun was so bright it hurt to look directly into it. It was late morning. Emma was wearing blue jeans, a white shirt, her favorite Nike sneakers, and a pair of plaid socks Ramsey had bought for her in the charming thatch-roofed village of Adare, where most of the picturesque cottages housed tourist shops.

Emma was feeding the ducks. Molly was crouched six feet from her, down on one knee, waiting for the late-morning sun to get to just the right angle for the perfect series of shots. She had a roll of thirty-six in her

Minolta, her film four hundred ASA. She didn't have her light meter with her, and wished fervently that she'd bought a new camera with the light meter built into it. But she'd shot Emma so often, with so many different backgrounds, different lights, and angles, she wasn't taking too much of a chance. It's just that she wanted one of these photos to be absolutely perfect. She wanted it for Ramsey, the man who'd saved her daughter's life, the man she was coming to know as well as she knew herself. There was more light than dark in Emma today, and in her surroundings as well. White ducks glossier than the shine on a brand-new Corvette were surrounding Emma, and Emma was laughing, and throwing single pieces of bread, hoarding each piece, choosing which was to be the lucky duck. One of the ducks was fast and cunning. He'd jumped and flapped wildly several times now in front of one of his cousins and ruthlessly snatched the bread from her fingertips. Molly quickly closed the aperture one f-stop and increased the shutter speed to 1/125 since she was hand-holding her camera and she didn't want to take the chance of blurring. Since the natural lighting was spectacular, she knew the background—the lake and the ducks—would be as clear and sharp as Emma's face. The sun was behind her so she could backlight Emma. She continued to meter off her face so she could get natural skin tones that would give her somewhat of a halo. The lake and the ducks would also be in focus, would show full stark color, full drama. She wanted fluidity, not a vaguely blurred motion shot with little detail, but the essence of constant motion captured at exactly the perfect moment. She wanted every crease in that shirt to be exactly as it looked, with no shadows or dimming, no unnecessary highlighting or overexposing. She wanted that incredible smile on Emma's face to be there just as it was at this moment, in one hundred years, sharp and warm and so real you could practically hear the laughter, feel its warmth. She snapped once, twice, three times, then shifted back on her heels for another series. Then she sat down on the slope, leaning back, looking up at Emma. The aggressive duck hopped high to grab a small piece of bread Emma had destined for the duck beside him. Emma jumped up and clapped, so pleased she thrust out a hunk of bread to the invader duck. The duck jumped up toward her, almost in counterpoint, his neck stretched out full length to get that bread. Molly snapped another series, ending up flat on her back, looking nearly straight up. She righted herself, and lay her Minolta SLR on her knee. She was out of film. The camera felt warm and comforting in her hand, just right resting against her leg.

She and the Minolta were old friends. She was used to the weight of it, the feel of it. The new cameras were something, doing everything she still did manually; some of them were so fine-tuned, they could probably even make coffee for the photographer. Nah, she didn't need coffee. Her Minolta had a lot of miles left in it.

She was pleased with the photos she'd taken. One of them would be perfect, she'd bet the farm on it. Maybe even two. For a moment, she wished she'd had a tripod. Then she shook her head, remembering what a pain in the butt it was to cart around all the extra stuff.

She saw a sudden movement out of the corner of her eye, off to the left in a stand of pine trees. She froze when she saw it, panic spiking in her. It was a man, leaning slightly around a tree, wearing a long brown coat, a brown knit cap on his head. He seemed to be staring at them. Molly was on her feet in an instant, her heart pounding, about to grab Emma when a man emerged from the trees, carrying a bag of golf clubs. The breath whooshed out of her mouth. The Irish and their incessant golf, surely a national addiction. There were courses everywhere, including here on the grounds of Dromoland Castle. She'd swear that the Scots, with their St. Andrews, couldn't be more golf-happy than the Irish. He saw her staring at him, and took off his golf hat, calling out a good morning.

She waved back, felt herself flush to her toes both with relief and chagrin that she'd panicked so easily.

But she knew she'd act the same way the next time a strange man suddenly appeared. She would until the man who'd taken Emma was caught. For now, he was still out there. He was still after Emma.

At the moment, Ramsey was making some phone calls, one of them to Virginia Trolley of the SFPD to see if she had anything to tell him. Emma's meeting with the police artist had shown a man in his forties, with thinning hair, a sharp chin, and whiskers heavy on his face. His eyes were a soft gray, and set wide apart. He'd had strange ears, large for the size of his head, sticking out a bit. Emma said that's why he wore a knit hat. He didn't like his ears. His bad teeth were the giveaway. Molly hoped the guy didn't make a trip to the dentist.

Molly had no idea—no one did—how accurate Emma's description was. But it was the best they had to go on. The drawing was in the hands of the SFPD and the FBI.

Having the picture out there would protect them somewhat, Molly thought, but he was still out there. She felt it deep in her innards. When they went back home, he would be there, waiting. Somewhere. She decided that when they returned to the U.S. she and Emma wouldn't go back to Denver. No, she'd take her to an entirely new city. She would change her name and Emma's. They would disappear. The man wouldn't be able to find them then. She had enough money from the divorce settlement. She was a good photographer. She would get better. She'd have to start over with her professional contacts, but that wasn't a big deal. Her biggest assignment had been photographing Louey for *Rolling Stone* magazine some six years before. They knew who she was, but that was about all.

She saw Emma molding her last pieces of bread in the shape of an apple. After she'd thrown the small glob to the ruthless duck, Molly called out, "Hey, Em. Maybe you can grow up to be a caterer."

The ducks stopped squawking. They knew the bread was gone. They were going back to the large pond, waddling gracelessly, flapping their wings, grooming themselves.

"What's that, Mama?"

"That's a person who's paid to cook for people on special occasions. You'd get to taste lots of different kinds of goodies. You'd get to be creative, make food look like different things, just the way you've made the bread look like an apple. You'd be a food artist."

"Would I have to feed all those people, too?"

"Emma, was that a joke?"

Emma thought about that, then gave her mother a small smile. "I don't think so."

"No, they wouldn't eat out of your hand. Well, they might, but not literally." Molly looked out over the beautiful grounds. She put her arms around Emma and drew her back against her. She desperately wanted to ask her what she was thinking, what she was feeling, but she was afraid that she wouldn't say the right thing if Emma were to tell her something awful. Instead, she said, her voice bright and warm with the overwhelming love she felt for her daughter, "We've got sun today, kiddo. What do you say we go to Bunratty Castle? Maybe have a picnic on the grounds? Since it was raining the other day when we went, you just got to spend ten minutes there. Ramsey says it's a great place to visit, when the sun's out."

Emma grinned every time someone mentioned Bunratty Castle, west of Limerick, where William Penn had been born in 1644, and where his father,

Admiral Penn, had surrendered in the civil war and sailed off to America. Ah, and that had led to stories of the Quakers in Pennsylvania, a good half dozen that Ramsey had been told growing up near Harrisburg.

Emma wiped her hands on her jeans as she said to Molly, "I'd like to climb all those steps. Maybe I'll get all the way to the top this time without Ramsey having to carry me. Yes, let's go, Mama. Tommy said that the tourist buses will start coming soon. But it's still early, he said."

Molly blinked. It was the end of May. Life had changed so irrevocably that Molly had forgotten the day of the week, much less the month. "Yes, it is very early in the tourist season. Isn't that something?" A month before she'd been taking pictures, trying to polish her craft, her life busy and fun. Not really full, but that was okay. Emma would be starting first grade in the fall. They'd both looked forward to that. Then Emma had been kidnapped and their lives had flown out of control.

Suddenly, Emma held out her left hand. "Tommy gave me this." It was a small elaborately worked dark silver ring with a purple stone in it. "Tommy said it was Celtic."

Molly held her daughter's small white hand and looked at the lovely child's ring on Emma's middle finger. "It's beautiful. He gave it to you this morning?"

"He said if I ate my oatmeal, he had a small present for me. It was yesterday."

Molly felt a sudden jolt of fear. She'd seen Tommy speaking to Emma, but when had he given her the ring? Was Tommy one of those monsters? Was he trying to seduce Emma into trusting him? For a moment she was so afraid she couldn't breathe. No, she was being ridiculous. He was a nice boy, no older than seventeen, hair as red as a swatch of crimson silk, face very fair and freckled. No, Tommy was simply a nice boy. Still, she found herself taking Emma's hand for no good reason at all.

"Mama, you're hurting me."

"What? Oh goodness, Em, I'm sorry. Look, there's Ramsey. Let's see if he wants to go to Bunratty."

They left Dromoland grounds an hour later, a picnic basket packed in the backseat beside Emma, with ham-and-cheese sandwiches, nothing else, because the Irish, Molly said, evidently didn't believe in mayonnaise or mustard or tomatoes or lettuce. They did, however, have potato chips. And lots of local cider.

The lanes were so narrow that if another car came along, they had to back up into one of the bulges, Emma called them, and park until the other car passed. "I'm nearly used to driving on the wrong side," Ramsey said as they passed a car on a turnout. "In the east of Ireland there are lots more people and better roads. By the time you get over Dublin way, you're pretty much used to all these strange things."

There was only one tour bus parked at Bunratty. They had nearly the entire shaded park to themselves. Emma climbed the castle's main stairs all on her own.

"WE think we've found him, or at least we know who he is."

Ramsey gripped the phone tight. It was midnight in Ireland, seven o'clock in Washington, D.C. Savich said again, "Ramsey, you there? Damned telephones. We got a poor connection?"

"No, it's fine. You really found him, Savich?"

"Yep. Well, we don't have him in the slammer yet, but we know who he is. His name's John Dickerson, aka Sonny Dickerson, aka Father Sonny. He's forty-eight years old, an ex-priest, finally booted out by the Church because he'd been so flagrant that the good bishops and the cardinal had to oust him. You remember how they used to ship the pedophile priests from one unsuspecting parish to another after having sent the offending priest off for spiritual and psychological rehabilitation?"

"Yeah. Thank God the Church now hands them over to be prosecuted."

"Yes, once they realized there were no cures. This guy was so over the edge that at the last parish they sent him to the people found out about him within a week of his arrival. Unfortunately, he had time to molest a little girl while her mother was in the church bathroom. There was a wedding rehearsal going on at the same time. Everyone came running out when they heard the mother yelling her head off. The bride and groom got an eyeful. He was in prison until about a year ago. He was supposed to register when he got out, but he didn't. He's been a fugitive, but no one ever really tried to find him, not enough cops, larger cases, until now."

"Does he look like Emma's description?"

"Have I got a surprise for you. I inputted the police sketch into what we call the Facial Recognition Algorithm program. The general public doesn't know about this program yet; I got it from a friend who helped develop it for Scotland Yard. I've made modifications and have been working on it for the FBI. We've already uploaded photographs of every convicted child molester in the United States, and several other groups of violent felons too.

"With MAXINE's help, we treated the police sketch like a photograph and ran the program. What this program does is compare the photo, or the sketch in this case, to the photos in the database. It compares, for example, the distance between the eyes, the length of the nose, the exact size of the upper lip, the distance between various facial bones, you get the idea. Since MAXINE and I are pretty flexible, we managed to make the comparisons and came up with a list of a couple of hundred who resembled the sketch. We found Father Sonny in the group in under an hour. He fits all the other characteristics: he's a heavy smoker, has rotten teeth, drinks too much, and he's been out of Folsom for about eight months. His prison records indicate he refused any dental care. He said, and I quote: 'I won't have any of those drill-wielding assholes in my mouth.' He's a real hard case, Ramsey, real hard. They only let him out because they didn't have a choice."

"Did he molest both little boys and little girls?"

Savich said, "Evidently he didn't have a particular preference, at least then. Obviously if Shaker hired him to kidnap Emma, in order to bring Louey into line, he's no longer on Shaker's payroll since Louey's dead, and since Emma managed to get away from him."

Ramsey said, "I can't imagine that Shaker would ever want to see this guy again, unless it was to have a little talk with him. No way Shaker knew he was a child molester when he hired him to kidnap Emma."

"So what Father Sonny did in San Francisco was all on his own." Savich paused a moment, then added, "He took a hell of a risk taking Emma right from under your nose. That's really out of control."

"Yeah, that's close to obsession. I'd say, bottom line, he's left common sense way behind."

Savich said, "Fixation, obsession, whatever the shrinks want to call it, Father Sonny's there. Our shrinks who deal with child molesters say it's common. A guy can come to believe that a certain child will save him. In this case, since the guy's an ex-priest, he might even believe that Emma can save his soul and cleanse him, heal him, maybe even make him acceptable to God again. Usually, though, after they're done with the child, they'll carefully select another child and believe the same thing all over again. Why does he want Emma back? Was it because she managed to escape him and so he wasn't the one who got to decide? He wants the control, the power? His can be the only voice?"

"Or maybe," Ramsey said, "he still believes that only Emma can save him, that she wasn't through cleansing him, so he's got to have her back. She said that he needed her more than God needed him, something to that effect. You know what? I want to kill him."

"Yeah, you and about a zillion other people. We've got everyone countrywide clued into Father Sonny. That's what most of the other prisoners called him. He'll surface sooner or later. Someone will see him, recognize him. We'll get him. Your cop friend in the SFPD, Virginia Trolley, she's heading things up out there. How is Emma doing? She love Ireland?"

"Oh yeah. She's big into feeding the ducks here at Dromoland Lake and into visiting castles. She hasn't had any nightmares since we've been here. You know, I was getting worried since she was always so quiet, so well behaved. Today she was a real kid, Savich. She finally whined this afternoon, didn't want to do something her mother told her to do. It warmed me to hear that fretful, obnoxious little voice. Molly says it's tough not to spoil her because of all that's happened to her. But we're trying." He paused, then said, "I saw Molly shooting photos of her this morning. Emma was feeding ducks, laughing, the sun bright, the ducks carrying on madly."

"And?"

"I don't know," Ramsey said. "I really don't know why I was telling you that." He saw Emma's beautiful face in his mind's eye, then, suddenly, saw her lying on her face in the forest, saw the marks on her small body, the blood on her legs. Vicious deep rage nearly overwhelmed him. It drummed all the way into his bones. He was clutching the receiver so tightly his knuckles showed white. "It's not right, Savich. This shouldn't have happened. Not to Emma, not to any little kid."

"You know how common it is, Ramsey. God knows you saw enough of it in your time in the U.S. Attorney's office, and probably some when you were a trial lawyer. And now as a judge."

They spoke of Paris, of Sherlock's continuing reaction to the word *pregnant*. Savich was laughing as he said, "I accidentally said the accursed word in a three-star restaurant on the Isle St. Louis. She nearly puked in her fancy French mushrooms stuffed with something I can't begin to pronounce. I'll bet it means something like 'greasy tourist innards' but I could be wrong. In any case, our waiter was wild-eyed, flapping his white waiter's towel around, but he got her to the women's room in the nick of time."

"The bathroom was very nice. It was too bad that I didn't make it to the toilet."

It was Sherlock and she was laughing. Ramsey said, "It shouldn't last much longer, should it?"

"The doc says another month. I'm thinking of taping Dillon's mouth shut to keep that word stuck in his throat, but then he couldn't kiss me properly. It's a tough call, downsides everywhere. How's Molly?"

"She's hanging in, taking lots of pictures, even of me. I look up and there she is, turning all these dials on her camera, assuming strange contorted positions, muttering about backlighting and the like. She's spending a fortune on film. You want to speak to her?"

Molly slipped out and came around to Ramsey's bed. Thank God Emma was sound asleep. She listened, then spoke to Sherlock. She laughed, a warm infectious sound that made Ramsey smile. She was humming to herself when she slipped back into her bed beside Emma.

TWENTY-EIGHT

Ramsey brushed his teeth, put the cap back on the toothpaste, and rinsed out his toothbrush, standing it bristles-up in a glass on the sink. He was leaning into the small shower stall to turn on the water. He heard something, straightened, and turned back toward the bathroom door.

Molly was standing there in her cotton nightgown, her hair tousled from sleeping, and her eyes were remarkably bright and focused. She was staring right at his cock.

"Molly?"

"Uh? Oh, Ramsey, I'm sorry. I wanted to go to the bathroom, I wasn't listening, I didn't realize you were in here and I—" Her voice fell like a rock off a cliff.

She continued to stare at him. Even when she'd spoken, she hadn't looked at his face. She hadn't even gotten as high as his chest.

She said now, still not looking at his face, "I guess I'd better leave now."

"I'll be out in a few minutes."

"I can hold it." She was out the door in a flash. He looked down at himself. He was getting erect, fast. Well, damn, he was a man and a man didn't have any say over that. It was the only completely independent organ of his entire body. Actually, given all the time they'd spent together, it was surprising this hadn't happened before. Actually, he rather wished, as he lathered soap on his chest and belly, that he'd been the one to walk in on Molly. He wondered how she'd have reacted if he'd stood there staring at her body, his eyes not getting above her neck. He also found himself wondering what she'd thought of his body. She'd seen him with a hard-on before, particularly in the mornings when they'd slept in the same room. But he hadn't been naked.

He hadn't worked out in a month except for that session with Savich in Mason Lord's state-of-the art gym. Sure he'd walked a lot, kept his cardiovascular system going at a fast clip through sheer stress, but it wasn't the same thing. He needed to work out. His body missed it. He flexed and stretched. He wondered if there were any gyms in Ireland. He'd just have to hike more, maybe carry Emma on his shoulders as a free weight.

He was whistling as he thought: So what'd you think, Molly? Did you like what you saw? He was whistling when he came out of the bathroom, completely dressed. "All yours," he said, and smiled at her.

She forced herself to look him straight in the eye and said, "Thank you."

LATE that afternoon, sitting on the Cliffs of Moher, waiting for that huge brilliant sun to sink down into the Atlantic, Ramsey took Molly's hand, lifted it to his mouth, and kissed her fingers, one at a time. She became instantly as still as a deer in the glare of headlights. He said quietly, still holding her hand, "Emma's not looking right now. I think she wants us to buy her another Celtic ring from that vendor over there. She's looking at every piece of jewelry he has. I've got my left eye on her. Don't worry. So, Molly, I think we should get married. What do you say?"

Molly jumped to her feet and took three quick steps back. Ramsey didn't move, just twisted around and looked up at her. Then he looked at Emma, who was now strolling not ten feet away from them, hovering near a man and a woman and their two young girl children.

Molly wrapped her arms around herself. She was shaking her head, her red hair a wild halo, corking out in all directions, simply beautiful. The sun, stark against her, turned her hair molten. She didn't look at him as she said, her voice low and strained, "Just because I saw you naked this morning and just stood there and stared at you, my little heart filled with lust, you think you've got to marry me? That doesn't make any sense, Ramsey. I know what men look like. I'll admit that you look the best of all the men I've ever seen—"

"And how many does that make exactly?"

"Two."

"You've made my day."

"Two, counting you."

"I take it back."

"Don't be ridiculous. I've seen lots of pictures, movies with men very nearly nude. You're as good-looking as the best of them, and you surely know it, you're not blind." She stopped suddenly, as if aware in that instant of what was coming unbidden out of her mouth. She pursed her lips, like a pissed-off grade-school teacher. "Just because I can still see you clearly in my head, it won't do to speak about you at any more length. No, I didn't mean to use that exact word. It was a slip of the tongue. Yes, enough about your body."

That was probably a good thing since he was getting hard and they were in public, and he wanted to laugh. "Okay, that's fine, at least for now. Incidentally, I didn't ask you to marry me because you happened to walk in on me. I was thinking it's kind of surprising that it hadn't happened before. Do you think if the shoe had been on the other foot, so to speak, you would have felt compelled to propose to me?"

"Oh, goodness. I would have sunk into the floor. I'm not beautiful like you, Ramsey. I'm so skinny."

He looked at her face, at her glorious hair, and said, "Don't you ever speak ill of yourself again. It really pisses me off."

She swallowed, looked down at her feet. "It's the truth."

"Bullshit." He looked back at the sun, getting lower now. He said, not looking at her, "Sit down. I don't want you to miss this."

"Then you shouldn't have said what you said at such a precious moment. It beat out the setting sun for sheer drama."

"I thought putting the two precious moments together was a bang-up idea."

Molly looked at Emma, who was playing now with the two children, the parents looking on. Molly waved to them. The woman waved back.

She sat back down, slowly, carefully, as if she were wearing a dress that he could look up if she wasn't careful. She sat Indian style, her palms flattened on her thighs. Her fingernails were short, blunt, like his. She was wearing black jeans and black half-boots. Her vivid yellow windbreaker was billowing out behind her as the stiff offshore early-evening winds swept in.

She didn't look at him, just stared at that bright red sun that was close enough to the water now to turn it a gleaming golden red. "Have you ever been married before, Ramsey?"

Getting down to it now, he thought. "Yes, when I was twenty-two and starting law school."

Her voice cynical, she said, "You knocked her up?"

"Nope. She was a marine, had just finished her basic training and was going to be shipped out to some god-awful place in Africa. We wanted to be married before she left."

"What happened?"

"We did well together. She was the one always on the road, off to someplace I'd never heard of, but it worked out okay. She wanted to wait on kids and I was agreeable. Then it was all over." He found his body tensing, becoming clammy, as it had that day he'd walked out of the courtroom, elated because he'd just won an important case, only to have one man and one woman, both in uniform, waiting for him. He'd known, oh yes, he'd known in that instant that Susan was dead.

"She was killed when her helicopter crashed in the Kuwaiti desert at the end of the Gulf War in ninety-one. She would have shipped home the very next week."

"I'm sorry," Molly said, "I'm so very sorry."

"Shit happens."

She laid her hand on his arm. "No, don't act like a man about it."

There was clean anger in his voice as he turned to her. "Why not? At least now I can sound all flippant and macho, but for a very long time I couldn't even say her name without stuttering or bawling. And you, of all people, Molly, know that shit does happen."

She didn't understand how he'd felt, given her own experience with marriage. She said, "You must have loved her very much."

"Yes, but Susan died a long time ago, Molly. Fact of the matter was that we didn't really know each other all that well. She was gone too much of the time. When she was home, it was nonstop sex until it was time for her to leave again. We talked, sure, but for the life of me, I can't remember many conversations. And, as I said, I know more about you than I did her. For example, I don't remember how she squeezed a tube of toothpaste, whereas I know that you flatten the tube in the middle. I don't know what kind of nightwear Susan really preferred. You love floaty silk nightgowns. I saw you rubbing the one you couldn't help but pack, you loved it so much. But with me around you wear only those cotton jobs that start at your throat and end at your toes. I never knew what her favorite breakfast was. You like to eat Grape-Nuts unless you're on the run—and I do mean that literally. She liked my body, she told me that whenever we were together, but I can't remember that she ever looked at me the way you did this morning. You licked your chops, Molly. I don't think you once got up to my face. I felt like a sex god. It was great."

"Isn't that strange? To be married for nearly three years and not really know your mate very well?"

He stared at the sun again, then over at Emma. He saw her laugh at something one of the kids said. After the man had taken her off the beach nearly right under his nose, he automatically checked on her every fifteen seconds, or less. Usually it was less, especially after San Francisco.

"Maybe, but I never knew Louey all that well either. Like Susan, he was gone most of the time. Unlike Susan, when he was home, he was usually a jerk." She sighed. "Louey's dead. It's just over a week. It seems much longer. Goodness, it feels as if I've known you forever."

"That's because we got thrown together in the same pot with the lid plunked down and lots of heat. No time-outs."

"I guess so." She studied his face in that special way she had, as if she were going to photograph him. "You're really meticulous with the toothpaste. You roll it up carefully from the bottom. When you're alone, do you sleep nude?"

"Most of the time."

"Listen, Ramsey, my father's a big-time crook and you're a federal judge."

"I deal all right with your father. I prefer dealing with your stepmama, but hey, I can make do."

She grinned at him. "Eve's something else, isn't she?"

"Yeah. Most of the time when I was around her, I would have sworn that she married your dad for his big bucks and power. Then, at other times, I'd be willing to swear that it was something else entirely." He shrugged. "Maybe we'll find out someday what she's all about."

"My father treats her like dirt."

"He does have that problem with women. But again, I have this gut feeling things are going to change." He looked over at Emma. She had started rigging up a kite with the other kids, the father showing them what to do. He smiled. Emma knew exactly what to do. Molly had taught her and done a really good job of it. He saw her then, flying her dragon kite in the meadow by the cabin. And then those men had come with their guns. It seemed an eon ago, another Ramsey Hunt. He shook himself. "Let's get back to us, Molly. There's nothing either of us can do about our families. We'll cope."

"Tell me about yours."

"My father's a dentist. First thing he'll do when he meets you is check your mouth, the way they do with horses. Because you've got great teeth, he'll probably fall in love with you on the spot. My old man's easy that way. Give him a beautiful tooth and he's in ecstasy.

"As for my mom, she's a retired schoolteacher, high-school history. I remember she cried when I announced I was going to law school. She believes all lawyers should be shot. She only forgave me when I told her I wanted to be one of the good guys. She approved of the U.S. Attorney's office. She still tells me all the lawyer jokes though."

"What about when you went back out to be a trial lawyer."

He ducked his head. "It was only for a year and a half. I hated it."

"So?"

"I didn't tell her. Since I'm a judge now, she treats me like I'm on the Supreme Court and asks me all sorts of questions about Sandra Day O'Connor and Ruth Bader Ginsburg, both of whom I've met only once, but that's about all. A neat woman, my mom. Uh, she doesn't look a thing like Eve. I also have two older brothers. One's career army, a two-star general, three kids. The other brother, Tony, is a political speechwriter. Tony's an okay guy, lives in Washington, D.C., nice wife, two kids, neither of whom takes drugs or is in jail."

He looked over at Emma at exactly the same time Molly did. Their eyes met. They smiled at each other.

"It will probably be a habit of a lifetime," Molly said, "checking on Emma. I'll probably have my antennae up when she's a little old lady."

"Do you want more kids, Molly?"

"Maybe. Two would be nice, maybe three. I like kids."

He realized he'd been holding his breath. He let it out and laughed. "Just the number I had in mind. I'm thirty-four. That's really young to be appointed to a judgeship, but as for my biological clock, it's running out fast. I heard it isn't good for a guy to father kids after he's forty. The risks are too great."

She poked his leg. "You mean you'll be too paunchy and too run-down to keep up with them?"

He leaned over, took her chin in his hand, and kissed her mouth. He pulled back, studying her face. "You've also got beautiful eyes. They're a bit on the vague side right now and I do like that."

They heard applause. They both jerked around to see Emma running away from the cliffs, her leprechaun kite high in the air. She was letting out the string perfectly, just as Molly had taught her. She was laughing, the wind whipping her hair, as the crimson shadow of the sun floated above the water before disappearing.

He looked at Molly then back at Emma. The look on his face was tender, filled with quiet joy. He said, not looking back at her, "We're both smart. We can work out any problems. Let's do it."

"Could you kiss me again, Ramsey?"

"My pleasure." He kissed her a bit longer this time, but he didn't let it get out of hand. He tasted her, nibbled on her bottom lip, wished she'd open her mouth, just a little bit. On the other hand, it probably wouldn't be smart to have his tongue in her mouth here on the Cliffs of Moher with Emma flying a leprechaun kite not thirty feet away. He pulled back. He wanted her a whole lot, maybe more than he'd ever wanted any woman before. The fact was, he really couldn't remember now what he'd felt like when he'd been with Susan. She was in the past, a past that held dear memories, a past that was becoming more blurred each day that passed with

Molly and Emma. He'd found a new focus, new feelings that were sometimes overwhelming they were so rich and powerful. He kissed her again, lightly, just a recognition kiss, and it was there, this knowing of each other. He smiled at her and said nothing, wondering what she was thinking.

Molly knew why he wanted to marry her, knew it, and accepted it. He wanted Emma. To get her, he had to make Mom part of the deal. She licked her bottom lip where he'd nipped her, saying, "You just want to keep feeling like a sex god."

He loved the humor in her, coming so seldom because life was so excessively grim. It made it all the more precious. He could look forward to her laughter for the rest of his life, he hoped, if she married him. "How'd you know?"

She looked at him a long time, studying his face, again as if she were setting her camera shot. She cocked her head to one side. "Sex is part of things. I know you like my hair, you even like my eyes. But I'm skinny, you know that. Will you mind having sex with me?"

He said, never looking away from those very nice eyes of hers, "I know it's expected, so I'll try."

She wanted to run her hand up his thigh but instead, she laughed, then almost immediately sobered. "What about Emma?"

"I guess at first we'll have to sneak around, that, or abstain for the time being. I spoke to Dr. Loo about Emma needing to sleep in the same room with either or both of us, that or in the same bed, and she said not to worry. She said of course it wasn't a good idea to have kids sleeping with their parents as a regular thing, but this was different. She said Emma would probably be the one to break away when she was ready. So, Molly, will you marry me?"

Molly got to her feet, dusting off her bottom with her hands. "It looks like the family is about ready to leave. Let's go get Emma and tell her she's going to have a new daddy." She started walking away, then said over her shoulder, a big grin on her face, "Yeah, I'll put you out of your misery, Judge Hunt."

"Say it," he called after her, raising his deep voice loud enough for several people to hear him and turn to look at Molly. "I want to hear you say the words."

She knew people were staring and listening and she laughed, shaking her head. She called out, "I'll marry you. It would be my pleasure to marry you."

There was some applause and a couple of groans from some men, who got punched by their wives.

"That sounds wonderful," he said, walking to stand beside her. "It sounds more than wonderful. We'll be a family for real now. Yes, I quite like that." He looked over at Emma and her new friends. "I think that man is going to give Emma the leprechaun kite. Let's go thank them for watching her." He stopped then, turned, and brought her against him. "Did I ever tell you that you're the most beautiful woman I've ever known? That you've even gotten more beautiful each added day I know you?"

"No. You only told me I had beautiful hair."

"That, too. That's your crowning glory, I'll admit it." He raised his hand and curled a thick strand around his finger. He smiled at her. "Feels like springy silk. Yeah, you're beautiful. I think every skinny little bone in your body is beautiful."

He looked over at Emma, who was panting from her run, dragging the kite behind her, looking tired and pleased. "You're sure you like me enough, Molly?"

"I like you enough." She looked down, scuffing the toe of her black boot in the dirt. She said then, making his eyes nearly cross, as she looked back up at him through her lashes, "I particularly like your body."

She thought for a moment that he was going to grab her, and she wouldn't have minded, but he didn't. He just smiled and said, "Excellent. That's a really good start. Let's get married, Molly, as soon as we get back home. We can stop off in Nevada. Let's have the honeymoon before the wedding. What do you think?"

What was love anyway? she thought, as she slowly nodded.

They didn't have the opportunity either to honeymoon in Ireland or to tell Emma that she was getting a new daddy. Waiting for them at the reception desk at Dromoland Castle were two phone messages and a fax from Savich.

THEY flew from Shannon to Chicago O'Hare in Business Class, in the middle section that holds three seats, putting Emma between them. She slept most of the way, propped up on three pillows on Ramsey's armrest, covered with a blanket, holding her piano close, the top keys sticking out from beneath the blanket. The piano had sat in the corner of their suite, seemingly forgotten by Emma, until the phone call had come, her mother had paled, Ramsey had cursed quietly, and they'd started packing quickly.

Molly saw that the shoelace from one of Emma's Nike sneakers was dangling. She stared at it, then finally reached down and simply pulled the sneaker off. She had a plaid sock on her small foot. Molly had washed out the pair the night before.

They'd said very little. Life had spun out of control again. Molly felt numb, nothing else, just a numb blankness that had taken over both her brain and her body. She supposed she should be grateful for it.

Finally, Molly said quietly, so as not to awaken Emma, "I'm having a hard time accepting it. I keep thinking it's a mistake, that someone really screwed up, that Eve was utterly wrong."

"I know."

"Will they get Rule Shaker now?"

"I don't know. We'll find out exactly what happened when we get to Chicago. Listen, your father's not dead yet. God knows how he's managed to survive so far, but he has. That's a good sign."

"Maybe he's already been able to tell the cops who shot him." She stopped, staring at the blank movie screen directly in front of them. "Or maybe by now it's over and he's dead."

Ramsey started to pick up the phone on the armrest. "No," she said, placing her hand over his. "No. I don't want to know, not yet. For the moment, I want to think you're right. He's told the cops who shot him. It will all be over by the time we arrive at O'Hare."

But Ramsey knew this wasn't likely. In fact it was well nigh impossible. He said quietly, "Remember I told you it was a distance shot, from a good seventy-five yards away, given the trajectory. The assassin probably fired from the roof of the four-story building across the street. Mason never saw his attacker. Savich said the preliminary ballistics report was that the bullet, a heavy 7.62 mm, was from a sniping rifle, like a SIG-Sauer SSG2000. That's a popular military rifle." He didn't tell her that the bullet had ripped through Mason Lord's chest, hurling him into a car parked at the curb. The impact had smashed the driver's-side window of a new blue Buick Riviera.

"Gunther was just a single step in front of your father. He wasn't touched."

Emma groaned in her sleep. Ramsey reached over and gently began to rub her shoulders and back. She pushed against his hand, then quieted.

"We had to tell her. She's not stupid."

"Yes, I know. This is her escape," Ramsey said, his voice pitched even lower than before. "First chance we have, let's call Dr. Loo again."

"He's not dead, Ramsey."

Ramsey didn't say anything. He kept lightly rubbing Emma's back. He leaned his head back against the headrest and closed his eyes. They'd just gotten over the jet lag of flying to Ireland when they'd gotten word. Now they'd get to do it all over again.

He wanted to get married.

He wanted Emma to know he'd always be with her, as in forever, as in she was his now. The woman who would be his wife as soon as it could be managed was two feet away from him. He didn't know what to say to her either. He wondered what the hell was going to happen now.

"Ramsey?"

"Yes, Molly?"

"We're going to have to wait until things are sorted out."

He looked over at her and said, "Well, hell."

TWENTY-NINE

Detective O'Connor was waiting for them at the Lord mansion. Miles was there, but no one else. Gunther and Mrs. Lord, Miles told them at the front door, were at the hospital. "Do come in. Mr. Lord is holding his own. He's not out of the woods yet, but he's holding steady. I'm sorry, Molly."

"Thanks, Miles. This is hard on everyone. Thanks for being here to hold down the fort."

"Hello, Judge Hunt, Mrs. Santera," Detective O'Connor said, stepping out of the living room and walking toward them. "I'm sorry you had to come back to this. It's unexpected. No one quite knows what to make of things. I hope you don't mind, Mrs. Santera, that I waited for you here?"

"No, Detective, not at all." Molly went down on her haunches in front of Emma. "You want to go with Miles to the kitchen and have a goodie to eat?"

"I made some chocolate-chip cookies just for you, Emma," Miles said. "They're still warm, right out of the oven."

Emma gave her mother a long, patient look. There was such weariness in her eyes that Molly wanted to fold her up against her and cry. "Your grandfather is in the hospital, Emma. He was hurt. We told you that. Now Detective O'Connor needs to speak to Ramsey and me. He wants to know what we think about things."

"All right, Mama, I'll go with Mr. Miles."

"Thanks, Em. I'll be in to see you soon. I want one of those cookies myself."

She got another long-suffering look. She didn't get back to her feet until Miles had taken Emma's hand in his and they were walking toward the kitchen, Emma holding her piano close against her chest. She rose and sighed. "Do come into the living room, Detective."

"It was verified," Detective O'Connor said. "The bullet was a 7.62 mm sniping round." He turned toward Ramsey. "You probably know that this bullet is heavier, to give it more energy and a flatter trajectory. That's particularly important over a long distance."

"Any sign of the shooter?"

"We went to the Ames Building, to the roof, which is the top of the fourth floor. We found a couple of cigarette butts, a to-go coffee container, and, wonder of wonders, there was this small wet spot."

Molly blinked at the detective. "Wet spot? Why is that a wonder?"

"He spit, Mrs. Santera. The shooter spit. That means DNA, if we're lucky. That means if and when we catch the guy, we'll have indisputable proof that he's guilty. The forensics folks think he's a smoker with a bad hacking cough. His vices might end up bringing him down.

"Since Mason Lord is a very powerful man, despite his more questionable associations and business practices, this case is very high profile. The press is starting to understand there isn't much to see around here. But they'll start showing up again at dawn, you can count on it. I'm glad you made it back so early. They'll find out soon enough that you're back, Judge Hunt."

"What do the doctors say about Mason's condition?"

Detective O'Connor checked his watch. "It's nearly midnight. I told his surgeon that you'd be arriving about now. He said you could call and he'd give you the latest word."

Detective O'Connor pulled out his cell phone and dialed. After five minutes of being sent from one person to the next, he handed the phone to Molly.

Ramsey watched her face as she took in what was being said to her. Her expression didn't change. That was odd. He watched her press the *Off* button, then hand the phone back to Detective O'Connor.

"He's alive. The surgeon, Dr. Bigliotti, says he's got a fifty-fifty chance—if, that is, he manages to survive the night. He already woke up." She looked at Detective O'Connor. "He whispered to the officer sitting next to his bed that Louey Santera shot him."

"You're kidding," Detective O'Connor said. "He must have been out of his head, what with the drugs."

"Yes, that's what Dr. Bigliotti said. My father hasn't said anything more. Dr. Bigliotti also said the media was all over him personally and the hospital in general. One of the night nurses nabbed a reporter who was carrying around a mop—as a disguise, I suppose—trying to find Mason Lord's room."

"Do you guys have any ideas? Any guesses that might help?"

Molly and Ramsey just looked at him. He knew defeat when he saw it.

THE hiss of the regulator was obscenely loud in the momentary quiet of the ICU at Chicago Memorial on Jefferson, the closest trauma center available when her father had been shot down in the street. Molly looked down at her father's white face, the tubes in his mouth and nose, the lines running into both arms, the bag emptying his bladder hanging from the side of the hospital bed. One officer sat not six inches away from him, a recorder on his lap, holding a police procedural mystery novel in his right hand. He nodded to them, then did a double take when he saw Ramsey. He nodded again, this time, his head going lower, a sign of excessive respect, Molly thought, to Ramsey.

The ICU was huge, impersonal, filled with high-tech equipment. There were six other patients, with just curtains around their beds, and they weren't quiet. Moans of pain mixed with that damnable hissing sound, low voices of relatives speaking to patients, curses from the bed in the far corner, a nurse's hurrying footsteps.

Her father was as still as death. If it weren't for the machine, he would be dead. She lightly touched her palm to his cheek. His skin felt slack and clammy.

She realized in that moment that she wanted him to live. No matter what was true, he was her father. She wanted him to live. The nurse motioned them to leave after five minutes.

In the corridor, Molly said to Detective O'Connor, "Has anyone called my mother? She lives in Italy."

He looked at her blankly, scratched his ear, and shook his head. "Can't say anyone has, Mrs. Santera."

"I'll do it then when we get back home." It was nearly two o'clock in the morning. Molly had wanted to come, to see his face, just to see for herself that he was alive. Life was there, huddling deep inside her father, barely.

There was no traffic on the drive back to Oak Park. Ramsey kept a hard focus on the road in front of him. He was nearly cross-eyed with fatigue.

Even if they'd managed to get married, he was so tired right now, he doubted he could even stay awake long enough to kiss Molly's ear, even if she offered her ear to him to kiss. She was in pretty bad shape herself.

When they finally drove to the gates of the Lord mansion, they saw a man jump from a dark car just up the road. A reporter.

"Just what we needed," Ramsey said, and quickly called out to the guard in the security box at the gate. "It's Judge Hunt, open the gates, quickly. A reporter is coming."

"Putrid little maggots," the guard snarled, and got the gate open before the reporter got to the rear end of the car.

"Wait!" the reporter yelled, but Ramsey roared through the open gate. The reporter started through, then saw the wild maniacal grin on the security guard's face in the lighted booth as the huge gates began to swing shut.

He stepped back, cursing. "Hey, haven't you heard of the First Amendment? You jerk!"

The security guard, still grinning like a mad scientist, said over the loudspeaker, "Sure, you little shit, and Prince Charles is a Tampax."

Ramsey heard that. It made no sense at all. It all of a sudden seemed hilarious. He began to laugh. Molly joined him. They walked into the house, holding hands, laughing their heads off.

"Oh, dear," Miles said.

BOTH Miles and Gunther had alibis. Warren O'Dell also had an alibi. So did Eve Lord. Of all things, three of her friends had come over for a visit.

They'd been drinking iced tea by the swimming pool at the time of Mason Lord's shooting.

The media had exploded. Since Eve was young, beautiful, extravagantly rich, she garnered immense sympathy and support, bolstered by the media, who always wallowed in beauty and money, particularly if it was possibly tragic beauty.

Molly's mother had expressed sympathy, but wasn't about to fly back to the U.S. "Why ever should I, my dear? I have no desire to hold his limp hand or let the paparazzi leap out of bushes at me. Just keep me informed, Molly."

Not unexpected, Molly thought, given that the new Mrs. Lord was young enough to be her daughter, and that her ex-husband hadn't been in her life for a good number of years.

Mason Lord, who lay unconscious, his life in the balance, was nearly forgotten. The attention was on the beautiful young wife, who just might at any moment become a widow. But then again, to be fair, what reporter wanted to risk his own neck questioning the background of Mason Lord?

He survived that night. They'd nearly lost him once, but they'd been able to control his blood pressure with a medication dripping into his IV, and he seemed stable. Molly and Ramsey hadn't gone back that morning, staying with Emma and watching as Eve Lord negotiated her way through the press when she visited her husband, all in glorious color on a special news bulletin on all three major local stations.

"I wish I had a clue as to what she was thinking," Molly said.

"So does Detective O'Connor," Ramsey said. He turned to see Emma walking slowly into the living room. "Hi, Em," Molly said. "Come on in and tell us what Miles is making for lunch."

Emma just stood there, holding her piano against her, looking bewildered. "Mama, when can we go home?"

Home, Molly thought. Which home?

"Where would you like to go?" Ramsey asked. He patted his knee. Emma went to him instantly. She carefully set her piano down on the floor beside the sofa and let him lift her onto his legs.

"Where?" he asked again.

"Home," Emma said. "To San Francisco."

"Ah," Ramsey said. "You got it right. What would you say, Em, if your mom and I were to get married?"

She turned to look up at him. She slowly raised her hand to lightly stroke his cheek. She said with all a child's appalling candor, "My daddy just died, Ramsey. He wasn't with us much, but he was my daddy."

"Yes, he was. He'll always be your daddy."

"I don't think so," Emma said then. She leaned against his chest, her cheek against his shoulder. "I can't take the chance, Ramsey, I just can't."

"What chance, sweetheart?"

"If you married Mama, someone might blow you up too."

"Oh, Emma," he said, and hugged her tightly against him. "No one's going to hurt me, no one."

"They already did. You got shot in the leg at the cabin and when my daddy blew up your back got hurt, too."

"Just minor stuff. A big guy like me can take lots of minor stuff. Don't worry, Em. Please."

She leaned down to pick up her piano.

Her security blanket, he thought, wondering what the hell to do. "You know something, Emma?"

She lightly stroked her finger on middle C, not looking at him. Afraid to look at him, he thought.

"I think when we're all a family and everything's okay again, we're going back to Ireland. Shall we all spend our honeymoon at Bunratty Castle?"

She gave him a small smile. She turned away from her piano and pressed herself against his chest. "I don't know, Ramsey. Will Mama be happy?"

"I can make her delirious, just ask her."

Emma raised her head and stared at her mother. "Mama, do you think we can keep Ramsey safe?"

This was a wallop in the gut, Molly thought, smiling at her daughter, whose piano was slipping off Ramsey's lap. She nodded. "Yes, I think we can keep him safe. You see, Em, he's right. He's big and strong. We're not as strong as he is, so we'll be thinking more. We'll be the brains of the operation. Yes, we'll keep him safe."

Emma nodded slowly. "Who shot Grandfather?"

"We don't know yet," Molly said. "But he's alive, Em, and they're taking care of him at the hospital."

"Look at the time," Ramsey said. "We've got to get going or we'll miss your appointment with Dr. Loo."

"I hope we can avoid the media," Molly said, worry lacing her voice as she looked down at Emma.

They did manage to lose the press, and in Dr. Eleanor Loo's office thirty minutes later, Emma said, "Dr. Loo, Ramsey and my mom are going to get married. What do you think?"

"I think," Eleanor Loo said, fascinated, "that I need to have my secretary go buy us a bottle of champagne. You, Emma, can have a Sprite, is that all right?"

"I'd rather have a Dr Pepper, Dr. Loo."

"That's great." Dr. Loo got on her phone for a moment, then turned back. "In half an hour, we'll have a toast. Congratulations to both of you. Now, Emma, tell me why you're worried."

"Because Ramsey could get killed like my daddy."

"That's true," Dr. Loo said slowly. "But you see, Emma, anything can happen to anybody in the world at any time. I'll never forget when Princess Diana died so tragically. I'll never forget the shock of it, the realization that none of us has any guarantees on anything. Life is one day at a time and trying to enjoy each day we're given. You've got to discover the knack for doing that. Do you understand?"

"That was different," Emma said. "Bad people are after us. It isn't just bad luck."

"You understand all too well," Dr. Loo said. "Okay, let's look at it this way. Ramsey and your mom want to give you a home. They want the three of you to be a family. They love you and want you to know that they'll always be there for you."

Emma sighed. She looked for a very long time at Ramsey, saying nothing, just studying him. Then she looked at her mother. Then, she turned back to Dr. Loo, and smiled. "I think Ramsey will make me a good papa. He already loves me bunches."

"He does, does he?"

"Yes. He went crazy in San Francisco when that bad man grabbed me again."

Molly had told Dr. Loo on the phone what had happened on the beach.

"Were you scared?"

"Yes, but it was over so fast. Ramsey said I saved myself again."

"What did you do?"

"The man hit me real hard, but I stayed awake. I bit him through his shirt, in the side. He's kind of fat around his stomach. I bit him real deep. He jerked and I got unburied, by his coat. Ramsey saw me and the man had to drop me." She turned to Ramsey. "I wish you could have caught him."

"Me too, kiddo."

Dr. Loo spoke alone to Emma for a while and then they drank champagne, Emma drank her Dr. Pepper, and they all accepted congratulations from the staff there and two waiting patients.

One of the patients, an old man with a severe eye twitch, said, "I saw a blurred photo of you, Judge, in one of the rags. You were hugging a little girl."

"No," Emma said loudly, holding her piano really hard to her chest, "he was hugging *me*. He was upset."

"NO. I didn't see anyone," Mason Lord said to Detective O'Connor. He paused, sucking in his breath with a sudden twinge of pain. He shot a hit of morphine into his vein by pressing the medication button.

Detective O'Connor waited until he saw the pain clear from Lord's eyes. "No shadows, no warning, nothing?"

"No. Gunther and I were just coming from a friend's office. We'd had a little chat with him. A good fellow, a politician."

"His name, sir?"

"State Senator Quentin Kordie. Don't worry about him, Detective, he wouldn't try to shoot me. We're simply friends, that's all."

"Very well. Now, sir, who knew where you would be?"

It was obvious to Molly that her father had thought about that. She hated the calculation in his eyes, the drawing of pain as he sorted again through the few people he believed had known where he would be at that particular time.

Finally, Mason said, "A number of people knew, but, of course, only people in my organization." He paused, pumped another hit of morphine into his vein, and said, "If I've got a traitor in my midst, I'll deal with it, Detective."

"No, Mr. Lord, this is a police matter. It's called attempted murder."

"Then you know who's behind it, Detective. Rule Shaker." He shook his head in bewilderment. "He's never been frankly stupid before. The moron."

Detective O'Connor rose from his chair. "It seems to me, Mr. Lord, that if indeed Mr. Shaker was a moron and did try to kill you, then you've got a big problem. You seem to be well protected for the moment. Naturally, I assume that Rule Shaker has heard that you're still alive. If you're right, I can imagine what he's saying right now."

RULE Shaker wasn't saying anything. He was standing close to the huge glass window in his office that looked out over an endless stretch of desert. He hadn't ever wanted a view of Las Vegas. He lived in a city of kitsch. He wasn't about to look at it unless he had to.

The desert was clean, the air pure, so hot that all life sheltered during the hottest part of the day. Including people. He couldn't see a single soul in that vast expanse. He turned slowly as Murdock said, "Rudy's still hanging out at that motel in Oak Park, waiting for orders."

"Let him continue to wait. I hear that Lord is getting stronger every day in that hospital. He's going to live."

"That's the word," Murdock said, uncrossing his legs. He'd gained weight since he'd gotten back from Germany. He hadn't liked following Louey Santera around, but that's what Mr. Shaker had ordered him to do and that's what he'd done. Now he was home and could eat all the KFC he'd missed in Germany. He'd put on six pounds since he'd returned.

"Is there anything you'd like me to do, sir?"

"I'm thinking about it, Murdock. For the moment, we'll just let him lie in his bed, feel lots of pain, and think about his transgressions."

"Mason Lord doesn't believe in transgressions," Murdock said. He studied his boss, the man who'd taken him out of the street six years before and trained him to be one of his forward men. Yes, he was one of the FM now, a group everyone important had heard of. He was respected and admired. He should get the six pounds off.

Mr. Shaker wasn't tall and aristocratic-looking like Mason Lord. Nature had shortchanged him, topping him off at a mere five foot seven inches. But he was a fit little man, hard and lean. He dressed beautifully, mostly in handmade English suits from Savile Row. But he was cursed with a swarthy complexion, flat black glass for eyes, scary eyes that made him look like a Middle Eastern terrorist or a religious fundamentalist, and a five-o'-clock shadow that started at nine o'clock in the morning. Actually, he looked like the Hollywood stereotype of exactly what he was: a crime boss. For all that, the man had more women than he could reasonably keep up with. Murdock suspected it was danger that brought the women. For all his smallness, Shaker looked like danger. He'd heard that Shaker had serviced two women the night before, and he was fifty-eight years old. Amazing.

Service. Murdock liked that word. He wished he could service women the way Mr. Shaker did. Maybe if he lost the six pounds, they'd come around him a little more here the way they had in Germany. Of course they'd wanted to use him to get close to Louey Santera, the little slime.

"He believes in transgressions, all right," Rule Shaker said. "Just not in his own. Let's just wait and see. Tell Rudy to keep alert. I'm going to have my helicopter fly out over the desert now. It's time to scatter Melissa's ashes."

"That's what she wanted, sir?"

Rule Shaker said, "Melissa was twenty-three. She didn't even know there was such a thing as death."

THIRTY

There were six bodyguards on duty around the clock, three shifts, one man always in the hospital room with Mason Lord and another outside his door. Mason Lord didn't trust the cops to do the job.

He said to Detective O'Connor, "If I'm not paying someone, then I can't be sure he's working for me."

"Fine by me," Detective O'Connor said. "It'll save the taxpayers some money. In Chicago, the good Lord knows they need a break."

The mainstream media finally got bored and left, but some paparazzi, hoping for another strike on Mason Lord, stayed on speculation of blood and gore. They were like a plague of locusts only not as benign, said one of the hospital administrators. They camped out at the Lord mansion, too. One of them got a shot of Emma sitting in the shade of a big rhododendron bush in the garden of the estate, playing her piano. It was taken from a goodly distance, a bit on the blurred side, from magnification, but it was still clearly Emma. She'd been labeled as the *Granddaughter of Crime Lord.*

When Mason Lord saw the photo, he said quietly to Gunther, "How clever the play on words is. Isn't it odd? It's this photo that has broken my patience, my indifference. Get the name of the paparazzo who took the picture."

JUST after lunch that day, Eve Lord came out of the living room into the grand foyer to hear Ramsey say to Molly, "There's no reason to stay longer. Your father is over the worst. We all know who likely shot him and there's not a thing we can do about it. As to the actual person who pulled the trigger, the cops are on it. Chances are slim we'll ever know. This could mean that the violence will escalate. I don't want us here if it does, particularly Emma. Let's get married. Let's go home."

And Molly, frumpy plain Molly with her wild red hair and too-skinny body, gazed up at the big man whom Eve would jump in a New York minute. Stared up at him like she wanted to eat him, and she probably did. Then she laughed and jumped into his arms. She clearly caught him off guard, but he was fast, managing to catch her and bring her tightly against his chest, his arms locked around her. She wrapped her legs around his waist. Then he laughed and swung her around. "Home," she said, kissing him once, twice, a half dozen more times. "I like the sound of that."

Slowly, he slid her down the front of his body. When she was standing, staring up at him, laughing, he leaned down and kissed her mouth. Molly's hands were on his shirt. She looked ready to rip it off him.

Eve cleared her throat. "I see there's more going on here than a little friendship."

"Yes," Ramsey said, lifting his head, releasing Molly slowly. The taste of her was still fresh, still drawing on him, the memory of her body was still warm against him. "You can congratulate us, Eve. Molly and I are going to be married." They hadn't told her before. It felt a bit on the indecent side to tell that to a woman who'd nearly been made a widow.

"Congratulations," Eve said. She looked down at Molly's waistline. "You pregnant already?"

"No, I'm not," Molly said. "Getting in that condition would be kind of hard, what with Emma sleeping in the same room, don't you think?"

"I would say that in my experience, men always find a way. My former fiancé nailed me once in the coat closet with his family not six feet away."

Ramsey laughed. "Then he deserves to be a former." He hugged Molly to his side. "Is Emma eating chocolate-chip cookies in Miles's kitchen?"

Eve pulled on soft pale cream leather gloves that matched her silk dress. "Not chocolate chip, but her new favorite—peanut butter. Mrs. Lopez was chattering about it. I'm going to see your father, Molly. Does he know about this?"

"Yes, we told him last night."

"I see. So I'm the last to know. Will you two be here when I get back?"

"Depends," Ramsey said. "You want to bring back something to celebrate?"

"Sure," Eve Lord said, then called out, "Gunther, I'm ready!"

IN the *Chicago Sun-Times*, on the bottom of page ten of Section A, there was brief mention of a man who had been found just off Highway 88 between Mooseheart and Aurora by a passing motorist. The man had been beaten severely, but was expected, in time, to make a full recovery. His cameras had been crushed and left beside him. The newspaper called him a freelance photographer, but bottom line, what he was, was a paparazzo.

"I think we should pack our meager belongings, grab Emma, and hop a plane to Reno. I was thinking Las Vegas, but Rule Shaker's there, and I can't quite handle getting married anywhere near to where he is. I don't want any more magazines or tabloids with pictures of Emma. She saw the one in the *National Informer*. She'd made out some of the words before I managed to get it away from her. I pray she hadn't gotten to the part about her playing the piano as well as her murdered father, Louey Santera. Can you begin to imagine the field day the media will have if we get married either here or in Harrisburg at my folks' place? They always find out, no matter how careful you are."

"Oh, God!" Miles came running out of the kitchen, a dishcloth in his hands. "Thank God you're both here. I don't believe this. Somebody tried to kill your daddy again, Molly. Oh God. Where's Gunther? Where's Mrs. Lord?"

"Is he all right, Miles?"

"Yes, he is. That was one of the guards we hired to protect him in the hospital. The guy fired from the building across the way—a good hundred and fifty yards—right through the window. He wounded a nurse who was taking your father's blood pressure."

"Is the nurse all right?" Molly asked.

"Took off a lot of her right ear; she bled all over everything, which made everyone believe that your father had been shot, but yeah, she's fine."

Ramsey squeezed Molly's hand. "I guess we'd better get to the hospital. Miles, will you make certain Emma is never out of your sight?"

"No problem, Ramsey." He'd been wringing his hands, but now at the mention of Emma, her need to be protected, he instantly calmed down. By the time Ramsey and Molly were out the front door, Miles had pulled himself together. Emma stood beside him. He was holding her hand.

Detective O'Connor from Oak Park and two detectives from the CPD were in Mason Lord's room when they arrived.

"Show them in," Detective O'Connor said. Introductions were made quickly. Miles was right. There was blood everywhere.

"Ears bleed like stink," one of the CPD detectives said. He pulled on his own ear and Molly realized the bottom part was gone. He'd never be able to wear pierced earrings. She nearly laughed. She was losing it.

She slipped her hand around Ramsey's. He looked at her briefly, saw her too-bright eyes, and slowly, very slowly, pulled her closer. "It's all right," he said quietly, his mouth nearly touching the top of her head. "It will be fine. Breathe slowly, that's it."

The hospital window was shattered. Two technicians were busy very carefully extracting the bullet from the wall about ten inches off the floor. The woman was using tweezers.

Detective O'Connor looked tired and harassed, but that wasn't anything new. She felt tension between him and the other cops. He told them in his concise way, "Nurse Thomas was standing right next to your father, taking his blood pressure. Suddenly he seemed to weaken and fall back against the pillow. Nurse Thomas immediately leaned over him, holding on to him, when the shooter fired. If your father hadn't gotten suddenly weak, if the nurse hadn't pressed him down even more, shielded him, all those things, then the chances are good that your father would have gone down this time, Mrs. Santera. At the very least he would have been wounded. The bullet went through Nurse Thomas's earlobe, downward. The bullet slammed into the wall less than a foot above the floor."

Molly leaned over her father. "Dad, Ramsey and I are here. You're all right, thank God."

"Yes," Mason said. "I'm fine, Molly. Actually, I've got to be the luckiest bastard in Chicago. As for Nurse Thomas, I'm going to cut her a nice check for her bravery."

They turned to see the technician holding up the bullet. "It's fairly intact," she called out. "Enough for identification."

"Excellent," one of the Chicago detectives said. "We'll do a comparison between this one and the one they found on the scene over on Jefferson after Mr. Lord was shot. Are you Judge Ramsey Hunt?"

"Yes," Ramsey said. "It seems likely the bullets will match, but unfortunately it won't tell us anything else."

"At least we'll verify that we've got just one perp here," Detective O'Connor said.

Molly, who was staring at that smashed window, said, "He blew out the window. I remember all of us mentioned the possibility, but the closest building is so far away."

"I'm not blaming Gunther," Mason said, the first words he'd spoken in a good ten minutes. There were seven people in the room, most of them talking. The instant he spoke, everyone shut up and turned toward him. He continued in that calm cool voice of his, "I remember when you were looking out that window, Molly. I remember you were one of the people who brought up the possibility, but none of us considered it a threat. We underestimated him. Technology keeps racing forward, and this time, our brains stayed behind. We're getting old and careless, Gunther. The guy had a clear shot at me through that damned window." He leaned back against the pillow, closed his eyes.

Gunther said, "That's why we've moved the bed away from the window." He was pale and tense, as close to distraught as Molly had ever seen him. He added, "One thing we do know is this guy is world-class. I've known of maybe a dozen guys who could have made that shot through a closed window."

Detective O'Connor said, "We'd like you to provide us with the names of all the men you know who would be capable of such a shot." He paused a moment, running his palm over his bald head. "You know, if Mr. Lord hadn't fallen back on the pillow at that particular instant . . ."

Gunther nodded, then said to Mason, "We're getting another room ready, sir. It's being seen to right now. No one will know the new room number. There won't be any window that has a building within a mile of it."

Mason laughed, then coughed. He was silent a moment, controlling the pain. "Gunther, you know a secret is impossible when more than one person knows about it. It'll get out, but it won't matter, because I'm going home."

"TELL me how you're feeling, Emma."

"About what exactly, Dr. Loo?"

"Well, your grandfather came home from the hospital this morning. How is he?"

"I heard Miles say he's really tired and weak. Eve didn't want me to get near him because I'm a kid and I make noise, only I don't, not much. I think she kept me away because she doesn't like me much. Then I saw his face when they were carrying him in on a stretcher. He looked all gray and old. I never thought he was old before. I always thought he looked like one of those movie stars in the old movies Mama likes. Yes, he's all black and white." Emma paused, easing her piano down across her legs. She added, "This morning he looked old. I didn't say anything. There were people everywhere. I think three of them were doctors and they were all around him."

"How is your mother dealing with all this?"

Emma thought about that. She lightly touched the piano keys but didn't make any sound. Her dark hair, normally in a French braid, was loose this morning. Emma had some of her mother's naturally curly hair. It swung over, hiding most of her face as she said, "Mama's really quiet. I think she's scared. She's been scared for a long time now. She's scared about me. She doesn't want to leave me alone. Neither does Ramsey." Emma sighed. "Sometimes I'd like to be alone, but I know they worry if I'm ever out of their sight. But that's not often." She raised her head, pushed her hair back, then looked toward the closed door. Molly and Ramsey were in the waiting room. "I'm really glad that we're getting married, though."

Dr. Loo smiled, unable not to. Despite everything, this child was one of the lucky ones. She figured that Molly and Ramsey would love Emma so much she'd have no choice but to heal. "When are you all going to get married?"

"I heard Mama say that we couldn't leave for another day or so." She lowered her voice. "I think we're going to elope." Dr. Loo nearly laughed aloud this time, restraining herself when Emma sighed again, that too-adult sigh that made Dr. Loo wish for a tantrum, or at least the threat of one. She remembered Ramsey saying the same thing. What was going on here?

"Do you want to elope, Emma?"

"Oh yes, Dr. Loo. I'd get to be Ramsey's best man and Mama's maid of honor. I'd get to be the flower girl, too."

"Then what bothers you?"

"My grandfather wants us to be married in his house. Miles said that he wants to give my mama away. But Eve wants us to leave. I think Eve will win."

"Why do you think that?"

"Because Grandfather is sick. He has to be standing to win." She lowered her head. "I heard Mama say that to Ramsey. They were talking really quiet so I snuck close so I could hear them."

"Well, you tell me tomorrow how everything is going, all right? Have you had any more nightmares, Emma?"

Emma shook her head. She scooted off the chair, her piano clutched close. "I think about him though, Dr. Loo."

"And what do you think, Emma?"

"That he's going to come back. I know when we go back to San Francisco there will be police officers close to make sure he doesn't get near us. I heard Ramsey talking to Officer Virginia on the phone yesterday. Ramsey told me his name is Sonny Dickerson. He showed me a photo of him. He's the man. I described him really well."

Dr. Loo had also seen the photograph. "Yes, you certainly did. Now, Emma, do you believe, deep down in your heart, and up higher, in your brain, that your mama and Ramsey will keep you safe?"

Emma thought about that. She looked hard at her Nike sneakers. She was wearing her favorite plaid socks that Ramsey had bought her in Ireland.

Dr. Loo patted her lightly on her arm. The child was still too thin, but that was all right, for now. She imagined that it worried her parents, though. Emma finally said, "My heart's sure, but my brain isn't."

Dr. Loo nodded. "That's smart. Until this Sonny Dickerson is caught,

Emma, it's really important for you to pay attention as well as your mama and Ramsey. Since there will be police nearby if he does come back, that should make you feel safer."

"I asked Ramsey to teach me to read more. Maybe I'll read about that man in a book."

"Yes, an excellent idea."

"Mama said I was so smart that I'd be reading about crime and punishment before I went to school this fall."

MOLLY looked at her father, who was slightly elevated in his hospital bed, a newspaper on his lap, his reading glasses on. He wasn't happy, but she wasn't about to back down. She wanted Emma out of here, as quickly as possible. He said in that particular mildly contemptuous way he always spoke to her, "You will marry here."

She just shook her head. She wasn't going to argue with him. She said mildly, "You've already seen me get married once. You don't need to do it a second time."

Ramsey said, "We'd like to get Emma out of here and safe."

"She's so safe in San Francisco?" Mason said, his sarcasm biting. "That bastard took her from right under your goddamned nose, Ramsey."

Eve said, "Mason, there are Ramsey's parents. It isn't fair to them."

He didn't even look over at her. "Keep out of it, Eve. This doesn't concern you."

She merely smiled down at him, seemingly untroubled. She said, "I think I'll go get some tea. Oh yes, Ramsey, the car's coming for you at three o'clock, if that's what you decide." She looked down at her Cartier watch, smiling a small but quite amused smile.

They left at five minutes after three, Molly's good-byes to her father curt. The media knew their plans, naturally, likely from a leak from the limo company. Ramsey and Molly watched the media take off after the town car with its thankfully tinted windows. He smiled. "Let's go, Gunther. Good idea. Well done."

I'M married, Molly thought, staring at her pale face in the mirror. Married again. Only this time I'm an adult, not a stupid immature kid. This time I married a good man and he's so sexy I don't think I can stand it. And he loves Emma to death.

She grinned at herself, touched on some lipstick, and slowly slipped the gorgeous peach silk nightgown over her head. Ramsey had presented it to her just ten minutes before, right in front of Emma, since there was no choice. "No more cotton tents," he'd whispered in her ear. "This is for both of us. Actually, tonight, I guess it's for Emma too." He looked as if he wanted to break into tears.

She walked out of the bathroom, leaving the light on for a moment, knowing it backlighted her very nicely.

Emma called out, sounding awed, which really pleased Molly, "Mama, you look like a fairy princess. Ramsey and I have been waiting for you. And waiting. I want to get married so I can wear that, too."

Emma sounded as bright as a new penny, enthusiastic, about as far from being asleep as a new puppy. So what? In the long run, it wasn't important when she had a wedding night, when she was finally alone with her new husband. Things would happen when it was time. She gave Emma a big hug, making her squeak she squeezed her so tightly. "We're married and we're all together," she said, smoothing her fingers through Emma's hair. "We're lucky, Em. I really like our man."

Ramsey was still wearing a beautiful dark suit and pristine white shirt. His tie wasn't as conservative. In fact, it was a psychedelic mishmash of purple, pink, and yellow squiggles. He looked big and tough, and his smile would have charmed the gold out of a miser's teeth.

"He promised me he wouldn't ever get fat, Mama," Emma said.

"That's right," Ramsey said. "I don't believe in it. However, to help me keep that promise, you've got to get me to a gym before too much more time passes. Well, Emma, we're married. Do you approve?"

There was a thread of fine tension in his voice. Molly cocked her head to one side, staring at him. Surely he knew that Emma was nuts about him. She understood. He had to hear it. He was waiting, all quiet.

Emma pulled away from her mom and walked to him. She held up her arms. He picked her up and held her close. She drew back and said not five inches from his face, "You're the best man in the whole world, Ramsey."

"Thanks, Emma. I think you're about the greatest little kid. And just look at your mama. She's not bad herself. I got myself a fairy princess." He hugged her again, then said to Molly, "Emma and I are going to wake you up every hour and tell you how beautiful you are."

"In theory I like the sound of that," Molly said, walking toward the king-size bed. "Now, you cutthroats, how about we play some Old Maid?"

"No, Mama, you know I like gin rummy better."

"Emma, you always win at gin rummy. I just got married. Can't you give me a break?"

"All right," Emma said. "We'll play five-card draw."

Ramsey hooted with laughter.

Emma looked quite pleased with herself. After she'd won the first hand with three jacks, she said, "This marriage thing isn't any different. We did this in Ireland. Nothing's changed. That's good."

"That's painfully true," Ramsey said, and shuffled the deck.

THIRTY-ONE

Just after midnight, Molly awoke slowly when Ramsey curled her hair around her ear, licked her earlobe, bit it gently, and said quietly, "If you want to join the game, it's best if you're in on the kickoff."

"I've always loved football, from the very first kickoff. Where's Emma?"

He moved on his elbow, above her. "Our little darling was sleeping so deeply I thought she'd start snoring at any moment. I tucked her in in the other bedroom. I left the door open a crack so we could hear her if she woke up, so no yelling from either of us. Okay?"

She raised her hand and touched her fingertips to his face. Her eyes were adjusted to the night. She touched his nose, ran her fingertips over his black eyebrows, touched his lips. "You're a beautiful man, Ramsey. When I walked in on you in the bathroom at Dromoland, I wanted to jump you."

He grabbed her and pulled her tightly against him. He groaned against her hair. "I wish you had. As you saw clearly, I wanted to be jumped. I was shaking I wanted to be jumped so badly."

She touched his shoulders, ran her hand down his back to his flank, realizing in that moment that he'd shucked off his boxer shorts. "Oh dear," she said, leaning up to bite his shoulder, "I'm overdressed."

He had that gorgeous silk nightgown off her in under ten seconds. She kissed his chin. "Do you want me to hang it up so it won't get wrinkled?" At the horrified look on his face, she lightly smacked his chest, and laughed. He rolled over on top of her, feeling the length of her against him. He breathed in her scent, feeling the textures of her flesh pressed up against him, the firmness, the softness of her belly. "I've thought about this so many times I nearly scrambled my brains. I surprised myself. I'd never thought I was such a horny bastard before, but with you, I am. I'm in a pretty bad way here, Molly."

"Will you try to nail me in the closet?"

He shook his head as he began kissing her, saying between kisses, "No, that's got no class. Well, maybe a closet would be all right if Emma's close by."

She arched up against him, found his mouth with her hands, and attacked him. "You don't know what a bad way is," she said into his mouth. "I want to eat you up." She was biting his neck, nibbling on his mouth.

"Nah, let me do that," he said against her breast. "That's my specialty. There's a whole lot of other stuff you can do. But later, Molly, a lot later." Then she opened her legs and he groaned in answer. He kissed her neck, her ear, her mouth, returning again and again. He balanced himself briefly on his elbow while his other hand went to her breast, then stroked down her ribs. "Well, hell," he said, his hand coming back up to her face, "I'm this big-time federal judge and we still can't do everything with Emma close. And the good Lord knows I want to very badly."

She was rubbing her foot along his leg. "Just keep trying. It's wonderful."

He lifted himself up onto his knees, shuddering with the effort to separate himself from her, and pushed her hands away when she would have brought him back down to her. He looked down at her, lightly touching her with his fingers, opening her legs wider. He brought his head down and began kissing her stomach. "This is a very good place to start," he said against her warm skin, moving downward until his mouth and his fingers stroked and pushed inside her, deep inside her, until, in about the same time it had taken Ramsey to get her nightgown off, she was lurching up, choking out, "Ramsey, oh, goodness, this is too much. I think a yell is coming."

He clapped one hand over her mouth and she yelled against his palm, wondering if she were going to die, knowing she wouldn't, and never wanting the incredible, shattering feelings to stop. When she slumped back, quivering as the aftershocks of that wild pleasure continued to career through her, he came inside her, deeper inside, until he was sealed to her. He froze over her, and in that instant, the knowledge that he was finally where he belonged, that she was his wife and his lover until they both left the earth, plucked him up, making him dizzy and hot, then shattered through him. He'd never realized there could be such a binding force in the world as what he was feeling now. He'd wanted Emma, wanted her safe, and he still did. Always it had been Emma and then, only after Emma, Molly had been in his mind. Now he didn't know. One thing he did know was that he hadn't expected being this consumed until there was nothing inside him but Molly and what she was making him feel. He shuddered like a palsied man as he climaxed deep inside this woman he'd known for less than two months, this woman who'd been married to a rock star and was the daughter of a gangster. Who knew about life?

Molly slowly opened her eyes only when she was certain she'd continue breathing if she tried such a violent movement. Nothing happened. She blinked. Nothing continued to happen. She concentrated on returning to life as she knew it. She couldn't believe the utter dizzying pleasure she'd just experienced. She said, "I'm going to try to talk now, not move, just talk. Yes, that was a complete sentence. Yes, I'm getting there, thank you. That was nice, Ramsey."

He was still deep inside her. It felt incredible. She closed her eyes again, just thinking about how amazing it was that they'd found each other. She lifted her hips. He groaned into her hair.

"What the hell do you mean 'nice'? Nice is a wussy word. It's close to an insult."

"Well, better than nice then. Really good. Maybe even getting close to superb."

He was quiet a moment, harder in her than he had been just the instant before. "What you need is a comparison. Now, you might think I would be ready right this minute, but I'm not. My spirit needs to revive. Give me at least five more minutes."

He was lying flat on top of her, his head on the pillow beside hers.

Molly stroked her hands up and down his long back. "I forgot to check your back. Is the burn healed?"

"Yes, it's all right."

"It feels pretty smooth. How about your leg?"

"My leg is as good as new. How about your arm? Are the stitches all gone?"

"All gone. Just a little scar ridge. Ramsey, would you mind if I admitted that I sort of more than just like you a whole lot?"

He was silent. She began to fidget. "No," he said, still unable to move. "Truth be told, I more than sort of just like you as well."

He finally managed to lift himself above her again. He leaned his head down and kissed her mouth. "For so long now I would look at your mouth and wonder how you tasted, what you'd feel like. I wanted to make love to your mouth. Then I'd think how I'd feel with your mouth on me."

Not even a minute later, Ramsey's spirit completely revived, and this time, he thought he'd die. It was close. It was wonderfully close. She could jump him anytime, anywhere.

At about four o'clock in the morning, Ramsey felt small hands patting his shoulder. He'd had the brains to put his boxer shorts back on, thank God, which he'd believed was a miracle. He'd even gotten Molly to put her nightgown back on, and she'd been only semiconscious.

He pulled Emma over his shoulder and scooted her down on the other side of her mother. Molly, still asleep, reached out her hand to touch him again. "Emma's here," he whispered. She quieted immediately. She smiled to herself in the darkness. She felt Emma's small arm come over around her waist. Emma said in her ear, "I know you're beautiful, Mama. It doesn't matter that I can't see you."

"Thank you, Em. You don't have to wake me every hour to tell me."

She settled again. Before she went back to sleep, she saw the justice of the peace pronounce them husband and wife, saw Emma grinning from ear to ear and announcing to the judge's wife who'd sold Molly a bouquet for ten dollars that they were all together now and wasn't that just perfect. The woman, bless her heart, had agreed, distracting Emma while Ramsey kissed her.

She fell deeply asleep, her spirit so very content that she forgot ex-priest Sonny Dickerson, who had gone so far around the bend, he would probably die before he gave Emma up.

THE next morning, Molly said over the breakfast table in their suite, "You know what I think?"

She spoke softly, for Emma was close by, sitting on the floor, practicing printing her name in a notebook Molly had bought her in the hotel gift shop.

Ramsey looked up from his hash browns. "I know this isn't serious. You're about ready to burst into laughter."

"No, you're wrong. I'm dead serious."

"All right, but I don't know what you're talking about. What do you think?"

"I think being with you was beyond superb. It was so wonderful, maybe it should be taxed."

He nearly lost it right there. He gulped. He took a quick drink of his coffee and scalded his mouth. Then he clearly remembered how she felt and nearly shuddered his way off his chair.

Emma looked up from her printing and said, "What's my last name now, Mama?"

Ramsey looked at Molly, sex forgotten, sudden fierce possessiveness in his voice as he said, "I'd like you to be Emma Hunt now. What do you think?"

"Could you print it out for me, Ramsey?"

He took her pencil and wrote out Emma Hunt. Emma went to work. She said finally, looking back up, "It looks pretty good all written out. It's okay with me." She held up the paper for them to see.

Both Ramsey and Molly examined her effort. Ramsey said, "Well done, even good enough so I can read it. *Emma Hunt*. It has a ring to it." Emma grinned and went back to her printing. Ramsey lowered his voice. "I'm sorry, Molly. We never discussed it, but I want this very badly. I want Emma to be mine, legally and every other way as well."

"I'm torn," she said, cutting another slice of her grapefruit. "Louey wasn't ever around, but he was her father. It's like he'll cease to exist now."

"Let me ask you a question. If Louey were still alive and you'd divorced him and then married me, what would you decide?"

She forked down the grapefruit, then picked up a piece of wheat toast. She said quietly, so Emma couldn't hear, "I'd say he was a bum and never even wanted to see Emma anyway. Maybe I'd say he didn't deserve for her to carry a name that meant so little." She shook her head. "But because he's dead, I feel she needs to hold on to something. How about Emma Santera Hunt? We could ask Dr. Loo, but that sounds like a good idea."

"Emma will always know that he was her father." Ramsey asked Emma what she thought of having three whole names. Emma approved.

Molly said, "Are you going to eat your bacon, Ramsey?"

"No, you take it. You need to keep up your strength. I'm brimming with strength. The more times a man gets jumped, the stronger he gets. He gets pumped up. All his muscles start to flex. His fortitude increases exponentially. I can't wait to prove it to you."

"How do you think it looks, Mama?"

Molly looked away from her new husband, wishing she could fling herself on top of him and screw his brains out. "Ah, Em, let's see. Ah, you've printed it another six times. Each is better. Very good, love. Oh yes, that looks just grand. When you start the first grade this fall, you'll be Emma Santera Hunt."

"Miss Emma Santera Hunt," Emma said. "I won't be a Ms. until I'm eighteen."

Molly looked over at Ramsey, who knew what she'd been thinking. "And I'll be Mrs. Molly Hunt."

"That makes all of us Hunts," Emma said happily, then frowned. "I never even thought about a Hunt before Ramsey found me."

Ramsey called his parents. His mother and father spoke to both Molly and Emma. It went well, though Molly heard the disappointment after they'd gotten over their shock. They agreed to go back for a reception in their honor sometime toward the end of the summer.

"By that time, everything should be resolved," Ramsey said as he put the receiver back into its cradle. "You'll see how my mom treats all her daughters-in-law like they're perfect and gives grief to her three sons."

"Makes sense to me," Molly said. "I guess I should call my mom."

THEY returned to San Francisco the following afternoon. It was close enough to midsummer to be chilly, with the fog from the Pacific rolling in through the Golden Gate.

Emma was wearing a sweater, walking around her new backyard, examining the flowers that grew well in the protection of a sturdy redwood fence. Her piano was on a chair in the kitchen. An unmarked police car was parked across the street.

"I'll get her a swing set," Ramsey said, coming up behind Molly, closing his arms around her. He leaned down and kissed her ear. "Maybe I can hang a tire from that branch on the pine tree over there."

She turned in his arms. "I want to have my way with you," she said, and so she did, right there in his study, their clothes on, ever watchful because Emma was close by. They were standing together, still breathing hard, when they heard Emma call out from the kitchen, "Mama, Ramsey's got a room that's filled with all sorts of cans."

Molly rolled her eyes. "Cans? All different sizes, I'll bet. You pervert."

"Mama? I can hear you laughing. Did you make a joke?"

"Oh yes," Molly said quietly. "Oh, yes."

AFTER a spicy dinner of Ramsey's favorite Chinese Szechwan Beef, and garlic noodles with eggplant, Molly said, as she watched Emma set down her fork, "It's time the three of us talked about this, Em. We've put it off long enough. You're ready to jump out of your skin." Emma's head came up. "Let me be real up-front with you. Ramsey's worried about you. He's worried because that awful man is still out there. We hoped he would have been caught by now, but he hasn't. This means, Em, that you're going to have to be super-careful. That means whenever we leave the house, you've got to stay really close to either me or Ramsey. If one of us ever walks ahead of you, you grab Ramsey's hand or mine. Do you understand? Does that make sense to you?"

Ramsey would never have brought it right out in the open like this. He felt as if they were standing over an active volcano. He barely managed to make his throat swallow the strong black coffee he'd just brewed.

Emma said, "Yes, I think it makes sense too, Mama. Dr. Loo told me that this man thought I could save him from going to Hell. She said that wasn't true, but it was stuck in his brain like that, and so it was true to him."

She was talking. He supposed he was astounded that everything out of that small mouth made such sense.

"She's probably right," Molly said.

"If he thought I could save him from going to Hell, then why did he hurt me so much?"

Molly said, "Mr. Savich told Ramsey that the doctors at the FBI think that just maybe he hurt you because he believed you should take his punishment for him, that by hurting you, his savior, he was cleansing himself of his sins, readying to give himself into God's hands."

"I don't understand that, Mama."

"No one does, not really," Ramsey said. "He's very sick and therefore he's very dangerous because he's out of control. That's why we've really got to be careful."

"I know he's still out there," Emma said. "He's just waiting."

Molly said, "I wish I could get him right this minute, but I can't. Until we do catch him, though, things are going to be tough for us. I'm sorry, but I can't change that. You're going to have to be on the lookout all the time and stick close. Now I want you to go to the front window and look at that light blue car parked across the street. Those are police officers and they're going to keep all their eyes open for that man."

"I see them, Mama."

Ramsey cleared his throat. But the reasonable sorts of words that had just come out of Molly's mouth were stuck in his throat. He tried to say something intelligent, something comforting, but what came out of his mouth was, "Emma, do you think you could come here a minute? I need to have you close to me. I'm not feeling so good."

Emma came running back to the table. Ramsey barely had time to push back his chair and lift her onto his legs. He drew her close. Emma was patting his arms. "It's going to be all right, Ramsey. We'll get through this. I promise."

He buried his face in her French braid. "I love you, Emma Hunt."

"I love you too, Ramsey. A whole lot." She kept stroking his arm and his shoulder, giving him all the comfort she could.

THAT weekend they went to Monterey to be tourists. They went first to the Monterey Bay Aquarium. Emma loved the jellyfish. The three of them sat on the bench facing the huge tank and watched the jellyfish for a good thirty minutes.

They walked through Carmel, played on the beautiful beach at the cove at the bottom of Ocean Avenue, drove down to Big Sur and picnicked off the road.

They kept Sonny Dickerson at bay in their minds for a good three days, at least for most of the time. Ramsey called Virginia Trolley once they'd reached their hotel, gave her their number, and told her that everyone was settled in. Molly called her father. He was improving by the day. Miles missed them, particularly Emma. Her father was sleeping, Eve said, but maybe they could call him next week and he'd want to speak to them.

"Bitch," Molly said quietly as she hung up the phone.

Ramsey looked up from the blackjack game he and Emma were playing. He'd taught her the game two days before. She was beating him, which both surprised him and made him so proud he couldn't stand it. He said over his shoulder to Molly with a grin, "It's easier for Eve to deal with your father when no one else is around, particularly if it happens to be a stepdaughter who's older than she is and a step-granddaughter who's smarter at gambling than she is, and a guy who's really handsome and witty who isn't at all interested in her. Darn it all, Emma, I can't believe you took a hit on sixteen. You should have held."

Emma looked so withdrawn, so apparently locked into herself, that it scared Molly until she realized that Emma was concentrating. Now Emma looked up and said in all seriousness, "I've been counting the cards real hard, Ramsey, just the way you told me to. I knew there were two more threes and two more aces in the deck. I don't remember how many twos there are."

He snarled, leaned over, and picked Emma up, falling onto his back and lifting her up over him, shaking her. She was screaming with laughter. "Molly," he called out over Emma's laughter, "can I go throw her in the jellyfish tank? Then you and I can sit there on that bench and watch her make friends."

"I remember now. There's one more two in the deck. It would be stupid to hold on sixteen."

"No, there aren't any more twos." He let her down. "Let's look. I'll prove it." There were twelve cards left. The very last card was the two of hearts.

THE next afternoon they were walking on the Monterey Wharf. Ramsey loved the smell of a wharf, a combination of salt and wood and creosote, a sealant used on the wood. Seagulls were thick and loud, begging handouts like the most aggressive panhandlers who flocked to Union Square in San Francisco. There were lots of fish stalls, and getting close to the stalls, particularly late in the afternoon, was nearly overwhelming—a putrid, briny odor that could bring tears to your eyes.

The smell of decaying seaweed was strong as well today. Flies swarmed over the seaweed. It wasn't an appetizing sight. Sea lions hooted near the wooden pilings, fat and bold, usually a dozen or so mesmerized children hanging around them, begging food from their parents to give to them.

And there were endless souvenir shops. Emma was wearing a Carmel T-shirt, white jeans, her Nike sneakers, and her plaid socks. Molly had told Ramsey she'd wished he'd bought Emma a good dozen pair since they were her favorites. She washed them out each night.

Because it was summer, there were tons of tourists. The sun was bright overhead, but it wasn't hot. It was rarely hot by the ocean. It was usually just perfect. Normally, Ramsey preferred to carry Emma. He knew she was safe when he was carrying her. But she was independent, and after a while, she'd given him a long look and said, "Ramsey, I'll be all right. I'm not going to go run off."

She was walking beside him, holding his hand, either trying to speed him up or slow him down. She had her eye on a particular sea lion who honked loudly at every person who appeared to look easy. He was immense, and Ramsey could see how he'd gotten that way. He asked one of the fishermen how long the sea lion had been in residence. "Two years," the man said. "Bloody beggar never stops eating. His name's Old Chester, the Gay Blade. Hey, what do you expect with San Francisco up the road? No one's supposed to feed any of them, but they do. You can buy cheap sardines right over there. The beggars, they got no shame."

Was he referring to the tourists or to the sea lions?

"All right," Ramsey finally said. "But you're going to have to toss the sardines to him, Emma. I draw the line at that. And don't get too close."

She gave him one of her tolerant nods and bought three sardines, thankfully dead, and was given a paper towel. Ramsey stood right behind her as she eased up until it was her turn to feed the behemoth. She yelled with laughter when he honked very loudly.

At the same moment, Molly yelled his name.

THIRTY-TWO

Ramsey nearly tripped, he swung around so quickly. A boy was trying to wrestle Molly's purse out of her hands. He ran full tilt toward the tussle, yelling, "Let her go, you little punk!"

Emma.

Ramsey jerked back around to see Emma standing there, her hand close to that sea lion, not realizing what had happened. There were people all around her. She was all right. Then, just at the instant when he would have turned back to Molly, Ramsey saw him slithering through a knot of kids and parents near the sea lions. He would recognize the man anywhere, both in his nightmares and in real life. Just a few more feet and he'd be close enough to grab her. He was nearly on her, not more than three feet away, moving quickly now since he knew the distraction he'd set into motion couldn't last much longer. He had his hand out when Ramsey grabbed him by his collar, jerked him around, and sent his fist into his jaw.

"Hey, buddy! Why'd you hit that guy? He wasn't doing nothing!"

"Yeah, you can't go around hitting people. What is it with you?"

There were half a dozen people swarming close now, pressing in toward him, but no one had grabbed him yet. He yelled, "Emma! Get over to your mother!"

Dickerson was stumbling to his feet, rubbing his jaw, spitting blood, yelling, "Why'd you hit me? I'm a priest! Why'd you hit a holy man?"

"Hey, buddy, you shouldn't oughta done that!"

Ramsey was shoved back. Another man punched him in the shoulder.

"No, stop! He's my papa and he was saving me!"

But they didn't hear the little girl. Just kept telling him what a bum he was.

Ramsey was desperate. He didn't want to, but he saw Dickerson going for Emma again. "Leave her alone!" he yelled, but Dickerson ignored him, so intent on Emma that Ramsey wondered if he'd even heard him.

"Sorry about this." Ramsey levered himself up and kicked one man high on the thigh, sent his fist into another man's shoulder, and one final kick into a man's belly. He was free. Dickerson was close to Emma again. This time Ramsey didn't yell. He wanted to get his bare hands on Dickerson and beat the living shit out of him. He felt rage pour through him, violent, pure vengeance. Dickerson was two feet away from her. The look on his face was calm, even serene, as if he were looking at a beautiful scene, and perhaps he was, somewhere in his demented brain. A man turned sharply and bumped into Ramsey. Ramsey couldn't stop himself, he shoved the guy hard out of the way. Then Dickerson looked up. Ramsey heard him curse, saw him weighing his chances of getting caught. He must have seen the death in Ramsey's eyes. He stumbled away down the wharf, weaving in and out of people. Ramsey yelled after him to stop. He stumbled faster, then straightened when the wharf was clear, and began running, Ramsey behind him, Emma running behind them both. People cleared from their path. Dickerson looked back, saw that Ramsey was closing, then turned sharply and jumped into the water. Ramsey grabbed up Emma, turned to a large woman who was surrounded by little kids and looked tough as nails, and said, "He's a child molester. He was after my daughter. Please hold her and keep her safe." He nearly threw Emma into the woman's arms. He jumped into the icy water of Monterey Bay after Sonny Dickerson.

He thought his flesh would freeze off his body. He felt as if his lungs had seized up. He got to the surface, looking for Dickerson. He couldn't see him. He couldn't be far. He felt as though he'd jumped right on top of him.

He heard Molly yell, "He's heading for the pilings, Ramsey. Hurry! Be careful! Damn you, be careful!"

He was a strong swimmer, but the surge was vicious, yanking one way, then the other. There were rocks around them, sharp and dangerous. The water was so cold his chest was tight and his arms and legs felt rubbery. Then, finally, he saw Dickerson, slipping in between the slimy pilings.

This time he wasn't about to let that monster escape him. Not again. He believed in the laws and in the courts, to his very fiber he believed in the order of law, but he knew that no lawyer was ever going to get the chance to represent this man, not if he could help it. He surged through the wildly slapping waves, nearly on him, when Dickerson, his hair plastered to his skull, suddenly waved a gun.

"Stay away from me!" he yelled, then got a mouthful of water. He choked and spat it out. "I mean it, Hunt. I'll shoot you if I have to."

Ramsey treaded water, yelling back, his voice strong and calm, even persuasive in his rage, "Listen to me, Dickerson, you'll never get Emma. All the cops have your photo and so does the FBI. Given what you've done, all of them want to shoot you down. You're not going to get Emma or any other little kid ever again. It's all over for you. Give it up." Ramsey grabbed one of the pilings, his palm slipping because it was so slimy. "Come on, Dickerson, don't be stupid. It's over."

"That's a lie. No one knows who I am. I'm an expert at makeup and disguises. All she saw was Clinton. It was good!"

"Not on the beach you didn't wear any makeup. Emma described you very well. It's not as if you'd just emerged newly hatched from under a rock. You have a record, fingerprints, photos, the whole shooting match. It's over. You're never going to get near her again. Did Rule Shaker know you were a child molester when he hired you to kidnap Emma?"

"I never met him, it was one of his men who hired me. He told me over and over that I wasn't to hurt the little girl, that she had to go back to her mother after her father cooperated with Shaker. Sure I agreed. I needed the money. But when I saw Emma, I knew she'd been sent to me.

"I knew she belonged to me. A week was only a beginning for us. But then she fooled me and ran away. It's just a matter of time and she'll be mine again."

Ramsey nearly lost it, but he wasn't stupid.

"You called up after she was gone and got those men up there to kill me, right?"

"Yes. I had to have her back, but you managed to escape."

"Yeah, and I got you too, didn't I?"

Dickerson yelled at that. He pushed forward, away from Ramsey, then veered toward a wobbly wooden ladder that looked as if it should have crumbled into the water years ago. He got himself halfway up before Ramsey was beneath him, grabbing his foot.

"Let me go! She's mine, do you hear me? I have to have her, she's all I've got. I can't survive without her. What I am is far more important than what she could ever be. I need her!"

Ramsey yanked as hard as he could on Dickerson's foot as Dickerson fired. Ramsey felt the heat of the bullet as it whizzed past his left ear.

An instant later there was another shot. It felt like a heavy blow striking his shoulder. He lurched backward, nearly losing his hold on Dickerson's foot. He didn't feel any pain, just more numbing cold. This numbness was different, colder than the water. It froze through his chest and down his arm, making it useless. He couldn't move his damned arm. He heard Molly's voice, Emma's voice. He heard someone scream out, "He's bleeding! That man's been shot."

Dickerson got his foot free. He kicked Ramsey hard in his wounded shoulder. Pain ripped through him and he fell back into the water.

He saw, as if from a great distance, Molly's white face, saw her raise her sneakered foot, saw her smash her sneakered foot into Dickerson's face just when he reached the top of the ladder. The force of her kick knocked Dickerson back. He scrambled wildly, trying to keep hold of the ladder, but the ancient rotting wood collapsed, each step crumbling when his weight hit it. Dickerson went flailing into the water, crashing beside him, struggling frantically, choking up water, trying to find the ladder whose rungs now hung down drunkenly. This time Ramsey had him around the neck and he never intended to let go. Dickerson was waving the gun around, yelling, water filling his mouth, still yelling, only it was gurgling now, and Ramsey felt him weakening. It was just a matter of which of them lasted longer now.

Ramsey felt the god-awful pain in his shoulder, the uselessness of his arm. He shuddered with the force of it, felt the pain pulling at him, felt light-headed and dizzy. But he didn't let Dickerson go. He only squeezed harder. Dickerson was twisting wildly, trying to turn the gun toward him. He tried to bring up his useless arm, but it just hung at his side, blood streaking down it, plastering his shirt to his flesh, hurting so badly his teeth were clenched. He was squeezing now as hard as he could. Why didn't Dickerson go down? Of course it was the force of the waves that prevented it. He couldn't get enough leverage. The gun waved in the air around them.

It didn't seem at all strange to him when he saw Molly scoot off the edge of the wharf to land in the water next to him. A moment later he thought he'd die of fear. He saw her grab Dickerson's arm, grab his wrist, and pull with all her might.

Dickerson screamed and yelled, but it didn't matter. Molly had the gun now. He saw her face was white, deadening fury in her eyes, saw her raise the gun to Dickerson's face, not a foot away from him. She was going to kill him. He realized in that moment that the last thing he ever wanted in his life was to have Molly kill another human being.

He said, "Don't shoot him, Molly, you might hit me. I've got him around the neck. See? I've got him. He's not going anywhere. It's all over for him. Please don't shoot."

She blinked, the blank rage receding. Dickerson heaved, shoving his elbow into Ramsey's stomach. The vicious surging water suddenly backlashed, shoving against them, giving Dickerson more power rather than slowing the force of his arm. Ramsey's hold loosened and Dickerson jerked free. He grabbed for the gun in Molly's hand.

There was a shot, wild, nearly straight up. Molly was heaving and struggling, but he was still on her. Ramsey kicked forward with his remaining strength to help her. God, he'd been a bloody fool to save the man's life. He was a fool and he was also losing. He heard Emma screaming his name.

Then there were two men in the water, and all of them were grabbing for that gun. When the gun went off another time, no one knew who had it, who had fired it.

All any of them knew was that there was an unconscious man on his face in the water, red streaked water flowing from beneath his body.

Ramsey said to the two men, "It's about time you two showed up. I'd about given up on you."

LIEUTENANT McPherson, of the MPD, a man whose face had come into focus just a couple of minutes before, said quietly, "Don't worry about anything, Judge Hunt. You're in Monterey. You're in a hospital room. The doctor and nurse just left before you woke up. You're going to make it, no problem. The only reason I'm here right now is I thought you'd want to know about Dickerson. He's still in surgery. The docs don't know if he'll make it. The bullet got him right in the chest. It's too soon to know."

"I wish they'd let the bastard die," Ramsey said. He couldn't move his right shoulder or his right arm. He looked down at a white sling. He remembered now how they'd wheeled him up to the operating room, side by side with Dickerson, Molly and Emma beside him, both of them white-faced and silent. He remembered Emma's small fingers lightly stroking his forearm. As for Molly, she'd held on to his hand for dear life. He vaguely remembered waking up in the recovery room. They'd just wheeled him into a private room, and he was alone with the lieutenant.

"Yes," Lieutenant McPherson was saying, "I hope he expires. It'd sure save the taxpayers a lot of money. Well, at least you're going to be all right, Judge Hunt."

"Do you know what they did to me?"

"The surgeon spoke to you in the recovery room. You don't remember?"

"No, just this voice that wouldn't shut up. Do you know anything?"

"Yes. They worked on you for a good two hours. When the surgeon came out, he said you were lucky. The bullet went through your pec, and all you've got there is skin, muscle, and fat. He said you'd hurt like hell because the bullet also broke your collarbone and grazed a rib, but there wasn't any bad damage, it would just take a while to heal. You should be ready to take out more crooks in your courtroom in three or four months. Oh yeah, the doc also said he was real pleased that the bullet hadn't hit anything important, said he didn't want any complications with a big-time federal judge. He gave a big belly laugh then."

Ramsey couldn't think of anything to say. His brain seemed to be going in and out on him. At least he felt blessedly numb, all of him. He wished Dickerson was dead. Surely it wasn't asking too much after what the bastard had done. If he lived, if they brought him up on kidnapping and attempted murder, he could still get out. Emma still wouldn't be safe.

He was losing it. Yes, she would be safe. By the time Dickerson ever got out of prison, Emma would be an adult. She'd be safe from predators like Dickerson because she'd keep accumulating birthdays.

"Judge Hunt? Can you hear me? Do you want me to get a doctor for you?"

Ramsey hadn't realized his head had fallen back against the very comfortable pillows. He opened his eyes to see Lieutenant McPherson looking very worried. He knew he'd been speaking, he'd felt the cadence of his voice, the underlying kindness, the concern, but he hadn't understood most of what he'd said. Ramsey managed to say, "I'm okay. I didn't think hospitals had comfortable pillows."

"These aren't the hospital's pillows," McPherson said. "These are from Mrs. Hunt, who's right now changing clothes along with your daughter. Actually they're from Mrs. Rallis, who went out and bought you pillows and your wife and daughter new clothes. She didn't like seeing them in hospital scrubs. Evidently she saw the whole thing on the wharf. She's a big name here in Monterey. If she says that you should have soft pillows, no one's going to argue with her."

Ramsey wanted to ask about Molly and Emma, find out if they were okay, but somehow, he couldn't get the words out. It was a weird feeling, this knowing words, feeling what those words meant to him, yet being unable to get them out of his mouth. He felt the man lightly pat his arm. "The doc gave you a shot of something really strong. He said you didn't seem like the sort to kick back and relax, so he said he'd lay you out, it would be the best thing. Did you hear me tell you about your daughter and Mrs. Hunt? They should be here soon. The last I heard, Mrs. Rallis insisted that your wife and Emma have coffee and hot chocolate. I tried to stop the doc from giving you that shot, but I couldn't. Can you talk, Judge Hunt?"

"No. I'm laid out," Ramsey said, but McPherson never said anything more, so he guessed he'd spoken to him only in his mind.

HE smiled at Molly and Emma coming into his hospital room. Emma was wearing a new outfit he'd never seen on her before. As for Molly, she looked like a fashion plate in a pale yellow silky-looking pants outfit and high-heeled shoes, of all things. Her beautiful hair was combed back, fastened with a fat gold clip at her neck. They both looked incredible to him. He wanted to shout to them that this time they'd won. He wanted to yell at Molly for jumping in the water like that. He also wanted to thank her for saving his bacon. He wanted to tell them he loved them more than he'd loved any two people in his entire life. But his mouth wouldn't say anything. He wondered again where the words were that would say what he wanted to say.

He heard McPherson say, "No, he's all right, ma'am, I promise. He's been in and out. The doc wants him to rest and so he's resting. You and Emma sure look like a million dollars. How do you feel, Mrs. Hunt? Would you like to give me a statement now?"

Then he heard Virginia Trolley's voice, telling McPherson to leave Molly alone, that she'd speak to him once she was convinced Ramsey would be all right. Boy, she'd gotten down here fast. He knew she'd take care of everything. He also knew she'd take a strip off her two cops who were supposedly protecting them. He thought he remembered one of the young cops telling him that he'd had to take a leak and that's why they'd been a couple of minutes late helping him. What about his partner? Ramsey had wanted to ask, but hadn't been able to.

He smiled now vaguely at Emma, who'd slipped away from her mama to come to him. "I'm okay, Em," he thought he said, but her face didn't change expression. He felt her soft mouth on his cheek. He heard her whisper against his ear, "We got him, Ramsey. Mrs. Rallis promised me he wasn't going to escape from her hospital." He wanted to laugh, but he didn't. He slid away. The last thing he felt was the touch of Emma's fingers on the back of his left hand.

"HE'S going to live," Molly said. "They spent hours on him in the operating room, and now he's going to live."

Virginia Trolley said from his other side, with a deep sigh, "They knew who and what he was. I wish they'd let him go. Now we'll have to try him, there'll be more garbage for you guys to go through."

"It's all right, Virginia," Ramsey said, his voice deep and gravelly this morning. He wanted a cup of coffee badly, but they wouldn't give it to him. The nurse had said he'd puke up his toenails if he drank coffee now. He wanted desperately to prove her either right or wrong. "Where's Emma?"

"I'm right here, Ramsey. Mama wanted me to pay attention to something else, but I told her I know what's going on. Does your shoulder hurt?"

"Nah, I'm a big guy, just like I told you. This isn't anything. I seem to be getting better at having my body parts shot all the time."

"I was afraid he would kill you, Ramsey," Emma said. "The water was all red. I would have gotten to you to help you, but that big lady wouldn't let go of me."

The thought of Emma jumping into the water like her mother had, maybe landing on Dickerson's head, nearly made his heart stop. He said, however, "Your mom saved my hide for you. Thanks. Now, Virginia, what's going to happen to Dickerson?"

"Your friend Dillon Savich is on his way out here. The kidnapping is federal so it's the FBI's call. He wants to speak to Dickerson himself. Also a profiler is coming. You know they're always interviewing sickos like Dickerson. He should be a gold mine of information for them. Are you up to giving the local boys a statement?"

He spoke to Lieutenant McPherson and his captain, Daniel Mapes. It took quite a while. He was white around the gills when Captain Mapes said, "That's enough, Judge Hunt. If we have more questions, we'll see you tomorrow."

"I didn't think they were ever going to leave," Molly said, coming to the bed. "You don't look so hot."

"I want a cup of coffee."

"I know. Here you are." It was a miracle. He avidly watched her pull the lid off a foam cup. He took three long drinks, then promptly wanted to die. It was close, but he wasn't about to let himself throw up. The nausea subsided, finally. Then he panicked. "Where's Emma?"

"She's all right. She's with Virginia, telling her exactly what happened. From a child's perspective, it should be very interesting. Now, you're to rest for a while longer. It sounds stupid to tell you how lucky you were when you're lying flat on your back feeling awful, but you are. You'll mend. The surgeon said you'd be ready to take me dancing by tomorrow night. Well, maybe Wednesday night."

Molly smiled at him, closed the door, and climbed up with him on the narrow hospital bed. She kissed his ear, his nose, his mouth. "You taste like hospital," she said, nuzzling his neck. "But since I'm dressed in silk, maybe it's that opposites-attract thing." She gave a deep sigh. "I wish we could play doctor."

"Molly, please don't make me hard. I can't begin to imagine what Nurse Hayman would do if she walked in and saw me pointing to the ceiling."

"She adores you. She'd probably pull me off you and take my place."

"Okay, enough of this newlywed stuff," said a man from the doorway.

"Not nearly as bad as Nurse Hayman," Molly said, and scooted off the bed.

It was Dillon Savich, grinning from ear to ear. Behind him was another man who looked as if he'd never smiled in his life. He looked like a medieval monk, all stiff and long and narrow, with a thin rim of gray hair circling his head.

"Hi, Ramsey, glad you're well enough to kiss Molly. Guys, this is Thomas Galviani, otherwise known as Tommy the Eye, a gentleman whose specialty is child molesters. He's one of the world's leading experts."

The man didn't change expression, just calmly nodded and shook

Ramsey's hand. He said, "Savich thinks I'm too serious, but I'm not. I'm glad to meet you, Judge Hunt. I read about what a hell of a good job you did on those drug dealers in your courtroom. Everyone in the Bureau is still talking about it. I'm more than glad this time our perp was caught before he killed. Congratulations on bringing him down."

"Thank you, Mr. Galviani."

"Tommy the Eye," he said without skipping a beat, his expression all bland, and Savich laughed.

"Where's Sherlock?"

Savich said to Molly, "She's in the women's room, cursing me. I said the P word to a doctor who was worried because she looked a bit on the pale side. I told him it had been a long trip and she was tired because she was pregnant. That was all it took."

"I hope," Tommy the Eye said, "that Sherlock doesn't shoot you before she stops having morning sickness."

They were still grinning when Sherlock came into the room. She walked up to her husband and punched him in the arm. Then she greeted Molly and Ramsey, all smiles. She said, "I stopped by the ICU. Dickerson is still out of it. They'll let us know if and when he wakes up."

"I would like to speak to him," said Tommy the Eye. "I've read everything we've got, all the reports from his first trial, the transcripts of what he said when and to whom. He's a preferential child molester, that is to say, he's a pedophile who sexually molests children. The preferential abuses up to as many as a thousand children in his life, not like a situational molester, who may just abuse a dozen or so children. This guy is a classic, with one exception. He brutalized Emma as well as sexually abused her. We call that a sadistic molester. Add to that the fact that with Emma he became obsessional. You don't see this all that often in child molesters, but it does happen. One particular child, the pedophile must have that child, no other. He lost all sense of survival. Most molesters would have shrugged and moved on to another child, but Dickerson didn't. He couldn't stop.

"He's not a stupid man, but he had to have known on some level that this obsession he had with Emma would bring him down. But he couldn't help himself, couldn't stop himself, couldn't leave and forget her. I understand he's also excellent at disguise and makeup."

"That's what he told me when we were in the water," Ramsey said.

"That's one of the reasons Rule Shaker's men hired him. Since Emma was going to be returned when Louey came around, the kidnapper couldn't be recognized, thus the disguise."

Tommy the Eye shook his head. "He must have thought he'd died and gone to heaven when he got the job."

Ramsey said, "How does all this get confused with his religious needs? He told Emma that he needed her, actually needed her."

"I would really like to talk to him about that. He seems like a boiling cauldron with all sorts of things tossed in indiscriminately, from beliefs of how Emma would save him to hurting her so that she would be taking his punishments for him. I can't wait to dig into his brain. But we're mostly thankful that he's out of commission now."

Molly said, "If and when you reach any understanding about him, Tommy, please tell us."

"I will, Mrs. Hunt."

He was rubbing his palms together.

THIRTY-THREE

By the time everyone had all the answers he or she wanted, Ramsey was feeling human enough to walk down to see Emma. She and Virginia Trolley were sitting in a corner of the cafeteria, their heads close together.

Emma looked up and saw him. She let out a yelp and dashed to him, wrapping herself around his leg. "It's all right, Emma," he said, patting her head. "See? I'm walking. It's for real. Nobody's holding me up. It was only another little bullet to a big macho guy like me. Now, let me pick you up so you can give me a proper hug."

"No, let me do it," Savich said and hoisted Emma up to eye level with Ramsey. She reached out and hugged him. He kissed her ear. "You smell good, Em. What is that? Oscar de la Renta?"

"No, that's the soap from the hotel." Emma drew back and said, "Was that a joke, Ramsey?"

Molly said to Sherlock, who was looking fit and quite beautiful and watching her husband with new eyes, "Ramsey loves her so much. Maybe someday he'll even love me."

"The man's found Nirvana and he knows it, Molly," Sherlock said in a matter-of-fact voice, still looking at her husband holding Emma, a besotted look on his face. "I've always liked Ramsey. Now that he's got you, everything will be just fine. What do you think, Molly? Does Dillon look like a natural holding Emma or what?"

THE orderly had brought two cots into Ramsey's room the night before. The whole family was together. They were sound asleep when the door suddenly burst open and Lieutenant McPherson ran in.

Ramsey was out of bed in an instant, ready to fight, and he nearly passed out cold. He fell back against the bed, breathing hard. "What's wrong?"

McPherson said, panting, "I was worried that something could have happened to you as well. Here, let me help you back into bed."

"What are you talking about?" Molly said, helping Ramsey herself. Emma was halfway to Ramsey's bed, intent, he knew, on protecting him.

"It's Dickerson," McPherson said. "They think somebody put something, maybe potassium, into one of his IVs. He's dead."

"BUT there are staff all over the place in the ICU," Virginia Trolley said, still looking utterly incredulous even though McPherson had been talking about it for a good ten minutes. She'd thrown on clothes and rushed to his hospital room when Ramsey had called her. Ramsey had never seen her without makeup before and her hair uncombed and her red blazer wrinkled. She looked cute. He'd never tell her that, of course, because she'd knock him out.

"How could anybody get in there," she continued, "stick a needle into the IV tube, and get out again, all without being seen by anybody? There weren't any guards on him, why would there be? He wasn't going anywhere on his own and no one ever thought he'd need protection. We've spoken to security and they've sealed off the hospital, but good luck on that. They're checking videotape right now to see if there's anything suspicious."

"Lieutenant McPherson said a nurse saw someone dressed in hospital whites," Molly said. "But that's no big deal. It's a little like wearing a uniform at the Pentagon. Nobody gives you much of a second glance if you appear to be someone who's supposed to belong."

"She's right," Ramsey said. "It's the only reasonable answer. Actually I don't think it's all that reasonable, but hey, this is a hospital, not a top-security area. The hospital staff weren't alerted to keep an eye out." He closed his eyes a minute. He was exhausted, his rib hurt, his shoulder ached like the devil, and he was ready to call in the cavalry for a pain pill.

He suddenly felt Emma's hand slip into his. He turned his head to see her studying him, knowing that he hurt, not knowing what to do about it. It was a lie, but he said cleanly, "I'm fine, Emma. But I like you right here holding my hand."

He also felt incredible relief. Dickerson was dead, long gone, no more threat to anyone. Emma was safe.

Lieutenant McPherson cleared his throat. "I also ran in here, Judge Hunt, because, to tell you the truth, you're the best suspect."

"I'm not moving too quickly right now," Ramsey said. "I nearly hung it up when you burst through that door. I think stealing a white coat, finding some potassium, since I don't carry any around with me, and walking nonchalantly into the ICU might have been beyond even my abilities, astounding though they be."

"That was a joke," Emma said to Lieutenant McPherson.

"I know. I'm glad all of you were here. It makes things easier."

Not an hour later, when the three of them were finally alone again, though they could see news vans below them in the street, they discovered they were all still too hyped to go back to sleep. The phone rang. Molly answered it, then, with a strange look on her face, she handed it to Ramsey. "I don't understand. It's my father. He wants to speak to you."

Ramsey thought briefly about pressing the speaker button. No, Emma was here. He picked up the phone and identified himself. It was indeed Mason Lord. He said, "I'm much better and I understand that you will survive as well, Ramsey. Oh yes, I'm also given to understand that there will be no more problems with that animal who was after Emma, and shot you."

Ramsey said very quietly, though he could feel the blood pounding through him, "How did you know, sir? Surely there hasn't been enough time for it to be on the news yet."

Mason laughed softly, then said, amusement lacing his voice, "I have friends everywhere, Ramsey. Of course I find things out very quickly. Actually, one could almost say that I find some things out almost before they happen."

Had it been Gunther who killed Dickerson? Or had Mason hired local talent for just this one assignment? Now that he'd had a second or two to think about it, he wasn't at all surprised. He didn't say anything. Why bother? What was there to say anyway?

"Now Emma doesn't have to be afraid, nor do you or Molly. I will expect the three of you here for Thanksgiving. That's my favorite holiday. No one expects extravagant gifts, just a great meal, which Miles always delivers."

"Yes," Ramsey said. "We'll be there." Slowly, he placed the phone back in the receiver. He looked at Molly and shook his head. She frowned a moment, then he knew she understood. She made a big deal out of yawning. "I'm ready to fold my tent. How about you, Em?"

"I'm sleepy too, Mama. What did Grandpa want, Ramsey?"

"He wanted to make sure we were all right. Nothing more."

"He was nice to call," Emma said, kissed Ramsey, and let her mother tuck her in.

Ramsey leaned back and closed his eyes. His shoulder was hurting like the devil. His fingertips tingled. His head ached. Now this. Molly leaned down to kiss him. He whispered, "He had Dickerson killed. What am I supposed to do?"

"Tell McPherson the truth. It won't matter, you know it won't. No one will ever take down my father. In fact I'll bet my father wants you to tell the cops. He's probably laughing right now, imagining it."

He suspected she was right. He called out, "Good night, Emma. Sleep well. You too, Molly."

IT was all over, Ramsey thought, as he walked up the stairs of their San Francisco home, Emma at his side. All over. He was thinking about Dickerson's mother in Duluth. She had paid for his cremation. Ramsey had actually gone, Savich with him, just to be sure, just to see the man before he was reduced to gray silt.

"Mama's asleep," Emma said. "She was really tired. I don't think she slept well last night."

That was true enough. He hadn't either. Emma had said she'd wanted to sleep in her own room, which was the reason neither of them had slept much. It was odd, but he'd missed her cuddling against them, at least in the morning he had.

"I hope she's not still asleep," Ramsey said. "I want to see her smile. She's done a lot of that since we got back home yesterday."

He stood in the doorway of their bedroom. Emma had left him, running down to her bedroom to fetch one of her toys. Molly was lying on her side, her back to him. She was wearing only a pair of white panties that were high cut on the sides. Her bottom leg was straight, the top leg was slightly bent. There wasn't a more seductive pose for a woman. He swallowed. Her hair was a glorious mess, tangled over a beautiful expanse of white flesh that made him want to walk right over there and begin kissing her back, starting at the base of her neck downward, until he could pull her panties away. They'd made love three times the previous night. He suspected there would have been a fourth time this morning, but Emma had had other plans.

"Mama kicked off the blanket," Emma said matter-of-factly beside him. She walked to the bed and gently raised the blanket to cover her mother. Molly stirred. She fell over onto her back and opened her eyes.

"Emma," she said, and raised her hand to cup her daughter's face. "Have you been taking care of Ramsey?"

"Yes, Mama. He's a lot better. He promised his shoulder only hurt a little bit. The best thing is he's not worried about me anymore."

"Emma, I'll worry about you until you're ninety years old. Now if we could just get rid of the press then everything would be fine and dandy," Ramsey said. "I'd really like to take you guys down to meet all the people in my office. We've also got a dynamite view." He sighed. "But you can bet the press is hanging out there." He walked to the bed, leaned down, and kissed Molly's nose. "You have a good sleep?"

She gave him a long lazy look that made him start to get hard again. "Yeah, no bad dreams, just oblivion. It's nice for a change. I'd best call my mom before it gets too late in Italy. She was concerned about Emma, and I promised."

Later in the kitchen, Molly put through the call, while Ramsey stood at the counter chopping some carrots and broccoli. Emma was setting the table.

Molly smiled into the phone, balancing it between her neck and shoulder as she stole a carrot. "Yes, Mom. How are you?"

"Fine, dear. Is everything all right?"

Molly told her, in a highly edited version, how the man had been captured. She finally told her he'd been murdered in the hospital.

Her mother was silent for a heartbeat, then she said, with affection, "Your father was always very efficient. Did he call you shortly after the man was dead to tell you that you were safe?"

Molly stared at the phone. "Yes, that's exactly what he did. The police still haven't located the person who shot potassium into Dickerson's IV."

"They won't either. Not a chance. Your father always hires reliable help."

"Yes, I suppose so. But I'm still very worried for him. He's been nearly killed, twice. That Rule Shaker doesn't seem like the type to give up."

"No, he never was. I doubt he's changed."

Molly jumped up from her chair, nearly pulling the phone off the wall. "What do you mean, Mom? Do you know Rule Shaker?"

"Certainly, dear. I knew him a very long time ago, when both he and your father were just getting started in their businesses. They were excellent friends, way back when. Our two families did everything together. I very much enjoyed his wife, Lorna, poor woman. She died in an automobile accident some fifteen years ago. I always believed Rule Shaker was responsible for that."

"But, Mom, they're bitter enemies now. It was Rule Shaker who blew up Louey, when Ramsey, Emma, and I were the actual targets. It was Rule Shaker who murdered a farmer in Colorado. He's tried twice to kill Father."

"These things happen, Molly. Just a moment." Molly heard her mother switch to her musical Italian. "What, Maria? Oh yes, put my tea on the table. That's fine. Do go to bed." Her mother returned, switching back to English. "Yes, dear? What were we speaking about?"

The good Lord give me patience, Molly thought, looking upward. "We were talking about the fact that my father and Rule Shaker are trying to kill each other. Why didn't I ever know about this? Why don't the police know about this? What happened between them?"

"I don't know about the police, dear. Surely they know. The split was no secret. As for you, why would you have ever known? The split happened when you were a little girl. Just before I left your father, actually. It was only a year later that Rule's wife left him."

"Do you know what happened?"

"Yes, dear. I don't suppose it matters now. You're all grown up with a daughter of your own. Rule Shaker wanted me to sleep with him, but you see, I was in love with your father. Too, I didn't really care for him. Rule looked like a gangster, if you know what I mean, the kind of gangster Hollywood put on the screen if they wanted no sympathy for the character, the kind who smokes. Your father never did look like anything but an aristocrat. He still does, in the photos I've seen of him over the years."

"But what happened?"

"Your father walked in on us. Rule Shaker was trying to force me, actually, and in a very crude way. Being a man, your father blamed me as well as his friend. It was the end of our marriage and the end of their friendship and business dealings. It was a very difficult time."

"I remember we went to Italy," Molly said slowly. "That was just after this had happened?"

"That's right. But it's a long time in the past, twenty years. Now, Molly, let me speak to Emma. I would like all of you to come to Italy for Thanksgiving. No worry about giving anyone a gift they won't like, just a very good meal. Our cook here, Magdalana, is excellent. She'd never cooked a turkey in her life until she came to me. Will you come?"

"I'll have to get back to you on that, Mom."

"Oh, yes, I did see a photo of your father in *Time* magazine, with his wife. It appears he's going to live, yet again. Well, I suppose that's good. After all, he did remove the threat from Emma."

"He had Dickerson murdered, Mother," Molly said, then realized she was a damned hypocrite and said quickly, "Although I wanted to kill him myself. You're right. No matter what else Father is, he did save Emma from a horrible experience in the courtroom, at the very least."

"Well, he still should be careful, don't you think?"

"Naturally," Molly said. "I don't think Rule Shaker is the kind of man to give up. I'm sure Father knows him well enough to realize that as well."

"Oh yes, he'll think he's being careful, but it isn't Rule I'm talking about. I just hope your father knows what he's doing."

"Doing about what?"

"Well, dear, it's his wife. I hadn't realized whom he'd married. In fact, it seems incredible to me that he would marry her, but evidently he didn't see any harm. Men are strange, don't you think? They think with their penises. That's what my mother always told me."

"I don't understand, Mom. What's strange about Eve? Admittedly she's younger than I am, but many older men have trophy wives, and yeah, I'd probably agree that most men do think with their dicks."

"Molly, dear, that's such a crude word. Now, that isn't what I meant. There was so much bad blood between your father and Rule Shaker and it kept getting worse. They went after the same deals. Sometimes one would win, sometimes the other, but the rivalry has gotten stronger over the years. That's why this is such a surprise."

"What's such a surprise?" Molly rolled her eyes toward Ramsey, who raised a black eyebrow.

"Your father's wife, dear. Eve. There was an excellent photo of her in *Time* magazine, just after your father was shot that first time. Didn't you know, dear? She's Rule Shaker's eldest daughter."

THIRTY-FOUR

Molly walked into her father's magnificent study and quietly closed the huge double doors behind her.

Her father rose slowly from his desk, raised an eyebrow, and said, "What is it, Molly? I wasn't expecting you. Is everything all right?"

He was dressed immaculately. Very few people who knew him would realize that he was thinner, that the flesh on his face was drawn more tautly, that his color wasn't exactly right, that, actually, he should still be in bed recovering from a gunshot wound to his chest. She smiled at him.

"Oh, yes, we're all fine. You're looking well. Miles said you've been up three hours today. He's worried, you know. He thinks you're overdoing it too quickly. He also said you ate a big piece of chocolate cake last night."

"Yes. There was some of Miles's homemade vanilla ice cream on top. I was growing mold in that bed. I'm fine. Where is Ramsey?"

"Both Ramsey and Emma are with Miles. I do believe Gunther is hovering, eating some of Miles's chocolate-chip cookies himself." She paused a moment, smiled at him, and said, "Actually, I wanted to see you by myself."

"What's this all about? Why are you here?"

The slant of his eyebrows, she thought, was identical to her own. She wondered that she'd never noticed that before. She'd have to ask Ramsey if he saw the similarity. "As a matter of fact," she said, "I'm here to do you a very big favor." He frowned at that, as she'd expected, since it was something he couldn't imagine. He waved her to a huge leather chair. "It's my favorite chair," he said, "but right now I can't sit in it. It's too difficult to get back out of it."

"Sort of like a pregnant woman."

"I doubt it. Now, what is this favor, Molly?" When she didn't answer immediately, he glanced at a paper he'd been reading, ignoring her. She'd seen him do this before. It really rattled a person wanting his attention. Odd how she saw and understood it, and was only tempted to tell him that he was a fine actor.

She let him scan a full page, then said finally, "Mother told me all about you and Rule Shaker, that you were best friends for so many years, your two families close. She told me how you blamed her as well as Rule Shaker when you came in on them."

His head came up with a snap. "I'll bet she told you how innocent she was, that Rule was trying to rape her."

"Yes, that's what she said. She said she didn't really like him, that he was crude, that she loved you, but of course, you blamed her as well as him. You threw her out. You kept my brother and I went with her to Italy."

He shrugged and winced a bit with pain. "It was a very long time ago. I can't imagine why she chose to tell you now. As for Rule Shaker, I've dealt with him over the years without much problem. Perhaps not as well as I'd like recently," he added, frowning down at a letter opener that looked as sharp as a stiletto. He looked up at her. "Actually, he's taken more business than I'd have liked over the past couple of years, but it's a temporary thing. He's become a thug, nothing more. He's always been jealous of me and what's mine. He had bad teeth when we were young. I'll bet he's got false teeth by now." He paused a moment, a frown settling on his forehead, looking beyond her, into the past, perhaps.

"I accepted him, made him my friend," he continued after a moment. "I can't believe I didn't see him clearly until I happened to walk in on him and your mother.

"He's tried to kill me, twice. I'm going to have to deal with him once and for all. I don't like having to constantly look over my shoulder. Gunther worries. He isn't happy about any of this either."

"Rule Shaker didn't try to kill you."

Her father looked at her with amazed contempt. "What did you say?"

"No," she said, very slowly, as if she were speaking to a dim child. "He didn't ever try to kill you. Actually, it was your wife."

Her father bounded to his feet, his face paling, then weaved where he stood. She saw waves of pain washing over him, started to go to him, then stopped, realizing that he hated anyone, particularly her, to see any weakness in him. He chopped his hand in the air, waving her back. "Eve? You're saying that Eve tried to kill me? You're trying to blame Eve? That's absurd, Molly, absolutely absurd." Then he turned to dial his private telephone. "We'll see about this. Where the hell do you get off accusing Eve of anything? You're jealous of her, aren't you, Molly? You can't stand her because she's everything you're not, you're—"

"She blew Louey up as well."

He slowly straightened and looked at her. He slowly laid down the receiver. He was shaking his head as he said, "No, it was Rule. He wanted you and Emma and Ramsey dead in order to bring Louey into line. That silly little bitch daughter of Rule's wanted the jerk. No, Rule blew Louey up by mistake. Because his intention was to kill you and Emma, I had to retaliate. He would have taken my daughter so I took his. Now, enough of your venom, Molly. I won't have any more of this. I'm getting Eve in here."

"She's not here. She left"—Molly looked down at her watch—

"probably about ten minutes ago. She's not coming back and you're not going after her."

She would swear she saw a fine tremor in his right hand. But his voice was calm with authority as he asked in that barely tolerant cold voice of his, "What is this all about, Molly?"

Slowly, Molly rose from the leather chair. She walked to her father's desk and splayed her palms on the rich mahogany surface. "Listen to me, Dad. Eve is Rule Shaker's daughter. After her mother's death, Eve continued her schooling in Europe, then went to school at Harvard. She didn't go back to live with her father and younger sister, which is why you never heard of her. Your wife has a master's degree in business, Dad. Her forte is financial analysis. She and Rule Shaker planned to take you for as much as they could. You just admitted that you'd lost more to him in the past couple of years than you'd wanted to lose. It wasn't just coincidental. Eve was feeding him business information."

She realized the instant he believed her. She saw his eyes go cold, saw the deep shifting of his eyes as images developed, changed, evolved in his mind. She said very quietly, "You're not going to kill Eve. It's over, all of it. No one will try to kill you and you won't try to kill Shaker."

His face was flushed, he was shaking his head. "No, it's impossible. I knew Eve. Do you think I'm stupid? I had her checked out completely before I married her. She's Swedish, from a little town north of Stockholm called Uppsala. I know all about her family. Her father's an engineer—he let her keep one of his diplomas. It's in our bedroom. Her mother is a schoolteacher. She teaches French, for God's sake. She has two younger sisters. I know everything about her. She's fluent in English because of an English nanny she had all during her childhood. I know she never went to college, that she—"

"Her name is Janice Claire Shaker. The last time you saw her, she was all of four years old, just a very little girl. You probably have no memory of her at all. When Rule Shaker and his wife divorced, Janice went with her mother to Boston and Rule Shaker kept Melissa, who was two years old at the time. They split their kids the way you did with me and Teddy.

"Janice married a Swedish engineer when she was only eighteen, her freshman year in college. Her husband was killed on a dam project a year later. She obviously got all her Swedish antecedents from her husband's family, including her husband's engineering degree that's hanging on your wall. In any case, somewhere along the line, Janice or her father came up with the idea to take you in. And they did take you in. Fooled you completely.

"She admitted to me that she murdered Louey. She hated him, didn't want her sister to be with him. She smuggled in the bomb that blew him up. Emma and I weren't the targets. And then when you killed Melissa, her sister, she tried to murder you. Maybe Eve would have tried to murder you eventually regardless of what happened. She didn't volunteer her plans. I don't know and neither will you. It doesn't matter. All of it's going to stop right now."

She watched him straighten, knew that the effect must be hurting his chest. Then he was utterly still, even his hands silent at his sides. He said, his voice as gentle as a soft spring rain, "If what you say is true, if she did betray me, then how could it possibly be over?"

She would have preferred rage, not this calm dead coldness. She didn't know where she found it, but she reached down deep inside her and brought up a very big smile. "Because, Dad, I've saved your life and now I'm going to end it all. No one is going to kill anyone. You try to harm Eve or Rule Shaker and I'm going to turn you in. It's true that I don't have much hard proof, but I know enough to make things excessively uncomfortable for you. If you refuse to end it, I also promise you will never see Emma or me again. I will not take the chance of Emma getting between you and Shaker.

"There will be no more attempts on your life or anyone connected with you, including me and Emma. Eve and her father have agreed to it. You took one of his daughters and you're giving the other one back. Louey is dead and you were nearly killed twice. They both know I could bring them down, because, you see, I taped my conversation with Eve and played it for them. One copy is with Dillon Savich of the FBI and the other is with the San Francisco District Attorney's office. I've got it all and I'll keep it safe. It's over. Believe me on this."

He slowly raised his hand. In an instant, Molly thought he was going to strike her. She stood her ground, waiting.

Slowly, Mason Lord lowered his arm. His voice was nearly a whisper as he said, "You're my daughter and you're threatening me with this?"

"Yes, I am. It's my only way to protect both Emma and you. I don't ever want to have to worry that Emma could be the next victim in your war with Rule Shaker. What's more, I don't want him or his daughter to kill you. Now, I want your word that you'll leave the Shakers alone."

Mason stared at the daughter who looked so much like her grandmother, who hadn't wanted Alicia to marry him, who'd looked at him like he was some sort of back alley scum. She'd looked at him and known what he was to his very soul. He'd seen the knowledge in those gray-green eyes of hers—Molly's eyes—and he'd hated her with everything in him. Now here was Molly, more her blood than she was his, telling him what to do. What was wrong with him? She was just a woman, nothing more.

He wanted to straighten her out but good, but instead, what came out of his mouth was, "I eliminated the scum who hurt Emma."

His voice was defensive, with maybe even a hint of a whine. It amazed her and heartened her. "Yes, I know. That's why I haven't already called the cops. Do you know something, Dad? I don't think you're all bad. You tried to protect family. That's something in your favor. A very big something. Do you agree, Dad? It stops here and now?"

Mason Lord looked down at his long white fingers. The flesh looked loose on the back of his hands. Slowly, he raised his head. Molly was standing quietly in front of him, her wild red hair pulled back and fastened with a gold clip against her nape.

Her ears, he thought, her ears were Alicia's. He'd always thought Alicia had beautiful ears. He heard her say again, her voice calm and low, "Do you agree, Dad?"

The phone rang sharp and loud beside his left hand.

"Answer it," Molly said, looking at her watch. "It's Rule Shaker, right on time. End it, Dad."

Maybe it was time to end it all. She had guts, his guts, to come in here and face him down.

Well, what the hell. He picked up the phone and said to a man he hadn't spoken to in twenty years, "Rule. It's Mason Lord."

EPILOGUE

"It's a boy," Ramsey called out. Both Molly and Emma came running into his study from the kitchen. He pressed the speaker button and put the phone down.

"Congratulations!" Molly and Emma shouted in unison. Emma's Dalmatian, six-month-old Kenny, barked madly, and jumped against Ramsey's leg. "When? How long? What's his name?"

Sherlock laughed, raucous and full-bodied, loud on the speaker. "His name is Sean Franklin Savich and he wailed his lungs out as he slid into Dillon's hands. He's big and healthy and everything's great. Dillon came through like a champ, kept me up and walking around until I finally told him I'd punch his lights out if he didn't let me lie down and yell at him."

Emma wanted to know when they'd bring Sean out so she could play with him. Soon, Sherlock told her, very soon.

When Ramsey hung up the phone, he sat down in his dark brown leather chair and pulled Molly onto his lap. Then he brought Emma down on Molly's lap, wrapping his arms around both of them. It was a routine all of them were used to. He looked at the wall across from his chair. There were three neoimpressionist paintings hanging there, selected by him and Molly together over the past several months.

"I got a request from my law clerks and my secretary today, all three of them—they want to see Emma," he said, kissing Molly's ear. "It's been at least a month, they said. They said I was being selfish with her. So, guys, would you like to come down to my office? Emma, you've got a holiday Monday so you won't miss any school. What do you say?"

"Will Mrs. Burger have some of her lemon bars?" Emma asked.

Ramsey laughed. "Greed always wins out. I'll ask her."

"If the answer's yes, then count us in," Molly said, and kissed Emma's ear.

When Emma jumped down to go play with Kenny in the backyard, Ramsey said to Molly, "I got a call from Lieutenant O'Connor from the Oak Park police. They found the man they believe shot your father in a dump site, somewhere in southern Ohio. He'd been dead quite a while, about six months. Rule Shaker didn't want any loose ends."

"Exactly. Eve must have told her father about the saliva the cops found and could do a DNA match on if they came up with a suspect. His spitting cost him his life."

"Yeah. Probably no big loss. That's over. No doubt it's a relief for your dad." He nuzzled her neck, fiddled with the small gold hoop in her left ear, and said, "Have you decided yet, Molly? Are we going to Italy or to Chicago for Thanksgiving? You'd best make up your mind; it's only a few days away and I imagine that there aren't many airline tickets left."

"No problem," she said, giving him a big grin. "We're going to Italy for Thanksgiving and to Chicago for Christmas. I told my dad that Emma wanted lots of really neat presents and that's why he got Christmas.

"He huffed and puffed, but then he laughed, said Gunther was already talking about getting Emma a G.I. Jane doll for Christmas, replete with appropriate weaponry. Can you beat that?"

"No, I'm not even going to try."

Molly rolled her eyes. "Well, since I still have my Detonics all safe and snug in a box on the top shelf of a closet, I guess I can't say much. Oh yes, I returned Mrs. Garcia's call. She said that Dr. Loo sends her love, that she's planning on spring skiing."

"What did she say about Emma?"

"She's pleased. She thinks it would be good for Emma to travel again. She's still very encouraged with the progress Emma's making. For now, she says that Emma's talked about it enough, and, in her own way, is ready to move on."

"Thank God for that. Am I spoiling her too rotten, Molly?"

"Nah, she's got a good head on her shoulders. She's spoiling you, actually. Imagine her running down here to the kitchen to make you some toast this morning so you wouldn't have to get your feet cold on the tile."

He laughed. "There are still crumbs in the bed. Oh yes, I forgot to tell you. You know how the district judges get their cases through the random lottery system? I just got handed another big-time drug case. I hope this one has a different ending than the last one."

"I think I'll hang out in the courtroom, just to make sure nobody tries anything."

He kissed her ear, her chin, the tip of her nose. "Emma spoils me and you protect me." He leaned back in the chair and gave her a big grin. "What more could a guy ask for?"

THE EDGE

PROLOGUE

Edgerton, Oregon

The night was black and calm, silent except for the mellow whine of the newly tuned Porsche engine, yet she heard the soft, sobbing voice pleading with her again, whispering low and deep. It never left her alone now.

No one else was near, it was just Jilly driving alone on the coast highway. The ocean stirred beside her, but with no moon out, it looked like an empty, black expanse. The Porsche, sensitive to the slightest touch of her fingers, gently swerved left, toward the cliff, toward the endless expanse of black water beyond. Jilly jerked the car back to the center line.

Laura's voice began sobbing in her brain, then grew louder, filling her, until Jilly wanted to burst.

"Shut up!" Jilly's scream filled the car for a brief moment. Her voice sounded harsh and ugly. It was nothing like Laura's had been, like a small child's sobbing, lost and inconsolable. Only death would bring peace. Jilly felt that voice, Laura's voice, build inside her again. She gripped the steering wheel and stared straight ahead, praying to herself, chanting for it to stop, for Laura to go away.

"Please," she whispered. "Please stop. Leave me alone. *Please.*"

But Laura didn't stop. She was no longer a child, speaking in a sweet, terrified voice. She was herself again, angry now, and this time foul words frothed from her mouth, spewing rage and saliva that Jilly tasted in the back of her throat. She banged her fists on the steering wheel, hard, harder still, rhythmically, to make the malevolent voice go away. She opened the window, pressed it all the way down and leaned out, letting the wind tear her hair back, and her eyes sting and water. She shouted into the night, "Make it stop!"

It stopped. Suddenly.

Jilly drew a deep breath and pulled her head back into the car. The wind whooshed through the car and she sucked in mouthfuls of the cold air. It tasted wonderful. It was over. Thank God, finally it had stopped. She raised her head, looking around, wondering where she was. She'd been driving for hours, it seemed, yet the dashboard clock read only midnight. She'd been gone from home for a half hour.

Her life had become whispers and screams until she couldn't bear it. Now there was silence, deep and complete silence.

Jilly began counting. *One, two, three*—no curses, no whispers, no small child's pleading, nothing, just her own breathing, the soft hum of her car. She threw back her head and closed her eyes a moment, relishing the silence. She began counting again. *Four, five, six*—still blessed silence.

Seven, eight—soft, very soft, like a faraway rustling of leaves, coming closer, closer. Not rustling, no, whispering. Laura was whispering again, begging not to die, begging and pleading and swearing she'd never meant to sleep with him, but it had just happened, he'd made it happen. But Jilly hadn't believed her.

"Please, stop, stop, stop," Jilly chanted over that feathery voice. Laura began screaming that Jilly was a pathetic bitch, a fool who couldn't see what she was. Jilly stomped down on the gas pedal. The Porsche lurched forward, hitting seventy, eighty, eighty-five. The coast road swerved. She kept the car directly in the center of the road. She began singing. Laura screamed louder, and Jilly sang louder. Ninety. Ninety-five.

"Go away. *Damn you, go away!*" Jilly's knuckles were white on the steering wheel, her head low, her forehead nearly touching the rim. The engine's vibrations made Laura's screaming voice convulse with power.

One hundred.

Jilly saw the sharp turn, but Laura yelled that they would be together soon now, very soon. She couldn't wait to get Jilly, and then they'd see who would win.

Jilly screamed, whether at Laura or at the sight of the cliff dropping some forty feet to the heaped and tumbled black rocks below. The Porsche plunged through the railing, thick wood and steel, picking up speed, and shot out to the vast empty blackness beyond.

One more scream rent the silence before the Porsche sliced nose first through the still, black water. There was scarcely a sound, just the fast downward plunge, the sharp, clean impact, then the quick shifting and closing over, the calm water returning to what it had been just a second before.

Then there was only the black night. And calm and silence.

ONE

Bethesda Naval Hospital
Maryland

I jerked upright in bed, clutched at my neck, and doubled over as a god-awful pain ripped through me. I'd heard a man yell, just beside me, nearly right in my ear. I couldn't draw a breath, I was suffocating. And a guy who wasn't even there was yelling at me and I was dying. I finally managed to heave inward and suck in a huge breath.

I'd felt a mountain of frigid water crash down on me like the whale had closed down over Jonah. But I wasn't drowning. I knew what drowning was, remembered it as clearly as if it had happened yesterday. I was seven years old, swimming with my older brother, Kevin, who was flirting with some young girls. I'd gotten tangled up in some underwater branches. It had been Jilly who'd jerked me out, smacked my back hard as I'd gagged and choked, until water gushed out of my mouth.

The dream wasn't like that. It was as if I'd been hit by that water just a moment before there was, quite simply, nothing. Nothing at all. Just stillness, no pain, no questions, no fear, just an utter blank.

I swung my legs over the bed and stamped them hard on the ancient linoleum, savoring the sluice of pain that rumbled through my shoulder, my ribs, my collarbone, my right thigh, and other parts of me that were healing well enough so that gradually I'd dropped them out of my inventory. That delicious sharp pain brought me fully into my favorite hospital room, planted me firmly in the here and now, out from under water in a nightmare that had left me being nothing at all.

Still, when my feet hit the linoleum, the shock of the impact punched me back, and I nearly fell. I grabbed the bed railing at the head of the bed, took a deep breath, and looked around. My feet were still on the floor, flat on off-white linoleum that I'd come to hate in the past two weeks as much as those pastel green and tan walls. Leave it to the military to pick those colors. But you couldn't hate when you were dead, so I was glad there was something there to prove to me that I was alive.

I'd been lucky, they'd told me. The blast hadn't zeroed in on my heart or my head or anything vital. It was like I'd gotten hit by a two-by-four all over—a bit smashed here, a bone broken there, a muscle twisted out down lower. My feet and my back had escaped, with faint bruises marching up my spine. The explosion missed my groin too, for which I was profoundly grateful.

I stood there by my bed, breathing and savoring all the air that was here, all of it mine.

I looked down at my messed-up bed. I wasn't about to fall back into that bed because I knew the dream still hovered, just beyond in the ether, much too close, waiting for me to sleep again. I wasn't about to. I stretched, slowly and carefully. Still, every move brought a jab of pain from somewhere in my body. I breathed in deeply and walked slowly to the window of my hospital room. I was in the newer hospital, built in 1980, a massive building attached to the original hospital, built sometime in the 1930s. Everyone there complained about having to walk miles to get anywhere. I wished I could walk even a part of a mile, and complain with them.

I saw a few starburst dots of light from the five-level open parking building across the way. The parking building as well as half a dozen support buildings were connected to the hospital by long corridors. I couldn't see more than a dozen parked cars from where I stood. Lights spiked up from lamps set at close intervals throughout the landscaped grounds. There were lights even in among the trees. My law enforcement instincts told me there were no places for a mugger or a terrorist to hide—too many lights.

There hadn't been any lights at all in the dream, just darkness, wet darkness. I walked slowly to the small bathroom, leaned over very carefully, cupped my hands under the water tap at the sink, and drank deeply. As I straightened, water ran down my chin and dripped onto my chest. I had dreamed I was drowning and yet my throat felt drier than that wool-parched, blistering air in Tunisia. It made no sense.

Unless I hadn't been the one drowning. Suddenly, deep down, I knew. I hadn't been the one to drown, but I'd been there, right there.

I looked around expecting someone to be there, close to me, right behind me, ready to tap me on the shoulder. For over two weeks since I'd been pounded into the desert sand by the bomb blast, there was always someone there beside me, speaking quietly to me, jabbing me with needles, endless numbers of needles. My arms ached from all the shots and my butt was still numb in places.

I drank more water, then slowly raised my head, careful as always not to move too quickly. I stared at the man in the mirror above the sink. I looked like oatmeal, gray and collapsed, like I wasn't really alive. I was used to seeing a big guy, but the person staring back at me wasn't at all substantial. He looked like a lot of big bones strung together. I grinned at him. At least I still had my teeth, and they were still straight. I felt lucky my teeth hadn't been blown out when that bomb exploded and hurled me like a bag of feathers some fifteen feet across desert sand.

When my friend Dillon Savich, another FBI agent, saw me in the gym, he'd probably shake his head and ask me where I'd stashed my coffin. I knew it would take a good six months before I could go toe-to-toe with Savich again and have a slim prayer of holding my own with him at the gym.

I took a deep breath, drank more water, and switched off the bathroom light. The figure in the mirror was shadowy now. He looked a lot better that way. I stepped back into the bedroom, to the stark outline of the single bed and the huge red digital numbers on the clock some friends had brought me, wrapped with a bright crimson ribbon. I looked at the clock. It was just seven minutes after three A.M. I remembered Savich's wife, Sherlock, also an FBI agent, telling me when I was floating between pain and the oblivion of morphine that every minute that clicked by on the clock meant I was that much closer to getting out of this place and back to work where I belonged.

I walked back to the bed and slowly lowered myself down on my back. I pulled up the single sheet and thin blanket with my left hand. I tried to relax, to settle and ease my muscles. I wasn't about to go to sleep again. I closed my eyes and tried to think logically and clearly about the dream. Yes, I'd felt water, but not really drowning, just a shock of water pouring into me. Just a taste of water. Then nothing at all.

I raised my left hand and rubbed my fist over my chest. At least my heart had calmed down. I pulled in more deep breaths and told myself to stop the drama crap and think. Think cold, that was the rule at the Academy. I had to stop the panic and think cold.

It took me another couple of minutes to wonder whether it hadn't been a dream at all, but something else. As clearly as I saw the face of the digital clock on the utility stand beside my bed, I remembered seeing Jilly's face.

I didn't like that at all. That was nuts, plain nuts. A strange dream where I was drowning, only not really, and for some reason Jilly was back there somewhere in my brain. I'd last seen Jilly at Kevin's home in Chevy Chase, Maryland, at the end of February. She'd acted a little strange, no other way to put it, but I hadn't really paid all that much attention, just tucked it away. Too much other stuff going on in my life, like going to Tunisia.

I remembered talking to Kevin about Jilly the day after she had flown in from Oregon. Kevin, my older brother, had just shaken his head. Living on the West Coast was making Jilly a little eccentric, and don't worry about it. Nothing more than that. Kevin was career army, had four boys, and not a whole lot of time to be thinking about the oddities of his three siblings. It had been just the four of us for eight years now, since our parents died in a car accident, hit by a drunk driver.

I remembered Jilly droning on about all sorts of things—her new Porsche, her dress that she'd bought at Langdon's in Portland, some girl called Cal Tarcher she didn't seem to like, and the girl's brother, Cotter, who Jilly had thought was a vicious bully. She'd even gone on and on about how good sex was with Paul, her husband of eight years. There didn't seem to be any particular point to any of it as far as I could see. Now what she'd said seemed more than just simply eccentric.

Was Jilly drowning in my dream?

I didn't want to let that thought dig itself into my brain, but it had weaseled in with that dream, and it wouldn't leave now. I was tired, but not quite as tired as the day before or the day before that. I was mending. The doctors would nod their heads and smile at each other, then at me, patting my unbruised right shoulder. They had talked about letting me go home next week. I decided I would make it sooner.

I knew I wasn't going back to sleep, not with that dream waiting for me, and I knew it was waiting, certain of it. I knew it was waiting because it didn't really feel like a dream, it was something else. I had to deal with this.

I decided then and there that I'd give my right nut for a beer. I didn't think it through, just pushed the call buzzer. In four minutes, according to my digital clock with its big red numbers, Midge Hardaway, my night nurse, stuck her head in the door.

"Mac? You okay? It's really late. You should be asleep. What's the problem?"

Midge was somewhere in her thirties, tall, with short honey-colored hair and a sharp chin. She was smart, reliable; you could count on her in a crunch. Whenever I'd drifted back to consciousness at the beginning of my stay here, she'd be right beside me, talking quietly to me, her fingers lightly stroking my arm.

I smiled at her with what I hoped was my best boyish smile, filled with irresistible charm. I wasn't sure she could even see it because the room was very dim, the only light coming from the corridor at her back. But I hoped she could at least hear all the effort I was putting into my voice. "Midge, save me. I'm in bad shape here. I can't stand it any longer. Please, you've gotta help me. You're my only hope."

The corridor light framed a smile that was at once sympathetic and filled with laughter that she didn't bother to hide quite enough. Then she cleared her throat. "Mac, listen to me now. You've been out of commission for over two weeks. I guess since you're feeling better, this could become more and more of a problem. But hey, hon, I'm married. What would Doug think? He's got this temper, you know?"

Forget boyish charm. I tried for pathetic. "Why would Doug care? He isn't here. He wouldn't even have to know if you think it would upset him, which I can't begin to imagine that it would."

"Now, Mac, if I weren't married, I'd be truly tempted, even though you're not even close to batting a thousand yet in the health department. Hey, I'm flattered. You're good-looking, at least you were in that photo they used of you in the newspaper, and you've got the use of both hands now. But the way things stand, Mac, I just can't do it."

"I'm really dying here, Midge. I'm not lying to you. Just this one time and I won't beg again—well, at least not until tomorrow night. Just one, Midge. I'll go slow. I've already got drool pooling in my mouth."

She stood there shaking her head back and forth, her hands on her hips, very nice hips I'd noticed nine days ago when I finally wasn't so dulled from painkillers. I sighed. "All right, if it's really against your ethics, or Doug's ethics. But I'll tell you, Midge, I don't see why it's such a big deal. And why your husband would care is beyond me. He'd probably be begging just like I am if he was in my shoes. Hey, maybe you could call Mrs. Luther. She's tough, but maybe she'll give in. I think she likes me, maybe—"

"Mac, are you nuts? Mrs. Luther is sixty-five years old. For God's sake, you can't be all that desperate. Ellen Luther? She'd probably bite you."

"Why would she do that? What are you talking about?"

"Mac," she said with great patience, "you're horny after two weeks of celibacy. I can understand that. But Mrs. Luther?"

"I think you've got the wrong idea here, Midge. I don't want Mrs. Luther. I want you in that way, but you're married, so I only think about that in passing, like any other guy would, you know, maybe once every five minutes or so during the day, maybe more the better I feel. No, what I'm dying for, what I want more than anything in the world, is a beer."

"A beer?" She stared at me for the longest time, then she started laughing. That laughter of hers grew until she had to come into the room and close the door so she wouldn't disturb other patients. She was doubled over with laughter, holding her sides. "You want a beer? That's what all this is about? A damned beer? And you'll go real slow?"

"Oh yes," I said, "oh yes."

She paused a moment in the open doorway, shaking her head and still laughing. Said over her shoulder, "You want a Bud Light?"

"I'd kill for a Bud Light."

The Bud can was so cold I thought my fingers would stick to it. There couldn't be anything better than this, I thought, as the beer slid down my throat. I wondered which nurse was hoarding the Bud in the nurses' refrigerator. I drank half the can in one long slug. Midge was standing beside the bed, looking down at me. "I hope mixing the beer with your meds doesn't make you puke. Hey, slow down. You promised you'd make it last. Men, you really can't believe them, not when it comes to beer."

"It's been a long time," I said, licking beer foam off my mouth. "I just couldn't help myself. The edge is off now." I heaved a thankful sigh and took a smaller drink, realizing that she wasn't likely to get me another beer. At least the terror of that nightmare was deep below the surface again, not sitting right there on my shoulder, waiting to whisper in my ear again. I had about a quarter of a can left. I rested it on my stomach.

Midge had moved next to me and now she was taking my pulse.

"My neighbor, Mr. Kowalski, waters my plants when I'm out of town or in the hospital, like now. He also keeps things dusted. He's a retired plumber, older than the paint on my great-aunt Silvia's house, and real sharp. James Quinlan—he's an FBI agent—he sings to his African violets. Healthiest critters you've ever seen. His wife wonders when she'll wake up some morning to find some plants cozying up to her in bed. Oh shit, Midge, I want to go home."

She lightly cupped my face against her palm. "I know, Mac. Soon now. Your pulse is fine. Now, let me take your blood pressure." She didn't tell me what it was, but she hummed under her breath, something from Verdi, I think, and that meant it was good. "You need to go back to sleep, Mac. Is your stomach happy with the beer? No nausea?"

I took the last pull of beer, kept the burp in my throat, and gave her a big smile. "I'm fine. I owe you, Midge, big time."

"I'll collect sometime, don't you worry. Your plants sound great. Hey, how about I get Mrs. Luther for you?"

I whimpered, and she left me alone, grinning and waving at me from the doorway. In the next instant, Jilly's face slammed back into my mind.

"You've got to face it, Mac," I said very quietly to myself in the still night, looking toward the window that gave onto the nearly empty parking lot. "All right. Let's just say it out loud. Was that a dream or some kind of prophecy? Is Jilly in some sort of trouble?"

No, that was bullshit. I knew bullshit.

I didn't go back to sleep. Truth was I was too scared. I wished I had another beer. Midge dropped by at four A.M., frowned at me, and shoved a sleeping pill down my throat.

At least I didn't dream for the three hours they gave me before the guy with the blood cart came by, shook my bruised shoulder to wake me up, and shoved a needle in my vein. He never paused in his talk—I think it was about the Redskins—slapped down a Band-Aid hard over the hole in my arm, and whistled as he pushed his torture cart out of my room. His name was Ted and he was, I thought, what the shrinks call a situational sadist.

At ten o'clock that morning, I simply couldn't wait any longer. I had to know. I dialed Jilly's number in Edgerton, Oregon. Her husband, Paul, answered the phone on the second ring.

"Jilly," I said, and knew my voice wasn't steady. "Paul, how's Jilly?"

Silence.

"Paul?"

I heard a shuddering breath, then, "She's in a coma, Mac."

I felt an odd settling deep inside me, the slow unwrapping of the package whose contents I already knew. I hadn't wanted this, but it hadn't really surprised me at all. I prayed as I asked, "Will she live?"

I could hear Paul fiddling with the phone cord, probably twisting it over and over his hand. Finally he said in a dead voice, "Nobody wants to even take a guess, Mac. The doctors did a CAT scan and an MRI. They say there's hardly any damage to her brain, just some tiny hemorrhages and some swelling, but nothing to account for the coma. They just don't know. They hope she'll come out of it really soon. Bottom line, we have to wait and see. First you getting blown up in some godforsaken place, and now Jilly in this ridiculous accident."

"What happened?" But I knew, yeah, I knew.

"Her car went over a cliff on the coast road last night, just after midnight. She was driving the new Porsche I gave her for Christmas. She'd be dead if a highway patrolman hadn't been passing by. He saw the whole thing, said she just seemed to let the car drift, then speeded up through the railing. He said the Porsche made a perfect nosedive into the water. The water isn't more than fifteen to twenty feet where she went over. The Porsche headlights were still on, thank God, and the driver's side window was open. He got her out on his first try, a pure miracle, he said. No one can believe he managed it, that she's still alive. I'll call you as soon as something changes—either way. I'm sorry, Mac, real sorry. Are you feeling better?"

"Yes, much better," I said. "Thank you, Paul. I'll be in touch." I laid the receiver gently back into its cradle. Paul had evidently been too upset even to wonder why I'd called him specifically about Jilly, at seven o'clock in the morning, West Coast time, the very morning after the accident. I wondered when Paul would think of it, wondered when he'd call me, asking about it.

At that moment, I didn't have a clue what I'd tell him.

TWO

"Mac, for God's sake, what are you doing out of bed? No way the doctors said you could leave. Just look at you. You don't look so hot. Your face is as gray as dingy old curtains."

Sherlock began shoving my chest lightly, pushing me back toward the bed. I'd managed to get my legs into a pair of jeans and had been in the middle of fighting with a long-sleeved shirt when she came in.

"Back into bed, Mac. You're not going anywhere. How'd you get those jeans on?" Sherlock tucked herself under my armpit, trying to turn me around, trying to force me down on that damned bed.

I stopped and she couldn't move me. "Listen, I'm all right, Sherlock. Let me go. I don't want you under my bare arm. I haven't had a shower yet."

"You're not that ripe. I'm not moving until you at least sit down and tell me what's going on."

"Okay, I'll sit," I said, and truth be told, it was a good thing I planned to sit quickly, though not on that bed. "Oh, all right. If you insist, Sherlock." I smiled at her. She was a tall, slender woman with a head of thick, curly red hair, confined this morning at the back of her neck with a gold clip. She had the whitest skin and the prettiest smile, warm and sweet unless she was pissed, when she could chew metal if it came right down to it. We'd come into the Bureau at the same time, all of two years ago now.

She managed a surprising amount of my weight, walking lock-step, veering sideways so she could push me down onto a hospital chair. Once I was seated I grinned up at her, remembering the two of us going up the ropes in our final physical exam at the Academy. I hadn't known if she'd be able to do it or not, and I hadn't been about to leave her. I'd hung beside her, encouraging her, calling her names, insulting her at a fine clip until she finally made it all the way up the rope with those skinny arms of hers. Sherlock didn't have a lot of upper-body strength, but she had something a whole lot better—guts and heart. She was more fond of me than I probably deserved.

"You're going to talk to me. The doctors are shaking their heads. They've already called your boss and I'll betcha they'll be here ready to roll you into the floor if you take so much as one step toward that door. Here's reinforcements. Dillon, come here and help me figure out what's eating Mac. Look, he's even got his pants on."

Dillon Savich raised a dark brow at that, his expression saying quite clearly to me, *The SOB better have his pants on.*

I settled back in the chair. What difference did five minutes make? I'd still be out of here soon enough. Besides, it was best that some of my friends knew what was going on.

"Look, guys, I've got to go home and pack. I've got to fly out to Oregon. My sister was in an accident last night. She's in a coma. I can't stay here."

Sherlock knelt beside the chair and took one of my big hands between hers. "Jilly? She's in a coma? What happened?"

I closed my eyes against immediate memories of that demented dream, or whatever it had been. "I called Oregon early this morning," I said. "Her husband Paul told me."

Sherlock cocked her head to one side and studied me for a moment. Then she asked, "Why'd you call her?"

Sherlock had this brain that could accelerate electrons.

Savich was still standing by the open doorway, looking fit and big and tough. His eyes were on his wife, Sherlock, who was still looking up at me, waiting for me to strip open my guts for her, which I was about to do. No contest.

"Sit back and close your eyes, Mac, that's right. I won't let anyone bother you. I wish I had some of Dillon's private reserve whiskey from Kentucky. It would mellow you out quicker than Sean can get Dillon up with his best yell."

"That didn't make a whole lot of sense, Sherlock, but let me tell you that Midge brought me a beer last night," I said. "I didn't puke. It tasted really good." An understatement. I couldn't imagine sex being better than that one Bud Light.

"I'm so happy for you," Sherlock said, and patted my cheek. And waited. I watched her look over at her husband, standing there just inside the hospital room, all calm and relaxed, his arms crossed over his chest. It was a pity there weren't more like him at the Bureau, instead of the clone bureaucrats who were too afraid to do anything that hadn't been sanctioned for at least a decade. I hated it when I saw it, prayed I wouldn't turn out to be like that in the years to come. Maybe I had a chance not to be, in the Counter-Terrorism section. The bureaucrats did their thing in Washington, but in the field the rules fell away. You were on your own, or at least you were if you were on the ground with a terrorist group in Tunisia.

"A dream," I said finally. "It started with a dream last night. I dreamed about drowning, or about someone drowning. I think it was Jilly." I told them everything I could remember, which was nearly all of it. I shrugged and said, "That's why I called so early this morning. I found out the dream, or whatever it was, had happened. She's in a coma." What is that going to mean? I wondered yet again. Will she live but be a vegetable? Will we have to decide whether or not to unplug her?

"I'm scared," I said, looking at Sherlock. "More scared than I've ever been in my life. Facing those terrorist goons with only a .450 Magnum Express wasn't even in the same ballpark. Getting blown into the air in that car explosion didn't come close to this, trust me."

"You wasted two of them, Mac," Savich said, "including the leader, and you would have been blown into a thousand pieces if it hadn't been for a bit of luck—the angle of the blast was sharper than they intended—and a well-placed sand dune."

I paused a moment, then nodded. "That I understand, but I don't understand this dream; it's just plain scary. I felt her hit the water. I felt pain, then nothing, like I was dead.

"I was with her, or I was her, or something. It's crazy, but I can't pretend it didn't happen. I've got to go to Oregon. Not next week or even in two days. I've got to go today."

Because Sherlock was right here with me, because I was so scared I wanted to howl and cry at the same time, I leaned over and pulled Sherlock up against my good side. One skinny little arm came around my neck. I felt tears clog my throat, but I wasn't about to let them out. I'd never live that one down, even if neither of them told a single soul. No, I held her close, felt that soft hair of hers tease my nose. I looked over at Savich. The two of them had been married a year and a half. I'd been Sherlock's Man of Honor at their wedding. Savich was well known and well liked in the Bureau. Both Savich and Sherlock were in the CAU, the Criminal Apprehension Unit, headed by Savich, who'd created the unit some three years before. I managed to get myself together and said, "You've got a good one here, Savich."

"Yeah, on top of everything else, she gave me the neatest little kid in all of Washington. You haven't seen Sean since he was a month old, Mac. It's time you did. He's pushing five months."

"I'll get over as soon as I can."

"See that you do. Hey, Sherlock, you okay? Don't worry about Mac. He'll go to Oregon and see what's going on. We'll be here if he needs backup, not more than a six-hour plane ride away.

"Mac, are you sure you're ready to climb back onto your horse? You still look a bit on the weedy side. How about coming to stay with us for a couple of days before you take off? We'll put you next to the baby's room. Too bad you can't breast-feed. That would make up for us having to take care of you."

AS it turned out, I ended up staying at the hospital for another day and a half until, frankly, I couldn't stand it anymore. I spoke to Paul twice a day. There was no change in Jilly's condition. The doctors were still saying there was nothing they could do but wait and see. Kevin and his boys were in Germany, and my sister Gwen, a buyer for Macy's, was in New York. I told them I'd keep them posted as often as I could.

I flew west that Friday, on an early morning flight from Washington Dulles. I rented a light blue Ford Taurus at the Portland International Airport without much hassle, which was always a pleasant surprise in my experience.

It was a beautiful day, not a hint of humidity, no rain clouds, a mild seventy degrees with a light breeze. I'd always liked the West Coast, especially Oregon with its raw, wild mountains and deep-cut gorges with rapids roaring through them. And the ocean, sweeping against the coast for some three hundred miles, all of it savage and magnificent.

I took my time, knowing my physical limits, not wanting to feel like I was going to fall down in a dead heap. I stopped at a Wendy's in Tufton, a little town near the coast. I saw the sign to Edgerton off Highway 101 an hour and a half later. There was only a spur west, 101W, a narrow paved road that ran four miles to the ocean. Unlike the scores of towns that were bisected by the coast highway, Edgerton was luckily situated west when they'd decided to take the highway more inland to the east. There were a few signs advertising three bed and breakfasts. The BUTTERCUP B&B sign was the biggest, shaped like a psychedelic flower and painted purple and yellow, announcing that it was right on the edge of the cliff, and showed a gothic structure that looked bleak and menacing on the billboard. If I remembered correctly, Paul had told me once that the folk here in Edgerton called it the Psycho B&B. There was another sign for a small diner called The Edwardian, claiming to have the best British cuisine, something I thought must be an oxymoron, based on my culinary experience during my year at the London School of Economics.

I remembered there had once been a small hotel on the narrow strip of beach at Edgerton, but it had been washed away during a winter storm in 1974. I tried to imagine such a thing and couldn't. I remembered the movie where a tsunami at least a million feet high had taken out Manhattan, and grinned. I remembered wondering if the Indians would be interested in buying back the island after that. I stuck my head out the window and smelled the ocean, tart and clean and salty. I loved the smell, felt something expand inside me anytime I was close to the sea. I sucked in that wonderful sticky, salty air. That really deep breath hurt me just a bit, nothing close to what it would have done if I'd tried it a week ago.

I slowed the Ford down to navigate a deep pothole. My brother-in-law, Paul Bartlett, Jilly's husband, was a man I didn't know all that well even though he and Jilly had been married for eight years now. They'd wed right after she'd gotten her master's degree in pharmacology. Paul had finished his Ph.D. the year before. He'd grown up in Edgerton, gone back east to Harvard. He'd always seemed to me a bit standoffish, a bit of a cold fish, but who really knew what another person was like? I remembered Jilly telling me how great sex with him was. No cold fish I knew of was into that.

I'd been surprised when six months before, Jilly had called to tell me that she and Paul were moving back to Edgerton, leaving Philadelphia and the pharmaceutical firm—VioTech—where both of them had spent the past six years of their professional lives. "Paul isn't happy here," she'd said.

"They won't let him continue with his research. He's really into it, Mac."
But what about you? I'd asked her. There'd been a brief pause, then she'd
said, "My clock is running out, Mac. We want a child. I'm going to lie low
for a while and we're going to try to get me pregnant. We've discussed this
thoroughly and we're sure. We're going back to The Edge." I smiled a bit,
thinking of that name. She'd told me a long time ago, before she and Paul
were married, that Edgerton had been discovered by an English naval lieutenant, Davies Edgerton, way back toward the end of the eighteenth century. The name had been corrupted over the years by the locals to the point
that most of its denizens now just called it The Edge.

I was nearly there. The four-mile drive to the ocean was rough, and that
was why the engineers had swung the highway to the east. There were deep
ravines and hillocks, a wide gully with a bridge over it, some stunted pine
and oak trees, and at least a dozen potholes that looked like they hadn't
seen maintenance since World War II. There was little greenery yet, too
early in the spring. A sign said EDGERTON—FIFTY FEET ABOVE SEA LEVEL
AND 602 RESIDENTS. My favorite resident was in the Tallshon Community
Hospital, some ten miles north of Edgerton, in a coma.

Jilly, I thought, my fingers tightening on the steering wheel, did you go
off that damned road on purpose? If you did, why?

THREE

*I was deep inside myself and it was comforting. When I first
realized I wasn't dead, I was shocked. How could I have survived?
I'd whipped the Porsche right off the cliff, hanging, hanging, before
it plunged clean as a stabbing knife through that black, still water.*

Then I didn't remember anything at all.

*I couldn't feel my body and perhaps that was a good thing.
I knew there were people around me, whispering as people do*

around those badly hurt, but I couldn't make out their words. It was odd, but they weren't really there, just hovering, insubstantial shadows. Like the shadows, I was here too, but not really. If only I could have heard and understood what they were saying. Now that would have been delicious.

At last I was alone. Completely alone. Laura wasn't here with me. Laura, I prayed, had gotten her revenge when I'd screamed like a madwoman and driven off the cliff. If she had come back with me, I thought I'd simply make myself stop breathing.

People came and went. I had no particular interest in any of them. I suppose they examined me and did things to me, but nothing really mattered at all.

Then suddenly everything changed. My brother Ford walked through the door and I saw him clearly. He was real, he had substance and an expression that was so filled with fear that I would have given quite a lot to be able to reassure him, but of course I couldn't. He was big and good-looking, my little brother, better-looking even than our father, who'd been a lady killer, our mother had always said fondly. Mother and Father were dead, weren't they?

Ford didn't look quite himself. Perhaps not as buff, not as commanding, not as massive. Hadn't he been hurt or something? I didn't know, couldn't grasp much of anything. But Ford was here, I was sure of that. I also knew that I was the only one who called him Ford and not Mac. He'd never been Mac to me.

How was this possible? He was here and I could see him, but I couldn't make out any of the others.

If I could have shouted to him, I would have. But I couldn't move, couldn't really feel anything at all except this quiet joy that my brother had come when I needed him.

I was shocked again when I heard him say close to my face, "Jilly, my God, Jilly, I can't bear this. What happened?"

I clearly heard his words, understood them. I was even more shocked when I felt—actually felt—his big hands covering one of mine; I'm not sure which one. I felt a shot of warmth from him, and the warmth stayed with me. It was remarkable. I didn't know what to think. How had Ford come so clearly to me when none of the others had? Why Ford and no one else?

"I know you can't answer me, Jilly, but perhaps somewhere deep inside, you can hear me."

Oh, yes, I wanted to tell him, I can hear you, yes I can. I loved his voice: deep, resonant, and mesmerizing. I think I'd told him once how much his voice warmed me to my toes. He'd told me it was his FBI interviewing voice, but that wasn't right. He'd always had that intimate, soothing voice.

He sat down beside me, always talking, deeply and slowly, never letting go of my hand, and the warmth of his hand was dizzying. How I wished that I could at least squeeze his fingers.

"I was with you, Jilly," he said, and I nearly stopped breathing.

What did he mean?

With me where?

"I was with you that night. Scared the shit out of me. I woke up in the hospital sweating my toenails off, so scared I thought I'd die. I went over the cliff with you, Jilly. I believed at first that I died with you, but neither of us died. That highway patrolman saved you. Now I've got to find out how this could have happened. Damnation, I wish I knew if you could hear me."

Ford paused, still staring down at me, and I wished with everything in me that I could give him some sort of sign, but I couldn't. I was just a lump lying there in that hospital bed that was probably very uncomfortable, if I could have felt it. I wasn't anything really but my brain and one of my hands that he was holding.

What did he mean that he'd been there with me going over the cliff? That didn't make any sense, not that anything happening right now made any sense.

A white shadowy figure came into my line of vision. Ford patted my hand, pressed it down against the bed. He walked to the figure and said, "Paul, I just arrived. I was talking to Jilly."

Paul. He was here in my room. I couldn't understand what he was saying to Ford, but from Ford's long silence, he must have been saying quite a lot. He and Ford moved away from me and I couldn't even hear Ford speaking anymore. I wanted more than anything for Paul to leave, but he didn't. What was he saying to Ford? I wanted my brother back. He was my only connection to what was real, what was out there beyond myself.

After a while I gave up and went to sleep. Before I slept I prayed that Ford wouldn't leave me here alone, that he would come back to me. I felt great sorrow for my Porsche, lying there at the bottom of the ocean, fish swimming through it.

I pulled the car into one of the six empty parking spaces in front of the Buttercup B&B, a whimsical name for the ugly, gothic Victorian house that was hanging nearly off the edge of the cliff. There couldn't have been more than twenty feet between the house and a thick stone wall that you could jump off of directly down to a narrow strip of rocky beach a good forty feet below.

Just as whimsical was the name of the main street in Edgerton—Fifth Avenue. The one time I'd been here before, I'd laughed my head off. Fifth Avenue, with four parallel streets running on either side of it, dead-ending at the cliffs, bisecting streets running north and south a good distance each way.

Nothing much had changed as far as I could see.

There were small cottages dating from the 1920s lined up like pastel boxes along Fifth Avenue. Ranch-style homes from the sixties sprawled, with larger plots of land, along the back streets. Wood and glass contemporary homes, the immigrant style from California, perched on higher ground lining the cliffs, while others dotted the shallow valleys that dipped away from the water. There were still a few odd shacks and cottages tucked in among the thick stands of spruce, cedar, and western hemlock.

I went into the Buttercup B&B and was told by a thin woman who sported a line of black hair above her upper lip that they had no vacancies. I thought about all the empty parking spaces out front, saw absolutely no one at all in the house, and said to the woman who was standing behind a stretch of shiny mahogany, looking wary and stubborn, "Busy time of year, hmm?"

"There's a convention in town," she said, turned pink, and studied the wall behind my left shoulder, papered with huge Victorian cabbage roses.

"A convention in Edgerton? Maybe they moved the Rose Bowl up here?"

"Oh, no, these aren't florists, they're, well, most of them are dentists, orthodontists, I believe, from all over the country. Sorry, sir."

I wondered what was considered the low season in Edgerton as I walked back to my car. Why hadn't the woman wanted me to stay there? Had it gotten around already that an FBI guy was in town? Nobody wanted a cop hanging around? It seemed to me that I was the safest customer to have sleeping in your house.

I turned left off Fifth Avenue and drove north up Liverpool Street, a steep winding road that ran parallel to 101 for a good ten miles before swerving eastward to join up once again with the highway. There were new houses along this stretch, spread far apart, most tucked discreetly out of sight from the chance runner or driver. At a particularly lovely spot, I saw a small hill that rose up some fifty yards back from the cliff. The hill was covered with spruce and cedar. At its base there sat a large dark red brick house. Except for a narrow driveway, the house was surrounded by dozens of trees, the outer perimeter trees partially stunted, leaning inward, battered by storms off the sea.

It was 12 Liverpool, Paul and Jilly's house. It couldn't have been built more than three or four years before. If I hadn't been looking for it I wouldn't have seen it.

I was surprised how much it looked like their home back in Philadelphia. It was then I saw a police car parked across the street from the house.

I pulled into the empty driveway, wondering how much longer Paul would be at the hospital. I walked to the cop car, a white four-door Chrysler with green lettering on the side: SHERIFF.

I stuck my head in the open passenger window. "What's up? You here to see Paul?"

She was a woman in her early thirties, wearing a beautifully pressed tan uniform, a wide black leather belt at her waist, a 9mm SIG Sauer Model 220, a sweet automatic pistol I knew very well, holstered to the belt. She said, "Yes. And just who might you be?"

"I'm Ford MacDougal, Jilly's brother, from Washington, D.C. I'm here to see her, and find out what happened to her."

"You're the FBI agent?"

There was deep suspicion in her voice. "Word gets around fast," I said. I stuck my hand through the open window. "Call me Mac."

She was wearing black leather driving gloves that felt very cool and soft to the touch when she clasped my hand. "I'm Maggie Sheffield, sheriff here in Edgerton. I want to find out what happened to Jilly as well. Did you just come from the hospital?" At my nod, she said, "No change?"

"No. I left Paul there with her. He's pretty upset."

"No wonder. It's got to be hell for him. It's not every day a man's wife drives off a cliff, ends up in the hospital rather than the morgue, and leaves her Porsche twenty feet underwater."

She sounded like she wanted to cry. About Jilly or about the Porsche?

"You've driven Jilly's car?"

"Yeah, once. Funny thing is that I never speed unless I have to, which isn't often. But I got behind the wheel, looked out the windshield, and my foot just hit the gas pedal. I was doing eighty before I even realized it. I was grateful there were no cops around." She smiled and looked away from me for a moment. "Jilly was so excited about that car. She'd drive it down Fifth Avenue, hooting and shouting and honking the horn. She'd swerve it from one side of the street to the other. People would come out of the grocery store, their houses, laughing, betting with her that she'd wreck the car with her shenanigans."

"She did."

"Yes, but it wasn't because of her having fun like a crazy teenager. It was something else entirely." Her voice had lightened up a bit, but now it was low and suspicious again. To my surprise, she suddenly smacked the steering wheel with her gloved fist. "It's nuts. Rob Morrison, the state cop who pulled her out, said she speeded up as she went toward the cliff. It's a pretty sharp incline at that particular spot, so that means she had to push down on the gas, like she wanted to go over. But that doesn't make any sense at all. Jilly wouldn't have tried to kill herself." She paused a moment, frowning over the steering wheel into the forest across the street. "I don't suppose you've got any ideas about this?"

I should have said no, because I didn't want this sheriff to think I was crazy, but what came out of my mouth was "Yes, I do. It's just that I don't understand my ideas either."

She laughed. It was an honest laugh that filled the car. "I think you'll need to explain that. Listen, you're a Fed when all's said and done. Sure you're Jilly's brother, but you're a Fed first. What's going on here?"

"All that's true, but I'm on leave from the FBI. I'm here as Jilly's brother, nothing more. I'm not going to throw my weight around, Sheriff." My stomach growled. "Tell you what. Paul's still at the hospital. Actually I'm going to stay here with him since the Buttercup B&B is filled up with the orthodontist convention. It's time for lunch and I'm starving."

"Orthodontist convention, huh? That's how Arlene got rid of you? The woman's got no imagination."

"She tried. I think I frightened her. Is it because I'm an outsider? A Fed?"

"Oh, yes. Arlene Hicks doesn't want you anywhere around her fine establishment. She's weird that way about cops."

"Word got around really fast."

"Yeah. Paul told Benny Pickle down at the gun shop that you were coming. That's all it took. Benny's got the biggest mouth west of the Cascades."

"But what's wrong with being a Fed? I'm clean, I'm polite, I don't spit. I wouldn't run out without paying my bill."

"Arlene doesn't even like me hanging around, and I'm a friendly face. You're not. She probably believes you're as bad as the IRS. You're from Washington, right? Place of sin and corruption."

"You've got a good point there. Maybe Arlene's on to something."

She waved that away. "Okay. You're here, Mac, and you want to find out what happened to Jilly. I want the same thing. It makes sense that we join forces, at least a bit. The thing is, are you willing to play level with me?"

I arched an eyebrow. "I hadn't really thought about playing with anybody. But if I do play, it's usually level. Any reason why it shouldn't be?"

"You're a Fed. You're a big footer. You're used to taking over, used to making local cops your gofers. I'm not a gofer."

"I told you, I'm not here as a Fed. I'm here only as Jilly's brother. Like you, I want to know what happened. Actually I'm pleased that as the local cop you haven't just kissed the whole thing off—attempted suicide—and called in a shrink.

"Sure, I'll play level with you. Do you know anything I should know? Is there any reason to believe Jilly didn't go over that cliff on purpose? You want to start sharing right now?"

She seemed to relax a bit. "When were you hurt and how?"

"How do you know I was hurt? Do I still look like week-old oatmeal?"

She cocked her head to one side, fully facing me, looking me over. I realized that she was younger than I'd first thought, probably late twenties. It was impossible to be really sure because she was wearing the dark glasses favored by highway patrol officers to intimidate the folk they stopped. I could see my reflection in the lenses. Her hair was thick, dark reddish-brown and curly, plaited into a thick French braid and pulled back up on top of her head, wound around itself and fastened with a clip carved as a totem pole. She was wearing pale coral lipstick, the shade my British girlfriend Caroline had favored. But Caroline, a clothing designer, had never looked as tough or self-reliant as this woman.

Of course she knew I was studying her, and she let me, saying finally, "I've always hated oatmeal. Fortunately, you don't resemble that at all, but you don't move all that easily, you know? You walk like you're twenty years older than you are. There are faint bruises along the left side of your face. You favor your right arm and you're a bit crabbed over, like you're worried you'll hurt your ribs. What happened to you?"

"I got in the way of a car bomb."

"I didn't hear about any federal guys being blown up."

"I was over in Tunisia. Bad place. You get hot sand in your mouth when you talk. The people I had to deal with weren't what you'd call very good-natured." I'd just told this woman, a perfect stranger, all sorts of stuff that wasn't any layperson's business, a local cop's least of all. Well, I was playing level, I was *sharing*, as politically correct folk would say. Even thinking that soppy word made me wince. If she knew anything at all, my spurt of openness—something I hoped wouldn't happen again—should help me worm it out of her.

"I'll take you to The Edwardian for lunch. It sounds like an English gentlemen's club, but it isn't. The food isn't great, but there's a lot of it, and you look like you could use the calories. You dropped what, a good fifteen pounds?"

"Yeah, about that," I said. It was only two o'clock in the afternoon and I wanted a soft bed, a dark room, and no interruptions for about three hours.

"Follow me. Fifteen minutes?"

"Thanks," I said.

I watched her turn the key in the ignition and smoothly do a U-turn on Liverpool Street.

Some twenty minutes later, once I'd ordered meat loaf, mashed potatoes, and green beans, and she'd ordered a huge chicken salad from Mr. Pete, a grizzled old varmint who was the only waiter for all ten patrons at The Edwardian at the moment, I leaned back against the hard wooden back of the booth and said, "I visited here about five years ago, as I said. I'd just gotten back from London, and Paul and Jilly invited me out here to meet his parents. I remember this place well. Nothing seems to have changed. How long have you been the sheriff?"

"Going on a year and a half now. The mayor of Edgerton is Miss Geraldine Tucker. Evidently she was going through a feminist phase, said she'd missed it when it first came around, and decided what the town needed was a female sheriff. I was a cop in Eugene at the time and had run into some bad trouble. I wanted out of there. This seemed a perfect opportunity." She shrugged. "I have one deputy and a secretary and about a dozen volunteers whenever I put out the call, which hasn't happened since I've been on the job. There's little crime, as you'd expect, just parking or speeding tickets, kids raising occasional hell, a couple of burglaries a month, probably by transients, normal stuff like that. There has been a rise in domestic cases recently, but nothing like it was in Eugene." She gave me a look that clearly said, *How much more level can you get?*

I smiled at her and said, "What happened in Eugene?"

Her lips were suddenly as thin as the soup an old guy was eating at the next table. "I think I'll keep that to myself, if you don't mind."

"Not at all. Hey, I'm just hoping that the meat loaf will stick to my ribs. They need all the padding they can get right now. What did you want to talk to Paul about?"

Before she could answer, an old man sauntered up, holding an Oakland A's baseball cap between his hands, big hands I saw, gnarly and veined but still strong. He had a full head of white curly hair, tobacco-stained teeth, and he was smiling at me. I put him in his seventies, a man who'd spent many years working hard.

"Charlie," Maggie said, leaning forward to take his hand. "How's tricks? You seen anything interesting I should know about?"

"Yes," he said, his voice all scratchy and thin as old drapes. "But it can wait. Is this the young feller from Washington?"

Maggie introduced us. He was Charlie Duck, a local who'd been here fifteen years. He nodded, never taking my hand, twirling that Oakland A's baseball cap around and around in his hands. "You're all tied up now, Mac, but later, when you've got some time, I wouldn't mind having a talk with you."

"Sure," I said, and wondered what kind of tall tales I'd be hearing.

He nodded, all solemn, and sauntered back to a booth where he sat down, alone.

"You see, not everybody doesn't like me."

"Charlie's a real neat old guy. You'll enjoy him if you two get together."

I said again, "What did you want to talk to Paul about?"

Maggie picked up her fork and began to weave it through her fingers, just like the old man had done with that baseball cap. She'd pulled off her driving gloves. She had elegant white hands, short nails, calluses on her thumb pads. "Just talk," she said. "I still can't believe how lucky Jilly was. Rob Morrison, the highway patrolman who saved her life, came in third in the Iron Man Triathlon over in Kona last year. That means a two-mile swim, a hundred miles on a bike, then twenty-six point two miles of running. He's in awesome shape. Anyone else, and they'd probably still be trying to get her out of the Porsche. The luck involved, it still boggles the mind."

I felt both grateful and envious. "The Iron Man. I had a friend who tried that. He made it to Kona, but he got cramps in the marathon leg. I want to meet this guy. I wish I had something more to give him than just my heartfelt thanks."

"After lunch." She picked up her glass of iced tea, just delivered by Mr. Pete, now wearing a bright red apron and chewing on a toothpick. He called her Ms. Sheriff. "Rob is working nights right now, sleeping during the day. He should be awake soon. I want to hear him go through what happened again so I'll take you with me. You very slickly asked me why I wanted to talk to Paul." She shrugged a bit. "I want to know who or what sent Jilly over that cliff. If anyone should know, it's Paul."

I couldn't face that, not just yet. "They've only been here about five and a half months. Paul grew up here, you know."

"Yes, but he has no more relatives here. His parents died about three years ago in a private plane crash over the Sierras near Tahoe. They were big-time skiers. Their bodies were never recovered, which is odd since most of the time planes that go down are found pretty quick. But not this time.

"Paul's uncle died of cancer about two years ago, and his cousins are all scattered across the country.

"Why'd he come back here? No offense, but it's the middle of nowhere and there isn't, frankly, much of anything here to interest two big-time researchers, which Jilly told me they both were."

My salad was delivered, a huge bowl filled with lettuce, red peppers, boiled potato chunks, and green beans, all topped with a heap of ranch dressing. I thought it looked wonderful. "Go ahead, get started," she said, and I forked down a big bite. "It isn't bad," I said, closed my eyes, and shoveled down six more bites. "Much better. When Jilly called me six months or so ago, she told me that VioTech—the pharmaceutical company where both of them worked—didn't want Paul to continue with the project he was involved in. Jilly said he was pissed and wanted to come back here and continue his work."

"What about Jilly? What were her plans?"

"She said her clock was running out. She wanted to have a kid."

"Jilly said that?" Maggie Sheffield was swiping butter on a dinner roll. She stopped cold and stared at me, shaking her head even as she said, "Oh, no, that's impossible."

"Why?"

"If she told me once, she told me half a dozen times, that neither she nor Paul had ever wanted rugrats. She said they'd been too selfish for too long a time now to think about changing to accommodate a child."

Well then, she'd obviously changed her mind since she'd spoken to me about it.

"Meatloaf's all gone," Mr. Pete announced, as if he was pleased as punch about it. "Pierre didn't make enough. It got eaten mostly by the breakfast crowd. How about some nice fish 'n' chips smothered in onion rings?"

All that fat swimming around in my arteries didn't sound like such a bad thing at that moment.

FOUR

Rob Morrison lived in a small wooden clapboard house tucked in among a good dozen spruce trees about two miles south of town. A narrow dirt road, posted as Penzance Street, snaked through the valleys and hills, and his house was at the end of the road. A wide gully lay just beyond. I turned when I got out of the car and stared over the western horizon. I felt a moment of deep envy. When Rob Morrison awoke in the morning, it was to an incredible view of the Pacific Ocean through the skinny spruce trees. It felt like being at the edge of the world.

Maggie knocked on the unpainted oak door. "Rob? Come on, wake up. You'll be on duty again in another four hours. Wake up."

I heard movement from inside the house. Finally, a man's deep voice called out, "Maggie, that you? What are you doing here? What's going on? How's Jilly?"

"Open up, Rob, and I'll tell you everything."

The door opened and a man about my age stood there, wearing only tight jeans with the top button open and a heavy morning beard. The sheriff had been right, this guy was in awesome shape. Thank God he'd been there at exactly the right moment.

"Who are you?"

I stuck out my hand. "Name's Ford MacDougal. I'm Jilly's brother. I want to thank you for saving her life."

"Rob Morrison," the guy said and took my right hand in a very strong grip. "Yeah, hey, I'm sorry it ever happened. How is she?"

"Jilly's still in a coma," Maggie said.

"Can we talk?" I said. Rob stood back and waved us in. "Mr. Thorne was here two days ago so the place is still as clean as a virgin's memories."

Maggie said to me, "That means there isn't anything of interest any-where, particularly dirt."

"A blank slate," I said.

"An unsoiled blank slate. Right. I'm making coffee. Any for either of you?" At my nod, he said, "Black and strong as tar?"

"That's it."

"Maggie, Earl Grey tea for you?"

She nodded. Both of us followed him through the painfully neat living room to the small kitchen just beyond.

"Nice place," I said. "Who's Mr. Thorne?"

Rob turned and smiled. "He's my housekeeper. Comes twice a week, keeps me from living like a pig. A retired salmon fisherman from Alaska. He calls my place his petri dish."

We sat on bar stools at the kitchen counter that separated the kitchen from the small rectangular dining area in front of two wide windows look-ing toward the ocean.

Soon the smell of coffee filled the air. I breathed in deeply. "The coffee at The Edwardian tasted like cheap watered-down instant."

"It was," Rob said. "Mr. Pete loves instant, makes it with lukewarm water, but only when Pierre Montrose, the owner, isn't there. I wouldn't be surprised if he stirred it with his finger." He poured the coffee and gently shoved a cup over to me.

He poured a cup of hot water over a tea bag. He added a single bag of Equal, stirred it, and gave it to Maggie.

We drank. I sighed deeply. "The best ritual in the world."

"Why don't you go get a shirt on, Rob?" Maggie said. "Mac and I won't move a muscle."

Rob shrugged his superbly muscled shoulder. "Nah, I've got to take a shower. Let's talk. I can get dressed after you guys leave."

I not only felt like a slab of cold oatmeal, I felt really pathetic. This guy could probably shove me over with one hand and walk away whistling. It was depressing as hell. At least the coffee was waking me up, aches and pains and all. I still wanted that nap, but with Rob Morrison sitting across from me, his legs crossed at the ankles, holding his coffee cup against his bare muscled belly, I wasn't about to slouch or yawn.

At least the guy had to have a housekeeper to keep from living like a slob in a cave.

"Rob," Maggie said, leaning forward, cupping the tea mug between her hands. "Tell us everything you can remember, every detail. I'm going to record it, okay?"

"Yeah, sure, but you already know everything."

"Let's do it again. I want it on record this time. Mac needs to hear it too." Maggie made preliminary comments into the recorder. After a couple of false starts, Rob sat forward and said slowly and very clearly, "It was nearly midnight on Tuesday, April twenty-second. I was cruising north along the coast road. I didn't see anybody or anything until I came around a deep curve and saw Jilly's white Porsche in front of me. I saw the car go toward the railing. It didn't slow, just kept going, right on through. Then the Porsche speeded up. I was right on its tail. When it went over the cliff I was there in just a couple of seconds. I saw the headlights through the water and dove in right at that spot. It went down about fifteen, sixteen feet, I'd estimate, before the car hit the sand and settled. The driver's-side window was completely open. I managed to pull Jilly through the window with no loss of time since her seat belt wasn't fastened. I kicked off the bottom and headed straight up. I estimate that she wasn't underwater more than two minutes, tops.

"I towed her to shore, made sure she was breathing. I climbed back up the cliff and radioed for an ambulance from my patrol car. They arrived about twelve minutes later and took her to the Tallshon Community Hospital. At least it was close by.

"That's it, Maggie. I can't remember anything else."

"Did you recognize Jilly when you realized it was a white Porsche?"

Rob nodded. "Oh, yeah, I'd know Jilly's Porsche anywhere, like everyone else in this town would."

"What did you think she was doing?" I asked.

"I didn't have a clue. I yelled and yelled at her but it didn't do any good. It was like she didn't even see me or hear me. Maybe she didn't."

"Did you see anything or anyone else?"

"No, no one."

Maggie said, "In your opinion, was Jilly Bartlett willfully driving the Porsche over the cliff?"

"It looked that way to me," Rob said.

"Is there any doubt in your mind," I said, "that Jilly was attempting to kill herself?"

Rob Morrison raised weary eyes to my face. He rubbed his fist over the thick dark whiskers on his chin. "No," he said finally, "I'm really sorry, but in my opinion, she was trying to kill herself."

"What about a mechanical problem that caused her to lose control?"

"Her car's still twenty feet under water, but I didn't see any signs of mechanical problems. No exploding tires, no smoke coming from the hood, no skid marks, nothing like that. I'm sorry, Mac."

Half an hour later, Maggie and I were sitting in her car outside Paul and Jilly's house.

"You look ready to fold in on yourself," she said. "Why don't you rest for a while before Paul comes home?"

"I don't have a key to the house," I said. "If it weren't for the big tooth convention in town I'd be at the Buttercup B & B. So I didn't think I'd be staying here with Paul."

"So no key?"

"No key. I figured I'd curl up on one of those chairs on their front porch."

"You're too big to do much curling," she said, and drummed her gloved fingers on her steering wheel. "Actually, since we're sharing information, why don't you tell me your ideas about Jilly? You know, the ideas you told me you didn't understand. Then you can head for that porch chair."

"You've got a good memory."

"Yes. What ideas, Mac?"

"Even if I tell you, you'll think I'm a nut case, or you'll dismiss it because I was in the hospital when it happened, and you'll think it was a psychotic reaction to a drug."

"Try me."

I looked away from her, then inward, back to that night. "I was in the hospital. I dreamed about Jilly being in trouble that night. Somehow I was with her when she went over the cliff." I wanted to laugh myself at what I'd just said, but I just shook my head. "You think I'm psychotic, right?"

She said slowly, staring at me, "I don't know what to believe. What did you do?"

"The next morning I called Paul right away, found out that my dream had actually happened. I've got no clue as to why I hooked up to Jilly like that, none."

"Jesus," she said.

"I had to come here."

"You shouldn't have left the hospital."

"There wasn't a choice. As it was, I waited another two days. The longest two days of my life."

She didn't say anything for a very long time. She rubbed her palm on her thigh. The crease in her tan pants was still sharp. The pants looked as fresh as if she'd just put them on.

"And you and Jilly never had any sort of link before this?"

I shook my head. "There are just us four kids now. Our folks have been dead for some time. Jilly's three years older than me. I'm the youngest. We weren't all that close really, both of us busy over the past several years, but that's normal I guess. Then this damned dream happened. The thing is, I feel like something made Jilly go over that cliff—or someone. She was alone in that car, but she wasn't, not really."

"That doesn't make much sense."

"I know," I said. "I know. At least it doesn't yet. You want the kicker? At the end of the dream I heard a man yelling." I drew a deep breath. "It sounded like Rob Morrison. I recognized his voice just now. There's no way I can accept this as a suicide attempt, not unless Jilly tells me it was."

I sipped a rich Pinot Noir from the Gray Canyon vineyard in Napa Valley.

"You like the wine?" Paul asked.

"It's darker than the deepest sin," I said, gently swirling the wine in its crystal glass, watching it glide smoothly over the sides. "I met Rob Morrison today, the man who saved Jilly."

"Yes," Paul said. "I met Rob just after Jilly and I moved here. He gave me a speeding ticket. I hear you also spent time with Maggie Sheffield."

"Yeah. I don't know what to think of her yet, but she seemed okay, once she got over her gut suspicions of me as an FBI agent."

Paul sat forward, his hands clenching. "Watch out for her, Mac."

"What does that mean?"

Paul shrugged his shoulders. "Please don't think I'm being harsh or a woman hater. I'll just come out with it. She's a bitch, a ball-buster."

"I didn't get that impression at all." I cut another piece of the thick sirloin steak. It was even better than the lettuce and green bean salad at The Edwardian. "She wants to find out why Jilly went over that cliff. I appreciate that. You should too. What'd she do to you? Give you a speeding ticket like Morrison?"

"No, nothing like that. She wants to blame me for Jilly's accident. She's never liked me, believes I'm not good enough for Jilly. I don't appreciate that at all."

It was my turn to shrug. "She didn't say a word about you, Paul. She was waiting here in her car when I drove up. She wanted to talk to you."

"I'd have her fired if I could talk Geraldine into it. The woman's a menace. She doesn't like men in general, always giving them grief. Have you seen that damned gun she wears on her belt? It's ridiculous. Edgerton is a small, peaceful little town. No one—man or woman—should be wearing a gun, but she does. Of course, I already spoke to her at the hospital after Jilly was admitted."

"It's not odd at all for a cop—male or female—to want to question someone more than once," I said mildly, surprised that Paul would spew out that sexist crap. I'd gotten no hint at all that she didn't like men. "In the excitement and stress of the moment, people tend to forget things. I'll bet even you will be able to tell her more now than you did then."

"About what, for God's sake? Jilly went over that damned cliff and I don't know why. She was a little depressed, but everyone's down once in a while. That's it, Mac. There's nothing more."

I took the last bite of my steak, sat back in my chair, rubbed my belly, and took another sip of my Pinot Noir. Paul looked pale, his skin drawn tight over his cheekbones. He looked ill, frightened. Or maybe I was just seeing myself in Paul. Lord knew I looked sick enough. "Are you certain there's nothing else, Paul? What was Jilly depressed about? Was she taking any medication for the depression? Was she seeing anyone professionally?"

Paul laughed, a tight, constipated laugh. "Just listen to you. SuperCop with his load of questions. No, she wasn't. I'm exhausted, Mac. I don't want to talk anymore. There's nothing more to say. I'm going to bed." He shoved back his chair and stood up. "Good night. I hope you don't mind the double bed in the guest room. It'll be a bit on the short side for you."

"I'll do fine, Paul. I slept some this afternoon on that big front porch chair of yours. I think I'll go to the hospital to see Jilly. Good night."

Ford was here again, holding my hand like he had before. The warmth of his hand was indescribable, just like before. Thank God I hadn't imagined it that first time. I didn't want to lose my brain the way I'd lost my body.

But when was before?

It could have been this morning or last year for all I knew. It was odd, but I had no sense of time at all. I knew what it was, but it had no meaning to me.

There were other shadowy creatures behind Ford, then finally they left, and we were alone.

"Jilly," he said, and I wanted to cry with the sheer relief of hearing his voice, but I didn't know if this body I couldn't feel was even capable of yielding up tears.

I wanted to ask him if they'd gotten my Porsche out of the ocean.

Ford said, "Sweetheart, I don't know if you can hear me or not. I hope somehow that you can. I spoke to Kevin and Gwen and gave them an update. They send their love and their prayers.

"Now, Jilly, tell me about why you were depressed."

Depressed? What was this about being depressed? I've never been depressed in my life. Who said anything about being depressed? I yelled it at Ford, but naturally, he didn't hear me because my words were only bouncing about inside my skull.

"I've got to find out why you drove your Porsche off that cliff, Jilly. I find it hard to believe that you were depressed. I can't remember when you were ever depressed, even when you were a teenager and Lester Harvey dumped you for Susan, that friend of yours who had the big breasts. I remember you just shook your head, said he was a worthless shit, and moved on.

"But things change. We haven't seen all that much of each other in the past five years or so. You've been with Paul. Dammit, Jilly, what happened to you?"

Ford was leaning his forehead on my hand. I could feel the soft whistle of his breath against my skin. I wasn't depressed, I wanted to tell him. He wanted to know what had happened to me so I said, "Listen, Ford, do you like sex? I didn't used to like it all that much, but then something happened. A wonderful something."

I wondered if my mouth was curving at all into a smile. Probably not. I heard Ford's quiet, steady breathing. He was asleep. Why had he fallen asleep? Then I remembered something about him being sick. Had he been injured somehow? I seemed to remember that.

I wish I could have run my fingers through his hair. Ford had lovely hair, all dark and longer than the FBI would like it to be. But it was his eyes I'd always liked best. Dark blue eyes, just like Mom's, at least I think they were like Mom's, she'd been dead for so very long. Yes, his eyes were deep and mellow and too intense on occasion. I remember hearing he was dating a woman named Dolores from Washington, D.C. Every time I thought of her name I pictured a Spanish flamenco dancer in my mind. I wonder if she liked sex with Ford.

When it comes down to it, who cares? I'm here, a prisoner, and Paul's alive, free to do whatever he wants. But it's not Paul I'm afraid of, goodness, never Paul. It's Laura. She was dangerous, wasn't she? I knew she'd betrayed me. She'd gotten into my head and nearly killed me. Oh, Ford, if she comes back, I won't be able to bear it. I'll die.

I'm lying here, just floating about, and I think of Laura. Laura, who betrayed me. Always Laura.

I woke up with a start some hours later at the touch of a nurse's hand on my shoulder. I raised my head, looked at her face, and said, "Always Laura. Laura betrayed her."

She arched her right eyebrow, sleek and black. "Laura? Who's Laura? Are you okay?"

I looked down at Jilly, silent, pale, her skin nearly translucent. "I'm fine," I said. Who was Laura? I looked up again at the nurse. She was very short, a tiny bird of a woman, and her voice was soft and sweet as a child's. I nodded at her, then looked at Jilly, whose features were barely visible in the dim light from the corridor. Evidently someone had come into the room, seen me asleep on Jilly's hand, and turned off the lights.

"It's time to turn her over," the nurse said quietly, "and to massage her. Bedsores will come eventually if we don't take care now."

"Tell me," I said, watching her untie the back of Jilly's hospital gown, "what you know about coma. The doctors spoke to me at some length, but it was difficult to understand exactly what to expect."

She began to rub thick white cream into Jilly's shoulders and back. "Remember that movie with Steven Seagal a while back where he'd been in a coma for seven years, then awakened?"

I nodded, remembering how much I'd admired Steven Seagal when I was a boy.

The nurse said, "He had a long beard and he was weak, had to practice to get his strength back, and of course he did. He was jumping around, maiming folk after only a week or so. Well, that's Hollywood. Actually, if a person's in a coma for longer than, say, a few days, the risk increases dramatically that something will be seriously wrong when and if the person ever comes out of it. I'm sorry to tell you if you don't know, but all sorts of brain damage is possible—retardation, inability to walk, to talk—any number of dreadful things.

"Most of the time, people come out of a coma very quickly, and they're usually okay. If Mrs. Bartlett comes out of this in, say, the next day or two, her chances are good that there won't be any terrible damage; but it's very possible there will be some. We just don't know. We make assumptions and predictions based on statistics, but in the end, everyone is different. We can hope and pray, and little else.

"In Mrs. Bartlett's case, there was no major damage they could see on any of her test results. Actually, she really shouldn't be in a coma at all. That just goes to show that there's so much we don't know about this sort of thing. I'm sorry, Mr. MacDougal, there's nothing else to say about it."

She'd given me a lot to think about. I fell asleep again, my head next to Jilly's hand. I dreamed about Maggie Sheffield. She was screaming that she was going to run Paul out of Edgerton.

FIVE

When I drove back into the driveway at 12 Liverpool Street at ten o'clock the following morning, I saw Maggie Sheffield's car parked across the street as it had been the day before, but she wasn't in it.

I heard her say as I walked quietly into the living room, "Paul, I called the hospital on my way over here. Mrs. Himmel told me there was no change. She said that Mac was still with Jilly, had been since last night."

I heard Paul grunt.

"Mac spends a lot more time there than you do, Paul. How's that?"

"Go to hell."

Paul didn't sound particularly pissed off at such a question, just incredibly tired. Personally, if she'd said that to me, I would have been tempted to slug her. I walked into the living room, a long narrow great room that ran the entire front of the house, facing the ocean. It was all windows across the front; where there had to be walls to hold up the house, they were stark white. Large square white pavers covered the floor, and all the furniture was black. It was a minimalist designer's wet dream—no compromises with kitsch or newspapers or photos anywhere. All those clean stark lines set my teeth on edge. I couldn't imagine cozying up with a good book in here or setting a nice big TV set in the corner and watching football. Actually, I didn't want to be anywhere near this room when I could help it. It was a testament—not to living, but to someone's idea of perfection. Even the paintings, all of the dozen or so abstracts, were made up of paint slashes, primarily black and white, lined up like perfect little soldiers along a long white wall. I couldn't imagine how anyone could live in this sterile space, particularly Jilly. I remembered Jilly's room growing up—bright teal blues and oranges and greens. Of course she'd also had punk-rocker posters on the walls. People changed, but this much? Was this all Paul's doing?

I said to Maggie, who was seated on a long black leather sofa, a small notebook open on her lap, "Sheriff, I hope you're well." She was wearing her tan uniform, running shoes on her feet. For an instant, I saw her without the tan uniform, as she'd been in my dream the night before. Her hair was ruthlessly pulled back, fastened with one of those things that my FBI friend Sherlock called a banana clip. Sherlock had a rainbow of colors in her banana clips.

"Mac," she said, rising. "I'm fine. How's Jilly?"

"The same. No change."

"I'm sorry. How are you feeling?"

"Fine, no problem."

"You're looking a lot better, not quite so ready for the grave as yesterday. Come sit down, Mac. I need to go over a few more things with Paul."

Paul hadn't stirred. He was seated forward in a black tufted leather chair, his hands clasped between his knees. He appeared to be studying a white paver at his feet. "There's a small scratch," he said.

"Scratch? What scratch?" Maggie asked.

"There," Paul said. "Right there, in the top right corner. I wonder how that could have happened."

"Tell you what, Paul," I said, not joking at all, "I'll get a load of newspapers and we can pile them up over the scratch."

"Yeah, Mac, sure. You're a philistine. You've got a messy, unsophisticated soul. Come join the fun. Let's get this over with. I've got to get back to work."

"Jilly told me that was why you left Philadelphia and VioTech—you wanted to continue work on this project and they wanted you to stop."

"That's right."

"What's the project?" I asked, walking over a black-and-white geometrical carpet to stand by one of the large glass windows that looked out at the ocean.

"It's all about the fountain of youth. I'm developing a pill that will reverse the aging process."

"My God, Paul," Maggie said, nearly falling off the sofa, "that's incredible! Why wouldn't they want you to continue on that? That would be worth not just a fortune, it would be worth the world."

Paul laughed at her. "Everyone bites big time on that one. Everyone wants youth back." He touched his receding hairline. "I'd rather come up with a pill to regrow hair myself."

"If Jean-Luc Picard on *Star Trek* is any indication, we still won't have a pill to grow hair even in the twenty-fourth century. You're out of luck, Paul."

"What are you really working on then, Paul?" I asked.

"Look, it's privileged information and it's really none of your business, either of you. It's got nothing to do with Jilly. Now please get off my back."

Maggie sat back down on the sofa and clicked her ballpoint pen. "I want to know what you and Jilly did last Tuesday night. Think back. It's dinnertime. Did you eat in or go out?"

"For God's sake, Maggie, why do you want to know what we did for dinner?"

"Did you eat in, Paul?" I asked, still standing in front of the window, my arms crossed over my chest.

"Yes, we did. We broiled halibut, squeezed on lemon. Jilly made garlic toast. I tossed a spinach salad. We ate. I had work to do after dinner. Jilly said she was going to drive around, nothing unusual in that. She loved driving the Porsche. She left here about nine o'clock."

"Rob Morrison said she went over the cliff at about midnight. That's three hours, Paul. That's an awfully long time to drive around."

"I went to work. I fell asleep at my desk, even left my computer on. If Jilly came back and left again, I wouldn't know. If she stayed out the full three hours, I wouldn't know that either. All I know is she left at nine."

"What was her mood at dinner?"

"Maggie, you know Jilly. She's never serious, always joking around. She told me a Viagra joke, I remember that."

"So what is it you're working on, Paul?" Maggie said. "You want to clone little Paul Bartletts?"

"No, Maggie, I wouldn't want to clone myself until I figure out how to regrow hair." He looked over at me. "Now you're a possibility. You've got good genes, Mac. The Germans would have approved of you, or the FBI. You interested?"

"So you put the FBI right in there with the Nazis, do you?" Why was he stonewalling? But how could a drug he was developing have anything to do with Jilly driving over a cliff?

Paul shrugged. "Lots of parallels, as I see it."

I let it go, shrugged. "Well, maybe I'll consider it three lifetimes from now if I turn real weird, but probably not. So you're saying that during dinner Jilly seemed perfectly normal?"

"Yes. She ate lightly. She wanted to lose five pounds."

Maggie said, "Was she taking any weight-loss pills?"

"Not that I know of. I'll check in the medicine cabinet and see what's there."

"Okay."

"Is it true you made love to Jilly every day, Paul?"

I'd swear that Paul turned red to his receding hairline. "What the hell kind of question is that, Mac? Why is that your business?"

"In February, Jilly told me about her love life. She'd never spoken so frankly about sex with you before that. Thinking back on it, something was off. She spoke about a number of things, going from one subject to the next, without pause, without emphasis on anything."

"What did she say, Mac?"

I looked at Maggie. In that moment, I would have sworn she had more than just a professional interest in what was going on here. Well, why not give her details? I said, "She spoke about her new dress, how Paul made love to her all the time, how she loved her Porsche, and she spoke about a brother and sister, Cal and Cotter Tarcher. Everything she said was in the same tone of voice, almost without emotion. Now, in hindsight, it wasn't quite right."

The doorbell rang.

Paul jumped to his feet. "Oh, God, what if something's happened to Jilly?"

He ran out of the living room. Maggie said to me, "I realize you don't want to hear this, Mac, but there was talk. Maybe it wasn't Paul she was having all that sex with."

I wanted to punch her. Jilly screwing around? I'd never believe that. Not Jilly. I didn't have time to question Maggie about it before Paul returned to the living room. Standing beside him in the doorway was a small girl—no, a woman—perhaps twenty-five. She had dark brown hair, thick and curly, pulled back with two plastic clips. Her skin was whiter than a pair of my boxer shorts fresh out of the drier. No freckles. She wore glasses with rounded gold frames. She was wearing jeans that were too loose on her and a white shirt, probably a man's, that hung halfway down her legs and was rolled up to her forearms.

"Hello, Cal," Maggie said, rising slowly. "What brings you here?"

Good grief. Cal Tarcher, in the flesh. The girl who was going to be jealous of Jilly's new dress. Sister of Cotter, the vicious bully.

I watched Cal raise her head, look furtively toward Paul, and say, "My father sent me. I'm glad you're here, Maggie. All of you are invited to our house tomorrow night." She looked toward me. "Are you Jilly's brother?"

"Yes. I'm Ford MacDougal."

"I'm Cal Tarcher. Is Jilly all right?"

"She's still the same. In a coma."

"I'm so sorry. I went to see her yesterday afternoon. The nurse told me to talk to Jilly, talk about anything—the weather, the latest Denzel Washington movie—whatever. Anyway, the party. Will all of you come?"

"Of course we'll come," Paul said, a hint of impatience in his voice. "Your father commands and we struggle to be first in line."

"It's not like that, Paul," Cal said, without looking at any of us.

Cal looked over Paul's right shoulder, toward a painting with two long diagonal slashes of stark black paint slapped on dead-white canvas. "We're all very worried about Jilly, Paul. Dad hopes you'll be able to make time and come to our house for at least a little while tomorrow night. He really wants to meet Jilly's brother. Maggie, do you know if Rob is working tomorrow night?"

"That's a loaded question. What makes you think I know his schedule?"

Cal Tarcher shrugged. "You're both law officers."

"Yeah, right."

Cal Tarcher was very uncomfortable with this, probably embarrassed. What was going on here? I felt as though I'd been dumped in the middle of a play and I didn't have a clue what the plot was. "I'll call him," Cal said in a low voice. Then she raised her head and looked directly at Maggie. "He's more likely to come if you ask him. He'll do whatever you ask. You know he doesn't like me. He thinks I'm stupid."

"Don't be ridiculous, Cal," Paul said. "Rob doesn't dislike anyone. It would take too much mental energy and he's got to conserve all he's got. I'll call him for you, all right?"

"Thank you, Paul. I'm off to invite Miss Geraldine. She's had a bad cold, but she's better now. I'm taking some homemade coffee cake to her. My father admires her so very much, you know."

"Beats me why," Paul said. He added to me, "Miss Geraldine Tucker is our mayor and a retired high school math teacher. She also heads up the Edgerton Citizen Coalition, better known as the BITEASS League. Its members range in age from in vitro to ninety-three—that's Mother Marco, who still owns the Union 76 gas station downtown.

"And no, there's no correlation between the letters and the name of the group. Didn't your dad come up with that, Cal?"

"It was my mom, actually."

"Your mother? Elaine?" There was surprise and disbelief in Maggie's voice.

"Why, yes," Cal said. "My mom's got a great sense of humor. She's also very smart. Actually you, Mr. MacDougal, are the only one coming who isn't a member of the League."

I said, "You need to come up with words to fit the letters."

"People have tried," Paul said. "Is that all, Cal? We're really busy here. Maggie is acting like I'm responsible, like I drove Jilly off that cliff. She's asking all sorts of questions."

Maggie waved her ballpoint pen at him, before turning back to Cal Tarcher. "Before you go, Cal, did you happen to see Jilly last Tuesday evening?"

"There was lots of fog that night," Cal said, looking, I thought, at her Bally shoes. "I remember Cotter's date canceling because she didn't want to drive in it."

"Jilly went over about midnight," I said. "Was there fog then?"

"No," Maggie said. "It was nearly gone then." She added, "It's very changeable around here—the fog flits through like a bride's veil or it settles thick as a blanket, then all of a sudden it vanishes. It was like that last Tuesday night. Cotter's date was driving to your house?"

Cal nodded. She was, I saw, finally making eye contact with me. "Cotter likes his dates to pick him up," she said, seeing my raised eyebrow. "He says it makes women feel powerful if they're the ones driving. If they get annoyed with him they can drop him off and leave him on the side of the road, no harm done."

"So did you see Jilly or not?" Maggie asked. She didn't like Cal Tarcher, I thought, looking from one woman to the other. I wondered why. Cal Tarcher seemed perfectly harmless to me, painfully shy, the opposite of Maggie, and that was perhaps why she didn't like her. Cal Tarcher made her impatient.

"Yes, I saw her," Cal said. She took two steps toward the door. It seemed that now she wanted to get out of there. "It was around nine-thirty. She was driving her Porsche down Fifth Avenue, playing her car stereo real loud. I was eating a late dinner at The Edwardian. There were maybe ten, twelve people there. We all got up and went outside to wave to Jilly. She was singing at the top of her lungs."

"What was she singing?" I asked.

"Songs from the musical *Oklahoma*. And laughing. Yes, I remember she was laughing. She shouted at everyone, told them she was going to go serenade all the dead folk in the cemetery. Then she did a U-turn and headed back east on Fifth Avenue."

"That's what everyone else said, more or less." Maggie added, "The cemetery is south of the main part of town, really close to the ocean, so it's possible that's what she did. But then, much later, she was driving north up the coast road."

I remembered Rob Morrison lived south of town. No, I thought, Jilly wouldn't break her marriage vows, not Jilly. She wanted to have a kid. She wouldn't screw around with anyone else. But I knew I wouldn't be able to leave it alone. I'd have to ask Maggie.

"Maybe she went to the cemetery and something happened to her," Cal said.

"Like what?" Maggie said, her words bitten out.

"I don't know," Cal said slowly, ducking eye contact with every one of us. "But sometimes you can see odd shadows there, hear things, soft-sounding things. The trees whisper to each other, I've always thought. The hemlocks always seem to be crowding in toward the graves. You can imagine that their roots are twisted around a lot of the older caskets, maybe cracking them open, maybe releasing—" Cal shrugged. Then she tried to smile. "No, that's silly, isn't it?"

"Yes," Maggie said. "Very silly. Dead people don't hold any interest, and that's all there is at the cemetery. Just moldy old bones. Now, Cal, Mac here doesn't know you're an artist and you have flights of fancy. Stop acting weird. You know you're not, really."

"I still wouldn't want to go there at night," Cal said. "Even if I was drunk. It's a creepy place."

"Are you saying Jilly seemed drunk when you saw her at nine-thirty?" I asked.

Cal was silent. Maggie said, "Nobody else said anything about her being drunk. High spirits, Mr. Pete said, and that was just Jilly. I asked the doctors at the hospital after they'd done tests on Jilly. Her blood alcohol level was consistent with a couple of glasses of wine. And the toxicology screen was negative. So forget the drunk thing. Now, Cal, you didn't see her after that?"

Cal shook her head. She took a step toward the door. I stepped forward. "Maggie, why don't you and Paul continue your chat. I'll walk Miss Tarcher to her car."

I thought she was going to make a mad dash for the front door to escape me. What was wrong with the woman?

"Wait, Cal," I said, and pitched my voice low, filled with cool authority, the perfect FBI voice. She reacted instantly to that voice and came to a dead halt. I cupped her elbow in my right hand and went outside with her.

It was a cool, very clear morning, a light breeze to ruffle the hair on your head. I breathed in the ocean smell, still new in my lungs.

I didn't say anything until we reached her car, a light blue BMW Roadster, its top down. She was looking at her feet again, walking quickly, eager to get away from me. I lightly touched her shoulder when she opened the car door and said, "Hold on a minute, Miss Tarcher. What's wrong? Who are you so afraid of?"

For the first time, she looked up at me with a straightforward look, no eye-shifting. I saw that her eyes were a pale blue behind the glasses, with shades of gray. Cool eyes, intelligent. And something else I couldn't pinpoint. She straightened, her shoulders going back. She wasn't as short as I'd thought. In fact she suddenly looked tall, standing there with a very conscious arrogance. Her voice was as cool and intelligent as her eyes. "That, Mr. MacDougal, is none of your business. Good day to you. I will see you tomorrow night, unless you decide to leave town before then." She looked back toward the house for a moment, and added, "Who cares?"

"I do," I said.

She gave me an indifferent nod, climbed into her Beemer and was around the curve in Liverpool Street in under ten seconds. She didn't look back.

Cal Tarcher seemed to be two distinct, two very different people. It drove me nuts not to know anything or anyone, not to be able to root about to put things together.

I stood staring out over the ocean. The water was calm, placid, reaching into an endless horizon. There was one lone fishing boat out some two hundred yards from land. I could make out two people from this distance, sitting motionless in the boat. I sighed and turned slowly to walk back to the house.

Maggie was putting her cell phone back in her jacket pocket as she came running down the stairs. "See you later, Mac," she said. "Doc Lambert just called to tell me someone struck Charlie Duck on the head. Thank God Charlie lives right next door to Doc Lambert. Charlie managed to crawl over just before he fell unconscious. Doc said it didn't look good. I'm heading over there now."

"He's the old guy I met at The Edwardian yesterday at lunch. I remember he wanted to talk to me. Who would hit him? Maggie, that doesn't make sense."

"I agree. I'm out of here. See you later."

I hoped the old guy would be all right, but serious head wounds seldom turned out well. I wondered what he'd wanted to talk to me about. I wondered why anyone would hit him on the head.

SIX

I picked up two sandwiches from Grace's Deli on Fifth Avenue and brought them back to Liverpool Street. I rousted Paul out of his lab and we sat down at the dining room table at twelve-thirty.

Paul set a cold can of Coors in front of each of us. "I accomplished next to nothing," he said as he sat down. "I can't seem to think, to solve the easiest problems." He peeled back the foil on his sandwich. "Ah, rare roast beef, my favorite. How'd you know that, Mac?"

"I remembered Jilly telling me some time ago. She said you would only eat it half-cooked and slathered with mayonnaise. The woman at the deli knew exactly how you liked it."

Paul's face became still. "I can't believe Jilly's not here, telling me I'm a jerk because I forgot to do something she'd asked me to do, telling me to leave her alone because she's working and who says my work's more important than hers? She could be yelling at me one minute, then she'd start laughing, lean over, and bite my ear. Damn, Mac, it's hard."

"Paul, who's Laura?"

I thought Paul was going to have a heart attack. He jerked and spilled his beer onto the back of his hand and wrist. He didn't curse, didn't say anything at all, just looked down at the beer dripping off his hand onto the shining mahogany tabletop.

I handed Paul his paper napkin. When he'd finished mopping up, I said again, "Paul, tell me about Laura. Who is she?"

Paul took a bite of his sandwich, chewed slowly, not looking at me, just chewed. He swallowed, took a long pull of beer, then said finally, "Laura? There isn't any Laura."

Paul Bartlett was thirty-six, skinny as a post, at home in preppy clothes—this morning a dark green Ralph Lauren T-shirt and khaki slacks, light tan Italian loafers with tassels.

He was a genius, Jilly had always said, simply a genius. Well, that could be, I thought, but he was a lousy liar. I wasn't about to let this slide. "Laura, Paul. Tell me about her. It's important."

"Why would Laura be important to this? How do you even know her name?"

"I heard it from Jilly," I said. I wasn't about to tell him that I'd come suddenly awake at the hospital, my face on Jilly's hand, saying Laura's name aloud. It sounded too off the wall. I leaned back in my chair and added easily, "She mentioned Laura's name. Didn't say anything else about her—just said her name."

Did Paul look relieved? I realized I'd blown it. I never should have told him the woman's name was all I knew. I was an idiot. I was supposed to be trained to lie and bluff well. I was losing it. But why did Paul feel he had to lie? And then of course I realized what Jilly had meant. Laura had betrayed her with her husband, Paul.

Paul took another bite of his sandwich. Some of the mayonnaise oozed out the sides and fell to the napkin. He chewed slowly, buying time, I knew, an old ploy to gain time to think, to make the other person begin to question himself. He said finally, after a long stretch of silence, "She's not important, just a woman who lives in Salem. I don't even know if that's the Laura Jilly mentioned. As far as I know, Jilly never even met Laura, never even heard of her. I don't understand why she'd say her name." He sipped his beer, his hand steady as a rock now.

"How did you meet her? What's her last name?"

"More questions, Mac, about a person Jilly only mentioned in passing? What's this all about?"

"Jilly said to me, 'Laura betrayed me.' What did she mean, Paul?"

Paul looked like I'd socked him in the jaw. He shook his head as if to clear it and said, "All right, dammit. There was a Laura, but I haven't seen her in several months. I broke it off. I lost my head for a while there, but then I realized that I loved Jilly, that I didn't want to lose her. I haven't seen Laura since March."

"Laura was your lover then?"

"You find that hard to believe, Mac? You look at me and you see a nerd who's a decade older than you are, and not a thing like you? No bulging muscles? No big macho cop with broad shoulders and a full head of hair who goes chasing after terrorists, for God's sake? The only thing good you can say about me is that I'm at least an evolved nerd since I attracted your sister."

I forced myself to take another bite of my tuna salad sandwich. So both this Laura and Paul had betrayed Jilly. I wanted to jump over the table and tear Paul Bartlett's head off. I made myself chew slowly, just as Paul had done. It gave me time to cool down. What I needed most of all was control. I said after just a moment, no anger at all in my voice, "Let's get something perfectly straight here, Paul. I find it hard to believe you'd sleep with another woman because you're a married man, supposedly a happily married man. A married man isn't supposed to screw around on his wife."

"I'm sorry." Paul rubbed his fingers through his light brown hair. "I didn't mean all that, Mac. I'm upset, you can see that."

"What's Laura's last name?"

"Scott. Laura Scott. She's a reference librarian at the public library in Salem. I met her there."

"Why were you at the Salem Public Library?"

Paul just shrugged. "They've got great science reference materials. I do some research there once in a while."

"How did Jilly find out about your sleeping with Laura?"

"I don't know. I didn't tell her. Of course Laura knows Jilly. They're friends."

"So Jilly went to the Salem Public Library too?"

"Yes, she liked to go there. Don't ask me why, but she did. Look, Mac, Laura is shy, withdrawn. She wouldn't have told Jilly. I can't imagine how she found out. The two of them, they're opposites. Jilly is beautiful, talented, outgoing, like all of you—you, Gwen, and Kevin. She never just plain walks, she struts. She oozes confidence, is immensely sure of herself. She believes she's the best. Laura isn't any of those things. She's so self-effacing she could be a shadow."

"Why did you sleep with her, Paul, if she's so damned self-effacing?"

Paul looked down at the remains of his roast beef sandwich. "What is that old saw about having steak all the time? Maybe I needed a change from Jilly for a while."

"Is Laura Scott still in Salem?"

"I don't know. She was upset when I told her it was over. I don't know if she stayed or not. Why does it matter? I tell you, Jilly should never have found out about her. Maybe I dreamed about her and happened to say her name, with Jilly overhearing. But it doesn't matter. It's not important, Mac. It wasn't important as of over a month ago."

I didn't let on to Paul that it was more than important to me. Jilly had known that Laura had betrayed her. Laura was so much in Jilly's mind that I'd somehow picked it up from Jilly when I'd been with her in the hospital. Was Laura the reason Jilly had driven her Porsche over the cliff?

An hour later, I was on the highway heading to Salem.

SALEM, the capital of Oregon, sits in the heart of the Willamette Valley, on the banks of the Willamette River. It's only forty-three miles southwest of Portland, a short hop as the natives say. I remembered Jilly telling me once, on her third glass of white wine, that its Indian name, *Chemeketa*, meant "place of rest" and had been translated into the biblical name of Salem, from the Hebrew *shalom*, meaning "peace."

When I reached Salem, I pulled off the road into a small park and dialed 411. There was no Laura Scott listed in the Salem phone directory. There was one unlisted number for an L. P. Scott. I asked for the main number of the Salem Public Library. Ten minutes later I found the big concrete building between Liberty Street and Commercial. It was only a short drive from Willamette University, just south of downtown. On the north side there was a big open courtyard that connected the library to City Hall. Too close to the bureaucrats for my taste. Once inside, you forgot how ugly the outside was. It was airy, lots of lights, the floor covered with a turquoise carpeting. The shelves were orange. Not what I would have picked, but it would keep students awake. I walked to the circulation desk and asked if a Ms. Scott worked there.

"Ms. Scott is our senior reference librarian," a man of Middle Eastern extraction told me in a thick accent, pointing to the right corner of the main floor. I thanked him and headed in the direction of his finger.

I paused a moment beside the Renaissance art section and looked at the woman who was speaking quietly to a high school student with bad skin. He looked ridiculous to a man of my advanced years with his pants pulled down to nearly the bottom of his butt, bagging to his knees and beyond.

The student moved away, ambling toward the magazine section. I got my first good look at Laura Scott. Paul had said she was painfully shy and withdrawn, that she disappeared, like a shadow. My first thought was: *Is the idiot blind?* Truth was, I took one look at her and felt a bolt of lust so strong I had to lean against the nineteenth-century English history section. How could he say that she was nondescript? She was slender, tall, and even though her suit was too long and a dull shade of olive green, it simply didn't matter. She'd look great in a potato sack. Her hair was made up of many shades of brown, from dark brown to a lighter brown to an ash blond. It was all coiled up and smashed close to her head with lots of clips, but I could tell that it was long and thick. Lovely hair. I wanted to throw all those clips in the wastebasket under her desk. I understood how Paul had taken one look at her and lost his head. But why had he said she was plain? Had he said it so she'd hold no interest for me? So I'd dismiss her?

Actually, Laura Scott looked restrained, very professional, particularly with her hair scraped back like that, and she shimmered. I leaned against the English history section again. Shimmered? I was losing it. Was her unremarkable presentation to the world calculated? To keep men in line around her? Well, it evidently hadn't worked with Paul.

It wasn't working with me. I said to myself three times: *She and Paul betrayed Jilly.* I said it a fourth time to make sure it got through.

I waited until the high school student in his low-slung jeans disappeared behind an orange shelf, a magazine in his hand.

I approached her slowly and said, "High school students today—sometimes I want to grab their jeans and give them a good yank. It wouldn't take much. That boy you were speaking to, I think if he coughed his jeans would be around his knees."

Her face was smooth and young and she didn't change expression for about three seconds. She stared at me blankly, bland as rice pudding, as if she hadn't heard me. Then she looked to where the boy was leaning down to pick another magazine off the shelf, the crotch of his pants literally between his knees. She looked back up at me and after another three seconds, to my surprise, she threw back her head and laughed, a big full laugh. That laugh broke through the silence like a drum roll.

The Middle Eastern guy at the circulation desk looked over, his mouth opening, his surprise evident even from across the room.

What was coming out of her mouth wasn't at all a nondescript laugh.

It was full and deep and delightful. I smiled at her and stuck out my hand. "Hello, my name's Ford MacDougal. I'm new in town, just started teaching at Willamette University. Political science, primarily Europe, twentieth century. I wanted to see what sorts of public resources the students had off-campus. I like the orange shelves and the turquoise carpeting."

"Hello. Is it Mr. or Dr.?"

"Oh, it's Dr. MacDougal, but I've always thought that sounded phony, at least off campus. To me, a doctor means doing proctology exams. I can't handle that thought. I'd much rather talk about the Latvian drug wars."

Again, she didn't move, didn't change expression for a good three seconds. Then she opened her mouth and a short ribald laugh came out. This time, she clapped her hands over her mouth and stared up at me. She got herself together. "I'm sorry," she said, nearly gasping with the effort not to laugh. "I'm not like this, normally. I'm really very serious. I never laugh." She cleared her throat, straightened her suit lapels, and said, "Very well, I'll call you Mr. MacDougal. My name's Laura Scott. I'm the head reference librarian here."

"You've got a great laugh," I said as we shook hands. She was strong, her hands narrow, her fingers long, nails well manicured.

"How long have you worked here?"

"Nearly six months. I'm originally from New York, came out here to go to Willamette. I graduated with a degree in library science. This is my first job here on the West Coast. The only bad thing about working here is the less-than-princely salary they pay me. It barely keeps me in cat food for Grubster—he's my sweetheart alley cat. There's Nolan too. He's got quite an appetite. Oh, he's my bird."

I'd heard every word she'd said. Grubster and Nolan. I liked pets. It was just that I couldn't keep from looking at her mouth. She had a full mouth, a bit of red lipstick left, beautiful. I cleared my throat. I was acting like a teenager. "You're right," I said, "money's always a bitch. Lucky for me, since I eat a lot, I don't have to share my Cheerios with a Grubster or Nolan. I only have to worry about feeding myself. The university is hard up too. My office has a view since I came in as a full professor, but the heating system is so antiquated you can hear the steam whistle when it comes out of those ancient pipes."

She blinked this time, rapidly, at least half a dozen times. She didn't burst into laughter, but she did giggle. I'd made her laugh. It felt good. Evidently, she found me amusing.

I'd come here ready to play a role, to get the truth out of this woman, to charm her, whatever. Instead, I wanted to scoop her up and take her to Tahiti. I hated this.

"Do you have plans for dinner?" At her pause, I added, "As I said, I'm new here in town and don't know a soul. I realize you could be worried I'm another Jack the Ripper from London, so maybe we could stay around here. That way I couldn't kidnap you or mug you or do anything else to you that you might not think appropriate. You know, fun stuff that isn't supposed to happen when you've only known someone an hour. How about the Amadeus Café I saw on the lower level?"

She looked over at the large institutional clock on the wall just above all the medieval reference books. She smiled up at me and nodded. "I know a great place a block down the street. Not the Amadeus—it's really good, but I eat there every day."

An hour later, after a solitary tour of the Salem Public Library, we walked down Liberty Street to the Mai Thai, which turned out to be an excellent restaurant even though it was so dark and dusty I was afraid to order any meat dish off the menu.

She'd taken her hair down before we'd left the library. I wanted my face and my hands in her hair. She was leaning toward me, her long hair falling over her left shoulder. Laura Scott hadn't shown me a single shy, withdrawn bone. She was open, responding to me with laughter and jokes, making me feel like I had to be the most fascinating guy in the known universe. She'd turned twenty-eight in March, she said. She was single, lived in a condo right on the river, played tennis and racquetball, and loved to horseback ride. Her favorite stable was five miles out of town.

She was at ease with me. I didn't want that to stop.

For myself, I made up a wonderful academic life, replete with stories that friends and siblings had told me of their college experiences over the years. She was down to the last few bites of her chicken satay when I knew the party was over. I was here for a reason, not to flirt and start a relationship with this fascinating woman. I said easily, watching her as closely as a snake watches a mongoose, "I have relatives down in Edgerton, a little town on the coast of Oregon, an hour from here."

She kept chewing her chicken, but I saw the change in her, instantly.

Her eyes, to this point rather vague and soft, were sharp, attentive behind her glasses. But she didn't say anything.

"My cousin—Rob Morrison—is a cop. He says everyone calls the town The Edge. He's got a little house very close to the cliffs. You look out the window and think you're on a boat. If you keep staring at the water, pretty soon it feels like you're really on a boat rocking back and forth. Have you ever heard of the place? Do you know anyone from there?"

Would she lie?

"Yes," she said, "I have, and yes, I do."

I nearly fell out of the booth I was so surprised she'd admit it, to me, a perfect stranger. Well, maybe that was why she'd admitted it—I was a perfect stranger. There was no reason to distrust me.

I said, "Do you know my cousin?"

"Rob Morrison? No, I don't believe I've ever met him."

"You wouldn't forget him if you had—he's a triathlete, a hunk."

She sighed deeply, her hands over her breast, and rolled her eyes. No one in the known universe could ever believe her to be nondescript. She sparkled. "No, sorry. I know the Bartletts—Jilly and Paul Bartlett."

"Small world," I said, wondering if my voice was shaking. "I know them as well." I took a bite of coconut soup and said, "You're younger than Jilly, so you didn't go to school together. How did you two meet?"

"We met about five months ago when she was here in Salem, at the library. We got to talking. She was looking for articles on infertility. I asked her about using the Internet, offered to show her how to go about it in the library, but she said that computers were beyond her. I saw her once or twice a week ever since then, sometimes here and sometimes in Edgerton. I met Paul about three months ago for the first time."

I sat back against the dark red vinyl of the booth. I picked up my fork and fiddled with it. Jilly told Laura that she didn't know anything about computers? Why had she told Laura that lie? Jilly was a whiz at computers, always had been. And what was this about infertility? Finally, I said, "So Jilly was your friend."

"Yes."

"You weren't Paul Bartlett's mistress?"

She cocked her head to one side, sending her beautiful hair spilling over her left shoulder nearly to her plate. "What is this, Dr. MacDougal? Did Jilly send you here? What's going on?"

"Ms. Scott, I lied to you. I'm not a professor at Willamette University. I don't know a thing about Latvian drug wars. I came into the library specifically to meet you. My name is Ford MacDougal; I didn't lie about that. I'm Jilly's brother. She's in the Tallshon Community Hospital, in a coma."

She dropped her thick-bowled white spoon into her soup. She turned perfectly white. I thought she was going to pass out. I was halfway out of the booth when I managed to stop myself. She was fine. I was the one who was the mess.

"I'm sorry I lied to you but I'd do it again no matter what I felt about you." If my boss heard me say that, he'd have laughed his head off.

She got hold of herself. "Jilly's in a coma? That's crazy. No, it's impossible."

"Why?"

"I saw her Tuesday night over in Edgerton."

SEVEN

I hadn't felt so stupid since my high school English class when Mrs. Zigler told me *Wuthering Heights* wasn't a fancy district of London.

I stared blankly at Laura Scott, and eventually my mouth moved. "You were with Jilly and Paul on Tuesday night?"

"Yes, it was a party of sorts, at least that's how they billed it. I had to leave so I don't know what happened after I was out of there."

"Who all was at this party?"

"Well, it was only Paul, Jilly, and I. I understand that other people were supposed to be coming by. When I left it wasn't very late. You see, Grubster—my cat—is on medication and I had to get home to give him a pill. But that's not important. Tell me about Jilly. What happened to her? Is she going to be all right?"

"She's in a coma. No one knows much of anything about her chances for recovery."

"But what happened?"

"She drove her Porsche off a cliff, landed in twenty feet of water, and a cop managed to pull her out. She told me a short time ago that you'd betrayed her. What did she mean by that?"

She shook her head, sending her hair perilously close again to her chicken satay. "What a strange thing for her to say. That's why you came to meet me? To see if I'd somehow betrayed your sister? I don't know what you're talking about. I just don't know." She was suddenly very still, staring down at her dinner plate. "It doesn't make sense. She was an excellent driver. I can't believe it. She was laughing the last time I saw her. Did someone force her off that cliff? Was it an accident? Was she hit by someone?"

Even I, the cop, hadn't first thought that someone forced her off the cliff. Why had Laura? "No, she went flying off a cliff some ten miles north of Edgerton right before the junction east back to 101. It would appear that she was trying to kill herself."

"How could she possibly have survived that?"

"As I said, a cop saw her go over and managed to pull her out before she drowned. No one disagrees that it was a miracle."

Laura Scott slowly rose and stared down at the platters still piled high with Thai food. She shook her head and stuck her hand in her purse. She pulled a fifty-dollar bill out of a very fat wallet and dropped it beside her soup bowl. She said, not looking at me, "She was always driving that car too fast, hooting and hollering, yelling at the top of her lungs. She liked danger, she told me. She said driving the Porsche at a hundred miles an hour was like flying, only without having to wear a parachute. Jilly wouldn't try to kill herself. She lost control of that damned Porsche. I want to see her. You said she was in Tallshon?"

"Yes, that's where she is." I rose to stand beside her. I lightly touched my fingers to her forearm, holding her still for a moment. "Before we go anywhere, tell me the truth, Laura. Are you or were you sleeping with Paul?"

She looked up at me like I'd lost my mind. "No," she said, "of course I wouldn't sleep with Paul. That's ridiculous."

I realized I was still touching my fingers to her forearm. I didn't stop. I didn't want to lose the connection to her. "Paul says you were his lover up until last month. Then he said he broke it off. And Jilly told me you had betrayed her."

She shook off my hand. I thought for a moment she was going to smack me, but at the last moment she held herself back. "No, I didn't sleep with Paul. He lied. Why? I don't know. As for Jilly claiming I betrayed her, I don't know what she meant."

"Why would Paul lie?"

"Ask him, damn you. I'm going to see Jilly."

"I'll drive you."

"No," she said. "You've done quite enough."

I couldn't believe it. Laura was here, standing beside Ford. I saw her as clearly as I saw Ford. I couldn't believe it was that betraying bitch, Laura. But it was. She was here and I saw her. She was saying something to Ford. What was she telling him?

I felt my flesh crawling, felt bile rise in my throat, felt the fear begin to wash through me, and yet I felt nothing at all. I was apart from her now and she couldn't hurt me. She was coming closer, and she was saying my name over and over. Why did I still feel the fear so strongly?

I wanted to scream that I would kill her, but I couldn't. Why in God's name was she here with me? How could she still have the power to terrify me? It shouldn't be happening. She should have been long gone by now, nothing more than a stupid memory. She was reaching out her hand to touch me as she spoke to Ford. I couldn't stand it.

"Her eyes are open. Look at that. Her eyes are open!"

"They usually are," Ford said. "It doesn't mean anything."

I felt her fingers touch my shoulder. Her fingers were cold as death.

I screamed.

I whirled around so fast I nearly landed on my butt. My heart was pounding out of my chest. I was at Jilly's side in an instant, shouting over my shoulder, "Laura, get the nurses, quick. And the doctors too. My God, hurry! Move it!"

I gathered Jilly up in my arms and pressed her tightly to me, trying to hold her steady. She was heaving against me, flailing her head from side to side, and she was screaming—screams that came out like low harsh bleating sounds. It sounded like someone was torturing her. She ran out of strength fast and slumped against me. I was relieved because I was afraid she would hurt herself. Very gently, I laid her back against the pillow. "Jilly," I said as I leaned down and kissed the tip of her nose. "No, don't close your eyes. Keep looking at me. Stay awake. Don't fall back asleep. You might not wake up again. Jilly, you've got to stay awake. Do you understand?"

"Yes, I can hear you, Ford," she said to me. Her voice was wispy, thin as a piece of paper, almost too faint for me to hear.

I patted her cheek, stroking my fingers through her hair. She felt alive, solid, back with me. I felt ready to burst with relief. "Good." I leaned closer. "Listen to me, Jilly. You were in a coma for four days. You've come out of it. You'll be just fine now. Jilly, keep your eyes open. Blink at me. Yes, that's good. Can you see me clearly?"

"Yes, Ford. I'm so glad you're here."

Her brain was all right, I was sure of it. Jilly was back with me, all of her. There was awareness in her eyes and she was staring hard at me, willing herself to be here, and she was. "You're the only one who still calls me Ford," I said, and kissed her cheek.

"You've never been Mac to me. I'm so thirsty." I quickly poured water from the carafe into the small glass on the table beside her bed and held her up while she sipped. I wiped the water off her chin when she finished drinking. She cleared her throat, swallowed a couple of times, and said, "When you first walked through that door I couldn't believe it. You were real, unlike all the others. To have you here was wonderful. I felt so alone."

I wasn't really surprised that she'd seen me, that she'd heard every word I'd said, seen the expressions on my face. Actually she could have told me what I'd eaten for breakfast, that she'd tasted it right along with me, and I wouldn't have doubted her for a moment. I said only, "I was real? Unlike the others? What do you mean exactly?"

"Oh, yes," she said, and managed a small smile. "You were very real. The others weren't. Everyone else who came in here was a white shadowy thing, but not you, Ford, not you. You were all here. You touched my hand and I felt warmth. Thank you."

I wasn't surprised, but I did wonder if I hadn't gone off the deep end after the car bomb in Tunisia. Psychic communication with my sister? I wondered what the FBI profilers would say about that.

I heard shouting and running feet. Two nurses and a doctor all tried to squeeze through the doorway and into the room at the same time. I nearly laughed, remembering the Three Stooges.

Things quickly degenerated from there.

DR. Sam Coates had a 1930s black pencil-thin mustache and a bald head. He said, "We'll be running lots more tests, but given how she appears now, I'm just about ready to say she's pulled through this with no physical or mental deficit." He sounded all cool and professional, but I could tell he was pleased beyond anything, the nurses too. They were hopping about beside him, nodding, smiling, looking ready to burst into song, probably the "Hallelujah" chorus. Dr. Coates continued, gesticulating with his hands, unable, I guess, to keep himself quiet, just like the nurses. "It really is a miracle, you know, Mr. MacDougal. No other way to say it. A miracle and we were all here to witness it. I've seen this complete recovery before with a drug overdose, but not after a head trauma. I'd begun to believe she wouldn't wake up."

He stuck out his hand and I obligingly shook it. I was grateful to all of them. Jilly's room was filled with people. Maggie and Paul had arrived not fifteen minutes before. I watched Dr. Coates shake Paul's hand. He nodded to Laura Scott and said to Maggie, "Sheriff. Now, I suggest all of you go home. Mrs. Bartlett will sleep soundly until morning. Go home."

"But what if she doesn't wake up again?" I asked, terrified when I'd seen Jilly close her eyes, her head falling to the side.

"Not to worry," Dr. Coates said. "Trust me on this. A coma's like a nightmare. Once you wake up, it's over. Memories of the nightmare or the coma might remain but it rarely comes back. Really."

Maggie said, "You're wrong about that, Doctor. Nightmares do come back."

Dr. Coates shrugged. "Sorry, I'll have to dig up another analogy."

"It's still great news," Maggie said, and shook his hand again. She said to Laura, "Why don't you come home with me? It's pretty late."

"No, thank you, Sheriff," Laura said. "My cat needs his medication. Also I have to work tomorrow." She walked to Paul, and I wondered if she was going to hit him. But she didn't. She frowned at him for a moment, then stepped back. I watched her walk out of the room. I was right behind her. I said over my shoulder to the doctor, "I'll be back in a moment."

I waited until Paul and Maggie were out of hearing distance, then I gave Laura's hand a tug and stopped her. I pulled her over to a window. "You said you weren't sleeping with Paul. Either you are a remarkable actress and liar, or you're really not sleeping with him."

"I'm a decent actress and liar when I have to be. One more time, Mac. I didn't sleep with Paul. I can't imagine sleeping with Paul."

I believed her and that raised more questions.

"Ask Paul."

"Yes, I will." I forced myself to walk away from her. I stopped to look out the window at the cloud-strewn dead sky. A stand of spruce stood beside the parking lot, thick leaves rustling. The wind was rising. It was pitch-black out there.

I heard her walking toward me. I could feel her. She vibrated with life. I wondered what she'd feel like if I touched her, really touched her.

"Good night, Mac. I'm glad Jilly woke up." She lightly patted my cheek, turned, and walked away. I watched her push open the exit door and ease through a small crowd of off-duty hospital personnel and a couple of late visitors. I couldn't stop myself. I came up behind her, my hand out to stop her when she suddenly turned back to me and said, "I understand from the sheriff that you're FBI. You're a big federal cop. She said you were here to help find out what happened to Jilly that night. Ask her. Find out what happened. Then tell me, please. You might consider believing me about Paul. Actually, truth be told, the only man I've met in the past year or so that I'd even consider going to bed with is you. Good night. Grubster is waiting for his pill. Nolan has probably torn the bars off his cage."

"He's sure been on those pills a long time," I called after her.

"Now you're a veterinarian? Give it up, Mac. I'll be back tomorrow to see Jilly."

"Why didn't Paul call you to tell you what had happened to Jilly?"

"I don't know," she shouted back, not turning. She kept walking. "Ask him. He's your damned brother-in-law. Don't you know him?"

I let her go. What else could I do? I watched her walk to her car without another word, without a backward glance at me. She was looking down as she walked, her shoulders slumped. I stood in the middle of the parking lot, staring after her until her Toyota turned out of the gated opening and disappeared into the night.

I found Paul in Jilly's room, sitting beside her bed, holding her hand. "I wish they'd kept her awake," he said. "It's like she's back in a coma. It's like she's gone again. I don't care what Dr. Coates said. I don't think any of them know much of anything. Why didn't you stop them, Mac?"

"She had a killer headache, Paul. They hadn't expected her to fall asleep so quickly, but Dr. Coates said it wasn't anything to worry about. Knowing the hospital routine, they'll be here to give her a shot in the butt at about three A.M."

"Yeah," Paul said, looking up at me. "You'd know, wouldn't you? How long were you in the naval hospital in Bethesda? Two, three weeks?"

"Too long, however long it was," I said, knowing that it was exactly eighteen days and eight hours. "I don't like to think about it. Jilly's awake now, Paul. Everything will be all right." He looked so painfully hopeful that I dropped my hand to his shoulder and squeezed. "Jilly's back with us. She'll tell us exactly what happened. It's over now, Paul." He looked like he was going to cry. For the life of me, I couldn't bring myself to demand that he explain Laura.

"Well, you look tired yourself, Mac. It's been a long day. You've been pushing yourself too hard. Why don't you have the doctors here check you out?"

I declined and sent Paul home. He looked ready to pitch forward onto his face. I'd nail him about Laura tomorrow. I wanted to know about the party on Tuesday night, the same night Jilly drove her Porsche off the cliff.

I realized that I didn't have to know any more about anything right now. Who cared what Paul had told me, what Laura had told me? It didn't matter. Jilly would live. She was the only reason I was here.

I was so tired my eyes hurt but I was too restless to sleep. I ended up wandering the hospital corridors, looking into every room that had windows, except for the morgue in the basement. I had a tough time dealing with the morgue anytime, but now, not a chance.

I went back to Jilly's room a little after one A.M., still wide awake, still restless. I sat down at the small table in front of the window, pulled out my notebook, and began to write. I wrote down what people had told me. I wrote down some of the questions I still had.

I laid down my pen. I shook my head. My written questions sounded like a soap opera. *Was Jilly sleeping with some other guy? Who is Laura Scott, really?*

I wrote one final question: *Jilly's awake. What am I still doing here?*

When Jilly awoke at two A.M. I was in a semi-stupor, feeling a strong pull from my cracked ribs because I was stretched out in a long deep chair pulled from the doctors' lounge, alongside her bed. I was holding her hand.

"Ford?"

It was her voice and it sounded to me like old knotted threads, ready to unravel at the first pull. She spoke again, and I knew she'd heard the weakness in her own voice and was concentrating on sounding stronger. "Ford?"

I gave her a big smile, which I didn't know if she could even see because the room was shadowy, with only a lamp in the far corner of the room lowered to dim. But my eyes were used to it. I could see her clearly. "Jilly, hi." I squeezed her hand, leaned up and kissed her forehead.

"You stayed with me?"

"Yeah. Paul looked ready to drop so I sent him on home. You want me to call the nurse?"

"Oh, no, I just want to lie here and be alive and start to believe it. The headache's gone. I just feel sort of weak, nothing more."

I gave her more water and rubbed my knuckles over her smooth cheek. "I was with you, Jilly. I was with you when you went over the cliff, when you hit the water. I felt that huge impact."

She said nothing, looked up at me, waiting.

"I was in the hospital myself, remember?"

She nodded. "The car bomb explosion, in Tunisia."

"Yes. That dream or vision—whatever—was more than real. I came awake and I couldn't breathe. It really scared me, Jilly. What I can't figure out is why you hooked up with me. How you were able to connect to my mind. Were you thinking about me at all at the time?"

She shook her head. "You told me about this already, Ford. I heard you clearly, that first time you came to see me. Do you believe me?"

"Of course I believe you. I'd be pretty stupid if I didn't, since I was with you in the Porsche, going over that bloody cliff."

"It's all very confusing, Ford."

"Jilly, the truth now. Were you thinking about Laura?"

I thought she'd pass out. She turned utterly white, her breath wheezed out, and she was shaking her head back and forth on the pillow. "You brought her here. She was with you. I saw her as clearly as I always saw you. No one else, Ford, just you. And then Laura was with you, and I saw her clearly too. And I started screaming—"

"And you came out of the coma screaming," I said slowly, my eyes never leaving her face. "You saw Laura and you couldn't bear to have her here, and then you woke up. Was she the one who brought you out of it?"

I didn't think she was going to answer me, then she whispered, "I had to get away from her, that's all I know. I couldn't believe she was still here. What were you doing with her?"

Only the truth, I thought, but what was the truth? There were so many lies swirling about that I couldn't be certain exactly where the truth lay, but I could at least tell her what I thought of things. "When I was here yesterday, I fell asleep holding your hand."

"I know. I saw you."

"We'll talk more about that later. I awoke suddenly and heard you saying that Laura had betrayed you. At dinner last night I asked Paul about Laura, said that you'd told me about her. It took a while, but he finally admitted that he'd had an affair with her, once he admitted that she actually existed. Then he said he'd broken it off. He told me she wasn't important. He didn't believe you knew about it. But you see, I knew that you had at least heard her name. I wanted to see her, so I went to the public library in Salem."

Suddenly, Jilly was nearly gasping for breath. She was wheezing. "Ford, you've got to believe me. Stay away from her. She's very dangerous."

And I was thinking: *I've never met anyone less dangerous in my life.* What was going on here?

"Did she sleep with Paul?"

Jilly shook her head, her skin so pale I thought she would faint. Then she nodded. Was it a yes or a no or more confusion? In any case, she was tired, upset, and I backed off. I patted her hand and covered her with a light blanket. I stood and felt my body creak. "You're exhausted. It's very late. I'll let you rest awhile. Let me get the nurse."

I watched her for a moment, seeing the waves of fatigue wash over her, dragging her under into oblivion. The nurse could wait. All my questions could wait. She needed sleep. I turned to see Nurse Himmel standing in the open doorway.

"Don't worry. I won't wake her up again. That's what you were coming to tell me, wasn't it?"

I nodded and stepped back so she could come into the room. I liked Nurse Himmel. She was short, built solid as a Humvee, and she'd always been kind to me, and to Jilly. Like Midge, Mrs. Himmel would have brought me a beer.

"She's sleeping, Mr. MacDougal," Mrs. Himmel said quietly as she gently pulled the blanket up to Jilly's neck. "She's just fine. Her pulse and oxygen level are normal. Goodness, it's wonderful to see a recovery like this. She'll be up and walking around soon. Now you should go home and sleep in your bed. You're looking a bit slack in the jaw."

"You're right, my jaw could use a rest."

She smiled at me.

Whatever. I knew she was right, but there was so much Jilly had to tell me. It could wait. It would be stupid if I got myself laid flat again. The people I called friends would never let me live it down. I could hear Quinlan, another FBI agent, calling me a wimp in that easy dark voice of his. I drove into Paul and Jilly's driveway twenty minutes later. I shucked off my clothes, down to my boxer shorts, and was in bed only five minutes after that.

I dreamed I was a waiter in a nightclub, with a white towel over my arm, carrying a tray of drinks, but I couldn't remember who had ordered them. I kept walking around this huge room, looking and looking, not knowing, and I was getting frantic. There were dozens of customer drink-tables, all of them circular, people crowded around them. There was Jilly, tap-dancing from one table to the next. She was dancing like a pro. People were whistling and clapping. She was also stark naked except for her black tap shoes. A man whose face I couldn't see clearly was running after her, holding a long cloak toward her, waving it at her actually.

When I woke up it was nearly nine o'clock the next morning. I hadn't slept so soundly since before I'd been blasted in Tunisia. For the first time I felt nearly back to normal. I stretched, flexed my muscles, even smiled at myself while I shaved. I didn't look like oatmeal anymore, thank God.

Paul wasn't home. I imagined he'd gone to the hospital to be with Jilly. I could speak to him there.

I was at the hospital a half hour later.

EIGHT

As I was turning the corner to the third-floor waiting room, I heard Maggie Sheffield's voice. "I can only tell you, Cotter, that someone hit Charlie Duck over the head and he died shortly after he managed to crawl over to Doc Lambert's house."

"You've got no clues? Nothing?"

"I'll tell you it's the damnedest thing, this murder of a harmless old man. It's not like this is Salem or Portland. This is Edgerton, small-town USA. I don't know if a murder has ever happened here before, but someone killed Charlie Duck and then ransacked his house."

I came into the waiting room to see the sheriff speaking to a young man I'd never seen before. He was about my age, on the short side, built like a bull—obviously a weight lifter—with a manner and look that were danger-ous. Strange that a guy would think that, but it was true. I disliked him on sight.

"Cotter Tarcher," the man said and nodded to me. "You're Jilly's brother?"

"That's right. Ford MacDougal. And you're Cal's brother?"

"Yes. I forgot you met Cal. She went over to Paul's house and caught all of you there. You're coming to the party tonight? It's Miss Geraldine's birthday and we always celebrate every year. My folks decided that we'd go ahead, despite Charlie Duck's death."

"It was murder, Cotter," Maggie said.

"To be honest, I forgot all about it," I said. "Jilly's awake. I've been think-ing about her." Cotter Tarcher looked dark from his dirt-black hair to the heavy growth of beard on his cheeks. I bet that women sensed danger in him and were drawn to it. At the same time they'd be wary, if they had half a brain. Cal had said that he let the women he dated do the driving, to make them feel like they had the power. It was a smart move on his part, the prick. He would need to mellow them out. I remembered that Jilly didn't like him either.

"Of course," Cotter said easily. "I saw Jilly a little while ago. She's looking really good. She got one of the nurse's aides to wash her hair. She looks normal. It's amazing."

I said to Maggie, "I heard you talking about Charlie Duck. It really is a shock for a little town like Edgerton. Did you bring in the crime-lab people from Portland? They're top-notch. The medical examiner—Ted Leppra—is one of the best M.E.s on the West Coast."

She shook her head. "I know how he died. He got bashed on the head, his brain filled up with blood and smashed bone, and that was the end of him. I don't see any need for an M.E. to translate that for me in medicalese—it's a waste of time.

"Poor old Charlie. He's been here for at least fifteen years. The funeral's on Tuesday. Everyone will be there at the League's Christian church."

"The League?" I asked.

Maggie said, "The BITEASS League, remember? Since everyone in town is a member, the League keeps up one central place of worship. Different religions can have the building at different times. In the case of funerals, it's an interdenominational service. Representatives from all the religious groups will take a few moments to speak. Since old Charlie was an agnostic, everyone will get equal time. If he'd been a Baptist, say, they'd get the lion's share of the time. Come if you can, Mac. You can meet the rest of the folk in town.

"Or are you heading back to Washington? Since Jilly's awake again, there's no reason for you to stay, is there? Has she told you about what happened Tuesday night? Does it match your dream?"

"I'm going to speak to her about it right now," I said, wishing Maggie hadn't said anything about it in front of Cotter Tarcher. But in the long run I couldn't see that it would make any difference. Who cared if anybody thought I was nuts? As for Tarcher, he hadn't acted like an ass, at least not yet.

"I hope she'll talk to you," Maggie said to me. "When I was in there this morning, she claimed she didn't remember a thing. She acted shocked when I told her we were worried because it looked to Rob like she'd driven over the cliff on purpose. She didn't say another word. If there's something more, maybe she'll tell you, Mac."

I said, "Maybe nothing's going on, Maggie."

"I hope you're right. I'm worried she might try to hurt herself again."

Cotter looked back and forth at each of us. "Try to drop by tonight, Mac. My parents would like to meet you." He shook my hand, harder than necessary, nodded to Maggie, gave me a look that said he could whip my ass anytime, and left. He was easy to dislike, on spec.

"Maggie," I said. "Were you invited over to Paul and Jilly's house on Tuesday night?"

"No. Why?"

"Laura Scott told me Paul and Jilly were expecting other people. She had to leave early, so she didn't know how many people or who they were."

Why did I have to know? It didn't matter. What mattered was speaking to Jilly, making sure she was okay now, that she wasn't depressed or bent on trying to kill herself again.

I thought about Laura, about how I'd never before met a woman who drew me instantly as she had. No, I wasn't going back to Washington yet. There was the Tarcher party tonight. It should prove interesting.

"Mac, before you go see Jilly, there's something else about Charlie Duck's murder, something that's really weird. I didn't want to say anything about it in front of Cotter, but hey, you're a cop too."

"You know something?"

"Yeah, but I don't know if it means anything. Someone killed Charlie, then ransacked his house. I've had my guy dust for fingerprints. I've made a search myself. I didn't find anything, nothing that might have been of interest to anyone. Whatever the murderer was looking for, he probably found it. He took the murder weapon with him."

She drew a deep breath. "Maybe you can help me figure this out. After Doc Lambert called me, he said that Charlie regained consciousness just a moment before he died."

My heart speeded up, I don't know why. I waited.

"Doc Lambert said Charlie was real frantic, mumbled a whole lot of stuff, but the only thing he could really make out was 'a big wallop, too much, then they got me.' Doc Lambert said he died then. Does that make any sense to you?"

"Have the M.E. in Portland do an autopsy," I said. "Do it right now."

"Why?"

"Because I've got this feeling, a real burning in my gut, that this wasn't a random killing and burglary. Charlie Duck wanted to speak to you. He wanted to speak to me. I wish he'd done it yesterday, but he didn't, obviously because he didn't think he was in any danger. But he was. Someone walloped him, it was too much, then they killed him."

"Mac, you make it sound like some sort of B movie. You know, the murdered guy trying to tell someone who it was who killed him? It doesn't happen like that in real life."

"Who was Charlie Duck?"

"He was a retired cop from Chicago. More than fifteen years ago."

My heart speeded up again. "Look, Maggie, Jilly goes over a cliff. Someone murders a retired cop. Maybe the two don't have anything to do with each other, but I'd rather know for sure than guess about it."

"Surely his death can't have anything to do with Jilly driving off that cliff. It doesn't make any sense."

"Have the M.E. do an autopsy. His name's Ted Leppra. Call him now, Maggie. Get it done."

A big wallop, too much, then they got me.

What was going on here?

Jilly was alone. She was reading a newspaper. When she saw me, she grew very still. I was at her side in two big steps. "What's wrong?"

She smiled up at me and laid the newspaper aside. "Nothing at all, Ford. I'm looking human again, don't you think? Did you come to tell me good-bye?"

"No, I came to talk to you."

Again she grew still, as if she didn't want to see me, didn't want to talk to me. Why?

"Jilly, you're my sister. I've known you all my life. I love you. If you tried to commit suicide, tell me why. I'll do what I can to help. I want to help. Please talk to me."

I knew her well enough to see the lie in her eyes and quickly added, "No, don't tell me you can't remember, like you told Maggie. Tell me the truth. Did you try to kill yourself, Jilly?"

"No, Ford, I'd never try to do such a ridiculous thing. Truth of it was that I lost control of my Porsche. I was singing as loud as I could, driving much too fast, and I lost control coming around a comer. That's it, Ford, I swear."

"Rob Morrison said you speeded up when you drove toward that cliff."

"He's wrong," Jilly said. "Absolutely wrong. I lost control. Maybe I hit the gas when I went through the railing, I don't remember. I suppose it's possible.

"Ford, I'm all right, truly. Go home now. You're still not back to one hundred percent. Better yet, take another week off and go down to Lake Tahoe and get some fishing in. You know you'd really like that."

"I'll think about it."

"Well, if I don't see you again, take care of yourself. You, Kevin, Gwen, and I—we'll get together at Gwen's in New York at Christmas."

It was a tradition, one we'd missed this past year and thus the get-together in February. I leaned down and hugged her hard against me. "I love you, Jilly," I said.

"I love you too, Ford. Don't worry about me anymore. Be sure to call Kevin and Gwen, tell them everything is all right."

THE Tarcher house sat on a cul-de-sac at the end of Brooklyn Heights Avenue. It clearly dominated the other three or four pretenders set far apart from one another, separated by spruce and hemlock. The mansion was a good three times larger than Paul and Jilly's place, and looked like an honest-to-God Victorian transplant straight from San Francisco. Its basic color was cream, but there were another four or five accent colors used on the various window frames and sills, door frames, balcony railings, arches, cornices, and various other whimsical things whose names I didn't know. It looked like a huge, fascinating, over-the-edge birthday cake. It had been designed by people with lots of money and an equal amount of imagination.

Four young guys dressed in red shirts and black pants were valeting all the guests' cars. By the time Paul and I pulled up in his Ford Explorer, there must have been thirty cars parked all along both sides of the winding avenue. It looked like the whole town had turned out for the event.

Jilly had wanted to come. She wanted everyone to see she was back in action again, even though her Porsche wasn't. She told me she'd already gotten a towing service to figure out if they could get her Porsche out of the ocean. I'd said fine, you can come if you can walk without assistance from here to the end of the hall. She made eight steps and drooped. But she was fine, according to all the tests Dr. Coates had done on her since early that morning. I'd asked him if he was coming to the Tarchers' party and he'd said he wouldn't miss it unless a set of triplets was ready to slip out.

My sister Gwen, who'd had three kids, none of whom, I was sure, had just slipped out, would have slugged him.

I turned to Paul as we stepped out of the Explorer in front of the Tarcher house. "Tell me about Tarcher, Paul."

"His full name's Alyssum Tarcher, and don't ask me where he got the weird name. He's been here some thirty years and he's filthy rich. I wouldn't be surprised if he owns half the state. Everybody here owes him, probably without exception. Nothing happens in this town that isn't run by him first. The mayor, Miss Geraldine, is at his beck and call. She'll do anything he wants. Actually, most of us will."

"Did you have to ask his permission to move back out here from Pennsylvania?"

"As a matter of fact, he helped me come back," Paul said, all cool and formal. "No secret there. He's invested in my current project. He sold Jilly and me our house."

"Ah," I said. So that's how he and Jilly were surviving. But that beautiful house and Jilly's Porsche were far above the survival line. "This is the fountain of youth formula?"

"Good try," Paul said, slamming his door. "Mac, I'm so relieved that Jilly lost control of the Porsche. If she'd tried to kill herself, I don't know what I would have done."

"Me either."

One of the young valets dashed up, out of breath, gave Paul a big purple ticket, and drove the Explorer away. "Some house, huh?"

"Incredible," I said, climbing up the deep half-dozen front steps. Lights and mellow chamber music poured out of the house. When we walked into the huge vestibule, I paused a moment, just breathing in the incredible smell of the house. It smelled like standing in the middle of a deep forest with a sliver of sunlight on your face—a hint of flowers, of water-drenched moss, of trees and light, pure air. I inhaled deeply as I turned to see a tall, hawk-nosed man walk toward us. It was, I had no doubt, Alyssum Tarcher, the patriarch of Edgerton, Oregon.

I am six feet, two inches tall, one hundred eighty-five pounds before the car bombing. He was at least two inches taller than me but not any heavier. He was probably around sixty years old, his hair thick, mixed black and white. He was a strong, vigorous man, no paunch, no softness on him. He looked potent. His son, Cotter, was standing behind him—thick-necked and dark, he looked like a thug. It was quite a contrast. He'd probably just shaved, but there was a hint of dark growth on his cheeks. He cracked his knuckles, his eyes studying my face.

"Ford MacDougal?"

Alyssum Tarcher's voice was as deep and rich as the smoothest Kentucky bourbon.

"Yes, sir," I said. He stuck out his hand and I shook it. An artist's hands, I thought, slender, narrow, long-fingered. Too smooth.

"You and Jilly don't look a thing like each other," Alyssum Tarcher said, looking through to my molecules, I thought. This was a dangerous man. Far more dangerous than his bully of a son.

"No," I said. "We don't."

"Of course you're both fine-looking young people and your general coloring's the same. You've met my son, Cotter?"

I shook Cotter's hand and smiled down at him, content to wait to let him begin the pissing contest, which he did, quickly. I managed to twist my hand slightly so that I had better leverage than him. I looked him straight in the eye and proceeded to crush his fingers. I let his hand go when I saw the strain around his mouth. I think Paul was the only one who noticed the locker-room behavior. As for Cotter, oddly enough, he looked both homicidally furious and curiously absorbed. He slowly rubbed his hand, staring at me. It was as if he was trying to get inside my head, trying to see how he could best go about smashing me. I knew I'd made an enemy, didn't really care, but I did wonder what he was thinking now. I hadn't met up with a verifiable sociopath in at least six months.

Cotter never looked away from me. I turned when I heard Alyssum Tarcher say, "Well, Paul, now that Jilly's back with us, you can get to work again. I understand all this has been hard on you, but now, finally, everything will be all right."

"Yes," Paul said. "Jilly wanted to come tonight, but she couldn't walk more than a few steps. Mac and I left her nearly asleep and disappointed. She wants me to assure everyone that she didn't go over that cliff on purpose. She lost control of the Porsche. She also swears that she won't go a hundred miles an hour around any more curves as long as she lives. She sends her love."

"That's a relief," Alyssum Tarcher said. He picked up two flutes of champagne from a waiter's tray and handed one to me and one to Paul.

Then he picked up one for himself, raised it, and said, "To the future. May our project succeed beyond our wildest imaginings."

"I'll drink to that," Paul said.

Neither Cotter nor I said anything, merely sipped the champagne, nasty stuff, I'd always thought, remembering fondly the Bud Light Midge had brought me in the middle of the night. Her husband, Doug, was a lucky man. I placed the flute back on the waiter's tray. Alyssum had a dark brow raised, but I didn't care.

Paul said, "It's a real tragedy about Charlie Duck getting killed. Not something you'd expect to have happen in a great town like Edgerton."

"Bad, bad thing," Alyssum Tarcher said, nodding that leonine head of his. "Everyone's been talking about it, trying to figure out who could have done such a thing, and why."

"He was a nosy old man," Cotter said. "He was always pissing people off when he pried into their business."

"A stranger went to his house and killed him, a random thing," said Tarcher. "It must have been. No one in Edgerton would have hurt a hair on his head."

"He didn't have much hair left," Paul said. He received a strained smile from Tarcher.

I turned to see Rob Morrison, looking like a hunk from Southern California in a black T-shirt, black slacks, and a black sports jacket, speaking to Maggie Sheffield. It was the first time I'd seen her out of uniform. She was a knockout. A red dress on a woman, especially one without much front or back, has an amazing effect. Her hair was piled up on top of her head and she was wearing three-inch heels. I had an urge to walk up to her, bite her earlobe, and go from there. Then I saw Rob Morrison's hand on her back, very low on her bare back. Very proprietary.

"Hello, Mac. You look very nice in that dark suit."

I turned to see Cal Tarcher, dressed like a frump in a long skirt with a black, high-neck, long-sleeved silk blouse and ballet flats. At least the skirt and blouse fit her, more or less. Her red hair was flat against her head, pulled back and tied with a black ribbon at the base of her neck. Her glasses had black frames. Well, at least she was color coordinated. "Hi, yourself," I said. I wondered what had happened to that young woman I'd seen briefly outside Paul and Jilly's house, the one who'd suddenly looked taller and arrogant and cold as ice. We were back to little miss prim and dowdy.

"I saw you staring at Maggie. She looks beautiful, doesn't she?"

"Oh, yes. I like a woman out of uniform. Maybe soon you can get out of your uniform. Maybe you could try a red dress like that."

The cold, arrogant young woman flashed across her face, then smoothed away. "Have you met my mother, Elaine?"

"No, not yet. The originator of BITEASS?"

"Yes," she said, and seemed delighted that I remembered. "I hear that Jilly is fine now. I tried to get to the hospital today but what with the party, I didn't have time. Mother had me running around all day long. You wouldn't believe how much food is going to be consumed tonight. Can you believe someone killed poor old Charlie Duck?"

"No, I can't."

"You hungry?"

"I can't wait to attack the food. Oh yeah, do you know if Paul slept around on Jilly?" I watched her eyes widen behind her glasses. Shock at what I'd said? It wasn't exactly acceptable party talk. Or was it surprise that I knew that? I realized then that I had to let it go. Jilly was fine. There was no crime here, except for the random murder of Charlie Duck.

"Paul loves Jilly," Cal said after a moment. "He wouldn't ever sleep with another woman. Besides, Paul's too skinny. He does enjoy sex, that's what Jilly told me. She said he was really good."

"Were you jealous of Jilly, Cal?"

NINE

She didn't skip a beat, just said in a very nice, indifferent voice, "Not at all. I liked Jilly. She was always so gay, always singing. Would you like a beer?"

I stared down at her a moment, waiting her out, but she beat me in that staring contest. Finally, I nodded.

"Let's go to the kitchen. Cotter and I keep our stash hidden behind

Father's mango supply. My mother hates mangoes so we have to hide the beer where she won't see it. She disapproves of beer, you know. It's low-class."

I followed her through the crowd of at least fifty people, all different ages, dressed to the hilt, all of them seeming to be enjoying themselves, digging into an incredible array of food—from oysters Rockefeller to trays of chilled fish smothered in limes to heaping platters of pesto pasta dotted with sun-dried tomatoes—set out on a wide table at least twenty feet long.

The kitchen was the command center. Cal didn't slow, just wove her way through the caterers to a huge refrigerator, opened it, and leaned inside. She was in there awhile, scrounging around. She came out holding two Coors. "Cotter's already been here. This is the end. We've got another six-pack out in the garage if we really get thirsty."

"This is great," I said, popped the lid, toasted her without saying anything, and drank. I loved beer.

"How old is Cotter?"

"He's twenty-eight, two years older than me. I know, I only look like I'm eighteen, but I'm not. You're also wondering what we're both doing still living at home at our age."

"I did wonder. But I'm not rude enough to ask."

"You were rude enough to ask me if I was jealous of Jilly. Why'd you even think of such a thing?"

"I heard something, I guess. Why are you and Cotter still living at home?"

She laughed, drank more of her beer, and led the way from the noisy, chaotic kitchen to a small back room, a library from the look of it. It was empty, dark. Cal shut the door and turned on a small Tiffany desk light.

She set the beer down on a desktop, then turned to face me. "Well, Jilly was wrong. I'm not jealous of her. Actually, I want to paint her. She keeps putting me off."

"Paul and Maggie said you were an artist. What do you paint?"

"I usually do landscapes, but people's faces fascinate me. Jilly has incredible bones. I want to paint them, and her eyes. Her eyes are the key to her. It's the same with you, Mac. You have beautiful eyes. Dark, stormy blue, romantic eyes."

"Don't make my beer go down the wrong way."

She stopped then, shook herself, and gave me a bright smile, a really fake smile. "How are you feeling? You're looking stronger and more fit than you did yesterday."

"I feel fine."

"Cotter lives at home because Father wants him to. He wants Cotter to learn all about his business holdings. He did allow Cotter to leave the state to go to UCLA, even pushed him. Cotter got his undergraduate degree in business and then an MBA, all in four years. The thing is, though, I don't believe Father will ever think Cotter competent enough to take over. He'll have to die before Cotter can get anywhere. Then, of course, it would be moot. But Cotter thinks our father will live forever."

"So Cotter wants out?"

"No, Cotter wants to run everything. I've told him he's too short. It would help if he'd wear elevator shoes. Tall men, like our father, like you, get all the respect. Cotter's too dark as well. He looks like a gangster."

"What did Cotter say to that?" I asked, fascinated.

"I believe he ordered some elevator shoes from a catalogue. He might wear them now for all I know. He still looks like a thug though. No way he can ever change that."

"You're very informative all of a sudden, Miss Tarcher. What's Cal stand for?"

"You don't want to know, trust me." She took two steps toward me and very slowly laid her open palms on my chest. "It stands for Calista. I like you, Mac."

I closed my hands over hers and lightly tugged them away. "Thank you. Actually, Calista isn't bad, but I like Cal better. It sounds more natural. I don't know what to think of you, Cal. I think that the picture you present to the world and how the world responds to that picture must amuse you tremendously."

She drew her hands free of mine and backed up until she was leaning against the desk.

"Don't bother to deny it. I saw the real you yesterday. You forgot to hide yourself for a moment there when I walked you to your car. I saw arrogance in you, certainty. I have this feeling that you're laughing at the whole town, that you think they're all fools. Maybe you are jealous of Jilly. Or maybe she's seen the real you and she's jealous of you. What do you think?"

"Is this the FBI speaking?" There was amusement in her voice and a smile on her mouth.

"Nope."

"You a profiler?"

"I'm in Counter-Terrorism. Jilly is very beautiful. Why would she be jealous of you?"

Cal shook her head, the abrupt movement clearly telling me that she was tired of this game. Standing there in the shadows cast by the Tiffany lamp, she said suddenly, "Please don't move. I want to sketch you. Is that okay?"

I was too startled to say anything. She dashed out of the room, leaving me there alone with two nearly empty Coors cans.

She came back into the room a couple of minutes later, holding a large sketch pad and a thick charcoal pencil in her hand. "Don't move, please," she said, walking quickly toward the desk.

I nodded. I looked at her as she flipped open the sketch pad, flipped through several pages, and propped the pad up on her thighs. Her face changed completely. There wasn't a hint of frump. I saw an intense woman who bristled with focus. This was a strong woman. I started to raise my hand, but she said, "No, Mac, don't move, please."

"I've never had anyone sketch me before. Can I at least talk?"

"Yes," she said, not really paying any attention to me, just drawing on the paper.

"Why do you dress like this?"

"Shut up."

"You said I could talk. The jeans you wore yesterday, they were huge, baggy. You were wearing a man's shirt. Why, Cal? Why were you hiding yourself?"

"I want men to desire me for my brain."

I laughed, I couldn't help myself. I tried to think of a less controversial question and said, "Do you think Maggie is sleeping with Rob Morrison?"

Her charcoal stopped cold in mid-stroke. She stared at me, her lips pursed. "He's so beautiful he could sleep with any woman he wanted. Why not Maggie?" She began sketching again, more quickly now, her strokes deep and fast, rather like really good sex, I thought.

She stopped suddenly, the charcoal pencil poised over the paper, and she stared at me. She was breathing hard. Her hands were shaking, her lips slightly parted.

"Done?" I asked, looking at her hands.

She didn't say anything. She set down the charcoal and the pad and flipped off the lamp.

"Mac," she said, in a voice low and harsh, and she jumped me.

I tried for about three and a half seconds to pull her off me, then a good wallop of lust changed my mind and I gave it up. She kissed me all over my face, ran her hands over my chest, then down, unzipping my slacks, and then her hands were inside my shorts. I nearly lost it when her fingers went around me. I felt a wildness in her, a frenzy, and I felt her fingers. Dear God, it had been too long and I was a mess. I pulled on her clothes, ripping her blouse, but she didn't seem to care. She pushed me down onto the carpet, climbed on top of me, and straightened over me. I could see her outline, her head thrown back, her throat white and smooth. I could hear her breathing—like someone running a race—hard and deep, jerking with effort.

"Cal," I said, trying to hold her still for a moment. "Cal, listen to me. I don't have any condoms."

"Don't worry about it. I'm healthy. You're an FBI agent. I'm on the pill."

In the next instant, she'd pulled down her panties, kicked off her ballet slippers, and spread her legs. She straddled me, and brought me up and into her. I went in high and deep and I could feel her, every slick bit of her, and I groaned with the effort of not coming right then. "No," I said, "no." I lifted her off me, nearly throwing her onto her back. I watched her raise her hand, jerk off her glasses, and toss them across the room. She stopped cold then, stared up at me. "I don't understand," she said.

"You don't have to," I said, and brought her up to my mouth. I wondered a few seconds later why the entire household didn't come rushing into the room, she screamed so loudly. I managed to fit my hand over her mouth, felt her hot breath lacing through my fingers, felt her cries nearly liquid against my skin. When she collapsed, all boneless, I came into her, wild and hard. I didn't stay long, I couldn't.

It always takes me a while to get my brain back together. I didn't really want to this time; I didn't want to think about any consequences. I just wanted to keep floating free, not thinking, simply mellowing, drifting away. Eventually she moved and then I did. She was wide awake, looking up at me in the shadowy light. "You came down on me," she said, unexpectedly.

I still tasted her, a lingering scent of dark promises and bone-deep lust.

It was amazing, that taste of hers, and it made me hard again. "Yes," I said, and managed to slide off to her side. I leaned down on my elbow, and kissed her mouth. I kissed her several times, lazy kisses, and I said against her lips, "You draw a picture and it makes you horny?"

"Not usually," she said, kissing me back, all the while stroking her fingers over my jaw and back into my hair. It was like she was drawing me all over again. "But you, Mac, you were different. I sketched your mouth, then your jaw, and it was all over for me." She sighed and curled onto her side facing me. "That was very nice, Mac. Come into me again."

"All right," I said. This time didn't last much longer than the first time, and I was ready this time to muffle her cries when she climaxed. I knew her scent, the taste of her, would stay with me for a while. I'd learned two very important things about Cal Tarcher: She really liked making love, and she had long thin legs that fit nicely around my neck.

I found out she wasn't much for conversation either, which I appreciated since I didn't have a thing to say. She kissed me once more, patted my cheek, and rose. I watched her blot herself with kleenex, watched her dress and slide her glasses up her nose. She left the small room first to go upstairs and straighten herself up, she told me. I moved more slowly. I finished my beer, now warm, and tossed it in the wastebasket beside the desk. I zipped up my pants, found a bathroom down the hall, and tried to wipe the just-fucked look off my face. It was difficult because it had felt so good, still felt good. So good if she'd been there I would have asked for more.

When I went back into the huge great room, confident that I looked normal again, except for the lingering glazed stupor in my eyes, the first person I saw was Maggie Sheffield, standing right in front of me. She frowned a moment, then looked me up and down. Then she smiled. "Well, Mac, who put you out of your misery?"

It was impossible. There was no way she could tell what I'd been doing. No way.

"You want to dance, Maggie?"

"I wonder," she said, tapping her fingertips on her cheek, her head cocked to one side.

"All right. No dance. I'd like to meet Elaine Tarcher," I said. "Could you introduce me?"

"Why not? Come along, Mac, that's Elaine over there, in the midst of that group of men. She's a middle-aged femme fatale. I think she's ridiculous with all her little coyness, a little pathetic actually. She's old enough to be my mother."

The first thought in my brain when I saw Elaine Tarcher up close was that if she wanted to jump me, I wouldn't have hesitated any longer than I'd hesitated with her daughter. The woman wasn't anywhere near her husband's age. I knew she had to be at least in her late forties, given Cotter's age, but still, she just didn't look it. There wasn't anything pathetic about her. I had nothing against cosmetic surgery, if that's what she used to stop the march of gravity. If so, Elaine Tarcher had an excellent cosmetic surgeon. She looked to be in her thirties, no older. She was wearing a black cocktail dress, sheer black panty hose, and black high heels. She had Cal's rich brown hair, short and styled in a mussed-up fashion that made her look very natural and, at the same time, eminently sophisticated. At least half a dozen men were standing around her in a circle, and she let them admire her. I heard her laugh, a charming sound, full and deep and very personal. I didn't agree at all with Maggie that any of her moves were ridiculous.

I heard Alyssum Tarcher call out Maggie's name. She shrugged, pressed my hand, and left me. I stood there observing Elaine Tarcher's magic.

"Everyone thinks my mother is just a silly, useless ornament, but it's not true."

I smiled down at Cal Tarcher, who'd come up behind me. I couldn't see any just-had-sex signs on her face. She was back in her frump mode, neat as could be, her glasses firmly in place. She had changed her blouse since I'd ripped hers. This one was just as bland.

"Introduce me, Cal."

She looked up at me, silent for a moment, and said, "I wish you weren't staying with Paul."

I felt her lurching upward, bringing me deeper inside her body, and swallowed hard. "I agree, but there's nothing to be done for it."

"Old Charlie Duck adored my mother. She'll be one of the main speakers at his funeral. I hope you'll be there? That's all she's talking about tonight, his murder. She's really mad about it."

"Oh, yes, I won't miss it. Perhaps Jilly can come as well."

"When are you going to leave? To go back to Washington."

"I don't know," I said. "Maybe I'll stay on a couple more days." I thought of Laura and felt a hard dash of guilt for having sex with Cal. I shouldn't, I knew that, but it was still there.

I met Elaine Tarcher, all of her gathered admirers, and Miss Geraldine, the leader of the town League and the mayor of Edgerton. She was a well-dressed old bat with a sharp tongue and faded blue eyes that I bet never missed a thing. She said, "Well, boy, I understand you came to see what happened to your sister. Well, I'll tell you what happened. She was going around a corner in that Porsche of hers and lost control. I've told Jilly a dozen times to be careful, but she just sings and dances away. She's fine now, I hear. That's good."

"That's exactly what Jilly said happened," I said.

"How long are you staying in Edgerton?"

"You'll make Mr. MacDougal feel unwelcome, Geraldine, and he's not," Elaine Tarcher said. She'd not said anything up to now. She'd been studying me, assessing me, calmly. There was nothing at all flirtatious in her manner. I wondered if she was seeing me as a possible mate for her daughter. I saw her group of friends fade back when her husband came over.

Alyssum nodded to his wife, then kissed Miss Geraldine's parchment cheek. "You've met our guest here, Geraldine?"

"He appears to be a good boy. Or maybe he's just tall and good-looking and nothing else interesting. I've heard he wants to solve the puzzle of our key letters."

"I've been working on it," I said.

"So did Charlie Duck," Elaine Tarcher said. "He told me a couple of days ago that he was getting real close. I know I never should have thought it up since I didn't have anything to go with it, and I've thought and thought, but without reportable results."

"BITEASS—not easy," Alyssum said. He was impatient with this nonsense, I could see. Where was that prick, Cotter?

"Edgerton Town League," said Elaine. "That would have been better. Simpler. Short and to the point."

"Not as clever," said Miss Geraldine. "I've always admired clever. Don't worry, Elaine. I'm counting on our nice-looking fellow here. So you're with the FBI. Is that right?"

"Yes, ma'am."

"I also heard you were in the hospital before you came here."

"Yes, ma'am. I'm fine now."

"Are you some sort of hero?"

"No way, ma'am, just in the wrong spot at the wrong time. How about Better Information Through Elucidation And Sober Selection?"

"That's not bad," Elaine said, nodding. She'd taken me seriously. No, I saw a flicker of amusement in her eyes.

"It doesn't mean anything," Alyssum said. "It's only nonsense."

Elaine Tarcher gave me a sweet smile. "Keep working on it, Mac. Do you mind if I call you Mac? Good. It's a nice solid name. Poor Cal, now she's got a burden to bear—"

"Please, Mother, don't."

"All right, dear. I forgot."

"Maybe," I said, "if you could tell me the purpose of the BITEASS League, I could come up with something better."

I know I didn't imagine it. Elaine Tarcher shot a look toward Miss Geraldine, who smiled and said, "We do a bit of everything, Mac. I originally organized the League to force a local chemical plant to clean up its waste. With Alyssum's help, we got them to do it. We discovered we had clout. With an entire town focusing on one specific problem, we could accomplish quite a lot. Now we use it whenever anyone in town needs help or there's another problem common to all of us. Nothing more than that. It's worked very well."

"Usually we're a big social club," Elaine said. "Tomorrow we'll hold a wake for poor Charlie. The funeral will be the next day. We want to give him a good send-off."

"Poor old man," Cal said.

"It's time for Geraldine to cut her birthday cake," Alyssum Tarcher said.

I walked with them to the long table where a large three-tiered cake sat, weighted down by more candles than I could count.

"Don't think we're insulting her," Cal said. "Geraldine always insists that the number of candles equal the number of years."

I saw Paul out of the corner of my eye, cutting through the crowds of people to get to me.

"What's the matter, Paul?"

"Mac, I just got a call from the hospital. Jilly's gone. They don't know where she is. Do you know anything? Did she tell you where she was going?"

TEN

It was after midnight when we'd all come back to Jilly's room. I stared down at her bed. It looked like Jilly had simply stood up, lightly smoothed her hand over the covers, and left the hospital room.

"She had no clothes," I said as I touched my hand to her pillowcase. "She couldn't have walked out of here in her hospital nightgown."

Paul said, "She asked me to bring her clothes this afternoon. I did. I didn't want to make her feel like she was some sort of prisoner. Believe me, she never said she was planning on walking out of here."

"This is weird," Rob Morrison said, walking into the hospital room. "Was she even strong enough to walk out of here?"

"Yes," Maggie said. "She was getting stronger by the minute. Her muscles hadn't given out on her. She was only here for four days, Rob. Does anyone here know anything?"

"Nobody saw a thing," Rob said, rubbing his hand across the back of his neck. His neck cracked. "Man, this doesn't make any sense. Why would she leave? Why didn't she say anything to the nurses? She's got to be here somewhere. I've rounded up everyone I could find to search the hospital, top to bottom. Two of the security guys have established grids in the parking lot and the grounds and are walking them off. They won't miss her even if she's hiding under a car."

"I'm talking to everyone," Maggie said. "Someone must have seen her leave. She's not a ghost."

Paul said suddenly, "Maybe somebody took her." It was the first time he'd said anything like that since we'd all run out of the Tarcher party more than three hours before.

I turned slowly to face Paul. "Why would anyone take Jilly?"

"I don't know," Paul said. "But somebody may have been afraid she'd remember everything that happened Tuesday night. She was gone for three hours. Where did she go? What did she do?" He added on a whisper, "Maybe it was Laura. I don't understand what was going on between Jilly and Laura anymore. Who else would have done it?"

I pictured Laura in my mind and I couldn't begin to believe she could have done anything like that. But Jilly had said that Laura had betrayed her, that Laura was dangerous.

"Fine," I said. I took Paul's arm and pulled him out of Jilly's room as I said, "Excuse us, Maggie, Rob, but I've got to clear something up with Paul, and it can't wait."

"Maybe Laura took her," Paul said again once we were in the empty hospital corridor.

"Let's say that Laura did take her. Did she have a gun to her head? Maybe Laura was carrying her over her shoulder? That means someone must have seen Laura with her. It's ridiculous, Paul, plain ridiculous. Now, I dragged you out here because I want the truth out of you and I want it now. Did you sleep with Laura?"

"All right, so I didn't sleep with her," he said, and my nerd brother-in-law actually flushed up to his eyebrows.

"Why would you tell a lie like that about an innocent woman?"

"I wanted to sleep with her, but she turned me down. I wanted to get even."

"That doesn't make sense, Paul. You never knew I'd even meet Laura Scott. How would that be getting even?"

"It wouldn't. Look, Mac, I wanted to sleep with her. It was a fantasy, nothing more really, lay off. It's not something I'm proud of doing, but I did it. Now I'm undoing it."

I said slowly, "Jilly told me that Laura had betrayed her. If you didn't sleep with Laura, if you made it all up, then what did Jilly mean?"

Paul shrugged. "I guess Jilly must have believed that Laura was my lover."

"I suppose you made some comments Jilly might have misinterpreted?" I wanted to slug him. It was hard not to.

"Look, Mac, Jilly and I were married for eight years. You can't be married that long and not have some problems. We had our share."

"According to Jilly in February when I saw her, you and she were in the sack all the time, having a fine time."

"Yeah, well, sex isn't everything."

"Paul, was Laura at your house last Tuesday night?"

"Of course she wasn't there. Why would she be? I already told you, Mac, it was only Jilly and me and the halibut we broiled. What the hell does that matter anyway? I'm going back to Jilly's room."

I watched him until he disappeared around the corner at the end of the hall. I heard Maggie speaking to Rob as they walked out of Jilly's room, over the security guards' voices, all of them talking over one another, making no sense really.

Mrs. Himmel caught sight of me and waved me down. I saw at least half a dozen hospital personnel milling about behind her. She was wringing her hands. I'd never seen Mrs. Himmel flustered before. She looked like she was going to burst into tears. Her pallor worried me. "Mrs. Himmel," I said, gently touching her shoulder.

"Oh, Mr. MacDougal, it's all my fault. Mrs. Bartlett is gone and it's my fault."

I pulled out my firm, very matter-of-fact voice that sometimes worked to calm things down. "Let's go someplace quiet, Mrs. Himmel. I need your help." I followed her to the nurses' lounge. There were two nurses inside, drinking coffee. I heard one of them say, "People said she'd tried to kill herself. Well, now she left to do it right this time."

The other nurse jumped to her feet when she saw me. "Oh, Mr. Mac-Dougal."

"Excuse us, please. Mrs. Himmel and I need to be alone for a moment."

The nurses were out of there in under two seconds. I led Mrs. Himmel to an old brown vinyl sofa that had seen better days maybe three decades ago. "Tell me what happened," I said, sitting down beside her.

She drew a deep breath, her fingers curling into a fist. I saw that she was a strong woman. Her biceps rippled as she clenched and unclenched her hands. She was regaining some healthy color. "Mrs. Bartlett was very quiet," she said finally. "I thought she had a lot on her mind, and no wonder. I've heard a lot of the stuff that's been going on, so many questions, so much that people wanted her to tell them. I heard her say today that everything from that night was blurry. Well, I suppose that's possible, but I really don't think so.

"Let me just get it off my chest. It is all my fault. If I hadn't eaten shrimp for dinner, I would have been at my station down from Mrs. Bartlett's room or actually with her in her room, tending her, and nothing would have happened!"

"Shrimp?" I must have blinked because she leaned over and patted my hand. She was in control again. "How could you possibly know? I've had a bad reaction to shrimp in the past, but it looked so good that I wanted to eat a little bit. Well, I did and it hit me really hard. I was in the bathroom most of the time, sicker than Mr. Peete down the hall who had a chemo session. Because I wasn't at my post, Mrs. Bartlett could have just walked out with no one stopping her or asking her questions, probably with no one even noticing her. And of course she had her own clothes. Dr. Bartlett brought her a suitcase this afternoon. She'd been fretting about it, you know, so he gave in and brought her the clothes she wanted."

Paul could describe what Jilly was wearing.

"When we walked in here just a few minutes ago, I heard Brenda Flack, one of the ICU nurses, talking about Mrs. Bartlett leaving to kill herself. I hate to say this, Mr. MacDougal, but it's possible."

"No," I said. "Jilly told me very clearly that she lost control of her car. She didn't try to kill herself. I believe her. Why did she walk out of here without telling anyone? I don't know. But count on it, I'm going to find out everything. Can you think of anything that happened today or this evening that wasn't quite right?"

"Well, there was a phone call from that young lady who was here yesterday."

"Laura Scott?"

"Yes, that's her. She asked to speak to Mrs. Bartlett, but there was a foul-up and she never got through to her. But why would that be important? They were friends, weren't they?"

At three in the morning we still had exactly zilch. No one had seen Jilly. No one had seen anyone carrying her out of the hospital or carrying much of anything, for that matter. Maggie Sheffield had an APB out on her. Since we had no clue about a car, there wasn't much to say other than to give a description of Jilly, and from Paul, a description of the clothes she was wearing, a gray running outfit with black trim and black-and-white running shoes.

I put pressure on the phone company and found out that there'd been a phone call to Jilly's room from the single pay phone on Fifth Avenue, downtown Edgerton, at 8:48 P.M. Laura's call had come in about eight, but she hadn't spoken to Jilly.

I found Paul sitting in the chair in Jilly's room, his head in his hands.

I said, "Someone called Jilly from a pay phone in Edgerton earlier this evening."

"There's only one public phone," Paul said. "It's on Fifth Avenue, right in front of Grace's Deli."

I said, "Anyone could have ducked out of the party to go make the call. You included, Paul."

"Yes," he said, not looking at me. "Cotter disagrees with me. He thinks Jilly was pissed off that everyone had assumed she was trying to kill herself. She wanted to make all of us worry that she just might try it again. She wants to make us suffer. She'll show up soon, laughing at us. Oh, yeah, Cotter was here earlier, helping look for her."

I said, "Let's get some sleep. It's late. My brain's scrambled. There's nothing more we can do until morning. Come on, Paul, let's go home."

I wanted at least three hours' sleep before I went to Salem to see Laura.

ELEVEN

It was just after seven the next morning when I pulled my car into a guest parking spot in front of a parkside condo complex. I got out and looked around. The complex didn't look more than three or four years old, designed in a country French style, three condos to each building, all of them garnished with pale gray wooden siding. The park was quite pretty, all pine and spruce trees, and playgrounds for kids, and even a pond for ducks and lily pads. As I walked into the complex, I saw a swimming pool off to the left, a clubhouse, and a small golf course. I remembered Laura saying that the library didn't pay much. That was interesting. This place wasn't cheap.

Laura Scott opened the door and blinked at me as I said, "Nice digs."

"Mac, what are you doing here?"

"Why didn't you go to see Jilly yesterday? You told me you were going to visit her."

She shook her head at me. It made her long hair swing and lift. She was wearing nice-fitting jeans and a loose T-shirt, and running shoes on her feet. I thought she looked elegant and sexy.

"Come in, Mac. Would you like a cup of coffee? It'll take me only a few minutes to brew."

"Yeah," I said and, having no choice, followed her into one of the most beautiful homes I'd ever been in. The foyer was small, tiled with country peach-shaded pavers and whimsical accent tiles of French country scenes. Off to the left was a beautiful oak staircase leading upstairs. I followed her through an archway into a living room that was octagonal-shaped, giving it complexity with lots of nooks and crannies. There were bright colors everywhere, window seats, small flashes of scarlet pillows, and richly colored South Seas–patterned material on a sectional sofa. There were lamps and chairs and small groupings and nearly every inch of the room was filled with something extravagant, brightly colored, and utterly useless. It coaxed you right in.

There were plants and flowers everywhere. A mynah bird stood on the back of a chair watching me. He squawked, then began poking under his wing feathers.

"That's Nolan," Laura said. "He doesn't talk—which is probably a good thing—just squawks occasionally."

"Squawk."

"That's his greeting."

"Hi, Nolan." I followed her through the dining room into a small kitchen that looked right out of *Bon Appétit* magazine. All in all, the condo was a good-sized place, not as big as my own house, but not bad.

"How many bedrooms?"

"Three upstairs and a study downstairs."

I accepted a cup of coffee, shook my head at the offer of milk or sugar. "You've got a really nice place here, Laura."

"Thank you."

"Did I see a two-car garage for each condo?"

"Yes. Before you raise that sarcastic eyebrow of yours even higher, let me tell you that my uncle George left me this condo in his will. About eighteen months ago, in case you wondered."

As, of course, I had. It was at least something solid and real that I could check out. "So Uncle George lived here?"

She nodded and sipped her coffee. Her head was cocked to the side, sending her loose hair hanging like a shining curtain beside her face. I wanted to roll around in that hair of hers, smooth it over my hands, let it tumble over my face. I'd noticed immediately that she wasn't wearing a bra. I noticed again, and swallowed.

I forced my libido back into its cage and got back to what I'd come for. "I was thinking that the complex doesn't look more than three years old."

"That's about right. My uncle George bought it when they began building. He died a year and a half ago. I'll never forget the first time I walked in here. The place was painted dark colors and filled with heavy, old pieces. I shoveled everything out and had the greatest time making it mine." She motioned toward the living room, and I followed her back out.

"Squawk."

"Nolan likes coffee but I only give him a tiny taste before bedtime."

I elected not to sit in the chair that was Nolan's current hangout. I sat opposite Laura on a pale yellow silk-covered chair. There was a hand-painted wooden magazine holder beside the chair. I saw two suspense novels, a world atlas, and three travel books. No magazines or newspapers to be seen.

"I didn't go see Jilly yesterday because I had to work. There was a meeting with the Board of Trustees in the afternoon and I had to make a presentation. I didn't go last night because, frankly, I didn't feel well. I'm going to see her this afternoon."

Ill? Had she eaten some of Mrs. Himmel's shrimp and spent the night in the bathroom?

"You look fine now, Laura. The flu bug gone? Or was it food poisoning?"

"No, it was a bad headache. Not quite a migraine, but still unpleasant. Maybe it came from all the stress. I came home about four in the afternoon and slept on and off until this morning. I called the hospital an hour ago to see how Jilly was doing, to see when I should come, but no one would tell me anything. Of course, it was only six o'clock. The most anyone would say was that Mrs. Bartlett was unavailable. Why are you here, Mac? Tell me what's going on."

"What was your presentation to the Board of Trustees about?"

Her mouth curved into a grin. "It was on library economics in the first decade of our new century and what the library should do to survive."

"I'm here because Jilly's gone."

She jumped to her feet, took two steps toward me, leaned down, and yelled in my face, "No! That's impossible, she couldn't have died. She woke up. She was bloody fine, the doctor said so. I called her last night. The nurse I spoke to said she was doing very well."

"You never actually spoke to Jilly last night?"

"No, there was some sort of screwup. One nurse answered the phone, then another picked it up instead of Jilly. What happened, Mac?"

"She's not dead. She's gone, disappeared out of the hospital."

She lurched back, knocking her coffee cup off the table. The cup shattered on the oak floor, the coffee snaking toward a small silk Persian rug. She made a small sound of distress in the back of her throat and stepped back, staring down at the coffee. I got up and moved the rug out of the way. Then I couldn't help myself. I took her left wrist and slowly pulled her against me. She resisted, then finally she came to me, wrapping her arms around my back. I said against her hair, "She's not dead, Laura, but she is gone. I came because I wanted to know if you knew why she left the hospital."

Laura was tall. She fit against me very nicely. I held her away from me. I had to or I'd never even be able to keep a modicum of objectivity.

"When?"

"About ten o'clock last night," I said, taking a step back from her. "We don't know where she is. I'd hoped you'd know."

She hadn't moved. She stood there where I'd put her. "Why should I know? Naturally I don't have any idea where she is. How could I possibly know? She's really missing? Just a second, Mac. I'd better clean that up."

I waited until she returned to the living room with a paper towel. She went down on her knees and wiped the floor clean. I said, "No one has a clue where she is. No one saw her leave, by herself or with anyone else."

She was cleaning up the shards of the cup, wiping more spilled coffee off the oak floor. She sat back on her heels and looked up at me. "And you think I'm involved," she said at last.

"I came here because I hoped you'd know. You called her last night." I raised my hand to cut her off. "Yes, I know, you never really spoke to her.

But hear this, Laura. Jilly didn't like you. She might have been afraid of you. I know she believed you betrayed her somehow. I know she didn't want to be anywhere near you. Surely you realize it was your being there that helped bring her out of the coma. She wanted to get away from you.

"Your story to me about meeting Jilly at your library—she was looking up articles on infertility of all things, you told me. I don't buy that, Laura. To the best of my knowledge Jilly only realized she wanted to get pregnant about six months ago, at the outside. She wouldn't even have started to worry there was a problem yet, would she?"

She rose slowly to her feet. She took a hard breath, her face set. "I'm not lying to you. That's exactly how I met Jilly. I don't personally know much of anything about infertility. How long does it take for someone to become concerned about not conceiving? I haven't a clue. Maybe she's been trying for quite a while and didn't tell you. That's certainly possible, isn't it? Jilly might not have been very well educated, but she wasn't stupid."

"You really believe Jilly was uneducated?"

"That's what she told me. She said she barely scraped through high school, said that one of her teachers wanted to get in her pants and so he passed her, helped her graduate. She was always talking about how brilliant Paul was, what a genius he was, and how she was content to be in the background and take care of him. I thought that was ridiculous, but it was what Jilly really believed, evidently what she really wanted. She said she wanted his child. She asked if I could begin to imagine how bright his child would be? Then she'd shudder and say that if the kid had her brains and her no-talent they'd all be in big trouble. I didn't tell her that I think Paul is too skinny, doesn't take proper care of himself, that he's losing his hair, and that I hope he doesn't pass that along to a kid."

If she was lying, I'd never in my life heard anyone better. I said, "This is all pretty strange, Laura. I guess then Jilly never told you she's a scientist, a researcher with a master's degree in pharmacology? That she'd completed all her course work for her Ph.D. but put it on hold because she was more interested in the projects she was doing than writing a silly thesis, her words?

"Why would she lie to you? Why would Paul back up her lie when you were with the both of them? Come on, Laura, if someone saw you last night, you'd better dredge him or her up because, frankly, I don't believe you. There's no proof of any crime yet, no proof that someone took Jilly from the hospital against her will, but as far as I'm concerned, I'd say you need an alibi."

"Wh-what?"

I thought Laura was going to pass out. She turned utterly white and leaned at the last minute against a white wall, barely missing a mirror with a brightly colored frame. She was shaking her head slowly, back and forth. The thing was, I wanted to comfort her, to hold her and pat her back. I wanted to bury my face in that long straight hair of hers.

"Squawk."

She looked wildly over at Nolan and spread her hands in front of her. "No, you're making that up, Mac. Jilly told me she was a housewife, that she didn't have a single skill. I always just laughed at her when she went off on those self-bashing kicks of hers. She was so very beautiful, you see, and she had this natural confidence that made everyone respond so eagerly and positively to her. She was bright, well spoken. I can't believe it. A scientist? A master's degree?" She looked suddenly as if she was going to cry. She was still shaking her head, her hair swinging. She looked shaken and confused. It couldn't be an act, I told myself. No one was this good.

"I was sleeping all evening, all night. I was alone. Why did Jilly lie to me?"

I said, "Paul told me there was no party at all last Tuesday night, the night of Jilly's supposed accident. He said that they ate dinner alone. He said Jilly left at nine o'clock to drive around in her Porsche and he was in his laboratory, working.

"He also admitted, finally, that he hadn't slept with you, that he'd wanted to but you weren't interested."

She looked like a blind person, feeling her way along the back of two chairs until she finally collapsed onto a section of the sofa. She lowered her head to her hands, her hair falling forward. "This is crazy," she whispered through her hands. "I don't understand any of it."

"That makes two of us. But the fact remains that Jilly is gone. Vanished." I had to attack straight on, I thought, whether I liked it or not. "I want to know where she is, Laura. I want to know how you convinced her to leave with you. I want to know how you managed to get out of the hospital without anyone spotting you."

She looked up at me, eyes focused and hard. Her voice was fierce. No more shock or palpitations out of her. "Listen up, Mac. I didn't lie to you, about any of it, the party included. I told you I had to leave early to give Grubster a pill. If there turned out not to be a party, that has nothing to do with me or with what Paul and Jilly told me."

"Where is Grubster?" I asked, looking around. Who would have a cat around when Nolan was sitting quite at his ease on the back of a chair, looking at my coffee cup?

She shook her head as she rose from the sofa. "Now you don't even believe I have a cat." She left the living room. I heard her light steps up the stairs. When she returned a couple of minutes later she was carrying a huge tiger-striped cat. "This is Grubster. As you can see, he likes his food. He weighs eighteen pounds. He doesn't move very quickly, unless it's a matter of food. He's nearly eight years old. He looks at Nolan and yawns. Sometimes they have staring contests. Sometimes Nolan even deigns to sit on his back and dig around behind his ears with his beak."

"Squawk."

Laura looked over at the bird. "Come here, Nolan, and say hello to Grubster."

The cat yawned and curled up next to Laura on the sofa. The mynah bird hopped from chair back to sofa section until he was finally looking down at the cat. Grubster cocked an eye open and regarded the bird with complete indifference.

"Would you like some more coffee, Mac?"

I nodded, staring from Grubster to Nolan. Someone was hanging me out to dry. Someone was playing a very big game with me and I didn't have a notion yet about the rules. I didn't know where the game left off and reality kicked back in. I also had no clue where Jilly had gone. Laura's claim that she'd had a bad headache and slept throughout the night was a good one, one I couldn't check out.

Laura handed me a new cup of coffee. Steam was snaking off the top of it. I took a sip. It was delicious. Maybe she'd tossed in a dash of Amaretto. I drank some more, trying to get my brain back on track. She handed me a chocolate chip cookie. She couldn't have known they were my favorite. I ate two, to help soak up the dash of alcohol in the coffee, then said, as I watched her drink her own coffee. "When you were at Jilly and Paul's last Tuesday night, what did you do after dinner?"

She took another drink of her coffee. "Very well. There were only the three of us. I got there about six-thirty. Jilly wanted fish. Paul made a salad, spinach, I think. I sliced and garlicked some bread. We ate, then listened to some music. Jilly and I even danced a couple of numbers. Paul drank a good bit. Jilly knew I couldn't stay late because I had to work at the library the next morning and because Grubster needed meds. She told me that some other people were coming, but later, so I'd have to meet them another time. We'd have another party in Edgerton real soon, she said."

I leaned forward in my chair. "Is this the truth, Laura?" She remained silent for a long time. I sipped more of my coffee, watching her.

"There's more, isn't there?"

She looked down at Grubster and began to scratch behind his ears. I could hear the cat purring from where I sat.

Finally she nodded. "Yes, there is more. I really don't want to talk about it, but Jilly's gone, and I know you won't be happy until you know everything, even if it doesn't have anything to do with what happened to Jilly." She sucked in a hard breath. "When Jilly went to the kitchen, Paul grabbed my breasts and pushed me down on the sofa. He started kissing me, tried to shove his knee between my legs. Then he heard Jilly call out something from the kitchen, and he jumped back away from me. He was breathing real hard. I looked at him and told him he was a creep.

"When Jilly came back to the living room, I made up the story about Grubster needing medication earlier than he really did. I wanted to get out of there. I didn't want Jilly to realize what her precious husband had done, the jerk. She adored him. She worshiped him. She wanted to have a kid with him. It was awful."

"And you never got the impression that Jilly was more than an infertile housewife?"

She shook her head, mute. "No. Neither of them ever said anything to make me believe what Jilly had told me wasn't the truth."

"Them's all the facts?"

"Yes, them's all the facts, the whole truth. I swear it."

"All right. Tell me, Laura, what kind of fish did you have for dinner?"

"Fish?" Her face was blank. "I don't particularly go for fish, so I really didn't pay any attention. Maybe it was bass, or halibut."

She'd gotten the fish right on the second guess. At least the rest of the meal was as Paul had described it to me, whatever good that did.

I felt suddenly so tired that I couldn't seem to think two words ahead.

It crashed over me, dragging me under. I stood up quickly and began pacing. It didn't help. I felt like I was slogging through mud.

"Mac, what's wrong?"

I kept walking around her living room. "I've got to go," I said. I needed to get out of there, breathe in some fresh air. What the hell was wrong with me? That was stupid, I knew exactly what was wrong. I'd been pushing my body too hard and now it was getting back at me. I hadn't felt this dragging sort of fatigue for more than a week, until now. I knew that I should keep questioning her, but for the life of me I couldn't think of anything else to ask.

"I'll see you later, Laura," I said and left. I heard her call my name, but I didn't stop or look around. I heard Nolan give a final squawk toward my back.

I rolled all the windows down in the Taurus, turned the radio onto a rock 'n' roll station, and cranked the volume up as high as it would go. I even stopped at a McDonald's and got more hot coffee.

I sang "King of the Road," and when I forgot the words, I hummed as loudly as I could. I couldn't keep my eyes open. I kept banging my forehead against the steering wheel. Three or four times I went off the road and scared the shit out of myself before I managed to twist the car back. I nearly hit a truck, which would have smashed me six feet under. The sound of his horn zinged through my head. Fear cleared out my mind for a few minutes. Then it was back, this overpowering, brain-numbing fatigue.

I knew that I wasn't going to make it back to Paul's house. I was sweating, remembering how close I'd come to biting the big one with that truck. The hospital, I thought. Yes, I could make it to the hospital. It wasn't more than six minutes away, maybe seven minutes. I managed to keep the car reasonably in my own lane. Only about half a dozen oncoming drivers honked at me. Finally, disbelieving that I'd really made it, I pulled into the Emergency Room parking area, clipping a bush on the way in. I watched my fingers try to turn the key off and fail. I felt like I was folding in on myself, that whatever strength I'd had until this minute was gone. I let go because I didn't really have any other choice.

Odd, but I heard a horn blasting in my eardrums. It was the last thing I remembered.

TWELVE

"Mac. It's time for you to wake up. Come on now, you can do it."

I didn't want to move. I didn't want to open my eyes. The voice came again, low and insistent. I recognized that twangy voice vaguely, and I hated it. It made my head ache. Finally, I managed to get words out of my mouth. I said, "Go away."

Twangy Voice said, "No can do, Mac. Open your eyes. Let me see that you're alive."

"Of course I'm alive," I said, pissed now, wishing I could lift my arm and punch the voice out. "Leave me the hell alone."

I heard the man speaking to someone else. "Slap his cheeks," a woman said. It was Mrs. Himmel.

Smack the man—that was a woman for you. "No," I said. "Don't hit me."

"He's coming around," Twangy Voice said, and I swear I could feel his breath on my skin. Skin? What did that mean? I felt something cold touch my bare chest. I didn't have my shirt on. How did that happen?

"Vitals are stable," another man said. I didn't recognize his voice at all. "Yeah, he's coming back now."

It pissed me off even more that this damned stranger would stick his oar in.

"Mind your own business," I said. "Nobody asked you."

Twangy Voice chuckled. "It will take him awhile to get back to normal. Give him a few more minutes. He's coming out of it fine."

"Yes," I said. "Go away." Then I opened my eyes and stared up at Dr. Sam Coates, Jilly's doctor, Mr. Twangy Voice.

"Ah," he said, smiling down at me. "You're back. Can you understand me, Mac?"

"Yes, I can understand you. What's going on? What are you doing here? Where's my shirt?"

"It seems you managed to drive nearly into the Emergency Room itself before you collapsed. You smashed down the horn with your forehead. There were a dozen nurses, orderlies, security, patients, and doctors with you within two seconds."

I remembered the loud noise. The horn blasting in my ear. "I've been pushing too hard, haven't I? My body's angry at me and finally shut down?"

"Paul told us you'd been in a terrorist attack out of the country, and in the hospital until very recently. But no, this had nothing to do with any relapse. Actually, you had a high level of phenobarbital in your system. You've been out of it for about three hours now. Once we guessed the problem, we began treating you, but this kind of thing takes time. You're going to feel groggy for a while."

I thought about the likely treatment and nearly turned green. "Tell me you didn't pump my stomach. I saw that done once and nearly puked."

"Sorry, Mac, we had to. We didn't have a choice. But hey, you were unconscious. We also put some activated charcoal in your stomach. There's still some flecks of black above your mouth and a bit dried on your chest. Pretty gross, but it soaks up all the poison. Don't worry about the IV and the oxygen. That's just in case something goes wrong. We'll keep them in for a while longer. Does your throat hurt?"

It did hurt. I nodded. My brain was finally kicking in again. "I was drugged, you said? With phenobarbital?"

"Yes. No one's suggested yet that you were trying to kill yourself. Who gave you the drug, Mac?"

I looked up at Dr. Coates, then over at Mrs. Himmel, whose face was shocked and still, and at a man I didn't know. "Well, damn," I said.

A few seconds later, Dr. Coates knew I was very much awake because I had his wrist in a vise as I said, "This is important. The cops need to get to Laura Scott's house in Salem. That's where I was this morning. She may have tried to kill me."

Dr. Coates wasn't a young man, but he could move fast. He was out of the room in a flash. Mrs. Himmel patted my hand. "You'll be all right now, Mac. Oh, this is Dr. Greenfield, he's the one you told not to butt in."

I looked at a skinny older guy who wore a thick black beard and sported a green and white dotted bow tie. "I'm alive," I said. "Thanks."

He said, "Your body's still not fully recovered. That must have been some terrorist, er, incident."

"Yeah, an incident."

"You're young and strong, Mr. MacDougal. You'll pull through this okay. I'll leave you in good hands." He turned on his heel, gave Mrs. Himmel a little salute, and left.

"He's our resident guru," Mrs. Himmel said. "Now you rest, Mr. MacDougal. Why would this woman try to kill you?"

"I don't know. I drove to Salem early this morning to speak to her. I'd like to think she had something to do with Jilly's leaving the hospital last night, but I didn't find out anything. I drank her coffee, then got really tired. I left." I wanted to cry or howl, I didn't know which. How could I have been so wrong about her?

"You almost didn't make it back, Mac," Dr. Coates said, coming back into the hospital room. "Why didn't you pull over and go to sleep?"

"I didn't think of doing that, for some reason. My only thought was getting back. I guess I was blurry because stopping wasn't an option in my mind."

"Well, you made it back. Some of that road you were driving is tricky enough when you're not drugged to the gills."

"A truck nearly got me and the adrenaline surge bolstered me up for a few minutes. I was singing, shouting, anything to keep myself awake. I couldn't go over a cliff in the car, like Jilly. I had to make it back." I drew a deep breath. "All right, what about Laura Scott?"

"Detective Minton Castanga will get back to us as soon as they get to her house and find out what's going on. I got him when I mentioned the words *attempted murder* and *FBI agent* all in the same breath."

"She could be long gone. If she wanted to kill me I don't think she'd hang around." Then I thought that if Laura had done it, she'd go to prison. I wondered: *In prison for what? What has she done? It had to be something bad enough to make her believe she had to kill me.*

Dr. Coates said, "As to that, there's no way to know if her intent was to kill you, unless she's caught and admits to it. You had a butt-load of the drug on board, but you probably would have survived the dose even without us. Your blood level was never that high, and you were never really unstable. They'll have to find her and see what she says."

I shook my head as I said, "I don't think they're going to find her.

She's a very smart lady. She won't be there and they're not going to catch her."

Dr. Coates listened to my chest again and Mrs. Himmel took my blood pressure. Then he said, "Oh, I nearly forgot. Dr. Paul Bartlett was here, pacing and upset, until finally we got him to go home. I'll call him and he can bring back the sheriff and some of your other friends who were trying to pile into your room. Maggie did tell me she was going to call the FBI and tell them what happened."

"Oh, no," I said. "I don't suppose you tried to talk her out of that?"

If Maggie did call the FBI, she would have gotten my supervisor, Big Carl Bardolino. I looked at the phone beside my bed. I didn't see much choice now. I made the phone call and got put on hold by his secretary. Big Carl was a man I respected, a twenty-five-year veteran, a canny team player but not a yes-man, and I really didn't want to talk to him about this.

"Yeah? Is this you, Mac? What the hell's going on? I get this call from a sheriff out there in boondocks U.S.A. telling me about your getting yourself poisoned."

"Yes, sir, that's why I'm calling. I wanted to let you know that I'm fine. The local cops are on it. No need to worry."

"Damnation, you got yourself involved with a woman, didn't you? How many times have I told you young people that you've got to be careful about letting your hormones go on a rampage and getting you compromised. Or should I say poisoned?"

"Yes, sir, you've told all of us that at least half a dozen times. That isn't exactly what happened."

"Yeah, right. I can hear the truthfulness in your voice. You're a lousy liar, Mac. How many times have I told all of you that only vigilance conquers lust?"

"At least half a dozen times."

"Right. And none of you ever listens. I'm fifty-three years old, thankfully beyond all that sort of thing, but you're not. You're supposed to be on leave. You're supposed to be taking care of yourself, not getting poisoned. How are you feeling? How's your sister?"

"Well, she was in an accident and she's okay, but she's out of the hospital right now, and I'm not sure where she is. I'm sorry the sheriff called you. I really don't think the drug I took was meant for me. There really wasn't any need to call you."

"Mac, I'm going to ream you if you get yourself hurt, you understand me? The FBI is a team, not a bunch of hotdoggers doing their own thing."

"I understand, sir. I'm not hotdogging. This is all about my sister, and where she's gone. It's not an official investigation. I'd appreciate it if you'd let me deal with it for now. I don't see any need to call in the cavalry."

He grunted. Finally, after I knew he'd chewed his unlit cigar nearly through, he said, "You will keep in touch with me, you understand?"

"Yes, sir. I understand."

I was so thankful I fell asleep, the oxygen still up my nose and the IV still dripping into my arm.

I woke up to see another man I didn't know staring down at me. His expression was thoughtful, and his long fingers stroked over his clean-shaven jaw. He had light hair, a narrow nose, and an obstinate look. He was dapper, no other way to say it, from his French-cuffed white shirt to his highly polished Italian loafers. I put him at about forty, on the lean side, probably a runner, with smart, dark eyes that had seen more than their share of the world. He didn't look at all like a doctor.

When he saw that I was back among the living, he said quietly, in a lazy drawl that shrieked Alabama, "I'm Detective Minton Castanga from the Salem Police Department. I understand your name is Ford MacDougal and you're an FBI agent here to find your now-missing sister."

"That's it exactly."

"Well, not all of it. You're flat on your back because someone laced your coffee with phenobarbital."

"Laura Scott," I said. "Did you find her?"

"Oh, yes, I was at her condo within ten minutes of Dr. Coates's phone call. However, she didn't tell us a thing."

"She's very smart. I doubted you would find her."

"You don't understand, Agent MacDougal. Laura Scott was lying unconscious on the floor of her living room, a huge cat curled up on her back and a mynah bird squawking on the seat of a chair just a foot from her head."

I couldn't take it in. "No," I said, struggling up to my elbows. "She's not dead. She isn't dead, is she?"

He cocked his head to the side, and I could nearly see his mental wheels turning. "No, no, she's not dead. She's at Salem General Community

Hospital. They're still working on her, lavaging her stomach, the whole bit you went through with the nasogastric tube, the oxygen up the nose, and the rest. They said she's going to make it.

"So, Agent MacDougal, she gave you coffee, you drank it, and she drank it as well, in front of you?"

"Yes." I thought back. "She had only about a half a cup, at least while I was there. I got more of the phenobarbital than she did. I drank two cups."

"Was anyone else there in the condo? Or was it just the two of you?"

"No, no one else that I saw. Just me, the bird, the cat, and Laura."

"One of two possibilities, then," he said, smiling down at me. It was a smile filled with irony and a good deal of understanding. "Someone wanted both of you dead, which doesn't ring true unless that person knew you were going to visit her."

"I didn't tell anyone I was going to visit her."

"All right then. It appears that you were an accident and it was Ms. Scott they were after."

"But who would want to kill Laura?" Saying the words made me crazy with worry, and guilt. Because I'd blamed her.

"Not a clue yet. We have to wait to talk to her. You don't think she did try to kill you and then gave herself just a bit of the drug to fool us?"

"No," I said. "Absolutely not. Now that I've got my brain back in gear, I realize there was no reason for her to try to kill me. As far as I know she isn't guilty of a thing. Don't get me wrong, Detective, there's lots of stuff going on here, stuff I haven't figured out yet. My sister, primarily. Why she went off a cliff and now has vanished. I know she believed that Laura betrayed her. She didn't want to see her. Perhaps she was even afraid of Laura. Or was that a lie? No matter how I slice it though, there's no reason why Laura would try to kill me."

"Maybe you were getting too close—to something, Agent MacDougal." I heard the tinny ring of a cell phone. He excused himself and walked over to the windows. He pulled a small cell phone out of his jacket pocket and spoke quietly.

I couldn't lie there like a piece of meat like I had back in Bethesda for more than two weeks. Slowly, I slid my legs over the side of the bed. They'd left me stark naked. I looked around for anything to put around me.

Detective Castanga said from behind me, "Ms. Scott is waking up. Oh, yes, I had my forensics folk check over her condo. They found a bottle of phenobarbital in the medicine cabinet of the second bathroom. It didn't have many pills left in it. It was prescribed to a George Grafton, and expired at least a year ago."

George Grafton had been her uncle George who'd left her the condo in his will. But how did it get in the coffee?

I said it aloud. "Laura isn't stupid. The more I think about it, the more certain I am that someone else did it. And whoever did it meant for Laura to die, like you said."

I stood slowly as I spoke, bringing the sheet and thin hospital blanket with me and wrapping them around my waist.

"Was Ms. Scott expecting anyone else to come see her?"

"Not that I know of."

"I'm going to speak to Laura Scott, Agent MacDougal, but first I want you to fill me in on everything so I don't have to start all over."

I told him everything I'd heard, everything I'd verified, and realized that there was precious little. For an attempted murder investigation, the tangible, solid facts in my pocket were pitifully few. "Bottom line, the first crime I can point to for certain is what just happened."

Detective Castanga jotted some notes and asked a few questions, but mainly he listened to me. I could feel the weight of his attention. He was good. He was putting his notebook into his pocket when I heard a sharp indrawn breath from the doorway.

I looked up to see Maggie Sheffield in her sheriff's uniform. She wasn't looking at me. She was stating at Detective Minton Castanga.

"Hello, Margaret," Detective Castanga said, taking a step toward her. He stopped cold at the look of mean dislike on her face, obvious even to me. "I wondered if I'd see you here."

"Of course I'm here," Maggie said. "I'm the sheriff. Where else would I be? The question is, what are you doing here?"

"We found Laura Scott on the floor of her living room, doped with phenobarbital, like Agent MacDougal here. You're looking well, Margaret."

"Yes. So are you, Mint."

Mint? Margaret? What was this all about? "You two know each other?"

Maggie Sheffield turned to face me as I stood beside my bed, a sheet and a single blanket knotted around my waist. "Hi, Mac. You've still got some impressive battle scars. You steady on your feet now?"

"I don't know about how steady my feet are, but at least they're holding me up."

Detective Minton Castanga finally answered my question, as he gave Maggie a long, cool look. "Margaret was my wife at one time, Agent MacDougal."

THIRTEEN

Laura was in room 511 at Salem General Hospital. I stood quietly by her bed looking down at her. She was breathing smoothly and slowly. They still had the oxygen tubes in her nose and the saline IV in her arm. She was alive and would recover, as I had. I was surprised that I'd never felt so thankful in my life as I was at that moment, except when Jilly woke up. Someone had smoothed down her hair and pushed it back from her face. All that beautiful hair was strewn over the hard hospital pillow. Unlike me, they'd put her in a hospital gown and pulled the light covers up to her shoulders.

I leaned down, lightly touched my palm to her cheek, and said, "Laura, I'll tell you what they said over and over to me when I was lying helpless flat on my back. It's time for you to wake up now. You've been sleeping long enough. Come on, come back to me."

Her lips moved slightly, forming my name.

I leaned closer, without conscious plan, and lightly kissed her pale mouth. "That's it. Yes, it's Mac. I like the way you say my name. Say it again. Come on, Laura. Come back to me."

"We were just coming in to wake her up again, but it sounds like you're doing a fine job." I turned to see a tall woman in a white coat. She smiled. "Keep encouraging her to open her eyes. Are you her husband?"

"No," I said, for the first time in my life thinking maybe that didn't sound so bad. I'd known Laura two days. Funny how that didn't seem to matter. "She's a friend," I said, smiling now. "I'm a friend."

"I'm her doctor, Elsa Kiren. Do you want me or one of the nurses to spell you?"

I shook my head. "No, I'll stay. I came out from under the same drug just a while ago. I know what's going on in her head."

"If you need any help, call out," Dr. Kiren said. "I'll be close by."

I turned back to Laura. I wondered if I'd been as pale as she was now before I'd come out of it. "Laura, listen to me now. I've been thinking about things and here's the bottom line. Somebody drugged you. I was an innocent bystander. Now it's time to wake up so we can figure this mess out. Come on." I lightly slapped her cheek. "Someone tried to kill you, Laura, wake up."

"Stop hitting me, you jerk."

I grinned from ear to ear and slapped her lightly on her other cheek.

She growled deep in her throat, probably like her cat. "After I leave you, I'll go back to your condo and take care of Nolan and Grubster. You've got to tell me what to do for them. Wake up, Laura, think of your bird and your cat."

Her eyes slowly opened. She looked at me without recognition, then I saw the light slowly rekindle in her eyes, saw memory return. I would swear that I could feel the exact moment that vivid intelligence of hers was under full sail again.

"Hi," I said. "Keep dialing your mind back in, that's it. It takes time, but you'll get there."

"I don't believe that you would drug me, Mac, but if you did, why?"

"Keep not believing it because I didn't. Until a couple of hours ago, I was lying on my back, like you are. Someone got both of us."

That opened her eyes really wide. Any vagueness was now long gone. "My head hurts."

"Yeah, I know. It lessens. Don't worry about it, my headache's nearly gone now. Who got us, Laura?"

"I don't know. It had to be in the coffee. Both of us drank it, you more than me, if I remember correctly."

I saw a shadowy movement off to my right and jerked around to see Detective Minton Castanga standing just inside the hospital room doorway.

I felt Laura tense, readying for battle, beneath my hand.

"He was here before but I was out of it. I don't like him. Send him away, Mac."

"I can't. But don't worry, Laura. This guy isn't bad. He's a cop, Detective Castanga, from the Salem PD. He's here to find out who dropped us both in our tracks. Detective, this is Laura Scott."

I straightened and turned to face him. "She just woke up again," I said. "Come on over and she can talk to both of us at once."

Detective Castanga stood on the other side of Laura's bed. He studied her silently for a moment, then said in that soft, endless drawl, "It's true I was here earlier. I stood right where I'm standing now, looking at you. I tried to imagine what you'd look like awake. I was off on all counts." He smiled then. "I'm glad you made it, Ms. Scott. You really do need to talk to me this time."

There was no expression whatsoever now on Laura's face. She was still pale, but her eyes were bright, focused. I couldn't begin to tell what she was thinking. She merely nodded her head very slightly and said finally, "All right, Detective."

"Agent MacDougal told me he believed that both of you were alone at your condo, except for the bird and the cat. Is this correct?"

"That's right. As far as I know, no one was lurking in a closet. If they were, they were certainly very quiet."

"You're right about the phenobarbital being in the coffee. It very probably came from an old prescription bottle in your medicine cabinet."

"No, I don't keep stuff like that. Oh, that's right, you're thinking about my uncle George."

"That's right. Why did you still have the pills?"

She shrugged. The covers slipped down just a bit. Without thinking, I pulled them back up and patted her cheek. She leaned her cheek against my hand.

"I don't know," she said. "They were just there. I've heard that phenobarbital is good if you really have a hard time going to sleep. I suppose I kept them just in case of insomnia. Not very bright of me, I suppose."

Suddenly, in the blink of an eye, Detective Castanga's Mr. Cool and Nice Guy was gone, and in his place was a hard-nosed son of a bitch whose voice and very stance were cold and sarcastic. "So, Ms. Scott, let me see if I get this right. Someone came into your house, rifled through your medicine cabinet, came up with the phenobarbital, stirred the stuff into your coffee, all without you ever seeing him or her?"

"I guess there's no other conclusion, Detective."

"Oh, yes there is. Seems just as likely to me that you're the one doing the drugging and that you tried to cover yourself by drinking a bit yourself."

I gave him a sharp look, but he was focused on Laura.

"From your tone I take it you want me to confess to feeding Mac the drug, then drugging myself. Or maybe you want us both to tell you it was a suicide pact between two lovers? Tell me, Detective, why would I want to kill Mac?"

"Because he knew something about you and he was going to take you down." His voice was like nails now. He leaned down, right in her face. I would give him three more seconds of this bullshit.

"Sorry, Detective. I don't have any fatal secrets like that," Laura said, and I could tell she was getting pissed. The three seconds were up. I was on the verge of interrupting this interrogation when she added in a voice as cold and sneering as Detective Castanga's, "Get out of my face, Detective. My head hurts. I'm cold and I still feel groggy. My stomach feels like it's caved in on itself, and you're treating me like I'm a failed murderer who ended up really fouling things up. Go away. I have nothing more to say to you. Go do your job and stop squandering precious time."

Detective Castanga slowly straightened. He was surprised, I could see it in the sudden twitch in his cheek, the slight hitch in his breathing.

"I think you tried to kill Mac, Ms. Scott. I'm going to prove it."

"Yeah, right. Run along, Detective, and search out every dead end you can find. Waste the taxpayers' money. You look like the type who would get off on that. That makes a lot more sense than finding out who drugged Mac and me. Cops like you make me want to spit."

Detective Castanga, very suddenly, with no warning at all, turned from a bad-ass to a man trying not to laugh, and failing at it. He did laugh. He rubbed his hands together. "You're very good, Ms. Scott. You're a reference librarian? At the public library? Hard to believe. You just took me apart very cleanly and smoothly." He was right. She'd sounded more hard-ass than he had.

Then Detective Castanga's laughter dried up. "Okay, so you were the target, Ms. Scott. I'll buy that now. Let's get down to business. Mac, pull up a chair, you're still looking pretty shaky. Hey, you were ready to belt me. Come on, she didn't need you to ride in and save her from the nasty cop. Now, Ms. Scott, do you want a couple of aspirin?"

Laura got her aspirin, Dr. Kiren finished checking her again quickly, nodded, and left us. Detective Castanga sat down with an open notebook on his leg. As for myself, I was trying to sit straight in the chair. "Talk," he said to both of us. "You two seem joined at the hip. Tell me why someone wants Ms. Scott dead."

Laura and I both remained silent as a tomb. Finally, I shrugged. "I already told you why I came here to Edgerton in the first place, Detective. It was all about my sister, Jilly. I just met Ms. Scott a couple of days ago."

Detective Castanga didn't believe me. He turned to Laura, a dark eyebrow cocked up a good inch.

"No, there's no reason I can think of. I'm a reference librarian, for heaven's sake."

In that instant, I knew she was lying. It was clean and fast, but it was a lie.

As for Detective Castanga, I don't know what he thought. He looked at her thoughtfully for a long time.

"It seems to me the shit hit the fan with your arrival, Mac. Give me names of people you've met in Edgerton."

Laura was relieved at that, I could tell. I hauled out the names of everyone I'd met in Edgerton. After I finished, he looked up and said, "All right, you've given me about twelve names. I'm going to read this list out loud. Add or subtract anyone you want to. Let's start with your heavyweight, Alyssum Tarcher. This guy is big bucks. His financial assets are far-reaching. He's got lots of power with a lot of folk here in our state government, and even in Washington, I'm told. You've got him on the list along with all his family members."

"Well, there's no way around it," I said. "Wait, obviously something else has happened since I came to Edgerton. There was Charlie Duck's murder a couple of days ago. Maggie can't find a reason either for the attack, or for why his house was ransacked." I shrugged, and because I was good, I looked him straight in the eye as I added, "She thinks it was a random killing, and she may be right, but who knows?"

Detective Castanga said, sitting back in his seat, "Yeah, it was a real shame. He had quite a reputation back in the bad old days. The old guy was a retired cop."

"Yeah, Maggie told me."

"He left the Chicago PD a long time ago. I'll speak to Maggie about what she's found out about it. She told me she'd sent the body to Portland to the medical examiner even though it was obvious old Charlie had been struck on the head. She was right. You never know what will turn up. She told me she was pushing to have his body back by Tuesday. That was the day his funeral had been set."

He turned his attention back to Laura. "Now, Ms. Scott, you claim you have no enemies. Still, I'll need a list of the people you know in Salem, and I'll need to go over that list with you."

Laura nodded, then closed her eyes. She looked pale and exhausted. I bet I looked about the same.

I wondered if I should tell Castanga all the rest of it, including Charlie's dying words. No, I'd leave that decision to Maggie.

I thought of Jilly and Paul. Could either of them hate Laura so much they'd want to murder her? Had Jilly left the hospital on her own, driven up to Salem, managed to get into Laura's apartment, and poured phenobarbital into the coffee can?

"Did Jilly have a key to your condo, Laura?" I asked finally, hating the words as they left my mouth.

"No," she said. "I don't think so. She visited me there, of course, from time to time. I need a better painkiller. My head is killing me."

Detective Castanga stood and slowly slipped his notebook back into the inside pocket of his coat. "We have time for this later, Ms. Scott, when you feel better. In the meantime, I'll post an officer by your door."

"Thank you, Detective," she said and closed her eyes again, turning her head away from him on the stingy hospital pillow.

"Mac, are you coming?"

I said, "I don't want to leave her here alone. Someone tried to kill her. It'll take a while for you to get someone over here."

"Not long," Detective Castanga said. "I got a guy who's a little burned out right now, but he'll guard her well." He said to Laura, "His name is Harold Hobbes, a nice guy, tough as nails, and he won't let his own mother into your room."

"Thank you, Detective," she said.

I went with Detective Castanga to the door and partway down the hospital corridor. Our footsteps sounded on a background of muted groans, one loud shout, the low hum of music, beeping machines, and an occasional curse. When I returned to Laura's room, I saw a tall woman bending over Laura.

"Hey," I said and ran forward.

The woman straightened and cocked her head at me in question. It was Dr. Kiren. "She's tired but wanted to ask me a question. I had to lean over to hear her."

"Sorry," I said.

Dr. Kiren smiled. "She'll be fine by this evening, maybe even ready to go home."

Home, I thought. No, that wouldn't work. I had to think about this.

Dr. Kiren's pager went off. On her way out, she told Laura to rest.

I thought about Charlie Duck's funeral. Hopefully Charlie would arrive back in time for his scheduled send-off.

I leaned over Laura and stroked my thumb over her eyebrows. I said very quietly, "I'll see you later this afternoon. Then we'll talk. Rest. Harold Hobbes will be outside your room. If anyone comes near you, it means they've gotten past Harold, so scream your head off."

"All right," she said, not opening her eyes. I'd nearly made it to the door when she called out, "Thanks, Mac."

"Sure," I said.

"I'm sorry I nearly got you killed."

"Yeah, I know."

I stopped at Laura's condo. Castanga's people had finished with it, but I still had to show my FBI badge so the manager would unlock her door. Grubster was standing directly in front of the door, waiting for Laura. He saw me, meowed once, then turned around and walked away, his tail high in the air. "I'm here to feed you," I called after him.

To my surprise, Grubster stopped, raised his left paw, licked it, and took two steps back toward me. Then he sat there. "Okay," I said. "Let's find your cat food."

I watched Grubster chow down an entire can of salmon and rice and a big handful of dried stuff that looked so bad I poured some non-fat milk over it. Grubster purred the whole time he ate. I gave him a ton of fresh water and eyed his cat box, which needed changing. Grubster watched my technique. He must have approved because on his way out of the kitchen he stopped a moment and swiped his whiskers against my leg.

"Now for you, Nolan." When I said his name, Nolan filled the air with loud, sharp squawks, probably a bird's equivalent to orders. I changed his water, crumpled up a thick slice of bread into small pieces, and sprinkled sunflower seeds on the floor of his cage. Nolan obligingly hopped in to dine.

I stopped at the front door, looked from Grubster to Nolan, sighed, and went back to scratch and pet Grubster while Nolan serenaded me with squawks between bread bites.

I'd always had dogs growing up. During the past four or five years, though, I hadn't had a pet of any kind around. As I left, it didn't seem strange to call back to the two of them, "I'll be back to get you guys later."

"Squawk."

Nothing from Grubster. He was asleep.

I got back to Edgerton in the early afternoon. I stopped at Grace's Deli and ordered up a tuna salad sandwich on rye bread, with lots of tomatoes and dill pickles. While I ate, I asked Grace how to go about renting a home or an apartment here in town or a bit out of town, maybe near where Rob Morrison's small clapboard cottage was.

Grace was strong-willed as a mule, tall and very thin, with a head of salt-and-pepper hair. She smiled at me and said, "Well, I reckon you could go over to the Buttercup Bed & Breakfast, but Arlene Hicks isn't really high on you being here. Never got it through her head that money is money. She already told you she was all filled up, didn't she?"

I nodded. "I should have told her that if she wasn't running drugs, she has nothing to fear."

"Well, she might be, you never know. Arlene's full of deep shoals, lots of secrets. I've got it, Mr. MacDougal. Mr. Tarcher owns a little house like Rob Morrison's. It's called Seagull Cottage, to the south of town, nearly right on the cliff. It's empty right now. The last tenants left about a month ago."

"Excellent." I finished off my sandwich and rose. "Are you coming to Charlie Duck's funeral?"

"Wouldn't miss it," Grace said. "I have a three-minute eulogy to give." She smiled, seeing my confusion. "I'm the town Buddhist."

"You're a Buddhist?"

"I haven't made up my mind, but I'm close enough. The thing is, though, that the Buddhists make it very simple for you to reach your heavenly reward. To reach Nirvana, all you have to do is live right, think right, and deny yourself just about everything. That's something, isn't it?"

"Where does the line begin?" I asked, looking around.

Grace cocked her head at me, and I smiled and left. I called the Tarcher house and was surprised when Alyssum himself answered the phone. I told him I wanted to rent Seagull Cottage and I told him why. If he was the one behind having Laura drugged, well, it hardly mattered. He'd find out soon enough anyway where she was. Besides, I wanted everyone to know that Laura and I were together and planned to camp right in their own backyard.

"So that's why I can't allow Ms. Scott to return to her place. It was Grace who kindly told me about the house you're renting down on the cliffs."

Alyssum Tarcher said, "Well, Agent MacDougal, this is a surprise. So you'll be guarding Ms. Scott then?"

I told him there'd be a lot of people near her, that Maggie was setting up a schedule, but I was going to be the main one baby-sitting.

"I'll tell you what, Agent MacDougal," Tarcher said, pausing for a deep, stentorian breath, "to do my good citizen's part, I'll grant you a month's free rent on the house." I didn't have a problem with that at all. I thanked him and made a date to pick up the house key. The only problem I foresaw was getting Laura away from her condo in Salem and down to Edgerton with me. And maybe getting the truth out of her.

I returned to Salem General Hospital, Nolan and Grubster on the backseat of the Taurus, the trunk loaded down with three suitcases holding about everything I could imagine she'd want and need.

I decided on my way up in the elevator how to get Laura to Edgerton.

FOURTEEN

Laura was sitting on the edge of the bed, her feet dangling, the green hospital nightgown falling off her left shoulder. When she saw me in the doorway, her face lit up.

"Mac! I was just going to get myself together. Would you mind taking me home?"

I told her I wouldn't mind at all. The clothes she'd worn when they'd brought her in were hanging in the closet. I spoke outside with Harold Hobbes while she changed.

"Hell of a thing," Harold said, as he nodded toward the door. "Some jerk trying to ice a pretty lady like that." I agreed that it was.

"No one even came by to sniff."

I knocked, heard Laura tell me to come in, and went in to fetch my new roommate.

Laura was still a bit on the shaky side, but she looked much better. They made her ride down in a wheelchair, which she didn't like at all. I put her in the passenger side of the Taurus and quickly shut the door.

"What is this, Mac?"—her first words to me when I slid in behind the steering wheel. I turned to the backseat and said, "Hi, guys. Everything okay?"

"Squawk."

"Grubster, you got any news from the front?"

Nothing from Grubster.

"What's going on here, Mac?"

I drove out of the parking lot. "You're on vacation as of right now, Ms. Scott. I've rented us a small house just south of Edgerton, on the cliffs. It's called Seagull Cottage, and Mr. Alyssum Tarcher has given it to us rent-free for a month. I'm going to be your roommate."

She chewed this over for about twenty-two seconds. "No way. I live in Salem. I'll lose my job."

"No. I got you a two-week vacation, without pay. I told them I was your brother and you'd come down with Lyme disease. They were suitably impressed. It was a Mr. Dirkson who cleared you. All right?"

"My condo."

"I told the manager you were going out of town. He's going to keep an eye on everything."

"I don't have any clothes."

"All in the trunk."

She was done, for the moment. We were out of Salem now, heading toward 101.

"It's okay, Laura," I said, giving her a quick smile. "Really, it's better this way. Except it's interesting about Alyssum Tarcher being our landlord. Hey, if he had anything to do with this, he would have found out that you'd flown the coop. Now everyone knows you're not alone, that you've got protection, namely yours truly."

"You don't know anything, Mac."

"I will, soon enough. I don't want you thinking that you're walking right into the bear cave, what with us going to Edgerton. I'll be in that cave with you and I'm mean. Besides, I've got a big spear. Running away is not the way to find out what's going on in Edgerton, or to find my sister." I waited, but she didn't say anything, nodded after a bit.

It had started raining, a drizzle at first, but now it was really coming down. "I didn't bring you a raincoat, sorry."

She didn't say a word for at least seven miles. Finally, I said, "Laura? Is this okay with you?"

"Are you really going to let people know—the whole town—that someone tried to kill me? Or are you going to leave it as both of us?"

"I already told Alyssum Tarcher that it was only you. When we get to Edgerton, I need to stop off at Paul's house to pick up my clothes. Then I need to see Maggie, find out if she's heard anything about Jilly. Also, Charlie Duck's autopsy report should be coming in soon."

"You think the old man's death is somehow connected, don't you?"

"My boss, Big Carl Bardolino, at the FBI, likes to say there's no such thing as coincidence, at least in our line of work."

"Squawk."

"Nolan's got some more sunflower seeds in that lunch bag on the backseat if you think he's still hungry."

A car came around to pass us, not too wise since we were on a curve. I slowed down a bit and gave it plenty of room to go around.

Laura started to say something as she turned around to reach for the bag of sunflower seeds. In the next instant, there was a popping sound, then another. I jerked back. I realized that a bullet had gone through her passenger-side window. It had crashed through my window and missed my neck by a couple of inches, leaving a spiderweb of cracked glass in its wake.

I pulled the steering wheel hard right, then corrected to the left, missing an oncoming car. I saw a man in my mind's eye, on the passenger side, raising what had to have been a gun. I saw the car just ahead of us, a dark red Honda. I gunned the Taurus and winced. In this rain, if I wasn't careful, we'd go skidding right off the road. The Honda roared ahead, cutting hard and fast around a sharp turn. I knew the Taurus wouldn't make it. I had to slow a bit. When I got around the curve, the Honda had widened the distance.

"My God, Mac, are you all right?"

"Yep. You?"

"I think so. If I hadn't turned in that moment to get Nolan some sunflower seeds—"

"I know. Laura, sit back down and fasten your seat belt."

"Squawk."

"It's all right, Nolan. Think of this as an adventure."

Laura was strapped in and I passed two cars, nearly skimming off the paint on the second one. Horns blared loudly in our ears.

We were getting closer. "Laura, I don't think we can catch them, but we can get the license plate."

"I can try," she said, and buzzed down what was left of her electric window to lean out. Rain flew in the open window, hard and heavy.

I tried to keep my hands loose and relaxed on the steering wheel even though my heart pounded faster in anger each time I saw that webbed bullet hole out of the corner of my eye. I passed another car, a Land Rover. The driver gave me the finger and shouted a curse. I didn't blame him.

There were about forty yards of highway between us and the Honda. I saw a man leaning out the passenger window, looking back. He had a gun. "Laura, down!"

She jerked back in and flattened herself against the seat as the man fired five or six rounds.

"Mac," she said, "you've got a gun, don't you?"

"Yes, but I've got to concentrate."

"Give it to me. I know how to shoot."

I didn't want to. It was the last thing I wanted to do, actually. I felt her hand pulling it out of my shoulder holster.

"Laura," I said, "I'd rather you didn't. Please, be careful."

"Get us closer to that damned Honda."

We closed to within fifteen yards of the Honda. This stretch of 101 was all curves and inclines and twisting hills. The rain had lightened up a bit, thank God. I'd be just on the verge of seeing the license plate when the Honda would disappear again around another curve.

Laura hugged the passenger door, waiting. She seemed very calm, perhaps too calm. Something was strange here. "Laura, are you all right?"

"I'm fine, Mac. Keep up with them. Yeah, a little bit closer." Suddenly, she reared up and halfway out the open window, rain curtaining her face. She shot off half the clip, fast.

The Honda's back window exploded. A man came out of the passenger-side window, a gun trained on us. Before he could fire, Laura shot off another three rounds. I saw his gun fly out of his hand and skitter across the highway. She'd got him. Then the Honda disappeared around another turn.

I gunned the Taurus. We came around the bend and skidded out to see the Honda disappear on the short straight stretch in front of us.

"Damn, I wanted to get a back tire."

When we last saw the Honda, it was weaving back and forth, the driver sawing the steering wheel to get it out of a skid. He straightened over a crest and the car shot forward. I gunned the Taurus. One more try. But the rain did us in. We hit a slick patch. The car spun in a full three-sixty. We ended up on the side of the road, about six feet from a ditch.

"We didn't get the license plate," Laura said. "Well, damn."

"After this I'm going to rent a Porsche. Bastards got away."

And Laura laughed.

We were still pumped with adrenaline. I started laughing too. It felt good. We were alive.

It took petting Grubster and calming Nolan to get ourselves back down.

"You okay?"

She nodded as she continued scratching behind Grubster's ears. "That was a close one, Mac. My heart's pounding louder than a runaway train. My adrenaline level was so high there for a while, I bet I could have flown right out of this busted window. Oh, Jesus, Mac."

She leaned over to me to put her arms around my back, her elbow hitting the steering wheel. Grubster was between us, purring loudly. I held her tightly, feeling her heartbeat against my chest, her warm breath against my neck, grateful that we'd survived this. It had been close. I took a quick survey of the Taurus. One busted window and a driver's-side window that was spider-webbed, with one small hole right in the middle. Too bad it hadn't stopped the bullet. Some sort of tangible evidence would have been nice.

"What are we going to do?" She didn't move while she spoke, and I liked that.

"I guess if I had my cell phone with me, I'd call Castanga, the President, and the Joint Chiefs of Staff."

"I don't have mine either," she said against my neck. "It's on the dining room table at my condo."

"Squawk!"

"Oh dear, I forgot about Nolan and Grubster."

She lifted Grubster off her lap and hefted him onto the backseat. She gave Nolan more sunflower seeds. I turned to see Grubster stretch his front legs against the front seat. I'd swear that cat was as tall as I was. Then he lightly jumped up front again and curled in Laura's lap.

I raised my hand and picked up a strand of hair that had come free of the clip at the back of her neck. I rubbed the hair between my fingers.

She grew very still.

"I'm glad we're both still alive."

"I wonder if you could be more pleased than Grubster here." The cat was purring so loudly she'd had to raise her voice. I sat back, tapped my fingertips against the steering wheel for a moment, and said, "That was excellent shooting."

"Thank you."

I smiled at her and wondered just how much of a smile it had turned out to be. "At least now I know what you lied about. You're a cop, Laura. Since you were a reference librarian at the Salem Public Library, it means you were undercover. Isn't that right?"

A myriad of expressions crossed her face, from doubt, to dread, to guilt. I guess she finally realized it was too late to go in any direction but toward the truth.

"Laura? You really can trust me. I have no intention of hurting you, or compromising your case, or blowing your cover, or getting you into trouble with your superiors. You've got to deal me in. We've been through too much together for you to leave me blowing in the breeze any longer. I don't want to be helpless, and that's what I am if you keep me in the dark. Come, it's time."

I took her hand as I watched her take a very deep breath. I watched her come to her decision. I swear her eyes turned two shades lighter because she knew the incessant lying was over. "Yes," she said. "Yes, I'm a cop."

I nodded for her to continue. Grubster continued purring at high volume, his tail thumping up and down.

"They wanted to kill me," Laura said, her fingers tightening in Grubster's fur. "If I hadn't turned to get some more sunflower seeds for Nolan—"

I quickly took my gun from between us on the seat and eased it back into my shoulder holster. "Meet me halfway," I said as I smoothed down my jacket, and she did. I pulled her against me, Grubster between us again, and lightly pressed her head against my shoulder. I pulled back, touched my forehead to hers, and cupped her head with my hands. "You've been alone in this for too long. You've got me in it now. Can you imagine what you and I can accomplish together?"

"There's really nothing more to accomplish. My cover's blown now. That's another reason for me to tell you the truth. My orders don't make sense anymore."

"Tell me then. All of it."

"I'm DEA, Mac. Even when I called my boss from the hospital and told him I'd been poisoned, that obviously my cover was blown wide open, he told me to lie low for a couple of days, that he'd try to find out what they know and how they'd found out. Of course I told him about you. That made him even more adamant. He said we'd worked too hard to have this case blown by the FBI. I'm sorry I had to lie to you, Mac."

"This guy sounds like a real winner. For God's sake, they tried to poison you."

"I was getting to be a pretty good reference librarian. I read about all the assigned texts for a degree."

"What's your real name?"

"I'm really Laura. They just changed my last name. My real last name is Bellamy. I've been undercover for over four months now. It involves drugs, of course."

"And it has to do with Paul and Jilly," I said slowly, looking closely at her. She paled and hesitated because what she was about to say was going to bring me pain.

"Just spit it out."

Grubster meowed loudly. "It's all right, Grubster. Take a nap. You've been through a lot." She closed her eyes a moment and ran her fingers through his fur. His loud purring soon filled the car again.

"About five months ago an electronic surveillance unit picked up a rumor that a new drug was being developed, one that is highly addictive and cheap to produce."

"A drug dealer's wet dream."

"Yes. A man called John Molinas was said to be bragging about it. We think Molinas is a major drug distributor, but we don't have anything solid on him. He's been in business in the past with a cartel headed by Del Cabrizo."

"I've heard of him."

"Del Cabrizo occasionally comes to the United States to shove a finger in our face. And now the reason I'm here. The word was that there was a wealthy local man involved. It's none other than Alyssum Tarcher."

I must admit I was staring at her now. "Tarcher involved with Del Cabrizo?"

"There's more. John Molinas is Alyssum Tarcher's brother-in-law. That's probably why Tarcher's involved in this thing."

"A real kicker," I said. "I knew Tarcher was powerful, but this? He's a crook too?"

"Evidently so. All of this came as a bit of a surprise to us too. You see, John Molinas hasn't been active for a few years as far as we could tell. Maybe he got religion, maybe he got cancer, we didn't know. But when we threw Alyssum Tarcher into the mix, it didn't take us long to find out that Dr. Bartlett and his wife, pharmaceutical researchers, had moved to Edgerton from Philadelphia into a house that Tarcher sold them for a nominal price. We put two and two together and put pressure on their employer in Philadelphia, VioTech, to tell us what they had been working on. Paul and Jilly had been working on some sort of memory drug. It sounded nuts, but still, our people went over all the research Paul and Jilly had submitted. It was obvious why VioTech had pulled the plug. Whatever else the drug did, it was very toxic, turned some lab animals completely nuts. They'd sunk millions of dollars into a drug that was going nowhere.

"Still, why had the Bartletts suddenly moved to Edgerton? We knew Paul had grown up there, but there wasn't anything to draw them back."

"Alyssum Tarcher was behind it," I said.

"Right. I set up in Salem posing as a reference librarian because there was no better way I could get closer to Edgerton, to the major players there. I did go to Grace's Deli to see if she needed help, but she didn't. I couldn't just move to Edgerton. Everyone would have known I was up to no good. It's too small and tight a community."

"Why the library?"

"I'm so sorry, Mac. The reason I became a reference librarian was that we found out that Jilly Bartlett was coming to the library in Salem. At least three days a week, like clockwork. Our surveillance showed—Mac, I'm so sorry about this—she was meeting a lover there, always in the reference section. If I became the reference librarian, I'd have a good chance to meet her, to make friends with her, and I did. The regular reference librarian got a very nice open-ended holiday, with pay."

I had only heard one thing. "A lover? Jilly met a man in the library three days a week?"

"Yes. He's a local thoracic surgeon. No one could find out how they'd met, but as yet we have no reason to think he's involved in anything going on down in Edgerton."

I looked up to see a police car cruising slowly by, felt eyes on us. I waved and turned the ignition key. "Let's go to that McDonald's we passed. I need some breathing space and then a cup of coffee."

The McDonald's was about three miles back up the highway off Exit 133. It was tucked between a Denny's and a Wendy's, with three gas stations completing the grouping.

Grubster slept through being put back into his carrying case. Nolan didn't even squawk once when Laura slipped his cover over the cage.

Over Big Macs and coffee, I said, "You've been undercover for four months. What have you come up with?"

"You mean against Jilly and Paul?"

"Believe me, I don't care about Molinas or Tarcher or this Del Cabrizo character."

"Again, Mac, I'm sorry, but the truth is that Jilly lied to me from the beginning, told me she was here because she wanted to get pregnant. She told me she was the uneducated one in the family. I don't know if she did this to protect herself or me.

"I like Jilly. When you told me she was in a coma, it really hit me hard because I do like her so much. She's funny, lights up a room when she swings in, her skirts swishing, her hair bouncing. We did get close, but not close enough that she ever really let me in."

"Bottom line, Laura, you didn't have squat on either Jilly or Paul, and that's because there isn't anything to get. I don't believe my sister would be involved with drug dealers. Both she and Paul are scientists, not criminals. They're moral people, not people who'd develop a drug to feed to kids. You're wrong about them, Laura. At least you're dead wrong about Jilly."

I was being a brother, defensive and angry, but I didn't care. I didn't want to accept it, couldn't accept it. I looked at Laura, felt mean as a snake, and said, "Did you sleep with Paul? As a sort of quid pro quo?"

"No," she said matter-of-factly, but I felt her surprise and hurt at my question. She dropped the french fry she was holding back onto her plate. "Jilly never mentioned anything like that to me. Actually, she's very fond of Paul."

I said slowly, "Jilly said you'd betrayed her. I assumed it meant you'd slept with Paul, but that isn't it at all. She found out you're a DEA agent, didn't she?"

"She must have but I don't know how. Maybe I gave myself away somehow, I don't know. But she must have found out that very night. Both she and Paul must have known since then. One of them may have made a phone call to Molinas. He's perfectly capable of everything that's happened since."

"So now you're saying that my sister conspired to commit murder. I'll never believe that. Probably Molinas found out about you. Jilly wouldn't blow the whistle on you."

She took my hand and held it between hers. "She came out of the coma, Mac, and disappeared as soon as she was able. She knew we were getting close. She went into hiding."

"Then why didn't Paul leave with her?"

"I don't know. There's still no direct evidence against either of them. I thought about that, a lot. Something else I wanted to tell you. Over the past couple of months, Jilly didn't seem quite right. She talked about sex a lot, how much more she liked it than before. Not just one conversation, she went on and on about it. And she seemed somehow off, the way she spoke of other things, mixing in non sequiturs, like she wasn't really with me."

"You think she was experimenting with her own drug?"

"I don't know what I'm saying, but she was different, Mac."

I let it go. It was just too close to my own memories of Jilly's visit the previous February. "Where is Molinas? Has he met with Jilly and Paul? Has he showed up at their house or at the Tarcher house?"

"No. But there's just no getting around the fact that it was Alyssum Tarcher who got Paul and Jilly back to Edgerton. He very nearly gave them the house, the price was so low. I'm sorry, Mac, but you don't do that for no reason.

"Our assumption is that Paul and Jilly are working on this drug, that they're trying to make it less toxic or more addictive, and then it'll be mass-produced and sold on the street."

"For argument's sake, let's say you're right about all of it. To get people hooked, a drug has to produce a high that will knock the user's socks off. Does this drug do that?"

"We don't know, but we think it has to do with sex."

No, I thought. Jilly and all her talk about sex to both Laura and me. No.

"You mean the user shoots up and lies there in a semi-stupor having orgasms?"

"Maybe. We don't know. Some of the VioTech data showed some very significant changes in lab animals' sexual drive. It went off the charts and frequently showed itself by intense sexual aggression. There's got to be more to it than that, of course. Jilly and Paul probably took some of their records with them.

"My boss told me to lie low, but I just can't do that. I don't know how close they are to perfecting the drug. If I can help it, that drug isn't going to make it to the streets. I don't know how to go about that anymore."

"I'm not going to stop looking for my sister, Laura. I guess I don't see any other choice but to join forces with you."

"You could get in big trouble with your people too, Mac. But more than that, I don't want you in any more danger. You've been an innocent by-stander in all of this and it nearly got you killed. I couldn't bear that."

I gave her a crooked grin. "We've known each other for two days."

"That's strange, isn't it?"

"Look, Laura, you know as well as I do that if you don't get on a phone and tell your boss you've been fired at in a car on a public highway, you can forget about your long-term career in the DEA. You're the one in jeopardy. You've got to think about covering your butt, driving to a motel on Bainbridge Island or somewhere and hiding until it's all over. That's what's safest."

"I don't want to call in the cavalry," she said. "I want to find Jilly. I can't head off to parts unknown and forget about this. If I call my boss, I'll be out of here for sure and the DEA will be all over town. These people are too smart. The DEA won't find a thing that way."

"And Jilly and Paul might get railroaded. I want to find out whether they're up to their necks in this, or if they're innocent bystanders, like I was two days ago."

Laura's eyes sheened, and her hands curled into fists.

"Laura—"

"No, this has to be my decision, Mac. I can't turn my back on Jilly. Or on you. I'm in this with you, for the long haul."

I smiled over at her. "All right. We're both professionals. We both know the risks we're taking." I took her hand, slowly smoothing away the fist. "You want to come to Edgerton with me?"

"Yes. I don't see anything else to do."

I took the last drink of my coffee. It was cold. I gave her a sideways look. "Did Paul really put the moves on you last Tuesday night?"

"Yes he did."

I sighed. "I thought so. Paul's not as good a liar as you are."

"That's because he's a scientist and not a federal agent. It's in our genes. I've had to weave so many lies in with the truth on this case that it's sometimes confused me. Mac, if we go to Edgerton, we're thumbing our nose at them."

"I honestly don't think they'll try anything in Edgerton, not when Alyssum Tarcher is our landlord and everybody knows we're there and I'm protecting you. It's our best cover."

"They could shoot us down on Fifth Avenue. That's not much more gall than trying to kill us on 101. This isn't your assignment, Mac."

"No, you're right. It's more than an assignment. This is about my sister. Give it up, Laura. Consider, you need me. Remember, I'm FBI. Now, I've got the beginnings of a plan. I'm calling two friends of mine in Washington, D.C., Savich and Sherlock, FBI agents."

I had to call collect since I didn't have enough coins for the pay phone. Thank God they were home. It took me fifteen minutes to cover all the ground.

When I returned to our table, I smiled down at Laura. "Our numbers are soon doubling. Sherlock and Savich will be here soon."

WHEN we reached the outskirts of Edgerton, I said, "We'll need to stop by Tarcher's house to get the key to Seagull Cottage. I won't bait him, at least not yet. But he'll know, Laura, he has to. I can't imagine that Molinas has kept him out of the loop."

It had started to drizzle again. Laura was beginning to shiver. I turned up the heater. "It'll be better in a few minutes, I hope."

"I'm fine." She leaned back and petted Grubster's head. She took him out of his carrier and he sprawled his full length along the backseat, his nose pressed against Nolan's cage.

Even the magnificent Tarcher mansion looked desolate in the thick dark rain. No hope for it, I thought, and sprinted from the car to the porch. I turned and waved to Laura to stay put, which she did.

Then I realized she was alone, vulnerable to attack. I dashed back through the rain to the Taurus, opened the door, drew my SIG Sauer, and handed it to her. "Keep it close," I said, and closed the car door again.

A maid, who was dressed in jeans and a sweater, let me into the large foyer and asked me to wait. It was better that I drip on the marble than on the highly polished oak floors in the living room beyond.

Cotter Tarcher was whistling as he came from the kitchen at the back of the house. He stopped dead in his tracks when he saw me.

"What's going on? Have you found Jilly?"

"No. I'm here to get the Seagull Cottage key from your father. Laura Scott and I will be staying there for a while."

"Why?" he asked, watching me drip on the floor. He was wearing sweats and running shoes. He was perfectly dry. I didn't answer him. "Do both you and your father work here at home?"

"For the most part. I usually knock off about five o'clock to either go to the gym or out running. Why are you and Laura Scott staying at our cottage?"

"Because someone tried to kill her and it seems safer if she's here, with me, than in Salem by herself. It's a bit on the wet side to go running, isn't it?"

"Yes. I'm working out downstairs in the gym. Where's Laura Scott?"

"In the car."

"Does she know Jilly?"

"Oh yes, she knows Jilly very well."

Alyssum Tarcher came striding down the stairs off to my right. He looked arrogant and intelligent, his eyes at that moment maybe even harder than his son's. He seemed somehow taller to me than he had just the night before.

"Agent MacDougal," he said, and shook my hand. "Here's the key to Seagull Cottage. I made sure the place was cleaned up and the phone works.

Given this weather, I checked to make sure there's heat as well. This Laura Scott, she's with you?"

"Yes, waiting for me in the car. Since someone tried to kill her, she's keeping my gun on her at all times." I suppose I should have mentioned Grubster and Nolan, but you never knew about a landlord, and I didn't want the pets to give him an excuse for us not to use his property. I thanked him and turned to leave.

"Agent MacDougal, call me if there's a problem—of any kind at all."

"Yeah," Cotter said. "My father chews on problems and spits out solutions."

Alyssum Tarcher laughed and buffeted his son's shoulder with a light shove.

"Who is it, Aly?"

Elaine Tarcher didn't wait for an answer, but came running lightly down the stairs. Like her son, she was wearing sweats and running shoes, and she didn't look much older than Cal. I realized I hadn't thought about Cal since, well, for a good while. "Mrs. Tarcher," I said, nodding. "Don't come any closer, I'm wet."

"I see that you are. We heard about your problem with that drug. Are you all right?"

"Yes, I'm fine. Did Mr. Tarcher tell you that Laura Scott and I will be staying for a while at Seagull Cottage?"

"Yes, he did tell me. He also told me that someone is trying to kill Ms. Scott. This isn't what we're used to, Agent MacDougal. You seem to have brought a good deal of trouble with you. We've never liked violence, only rarely seen it here in Edgerton. Until poor Charlie Duck. Have you heard anything about Jilly?"

I said no and left three minutes later, sprinting back to the car under thick, cold rain that was coming down harder than ever and had me shivering even after five minutes with the car heater turned on high. Laura had put one of her jackets up against the shattered window. It kept the rain out, but the heat from the car seeped out quickly.

I stopped off at Paul's house. I was relieved when he wasn't at home. Truth be told, I wasn't ready to confront him. The last thing I wanted to happen was to scare him into running, maybe even disappearing like Jilly.

I packed up my clothes, left him a note telling him where I was, and didn't give him any explanation at all.

We drove to a small grocery store called The Cove to stock up. Laura remained in the car both times, my SIG Sauer on her lap.

It was dark when we arrived at Seagull Cottage, not more than fifty feet from the cliffs with, I imagined, a sweeping view up and down the Oregon coast. But not tonight. Only heavy, cold rain tonight that covered everything, leaving the ocean black and flat. There wasn't any wind at all and surely that was odd. The rain came straight down, striking the ground hard as a slap. There were only about half a dozen spruce trees to soften the barren landscape.

I unlocked the door, checked out the inside, and waved Laura in.

FIFTEEN

At seven that evening we ate our dinner in front of the fireplace, chicken noodle soup and English muffins with butter dripping over the sides. Grubster lay sleeping at Laura's feet, sated from two cans of cat food, with an occasional twitch. Nolan was under wraps for the night. "That was delicious," Laura said as she sat back on her hands and yawned.

"Yes, it was," I said, barely managing to stifle my own yawn. "It's been a long day."

She cocked an eye open. "You're being the master of understatement here?"

For the life of me I was too tired to think of something clever to say to that wonderful straight line. I said, "You ready to hang it up?"

Laura looked toward the cottage door. I could see the tension in her. "No," she said. "They wouldn't dare try anything here, in Edgerton."

"I don't think so either. Tomorrow is Charlie Duck's funeral. I want to introduce you to everyone and start getting in Tarcher's face. As for Paul, I want to handle him very carefully. I don't want him running."

"He'll never admit to anything, I'd swear to it. He'll protect Jilly."

She was probably right. I was imagining what it would be like to put my hands around his neck, lift him off the floor, and shake him.

"When Savich and Sherlock get here, we'll all discuss what's the best approach. They know we've got to act quickly."

"Your friends sure have a lot of flexibility."

"Yeah. They're both in the same unit and he's in charge. Savich's boss, Jimmy Maitland, usually gives him as much leeway as he wants. Besides, they're coming as my friends, not an official assignment.

"Sherlock and Savich are first-class agents and very good friends. It's possible they'll see things as outsiders that you and I have missed. They'll have some great ideas, you can count on that."

"I don't know anyone like that in the DEA." She put her fingers on my lips. "No, don't you dare start up with cracks about my agency."

"I wouldn't dream of it, Laura. Now, I'll hook a chair under the doorknob and I'll put my SIG right beside the bed. We've got the curtains pulled over the windows and everything's locked up tight. It'll be okay."

"I guess there's nothing more that we can do. Goodness, it's only eight-thirty. It feels like it should be at least midnight, I'm so tired."

"Why don't you take the bathroom first? I want to check around outside."

"Be careful, Mac." She lightly touched her fingers to my face. "I mean it, be very careful. You've gotten kind of important to me, real fast."

I wanted to kiss her and not stop, so I got out of there fast. The rain had stopped for the moment. Low-lying black clouds were shifting in thick, grotesque shapes across a huge fat full moon.

It looked like a werewolf kind of night.

In that instant I heard something, something not far away, off to my left, away from the cliffs, something rustling, then moving, perhaps a heavy foot thudding on the ground, then silence, then more rustling.

I waited, so still I could hear my own breath. Nothing more, as if whatever it was that was coming toward me had stopped. I waited longer, then longer still. Still nothing. I wondered if my brain had obligingly conjured up the bogeyman.

I remembered Cal saying that she never wanted to go anywhere near the cemetery, that the trees were growing inward, pushing so close that the roots probably had split through the coffins. I'd thought she was nuts then. Now I was hearing things, and terrifying myself. I was losing it.

I walked to the cliff and stood looking out over the flat, black water. It went forever, well beyond those distant low dark clouds that tricked the eye, making it appear that the water simply disappeared into them. Looking north and south, I could make out the coastline—primeval mists, driftwood strewn over and sprawled out in piles on the beach. Black rocks rose out of the water like misshapen sentinels, groups of them hovering below me, the water scaling them, then crashing back, gushing white foam. Again and again, never stopping, never changing. I thought about what it would be like to be here every day of my life and wondered if my soul would be calmed, or if I'd go mad.

I turned to go back, pausing a moment to get my bearings. Seagull Cottage sat at the very end of a narrow, rutted dirt road, winding south and west toward the cliff, only to this small cottage. I couldn't see the half-mile back to the road this one split off from. There were no car headlights that I could see even in the distance. I walked to the back of the cottage, checked the windows, and looked south to the wild barren hills that rose and fell as far as I could see. Anyone could hike to the cottage over those soulless hills. I didn't like it. I wondered if we weren't the biggest fools in Oregon, staying here right in Tarcher's face. I was putting my life on the line, but more important, putting Laura in danger as well. I shook my head. I wasn't going to back down and I couldn't imagine Laura backing away now either.

I looked at the cottage. All the windows were secure, covered with patterned cotton curtains, faded from many years in the sun. There was nothing else I could do.

My head had started aching again. No wonder. My body felt like it had been hit by a wrecking ball. I was so tired I could barely stand. But I also felt jumpy.

When I walked into the small bedroom, Laura was standing in a long nightgown by the side of the bed, looking at me.

"Hi," she said, her voice deep and rich, making that small word sound far too sexy. I was at her side in just under four steps. She moved against me, raised her face, and kissed my mouth.

In an instant my fatigue was gone. I'd known this woman for a matter of days and I wanted her more than any woman I'd ever met in my life. There were no more lies between us, I thought, not a single one.

My hands were all over her, in her hair, stroking and rubbing that thick smooth hair on my face even as I kissed her, and down her back, cupping her tightly against me.

"This is crazy right now," I said, and smiled at her beautiful face, now flushed with color. She was breathing fast, as excited as I was.

"Crazy is as crazy does," she said, bit my ear, hooked her leg behind mine, and knocked me onto my back on the bed. She fell on top of me, kissing me, yanking on my hair to get more of me. I was kissing her and laughing at the same time. I was roaring with power.

I had my clothes off in just under a minute and her nightgown over her head and tossed to the far corner of the small bedroom in another two seconds flat. "I don't believe this," I said, looking at her, wanting all of her at once, not knowing where to start. She laughed as she kissed me and then her hands were all over me.

We were laughing and moaning together when I came into her and she arched up sharply, biting and licking my neck, nipping me with little kisses. I forced myself to stop. "I've got to get a grip here," I said, "I want to feel you around me. I've wanted to make love with you from the moment I saw you talking to that teenage boy in the library."

"I wanted you over the chicken satay," she said and tightened her arms around my back. "Yes, hold still, Mac, and let me feel you. I hadn't imagined this tonight, I really hadn't, I—"

She climaxed. I watched the pleasure take her, felt her tightening around me and knew I couldn't hold on much longer. Wonderful thing was, it didn't matter. In a frenzy, I joined her.

"It's the two of us now, Laura."

"That's more than fine by me," she said. "I'm really glad you came to the library, even if you don't know a thing about Latvian drug wars."

At ten minutes after one o'clock in the morning, we were both awake again, still not going slow and easy but frenetic and urgent. There wasn't any laughter this time, only the darkness surrounding us, Laura's lovely flesh, and the sweet groans coming from her mouth. Afterward I came up on my elbows and touched my forehead to hers. "It's all over for me, Laura."

"Yes, I can feel that it is."

The woman had the gall to laugh.

"That isn't what I meant."

"I know." She kissed my chin, bit my earlobe, and polished it by chopping my elbows so that I fell on top of her again. She wrapped her arms tightly around my back and held me close. "It was over for me, Mac, when you walked into the reference section and made me laugh with the first thing out of your mouth. The truth is, for me, this is a rather incredible thing."

"Yes, for me as well. I just wish we could have met in a more normal way. Getting poisoned and shot at during the courting period tends to make a guy look over his shoulder a whole lot, and it wasn't even your dad."

"I forced it on you. Every time I think of all the lies I told you—had to tell you—it makes me furious and sad. Promise me that you've forgiven me."

"Since I'm lying naked on top of you and you've kissed me everywhere, I guess I'll have to. But no more lies or evasions, Laura, ever. Okay?"

"I promise. Now you make me a promise, Mac. Promise me that everything's going to turn out okay."

"I can promise you that we're going to survive this, Laura. But how can it ultimately end well if Jilly's involved?"

She kissed me again in answer, and we fell asleep, her warm breath against my neck.

I had incredible dreams.

There were werewolves prowling around outside the cottage, but they weren't trying to peer in.

I came awake suddenly to the sound of loud banging on wood, and a voice calling out.

My brain woke up in high gear. I pulled on old cotton sweats, grabbed my SIG off the nightstand, and eased out of bed. Laura was still asleep, sprawled on her back. She was naked and my hands were on her before I could stop myself. I covered her quickly.

Daylight hadn't made it through the curtained windows. It was dull gray and cold in the small living room, the fire in the grate long cold. Where was Grubster?

Someone banged on the door again. "Open up. Come on, Mac, open the bloody door."

I recognized that irritated, sweet voice. I jerked the chair away from under the doorknob, turned the lock, and pulled open the door. Standing on the small porch was Sherlock. Early-morning sunlight backlighted her. With all that red hair, she looked like a Titian painting come to life.

She was on me in an instant, hugging me tight. "Hi, Mac," she said, drawing back, giving me a big smile.

"My angel," I said, grabbing her up in my arms, and swinging her around. "I hadn't expected you this soon. What did you do, immediately hop a plane?"

She kissed my ear. "Yes, we took the red-eye." Then she said over my shoulder, "Hello, who are you?"

I let Sherlock slowly back down on her feet. We turned together to see Laura, in her sweats, her hair tangled around her flushed face, Grubster curling around her bare feet.

"So soon, Mac?"

"This is Sherlock, Laura. I got her through her final physical exam at the Academy. She would have failed miserably if I hadn't been there."

"Ha. He was noted for his magnificent brawn, but I had the brain power." Sherlock and Laura shook hands, Sherlock eyeing Laura like you'd expect a mother to do.

"Where's Savich?" I asked, giving Sherlock a final hug. "You did let him come with you, didn't you, Sherlock? I mean rather than leaving him home to take care of Sean? He's come in handy before, hasn't he?"

She laughed and poked me. "That man is a dream and don't you ever doubt it. We took Sean over to Savich's mom, who couldn't wait for us to leave so she could spoil him rotten.

"Hey, it's after eight o'clock in the morning, Mac. Dillon is walking the cliffs, checking for any recent signs of people close to the cottage. He wanted me to wait, to give you more sleeping time, but hey, I couldn't. I was worried about you. You're okay, Mac, really? And you too, Laura?"

I was wondering if Savich knew werewolf tracks when he saw them. "No one came back last night. Maybe the bears are hibernating."

"Both Dillon and I are good at finding bears. We're all together now, Mac, not just you two alone anymore." Sherlock began to examine me, not saying another word, lightly touching my arms, my face. She pulled up my sweatshirt and began looking me over. "Your ribs okay now?" I felt her fingertips lightly brushing over my still-bruised middle.

"Yeah, I still get tired quicker than I used to, but it's better every day. Hey, Sherlock, don't pull down my pants."

"Oh, all right." She straightened again, then gave me several long looks. "How do you guys feel now after all that phenobarbital?"

Laura said, "I'm still just a bit on the groggy side, but it's nearly gone."

"Since I'm a manly man, I had almost no aftereffects."

I got a punch in the arm.

"I'm off to make some coffee," Laura said. "Everyone want some?"

I heard her moving around in the small kitchen that was separated from the living/dining room by a bar with three stools bellied up to it.

"Squawk."

"That's Nolan, and his first word of the new day," Laura had pulled off his cage cover.

Laura called out, "You can open his cage if you want to. All the windows are closed, he'll be just fine. Also, if you could sprinkle some sunflower seeds for him. I'm making him some toast right now. Yes, Grubster, I hear you, the world hears you. I'm going to open some cat food for you. Don't fret."

I watched Sherlock open Nolan's door, saw him stare at her a moment, then, a step at a time, venture outside his cage. He cocked his head at Sherlock. "Squawk."

He jumped to the back of one of the love seats. He took a sunflower seed from Sherlock's outstretched fingers, carefully dropped it on the sofa back, then hopped up on Sherlock's shoulder and began chewing on her hair. Sherlock began to laugh.

"Squawk."

"Eat your breakfast, Nolan," Sherlock said, and set him on the sofa back.

Grubster was meowing his head off. Then, suddenly, there was silence from him. He'd doubtless buried his face in a bowl of cat food.

"Come sit down, Sherlock," I said. "I don't remember how you like your coffee."

"Just a bit of fake sugar and a dollop of milk," Sherlock said to Laura. "Oh, if you don't have any of that stuff, black is just fine."

"No, we're in luck," Laura said. "That's the way I drink my coffee too. Mac?"

"Don't pour me any yet, Laura," I called from the cottage door. "I want to see what Savich is up to."

"Put on some shoes before you head out," Sherlock said, absorbed with putting another sunflower seed in Nolan's mouth.

When I walked outside, I was surprised to see a beautiful clear morning, the sky as blue as Sherlock's eyes, with just a light breeze. I turned south to see Savich striding toward me. He saw me and waved.

Like his wife, when he reached me he studied me closely. "You okay?" Thank God he didn't feel it necessary to feel me up.

"Yeah, nothing to worry about. Did you see anything? Sherlock's already inside drinking coffee. Come on in. I'm surely pleased to see both of you."

"I didn't see any signs of anyone out here. The ground's still soft from all the rain. There would have been footprints if anyone had come close. But you've already checked out here, haven't you?"

"Not this morning."

"Now you don't have to. Sounds like you guys are in a bit of trouble. I'm glad you called us. But it's going to be sticky, Mac. We're both really sorry about Jilly and any involvement she may have in all this. I want you to know, too, that we talked it over on the way here, and for Jilly's sake, we're with you for a day or two. I agree with you we should be safe enough for that long. Someone would have to be crazy to come after four federal agents when everyone knows why we're here.

"I said as little as possible to Jimmy Maitland. For the moment, at least, since you're on leave and have already talked to your boss, Carl Bardolino, he's going to let us go with this. As I said, Sherlock and I discussed this situation thoroughly on the flight to Portland. We've got more questions. Then we can discuss strategy." He paused a moment and gripped my shoulder. "I'm very sorry about Jilly, Mac. No word about where she is?"

"No. I'm sorry about your having to leave Sean."

"He'll do fine. Sherlock says he's too young to be ruined yet, so it doesn't matter how often my mom tickles his stomach and tells him he's the prince of the world. I sure hope she's right."

It sounded so normal, so very unlike the past four days of my life. I sighed. "Come meet Laura Scott."

SIXTEEN

After we'd each drunk a cup of coffee strong enough to cut through sludge and Savich had finished his tea, I said, "There's a whole lot we need to do today. Since we don't know how long we can count on staying here, we've got to make good use of every minute."

I looked over at Savich, who was staring into his empty tea cup. He looked every inch a mean son of a bitch, big and muscled, wearing jeans and a dark blue turtleneck sweater, short boots. You could count on him to cover your back. "It's fifteen minutes after eight o'clock in the morning, Mac. I ain't going nowhere until I get food in this empty belly."

Sherlock said, "Before we do anything, you guys need to go shower. A shave for you, Mac. Your hair's standing on end. Actually, both of you could use some more sleep. But it's odd. You both look real relaxed." She raised her eyebrow, blinked twice, and walked quickly into the kitchen.

"She knows," Laura said to me.

"I hope she approves of you."

Laura and I didn't share the shower, but it was a temptation. We brushed our teeth together. When we returned, I inhaled the smell of bacon and eggs and nearly cried. I saw that Nolan was riding around on Savich's shoulder. Grubster was sitting on Sherlock's lap.

"Quite a menagerie you've got," Savich said, and lightly stroked his fingertip down Nolan's breast.

"Squawk."

The table was set. We all sat down like grown-ups. Savich brought out the plates of food he'd kept warm in the oven. "Eat up." Savich ate for five minutes, then said, "Mac, you mentioned this old fellow, Charlie Duck, who was murdered. What about him? How does he fit into all of this?"

"All we have is his dying words to Doc Lambert: 'a big wallop, too much, then they got me.' He knew something about Laura's drug case, no question at all in my mind about that. But what?"

Laura said, "There hasn't been a whole lot of time to think since I met Mac, but I agree with him. Charlie found out something he shouldn't have and that's why they killed him."

I said, "After breakfast I want to call the M.E. in Portland and see what he has to say. I want to speak to Maggie Sheffield, the sheriff, and see if she's learned anything. I'd assume that she would have called here if she'd gotten any leads on Jilly."

"Charlie Duck's funeral is this afternoon," Laura said as she fed a sunflower seed to Nolan, who was seated on a chair arm. "We can go see what's in the pot and maybe stir it up."

"We're going to start stirring the pot much sooner than that," I said. "Paul's first on the list."

Savich reached down and fed a bit of bacon to Grubster. He said to Sherlock, "Do you think they'll keep us as interested as Sean does?"

"He's already a hell-raiser," Sherlock said. "Dillon is trying to find some weights light enough for him so he can begin his training." She looked at Grubster, who was now washing himself on one of the love seats. "That's some cat," she said. "You're a big varmint, aren't you?"

"I found him when I was a sophomore in college. He was so tiny and skinny then, not larger than one of his legs is now. The vet thinks he's about seven or eight years old. Once Grubster trained me with a can opener, he never stopped eating."

Sherlock made more coffee. I lit the logs in the fireplace. The room was soon warm and cozy. Sherlock said unexpectedly, "It was probably a good thing you saw Laura use a gun. She was forced to tell you everything. I hate to go into situations blind."

"My wife," Savich said, patting her thigh, "can find a silver lining in a ditch. But you know, it's probably better that the shooters got away. If you'd taken them in, the shit would have hit the fan and you'd be sitting here watching yourself on national news. The agency directors would be arguing about who should be in charge, and the criminals would probably disappear while all the bureaucratic chaos was going on. You and Laura would be separated and sent to different sides of the country for endless debriefings that would ultimately lead nowhere. So Sherlock's right, as usual."

He stood up and picked cat hairs off his jeans. "I do have an announcement to make. Laura is nuts about you, Mac, so there's one good thing in all this mess. Now, let's get this show on the road."

I heard a car coming down the dirt road. I reached automatically to my belt. "Where did you park your car, Savich?"

"Behind the cottage."

"Good," I said. "Everyone stay put." I pulled out my SIG, eased open the front door, and stepped outside, pulling the door closed behind me.

SEVENTEEN

Cal's light blue BMW Roadster convertible roared toward me. The earth was still damp from the rain, so the car didn't kick up any dust though she'd jammed on the brakes to do just that. I remembered our own party at her parents' house and winced.

I quickly tucked my SIG into the back of my pants, called out, and waved to her. Cal got out of the little car and looked at me, but didn't wave or say anything, just waited for me to come to her. She was wearing baggy jeans and a huge sweater that came nearly to her knees. Her glasses were firmly on her nose. Her hair was scraped back in a ponytail.

When I was nearly to the car, she jumped me, just as she had the night of the party. Her legs went around my waist, her arms around my neck. She started kissing me enthusiastically all over my face.

I gave her a hug and peeled her off me. "Hi, Cal, what's cooking?"

"What's wrong, Mac? Don't you want to make love? How about over on the edge of the cliff. It's warm enough, or I'll get you warm soon enough. How about it?"

"I've got company, Cal."

"Oh yes, Mom told me you were here at Seagull Cottage with Laura Scott, that you were playing FBI agent and protecting her. That right?"

"Yeah, that's right. It's early, Cal. What can I do for you?"

"I came around to see if there was anything I could do to help. Where's this Laura Scott you're protecting?"

"I'm right here."

Sure enough, Laura was standing on the single step that led to the front door. "Hi," she said. "I'm Laura Scott."

"I'm Cal Tarcher. No one can figure out why anybody wants to kill you."

"Easy enough," Laura said. "I'm a DEA agent. I was undercover until last week, when my cover broke down. See, I was getting too close to something. Would you like to come inside? I think there's some breakfast left. You and Mac seem to be great friends."

"You're a DEA agent? That mean you're a drug cop?"

"That's exactly what I am."

"What are you doing here, with Mac?"

"That's a very long story. Would you like to go on in?"

I said in Laura's ear after Cal passed us both and went inside the cottage, "You didn't have to invite her in, you evil woman."

"Why not? You two sure do seem on very good terms. I'd be almost tempted to say intimate terms. Sherlock and Savich are holed up in the bedroom. Can we expect any more of your conquests to show up, Mac?"

"Cut it out, Laura. It's not what you think. Besides, I'd barely met you when Cal nailed me."

"She nailed you? Usually it's said the other way around. Poor Mac, all these women after your body."

"You're the last so you'd better not put too many holes in me."

She lightly patted my cheek and followed Cal into the cottage.

Laura had removed all signs of Sherlock and Savich. I wondered why they hadn't wanted to stay out here. "How about some bacon and toast, Cal?"

"Thanks, Mac. Hey, who's this?"

"That's my cat, Grubster."

Cal immediately broke a piece of bacon in half and fed it to Grubster. "He's a pig." Having said that, Cal took a big bite of toast. She leaned down and gave Grubster the other half of the bacon.

"He'll kill for you now."

"He's beautiful. Who's that?"

"Squawk."

"That's my mynah bird, Nolan. Would you like some coffee, Cal?"

She nodded and Laura soon returned with the coffeepot and poured, then went back into the kitchen.

Cal took a drink, then sat forward on her chair and whispered in a very loud stage voice, "I know you have to protect her, Mac, but maybe we can get rid of her for a while? She seems nice, she'll probably want to take a walk on the cliffs. She won't have to stay out long. I figure I can have you out of those pants in under three seconds."

Stones were piled on top of my tongue.

"It might be nice to have a bed this time instead of the floor. What do you think?"

"Cal," I said, "this isn't the time, really. Laura can't be alone. This isn't a game—someone's trying to kill her."

"Oh, I don't know, Mac," Laura said, grinning, not six feet away. "I think I'd like a walk on the cliffs. You two can go tangle up the sheets. Would you like me to make the bed before I leave?"

I knew it. I just knew it. There was no justice, no fairness in the world. What there was, was Laura standing two feet away from Cal, no expression at all on her face, and I knew that was a bad sign.

"You see, Mac?" Cal said. "Laura doesn't mind. You'd really make up the bed for us?"

"It's not all that messed up," said the woman I'd made love to the previous night, the woman who Savich said was nuts about me. "We both slept like logs, little movement. Hey, I could spread the covers and you two could tussle on top. How about that?"

Cal was suddenly very quiet. "You two slept together last night?"

"Yes," I said, standing. "We did. Now, Cal, we've got lots of stuff to do. Was there anything specific you wanted?"

"No, just you, Mac." Cal slid off the bar stool. She took the last bite of her toast. She wiped her hands on her jeans' leg. "I thought this was only a cop assignment for you, Mac," she said slowly.

"It's a lot of things, Cal. Is there any word on Jilly?"

Cal shook her head. "Surely Maggie would call you first if she found out anything." She looked over at Laura, for a very long time. "Do you know what, Laura?"

"No, what?"

"I sure would like to paint you. Your face isn't all that interesting, but

your clothes are so tight I can tell you've got a great body. How about it?"
I pictured Cal jumping Laura after she'd sketched her body.

Laura stared at Cal like she was two boards shy of a floor. Then, slowly, she turned to me. "What do you think, Mac?"

"Cal's a good artist," I said.

"No, do you think I've got a great body?"

"Yes, and Cal's still a good artist."

"Okay," Cal said, rubbing her hands together. "We can set up a time for next week. About us, Mac, we can talk about it another time, since you say you're so busy. Oh yeah, I got some of those French condoms, you know, the ones that are real slippery and ribbed?"

I thought I'd be smart and not say a single word to that. I don't think I even breathed for at least ten seconds. I watched Cal leave the cottage, heard the soft roar of the BMW's engine.

"Well," Laura said, eyeing me, then the toast crumbs all around Cal's plate. "I guess that took care of my idea of actually questioning her."

I grinned at her, grabbed her, and jerked her into my arms. I was kissing her when Savich and Sherlock walked back into the room.

I kept kissing Laura until I saw that she was laughing. "Good," I said, and rubbed my hands down her arms. "I barely knew you, Laura. It just happened. Okay?"

"No, it's not at all okay, but I won't break you into parts about it now."

"What sort of punishment do you have in mind?"

She laughed again and poked me in the belly.

I said to Savich, "Why didn't you guys stay out here to meet Cal?"

"You had a great dynamic going there, Mac. If we'd come out, everything would have changed."

"Thanks for the entertainment," Sherlock said.

"You guys just keep enjoying your own jokes," I said as I dialed Ted Leppra, the M.E. up in Portland.

A minute later, Ted Leppra, boy wonder, told me it was indeed a blow to the head that had killed Charlie Duck. "He survived maybe ten to twenty minutes after someone hit him," Ted said in his smoker's hacking voice, "and bought it, I was told, on the floor of the local doctor's house. It was a pretty fast bleed into and around his brain. His brain was crushed by blood, if you prefer a more colorful description."

"You're sure?"

"Oh, yes. Funny thing though, Mac. As you probably know, the old guy was a former cop from Chicago. One of the detectives was cruising through here during an autopsy and we got to talking about him. Do you think there's a tie-in? Someone out for revenge after he got out of the can?"

"Could be," I said, all neutral. "The local sheriff is looking into all of that, naturally."

"Hey, you don't sound happy, Mac."

"No, I'm not. I was hoping there was something else involved here."

Ted coughed, holding the phone away while he hacked. "Sorry," he said. "I know, I've got to stop smoking."

"You of all people have seen enough smokers' lungs," I said mildly.

"Yeah, yeah. Listen, maybe there was something else."

"Hang on a minute, Ted. I'm going to put you on speaker. There are some other folk here who need to hear what you've got to say."

"Okay. Mac, you were right about that. We found some sort of drug in his system. It appears to be an opiate or related to an opiate. At least it tested positive on the opiate screen. I haven't been able to identify it yet. It's maybe some sort of drug we've never seen before. Weird, huh?"

"Not really," I said. "It's very possible it's a brand-new drug that isn't on the market yet. When will you be able to give me more information, Ted?"

"Give me a couple more days. Call me on Friday. If I find out anything sooner I'll let you know."

"Stop smoking, you moron."

"What did you say? I can't hear you, Mac."

I hung up the phone, turned, and looked at everybody. "Charlie was on to them. He had some sort of drug in his system."

"He either found out about it and wanted to see what it was, or someone forced it down him," Laura said. "Remember what he said when he was dying—'a big wallop, too much, then they got me.'"

Savich was scratching Grubster's ears. "Or maybe lots of people around here want to try it and ignore the side effects."

"More likely he discovered something and that's why he wanted to talk to me. But he didn't think it was all that urgent."

"He was wrong," Laura said.

"Yes, the poor old man," I said. "Now we know that they killed Charlie

Duck. The drug in his system pretty well proves that. I wish I'd collared him that first day, but you know, I thought he had some fishing stories to tell me. I was an idiot."

"He did try to tell the doctor what had happened," Laura said. "It's too bad he couldn't say more before he died."

I picked up the phone again. "Maybe he's got some friends he still talks to in the Chicago Police Department."

I identified myself to three indifferent people at the Chicago Police Department, in three different departments, including Internal Affairs, and finally ended up in Personnel, where I identified myself to yet another indifferent person. Finally, I got hold of Liz Taylor. She was a real charmer, no sarcasm, she really was.

"Nope," she said cheerfully, first thing off the bat, "I'm no relation at all, so you don't have to wonder. Now, you say you want to know about Charlie Duck?"

"Yes, please. I understand he was a detective with the CPD until about fifteen years ago?"

"Yeah, I remember Charlie well. He was a homicide detective, sharp as a tack. It's funny, you know? Usually, the bosses want the old guys to retire as soon as they can plunk a gold watch on their wrist and push them out the door. But not Charlie. Everybody wanted him to stay. I bet he could have continued here until he croaked, but he wanted to leave. I'll never forget on his sixtieth birthday, he gave me a big kiss and said he was out of here, no more dealing with scumbags, no more weeping over plea bargains that let criminals back out on the streets faster than it took the cops to catch them. He didn't want any more winters in Chicago, either. They aged his skin, he said. He was gone by the following week. Hey, who are you anyway? I know you're FBI, but why do you want to know about Charlie?"

"Charlie's dead," I said. "He was murdered. I'm trying to find out who killed him and why."

"Oh no," Liz Taylor said. "Oh no. I got a Christmas card from him this last December. Sweet, sweet old Charlie." I heard her sniff.

"Tell me about him," I said. "I heard he wasn't exactly the trusting type."

"That was Charlie," Liz said, sniffing some more. "Some people didn't like him, called him a snoop and a son of a bitch, and I guess he was. But he'd never hurt you if you hadn't done anything wrong. He had the highest homicide clearance rate of any detective in the department. In fact, he still holds the record. Poor Charlie. I'll tell you, nothing could stop him if he smelled something rotten."

Not only had he been a detective, he'd been in homicide. He was smart and relentless. It had been a deadly mix for the old man.

"I need the names of friends he's still close to in Chicago. Some other cops. Can you give me some names?"

"Wait. Is that what happened? He smelled something rotten? And that's why someone killed him?"

"Probably," I said. "Do you know of any family or friends he still kept up with? Maybe confided in?"

"No family left," she said. "His wife died before he left the force. Breast cancer, poor woman. He went out west somewhere when he retired, to live with his parents, somewhere on the West Coast. In Oregon, right?"

"That's right," I said, my jaw nearly locked with impatience. "Liz, any friends?"

"Just a couple of older guys still on the force. But I don't think they've spoken to him in years. I can ask around, see if any of them have spoken to him recently."

"Yeah," I said, "I'd really appreciate that." I thanked her profusely, gave her my phone number at the cottage, and hung up.

"Interesting," Laura said. "Too bad she couldn't give you anything."

"She's got to come up with something pretty quick," Savich said, "or it'll be too late."

"Amen to that," Sherlock said, turning to her husband.

I walked to Laura, lightly lifted her chin in my palm, and said, "Forget Cal Tarcher. Forget all those hundreds of other women."

She laughed so hard I had to squeeze it out of her. She still thought I was funny.

AT two o'clock, Laura and I were seated next to Savich and Sherlock in the League's Christian Church on Greenwich Street, just off Fifth Avenue. There was a small park opposite the white brick church, and lots of parking space. The building itself looked strangely unchurchlike, I supposed because it housed so many different religions.

I'd introduced Laura to everyone as a DEA agent I was currently working with, Savich and Sherlock as FBI agents who were here to help us look into things. What things? Who had tried to kill Laura? I'd been as vague as possible as I'd smiled into Alyssum Tarcher's face with that news. It was an I'll-get-you-later smile and I'd swear he knew exactly what I was thinking.

Charlie Duck held the place of honor in the nave of the church, his beautifully carved silver urn set in the center of a circular piece of glass balanced on top of a hand-carved rosewood pyramid at least five feet tall. I couldn't tell how that round piece of smoky glass balanced on that pyramid point.

While we sat waiting for the service to begin, I gave them all a running commentary on the people I'd met.

Paul came in, but he didn't sit down beside me. In fact, he didn't even acknowledge me or Laura. He looked tired, his face gray, harsh shadows scored deeply beneath his eyes. More than that, he looked scared.

I looked around to see that every pew was filled. There were at least a hundred folk, a good two dozen more lining the back of the church. Everyone had left work and come here. All of a sudden conversation stopped.

Alyssum Tarcher, dressed in a black suit that quietly announced English bespoke, strode to the pulpit, which really wasn't a pulpit, but rather a long, thick mahogany board set atop marble pillars. The interior of the church was all like that—a mixture of styles and materials, announcing all sorts of possibilities but nothing specific, like an onion dome or a menorah.

Alyssum Tarcher cleared his throat and raised his head. Sunlight poured through the high windows and flooded over him. The air was perfectly still. There wasn't a sound.

He gave an almost imperceptible nod. Bagpipes sounded, low and raw and savagely beautiful. No one seemed surprised, evidently used to this. The pipes played a wrenchingly sad set of chords, then grew more distant, softer, leaving only echoes.

"Charles Edward Duck," Alyssum Tarcher said in a rolling, powerful voice, "was a man who lived a full and rich life."

I tuned him out, studying Paul's face in profile. What was going on?

"He was a police detective in Chicago until he retired to Edgerton to live with his aging parents, now deceased, some sixteen years ago. We will miss him. He was one of us."

I heard the scrape of bagpipes again, minor chords sliding into one another, then nothing. Alyssum Tarcher, the patriarch, returned to sit in the first row.

Elaine Tarcher rose next. She looked slim and well groomed and rich.

Her dark suit was elegant, somber. She wore pearls. When she spoke, her voice was full and deep with emotion. "I met Charlie Duck his first day in Edgerton, I nearly hit him with my new car. He gave me a big grin and said he wouldn't arrest me this time. He then told me I was as pretty as his wife. Charlie played his guitar for all of us. Good-bye, Charlie."

A dozen townsfolk followed, the first representing the Anglican Church. It was Rob Morrison. He spoke briefly of Charlie's good nature, his acceptance of others, his tolerance.

Miss Geraldine, the leader of the town League, mayor of Edgerton, represented the Jewish religion. She spoke of Charlie's lack of anger toward anyone, his gentleness.

It appeared that everyone had seen Charlie Duck differently.

The final speaker was Mother Marco, ninety-three, who owned the Union 76 station. She was small and frail, and her pink scalp showed through soft, sparse white hair. "I don't represent any religion," she said in a surprisingly strong voice. "Well, maybe you could say I represent old age and the brink of death. I feel older than the rocks on the shore below Edgerton." The old lady grinned out at us all, showing big, very white false teeth. "And I'm proud of it. I knew Charlie Duck better than any of you. He was smart, was Charlie. He knew a bit about everything. He liked finding things out. If he didn't understand something, he dug and dug until he found his answers. Because he was a police detective in Chicago, he didn't have a high opinion of anybody. He wasn't blind about people."

Of all the speakers, I thought that old Mother Marco had hit Charlie right on.

Alyssum Tarcher walked to the wooden pyramid and picked up Charlie's silver urn and held it over his head. "To Charlie," he shouted. Everyone cheered, filed in behind Alyssum Tarcher, and marched out of the church.

"My, oh my," Sherlock said.

"Some show," Savich said.

I felt Laura's fingers close around my hand. "I don't want to go there," she said. "To the cemetery. I don't want to go."

"No, we don't have to. No one will expect us. After all, we are outsiders." I saw Rob Morrison beside Maggie Sheffield, and I thought of Detective Castanga. *Margaret was my wife at one time.*

"Who the hell are you?"

"This is Cotter Tarcher, guys. He's Alyssum's only son."

Cotter dismissed the two women and eyed Savich, his eyes dark and hot. Savich arched a dark eyebrow.

"Here we have the weakest link," I whispered to Laura.

"I asked you a question, buddy. What are you doing here? You don't belong here. Nobody invited you."

"Actually, I did," I said. I nodded toward both Sherlock and Savich, and showed Cotter that I was holding Laura's hand. "They're friends of mine."

Cotter said, "None of you should be here."

Savich smiled, a kick-ass smile that should have alerted Cotter but didn't. Savich knew exactly what he was doing. He'd taken Cotter's measure very quickly. "I enjoyed the performances, sport. Everyone who spoke was very talented. Why didn't you speak?"

Cotter's eyes flamed. He was quickly going beyond anger, to nearly out of control. What had happened to him? Cotter had a hair trigger, but no one was more surprised than I was when Cotter took a swing at Savich. I didn't move; I even felt a bit sorry for Cotter. As for Sherlock, she said, "Oh, no. You idiot," but not in time.

Savich smoothly caught Cotter's wrist and squeezed it back down to his side. Cotter tried a kick but didn't make it. Savich grabbed Cotter's leg just behind his knee and flipped him into the air. He released Cotter's wrist only at the last minute before he landed on his back in a marigold bed, the move smoother than a twelve-year-old scotch.

Sherlock looked down at Cotter, her hands on her hips. "Why are you acting like an adolescent?"

"Get a grip on yourself," Savich said. "Consider growing up."

"None of you is worth a piece of shit. Big federal agents, that's a laugh. You'll never find out anything." Cotter dragged himself out of the flower bed and stomped away.

"That man has real problems," Laura said.

"He's the local sociopath," I said. "So he doesn't think we're going to find out anything, does he?" I watched him speak to Alyssum Tarcher, and the older man shook his head. "When I first met him I thought he was just an immature hothead. But after seeing him perform today, I wonder if he's involved in all of this, his daddy's right hand?"

"His father looks like an aristocrat, a sleek greyhound among a pack of mutts," Sherlock said. "As for Cotter, he looks like a little bulldog."

"I think Cal and Cotter are different," Laura said. "Cal acts weird too, but Mac's never called her a sociopath."

"Hey," I said. "At the very least we know that Cal's got great taste in men."

I saw Alyssum Tarcher look back at me. His face was cold but his eyes were suddenly as hot as his son's.

EIGHTEEN

It was just after five-thirty in the afternoon when Savich and I pulled into the driveway of 12 Liverpool Street. Paul was indeed at home. Actually, both his car and Maggie Sheffield's sheriff's car were side by side in the driveway. We heard them yelling at each other from the front porch and stopped a moment beside a hanging plant that looked a lot happier than I did. We stood quietly outside the front door, listening.

"You little worm," we heard Maggie scream at the top of her lungs. "Don't say or do anything like that again, Paul, or I'll take your head off. Are you nuts? How long has Jilly been gone?"

"What do you know? You don't know anything. You like to play at doing a man's job, but you don't do it well. But as a woman, Maggie, you really suck. Maybe this is the ideal job for you. What are you, a dyke?"

We heard a crash. I sighed, opened the door, walked into the small foyer, and looked to the right, into the living room. There I saw Maggie straddling Paul, who was lying flat on his back in his black-and-white living room. She had him by the neck, his head pressed against the floor.

Savich calmly walked over to her, grabbed her under her arms, and pulled her straight up. She turned on him, fists raised. He held her up by her armpits and said in that deep, smooth voice of his, "Not smart. Don't do it."

"Enough, both of you," I said, and gave Paul a hand up. "Now, what's this all about? We could hear you screaming at each other from the front porch."

"He's a stupid prick," Maggie said. "Let me down, you jock. I'm the sheriff. I'll arrest you."

"I'm not a jock, ma'am. I'm a Special Agent. Dillon Savich, FBI."

"Oh," she said, and immediately went still. "I'm sorry. You're here for Mac, aren't you? I saw you at Charlie Duck's funeral but I was late and didn't have a chance to meet you."

"That's right. Can I put you down now?"

"Please do. I won't hurt that little wimp." She looked over at Paul like she wanted to spit on him.

"Paul," I said, "go sit down. We need to talk. Maggie, you sit over in that chair. Either of you makes a move toward the other and Savich or I will flatten you. Well, Savich will for sure. My ribs are a bit on the sore side. Got it?"

"I'm the sheriff," Maggie said, tucking her blouse back in. "I'll do whatever I want to."

"Fine," Savich said. "That's the spirit. What we'd really like is for you to sit down and tell us if you've heard anything about Mac's sister."

"Not a blessed thing," Maggie said, looking over at Paul. "I even spoke to Minton this morning, not something I was crazy about doing, but he didn't have anything new, just sputtered and whined about not knowing what you and Ms. Scott are up to. I told him that if it had been any of his business, you would have told him." She smiled. "He called me a bitch. Made my day. I'm leaving now. If I stay in the room any longer with this jackass, I'll lose it. Call me if you find out anything, Mac." She nodded. "Agent Savich, thank you for your generous help. I'm sure you'll let me know if you need anything."

"Wait a minute, Maggie, I'll walk you out," I said.

"He's a pathetic jerk," Maggie said in my direction as we walked out of the house. "What did he say this time to make you blow up?"

"You won't believe it, Mac. He tried to get in my pants. Well, to get under my uniform so he could find my pants. The little jerk. It took me a while to get him off me, so I could beat the crap out of him."

"Why would he do that?"

"God knows. I've always thought he was weird."

"Okay, Maggie. We'll keep in touch."

I waited until she drove off, waving at me. When I came back into the living room, Savich was waiting. "All right, Paul," he said as I came in, "tell us about the drug you've developed."

"Yes. We're real interested in that, Paul."

Paul sat there, staring down at his hands that were clasped between his legs. "I don't have a damned thing to tell either of you. Go away."

"No, we're not going anywhere until you tell us about it."

Paul looked as if he wanted to fold in on himself. Again, I thought he looked scared. "Talk," I said.

He walked around the room a couple of times, pausing in front of one of the stark modern paintings. We waited until finally he turned back to us and said, "It's all experimental, Mac. It's doubtful anything will come of it, truth be told. You know the odds against developing successful drugs these days. The business of pharmaceutical research is astronomically expensive, demands incredible numbers of man-hours and highly specialized computer programs. And then there's the FDA to contend with."

He paused a moment and pulled at a loose thread on his tweed jacket. "I wanted to continue along a certain line of research. The people at VioTech deemed it too expensive to continue the research, not enough projected payback even if the drug could be perfected, and so they canceled it. They wanted Jilly and me to go into AIDS research. Our interests just don't lie there. When Alyssum Tarcher offered to finance us, we took him up on it."

"What exactly is the drug, Paul?" I asked.

"It's a memory drug, nothing more than that."

"I don't know what you mean by a memory drug," Savich said. "We know so little about the mind, about how memory even works. What does it do to the memory?"

"It's meant to take away the physical responses to bad memories when they surface. You see, the drug seems to be activated when there are sudden physical manifestations of distress—heightened adrenaline levels, rapid heartbeat, dilated pupils—things like that. Its purpose is to shut down the power of the memory by reducing the physical distress and substituting a sense of well-being.

"The benefits might be enormous in treating someone who has lived through something terrible, for example, soldiers surviving battles, or physical or sexual abuse as a child. Once the emotional baggage of the memory is dissipated, so is its physiological power."

I sat forward on the sofa, my hands clasped between my knees. Finally he was talking. I had to keep him going. "The physical reactions you're describing, Paul, aren't only prompted by a bad memory. They can happen with a whole lot of things, like fear, excitement, tension."

"True enough, but you see, the drug is meant to be given in a controlled setting in which the memory is repeatedly triggered. So the drug is focused."

"It sounds incredible," Savich said slowly. "But how can you continue research by yourself, in a home laboratory?"

"I was very close to success when I left VioTech, although none of the decision makers at VioTech agreed. It's just a matter of fine-tuning some of the drug's side chains."

"Would the drug be addictive?" I asked.

"Oh no," Paul said, shaking his head. "Oh no."

"What about military uses?" Savich asked. "After all, if you can lessen all the physical manifestations of distress, why, then you could give your soldiers a shot and produce a battalion of heroes."

"No, I won't ever have anything to do with the military."

Paul looked incredibly tired, his voice flat, as if he simply didn't care about anything anymore.

"When I asked you about this before," I said, "you laughed it off as a fountain of youth drug. This is something else entirely."

"It doesn't matter. None of this has anything to do with Jilly's disappearance. It doesn't have anything to do with anything at all. Go away, Mac. I don't want to talk to either of you anymore. Please leave now."

"Oh?" I asked, an eyebrow up. "You merely want to attack women who happen to wander into your house?"

"Maggie told you about it all wrong. She was coming on to me and when I decided to do something about it, she turned on me. A man gets horny, you know that. Maggie's nothing but a tease, Mac."

"Tell me where Jilly is, Paul."

"I don't know. If I did, I'd be with her."

"Look, Paul," I continued after a moment, "it's time to drop the pretense. Laura told me she's DEA, that she was undercover. They know about this drug. They know about Molinas. There were then two attempts on Laura's life after Jilly disappeared. Who ordered them, Paul? You? Tarcher?

This arch criminal, Del Cabrizo? Tell us how Tarcher's involved. Tell us about John Molinas."

"I don't have to talk to you, and I want you to go away, both of you." With those words, Paul got up and walked out of the living room.

I went after him. When he heard me coming, he broke into a run, took the stairs three at a time. By the time I caught up to him, he was locked in his laboratory. This was nuts. It was a steel-reinforced door. I didn't have a prayer of breaking it open. I told him to let me in, pleaded with him to tell me what was going on before they came in with a search warrant, but he remained completely silent.

After ten minutes, I felt Savich touch my arm. "Let's go," he said. "We need to regroup. Maybe it's time for Laura to call her boss at the DEA and let them take over. A search warrant doesn't sound like such a bad idea. They can haul both him and Tarcher in and interrogate them big time. I'm tired. That late flight is catching up with me."

"Maybe you and Sherlock can rest a little when we get back to the cottage."

NINETEEN

Laura and I held hands while we watched the sun sink into the ocean. The evening was mild with only a light breeze coming off the ocean. We walked along the cliffs, stopping every couple of steps to talk or kiss.

"You're right," she said, her arms clasped tightly around my back.

"About what this time?" I kissed her silly before she managed to pull back.

"We've talked to almost everyone today. You baited Tarcher. You went after Paul and he's locked himself up. It's hard to know how to make any more progress. Unless you've got a better idea, maybe it's time to call my boss and let the DEA come on out and kick butt."

Savich agreed with her. I agreed with her. But what hit me full in the gut in that moment was that I had met Laura less than a week before. Yet I knew she was honorable and, I'd wager, as loyal as a tick. After less than a week, I knew I didn't want to let her get away from me.

I couldn't stop looking at her. She was wearing Nike running shoes, tight jeans, and a long, loose white shirt. She'd pulled up her long hair and fastened it with a banana clip. She wore a bit of coral lipstick and no other makeup. I'd nearly kissed all of it off. I looked at her mouth and decided it was my duty to get the rest of it. I closed my hand over her forearm and pulled her to a stop. We looked out over the ocean, following the flight of several seagulls that were cruising for dinner in the water below. It was quiet and peaceful, tastes of salt blowing in the wind.

"Let's sit down," I said. We found a trio of rocks leaning into one another, back about fifteen feet from the cliffs.

"Talk to me," I said.

"You want me to tell you how sexy you look?"

"Yeah, but it can wait a minute. Tell me about yourself, Laura."

"Nothing wild in my youth, Mac. Actually, I had a pretty normal life growing up in Tacoma, Washington. My mom and dad were close to me and my older brother.

"I played the clarinet growing up. I had great technique but my tone wasn't very good. I could never be first chair because of that."

"You couldn't play those sweet solos, huh?"

"Only once in junior high. I was a pretty sight, my mom said, but my clarinet wasn't a pretty sound. I went to Boston College, dropped the clarinet—no loss to the music world—and got a degree in psychology. I always knew I wanted to be a cop. I love my job, Mac. My older brother, Alan, is a homicide detective in Seattle. My dad was a cop. He's dead now. My mom lives near my brother and his family in Seattle."

I noticed how the wind, stiffer now than just five minutes before, lifted some stray hair and blew it across her face. I watched the fading daylight shadow-play across her face.

In that instant, a bullet struck the rock not an inch from her hand, spewing out sharp shards. She looked at me blankly as I grabbed her and hurled her to the ground, rolling back behind those rocks. Not much cover, but it was all we had.

Two more shots rang out, one striking the rocky ground and flinging out clumps of dirt and shards of stone, and the other probably high and wide. I grabbed Laura's head and flattened her face against the ground. I had all of her covered with my body, I hoped.

I leaned close to her ear. "We're about twenty feet from the cottage and there's not even a stump for cover."

There was another shot, this one thudding solidly into the ground beside us. I pulled her back farther under me.

I looked back at the cottage, beyond that huge expanse of naked ground, and saw the front door slowly open. "Sherlock, Savich," I shouted. "Keep inside. Call the cops."

I saw a good half-dozen bullets slam into the cottage. Those shots came from my right, near the cliff. I squirmed around, pulled my SIG Sauer, rose up on my elbow, and fired off six rounds in that direction. I heard a yell.

I smiled. "Maybe I got one of the bastards. Now they know we're armed, they won't take the chance of rushing us. They might have heard me yell for Sherlock and Savich to call for the backup. Hold tight, Laura. Think of me as your Kevlar vest."

Her face was covered with dirt. She spit some out. "That was close. This is incredible, Mac. Who are these people coming after federal agents? What good does this do them?"

I was lying only half on top of her now. Three more shots sounded, these toward the cottage. I wasn't surprised to hear return fire from the cottage, fast, an entire clip in a matter of seconds. I knew I wasn't mistaken— there was a shout of pain. Sherlock or Savich had hit one of them. How many were there?

There was silence now. Even the seagulls were quiet. Laura began to squirm away. "No," I said, grabbing her shoulder. "Don't move, not yet. Wait a few more minutes."

I yelled, "Savich, did you get through?"

He yelled back, "The cops should be here in three minutes, no more." But there was something about his voice I didn't like, something that didn't sound right.

"Those guys must have thought they'd died and gone to heaven when you and I came trooping out here."

I looked up at the sky. We had another fifteen minutes of daylight. Laura and I had three rocks for cover. A piece of cake.

She twisted about to get more comfortable, lying fully beneath me now, and said, "How many are there?"

"I don't know. At least three. Two of them may be hit. Now we wait for Sherlock and Savich. It shouldn't be long."

We waited stiff and silent for two more minutes. Laura spit out some more dirt.

The door to the cottage opened. I heard Savich yell, "Come on in, Mac. Run!"

We ran hunkered over, zigzagging over the ground as we'd been trained to do, Sherlock and Savich covering us. They fired off another clip each, fanning the area behind us. There were three or four stray shots that didn't come near us, several more that struck the cottage, then silence again.

I literally threw Laura through the door, turned and fired as Sherlock and Savich eased back into the cottage. I slammed the door, crouched to the floor, and turned to see both women laughing.

"Well done, you two," Laura said, her arms around Sherlock. "You really saved our hides."

Well, I thought, staring at the women, everyone reacts differently to being shot at. I checked out the other narrow window that looked toward the cliffs. Nothing. I pulled the curtain tightly over the window. Savich nodded. "All clear from here." He was staring from his wife to Laura. Laura's face was dirty, her hair hanging in tangles. Sherlock was grinning at her like a loon.

"You've got a clot of dirt in your ear," Sherlock said and picked it out.

"So who did you call, Savich?" I said.

He pulled the curtain back into place. "They cut the phone lines, Mac. It's just us in this little box of Cracker Jacks. Our cell phones don't work here."

"Yeah, I tried mine earlier. Nothing," I said. "These guys are good." I got to my feet and went into the kitchen to check the back of the house. I brought the two beers left in the refrigerator back into the living room. I looked from Laura to Sherlock, knew there was no hope for it, and pulled a quarter out of my pocket. "Call it in the air, Sherlock," I said.

So much for fairness. They started on the beers without the slightest guilt.

"They sure seem committed," Savich said, looking up from cleaning his gun by the window. "They can't shoot worth spit, but they're very serious about this."

"Please tell me our rental car has a cell phone, Dillon," Sherlock said.

"I'd tell you so if it were true," Savich said. "It won't work here anyway."

"This is very depressing," Sherlock said. "I wish I hadn't finished my beer off so fast."

I checked the dead bolt again and shifted the chair more firmly beneath the knob. "When it's dark we've got to try to get out of here."

"It's dark enough," Laura said. "We'll all go right now. Let's try to make it to your car, Mac. We can get the hell out of Dodge." I saw she was chewing on her bottom lip, looking toward Savich, who'd been silent. He said finally, "I agree. It's been nearly a half hour that we haven't heard a thing. If they wanted to kill us, they'd still be shooting. Yeah, why not try to get out of here?"

I opened the front door very quietly. I waited, then eased outside, looking toward the cliffs, sweeping my SIG Sauer slowly around in a wide arc. There was a big moon floating over the water, but roiling dark tattered clouds kept sliding in front of it. The night was blessedly dark. I waited until the moon was covered, then ran low to the Taurus, Savich, Sherlock, and Laura on my heels.

Both women were in, down on the floor of the backseat, Savich in the passenger seat as I turned the key in the ignition. Nothing. I tried again, then stopped. "Somebody disabled the car," I said.

"They must have been very quiet about it," Savich said. "Let's get back inside. I'll cover you."

No one tried to shoot us on our mad run back.

Once the four of us were back inside the cottage, the front door closed and locked, Savich said, "This is interesting. We're in America and we're as effectively cut off from help as you were, Mac, in North Africa." I remembered that day when I thought my ticket was punched. There'd been help there though.

Laura shook her head, her face drawn. "This should have been just me. It doesn't matter that you're cops too, this wasn't your assignment. You're innocent bystanders. I'm sorry you got tossed into the middle."

"I made the decision with you," I said. "It's Sherlock and Savich who are the innocent bystanders."

"Shove it, Mac," Savich said.

"Coffee," Sherlock said. "We might as well start making some. We're going to have to wait for the sheriff. You do think she's coming to check on us, don't you?"

"I don't think they're going to let us sit here and snooze all night, Sherlock," Savich said. "They're going to come for us."

"Interesting how they got off at least a dozen shots at us, Laura, and missed. Don't you think that's strange?"

"They don't want us dead for some reason?" Savich said, a dark eyebrow hoisted up an inch.

"Maybe not," I said.

In the next instant, all three windows across the front of the cottage imploded, spewing in shattered glass, tattered bits of curtains, and heavy metal canisters that struck the floor and rolled. They made loud popping noises and gushed out smoke. The smoke was something caustic, bitter, something that burned the very air, something that burned the breath in your mouth.

There was no time. I looked at Laura, who was staring down at one of those small egg-shaped gray cylinders that was releasing a steady stream of the pale blue smoke not six feet away from her.

"It's ice acid," she said. "I'm sorry, guys. I'm very, very sorry."

I wanted to tell her it wasn't her fault. I opened my mouth, inhaled some of the ice acid, and thought my tongue would burn off. I wanted to yell with the pain, but my throat was burned closed. I was shutting down and it was the strangest feeling. I was beginning to feel cold, my mouth was numb, my teeth chattering. That's why they called it ice acid. It did that to you before it laid you flat.

Before I closed my eyes, I saw Savich holding Sherlock tightly against him, his head against the top of hers. Laura was on her side on the floor, her legs drawn up. She wasn't moving. I tried to get to her. Then I couldn't see her. My eyes were freezing shut, tears seeping out, ice cold on my cheeks. I wanted to tell Savich that we had to get out of here.

Then I didn't feel a thing.

TWENTY

I knew I was awake because I heard myself moaning. But there wasn't any pain. Laura was calling my name, over and over. "Mac, don't do this. Please, please, Mac, stop. Wake up!"

I opened my eyes and stared down into Laura's face. "Oh God, you're awake. Mac, you've got to stop."

For a moment I didn't know what she was talking about. Stop what? "Mac, please, get away. Stop it, Mac."

No, I wasn't feeling any pain, but what I was feeling was harsh and real. It was shattering me. I didn't understand it.

"Mac, wake up!"

I was on top of her. She was naked and I was naked as well and between her legs. I was poised to come into her. I felt such overwhelming lust, I didn't think I could stop.

"Laura, my God, Laura."

"Mac, stop!"

"Oh, God, I don't think I can." I was panting, trying to slow the movement of my body. The urge to come into her was killing me. I locked my muscles and yelled. I wasn't going to rape her. I wasn't. The need to do just that was beyond what I could understand. It was pushing me, driving me, and I yelled again, trying to get hold, to get my mind, my will, back. I could feel her flesh against me and I didn't think I could hold back.

I looked down at her, saw she was crying, tears rolling down her cheeks.

"NO!" I yelled, my head thrown back.

I jerked myself off her, falling beside her on the wooden floor. I lay there panting, cursing, feeling the urge to come inside her pounding through my body.

"Mac."

Her voice seemed a long way away, but I knew she was lying beside me. "Are you all right?"

There wasn't any more fear in her voice, just relief. I turned onto my side to face her. She was looking at me, and she was smiling. It was then I saw that her hands were tied over her head, her legs open and tied at the ankles. She was helpless. I wasn't. I wasn't quite naked. I still had on my running shoes and shirt.

I took deep breaths, over and over, kept sucking in air and blowing out, trying desperately to clear my mind.

I reached out my hand to touch her, then pulled it back. I wasn't strong enough yet.

Tears were still on her cheeks. I couldn't bear it. I touched her then, wiping the tears away with my fingers. "I'm so sorry, Laura. What happened?"

"They drugged us."

I made the mistake of looking down her body. I gritted my teeth and rolled away. I was still hard. I jumped to my feet, grabbed my clothes off the floor, and quickly pulled my shorts and pants on.

I felt more normal now that I was dressed. Fight it, I said to myself over and over. Just fight it.

I came down on my knees beside her. Her legs were wide apart, her ankles tied to small rings fastened in the floor.

"I'm sorry," I said. "I didn't realize, didn't know—"

"You weren't the one who tied me down, Mac. I'm all right. You managed to stop."

My hands were shaking. It took awhile for me to untie the knots around her wrists and ankles. Slowly, she pulled her legs together and sat up. She was rubbing her wrists. "Thank you, Mac."

"Where are your clothes?"

"I don't know."

I stripped off my shirt and handed it to her. As I watched her pull it on and fasten the buttons, my mind started to feel heavy and dull. The urge to have her was receding now. I could control it.

She rose and walked to the narrow bed in the corner of the small room we were in. My shirt came down to her thighs. She sat on the side of the bed, rubbed her wrists.

I sat beside her. I wasn't about to touch her. I was afraid that if I did, I'd lose it again. "Tell me what happened. Where are we?"

"I couldn't catch what they were saying. You were awake but still very groggy. I watched them inject you." She shuddered.

I pulled her against me, holding her tightly. "We beat them," I said as I rubbed her back, "we're both all right."

She said against my shoulder, "I think it was all a game to them. They wanted to have some fun. They took my clothes and tied me down. Then they set you on me like a stallion over a mare. They put your face between my legs. When they pulled you back, they were laughing. Then one of the men, probably the leader, said something and they left us alone." She was silent again. I kissed her hair, kept rubbing her back. "It's all right," I said.

"Only because you came out of it enough to see what you were doing. I didn't think you'd be able to stop, Mac, it was awful."

She'd been tied down, naked, helpless. I closed my eyes a moment against the enormity of it. If I hadn't been able to stop myself, then— "They wanted me to rape you?"

"Apparently. Funny thing, knowing it was you but that you weren't really there made it worse. You weren't my Mac. You were a stranger who didn't care who I was. You had my scent, knew I was female, and that was enough. That drug was in control."

"The drug," I said slowly. "Remember you told me the drug had some effect on sex?"

"Yes. This had to be it, what we've been looking for. They used it on you to see what it would do to you."

I wanted to kill them. They'd treated us like animals. We'd been used for sport.

"They probably gave you a lot more than one would inject for a sex high."

"That figures. I didn't really feel like I was having the time of my life."

I felt her smile against my shoulder. I squeezed her. "Did they hurt you?"

"Not that I can tell. I don't know how long we've been out. But they brought me out of it with smelling salts. They wanted me fully awake when they set you on me. Mac, I couldn't do anything and you were gone. Then I saw you come back, just a bit, and that's when I talked to you until finally you got control back."

"Do you know where we are?"

"No. I've only been clearheaded for about an hour. It's night, I do know that much. My watch says it's a bit after ten."

There were no windows in the small room. It was nearly square, not more than twelve by twelve. There was one single bed, an ancient rag rug beside it, and a toilet and sink in the far corner.

"It was about eight at night when they threw the ice acid into the cottage," I said.

"So how much time has passed? Hours? A day? I don't know, Mac. But I'll tell you one thing. Right now if I had my gun, I swear I'd blow off the head of the first man who came through the door. I can't believe what they did. And they laughed about it."

"How many?"

"There were three men, then the man I think was their leader came in and made them leave." She paused a moment, then added, "They were all speaking Spanish. I doubt we're still in Oregon."

"Mexico, maybe," I said.

"Could be," she agreed. "Or Colombia. Remember the DEA agent who was tortured and murdered in Mexico some years ago? And nothing at all happened?"

I held her away from me. "Listen up, Laura. Don't think like that. It does no good. You haven't seen Sherlock or Savich?"

She shook her head. "When I woke up, I was alone. When they brought me here to this room, it was empty. I don't know where they were keeping you, but two of the men half-dragged you in here. It was like you were in a stupor. They tossed you on that bed and injected you. Five minutes later they put you on me. They're animals."

"I wonder what would have happened if I hadn't gotten control? The way I felt, I would have kept at it until I was dead or the drug finally wore off. Maybe that's what they wanted to see. I wonder if they were laying bets."

She pulled back. "But you stopped yourself, Mac."

I kissed her mouth. I smoothed back her hair, lightly ran my thumb over her eyebrows. "I finally realized it was you. I love you, Laura. I couldn't have hurt you."

"Well then, let's take care of this mess and then get married. Can we do that, Mac?"

I couldn't believe it had taken me until I was twenty-nine years old to find this woman. I kissed the tip of her nose. "In exactly that order."

I looked over to the small rings screwed into the wooden floor. Had they done this before? Brought in some women and taken turns, enjoying the hell out of it? The drug was something. I was still hard.

I looked at Laura again. Her hair was curtaining her face, hanging long and loose, real shiny. I couldn't believe it. "They combed your hair?"

"Yes," she said, not looking at me. "More than that even. They bathed me, washed my hair, and sprayed some perfume on me. They let two women do this while they watched. Neither of the women spoke any English. Then they brought me to this room. I got the feeling they've done this before with other women."

I pulled her close again, and this time I really smelled the musk on her. I felt a wave of lust. It wasn't overpowering, but I didn't want to test myself. "I'm thirsty," I said. Having a bit of distance between us made it easier. I walked to the sink. It was as ancient as the rug by the bed, cracked and rusted. But the water was cool enough and clear. I washed my face. Laura's scent was gone. The heavy feeling in my brain was easing. I could think more than one thought at a time now, glean more than one impression. But my only thought was that I wanted to kill them. I couldn't seem to get beyond that and I knew I had to. We had to get out of here.

Laura stood up. "Did you walk away because the drug hit you again?"

"Yeah, but it's better now. Don't worry about me." Then I shook my head and said, "No, forget that. If I start looking at you funny, or talking funny, anything that isn't right, you get away from me, fast. If you can't, knock me silly. Protect yourself. All right?"

She studied my face for a long time, then nodded. When she walked toward me, I took an outside route back to the bed. I said while she was cupping water in her hands, "We've got to figure out how to get out of this bloody room."

We both looked at the one door, no windows.

"Do you think they'll feed us?" I was starving, my stomach nearly beyond the growling stage, but that wasn't the point. "If they bring us food, we'll have a chance to get out of here."

They fed us, not ten minutes later. The door simply unlocked, very quickly, and a young boy carrying two big plates in his skinny arms walked in. Behind him stood another man holding an AK-47 at the ready. He didn't come into the room, just stood there in the doorway, aiming his weapon at my belly, watchful and ready.

I don't even think I heard them close and lock the door. My eyes were on the food. There were stacks of soft tortillas and beans, strips of beef, and thick pepper-and-onion-filled potatoes. I was so hungry it tasted as good as anything I'd ever eaten.

They left a large pitcher of cold water. We drank the whole thing since the peppers were hotter than pitch. There wasn't a bit of food left. Laura looked down at the empty plates and said, "I hope we don't get sick from stuffing ourselves."

"Not a pretty thought," I said, remembering the Montezuma's revenge that had me dehydrated and ten pounds lighter a couple of years before when I'd been fishing off Cozumel. "One guy with an AK-47. I think we should move over by the door so that if he comes alone again, we'll have a chance at the guy with the gun."

Laura nodded. "There's only this one skinny pillow and the blanket. I'll mold them under the sheet. Maybe for an instant they'll think we're on the bed, asleep."

We did that and stood back to look at our handiwork. "Not very good," I said, "but hopefully it'll work. Which side of the door would you like?"

I ended up on the side of the lock, Laura behind the door. She'd taken off the heavy porcelain toilet lid and held it against her chest.

"They must know that we won't be sitting here idle," she said. "They'll expect us to try something. It's even possible that they're watching us even now."

I'd thought the same thing. I got up and went over that small room, inch by inch. I didn't see anything that remotely resembled a camera lens or a peephole. I sat back down. "I sure hope that Sherlock and Savich are all right."

"Maybe Sherlock's sitting by the door as we speak, a toilet lid hugged to her chest."

We waited. For a very long time. We slept. We awoke early the next morning. My watch read about 6:30 A.M.

We took turns using the toilet and washing up. At exactly seven o'clock, we heard them coming.

TWENTY-ONE

A key turned in the lock. The door slowly opened. But no one said a word, no one moved in. A canister of gas rolled through the doorway. I jumped to my feet, grabbed the thing up, and threw it in the toilet. I flushed it. Smoke gushed out of the bowl. I slammed down the toilet seat. Thankfully it contained most of the smoke. I'd inhaled only a bit. I didn't feel a thing.

I heard a man laugh. I turned to look at the two men who stood watching me from the doorway.

"*¡Así se hace!*" one of them said. He had a deep bass voice. He was a short, wiry, dark man, dressed in army fatigues, like his partner. He said in strongly accented English this time, "*Sí*, that was well done. We knew you would be waiting for us. And now you have finished. Move." He waved the AK-47 toward me. "The woman is still sleeping? You wore her out, eh?"

I took a step, watching the men. The man with the bass voice raised his weapon, but he didn't say anything more because Laura rose up, whipped around the side of the door, and smashed him in the face with the porcelain toilet lid.

The other man leaped through the doorway, his eyes on Laura, his AK-47 up, ready to fire.

I yelled and ran straight at him. He whipped the gun around, only to moan and fall hard to the floor when Laura hit him hard on his temple with the toilet lid.

The first man tried to struggle up. Laura calmly leaned over and smashed him hard again. Then she kicked both of them hard in the ribs.

"Close the door quick," I said. I grabbed the larger man under his arms and began dragging him inside the room. Laura grabbed the other guy.

I picked up one of the AK-47s and looked out the door. There was a long narrow corridor on either side of the room. No one else was in sight.

"We need their clothes," I said.

Five minutes later, we were buttoning our camouflage pants and lacing up our combat boots. Laura had ripped the sleeves off my white shirt to stuff in the toes of her boots. She stamped her feet a couple of times and smiled at me. "Good fit now. I'm glad one of the men was bigger. The fatigues nearly fit you."

It took us longer to tie up the men. Laura stripped them both to their skin and tied one of each of their legs to the rings in the floor where she'd been shackled. She rose and dusted her hands and looked at me.

"Okay, let's get out of here. Savich and Sherlock have got to be somewhere close by."

We locked the door and turned to the left, for no other reason than I am left-handed and that was the way I'd turned first. We each had a full magazine in the AK-47s and another magazine from each man's belt.

I was armed and dangerous, feeling more pissed than prudent. Laura had tucked her hair up beneath the army camouflage cap. From a distance of ten feet, I guess she could pass for a man for at least a few seconds.

"The stupid goons," she whispered, "dressed up like army militia."

"Don't complain. It might help us if we get out of here." My boots were hurting my feet already. I was going to get blisters.

We heard booted feet tramping toward us. There was a door on our right, the third one along this side of the corridor. I opened it as quietly as I could and we slipped inside. We listened. Then we heard a noise, just the clearing of a throat.

Both of us whipped around to see an old man sitting at a small table in the corner, tucked away in shadows, beneath a narrow, high window, eating a bowl of soup. He was bald and his face was scored with lines, the color of brown leather. He had a long dirty-gray beard. He was wearing an old dark brown wool robe, a rope tied around his waist.

He was staring at us, a tortilla halfway to his mouth. I whispered in Spanish for him not to move, "*Quédate*, Father. Don't even twitch your beard."

I looked up at Laura. She was standing pressed to the door, still listening, her fingers pressed against her lips for quiet. The boots marched by. No one stopped. The priest didn't move.

"Who are you?" he asked me in Spanish in a deep and ancient voice.

"We're American federal agents. They drugged us and brought us here as prisoners. They're going to kill us if they get ahold of us again. We're trying to get away. Are you a prisoner too, Father?"

He shook his head. "No, I come to the compound once a week to minister to all the people. When I arrive, one of the women gives me breakfast." His words rolled into one another, nearly slurring. It was hard for me to understand him. But I understood enough.

"What day is it?"

He had to repeat it twice before I understood. Thursday. We'd lost a day.

"Where are we, Father?"

He looked at me like I'd lost my mind. "You're outside of Dos Brazos."

More boots were marching this way. They were slowing. We were trapped. The one narrow window wouldn't let a skinny kid through it. The old man looked at us, then said slowly, "There's no more time. Both of you, get under the bed, quickly. I will deal with the men."

If he betrayed us, we had less of a chance pinned under the narrow sagging bed in the far corner. We had no choice. Laura and I scooted under it. At least the stringy blanket fell over the bed nearly to the floor. We fit, barely. I was nearly lying on the AK-47, Laura pressed against my back, her weapon pressed against my spine.

The door opened, no knock. I saw at least three pairs of boots. I heard a man with a shrill voice say in Spanish, "Father, have you been here long?"

"*Sí*. I am still eating my breakfast."

"You haven't heard anything, no people, no running?"

"Just you, *señor*, and your men. *¿Qué haces?* What is the matter? Is there a fire?"

"Oh no, nothing like that. Some people—a man and a woman—we were holding them for the *policía*. They've gotten away. Don't worry, Father. We'll find them."

The priest didn't say anything. Was he giving them a sign? No. The men turned and marched back out the door. Then, suddenly, one of them said, "Father Orlando, the woman Hestia told me that her son is in great pain. She wants you to see him now. Can you come? My men will escort you to keep you safe from the foreign man and woman."

"I will come," said the priest. He was wearing old Birkenstock sandals, no socks. His feet were as worn and scarred as a tree trunk.

The door finally closed. We slowly moved out from under the bed.

"That was close," Laura said, wiping herself down. I stared toward the small table. There were three soft tortillas lying there. I was still hungry. I grabbed them up, rolled them, gave Laura a big bite, and stuffed the rest in my mouth.

"I'm starting to feel human again."

TWENTY-TWO

We were in some sort of old wooden barracks that turned and twisted about like a rabbit warren. The first two rooms we looked into were empty, but in the third one there was a man sleeping in a lower bunk, his back to us. He didn't stir. We quietly closed the door and kept looking. Savich and Sherlock had to be in one of these rooms.

We eased out into the corridor again. We came to a corner, and I motioned Laura to stay back while I went down on my haunches and took a quick look. I nearly lost my tortillas I was so startled. Not fifteen feet from me were at least ten men of all ages, dressed in fatigues and combat boots, all at stiff attention, their weapons held against their shoulders, their backs to me. They were silent, not a single twitch. I couldn't even hear them breathe.

An older man, in his early fifties, stood in front of them. He wore civilian clothes, a white linen shirt open at the neck, tan slacks, and Italian loafers. He was perfectly bald. It looked like he shaved his head for effect. He was a large man, nearly as tall as me, and solid with muscle. He was carrying a white lab coat over his arm. He was speaking quickly in Spanish. I understood most of it. I slowly eased back as he said, ". . . we must find the man and the woman. They are dangerous American agents here to destroy us. If you see them, you must not kill them. That is forbidden."

I whispered to Laura, "A dozen soldiers ahead. The man who called the others off us, was he really big, muscular, and bald?"

"No, it was another man."

"This one seems to be the boss. He's giving them orders about us. He doesn't want us killed. I suppose that's good news. Oh yeah, he's a sharp dresser."

"Let's get out of here." We came quickly to the other end of the long corridor, to a big double door. I tried the shiny brass doorknob.

It turned easily and silently. I went in low and swung around, fanning the room with my weapon. It was a very fancy office at first sight, with lots of gold-trimmed antique furnishings and several incredible Persian carpets. It wasn't much of an office. There wasn't a telephone or a fax or a computer, nothing to use to get help.

We eased inside and closed the door. I turned the lock. "*El jefe's* office," I said. "The boss of this place. Probably it's the bald guy out there with the soldiers. I wonder who he is. I don't even see a phone. They must communicate by radio."

Laura was already behind the huge Louis XIV desk, going through the papers. Behind her was a large glass window looking out over a small walled-in, English-type garden filled with tropical flowers and plants. "It's all in Spanish and I can't read it," she said. "Quick, come here, Mac."

Someone tried to turn the handle on the door.

I heard shouts. More pounding. A gun butt smashed against one of the doors, then another. The expensive wood splintered.

No time. I prayed and grabbed Laura's left hand. We took a running start, crossed our arms in front of our faces, and crashed through the huge glass window behind the Louis XIV desk.

We thankfully landed on grass, rolled, and came up instantly into a run. We were in a private flower garden, perfectly manicured and maintained, and I, who loved flowers, couldn't care less.

Ain't nothing easy, I thought, as I smashed the butt of my weapon against a small gate in the far corner of the garden. The aging wood splintered and fell outward. We were out of the compound, only to stop cold. There was absolutely nothing in front of us except jungle and a three- or four-foot-wide moat of sorts, probably to keep the jungle from encroaching into the compound every few days. It was filled with brackish water that looked like it could kill anything that even got close to it.

I took her hand again, and we jumped the moat. We heard shouting behind us. Guns were fired over our heads. Good, they hadn't forgotten *el jefe* had told them to keep us alive.

We ran into a dense green wall of vegetation that blocked out the sun within a couple of minutes. It was going to be a race, us against a dozen men native to this place.

I'd never been in a jungle before. The floor wasn't a thicket of plants and trees and bushes as I'd expected. We didn't need a machete like the movies I'd seen had portrayed. It was nearly bare, only a single layer of leaves covering the ground. But that single layer was rotten. Everything around us was alive and green or rotting.

It got darker as we ran, the green over our heads forming an opaque canopy. Only the thinnest slivers of sunlight managed to get through. No wonder everything rotted so quickly—there was no sunlight to dry anything out. People would rot too, I thought, and there were a lot of creatures to help them. This was not a good place to be.

We ran another twenty feet into the jungle and came to a dead stop. We couldn't go farther without a machete after all. It was impossible to pull away the branches and vines that were in front of us, an impenetrable wall of green. I'd never imagined anything like this. We stopped and listened. For a few moments, we didn't hear anything, then I heard a man shout. It was in very fast Spanish and I couldn't make it out. I heard men crashing through the dense foliage, not paying any attention to where they stepped, just coming toward us.

"It's time to try to hide," I said. We went exactly ten big steps to the right, careful not to leave any signs of our tracks to this spot, and hunkered down behind a tree. I looked up and saw a frog staring me right in the eye. At least this little guy wouldn't try to eat us. He looked like he belonged on that old Bud commercial.

We were ill equipped, just our clothes and guns. There was no way we could survive for any time at all in this alien place. I didn't want to think about it. I had no intention of staying here any longer than necessary.

The men were close now, not more than twenty feet away from us. Two of them were arguing about which direction to take. Ants were crawling over my feet. Laura swatted the back of her hand. A coral snake, its beautiful bright bands announcing that it could kill you fast, slithered by not six feet from Laura's foot. I wrapped my arm around her shoulders.

I realized I was so hot my blood seemed to swell in my veins. Sweat pooled under my arms and at the small of my back. I hated the heat. Why couldn't drug runners deal out of Canada? A lovely little insect the size of a fifty-cent piece dropped from a branch above my head onto my forearm. It took a good-sized bite out of me, then lightly dropped to the ground where it scurried off to hide beneath a leaf.

Finally, the men fanned out, several coming our way. It made sense. I would have done the same thing. I listened carefully to every boot crunch.

Only two men were coming our way. I raised two fingers to Laura and she nodded, readying herself.

I pointed to the guns and shook my head. She nodded again. A minute later they were not a foot from us, sweeping their guns around, swearing at all the bugs, all the dripping leaves overhead, all in Spanish. If they found us, I knew we had to be fast and quiet as the dead. One of the men yelped. Maybe the insect that had just bitten off half my forearm had gotten him.

Then one of the men looked down and we stared at each other. Without a sound, I reared up and smashed the butt of the AK-47 under his jaw. It cracked real loud, but he only let out a whiff of a yell before he fell.

Laura moved fast. She butted the other man in his gut, then raised her weapon and slammed it down against his temple.

We stood over the two men, trying to control our breathing.

We heard men calling to one another. They apparently hadn't heard these two go down, thank God. Of course they'd be missed soon enough. We quickly stripped the man Laura hit, because he was very small. Laura pulled on his pants and his boots and threw the pants and boots she'd been wearing into a bush that, I swear, quivered when the boots struck it. We relieved both of them of their weapons.

It took three minutes, no longer. We began to make our way due west, going by small glimpses of sun. Every dozen or so steps, we wiped away the marks of our passage. Our progress was slow. Both of us were dripping wet, so thirsty our tongues felt swollen. We heard the chattering of monkeys high above our heads in the interlocking tree branches, and the constant calls and shrieks of animals we'd never heard in our lives. We heard a low, warning growl. A puma, Laura whispered. They knew we were there and were announcing it loudly to their cousins.

Birds checked in—squawking louder and more ferociously than Nolan ever had even at his crankiest.

"Listen to them," Laura said. "They're all around us and loud as can be. Oh, Mac—what do you think the ice acid does to animals? Like Grub-ster and Nolan?"

I stopped cold and stared at her. I hadn't thought about them. I said, "Doesn't it make sense that they'd sleep like we did? That they'd wake up, like we did? That they'd be all right?"

I thought she was going to burst into tears.

"That was a stupid question," I said without hesitation. "I'll wager my AK-47 that they're fine." The panic calmed in her eyes. "Maggie's probably feeding them. Don't worry, Laura."

We kept walking, looking carefully down and around before we took each step. To walk a mile would take three hours, I figured, cursing at the boots rubbing my heels.

Then, suddenly, with no warning, it started to rain. We looked at each other, tilted our heads back, and opened our mouths. The water tasted won-derful. Suddenly, something with a dozen skittering legs landed on my cheek. I shook it off, cupped my hands together, and drank.

The rain was so heavy, even coming through the dense canopy of green overhead, that in only a minute or two we weren't thirsty anymore. We were also sodden and nearly steaming, it was so hot. It felt miserable. I couldn't wait to be on a ski slope, puffs of cold air streaming out of my mouth.

I raised my hand and rubbed my fingers over a dirty smudge on Laura's cheek. "You know, Laura, when I flew from Washington a week ago, I never imagined ending up in a rain forest with the woman I love, the woman I had to come three thousand miles to meet."

"This isn't anything I'd anticipated either," she said, and kissed my fin-gers. "We'd better get to work on finding Savich and Sherlock."

I laid my weapons on the ground and buttoned her shirt up to her neck, then raised the collar. It touched her chin. "Let's keep as much covered as we can," I added, and buttoned my own shirt up to my chin. Our sleeves were fastened at our wrists. At least our fatigues were tucked inside our boots and the boots were sturdy. It was good protection from all the crea-tures that slithered close to us.

We started walking northeast, roughly parallel to what looked like clear-cut land just outside the rain forest, not more than a hundred yards distant. We wanted to stay hidden until we were well beyond the com-pound. After another hour, we turned south again. It didn't take more than twenty minutes to reach the edge of the rain forest. The thick foliage suddenly thinned. The sun was bright overhead, the air immediately drier. The difference in the landscape couldn't have been more dramatic. The lush, dense forest simply gave way to an indistinct barren patch.

I figured we were at least a hundred yards northeast of the compound.

TWENTY-THREE

There were mountains in the distance, their tops shrouded with clouds.

There was no sign of people, of any habitation at all. We'd stepped out of a green world filled with more creatures than anywhere else on the planet into desert terrain. The sun dried our clothes in less than fifteen minutes. It also made us thirstier.

"We need water," Laura said. "Then some shelter." She pointed toward a copse of trees not too far away. The copse was on a small hill. From there we might see some sign of life, perhaps even the compound.

"Listen," Laura said. She pointed up. Above, a small plane was coming closer.

It was then I saw the empty airstrip a few hundred yards from where we stood. A four-seat Cessna was coming in.

We ran back into the rain forest until we heard the plane land, then slowly eased out on our bellies. We could barely make out three people getting off the plane, walking to a jeep, and getting in. Men or women, we couldn't be sure. The jeep drove off, due east from the airstrip.

To my disappointment, the Cessna was in the air and gone beyond the mountains in a matter of minutes.

"I wish," Laura said, "that the plane had hung around. We could have persuaded the pilot to get us out of here."

"All we need is Savich," I said. "He's got a license. He can fly anything."

Laura and I walked slowly out of the rain forest again. The dry air felt wonderful on my face. I saw Laura raise her face to the baking sun high overhead.

"It's around midafternoon," I said. "At least four and a half hours until it gets dark."

"We can scout around, try to see the best way to get back into the compound."

"I'm hungry," I said, and rubbed my fist against my belly. My hand stopped. I saw her eyes follow my hand, then widen with alarm. Coming from nowhere, just suddenly upon me, I felt a bolt of incredible lust. I was almost instantly as hard as the rocks I was standing on. I was losing it. Laura was staring at me.

"Mac, what's wrong?"

I grabbed her, flattened my hand over her mouth, and said in a raw voice, "Laura, there's time for us to make love. Let's do it right here, right now. I've got to—"

"Mac, stop it!"

I heard her voice, but what she said made no difference. There was only one thing I wanted, only one thing I was going to do. I was trying to pull her shirt off and unzip my pants at the same time. I didn't even think about touching her, no, I just had to get inside her, right that instant. She twisted away from me.

I grabbed a moment of reason and choked out, "It's hit me again, Laura. I don't know if I can control it. I'll hurt you. Get out of here, now. Run!"

"Mac, you can control it, you did it before!"

"Please, Laura." I was on her again, knocking her backward. She hit a tree but didn't fall. Instead of running, she stepped forward and kicked me in the balls. My breath whooshed out. The pain blanked anything in my brain. And I stood there, bent over like an old man, knowing the pain was going to get worse, much worse. And it did. I moaned, clutched myself, and folded over. I waited for the god-awful agony to lessen. I simply tried to breathe and not fall on the ground and weep like a baby. Laura was standing not three feet in front of me, not saying a word.

"Good shot," I said when I could get the words out.

Neither of us moved. I stood there, still hunkered over, trying to get hold of myself.

"It's not so bad now, thank God," I said, slowly straightening. "I can't believe a drug can do that. You feel like an animal in pain, and just have to get out of it. You might have had to kill me to stop me if you weren't so smart. You knocked every thought, every urge, out of my brain."

"I didn't know what else to do. You sure you're all right, Mac?"

"You don't have to kick me again, at least for the moment. I'm back together again. It was there for a moment that I wanted sex more than I wanted life. I thought having sex at that very moment *was* life. How can there be people who would pay for this drug?"

She lightly touched her fingertips to my mouth. "Let me know if I have to kick you again."

"I don't think so," I said slowly. We sat down and leaned against a scrubby tree I couldn't identify. It gave about as much shade as a single leaf on one of the trees I couldn't identify in the rain forest.

"They didn't kill us, Mac. They brought us down here and they haven't done anything but play with us, ugly games, but no torture. Drug dealers don't do that. Drug dealers eliminate anyone they perceive as a threat to their operation. When they fired on us at Seagull Cottage, they weren't trying to kill us. They just wanted us under wraps, inside the cottage, so they could use the ice acid and bring us to wherever we are."

"Maybe they took us because they wanted guinea pigs for the drug."

"They can pull people off the street to experiment on. They wouldn't take four federal agents to do that." She took my hand. "I know this is tough, Mac. But someone gave them orders not to kill us. The only person I can think of who cares whether or not you live or die is Jilly. If you weren't involved, I think we'd be dead."

"No," I said. "It had to be Paul. He gave the order because he knew how much Jilly would be hurt if I was killed."

She swatted an insect off her knee. "I'm sorry, Mac. But you've got to think objectively about this. Four federal agents are in Edgerton, Oregon. Things are getting too hot. It's Jilly, Paul, Molinas, and Tarcher whose butts are on the line. They've got to buy some time so they can shut things down and clear out before the cops come to get them. There's another guy I told you a little about: Del Cabrizo, the head of the Maille cartel. We believe he's the kingpin behind the development of this drug. John Molinas is just one of his flunkies. He probably used Molinas to get to Tarcher and to Jilly and Paul. As to Alyssum Tarcher's exact role, I'd say he cut himself in by getting Paul and Jilly out to Edgerton.

"But I do know that Jilly is the only one who has the power to keep us alive. She's the only one with the leverage. We're kept alive or the problems getting the drug ready for the streets won't get solved.

"She left the hospital to get away from you, Mac. She knew you wouldn't stop pushing. She had no choice but to leave and hide out, and hope you went home."

"My sister, no matter whatever else she possibly could have done, wouldn't drug me and set me over you like a dog in heat. She hates you because you betrayed her, not me."

"Jilly doesn't have a clue what they'd do to us. She's in Oregon, not here. But I'll tell you, Mac, she knows what kind of people they are. She had to have guessed they wouldn't treat us as valued guests."

She knew I didn't want to hear this. Bless her, she didn't say anything more about Jilly's role in all this mess. She knew I'd think about it.

"Who is that bald man in the compound?" I asked.

"I've been thinking about that. From your description, I'd say it has to be John Molinas. In the photo I saw of him he had a lot of thick black hair."

"I guess he thinks the shaved head is more intimidating."

Laura said, "If it is Molinas, I think he's here to make sure no one kills us. Maybe Jilly demanded insurance, insisted he be here to run the show. She wanted to make sure that Del Cabrizo wouldn't have our throats cut. Maybe it was her way to protect you."

I rested my head on my crossed arms. I felt a huge wave of fatigue wash over me. No sex in this, no prodding lust, just sudden, utter exhaustion. "Laura," I said, trying to raise my head. "Laura, what the hell am I feeling now?"

I heard her voice, thin, far away, calling my name. I tried to look up but I didn't have the strength to lift my head. I clearly saw the terrorists in Tunisia, heard their voices, wondered if I would ever escape this mess alive, then there was the car, driving toward us, only there was no driver, and then it was a ball of flame and I was gone. Unholy fear ate into me. It seemed stronger, more corrosive now than when it had actually happened.

It was the effect of the damned drug again, I thought, but it didn't make any difference. The sun grew hotter, the air even drier. The heat was inside me, filling me. There was desolation everywhere and I was part of it. I had flown to the sun and fallen in.

"Mac!"

Laura's voice was high, terrified.

I tried to look at her, but her face blurred, then faded into a strange sort of gray whiteness that seemed endless and cold, but it wasn't any of those things, and on some level I knew it. I didn't know what it was, and I didn't care.

I was floating now, and it was very strange to be staring down at a large man, and I knew the man was me, only he was lying there, his eyes closed, his chest heaving with the effort to breathe. Then I knew he was me because suddenly I couldn't breathe. I was dying.

Then there wasn't any more pain, just a gray-white void that didn't go anywhere. I was cold. That made sense, I was naked. I wanted covers but couldn't seem to move my arms.

I felt fingers on my forearm, soft fingers, loving fingers, fingers so gentle I wanted to see who they belonged to. It became more than that. I had to know who was touching me like that. I forced my eyes open, forced myself to look through the gray-white, to find the person whose fingers were so gentle, so tender.

I saw Jilly standing over me, looking both frightened and angry. Why would she be frightened? Or angry? It made no sense at all. I had to know. I concentrated with everything in me and whispered, "Jilly? You're all right. Thank God. I've been so worried about you. Why are we here, Jilly? Where are we?"

She smiled down at me and lightly touched her fingertips to my cheek. "It'll be all right, Ford. Listen to me now. You're coming out of it, very soon now. No, keep your eyes open, Ford, listen to me. You mustn't drink or eat anything. Do you understand me? *Don't even drink out of the tap. Nothing.*"

"Laura, Jilly? Where is she?"

"It will be all right, Ford. Laura's here. Get strong, Ford. Lie still and get strong."

And then her fingers left my arm. When I looked up, she was gone. The gray-white void thickened around me until I disappeared into it, eased into it and let it swallow me. I wondered why I wasn't cold any longer.

I opened my eyes and realized that no one was standing over me. I felt clearheaded, but so hungry I could have eaten just about anything. I shook my head. What had happened? "Laura?"

I saw her lying on her side on a folded blanket on the floor beside the bed I was lying on. She was naked, like I was. I was down on the floor next to her in an instant, panicked. "Laura?" I lightly pressed my fingers against the pulse in her throat. It was strong and steady.

I knelt over her, wondering what to do, then wondering where we were. Something was very wrong here but I just didn't get it yet. I lightly stroked my hand over her shoulder and turned her onto her back.

"Laura," I said again, and leaned down to kiss her mouth. Her lips were dry. She was so pale. "Laura," I said, and watched her eyes slowly open.

I saw the scream in her eyes and quickly pressed my palm against her mouth. "No, be quiet. I don't know what's going on here yet. Are you all right?"

She looked confused, her brows drawn together. Her long hair was in tangles around her head. "Mac," she said at last, and her voice sounded beautiful to me.

"It's all right, sweetheart. We're both alive. I don't know where or why. Somebody stripped both of us naked."

She didn't move, didn't try to cover herself. I saw her draw in a deep breath and knew she was searching for control, for something to latch onto, something that made sense.

"I saw a man, standing behind you. He was there, suddenly. I never heard him coming. And he sprayed something at me. Before I went out, I saw him strike you on the back of your head. I don't remember anything else. I want to get up now, Mac."

I gave her my hand. She was looking at me and I realized that I was hard again. I was embarrassed and frightened as hell. Pain was one thing, but not knowing what was real and what wasn't, that was beyond anything I'd ever experienced in my life. I hated it.

I turned away from her, grabbed a blanket off the bed, and wrapped it around my waist. There was only a dingy sheet for Laura. I pulled it off the small bed and handed it to her. She wrapped it around herself, tucking in the ends over her breasts.

She sat beside me on the bed. "I'm dying of thirst," she said, not looking at me but down at her bare feet.

I said without thinking, "We're not going to drink anything at all. Not even tap water."

"Why?"

I turned to face her. I lifted her hand and held it between mine. She leaned forward until her cheek was touching my shoulder.

"Listen, Laura. Jilly came to see me. She's here. She seemed upset. She told me not to eat or drink anything."

"Jilly, here? But when could you have seen her, Mac?"

"I don't know but it makes as much sense as you and me being here, wherever here is."

"It means she is involved," Laura said finally. "You see that now, don't you, Mac? If she was really here, with you, then she's in on all of this, somehow."

"Yes, I know," I said.

"They've got us again, haven't they? What are we going to do?"

But how did they have us again? They just walked up to us and turned off the lights? What was going on here? Was it all somehow planned with a drug whose effects diminished, then came roaring back?

I stood and began pacing the twelve-by-twelve room. "We've got to find Sherlock and Savich," I said over my shoulder. "We know they're real."

It was odd but even though I was walking around and speaking to Laura, I knew that somewhere inside my brain something still wasn't right. I remembered reliving that horrible few moments in Tunisia, how it had somehow been magnified.

I looked over at the tap in the small sink.

Neither of us was going to touch another drop of water, at least not in this place.

TWENTY-FOUR

What about the food? Jilly hadn't said anything about food, had she? Yes, she had, I remembered. I looked down at the plate of steaming rice, tortillas with small pools of melted butter, and the small bowl of beef in some sort of red sauce. I held out my hand and stopped Laura from using her fork.

"We just can't take the chance. They could put drugs in the food as easily as in the water." I smelled those tortillas and wanted to curse, which I did under my breath.

Two men had stood in the doorway, their weapons pointed right at us, as a young girl, not more than twelve years old, looking so scared I thought she was going to pass out, brought us the meal.

"There's something else," I said, and got to my feet. I gently put the two trays of food on the floor. "Let's look around again for cameras or listening devices. There weren't any last time, but who knows?"

We didn't find anything. Even so, I kept my voice down. "We need to get ready for any opportunity, just like the first time."

"Can we be so lucky again? There were two guys this time with AK-47s." She looked over at the toilet. "The porcelain lid is gone."

"I never said they were stupid. We'll have to find something else. We do have an advantage here."

"I'd bet the farm they put drugs in the food and water. Someone will come sooner or later to see how we're reacting. It won't occur to them that we wouldn't eat or drink anything. They'll be expecting us to be out cold or having sex on the floor or whatever else this drug does to you."

Her shoulders were slumped. I'd never seen her look so defeated. "Laura, listen to me. Our brains will straighten up again. No more drugs. We're pros. If anyone can get out of this place, we can. Now, come here and hold me. I'm feeling a bit off balance right now. I need you."

She came to me, clutching the sheet over her breasts. She didn't say anything, just held me against her. I felt her kiss my bare shoulder.

Suddenly I was so pissed I could have easily killed the first person through that door. I kissed Laura and set her away from me. I got up and tore off a leg of the bed. My blanket fell off but I didn't pay any attention. I hefted that leg. It made a solid club. I handed it to Laura. "Hit me if I try to take you down again. Please, I'd much prefer that to being kicked."

She took the club and hefted it. Then she smiled at me. "Give me a bad guy instead."

It was such an excellent weapon that I took off another leg for myself and swung it around a bit, liking the solid weight of it in my hand. I smiled at Laura, standing not six feet away. She still had that old threadbare sheet wrapped around her, her hair was in tangles, and she looked ready for anything. The woman was tough. I realized then that she wasn't looking at my face. I picked up my blanket and wrapped it around me again.

"You're the best, Laura," I said. "I can't imagine having a better partner. Now we wait again."

We waited.

We dozed. Since there were no windows, we had no clue if it was night
or day. There was a lamp in the room and it gave off a sluggish sixty-watt
light.

The sound of at least three pairs of boots thudding on the wooden floor
snapped me alert. I couldn't wait to get a shot at the bastards.

I raised a finger to Laura. She nodded. I could see she was ready. I wondered if she was as angry as I was, and imagined that she was.

The door handle turned. There wasn't a sound. Both Laura and I were
staring at that turning knob.

A woman wearing a white lab coat stepped in. She had a small silver
tray in her right hand. I moaned loudly and clutched my throat.

She came down to her knees beside me, and I moaned again. But I was
looking behind her at the same two men who'd accompanied the breakfast
or lunch or whatever meal it had been. When the first man came through
the door, his gun was down because he was staring down at me and the
woman. I grabbed her under the arms and threw her at him. She yelled as
she hit him squarely in his AK-47.

He screamed out the other man's name: "Carlos!"

Carlos was through the door in an instant, the weapon raised to mow
me down. Laura rose up behind him, and the club came down in a hard,
graceful arc against the side of his head. His eyes bulged. Blood poured out
of his mouth, then he fell against the door. The other man had gotten his
AK-47 free of the woman and was swinging it up. I wasn't in a good position. I managed to roll to my left side and kick up as I moved. My foot
struck the weapon but didn't knock it from his hands. He fired two rounds,
a loud, obscene sound. One bullet smashed into the floor beside my head,
spewing splinters of wood into my arm and chest. The other bullet struck
the woman. I heard her cry out as I gained the leverage I needed. I kicked
him solidly beneath his chin at the same time Laura clubbed him in his kidneys.

His eyes rolled back in his head and he went down like a stone. I slowly
rose. "These guys were serious." I knelt beside the woman. The bullet had
struck her forearm. She'd be all right. I told her in Spanish to be still. As for
the two men, all I wanted from them were their clothes.

Laura went right to the smaller man and stripped him. We both tucked the legs of our fatigues into the boots at about the same time. I saw Laura lean down next to the woman. "What is it?"

"Look," she said, raising a pistol, a Bren Ten, a 10mm automatic that held eleven rounds.

"The woman had it on her tray along with some needles and bottles. I haven't seen one of these guys for a long time. It's a good combat weapon."

I grabbed the two small vials on the tray.

"Good idea," she said, smiling at me. "You ready?"

I turned left and stopped cold.

"What's wrong, Mac?"

"Just an attack of déjà vu," I said, and slithered out the door. We left the men completely naked and tied up as best we could with strips of the bed sheet Laura had been wearing. Laura had tied the woman up with her underwear.

"Let's go to Molinas's office," I said. "If there's someone there, we can force them to take us to Sherlock and Savich."

We passed a window. It was dark outside, and that was good. How much time had passed?

The office was empty. They'd boarded up the glass windows behind the desk. "Maybe they've hidden a phone," I said, and began opening drawers.

Suddenly I felt dizzy and unfocused. I stood there, waiting to see what would happen. Was this death coming? A numbing cold overwhelmed me. I felt it chewing at the edges of my brain. My heart pounded. Laura was staring at me, her hand out. I knew she was talking but I couldn't make out her words. To die like this, I thought, as I went to my knees.

I wasn't dying. It was the drug again. I fell back against the wall. I saw Laura over me even as I sat there, my head to one side.

She was shaking me as hard as she could. "Mac, listen to me. I know you can hear me, you're looking at me. Blink at me. Yes, that's right. Whatever's going on in your head, you've got to control it. We've got to get out of here."

I looked over at the glass windows. They weren't boarded up. The glass was solid, whole. And I wondered: Did we really crash through it the first time?

"Mac, blink at me again."

I evidently did because she started speaking again. Her voice was low. She was close to me. I could feel her breath on my face.

"I want you to raise your hand now, Mac."

I looked down at my hand lying limp on the floor. I looked and looked at it and then I thought, Raise your damned hand. My hand came right up. I cupped Laura's face with it. "Whatever it is, it's going away. It's a weird feeling. Laura, we didn't use anything when we made love at Seagull Cottage. If I made you pregnant, I don't want you to worry about it, okay? We're going to get married. It'll all be okay."

She grinned at me, leaned down, and kissed my mouth. It was a sweet kiss and I felt it throughout my body, and the feeling was healthy and real. "I'm better," I said.

"Good. I want you to stand up now, Mac. Do you think you can do it?"

I felt the journey of coming back into myself, of retaking control. I doubted in that moment if I would ever again even willingly take an aspirin. There is nothing more terrifying than losing control of your mind.

I got up. I stood staring at the boarded-up windows. "My memory went haywire. I felt numb and everything was different. This damned drug is a killer."

"Let's find Molinas, Mac."

I picked up my AK-47. I felt strong again. In control. But for how long this time?

TWENTY-FIVE

I was frankly surprised when we went through a corridor on the far side of the office and found ourselves in an antique-filled bedroom. The man we believed to be Molinas was sitting on the side of a bed, leaning over a woman. Not a woman, she was young, perhaps eighteen. She had a white sheet pulled to her chin. Thick, shiny dark hair fanned around her face on a white pillow.

Molinas hadn't heard us. All his attention was focused on the girl. He was wearing black pants, a loose white shirt, and his bald head gleamed beneath the mellow bulb above the bed.

He was speaking quietly, but I couldn't make out his words. I watched him stroke her hair, lean down to kiss her. He continued speaking in a low, warm voice even as he straightened again. I couldn't tell if he was speaking Spanish or English. I saw the girl's hand come up and lightly touch his shoulder.

I nodded to Laura and pointed to the Bren Ten she held lightly in her right hand. She frowned a moment, then reluctantly handed it to me. How could she know what I intended?

"Take the girl, Laura," I whispered.

She nodded again. I left my AK-47 on the floor outside the door. We went as silently as we could into the still air of the room. It smelled sweet in the bedroom, a vague rose smell. I didn't like it. It was cloying.

He was completely focused on the girl, leaning over her, speaking. My boots creaked. I froze, but he didn't move. What were they talking about?

I gently pressed the Bren Ten against his left ear. "Hello," I said. "¿Cómo le va?"

The girl was sitting up now, pressed against the bed's headboard, her eyes wide, silent as death. She was terrified.

I felt him coil then relax again. He said, "If you kill me you'll never get out of here alive."

"It won't matter to you, Molinas," Laura said very calmly.

"How do you know who I am?"

"Who else would they send down here?" Laura asked. "You were assigned to keep us. As for all the fun you had with us, that was your own idea, wasn't it?"

"Some of the men are animals. I protected you."

I looked over at the girl, who still clutched the sheet to her throat, her narrow hands clenched. I said in Spanish, "Don't be afraid. We're not going to hurt you."

Slowly she nodded and said in perfect English, "Who are you?"

"My name's Mac. What's yours?"

"Marran."

Molinas moved and I gave him all my attention. "Keep an eye on her, Laura."

I came down beside him and raised the pistol. "You're going to take us to where you're holding the other two agents."

"They're dead," he said.

"Then so are you." I pressed the pistol against the side of his mouth and cocked it.

"No, don't," he choked out. "They're not dead, I swear it. I'll take you to them."

"Did you drug them like you did me?"

"Yes, but not in the same way. They're all right."

"You'd better hope that we agree. Now, I want you to get up real slow."

"We should probably bring the girl along," Laura said.

Molinas lunged for me as he rose, but I brought the pistol down on the side of his head. The girl groaned. Laura clapped her hand over the girl's mouth, pressing her head back against her pillow.

Molinas went down but not out. He landed on his knees, moaning, holding his head. I knew the pain must be bad, the bastard.

"If you try that again, I'll kill you." I said it in a near whisper. I didn't want the girl to make any more noise. I thought about hauling her with us and decided it wouldn't improve our odds. We'd leave her here. I opened my mouth to tell Laura when I saw that she'd already begun ripping up the sheet. I waited for her, keeping the tip of the Bren Ten against the back of Molinas's head. The girl was silent now. I saw tears running down her cheeks.

"Who is she?" I asked Molinas, who was still holding his head in his hands.

He tightened like a spigot in January. "Touch her, you bastard, and I'll rip your head off your shoulders." I believed him.

It took Laura a few minutes to tie the girl firmly. I noticed she had skinny arms. They were pale with sharp blue veins running beneath her flesh. Her beautiful shiny hair streamed across her face. Laura smoothed it back after she'd fastened the gag in her mouth.

I hoped Molinas could walk. I started to help him to his feet. He snarled at me and made it himself. A proud man, I thought. I looked back at the girl, who was staring at him, her eyes large and frightened.

"Turn out the light, Laura."

The room went dark.

We heard a whimper from the bed.

I could feel him resist when he heard the girl's distress. "We didn't do anything to her," I said. "She'll be all right, if you don't do anything stupid. Now walk."

The moment we had him back in his office, Laura motioned for me to stop. I kept three feet between me and Molinas. She walked to the door, opened it quietly, and leaned out. She turned back to me and nodded.

"Now," I said quietly, "you're going to take us to the other agents."

He said nothing, merely walked from the office and turned left down the corridor. "You're dead if one of your soldiers tries to take us out."

He stiffened but didn't say a thing.

"If you're dead, what will happen to the girl? She's already tied down. A regular offering, I'd say."

He nodded, and I heard him curse, low and fluently. Even with a Spanish last name, those curses were pure American.

"Who is that girl?"

He kept walking.

"You might as well tell me."

Finally, not turning to face me, he answered, "She is my daughter."

TWENTY-SIX

"Where are your men, Molinas?" I said near his left ear. "Some operation you run here. Hard to believe you haven't been kicked out of town."

"The men are not professionals," Molinas said, and I could tell that disgusted him. "They have courage but no discipline."

"I buy that," I said. "Now, tell us where we are."

"No, you can't kill me. If you do, you won't ever get your friends out of here. I can't tell you anything. If I did, I would be dead and so would my daughter. Very few people know about this place. If you find out on your own, I cannot be blamed. Your friends are around that corner. There are three guards around the door."

Suddenly, Laura put her finger against her lips. We heard a man talking in a low voice. She walked quietly to the corner and looked around it. She came back. "There are three guards up ahead, like he said. They're sitting on the floor outside a door. Their heads are down, but I'm not certain they're asleep."

"The other agents are behind that door?" I asked.

"I wasn't lying."

He was pale now, but he didn't say anything more.

"Del Cabrizo's behind the whole operation, isn't he?" Laura asked Molinas.

"I can't tell you anything. You can kill me if you must but I know you won't harm my daughter."

"We'll do whatever we need to," I said. "I want you to walk ahead to the men and tell them that you intend to speak to the prisoners. You will tell them to go outside until you come to tell them to return. If you screw this up, Molinas, I will personally shoot you. I won't harm your daughter, but I will shoot you. Trust me on this."

He looked me straight in the face. He had dark blue eyes, and there was something familiar about them. The shape, perhaps, slightly tilted at the corners. They were his sister's eyes, Elaine Tarcher's. He said in a low voice, "My daughter is innocent. She has suffered enough. If I release your friends, will you leave here?"

"You can hardly expect things to go on as they have."

"No, once you escape, my job here is over. Then I will deal with what will happen."

I shrugged. "Your daughter, who is so precious to you—why is she here with you? Have you let her watch you pump drugs into people?"

"No. We have only been here for a short time. We arrived just before you did. I couldn't leave Marran back home. She needs me. You cannot take me with you as a hostage. You cannot leave her here alone. She would be savaged by these men. She would kill herself. She's tried before. I will do as you ask, Agent MacDougal."

He was pleading with me, his expression as raw as his voice. His daughter was more important to him than his pride, certainly more important to him than his own life. "Let me see what kind of shape my friends are in. Then I'll decide what to do with you. You try to screw me, Molinas, and you're dead. Think of your daughter before you decide to betray me. By the way, I speak Spanish."

Molinas nodded and straightened. As he walked forward, he looked like a man used to command, a man in charge. Laura and I watched him kick one man in the knee. The man cried out. The other two awoke. The man Molinas had kicked scrambled to his feet, excuses tumbling out of his mouth. I understood only that they were excuses. Molinas raised his foot and kicked another man in the ribs. The third managed to jump away.

He used his hands while he spoke to the men, and his voice was low and angry. If he'd had my gun I wouldn't have been surprised if he'd shot all three of them. He motioned for them to pick up their weapons. He stood there watching them scurry away. He had told them to go outside and stay there. Then, after just a slight pause, he turned and walked back to Laura and me. He held up a key ring, pulled out a long brass key and handed it to me.

"This is the one."

I gave the key to Laura. "Be careful. There might be a man inside."

She nodded. I remained behind with Molinas, the Bren Ten pressed against his neck. "Nice clothes," I said close to his ear while we waited. "I guess dealing drugs to kids lets you hobnob with a lot of Italian designers."

"I haven't been involved in drugs for five years," he said. "I am doing this for other reasons."

"Yeah, right. And you keep American federal agents for the fun of it." I focused on the slowly opening door. Laura eased inside, crouched low. I saw a light come on, then nothing. "Let's go. One try at me and I'll pull the trigger."

Savich was half-crouched, ready to attack. He looked pale and drawn, his clothes torn and dirty, and there was such rage in his eyes that suddenly I didn't want to know what had been done to him. "I was hoping you'd come," he said, as he slowly straightened.

I came into the small room, pushing Molinas in front of me. Savich's hands closed around his throat and he shook him like he was a rag. Molinas did nothing to defend himself.

"Savich, stop it." I tried to jerk Molinas away from him, but Savich was out of control.

Laura cried out, "Sherlock. Oh, God!"

Sherlock was the only thing that could have distracted him and Laura knew it. Savich dropped his hands and whirled about, dropping to his knees beside Sherlock. She was unconscious, huddled on her side.

He gathered her against him and rocked her back and forth, back and forth, kissing her dirty hair. Savich looked up. His face was battered. He'd been beaten. I nearly pulled the trigger. "By God, what have you done to him? You damned bastard. I should have let him strangle you."

"He is all right," Molinas said, and I knew his throat hurt. Savich was strong, very strong, no matter what they'd done to him.

I shoved Molinas to the floor and closed the door, then walked to where Savich sat, still rocking Sherlock on his legs.

"Thanks for coming, guys. I'm glad to see you, to say the least. I did try, but I couldn't get us out of here. I failed. I took out a couple of them but then four others came in and I got the crap kicked out of me for my efforts."

He was coherent. He was himself.

"They didn't drug you?" I asked.

"Not after I woke up when we first got here, wherever here is. They took Sherlock. I guess they wanted me to be clearheaded enough to see what the drug did to her."

"What happened to her?"

"When she's awake, she keeps reliving that awful time in the past when she was hunting down that serial killer, Marlin Jones." I was nodding. I knew all about Marlin Jones. Savich explained for Laura. "She was his prisoner. It was terrifying for her. She had nightmares about it for months. With the drug, it's come back, only worse. You can feel her terror, her confusion." He looked over at Molinas. "I'm going to kill that sadistic bastard."

But he didn't move, just kept rocking Sherlock.

He said even as he rubbed his cheek against Sherlock's hair, "After they beat me, they left me alone. They never did shoot any drugs into me."

I looked down at Sherlock, and then I struck Molinas, I couldn't stop myself. I must have gotten him just right because his head fell back against the wall. I drew a deep breath. "I'm sorry, guys. He'll be back with us in a minute. He's going to get us out of here. There's an airstrip out there."

"Thank God," Savich said. He was still clutching Sherlock tightly against his chest. "They drugged you again, Mac?"

I said, as I watched Molinas open his eyes, "I'll tell you about it later." I hunkered down into Molinas's face. "You're going to get on your radio. You're going to get a plane in here. Now."

Savich said, "I want to take him back with us. I want to strap him down and give him the lethal injection myself."

Molinas smiled. "Sorry, Agent Savich. That won't be possible. The plane carries only four passengers. I gather one of you is a pilot?"

"No problem," Savich said. He rose, Sherlock in his arms. "I can kill you myself if I can't take you back. I don't want to think how much dirty money you've got for lawyers. Yes, this is better. I don't want to let the law dick around with you."

"Your wife will be all right," Molinas said. "It will be a bit longer before she comes around, but she will be all right. There are two separate drugs that can be mixed together in varying amounts. We were having trouble with the balance and the dose. Everyone reacts differently. Some people are particularly sensitive. Your wife is one of them."

Very slowly, Savich turned and laid Sherlock on the tattered black blanket spread on the wooden floor. He rose, then faced Molinas and smiled. It was a terrifying smile.

I didn't move. This was up to Savich. I looked over at Sherlock. Laura was kneeling beside her now, stroking one of her hands.

"Get up," Savich said.

Molinas slowly rose.

There was no graceful display of martial arts, only the raw power of Savich's fist into Molinas's belly, then his knee into his groin. Molinas went down like a stone.

"Good," Laura said. "He deserved it, but now we've got to get him into good enough shape to get to a radio and order up a plane."

"I want Jilly," I said.

Savich stared at me. "What did you say, Mac? Jilly? She's here?"

"She came to me when I was just coming out of a session with their drugs. She warned me not to eat or drink anything. Whatever she's doing here, Savich, she kept Laura and me away from another round of drugs."

Laura didn't argue with me, only said, "If she's here then we'll need a bigger plane."

"Jilly's small," I said. "We can fit the five of us in a Cessna."

"Mac," Savich said, lightly touching his bruised fingers to my forearm. "Is your brother-in-law, Paul, here too?"

"I don't know," I said. "If he's here I say leave the bastard. He's the one who developed the drug with all its charms. I just want Jilly." I looked over at Laura. She was staring at the floor, and I saw her eyes narrow in fury.

I followed her line of vision. Savich was shackled to a ring in the floor. It was Molinas's bad luck that I'd pushed him far enough into the room for Savich to reach him.

No wonder Savich hadn't escaped. As simple as that.

"Savich, I don't believe this."

"They enjoyed the fact that I could strain and curse, but not reach them. They laughed about it. They knew exactly how far the chain would let me reach. Thanks for bringing that big bastard close enough so I could get him."

"Savich," Laura said quietly, as I tried all the keys on the ring Molinas had given me. "He's Alyssum Tarcher's brother-in-law, John Molinas."

"I remember."

Finally, Laura found the key that fit the shackle on Savich's right ankle. When it fell open, he knelt down and rubbed his ankle. He pulled down his sock. There was dark bruising but no broken skin. "I have Sherlock to thank for these thick wool socks. It's good to get that thing off me." He sounded like himself, which was a big relief.

We had no choice but to wait for Molinas to come to his senses. There was a bucket of water on a rickety table in the corner. Laura threw it on him.

Savich pulled Sherlock up against him. "Sherlock. Come on, love, wake up. You can do it. Wake up." I watched Savich lightly slap her cheeks. "Come on, sweetheart, open your eyes. Hey, I'll let you throw me the next time we're in the gym, but you've got to wake up for me now."

Finally, she did open her eyes and look up at him. She looked drugged, strung out, and when she whispered, "Dillon?" her voice was slurred.

"She recognizes you," Laura said. "That's a good start."

"It's me, Sherlock. It's all right now. Mac and Laura are here. We're leaving."

"He's here, Dillon," she whispered, rubbing her fingers against her temple. "He's tucked right behind my left ear. He's laughing. He won't leave me alone, and he's still laughing. He won't stop. Please, Dillon, please make him stop." She closed her eyes again and slumped back against Savich's arm.

"Is she talking about Marlin Jones?" I asked, kicking Molinas lightly in the ribs. He was still trying to catch a breath.

"Yes," Savich said, never looking away from Sherlock's chalky face. "The drug they've been giving her brought him back, planted him in her mind and magnified him, made him into even more of a monster than he really was, and that's saying something. He's there in her head, as real as you are."

"It did the same thing to me," I said slowly, "but it happened only once. I relived the car bomb in Tunisia. You're right. It was worse remembering it than when it actually happened. Paul said the drug was supposed to lessen the power of a bad memory."

Molinas struggled to sit up. "Yes, the drug is supposed to relieve the physical symptoms. They promised me it would. But there's something wrong. The drug shouldn't bring the memory to the forefront.

"It's like you said, the drug is supposed to dissipate the physical symptoms, and with repeated doses finally remove the horror of the memory. But it doesn't work. I tried different doses and even different additives to see if I couldn't fix the drug. But it doesn't work."

I went down on my haunches in front of Molinas. "What happened to your daughter?"

"She was raped three years ago right on campus at her private school. She was only fifteen years old. Four older boys raped her. It destroyed her. They promised me the drug would help her, that's the only reason I got involved with Alyssum and Del Cabrizo in the first place, to help my daughter.

"That's why I gave her the drug. I injected her myself. But it hasn't worked. Her memories of that night have grown worse, not better. The drug is killing her!"

"So you gave Sherlock an even larger dose and mixed in other drugs?" I asked.

Molinas stared into Savich's eyes and saw his own death there. He leaned over and vomited on the wooden floor.

SAVICH carried Sherlock in his arms. She was conscious now, but her eyes were heavy and vague. He'd wrapped her in all the blankets that were in that cell. She was disturbingly silent, quiescent. That really worried me. My mouthy Sherlock, whose big sweetheart smile had everyone around wanting to do whatever she wanted, including her husband, was lying like a ghost, not really there. Laura walked behind them, carrying two AK-47s.

I marched Molinas in front of me, the Bren Ten pressed against the small of his back, another AK-47 slung over my left shoulder.

"Take me to Jilly," I said to Molinas. "Now. I want to see my sister. She's coming out with us."

"Your sister isn't here," Molinas said. I could tell it hurt him to speak.

I smiled at him. "I don't believe you. She came to me. She spoke to me, she warned me."

He said slowly, "It must have been the drug. Your sister was never here. Never. I have no reason to lie to you about that. It was the drug. It's unpredictable. But I have never heard of it doing that before."

Was that possible? Jilly had been standing over me, clear as day. She'd been with me, speaking to me, dammit.

"She's never been here," Molinas repeated.

"But you know her?" Laura said.

"I know who she is," Molinas said carefully. We stopped and kept silent. There were men speaking not fifteen feet away. About three minutes later their boot steps faded down the long wooden corridor.

We went back to his big opulent office and the huge adjoining bedchamber only to find it empty. His daughter, Marran, must have gotten herself untied because she'd locked herself in the bathroom. Molinas told her to stay there until he came back. We heard her crying.

"Look what I found."

We turned to see that Laura had opened a closet door that I hadn't seen before. "Guns, clothes, and look at this—two more AK-47s."

She turned around, grinning really big. She was holding up a machete. "You never know if we might need it. They all carry knives. Maybe we should have one too." She looked over at Savich. "You guys need to get out of those clothes. I'll help change Sherlock."

She clipped the machete to her own belt. "There," she said, patting it. "I guess I'm ready now for just about anything."

"I know you've got to have a radio somewhere. Get it." Molinas opened the third drawer of the huge desk and pulled out a small black radio.

"Get the plane here, now."

We all watched him set a frequency and listened to his rapid Spanish, some of which I couldn't make out. He looked up when he finished. "I didn't betray you," he said.

Savich walked to where Sherlock was sitting on the floor, Laura holding her hand. He bent down and picked her up. "Let's get out of here."

"You'd better pray that the Cessna comes," I said against Molinas's ear.

"It will come," he said. I saw him glance back at the radio.

He didn't look happy.

TWENTY-SEVEN

We reached the airstrip at about five-thirty in the morning, according to the
watch I'd taken from Molinas. The half-moon was fading quickly, but still
hanging on, and behind it a few scattered stars dotted the gray sky. The
mountains in the distance looked like ghosts, stretched up into broad sword
shapes, others hunched over, all of them unearthly in the vague dawn light.
There would soon be enough light to use the airstrip. Three days ago, I
thought, we were in Edgerton, Oregon, buying sandwiches from Grace's
Deli.

The silence was profound, just the crunch of our boots on the rocky
ground. The rain forest began not a hundred yards to our left, stretching up
the flank of the distant eastern mountains. The compound was directly
behind us. If anyone was following us, they were staying out of sight. I
thought of snipers and moved closer to Molinas. I hoped we covered the
others' backs well enough so if there were snipers, they'd be afraid to shoot
for fear of hitting Molinas.

When we reached the edge of the airstrip, the sky was a soft gray, with
strips of pink streaking to the east. There was no cover. We crouched down
against the stark landscape, still too well silhouetted for anyone with a gun.

Savich turned, a black eyebrow raised. "The rain forest begins right
over there? Yet it's hot and barren here. How can that be?"

"It's called deforestation." Molinas said. "The people are very poor."

"Mac and I were already in there," Laura said. "It's incredibly beautiful but the humidity strangles you, and there are so many creatures you can hear but can't see, it's also terrifying. I'm grateful we don't have to go back in."

Sherlock laughed, shaky, but it was a real laugh. "I think I need to kill Marlin again. I can hear his laughter, his shouting. I'm just going to kill him. I'll see if he can come back from the dead a second time."

"Yes, kill him," Savich said, looking directly into her eyes. "Kill him again, Sherlock. You're the only one who can do it. You did it before, you can do it again. Kill him and kick him a couple of times, then come back to me and stay. I need you here."

"I need you too, Dillon," she said and closed her eyes. The look on Savich's face was terrifying. I gripped his shoulder.

It was in that moment that I knew Jilly had been taking the drug when she went over the cliff. I'd been there with her and the drug had driven her mad, like Sherlock. When she'd discovered Laura was a DEA agent, that she'd been betrayed, she'd been haunted by Laura in her mind. She hadn't been able to bear it. And that's why she'd driven her Porsche off the cliff.

I looked over at Laura. She was still staring toward the eastern mountains, not moving, just staring. I wanted to tell her that everything would be all right, but there was something about the way she was focused on those mountains, her silence, that kept me quiet. Laura had it together. She was fine. I smiled at her, knowing in my gut that this woman I'd known for less than a week would decide that living with me was better than living without me.

We tried to limit our risks. We sat closely pressed together, Molinas facing back toward the compound. I didn't think any of his men could have gotten beyond us, but I couldn't be sure.

A small plane was coming in, the buzz of its engine sounding rough. I saw Savich frowning at that sound, looking toward the mountains. In a couple of minutes, a sleek little Cessna 310 appeared over the top of the closest peak, banked sharply, and started in to land, the sunrise a halo around it.

I didn't like the sound it was making—the engines sputtering, missing, as if barely hanging on.

Had Molinas screwed us?

I was turning to him when suddenly two helicopters burst over the mountains.

"My God," Savich said, shading his eyes, "they're McDonnell Douglas—

Apaches, AH-64 Apaches. They're ours. They've got an M230 Chain Gun, Hellfire missiles, and a stinger. Down! Everybody, DOWN!"

We all hit the ground. In a blink one of the Apaches fired on the Cessna. The small plane sputtered above the ground. I saw two men inside, one of them screaming. I watched the plane explode, showering debris into the dawn sky. Twisting shards of metal, parts of the engine, the seats, one of them holding what had been a man still strapped in, scattered over the airstrip and the land around it. A part of a wing crashed into the ground not twenty feet from us.

Savich said. "Good old USA Apaches. What are they doing here?"

"Somehow they must have found out where we were." Laura was yelling at the Apaches, waving her arms. I held Molinas close.

I looked up at the helicopters. They came closer and hovered, making no move to land.

"Laura," I shouted, "get away from there! Run!"

Without warning, they fired on us.

"The rain forest!" I grabbed Molinas and shoved him ahead of me. They came around again, firing, the hail of bullets kicking up dirt all around us. We made the rain forest, barely. Then I realized the last thing we needed was Molinas holding us back. He'd betrayed us.

I jerked him around and yelled in his face, "You damned bastard!"

"I didn't betray you." He was panting now. "You saw them. They shot down the Cessna. One of my men must have radioed Del Cabrizo and told him you were escaping. The cartel ordered it. I didn't."

"That makes me feel a whole lot better," I said. "Well, you can stay and talk to him about it." I shoved him down behind a tree, took off his belt, and tied his hands behind him to the skinny tree. I ripped off his very nice Italian silk shirt and stuffed it into his mouth, tying the rest behind his head.

"You'd better pray they don't think you're disposable. That's about the only thing that would save both of you."

I turned away from him and shouted, "Savich, we're heading north. Keep going, but veer to your left, to the west." Thank God it was light enough now to see where we were going. Northwest, we had to go northwest. Molinas's soldiers would be searching for him and then come after us.

Savich nodded, holding Sherlock close. I looked at Laura, wondering why she hadn't come to help me. She was standing about ten feet from me, not moving. I watched her weave where she stood, then drop one of the AK-47s.

"Laura?"

I heard the Apaches overhead, incredibly loud, heard their automatic weapons firing into the forest. Chances were that only an incredibly lucky shot would find us through that thick, nearly impenetrable canopy overhead. But given how our luck had gone so far, I didn't want to take any chances.

"Laura?" I yelled again. "Come on! We've got to hurry. I'll take the other weapon. What the hell's wrong?" She didn't answer. I saw her lean back against a tree, gripping her shoulder.

"Laura?"

"Just a minute, Mac." Her eyes were closed, her teeth gritted.

Oh, God, she'd been hit. The guns kept sounding overhead, the bullets smashing down through the foliage. We were too close to the edge of the rain forest. We had to go deeper. Without a word, I pulled her hand away from her shoulder. "It went through," she said, and I saw she was right after I'd opened her shirt.

"Hold still." I unbuttoned my fatigue shirt and jerked it off. At least it wasn't as sweaty as my undershirt. I wrapped it as best I could over the wound, tying it under her breasts. It was still bleeding. She was trembling. Her blood streaked over my hands. "Can you hang on for a while?"

She gave me a smile that made me want to cry and said, "I'm DEA. Of course I can hang on."

I smiled at her as I rebuttoned her shirt, picked up both AK-47s, and hoisted her over my shoulder.

"Mac, no, I can walk."

"It's time for the DEA agent to keep her mouth shut," I said, and to Savich, who'd turned back, "Laura's been shot. It's clean, through the upper shoulder. But we've got to take care of it, we've—"

An Apache was coming in fast and hovered right over us. It sounded muffled through all the greenery overhead, but it was close, too close. If it fired downward, it could hit us.

I laid Laura on the floor of the forest, cupped her cheek with my palm, and said, "Don't move, I'll be right back. I'm going to get you a first-aid kit and then I'm going to play doctor."

She looked at me like the drug had captured my brain again. I smiled at her, grabbed one of the AK-47s, and ran for a small, light-filled clearing inside the forest belt. I looked up. An Apache was hovering not twenty yards overhead, its rotor blades fanning the thick upper canopy of the rain forest. I heard birds screeching, heard their wings flapping madly to escape. The growth was so thick off to my left that I couldn't see them. I could make out a man staring downward with binoculars.

"Hey, you bastards!" I fired upward. When I cleared the magazine, I pulled it out and shoved another in, and waited. I needed them closer, and lower. The Apache weaved, plunging side to side. Yes, I thought, you've seen me. Now, come and get me. I could hear a man yelling. They were right over me now. I fired off another twelve rounds, directly into the gut of the helicopter.

I could see the pilot fighting the controls, trying to regain control. I heard the other man yell. Then, like it was released from a slingshot, the Apache rose straight up and then dipped sharply to the left. I fired another half-dozen rounds. It trembled, the rotor grinding, those amazing General Electric turboshafts sputtering, dying now from all the damage my bullets had caused. The Apache lurched and went straight up again, its nose aimed at the sky. It stopped, trembled some more, turned nose toward the ground, and came down fast. I beard the two men screaming.

The helicopter plunged into the rain forest, slashing through leaves and trees. I heard a loud ripping sound—its rotor being torn off. Then silence. I heard the other helicopter, but it wasn't close. Wouldn't it come over us like this one had? Because they saw it go down?

I waited a moment, then ran as fast as I could to where the helicopter lay, nose buried some two feet into the ground, its rotor broken off halfway down, gleaming sharp blade edges embedded in the foliage. Monkeys shrieked overhead. I saw several of them leaping from tree to tree some six feet above my head. I knew the helicopter could explode, but I had to get my hands on a first-aid kit. I couldn't face the thought of Laura wounded in this living hellhole without any medical supplies.

The gunner and the pilot were both dead. They were wearing fatigues, like the rest of Molinas's men. They were in an American helicopter but they surely weren't Americans. They were probably Del Cabrizo's men, sent to take us out, just as Molinas had said.

To my relief, I found the first-aid kit shoved beneath the pilot's seat. On the back of the pilot's chair, to my amazement, were half a dozen containers of bottled water in a net fastened to a strap. There were several blankets strewn over the backseat. I grabbed them up, smelling the fresh, thick scent of sex. Now I knew what these guys had been doing before they'd taken off.

I unfastened the net that held the water from the strap, threw the blankets over my shoulder, and shouting like a madman, I ran back.

We were still too close to the edge of the rain forest. I didn't hear anyone coming, didn't hear the other Apache. But it was stupid to take any chances.

Savich said, "You've got your first-aid kit, and water. I'm going to make sure you get a promotion and a raise, Mac."

"Can you hold out a bit longer?" I said, coming down to my knees beside Laura.

"Yes, but then I want to relax by the pool with a good book."

"You got it. Let's see what we've got in here. There should be some pain pills to help take the edge off." I found them and gave her three, and all the water she wanted from one of the bottles. Savich had gotten the bleeding stopped, thank God. It was as good as we could do for the moment. I rose quickly. "Let's go northwest about fifty more yards, then I'll backtrack and erase our tracks. The good Lord is looking out for us, guys. Look at all this bottled water. And it isn't even drugged."

Another fifteen feet ahead and we couldn't get through the twisted and intertwined vines and trees. It was a wall of green. The first time we'd been helpless, but this time we had the machete Laura had taken.

I unfastened it from her belt, kissed her cheek. "You're brilliant." I said. "I can't promise anything, but it seems to me that just maybe you've got the makings of an FBI agent."

"You really think so?" She managed a smile. Laura had to walk since I was carrying the water and the first-aid kit and one AK-47 and hacking our way through the dense green foliage. So much of it. I held her up, my arm around her waist. "You're doing great, kiddo. Just hang in there. Another fifteen steps and we'll rest. That's good Laura, ten more steps." I took another whack at the twisted vines in front of us. "The sucker's nice and sharp, thank God."

"I'd rather have a margarita, Mac."

"Me too, but I'd rather know for sure where we are. I should have wrung that out of Molinas."

"He got us out of there. We're in Colombia, Mac. We have to be."

I heard Sherlock moan, heard Savich's low voice, but I couldn't make out his words.

He hefted Sherlock over his shoulder and took the machete from me. I was grateful. We kept going, at least another fifty steps. It was Savich who pulled up. He was panting hard. He gently eased Sherlock to the ground and balanced the big machete and an AK-47 against a tree trunk beside her.

"Mac, spread out those blankets and let's lay our patients on them. Shush, Sherlock, it's okay."

Sherlock opened her eyes and looked over at me, at the AK-47s I was laying next to Savich. The only thing was, Sherlock wasn't behind those eyes. I looked away, I couldn't stand it. I wished I'd killed Molinas.

I leaned Laura against a tree, unwrapped the blankets from around her, and spread them out. I eased her down onto her back. Her eyes were nearly black with pain.

I leaned down and kissed her dry mouth. "Now, you just lie here, make Savich give you some water." I unfolded the other two blankets that I'd been carrying over my shoulder and spread them out over her. I said to Savich, "We've been using the machete, but maybe there's something I can do to lessen their chances of tracking us." Before I left I gave Laura another pain pill.

When I returned some five minutes later, I heard Laura whisper, "I'm sorry, really sorry. I should have dodged better. Maybe I'll be demoted to the FBI."

"You'd have to do something a lot worse than dodge the wrong way to be consigned with the likes of us," Savich said. "Rest now, Laura."

"And hold still," I said. I flipped up the metal clip on the first-aid kit. "I'm going to play doctor now." I looked through the medical supplies. Alcohol, an oral antibiotic, aspirin, gauze, bandages, tape, needles, matches, thread, the pain pills—thank God the helicopter hadn't exploded. I had a feeling this was the luckiest find I'd ever make in my life. After Laura.

Laura focused her eyes on my face. "We could be in Thailand right now. Any place there's a jungle."

"Not with a town called Dos Brazos," I said. "Hold still and swallow these pills. It's an antibiotic and another pain pill." I waited a couple of minutes for the meds to start taking hold, then stripped her shoulder down and examined the wound. It was just a small hole in the front, sluggishly oozing blood. "Hold still," I said again. I wet one of the bandages with alcohol and pressed it against the wound.

Laura didn't make a sound. Her eyes were tightly closed. She was biting her lower lip. "It's all right. I'm not in shock, at least not now. You don't have to look at me like that. I was shot two years ago. I know what shock feels like. Really, it isn't bad this time."

"Where were you shot?" I asked her.

"In my right thigh."

I could only shake my head. "You're doing really good. Don't move." I lifted her up and looked at the exit wound. It was raw and big and covered with shredded, bloody flesh and material from her fatigue shirt.

I said, "I can't put stitches in to close the wound, Laura, there's no way to get the wound sterile. The chances are the wound would get infected and that would be worse. So I'll just clean it and lay a bandage over it. We'll change the bandage every day. Okay?"

"Yes. I hate needles."

I laid a cloth soaked with alcohol over the wound in her back and gently cleaned the area as best I could. There was an antibiotic ointment, and I smoothed it on. Savich unwrapped a sterilized square of gauze and handed it to me. I removed the alcohol pad and pressed the gauze over the wound and pressed strips of adhesive bandage over it.

I repeated the procedure on the small entry wound. I washed the blood off her breast. The dried blood was dark red, nearly black now against her white flesh. I hated it.

I wrapped her shoulder, tying the thick bandage beneath her breasts. I'd done all I could think of. I'd done the best I could.

"Hey, Sherlock, you still there, sweetheart?"

"I'm here, Dillon."

"Do you think we're doing things okay here? Concentrate, Sherlock. You wanted to do it, and it's time. Talk to me."

"I'm here," she said in a thin, nearly transparent voice. "I'm concentrating really hard."

After a few minutes, I asked Laura if it still hurt.

"Just a bit," she said, and I believed her. She sounded vague and pleasantly surprised. "Isn't it wonderful how that stuff works? No, it isn't too bad."

TWENTY-EIGHT

I had to keep her warm. I got her back into her shirt and covered her with blankets. "You hunker down and take it easy now." Since she'd taken a bullet in the leg, she knew what that sort of pain felt like. I had no doubt she could deal with it. The thing was to keep her alive in this damned rain forest with more possible ways to die than the L.A. freeways.

Savich had turned back to his wife. "What do you say, Sherlock? Were we efficient enough for you?"

"I don't know, Dillon. I'm sorry, but I can't seem to concentrate, I—" She was gone from us.

"She'll dream of that lunatic now," Savich said. "It isn't fair, Mac, it isn't fair."

"She was with us longer this time," I said.

Laura said, "Maybe this time she'll kill Marlin Jones. That would be best for her."

"I hadn't really believed that such a thing was possible, but maybe," Savich said thoughtfully. He leaned close to his wife's face. "Did you hear that, Sherlock? Kill the bastard if he dares to come again. Shoot him right between the eyes. Try really hard to do that, okay?"

He stopped talking and looked up. We listened to the distant sound of an Apache. Not hovering or firing down, just cruising, it seemed to me.

Since there was no way they could ever see us through the thick canopy of green, there was no reason to fire.

I told them what I thought had happened to make Jilly drive off that cliff. "There's no doubt in my mind that Jilly was on that drug. I think the night she went over the cliff she was trying to get away from Laura. Laura was in her head, like Marlin Jones is in Sherlock's head, just like when I relived being in Tunisia. But there's a big difference here. Sherlock will come out of this, like I did. Maybe Jilly took too much of the drug, maybe she was really hooked, because she was still obsessed with Laura when she woke up in the hospital.

"Did she run out of the hospital herself because she didn't want to see me again? I don't know. Maybe. When we find her, we'll get the answer."

"The truth is," Savich said, "we don't have a clue about what the long-term effects of the drug are."

"I'm afraid that even Paul doesn't know that," I said. I saw a beetle, black and orange and green, pause a moment, wiggle its antennae at me, then hurry behind some small orange leaves. I saw several other leaves move. Critters everywhere, I thought, all of them hungry. Everything was alive in this place, everything was hungry, everything was hunted by something else, that or dead and instantly rotting or eaten.

I turned to Laura and lightly stroked my fingers over her mouth. "Since you've been cooperative, I'll give you some more water."

She drank down a good bit. I looked at the half-dozen bottles. Should we conserve? I wondered how long we'd have to survive in this place. Laura was shivering. I started to take off my shirt, but she stopped me. "Not here, Mac. You've got to keep as much of you covered as possible. There are lots of nasty things around here to bite you. And there are leeches too."

Leeches. Good lord. She was right. I doubled one sex-scented blanket and tucked it around her chest and neck.

"We've got to be very careful," she said. She paused, then frowned. I knew she was trying to get her thoughts together.

"It's okay, Laura. Take your time. We're not going anywhere."

"I was just thinking about my boss, Richard Atherton, wondering if the DEA is all over Edgerton." She stopped then. I knew she was in pain. I couldn't stand it. I gave her another pain pill.

After a few minutes, she opened her eyes, smiled at me, but her face was flushed. From fever or the heat or the tremendous weight of the humidity, I didn't know. "Breathe deeply, Laura," I said. "Think about that margarita I'm going to make for you. Think of me rubbing oil on your back, massaging your shoulders until all the knots are out. Now won't that feel good?" I lightly stroked my fingers over her cheek.

I smoothed the hair back from her face. After a few minutes she looked woozy. I didn't want to kill her with too many pain pills. I looked down at my watch. Nearly eight o'clock in the morning. No more pills until noon. I said, "Be quiet for a while, Laura. You can tell us all this stuff later, after you feel better. Are you warm enough?"

She thought about it but didn't say anything.

Sherlock was far off in a stupor, no doubt troubled by visions of Marlin Jones.

"How long has it been since they drugged her the last time, Savich?"

He thought a moment. "Actually, she was back with me only about thirty minutes before you and Laura arrived with Molinas."

"So it's only been about six hours."

Savich was staring up into the canopy of trees over our heads. I heard monkeys shrieking, a bird's wings flapping wildly, and other sounds I'd never heard before.

"What is it?" I asked him.

"I hear something," Savich mouthed to me. "Someone's coming this way. We knew they'd come after us. I wonder if they found Molinas."

I squeezed Laura's hand to keep her quiet and listened. Yes, someone was coming, several someones. They were searching blind, not too far away now. Savich had lifted one of the AK-47s. I eased the Bren Ten out of my waistband. "Don't move," I whispered against Laura's ear. She looked at once alarmed, then almost instantly quite calm again. "I might be down, Mac, but I'm not out. Give me a gun."

"Not on your life. You're a patient. You're not to move. Think about that shoulder opening. It wouldn't be good, Laura. We've got to survive. Now, lie still and—"

"I don't want Sherlock or me to die because I'm helpless, Mac. Sherlock's out of it. I'm all she's got. Give me the Bren Ten."

I gave it to her without another word.

"They're close, Mac," said Savich. "Let's go."

I slung the other AK-47 over my shoulder, slid the machete through my belt, checked the other magazine in my waistband, and fell in behind

Savich. If something happened to us, Laura had the Bren Ten. No, I wouldn't think about that, but I still took one backward look. Laura's fingers were curled around the pistol. I gave her a thumbs-up.

We were nearly on their heels fifty steps later. They weren't trying to be quiet. They were speaking loudly in Spanish, cursing, from what I could make out.

We waited, crouched down beneath some broad green leaves larger than my chest. The heat was rising. The air was becoming so heavy, so filled with water that moving through it was like carrying weights. It was tough to breathe. Thank God for that water I'd found in the Apache. The men kept complaining, coming within a dozen feet of where we were crouched on the floor of the forest.

"Let's get behind them," Savich said.

They were walking single file only about eight yards ahead of us. Their heavy steps covered any noise we made. I saw Savich's profile. He looked carved out of stone. Mean, dangerous stone. There was death in his eyes, and utter concentration.

He took the last man down so quickly I heard only a hoarse gurgle. The men ahead didn't hear a thing. Savich sliced his throat with a small scalpel he'd taken from the first-aid kit, then quickly dragged him out of sight. There were two others, who could turn around any minute. We didn't want to be standing there staring at them. He looked up as he laid the guy on his back.

"Let's get the other two."

We heard the two men talking just ahead of us in rapid Spanish. I paused a moment, listening carefully. I said behind my hand to Savich, "They think Leon stopped to piss."

"We'll take them both together," Savich said.

It happened fast.

Savich took one of them cleanly with the scalpel, just like the first man. I quickly sidestepped them when the other one turned, alarm firing his face. He yelled and lunged at me, bringing up his AK-47. I brought up my hand and smashed it into his throat. His head snapped back. He dropped to his knees, gagging and choking. I finished it with a blow with my rifle butt.

I raised my head to see a big cat staring at me calmly. He was stretched out along a low-lying branch, watching the two of us, unmoved. He looked down at us with, at best, mild interest. Was he waiting to eat the guys who lost?

Savich said, "It's a jaguar, Mac. He won't risk tangling with you. But he might take your prey. Hey, you okay?"

"Yeah," I said.

"Don't worry about him. Now, let's see what we can salvage here."

"Look," I said. "There's a couple of Baby Ruth candy bars here. Hot damn, we need those. We should check the other guy too. You know, Savich, these wrappers aren't written in Spanish. Neither is anything in the first-aid kit I got out of the helicopter, which was also American. Everything's American except for Molinas's men. Who are these guys? What do they do around here?"

Savich answered me with a shrug. He was right. At the moment, who these goons were wasn't important.

I felt strangely detached from the three dead men, poor bastards. "We got it done. Let's get back to Laura and Sherlock."

When we came through the trees to Sherlock and Laura, I nearly lost it. A man was standing over the women, his AK-47 pointed down at Laura's chest. Laura's eyes were closed. I didn't see the Bren Ten.

He didn't seem to know what to do. He saw us and said, "You will not move, *señor*, or I will shoot the women. That's right, lay down the weapons and step away."

They were the last words he ever said.

Laura pulled up the Bren Ten in a single motion and shot him through the forehead.

TWENTY-NINE

"That was well done, Laura," I said.

She laid the Bren Ten back against her stomach. "One minute we were alone, the next, he just appeared. You rattled him. It gave me the chance I needed."

We took his weapon and three candy bars from his pants pocket. Soon Savich was stamping his feet into new boots. "They fit perfectly," he said. "And he has water too."

I said, "That shot could attract anyone else out there. Savich and I should look around. We shouldn't be much longer than ten minutes."

Laura said, "Go. We'll be all right."

Savich and I went together, back toward where they'd come from. We saw a green boa wrapped at least three times around a tree we passed. I felt a chill slide over my flesh. "There are too many things alive in this place. Every step you take you've got to look everywhere, up and down and side-ways, all the time. I just touched a tree that was covered with spikes. It's all so bloody wild and we're not in control here."

"If Laura hadn't taken that machete," Savich said, "we wouldn't be here at all."

I traced the flight of a scarlet macaw, its brilliant red feathers blending down its back into yellow, then blue. He landed, hovering on the very end of a branch not three feet from us that pumped up and down with the bird's weight. I wondered what Nolan would think of this otherworldly bird.

"A trail or two might be nice," Savich said. "There's no sign of anyone else. Let's get back."

It was so hot now it was hard to breathe. The humidity was crushing. Our shirts were soaked with sweat. The sweat was so deep on my forearm I could see insects drowning before they could bite me.

"It's still morning," Savich said. "I can't wait to see how much hotter it gets by this afternoon. Look at this damned soil—it's clay. I don't want it to rain. Maybe it's not the rainy season, you think?" He laughed, shaking his head at himself.

I said to Savich, "It's not even ten o'clock yet, but we shouldn't stay here. What do you think? Carrying Sherlock and Laura and all the supplies, can we make maybe half a mile before collapsing under a tree?"

"At most," Savich said. "If we have to use the machete to get through, we might not make more than a couple of miles all day."

"Better the women are down than us. I can just see Laura trying to tote my carcass over her shoulder."

Savich laughed, then sobered. "If Laura's wound gets infected, she's in major trouble."

"We've got some more shirts. We'll cover every naked bit of her. The shirts might not smell real sweet, but they're blessed protection against the filth and the bugs."

I looked up at the dense canopy overhead, saw a big reddish monkey staring down at us. "There are so many colors," I said, "everywhere. Look, Savich, mangoes. They're even ripe. We can eat our Baby Ruths, then have mangoes for dessert." I picked about half a dozen of the best. I was surprised that some of the critters hadn't already nabbed them.

AT one o'clock in the afternoon, we broke into a small clearing, maybe two square meters, that wasn't overflowing with growing green things. The canopy wasn't as thick here and more light came through. That light brought us some breathing space, literally. I stood a moment, Laura in my arms, under a thick shaft of hot, clear sunlight. I laid her on a blanket right beneath that blessed shaft of light. "Soak it up," I told her. "Let it dry you to your toes."

I dragged the thick net that held the water bottles over the last thirty or so yards. Two snakes flashed across the ground so fast I couldn't imagine any predator catching them. I had no idea if they'd kill you with a bite or not.

I spread out the blankets, then scraped away more foliage to create a small perimeter. Laura had been largely silent for the past two hours. I think she'd slept part of the time, so drugged that she couldn't stay awake. I laid my palm across her forehead. She was hot, but maybe that was normal in this hellhole. It had to be near one hundred percent humidity on the floor of the rain forest. At least her skin didn't feel clammy.

Sherlock was finally awake. She was sitting cross-legged in the middle of a blanket, staring over at Laura. "Don't let her die," she said to me, and began shredding the ragged edge of one of the shirts she was wearing. She'd torn off a strip of shirt and tied her thick red hair back from her face. Still, strands were curling haphazardly around her ears. "I couldn't have imagined a place like this. I just saw a frog that flew from one tree to another tree. They were at least ten feet apart. It was long and skinny and just about the ugliest thing I've ever seen. I think it was red, maybe orange, I can't be sure, it flew so fast. This place isn't meant for people, you know?"

"I know," Savich said. "Maybe we should think of our little sojourn here as a bizarre sort of vacation. Maybe Club Med would be interested. Mac and I saw a jaguar. You rarely see them, even here. Drink this, sweetheart. No, don't just give me ladylike sips. Gulp it down. That's right."

When she'd drunk her fill, Savich wiped her mouth. She raised her hand and touched his fingers as they lay against her cheek. "Dillon, my brain feels like it's coming back to me. Is that a lemon I see?"

"Good," he said. "That's good. Yep, Mac and I found some lemon and lime trees. We picked both. If we run out of water or need to wash up, we can use them."

"We can use the lime in Laura's margaritas. I can see you now, Dillon, see exactly who you are. I didn't like being away from you like that."

"I didn't like it either," Savich said.

"You don't have to carry me anymore now."

He leaned over and kissed her hard and quick. "Good. That means you can help carry the water bottles."

She laughed, a real Sherlock laugh, and again, it made me wish I'd killed Molinas for what he'd done to her. And what he'd done to me.

Laura's eyes were closed. I knew she was in pain, but I needed to ration the pain pills. I gave her water, antibiotics, and two aspirin.

"It's time for lunch," I said. "It's all sugar and fat. My two most favorite things in the world. We'll be on such highs, we'll be jumping around up there in the trees with the monkeys."

Savich said, "I saw half a dozen red howler monkeys about seventy-five paces behind us. They were swinging around, high above us, interested but not going crazy at the sight of us. It was like we were neighbors they just didn't like. It made me think they've seen a number of people here in their territory. Maybe we aren't deep in a rain forest in the bowels of Colombia, a hundred miles from civilization. Maybe we're close to a village or a town. Though I don't know who would live in a place where taking a breath feels like sucking on a blast furnace."

I frowned over at him, nodding. "You're right. That jaguar we saw seemed bored, like we were no big deal. Like he'd keep an eye on us because it was part of his job but he wasn't at all worried."

"That's probably how they look just before they spring," Savich said, laughing at my expression. "Nah, I wouldn't worry about the cats. Who knows? Hey, are you guys ready for some lunch?"

"I want my margarita," Laura said, her voice slurred. "I know you picked some limes. I heard Sherlock talk about it." I opened her two shirts and looked at the bandage. No blood, thank God. What should I do for it now? I'd been through some basic survival training, but that was it. I saw a small pool of dried blood on her right breast that I'd missed when I'd cleaned her with the alcohol. I didn't think, just lightly scratched up the dried blood. Her eyes opened.

"Blood," I said. "I couldn't bear to see it on you, Laura."

"How do I look?"

I wanted to tell her that despite everything I was still a guy, with guy thoughts, and I wanted to look at her breasts and smooth my fingers over them while my eyes were closed, and tell her she was beautiful. I felt an insect bite the base of my index finger. "No new bleeding. The bandage is nice and clean. You're sweating and that's good. A nice dry, hot sweat from the sun. I think the best thing is to leave everything alone. Tomorrow morning I'll change the bandage and see how the wound looks. Now, since you're such a good patient, you get a reward." I peeled a Baby Ruth candy bar and broke off a small chunk. I waved it under Laura's nose. She didn't say a word, opened her mouth. She smiled while she chewed. I fed her the entire bar. "You're going to want to start dancing from this sugar high," I said.

"She can dance with Sherlock," Savich said. He was sitting on Sherlock's blanket, licking chocolate from his fingers.

"Sherlock, you okay now?"

"I'm a lot better than you are, Laura. Is the pain bad?"

"I can control it. I'm forced to lie here and watch Mac eat one of my candy bars. It's tough. My mouth is watering. If I had the strength, I'd rip it out of his mouth."

I broke off a little piece and put it in her mouth. She closed her eyes in bliss and chewed.

I counted. We had five more candy bars. We needed to find some fruit besides the mangoes. I thought bananas should be all over the place, but I hadn't seen any. I'd seen a small anteater scraping along on the floor, and I tried to imagine baking him over a fire. I said, "Everyone, keep your eyes open for some edible stuff, probably fruit, that we can pull off a tree, peel, and eat, okay?"

"We might as well start on the mangoes," Savich said, as he began peeling mangoes and handing them out. "Nice and ripe. Eat up."

"I've got matches," Sherlock said, mango juice dripping off her chin. "When we stop this afternoon, we'll build a fire. It'll keep the creepy things away."

"I know all about how to do that," Laura said. "I spent lots of my childhood at campgrounds being ordered around by Dad and an older brother. I've seen some birch and beech trees. Even some oak. That's hard wood, good for burning in a fire."

Sherlock crawled over to Laura. "I've got another strip of shirt. Let me braid your hair, it's kind of all over the place."

I watched Sherlock try to make a French braid of Laura's long, very matted hair. She smoothed out most of the tangles and picked away half a dozen insects. The best I could say about the result was that her hair was away from her face.

"How is it?" Laura asked.

"You're gorgeous. Sherlock's got a real talent with hair, particularly really long hair like yours." I dabbed a piece of wet shirt over Laura's mouth to get rid of the sticky mango juice. I could just imagine how all the flying critters would love that stuff.

She smiled and closed her eyes.

I got to my feet and stretched. I packed everything up, then lifted Laura into my arms. I was used to her weight now. It felt good. I looked all around me, carefully. Nothing lethal in sight, man or beast.

Sherlock, thank God, was walking on her own. She kept up with Savich, right on his heels, carrying the first-aid kit and an AK-47. "Sleep, Laura," I said. "I won't tell any bad jokes to keep you up."

"That's good, Mac," she said against my shoulder. Her voice was weaker.

We kept moving. Laura seemed lighter than she had an hour before. It was as if she were fading away, slowly, and there didn't seem to be anything I could do to stop it. Except find help.

Savich kept up a steady stride, chopping away the undergrowth ahead of us. We saw very little but we heard scurrying sounds all around us.

Suddenly we heard screaming and barking sounds, high above us. A family of spider monkeys, about ten of them, were jumping up and down, rattling branches. Savich got hit in the middle of his back with a shriveled piece of brown fruit we couldn't identify. They hurled other vegetation and small branches down at us, but nothing that hurt us. I hurried and got a thick, sharp-edged leaf in my face for my trouble. They weren't afraid of us, only pissed that we were in their territory. Once we had moved sufficiently on, they ignored us.

When the rain came in the middle of the afternoon, hot, thick sheets of rain, I would have given two of my candy bars for a big umbrella. Then we discovered that parts of the canopy overhead were so thick, we were able to stay relatively dry if we stayed in the right spots. I covered Laura as best I could. Steam rose off the ground when the deluge finally stopped. The humidity didn't lessen, it just wasn't liquid anymore. Steam rose from our clothes again.

We all smelled very ripe.

I eased Laura onto her feet, holding her upright against me.

"Can you imagine what a cold shower would feel like, Mac?" she asked.

"Right now," I said, and closed my eyes briefly, "it would be on my top-ten list. Maybe top three. I want you in that cold shower with me, Laura, laughing and fit again."

She didn't say anything and that scared me. We kept going.

Now, to add to the impenetrable undergrowth in front of us, the ground was mud. The nicely packed clay was slippery and wet through to a depth of a good six inches. Mud covered us to our knees. It made walking as hard as sucking one of our limes through a straw. I nearly fell once. It was Sherlock who steadied me.

Sweat poured off us. Savich was grunting with each swing of the machete. Monkeys and birds shrieked and howled above us. We couldn't see even one of them. The racket was nearly deafening at times.

When I wanted to stop, go down on my knees, and never move again, I saw butterflies sporting the most amazing colors—reds, yellows, greens. I pointed at them. One followed us a good distance, gliding beside my face, wide-winged, the brightest blue imaginable, its wings rimmed with solid black. When the butterflies disappeared, taking their beauty with them, I realized we'd moved at least another twenty feet west. The rain forest was deadly, horrific, and those butterflies were the most beautiful things I'd ever seen.

Sherlock spotted two coral snakes. She came to a stop and stared two feet to her left into some undergrowth. There was no way a coral snake could go unnoticed. The vivid orange-and-white stripes slithered away from us and into deeper cover.

I checked to see that everyone's boots were tightly laced up, the ends of their pants firmly tucked inside the boots. It was hard to tell with all the mud covering everything. At least we didn't have any mud on our skin. Talk about itching. But no insects could get inside, and no snakes. I noticed bites on the backs of my hands. No hope for it.

Survival, I thought. We just had to survive. We didn't hear any helicopters for the rest of the afternoon, or the noise of any other humans. It was only the four of us, alone in this living oven.

"Hot damn," Savich shouted. "Look what I found. Ripe bananas, to go with our mangoes. Now the Baby Ruths can be our dessert."

We also found some *pipas*, a green coconut you can crack open and drink out of. Since Sherlock had taken one of those huge leaves and fashioned it into a funnel to catch rainwater during the downpour, both the empty water bottles were full again. We picked half a dozen *pipas* just in case.

I was doing the hacking now, Savich carrying Laura. I said over my shoulder, after I'd had to whack a welter of green intertwined leaves three times to get them apart, "I wonder if they found Molinas, the bastard. Maybe they didn't. Maybe a coral snake got him. Or maybe he's still lying there with insects crawling all over him."

"Or maybe," Savich said, "this Del Cabrizo character was so angry that we escaped, he killed him."

I didn't want to think about what could happen to Molinas's daughter.

We stopped to make camp when we came to another small clearing. When we stepped into the sunlight, we saw a flock of wild turkeys running through the deep grass to the other side. They disappeared into the forest. It was late in the afternoon, time to stop anyway.

Laura was getting weaker. It required too much energy for her to talk. I gave her more antibiotics, more aspirin, and two more pain pills. There were only four left. She didn't have a fever, and the bandages looked clean, but she was getting weaker.

Sherlock swept our small campsite clean with the thick net. The ground here was nearly dry because of the direct, hot sunlight. She managed to get it completely bare. "It's important that we leave room so lots of oxygen can circulate. Once we build a fire, it will stay brighter and hotter." I collected tinder: low, dead hanging branches, rotted pieces of tree that were dry. We managed to find some birch that Laura said was good for fires. Sherlock began digging a moat around our campsite. She said it would keep the critters out.

Savich used the scissors from the first-aid kit to make several fire sticks. He shaved the sticks with shallow cuts to "feather" them. "My granddaddy taught me how to do this," he said. "It'll make the wood catch fire more quickly."

We mixed birch bark and dried grass. I stood back and watched Sherlock build a teepee of kindling over a pile of tinder. I handed Savich the matches from the first-aid kit and watched him light one of his fire sticks, let it burn brightly, and touch it to the tinder. I couldn't believe it actually worked. It bloomed up bright and hot. It must have been ninety degrees, and there we were, sucking up to it.

"A hot dog might be nice," Sherlock said. "Potato chips, some dill pickles."

"Tortilla chips and hot salsa," Savich said, rubbing his hands together, and grinned. Behind him, a branch shimmied. A brown-spotted gecko poked its head around a tree, looked at us, then pressed itself flat against the bark. I swear it disappeared.

"Maybe some pickle relish on the hot dog," Sherlock said. "Forget the dills." As she spoke, she was looking over at Laura, who lay quietly.

We were trapped in a Hieronymus Bosch painting and we'd managed, for a moment, to superimpose normalcy. As evening settled in, the beetles began to move around. You could hear them scuttling to and fro. So many of them, all hungry. I smiled over at Laura. "We're geniuses. Look at that fire."

But Laura wasn't looking at either me or the fire. She was staring to her right, beyond the perimeter of the campsite, beyond Sherlock's moat. Her face was whiter than boiled rice. I heard her say my name, her voice just above a croak.

I pulled the Bren Ten out of my waistband and slowly turned.

THIRTY

There, reared up on its hind feet, its claws extended, claws so ragged and huge that one swipe could have taken off my face, was a golden brown armadillo. Not one of those small guys you see as road kill on the west Texas highways, but a giant armadillo. I'd never even seen one in a zoo. I'd only seen pictures of them. It had a long snout and small eyes that never left us. The hoary flesh seemed to retract farther, showing more of its claws.

"It doesn't eat people," Laura whispered. "It eats worms."

"That's a happy thought," I said as I lowered the Bren Ten. Who knew if men were out there to hear the noise? Savich tossed me a rock. I threw it, kicking up leaves and dirt not six inches from where the armadillo stood. It made a strange hissing noise and disappeared back into the undergrowth.

I heard a collective sigh of relief.

It was time to eat. Savich peeled mangoes with the first-aid scissors. A great find, those scissors. Savich assigned me the task of peeling bananas.

I eyed my slice for just an instant before eating it. I didn't think we could get food poisoning or diarrhea from something we had just peeled. We each ate only two mangoes, followed by one banana, and polished it off with one of the precious Baby Ruths.

"It's only eight o'clock," Sherlock said. "Does anyone know what day it is?"

"If it's Friday," Savich said, "you and I would be putting Sean to bed, then curling up downstairs with a Hitchcock movie."

Sherlock grinned at the thought, then she scooted over to Laura. She lightly laid her palm on Laura's cheek, then her forehead. "Mac, when did you give her aspirin?"

"Two hours ago."

"She's getting a fever. We've got to dump water down her throat and keep at it. That's what the doctor told me to do with Sean when he had a high fever."

I'd endured long nights before, but this was the longest. At least three dozen different beetles kept up an endless dissonant concert throughout the night. We heard things slithering all around us. I'd swear I heard at least a dozen winged things fluttering over my head. But the noise of those beetles, there was nothing like it.

Savich kept the fire burning bright. No more giant armadillos came to visit. No snakes slithered in to get warm. Only the four of us and the fever that was burning Laura up inside.

I was sleeping lightly when I felt her trembling beside me. The shakes, I thought, from a breaking fever. I got all the water I could down her throat, then eased her tight against me, and perhaps it worked because she stopped moaning and eased into fitful sleep for several hours.

We had to find civilization.

With our luck, we'd probably go loping into another drug dealer's compound.

THE next morning, we drank a bottle of our precious water, ate two more mangoes, three more bananas, and savored the last of our Baby Ruths.

When we were ready to head out, Savich looked at me and held out his arms. I shook my head and pulled Laura closer to my chest.

"Give her to me. You're driving yourself into the ground, Mac. It hasn't been that long since Tunisia. You do the chopping for a while. I'll carry her until noon, then you can take over again."

It was clear ahead, no need for the machete. It was an unexpected blessing.

Laura's fever had fallen close to morning and hadn't come back, as far as any of us could tell. But she was weak. The wound was red and swollen, but there wasn't any pus. I rubbed in the last of the antibiotic cream. Her flesh felt hot beneath my fingers. I didn't know how serious it was, but I knew we had to get out of this damned hellhole. I had very little of anything left. I prayed that a real live doctor would suddenly appear in the path ahead of us, waving a black bag and speaking English.

When Savich was holding her, I took the edge of one of the shirts she was wearing and wet it. I dabbed it all over her face. Her mouth automatically opened. I gave her as much water as she wanted.

"I figure we pulled a little south before we stopped yesterday," I said, once I'd gotten my bearings. "Let's go due west and hold to it."

"Look, we've got to be somewhere," Sherlock said, swiping an insect off her knee. "It's a small planet, right?"

"You're right," Savich said. "Sherlock, lead the way. Mac, you take the rear. Everyone, eyes sharp. I've got a hankering for a banana, so keep a lookout for some ripe ones."

When it rained late that morning, Sherlock managed to capture a good half bottle of fresh rainwater, again using one of those big leaves as a funnel. She stood holding that half-filled water bottle, hair streaming down her face, covered with bite marks, puffed up proud as a peacock, grinning like a fool.

We were wet, but there was nothing we could do about it. Savich managed to keep Laura's wound dry.

The ground turned to mud again and the undergrowth suddenly thickened. I pulled out the machete and began hacking. My arms felt like they were burning in their sockets. When we found a small area that enjoyed, for some reason unknown to me, a patch of clear sunlight, Savich laid Laura on her back on a blanket and wrapped another blanket around a water bottle to put under her head.

We got a small fire going within ten minutes this time. With that sun overhead, we found dry tinder quickly. With the fire burning brightly, the insects backed off.

Savich began peeling mangoes with the first-aid scissors. "I always liked these things," he said. He gave a slice to Sherlock.

He cut off another thick slice and handed it to me. I waved it over Laura's mouth. She opened up. She was still eating. The food seemed to rouse her. She said suddenly, "Sherlock, have you felt any sort of withdrawal signs? Like you wanted more of that drug?"

"No, thank God." She shuddered. "Why do you ask? Oh, I see. If a drug's not addictive, it wouldn't be worth the drug dealer's time to sell it. No repeat customers."

"Right. Mac, how about you?"

"I haven't felt anything either."

"Maybe you guys haven't had enough of it," Laura said. "Maybe it takes more than three doses to get hooked."

"Do you think Jilly was hooked, Mac?"

I hated to say it, but I did. "Yes."

"I wonder who else in Edgerton has tried the stuff and what they're doing now," Sherlock said.

"I'll bet you Charlie Duck tried it. The coroner told me there was something odd in Charlie's blood. He was going to run more tests. Maybe he even tried it on purpose to find out what was going on. He was a retired cop, remember."

"Maybe that's why someone killed him," Laura said.

"That works," Savich said, nodding as he ate a bite of banana.

"Mac," Sherlock said suddenly, "you had that hookup with Jilly when she went off the cliff and you were actually in bed in Bethesda. You didn't understand it. Well, maybe it happened again. Maybe Jilly was in your mind, warning you."

"There's really no other explanation," Savich said, folding up the banana peel. "Unless you dreamed it up because you were drugged out of your mind."

"I was drugged for sure. Whatever it means, I hope it also means that Jilly is alive. This is tough to take," I said, leaning over to feel her forehead. "How do you feel?"

"There's something crawling up my leg—on the outside, at least."

I swiped off the salamander, who flicked its skinny tail, then flitted off into the undergrowth.

Savich was carving another feather stick with the scissors. The damned thing looked like a piece of art.

Laura moaned. She was lying on her back, her eyes closed. Her face was paper white, her lips were nearly blue. I shoveled more aspirin down her throat.

There wasn't much of anything left in the first-aid kit. My eyes met Savich's across her body. He was frowning. He was also holding Sherlock's hand, tight.

We slogged through the mud at least another couple of miles before we stopped for the night.

Laura was about the same the following morning, weak, shaky, and feverish. The wound was redder, more swollen. There was no kidding anybody now. It was bad. We had to get her to a hospital. We were up and walking, Savich carrying Laura, by sunrise.

"Due west," I said again, and began hacking.

We found a stalk of ripe bananas at nine o'clock. Savich tore them off the stalk to the accompaniment of screaming monkeys, whose breakfast we were stealing. I was relieved they didn't dive-bomb us.

It was nearly noon when I smelled something. I stopped dead in my tracks, lifted my head, and smelled. It was salt, so strong I could taste it.

I started to let out a yell when I heard men's voices, loud, not twenty feet away from us.

"Oh, no," Sherlock said, and backed up, dropping everything except her AK-47. "How could they have found us?"

Savich held Laura, who was either asleep or unconscious. He didn't put her down, just drew back so I could come up alongside Sherlock.

"They don't care that we can hear them," I whispered. "Are there that many of them? Have they fanned out?"

"I can smell the salt now, Mac. We've got to be near the ocean."

The voice moved away. Then, to my shock, I heard women's voices. Then laughter. Lots of laughter, yelling, more laughter. I heard screaming, but not in terror, screaming and shouting in fun, and all of it was in English.

Something was very strange here.

The thick foliage melted away, everything suddenly thinning out. I took the lead, my Bren Ten in my hand, Sherlock in the rear, Savich carrying Laura between us. We moved as quietly as we could. I saw a troop of green parrots flying from one banana tree to the next, a phalanx of green with flashes of red and yellow. The salt smell grew stronger, and the sun slashed down through the trees above us as the thick canopy above disappeared.

I felt a breeze on my face. I broke through a final curtain of green leaves and stepped onto white sand. Savich inched out behind me. I heard Sherlock suck in her breath. We stood there, staring.

We were standing at the edge of the rain forest, a good fifty feet of pristine white sand stretching between us and the ocean. It was the most beautiful sight I'd ever seen.

Some twenty yards up the beach were at least twenty men and women in swimsuits, playing volleyball.

There were beach towels strewn over the sand, a couple of sand castles, half a dozen umbrellas and beach chairs. To top it off, there was a guy on a seat set up some twenty feet above the ground, an umbrella covering him. He was a lifeguard.

Laura made a soft noise in her throat. She opened her eyes and looked at me. "What's happening?"

"I'd say we lucked out, sweetheart. Hold on. You and I are going to be in that cold shower before you know it."

The laughter slowly died away. The men and women were looking down the beach at us. Two of the men waved the others back and came walking toward us. I dropped the Bren Ten to my side. Sherlock eased down on the AK-47, trying to look a little less terrifying.

I yelled, "We need some help. We've got a wounded person here."

The women came trotting up behind the men. One of the guys sprinted toward us. Short and fiercely sunburned, he was wearing glasses and a slouchy green hat. "I'm a doctor," he said, panting when he stopped in front of us. "My God, what happened to you guys? Who's hurt?"

"Over here," Savich said. He carefully laid Laura down on a blanket Sherlock quickly spread beneath a palm tree.

She was barely responding. I unbuttoned the two shirts and bared the bandages. As he knelt down beside her, I said, "It's a gunshot wound through the shoulder, happened two days ago. I had a first-aid kit, thank God. I didn't set any stitches for fear of infection. I changed the bandages every day and kept the wound as clean as possible. But it looks like it got infected anyway."

In the next minute, at least a dozen men and women circled around us. Savich rose and smiled at them, looking ferocious, I realized, seeing how dirty he was, with mud dried to his thighs and his growth of beard. He looked like a wild man, filthy and dangerous.

Then Sherlock laughed. She tossed the water bottles in their net to the ground and let out a big whoop. "We've been in the rain forest for over two days. Is this Club Med?"

The men and women looked at one another. A man in a loose red-and-white-striped bathing suit said, "No, we're on a day trip here from up the coast," he said, eyeing us closely. "You got separated from your guide?"

"We didn't have a guide," Sherlock said. "Where are we?"

"You're in the Corcovado National Park."

"Anywhere near Dos Brazos?" I asked, and slapped a bug off my neck.

"Yeah, it's at the southeast end of the rain forest."

Laura opened her eyes and looked up at the man who was carefully lifting up the bandage on her shoulder. "It's all right. You hang in there. It's not bad. But you need a hospital. What's your name?"

"I'm Laura. What's yours?"

"I'm Tom. I'm here on my honeymoon. It's a great place. Well, maybe it wasn't such a great place for you. What happened?"

"I'm a federal agent. All of us are. I got shot by some drug dealers. We've been in the rain forest for the past two days."

Tom the doctor sat back on his heels and turned to a woman who had to be close to six feet tall. "Glenis, go tell the lifeguard that we need a helicopter here fast. It's a medical emergency."

"And the police," I said.

Tom said to all of us, "The Sirena Ranger Station is up the way a bit. It shouldn't take too long. The wound's infected, but it doesn't look too bad, considering. You guys did really well taking care of her."

"Thanks," I said.

"I want a margarita," Laura said. "With lots of lime. We'll even provide the lime."

I looked around at everyone in that circle. "I've heard of Corcovado," I said slowly. "Isn't it in Costa Rica?"

One of the women who was wearing a bright red bikini nodded. "Where did you think you were?"

"Maybe Colombia," I said. "Hey, I've always wanted to visit Costa Rica."

"No wonder the animals were bored with us," Sherlock said.

One of the men said, "Didn't you see anyone?"

"Just the bad guys," Sherlock said. "And some footprints that led off into the undergrowth. We couldn't take a chance of getting more lost than we already were. We've just been making our way west."

"You didn't see the tram overhead?" Tom asked. At our blank looks, he said, "Hey, we all took a ride through the rain forest on it yesterday. It was awesome. Well, I guess you must have missed it." He stuck out his hand to me. "Welcome to Playa Blanca."

THIRTY-ONE

I was staring at the man when I heard Laura wheezing and choking. I was at her side in an instant, grabbing her arms, lifting her against me. She was trembling violently. "Laura," I said.

"No!"

Tom shoved me out of the way. He peeled back her eyelids, checked her pulse, then immediately yelled for beach towels. Beach towels?

Men and women came running, their arms loaded down with colorful towels with parrots and leopards and bright suns on them. Tom covered her with a good half-dozen beach towels, wet down the end of one of them and spread it over her forehead. He sat back on his heels and said, "Bring me cold drinks, not the diet ones, the ones filled with sugar."

Someone slapped a Dr Pepper into his hand. He peeled back the tab and said to me, "Hold up her head. We need to get this down her." I didn't think she'd take any, but she did. On some level she must have known she had to drink. "The sugar's really good for her," Tom said. "And she needs the liquid badly. Let's keep getting it down her throat. We've got to keep her hydrated."

The beach crowd gave her some room.

"Where's that helicopter?" Tom called out as he poured more Dr Pepper down Laura's throat.

"The lifeguard says another ten, fifteen minutes," someone yelled back.

The men and women seemed to have assigned themselves tasks. Some of them brought us drinks, others food, still others brought insect repellent and more beach towels. One woman wearing a thong bikini that was an eye-catcher dragged up a huge umbrella and positioned it so that Laura was well protected from the sun.

It seemed like an eternity had passed when—no more fluttering eyelids, no moans, no twitches—Laura opened her eyes and looked straight up at me. She was dead white but her eyes were focused. She was back again. She smiled at me. Tom gave her more Dr Pepper.

"You're doing great, Laura," he said. "Hang in there. Breathe slowly and lightly. Yes, that's it. Don't let yourself go under again. Okay?"

"Okay." It was her voice, frail and paper thin, but she was back.

"I can hear the helicopter," I said. "Don't leave me now, Laura. No more going back into the ether. It would really piss me off. I think Tom would freak out. Smile at me every couple of minutes while you concentrate on breathing. I need reassurance. Okay?"

"I'm all right," she whispered. "It hurts really bad, Mac, but I can deal with this. How's this for a smile?"

"It's the most beautiful smile I've ever seen. I'm sorry, but I don't have any more pain pills. Squeeze my hand when it gets really bad."

When the helicopter landed some twenty yards away from us down the beach, I was nearly a basket case. Two men, each with a gurney slung over his back, and one woman carrying a black bag ran to us. For the first time, I began to really believe that Laura would make it. I wanted to cry with relief.

When the helicopter lifted off, I was holding Laura's hand and waving to Dr. Tom and all the men and women vacationers who'd helped us out. One of the medics was sticking an IV into her arm, saying as he did so, his English beautifully deep and soothing, "It's sugar and salt water. Nothing to worry about. The doctor said she's been drinking soda. This is even better."

"She's dehydrated," another medic said, a young woman wearing a Mets baseball cap backward on her head. She fit a plastic oxygen mask over Laura's nose and mouth. "Is she allergic to anything?"

I shook my head. "I don't know."

The woman said nothing, nodded. "I'm going to give her an intravenous antibiotic called cefotetan. It's very rare that anyone's allergic to it." She added, slanting a look at me, "She your wife?"

"Not yet," I said. Another of the medics was checking Sherlock. The helicopter rose well above the treetops and we got a panoramic view of the rain forest. Dense, forbidding, so green you felt like you were growing mold just looking at it. Low, thick fog was hanging over parts of it, like a wispy gray veil. It looked mysterious, otherworldly. It didn't look like a place where human beings belonged. Far off to the southeast must have been where we ran into it to escape the helicopters shooting at us. The town of Dos Brazos was over there, I guessed, somewhere, and a few miles southwest was the compound and Molinas, the bastard, and his men who had balls but no discipline.

We'd survived. Odd to think that trams ran tourists through the rain forest, all snug and safe, hands holding cameras and soft drinks.

It was too difficult to be heard over all the noise of the rotors, so we sat there, looking down at the huge stretch of rain forest that had been both prison and haven.

The woman paramedic lightly touched her hand to my shoulder. I leaned close. "We're going directly to San José," she said. "The *señorita* needs the best facility."

"How much longer?"

She shrugged. "Maybe an hour."

I took Laura's hand. She was still mumbling, still out of it. It was a very long hour.

I'd always wanted to visit Costa Rica, but not like this. Another five minutes and the helicopter set down in the parking lot of the Hospital San Juan de Dios.

There were medics with a gurney waiting. The last I saw of Laura was her long hair hanging off the side of the gurney—tangled and damp from the cold wet towels they'd kept on her forehead—beautiful hair, I thought. Hell, I was in love. She could have been bald and I'd have admired the shine.

The woman medic turned, smiled, and said, "Go to the third floor as soon as they've checked you all out. She'll be in surgery there."

Sherlock took my arm and led me toward the emergency room. "We made it," she whispered. "Don't worry, Mac. Laura will be fine."

An hour later we'd been examined, cleaned up somewhat, but Savich and I still looked like wild men, with stubble on our faces, torn fatigues, and swollen insect bites covering our necks and the backs of our hands. As for Sherlock, she looked like Little Orphan Annie before she hit the big time, her red hair a wild nimbus around her head, her face pale, her clothes stiff with dried mud. I leaned down and kissed her cheek. She tasted like insect repellent.

But at least we looked human again, and that was a good start.

I called Laura's boss, Richard Atherton, of the DEA. Savich set up a conference call with his boss, Jimmy Maitland, and Carl Bardolino, my chief. We went over every detail of what had happened. It took at least an hour, some of it peppered with curses from Atherton. We agreed they would fill in our embassy and contact the local authorities to get us protection. They all wanted to come and bring agents with them. Bottom line, no one was going to take four federal agents and haul them off to another country and get away with it. They were arranging for an assault on the compound with the Costa Rican military. Edgerton was already covered with agents, searching for us, questioning everyone, turning the town upside down. I thought of my sister. I was worried and scared for her.

I listened as Sherlock and Savich called his mom and talked baby talk to their son.

Dr. Manuel Salinas came to us in the waiting room and said in only slightly accented English, "You did very well. Two days in the rain forest with a bullet through her shoulder, I will tell you that I am surprised Ms. Bellamy survived. You took very good care of her. We went in and cleaned the wound. There was not any deep infection, which is a big relief. We were able to stitch the wound. She will be all right. She is still under the effects of the medication. You can see her in another hour or so." He shook my hand. "You did an excellent job, all of you. I would like her to remain here for another two days to be sure there are no complications. Then you may fly back to the United States."

I wanted to kiss him.

After assuring myself that Laura was going to be all right, I left with Sherlock and Savich to buy new clothes. Since we had no wallets, no ID, and not even a dollar bill among the three of us, Dr. Salinas loaned us money. Once Savich and I had shaved and no longer looked like desperadoes, they let us into the stores. When we got back to the hospital, we all showered again and changed in the doctors' locker room. Then we ate, wearing our new duds, and waited. Local police authorities arrived to question us and to provide protection, which made us all feel better, given the tenacity of Molinas's soldiers. They agreed to wait until representatives from the DEA and the FBI arrived. They seemed concerned and cooperative. One police lieutenant told us that he'd heard about an old army compound near Dos Brazos. He was surprised someone would try to use it for the drug trade into his country. They wouldn't get away with anything like that in Costa Rica.

The day seemed to last forever. Laura awoke briefly, but mostly slept. We all elected to stay at the hospital that night, at the urging of the six police officers there to protect us.

The next morning we were seated in Laura's room, speaking quietly since she was sleeping. I heard a man's voice but didn't look up. Then the hospital room door opened and Savich roared to his feet. "Good God, sir, am I glad to see you!"

Assistant Director Jimmy Maitland, Savich's boss, came into the hospital room like a tackle bursting through the line, grinning from ear to ear when he saw Sherlock and Savich.

"S and S, good to see you guys on your feet. I don't mind telling you though that I'm glad this sort of thing is mostly behind me." He hugged Sherlock tightly and shook hands with Savich.

Behind him was my own boss, Big Carl Bardolino. He was a man I'd walk over coals to work for, a man who was ferocious in his loyalty to his people, just as Jimmy Maitland was to his. Big Carl came in at just under six feet five inches and weighed a lithe two hundred and twenty pounds. I'd never yet seen an agent who could take him in the gym. "Sir," I said. "Welcome to Costa Rica."

"Good to see you in one piece this time, Mac."

Another man I'd never seen before walked over to Laura's bed. I knew he wasn't FBI. Funny, but I knew that immediately. I also knew that I wasn't going to like him.

"We met this fellow at the airport," Jimmy Maitland said. "He's DEA. We let him come with us because he's Laura Bellamy's boss, at least that's what he says. His name's Richard Atherton."

I looked him over. He was tall, thin, too well dressed for a Fed, very blond, and looked supercilious. He was wearing loafers with little tassels on them. I said to him, "I was not in Edgerton on assignment for the FBI. I was there on a personal matter, to help my sister. You were dead wrong."

"That's what you told me on the phone," Atherton said, looking at Big Carl. He ignored all of us and looked down at Laura a moment, then said to Savich, "I suppose you were there just to visit with him." He nodded in my direction.

"That's right. As I'm sure he told you, someone tried to kill him. Sherlock and I don't like it when folks try to kill our friends."

A too-blond brow arched up. "You're Sherlock? You're the agent who took down the String Killer?" There was stark admiration in his voice, and Savich frowned.

Sherlock flinched and I knew she was remembering the drug-induced nightmares filled with Marlin Jones. Ignoring him, she addressed Big Carl and Maitland. "The local cops want to take out that compound as much as we do. Shall I tell them that you're here and ready to go?"

"It's okay, Sherlock," Maitland said. "We've already set things up."

"This is DEA business," Atherton said. "It's not in FBI jurisdiction. Anything you have to say, you say it to me first, not these guys."

"Are you always an asshole?" I asked him.

Atherton took a step toward me, looked uncertain, then stopped. I wanted him to take a shot at me, I really did, and so I added, "Laura said you were ambitious, but she didn't say you were an asshole. Surely that isn't a requirement for supervisors in the DEA?"

I heard Maitland cough behind his hand. Atherton took another step toward me.

Savich took his forearm. "Don't do it," he said to him quietly, very close to his left ear. "Trust me on this, Atherton. It wouldn't be smart. We're both pretty pissed at your attitude. I suggest if you want to keep your nice capped teeth intact, you sit yourself down and listen. It's time for full cooperation. This isn't some sort of game. Look at Laura. She nearly died."

"Yeah, because she disobeyed my direct orders."

And that, I knew, was the truth. I said, "Yes, she did. As a matter of fact, we were all hot dogs, but believe me, we paid for it."

"You wrecked my operation."

"That remains to be seen," Maitland said. "We've got about a dozen FBI agents in Edgerton as we speak, turning over every rock."

"We were about to holler for help," Sherlock said. "We just didn't have time. They got us that very first night."

Maitland said, raising his huge hands, "What's done is done. Carl and I will deal with our agents later. As for Mac, he wasn't there on the job but on personal business. We're all in Edgerton now tearing the place down to the ground. If there's still anything there to tie Tarcher and Paul Bartlett to this drug operation, we'll find it."

Atherton stepped back from me, looked hard at Maitland, and sighed. "Well, hell. If there's a chance we can get anything on Del Cabrizo, I want to be there with you to find it. But I think they must have hit you guys so quickly to give themselves time to close down shop, to destroy evidence."

Maitland, always a diplomat, said, "If you can nail Del Cabrizo it would be quite a feather in the DEA's cap. We can use all the help we can get."

"As of right now," Big Carl said, "this is an interagency operation. All right with you, Atherton?"

Atherton nodded. He was looking at Laura, oxygen in her nose, an IV in her arm, lying there pale and silent. He walked over to her and lightly touched her shoulder. Maybe he really gave a damn about her.

Laura, her voice a thread of sound, said, "Please get Molinas. He tried to make us think he was so noble, trying to make his daughter well, but he isn't. He would have done anything to us. He wouldn't have cared if we died or just went crazy. He's as bad as Del Cabrizo." She blinked, closed her eyes, and turned her cheek into the hospital pillow.

Maitland stood up. "It's time for the FBI and the DEA to mount a joint operation. We'll all go down to this compound to see what's going on."

THIRTY-TWO

"Out with it, Mac. What happened?"

"Molinas is dead," I said to Laura. "It wasn't our side who killed him. Del Cabrizo's people arrived before we did and executed him."

"He was afraid of Del Cabrizo."

"He was right to be. Unfortunately, we didn't find Molinas's daughter. By the time we and the Costa Rican people got to the compound, it was deserted. The police burned it to the ground to prevent any possibility that it could ever be used again as a halfway point. They're going to patrol the airspace too."

"Any word yet from Edgerton?"

"They searched the Tarcher house from top to bottom, and they're going through his business records. Nothing yet, no financial records to indicate anything concerning drugs.

"Paul's gone, everything in his house including his computer, gone as well. Tarcher says he doesn't have any idea what all this is about. They can't hold him, at least not yet. They're still looking for Jilly too. But as of two hours ago, we've got nothing on anybody."

I helped Laura move herself higher on the pillow. "There, that's better. Now, what about Charlie Duck and the traces of the drug the M.E. found?"

"Tarcher said he hadn't any idea how Charlie Duck had gotten ahold of Paul's drug. Maybe Paul killed him, Tarcher said." I lightly kissed Laura's hand. Her skin was smooth and soft. Her fingers clasped mine. Her grip was stronger. "As you can imagine, the local sheriff, Maggie Sheffield, isn't a happy camper. She and Atherton are going at each other like two cocks after the same hen."

Laura laughed.

"Well, two dogs after the same bone. You get the idea. Since I got this from Atherton, he didn't quite phrase it like that, just complained that this cop in Edgerton was a pain in the butt."

"What are we going to do, Mac?"

I kissed her mouth and the tip of her nose. I got her earlobe on the third kiss. "We're going to stay right here until you're well enough to travel. Then"—I drew a deep breath—"I've got to go back to Edgerton. I've got to find Jilly."

"Give me a couple more days, Mac. We'll go together."

FOUR days later, all four of us landed in Portland, Oregon. Sherlock and Savich wouldn't let us go alone.

Savich rented a Toyota Cressida and I rented a Ford Explorer at the airport. They remembered us from last time and gave us a distrustful look, but our original rental cars had been returned to the rental company, the repair bills paid, everything right and tight.

I laid back behind Savich's car, bright red and in-your-face, on the road to Edgerton. We pulled into Paul's driveway on Liverpool Street a little over an hour later. It was two o'clock in the afternoon, a Thursday, in early May. A thick wet fog hung over the coastline. Since Paul and Jilly's house wasn't even fifty feet from the ocean, the fog was thick, so thick I could barely see Savich's red car right in front of me. I ached all over in the dampness, a lingering present from my injuries in Tunisia, I guessed. I wondered if this bone-deep damp made Laura's shoulder ache and pull.

There was no one around to see me pop the lock on the front door.

"It's not really breaking and entering," Savich said, providing me some cover as I broke in. "This is your sister's house, after all."

The house felt as cold and hollow as ever.

And empty. If Paul had left any notes or journals or equipment, the cops had taken it. I imagined that he'd taken everything.

"We might as well look," Laura said beside my elbow. "You never know."

Sherlock, humming, went off to the back of the house. I stood there quietly in the living room, wondering where Paul would have hidden something he hadn't taken.

I turned slowly, taking in the modern art, the glass and furnishings, all cold whites and blacks that filled the long room. I still hated it.

Thirty minutes later I joined Savich upstairs in Paul's laboratory. Savich was looking through an empty closet, singing a country-and-western song under his breath.

I smiled as I carefully scanned the long narrow room, looking, I suppose, for anything that might be out of place, or something that wasn't quite in the right place, like a seam in the wall. Anything that felt even slightly unusual to me.

Nothing.

Savich was singing about *Tommy breaking out of that hot, dark Mexican jail* . . .

He stuck his head out of the closet. "I even tapped around the walls. Nothing."

He rose, wiped his hands on his pants, and said, "Well, I say we go over to the Tarcher house and see how glad they are to see us."

I said, "This is probably off the wall, but once Maggie told me that Jilly was sleeping with Rob Morrison. How about we go see him first?"

Morrison's cottage was deserted, not even a car parked in front. No fresh tire tracks. The place looked like it had been empty for a good number of days.

Savich tried the front door. It was locked. Savich looked at me and said, "This is personal, Mac." He pulled out his small pick set and went to work. He couldn't get it open. "Interesting," he said.

"It is," Sherlock said, crowding in on him. "Why would you have a Fort Knox lock on a shack?"

"Good question."

I walked around the cottage to the large glass window behind the sink in the kitchen. I whistled as I gently broke the glass. Now this was breaking and entering, for sure.

I managed not to cut myself as I came in over the sink and jumped to the linoleum floor. The lock on the front door was elaborate, state of the art. It took a minute to figure out. Finally, I flipped three switches and opened the door for Savich and Sherlock.

"A guy lives here?" Sherlock said, looking around. "Alone? This place is as neat as ours, Dillon, just after Julie our housekeeper's been there."

"Morrison's got a housekeeper too, a retired Alaskan fisherman named Mr. Thorne. I've never met him, but he sure does good work."

We got to it. Twenty minutes later, we gathered in the living room, not a whit wiser than twenty minutes before. We'd found a file drawer that held his insurance papers, medical records, car repairs from three different mechanics, and a few odd letters from relatives, nothing interesting or informative. There were a few framed photos around, but the only one that made me stop cold was one of Jilly, set in a gold frame, facedown on the bedside table. She was standing on a cliff, smiling big, wearing a sundress and big sunglasses.

"The shed beside the house," Savich said. "I want to take a look in there."

The shed looked as old as the dirt it sat on, the wood rotting and smelling of damp, the door rickety. It was locked. Savich gave it a solid thump with his fist. The door shuddered off its hinges and fell inward. An ungodly odor slammed out at us.

"What is it, Dillon?" Sherlock was crowding him.

Savich turned slowly, taking her arms. "Stay back."

We hadn't found Jilly.

We'd found Rob Morrison.

THIRTY-THREE

I looked on as Maggie watched them put her lover into a body bag. Two men heaved the body bag up into the coroner's van and slammed the doors. She stood there, watching the van disappear around a curve about half a mile away from Rob Morrison's cottage.

She'd looked only once at his body, her hand covering her nose and mouth, then walked away and said nothing to any of us for at least ten minutes. Then we'd waited for nearly an hour before the Salem coroner's office and forensic guy showed up, Detective Minton Castanga in charge. Until now, he'd said nothing at all to Maggie, done nothing more than greeted us.

It had started raining as the coroner's van pulled away. Castanga motioned all of us into the house.

"Talk to me," he said, and sat down on Rob Morrison's sofa.

We told him everything, except we told him we broke into the house after finding the body.

Castanga scratched his chin with his pen and said, "Now, let me get this exactly straight. You federal people have been all over this town for nearly a week now, then you four came here expecting to find Mac's sister, Jilly. Or because Morrison might know where she is?"

"That's right," I said. Laura sat beside me, listing slightly to the left, against my shoulder.

"Do you have any idea who killed Rob Morrison?" He lifted a beautifully polished red apple from the full bowl on top of the coffee table, rubbed it on his jacket arm, and took a big bite.

"None of us know who killed Rob Morrison," I said. "None of us know anything about this. His murder must somehow be connected to the drug operation that's being investigated, but we have no direct knowledge of that. We were just looking around, saw the shed door hanging open, and checked it out. There was Morrison, dead." So the door hadn't been exactly open. I didn't think Castanga needed to know we were searching Morrison's property.

"Two gunshots in the middle of the back," Castanga said. "Someone wanted him gone and took care of it efficiently. It appears he's been dead for at least four days." Castanga put down the apple core on the polished coffee table, frowned, then gently set it atop the other apples. "Don't want to stain the wood," he said.

"You never cared about staining wood when we were married," Maggie Sheffield said.

"I was young and foolish then."

"Yeah, no more than thirty-five." Maggie stood.

Castanga said gently, "Maggie, I understand that you were seeing Rob Morrison. Hadn't you wondered where he was?"

She shrugged. The pain in her eyes was there for all to see. "He's not known for fidelity. When he didn't call me, I tried to get him a couple of times. Then I just stopped."

"We're really sorry, Maggie," Sherlock said.

"I am too," I said. "He saved Jilly's life."

Maggie's chin went up. "Thanks. Now, I'm going to start interviewing to see what I can find out."

Castanga looked as if he'd object, then he shrugged. "Go easy, Maggie, and be careful. I'm not being overprotective. People are in the habit of dying around here."

Maggie said, "I should have stayed in Eugene."

Castanga turned to Laura, who was still leaning against my shoulder. "Take care of her," he said to all of us. "She should be in bed."

Castanga closed his small notebook and shoved it inside his jacket. He rose, wiping his hands on his slacks. "Oh, yeah, not a clue as to who drugged you two. As you probably know, the DEA also slammed the lid down on our investigation. It wasn't going anywhere, anyway."

We had lunch at Grace's Deli on Fifth Avenue. I think Grace was the only person in Edgerton who was actually pleased to see us. She took one look at Laura, started patting her, and led her to a chair.

While she made us sandwiches, she talked nonstop about all the trouble. "Must have been thirty federal officers. They blanketed Edgerton, even tucked in the corners. No one could get in or out. They were everywhere, talking to everyone. You know what?"

She handed Laura her tuna salad sandwich and answered her own question.

"No, of course you don't know anything. You poor people were down in a drug dealer's camp, being tortured."

"How did you know about that?" I asked and, unable to wait, took a big bite of my corned beef sandwich on rye.

"Everybody knows everything. There was a meeting of the BITEASS and we all talked about it. Isn't it something about that drug that Dr. Bartlett invented? And Rob Morrison, murdered because he knew about it and was going to turn those dealers in, whoever they are. Poor boy. Of course, Cotter Tarcher was telling everybody it was all ridiculous, that the drug just gave you great sex, and what was wrong with that?"

"Great sex," I said, shaking my head.

"I wonder," Laura said, "if there has been an increase in rape reports around here lately."

When we pulled into the Tarcher driveway, it was like an alarm went off. Laura straightened up, blinked, and insisted she felt wonderful and renewed after her tuna sandwich and nap.

"A five-minute nap."

"I'm a woman. I can do more on less."

Sherlock and Savich pulled up behind us in the driveway.

My knock brought an immediate response.

"Not you clowns again. What do you want?"

I smiled at Cotter Tarcher, who was blocking the front door, dressed like a thug in black jeans and a white T-shirt. He was even wearing black boots. He looked as dark as a night in hell, spoiling for a fight.

"Hi, Cotter," I said. "You remember Savich and Sherlock, don't you? And Ms. Scott? Sure you do. Savich and you caused a little ruckus."

He stepped back to slam the front door in my face. "I don't think so," I said. I slammed the door open, sending him onto his back, skidding across the black-and-white Italian marble floor.

"Control yourself, Cotter. We're here to speak to your parents. It's time for you to show some manners." I walked into the house, with Laura, Savich, and Sherlock right behind me. "You've really got to change that bad-boy image."

He started to get to his feet so he could come at me, but a woman's voice stopped him.

"No, Cotter, don't waste your energy on the federal agents. There are four of them and only one of you, although the women probably aren't that tough. I'm sure you could deal with the one wearing the sling. Don't forget too they can always arrest you."

She turned to us. "I see you've come into my house without invitation. Since I do have some manners, quite good manners, you may stay for a while. You said you wanted to speak to me?" At my nod, she waved her hand. "I suppose you will come into the living room. Goodness knows, we've had more federal agents trooping through the house, tearing everything apart, making huge messes and not bothering to clean them up."

Elaine Tarcher looked elegant in a pair of tight white jeans and a loose pale peach cashmere sweater. Her rich brown hair was tousled around her face, and she wore cream-colored ballet slippers on her feet. She led the way, not looking back to see whether or not we followed her.

"Poor Maggie," she said as she gracefully displayed herself on an elegant wing chair that looked at least two hundred years old. "Is she dreadfully distraught over Rob's death?"

"How did you find out so fast?" Sherlock asked, uncrossing her legs and sitting forward.

Elaine shrugged elegantly. "One hears things so quickly in Edgerton. Perhaps it was our postman who told our housekeeper who told me, just minutes ago. I can't be expected to remember everything."

"He didn't just die," I said. "Someone murdered him. Two shots in the back. They threw him in the shed and left him there. We found him by accident."

"Yes, I know. Rob wasn't at all faithful to Maggie, you know. It wasn't Maggie's fault. Actually, I've never known Rob to be faithful to any woman for longer than perhaps two and a half weeks, maximum."

I leaned back in my chair, a match to hers, my elbows resting on my thighs, hands clasped between my knees. "He was only faithful to you that long, Elaine?"

"I suppose there'll be an investigation," she said, giving me a sad smile. "It was two and a half weeks exactly. I'll tell you, I was very surprised when he patted my cheek one evening after we'd made love and told me he was moving on. He was speaking metaphorically, of course, since we were at his cottage and so I was the one who had to leave. It was always so clean, that precious little house, what with Mr. Thorne taking such good care of it. I never even questioned if the sheets were fresh. I knew they were." She sighed and dabbed a very pretty swatch of white handkerchief to her eyes. "Rob was such a lovely young man. I could be with him for hours, not saying anything, content to touch his beautiful body." She actually sighed again. "Such endurance he had. And he just got more and more devoted as time went on." She looked over at me through her lashes. "In matters of the flesh, I mean."

"Who did he move on to?" Savich asked. He'd remained standing behind Sherlock, who was sitting on a low blue brocade love seat, his hand lightly resting on her shoulder.

"To Maggie. I tried to tell her he was a Teflon kind of guy, but she just laughed and said just because I was rich didn't mean Rob would stay with me."

"Mother, get rid of these creeps. Tell them to get out. They don't have a warrant. They have no power to make us do anything."

"Now, Cotter, there's no call to be rude," Elaine said. She looked at him like she really loved him, but she also let him see her parental disappointment. "You did learn manners and good breeding when you were growing up, remember? I don't know what happened to them though."

"You can take the boy out of the loony bin," Sherlock said, giving Cotter a small salute, "but you can't take—well, you know the rest of it."

I thought Cotter would leap on Sherlock, but then he saw Savich's face.

"I'm not crazy."

"No, of course you're not, dear. You're just high-strung, like I was when I was your age. I want you to keep yourself calm. Our guests are nearly ready to leave."

"Do you know anything about Rob Morrison's murder?" I asked him.

"Not a damned thing," Cotter said, his voice savage. "But no big loss. The bastard's dead. No one wants the prick now."

Savich said in that deep, calm voice of his, "I'm tired of your foul mouth, Cotter. You're an undisciplined boy in a man's body. You're offending me."

Cotter stared at Savich for a long moment, then he took a step back.

"I can say whatever I want to, you fuckhead."

"That's quite enough," Elaine Tarcher said, rising gracefully to her feet to face the man who was her son, and who was also certifiable. "You're not off in the woods with them somewhere, Cotter, you're here in the living room of my house."

To my wonder and relief, Cotter said in a calm, controlled voice, "I'm sorry, Mother. I don't want to make a mess in the living room. You have so many nice things in here." He'd made the right choice.

"Yes, dear. It's kind of you to remember. Go find your father now."

Cotter walked out through the elegant arch of the living room doorway. He turned and said, "Rob Morrison was a fool. He only wanted you for two and a half weeks, Mother. Was he blind? You're so beautiful the bastard should have been crawling to you. Rob was the crazy one." Then he was gone.

"I apologize," Elaine said with a charming smile to all of us. "Cotter gets overstimulated sometimes. My mother was exactly the same way. I believe it's drinking too much coffee. He doesn't mean any harm. Now, are you all ready to leave? It's time, you know. I do have a lot to accomplish this afternoon."

Sherlock shuddered. Laura said, "Mrs. Tarcher, your son is very seriously disturbed. He's a sociopath. He needs professional help before he hurts someone or himself. Surely you see that?"

"She's right," Savich said. "He's dangerous, ma'am, and one of these days he won't back down."

"I'll deal with it if and when that day comes," she said. "He doesn't need a shrink. That's absurd. Actually, I believe he got himself involved with that terrible drug of Paul's. As soon as some time passes, I'm sure he will be all right again.

"I'd like you all to leave now. I've been very cooperative, but enough is enough. Why are you staring at me, Agent Savich?"

"You said your son was taking Paul's drug," Savich said, his hand still on Sherlock's shoulder.

"Yes, I'm afraid so. I'm not sure what it was, but he's seemed more aggressive, not always in control of himself."

"What we gave Cotter, my dear, was a simple tranquilizer that Paul recommended, nothing more." Alyssum Tarcher had entered the room speaking these words. He stood tall and imposing in tailored Italian slacks and a white shirt open at his throat. How much had he heard his wife spill?

He continued, "Well, if it isn't more federal agents, in my living room, threatening my wife and bullying my son. Poor Cotter is in a state. Now, I've had it with all of you. If you don't have a warrant, I want you out of here."

"Sir," I said to Alyssum Tarcher, "we came to ask you about Jilly. She's still missing. I'm very worried about her. Have you seen her? Do you know where she is?"

"We haven't seen Jilly since before her accident," he said.

"Do you think Jilly was taking Paul's drug?" Savich asked. "Do you think she was taking too much of it? That it made her mentally unstable and that's why she drove off the cliff?"

"I don't know what you're talking about. You are upsetting my wife."

Laura was hurting, I could tell, but she was controlling it well. She said, "Did you know that John Molinas was murdered in Costa Rica at a drug compound run by Del Cabrizo?"

"It was on the national news," Alyssum said slowly, one eye on his wife. She was sitting very still, her eyes on her ballet slippers. "Neither Elaine nor I have seen John in a very long time. We were saddened to hear of his death."

"Unfortunately, your niece is missing," Sherlock said.

"My brother loved his daughter very much," Elaine said, rising slowly to stand by her husband. "He wasn't a bad man."

"I want you to leave now," Alyssum Tarcher said. "I am innocent of any drug-trafficking charges, these horrible murders that you and your sister, Agent MacDougal, seem to have brought to us. There is nothing for you here. I don't plan to fall apart and confess because there is nothing to confess. Get out now."

We were nearly to the front door when he said from behind us, "I'll be sending you a bill for the repairs I had to have done on Seagull Cottage. You left it in a mess."

He had wonderful gall.

"That was a good touch," Savich said as we left. "That man's something."

I turned to look back at the house. I saw Cotter staring at us through one of the upstairs windows. When he saw me looking up at him, the curtain fell back over the window. I knew exactly what the drug had done to him. But he'd probably loved it. Had his father taken the drug as well? His mother? I didn't think so. As for Cal, I'd probably never be certain one way or the other.

I felt empty. Coming here had been a waste of time. Jilly was gone and I had no idea now where to look.

"Let's spend the night in Salem at my condo," Laura said. "I want to see Grubster and Nolan. When I called the super from San José, he said they were eating well, but not happy that I was gone. It was very nice of Maggie to take them back home."

"Will they sleep with us?"

"It's a queen-size bed," Laura said. "There'll be room enough for all of us. Oh, yes, I've got a nice guest room for Sherlock and Savich."

I called Maggie Sheffield and told her where we'd be if anything happened to turn up, which I strongly doubted. So did she, but she was nice enough not to say so.

I fell asleep in Laura's very comfortable bed, at arm's length from Laura because Grubster had decided to purr the night away snuggled against her side.

I dreamed I saw headlights, bright and sharp, piercing through a dense fog that seemed to cover everything in a thick veil of white.

Odd, but I could clearly see the road ahead. It was coming at me quickly, too quickly. I wanted to yell and smash down on the brakes, but I couldn't. If there were brakes, I didn't know where to find them. I wanted to get away from that highway that was moving so quickly, but I was helpless. I was trapped.

I couldn't draw a breath I was so afraid. Suddenly, I heard a soft keening sound from beside me. It was a woman moaning as if she hadn't anything left, as if there was nothing more for her and she knew it and accepted it.

I wanted us both to stop, but the road kept coming up through those bright headlights, faster and faster. I tried to tell her I was here with her, that I would help if I could. But she couldn't hear me.

I heard her speaking now, quietly. She was praying. I was nearly part of her in those moments when she prayed for forgiveness.

I knew I was dreaming despite what I thought, what I felt. I wanted to wake up but I couldn't.

The road disappeared. I was thrown forward hard, but then everything seemed to fade away. We were flying out into the fog, sailing high, then dropping toward the water.

I was aware of immense pain slamming through me, a tremendous pressure against my chest that didn't really hurt but was just there. Then it too was gone. There was an eerie sense of calm, of finality. So easy, I thought, it was so very easy. I smiled at the gentleness of it, smiled even as everything simply went black, and I felt nothing at all.

THE next morning the four of us stood together on the cliff, looking out over the water. It didn't take long. A man in scuba gear split the surface of the water and yelled, "She's down here!"

I'd known Jilly would be. In my dream I was down there with her.

Another man came up beside him. He called out, "There are two cars down there, next to each other. There's a white Porsche that looks like it's been there awhile and the one she's in looks like a rental car."

EPILOGUE

Washington, D.C.
Three Months Later

"Squawk."

"Keep your feathers on, Nolan." I dumped a pile of sunflower seeds in my palm and reached inside his cage.

"Squawk."

"Here you go."

Grubster rubbed against my bare leg. "Yep, you're next, fella."

You'd look at Grubster and believe he'd eat anything that didn't move out of his path he was so big, but it wasn't true. Grubster ate only gourmet cat food. That had started the day we'd all moved into a new town house in Georgetown.

"He thinks he's upscale now," Laura had said. "It's his statement of self-worth."

I put a slice of bread into the toaster and got out the can opener. I forked out an entire can of salmon and rice into Grubster's big white bowl, with a smiling cat face on the bottom, petted his back, rubbed his ears, and listened to him purr as he chowed down.

"Squawk."

I waved a hot slice of toast until it cooled and broke off small pieces for Nolan.

"Everyone happy now?"

There was blessed silence.

It was Saturday morning, already warm and promising to be hot by noon, and Laura was still asleep. I was about to go back to bed to kiss her awake when the doorbell rang.

"Just a minute," I called out and went into the bedroom to pull on a pair of jeans.

"A registered letter. Are you Mr. MacDougal?"

I nodded. "Who is it from?"

"It's from Oregon, that's all I know."

I don't know what I expected, but this wasn't it. It was a short note from a lawyer in Salem, Oregon, telling me only that my sister wished this to be mailed to me exactly three months after her death had been confirmed.

My hand shook as I smoothed out the pages.

My dearest Ford:

I wonder if you will be with me tonight. If so, you will know what it is I have done. I am so sorry to cause you this pain, but I will be grateful if you are there with me.

How can I begin? At the beginning, I suppose. Paul and I had such great hopes for my brainchild. I managed to bond a neuro-transmitter involved with memory to an opiate, and was surprised when the compound proved stable. We thought we would accomplish so much with it when it seemed not to be toxic and had such profound effects in our laboratory. We thought we'd found a key to how memory works, and maybe sexual drive too. But no matter what we tried, we couldn't control it or predict its effects well enough, and the bastards at VioTech pulled the plug on us.

Actually, Ford, they pulled the plug because both Paul and I had tried the drug ourselves, and they found out about it. It was the stupidest thing I've ever done. It was so wonderful at first. The sex was simply incredible. By the time we left VioTech, I was badly hooked. Paul was always afraid of it, even though he loved what it did to his sex drive, and so he kept his doses in check, and it saved him.

But we had to be able to make more of it by then, and I wanted to keep trying to alter the drug, or control it better. We approached Cotter Tarcher in Edgerton. Paul knew the vicious little bully well enough to think he'd be interested. After Cotter tried the drug, he was willing to help talk his parents into supporting us. Cotter thought he would get rich beyond his dreams. We didn't know his uncle, John Molinas, was a drug distributor, and that Cotter would tell him about us. Nor did we know that he'd bring that big drug lord in on it—Del Cabrizo.

We didn't make any progress, and I got worse. The drug just took over. It still has control. I'm not proud of what I've done in the last six months, Ford, the men I've been with, including Del Cabrizo. When Del Cabrizo had Molinas tell us Laura was DEA, it turned me completely psychotic. She was inside my head, tormenting me, and I couldn't stand it. I tried to kill myself so that I would be killing her too.

And then you arrived. You were such a comfort to me. I left the hospital because Cotter called to warn me that Del Cabrizo knew you'd found Laura, and he was threatening to kill both of you. I don't know how he found out, but he did. I was so afraid for you. There was nothing else I could do, so I left the hospital and went into hiding. I stayed with Rob Morrison for a little while, another man I'm not proud to say was my lover. Because Rob crossed them by hiding me for just that first night, they killed him.

Del Cabrizo needed me to make progress on the drug, you see, and it became a sort of standoff. I told them I'd keep working on the drug if they didn't kill you. But I couldn't stop them from taking you. They promised not to kill you if I helped them clear out all the evidence and move the operation to a cabin outside Spokane. They wanted me to get back to work once we moved everything to Spokane out of sight.

They also killed Charlie Duck, an old man who dug and dug once he suspected what was going on. I told Molinas I was afraid of what he'd found out and that he'd talk. With those words, I signed his death warrant. Del Cabrizo sent some goons to his house to search for anything he'd written down about what he'd found out. Paul told me they'd forced a lot of the drug down him, then killed him when he tried to break away.

I'm so sorry about what they did to you, Ford. Please forgive me. I heard about your escape. Good for you. My brother the cop, you were always my hero.

I've been responsible for so much death and pain. It's all my fault.

As you know, I got away from them. But they've still got Paul. I know you can track him down if you want to, but they will kill him in a heartbeat if you do. They will probably kill him anyway when they realize he can't help them. He just doesn't know enough. Please, don't you be the one to go after him.

I wanted you to know what happened so you could put me away, maybe tuck me in the back of your mind as at least a bitter-sweet memory. No matter what I was, what I became, I loved you, Ford.

By the way, you should get together with Laura. She's perfect for you.

Good-bye, my dearest. Jilly

I slowly folded the pages and eased them back into the envelope. I lit a fire in the fireplace. When it was going strong, I gently placed the envelope on top of the flames.

I sat on my haunches and watched as it burned. I didn't move until it was completely gone.

"Mac? It's got to be ninety degrees in here. You lit a fire?"

I rose slowly and walked to my wife. I hugged her tightly against me. "Would you believe that I found an old photo of me hugging a girlfriend and I burned it before you saw it and got jealous?"

"Squawk."

"Nolan believes me."

"Sure, Mac," she said. I knew she didn't understand, but she was willing to accept that I didn't want to explain.

I hugged her for a very long time.

Catherine Coulter is the #1 *New York Times* bestselling author of more than eighty novels, including the FBI Thriller series and A Brit in the FBI international thriller series, cowritten with J. T. Ellison. She lives in Sausalito, California, with her Übermensch husband and their two noble cats, Peyton and Eli.